Praise for

The House on Durrow Street

"Beckett's enchantingly gothic voice is in evidence in this second in the series; [the] protagonist Ivy is as enchantingly strong as ever, with a beguiling Austen-esque personality, which really carries the novel. The backdrop of quirky characters, a fascinating magic system and the mysterious nature of the house all wrap up a delightful . . . novel."

—*RT Book Reviews*

"*The House on Durrow Street* (A++) is one of those novels that stay with you for a long time and I plan to reread the whole series across the years." —Fantasy Book Critic

"I highly recommend *The House on Durrow Street* as a splendid fantasy that is both magical and very proper." —SFRevu

Praise for

The Magicians and Mrs. Quent

"*The Magicians and Mrs. Quent* by Galen Beckett is a charming and mannered fantasy confection with a darker core of Gothic romance wrapped around a mystery. Fans of any of these will enjoy it. Readers who enjoy all these genres will find it a banquet."

—ROBIN HOBB, author of *Dragon Haven*

"*The Magicians and Mrs. Quent* is a charming and accomplished debut, sure to delight fantasy aficionados and lovers of gothic romance alike." —JACQUELINE CAREY, author of *Naamah's Blessing*

ALSO BY GALEN BECKETT

The Magicians and Mrs. Quent
The House on Durrow Street

The Master
of
Heathcrest Hall

The Master of Heathcrest Hall

Galen Beckett

BALLANTINE BOOKS ✦ NEW YORK

A Spectra Trade Paperback Original

Copyright © 2012 by Mark Anthony

Published in the United States by Spectra Books,
an imprint of the Random House Publishing Group,
a division of Random House, Inc., New York.

SPECTRA and the portrayal of a boxed "S" are trademarks
of Random House, Inc.

LIBRARY OF CONGRESS CATALOGING-IN-PUBLICATION DATA
Beckett, Galen
The master of Heathcrest Hall / Galen Beckett.
p.   cm.
ISBN 978-0-553-80760-8 (pbk.)—ISBN 978-0-345-53248-0 (eBook)
I. Title.
PS3602.E27M37 2012
813'.6—dc23   2012000361

Printed in the United States of America

www.ballantinebooks.com

2 4 6 8 9 7 5 3 1

This is for all the witches,
magicians, and illusionists who stand
against the shadows in this world.

BOOK ONE

———— ❧ ————

The Gallows Game

CHAPTER ONE

$\mathfrak{T}$HE PEOPLE HUDDLED in the cave as the wind shook the branches of the trees outside.

The cave was damp and musty from disuse, for it had been a long while since they had last journeyed to it. In years past, they would dwell here during the darkest winter months, when the thick stone offered protection from the winds that swept out of the north—and from the wolves that prowled the frozen land, their fur ragged, desperate enough to brave fire and arrow in search of something to fill their shrunken bellies.

For most of the year, the people lived five days' walk to the south of this place, in a camp by the blue sea. There they would spend the long days as they had for time out of mind, prying mussels from the rocks and spearing fish and cormorants, until they became as sleek as the otters that basked on the shore in the sun.

At least, that was how things used to be. Layka still remembered what it had been like when she was smaller. She would spend the warm evenings walking along the beach, clad only in a supple doeskin, choosing shells that might be strung on a piece of leather—saving them for the day when she was old enough to begin making herself beautiful for the young men who visited on occasion from the other camps down the shore.

But that was before everything changed.

It began one day with a violent shuddering of the ground. An awful groaning noise filled the air, and the sea pulled away from the shore. All knew this was a sign to flee to a higher place, but even as they did so a sudden night fell over the world. It was as if a fist had closed around the burning ember of the sun, snuffing it out. The people looked up and, for the first time, saw an unfamiliar red spark smoldering among the stars. What this new object in the night sky was, no one knew—not even Nesharu, who of all the people was the oldest and wisest.

At last the trembling of the ground ceased, and the ocean roared back upon the beach. Dawn came, and the day seemed to pass as usual. But when it ended, the red spark again shone in the sky, a little brighter than before. The night that followed lasted too long. The world grew cold, and though it was yet early summer, stars that should only have risen in autumn spun into the sky. By morning, when Layka walked along the shore, she found it rimed with frost. She shivered despite the aurochs hide she had thrown over her shoulders, and had to use her nails to pry up shells from the sand.

After that, the days no longer continued their gradual and steady lengthening toward midsummer. Instead, one night might flit by, swift as a bat, followed by a day during which the sun seemed to hang motionless overhead, blazing so fiercely that the otters were forced to slip into the sea to escape its heat. Then, without warning, the heat would give way to bitter cold after the sun failed to show itself for what felt like days.

A fear came over the people. Plants wilted and shriveled in alternation. Animals grew torpid and confused, wandering across the land as if they did not know which direction to go. Many dead fish washed up on the shore, carried by currents that had gone too hot or cold to sustain them. Sometimes other things washed up on the beach as well: gelatinous remnants of unknown creatures that smelled so foul even the dogs would not touch them. And all the while the red spark grew larger in the sky, glaring like the eye of some angry beast.

That had been three years ago. Or at least so they guessed, for they could no longer count the years by the passage of the seasons. Winter no longer gave way to spring; bright summer never dulled to autumn. Instead, the sequence of days was as patternless as a handful of fish bones thrown on the midden heap. Yet it must have been three years since everything changed, or close to it, for Layka had been just past her thirteenth winter then, and now she was nearly a woman.

Not that it mattered. Young men never came from the other camps anymore. Nobody did, not since the red eye had shown itself. The pretty shells Layka had gathered remained unstrung, piled in a corner of the hut she shared with her parents and her brother. Anyway, there was no time to think about making herself beautiful. It was all she and the others could do to survive. Those first months had been especially awful. Game perished. Springs and rivulets went dry, and the sea grew barren of fish. The people froze and sweltered in alternation, and many succumbed to hunger or fever.

That any of them managed to live was due to Nesharu. For hours she would stand watching the sky, observing the movements of birds or listening to the wind. Then she would tell the people where to look for water or animals to hunt. At first they found little to sustain them. Yet over time some plants began to sprout again, spindly but green. A few animals returned, as did the fish in the sea. And though these were not nearly so plentiful as before, they were enough. The days and nights came and went, sometimes short, sometimes long. For three years the people struggled and endured.

Then a young man came to the camp.

It was one of those endless afternoons when the sunlight went flat and turned everything to white. The people looked up to see a hunter they did not know just beyond the huts. At once the men rushed toward him, spears at the ready, but it was soon obvious that he posed no threat. He was thin, his beard crusted with salt, and despite the heat of the day he was shivering. The people gathered around him and saw that the man bore deep gashes on his arm and side. The flesh around the wounds had turned the color of ash and gave off a rank odor.

The hunter fell to the ground and started to mutter, but it was difficult to understand him. By the ochre that stained the hides he wore, he came from one of the camps around the great curve in the shoreline many days' walk to the south, and the language spoken there was not entirely like that of the people. However, they gave him water, and after a time Nesharu made out some of his speech.

They came during a long night, the hunter told them. Shadows that stalked, shadows with pointed teeth. They ate men from the inside out and put on their skins, so you could not tell what they were. Then, when darkness fell, they cast off the skins to feed, and no arrow could pierce them.

The people were frightened by these words. Layka looked at his wounds, counting the parallel lines in his flesh, and wondered what kind of animal had seven talons upon each of its paws.

"If an arrow will not pierce them, how can these shadows be hunted?" Nesharu asked as she knelt beside the man, a listless wind stirring her hair like the white tendrils of an anemone in the shallows.

"Take their heads," the hunter croaked through cracked lips. "While they still wear a man's skin, take their heads."

Nesharu sat with the hunter for many more hours, her weathered face grim as she leaned close, trying to make out more of the man's words. But the hunter's voice grew fainter, until his lips moved without making any sound, and his eyes stared blindly. Then, as the sun at last dipped below the edge of the sea, his spirit left him.

The people gathered wood, and upon Nesharu's direction they burned the body far away from the huts as the red eye looked down from above. It was a circle nearly as large as the moon now, its light staining the ground like blood after a hunt.

That night was short, but by the time a swift dawn swept across the land, three men were already heading out from the camp. They were the fastest runners among the people. Since the red eye appeared in the sky, no one had gone more than a long day's walk away from the camp. Now the men intended to go all the way around the great bend of the shore, to the southern camps, to see if they could learn more about the things the hunter had spoken of—and what danger they might pose to the people. The runners quickly became small specks on the horizon, then were lost from view.

For five alternations of light and dark, the people waited. Then, just as the sun heaved into the sky at the start of the sixth day, a single runner stumbled into the camp. It was Layka's brother, Tennek.

"You are a good runner," Nesharu said as the people gathered around Tennek, "but it is still much too soon for you to have gone all the way past the great bend and back. And where are the others?"

Tennek shook his head, unable to speak. His breaths came rapidly, and his eyes were wide, as if one of the long-fanged cats pursued him. Layka came forward bearing a shell filled with water and gave it to her elder brother. He drank it, and at last his breathing eased so that he could speak.

The others gathered close. Despite the rising sun, a coldness crept over them as Tennek described how, on the second day out, the runners came to a camp along the shore just where it began to bend to the east.

Who dwelled there, they did not know, for the small lodges made of sticks and mud were all empty. There was wood in the fire pits and a rack of drying fish, as well as a large chunk of flint set out on a flat stone, ready to be struck and knapped into points. It looked as if the people who had made this camp planned to return at any moment.

By then a sudden twilight was descending, and as there was no other shelter, the three runners retreated into one of the empty lodges. They took turns keeping watch, only at some point during the night Tennek and Haleth both woke to discover that Davu was gone. They called out to him from the entrance of the lodge, but there was no answer. When dawn broke, they went out to look for him.

They spent the whole day searching, but there was no sign of Davu in the camp or anywhere around it. Still they kept looking until night fell, when again they had no choice but to retreat into one of the lodges in the camp. This time, neither of them slept, and when morning at last came they agreed they must continue their journey south and hope that Davu would either find them or return to the people. They took some of the dried fish and the flint core, then left the camp.

As they did, they saw Davu walking toward them along the shore. Surprised and happy, they hurried to him and asked him where he had been.

He did not answer. His eyes were hard and dull as pebbles, and there were strange marks on his hand, like a tattoo made with charcoal and a bone needle, only sharper and darker. Haleth asked Davu to hold out his hand so he might look at the tattoo more closely. Davu did not respond, so Haleth reached out to take his hand.

And Davu lunged forward to clamp his teeth upon Haleth's throat.

So astonished were both Tennek and Haleth that for a moment neither of them moved. Only then came a great gush of blood, and Haleth cried out. He pulled away from Davu's grasp, his hands fluttering to his neck, but they could not stanch the flow. As Tennek watched, Haleth sank to his knees, then collapsed into the sand.

Tennek tried to run, but his feet would not move, and then Davu was before him, his eyes as dark and empty as a shark's, his mouth wet with red. He reached out a hand, the one marked with black lines, and wrapped its fingers around Tennek's throat.

Pain at last freed Tennek from his torpor. He tightened his grip around the flint core in his hand, then swung his arm around and brought the heavy chunk of stone crashing against the side of Davu's face. There was a crunching noise as Davu's head turned halfway around on his shoulders.

Yet despite this, Davu's hands continued to grope blindly. Tennek shoved him backward, so that he fell to the sand, then knelt and brought the sharp end of the flint core down upon Davu's spine, again and again, until at last it was done and Davu's head rolled free. No blood came from the stump of his neck, and Tennek did not see muscle or tendon or bone. There was only a gray substance, thick as sea kelp, oozing from both body and head. For a minute Tennek stared at the two corpses on the beach.

Then he threw down the flint and ran, hardly stopping for breath or water, until he returned to the camp.

Many of the people cried out as Tennek finished describing what had befallen him, but Layka could think only that her brother was weary, and that he needed more water. Before she could bring it to him, Nesharu took up a small flint knife and flicked it against Tennek's arm. Tennek let out a cry. All gazed expectantly at the cut on his arm.

A stream of bright red welled forth.

Nesharu nodded, then let Layka bring another shell of water to her brother.

"It is no longer safe here," Nesharu said then. "We must leave this place. We will make for our winter-home." And before the sun had reached its highest point, the people were marching away from the shore, their few belongings on their backs.

That had been seven sunrises ago. It had taken them longer to reach the cave than they expected, for a number of the days passed swiftly, while one of the nights went on so long that snow began to drift down before the sun rose again. Several times they saw plumes of smoke rising in the distance, and they gave these a wide berth. And once, as they huddled together in darkness, they heard distant screams borne on the night wind—though whether they were the sounds of humans or some animal, they could not be certain.

Their trek was nearing its end when they encountered a band much like their own: a collection of some thirty women, children, infants, and men. By their shell necklaces and wristbands, and by their speech, they were from one of the other camps along the western shore. This was one of the bands that the people some-times traded with, and from whose young men Layka might pos-sibly choose a mate.

On this occasion their meeting was not so friendly as it would have been for trading goods or seeking partners in years past, and the two bands approached one another slowly, spears at the ready. However, their wise one was with them: a woman who, like Ne-sharu, had seen at least forty winters. She and Nesharu came to-gether and spoke for a time, their heads bowed together. Then the other band turned and continued northward.

Nesharu said the others knew of the shadows. The band had come upon a camp that had been empty save for scraps of skin. Their own band had been attacked two nights before, and they had lost four to swirls of darkness that lunged and bit, dragging them into the night.

"Where do they go now?" Tennek asked, looking after the oth-ers.

"They go to find shelter, as we do," Nesharu said, taking up her walking stick. "Come, Layka, walk with me for a while. There are plants here that do not grow by the shore that I want to show you."

Layka hurried after the older woman. She always liked it when Nesharu singled her out. The older woman would tell her what things were good to eat, and which would make a man go numb and stop his heart, and whether the patterns of kelp and shells on the shore meant there would be good fishing or a storm was com-ing.

Usually Layka was quick to remember these sorts of things. Only now she seemed to forget the names of the plants as soon as Nesharu told them to her. She kept thinking of the band of people marching to the north, seeking shelter. Only what place could provide shelter from the dark? When night fell, did not even the brightest of fires cast shadows? Layka wanted to ask Nesharu these things, but instead she chewed a piece of dried fish as she walked and listened to the older woman speak.

The next day, they reached the cave.

All of the people felt a relief. They had arrived none too soon, for as they marched up the slope to the familiar jumble of rocks, clouds gathered in the sky: black tinged with livid red. Streaks of yellow lightning stabbed down from the clouds, and thunder shook the ground.

Not far past the cave was a tangled green wall—the edge of the great forest that stretched, Nesharu had said once, to the end of the world. The trees swayed in the gale, and the wind roared through their branches. To Layka, it almost seemed that the trees were speaking in agitated voices. Hurrying before the strange storm, the people ascended the slope and climbed through the open mouth in the rocks.

The floor of the cave was littered with old leaves and splinters of bone. The people had not been here in three years, but it was clear animals had used it as a home at some point. Now the cave was empty and cold. A fire would have warmed the musty air, but there had been no time to gather wood. Not that Nesharu would have allowed them to do so anyway. In the past they had dwelled in the cave only during the winter months, when the trees were barren, and their branches stiff and brittle from cold. At such times, the people would dare to venture to the edge of the forest to gather wood, or perhaps to hunt rabbit or roe deer, all under Nesharu's watchful eye.

As they approached the cave, Layka's gaze had been drawn to the trees. Some branches were shedding yellowed leaves even as others bore green, as if the trees did not know whether it was autumn or spring. Regardless, their branches were lithe and supple as they tossed in the wind—which meant it would not be wise to venture too close to the trees. Some of the older men told stories of foolish hunters who had gone into the woods in summer, pursuing a fat buck, and were never seen again. And in winters past, as they gathered around a crackling fire in the cave, Nesharu would speak of the time when the leviathans walked the land. This was long ago, before there were any people. So large were these great beasts that their shoulders stood as high as the tallest tree, and they grazed upon the forests as aurochs graze upon the grassy plains.

But just as a berry bush grows sharp thorns to ward off bird and squirrel, so the trees grew their own defenses. They learned to strike with branch, to bind with root, and to beat back the great animals that would feed upon them. In time, the leviathans dwindled in number, until there were none left upon the land. Though whether this was due solely to the actions of the trees, or to some other change in the world, Nesharu did not know.

As a girl, Layka had wished she could have seen the great beasts, and wondered if any yet lived. Once, while wandering far along the shore, she had come upon a massive bone jutting out of the sand, and she had thought maybe it was from a leviathan. But when she described the shape and size of the bone to Tennek, he had said it was only a whale jaw.

Now, as the people huddled together in the darkness, Layka listened. The wind rushed past the mouth of the cave, carrying the sound of the trees with it. The noise sent a thrum of excitement through her, though she did not know why. Perhaps it was because she had never been in the cave when the trees were not bare with winter, and she had never before heard the sound of wind passing through the forest. The noise was like the surging of ocean waves—except that she had never been able to hear words in the sound of the waves against the shore.

Something is wrong, the trees were saying. *The light has changed. The ground trembles. The rain is bitter. Something is wrong. . . .*

There was a shout, and this time the voice that rose on the air was not that of the trees, but rather belonged to Tennek. Layka opened her eyes and let out a gasp as a flash of yellow lightning illuminated the shapes of a man and a woman standing at the cave's mouth.

Tennek had been keeping watch at the entrance of the cave, but the gloom of the storm had made the world outside as dark as within, and he had not seen the others approaching. Now he fumbled with his spear, but before he could thrust it, the woman lashed out an arm, quick as the strike of a snake, and caught the wooden shaft, stopping him. The lightning faded, but as the thunder followed, Layka realized she could still see the strangers, for the man held a burning brand in his hand.

No, it wasn't a piece of burning wood, she realized as her eyes adjusted to the light. Instead, it was from a clear stone that the red glow came. The people shrank back from the unnatural light. Tennek tried to pull his spear free, but the woman flicked her dark gaze at him, and he let go, staggering back as if struck.

"Who are you?" Nesharu said, leaning on her walking stick as she approached.

"We mean you no harm," the man said. "You need not fear us."

His words were peculiar. They were spoken in the tongue of the people and were easily understood, but the cadence and tone were wrong. Or rather, they seemed too carefully, too exactingly formed. All the same, his voice was deep and calming, and Layka felt her heartbeat slow. The man was taller than any of the men of the people, and his face and body were well made. He wore the gray fur of a wolf across his wide shoulders.

"Why should we not feel fear?" Nesharu said.

The woman made a low sound: like a laugh, but not. "He said you need not fear us. He did not say you shouldn't feel fear."

Layka's heartbeat quickened again. The woman's face was as pale, smooth, and hard as the inside of a cockleshell. Her black eyes reflected the strange crimson light, and she wore supple hides that had been cut and laced together, tightly fitting the curves and angles of her body. Layka had never seen anything like them.

"What do you want of us?" Nesharu said, squinting against the light. "If you need food, take some fish, and then go."

"We do not need food," the man said in his soothing voice. "We need your help."

"Our help? For what?"

"To fight against the shadows."

Nesharu frowned. "Why should we help you when you come in the night like shadows yourselves?"

The man hesitated, then reached into the pouch at his belt and took out a small flint knife. He drew the knife across the palm of his hand, so that a line of dark red blood welled forth. The people let out a sigh.

Nesharu studied him a long moment, then nodded toward the white-faced woman. "What of her?"

The tall man grinned. "You can try to cut her if you wish, but I do not think you will succeed. However, she is with me, so you need not be wary of her."

"I think you are wrong in that," Nesharu said, eyeing the woman. "But you should come in from the storm."

And the strangers did.

The man spoke a word, and the red stone in his hand grew brighter. He set it within the fire ring on the floor so that its glow filled the cave, pushing back the dark, and despite its peculiar source the people were glad for the light. Layka dared to reach out a hand toward the stone. She could feel no heat coming from it, but before she could touch the stone to be sure, the tall man gave her a look. It was sharp, but not angry. Indeed, the corners of his mouth seemed to curve upward a bit.

She quickly drew her hand back and found herself smiling as well. He was, she thought, more handsome than any of the men in her band. Even more than her brother, Tennek, who all agreed was good to look at.

Nesharu offered the strangers food, and they accepted it. However, while the man sat around the fire ring with the others, the pale woman took her fish and went back to the mouth of the cave to stand there, gazing outward with black eyes.

"I have never seen a coal like this," Nesharu said, gesturing to the red stone. "It gives light but not heat, and it seems never to burn up."

The man nodded. "You are right. It is—"

He spoke a word Layka did not know, one whose strange sound struck her ears harshly and caused her to flinch.

"Magick," Nesharu said, doing her best to repeat the word, though her lips could not exactly reproduce the odd sound of it.

The man smiled. "Close enough."

"Is it like the *wayru*?" Tennek said, using the word of the people that referred to that kind of wisdom that Nesharu had—knowledge of the pattern of the seasons, and the habits of animals, and which plants could ease pain or cool a fever or make a poison.

"No, it's different from that," the tall man said.

Tennek squatted by the fire ring, his face bathed by the crimson light. "Can it cause harm to the shadows?"

"It can. But there are many shadows, and I am only one."

"What of her?" Nesharu said. "She looks as if she could fight things. Your *sar valak*."

She used the words of the people that mean *pale, white* and also *pointed barb, thorn*.

The man laughed. "*Sar valak*," he murmured. "I like that name. Yes, my White Thorn can fight these things. She can fight many of them. But again, she is only one."

"And how many shadows are there?"

His face grew grim, and he held up one of the small dried fish. "How many of these dwell in the sea?"

The people stared at him, and some trembled.

Nesharu, however, kept her gaze firmly fixed upon the tall man. "If there are so many, how have they not overcome us all?"

"Because they are not all here yet. There is yet time—time before the night wanderers stand as one in the sky."

There were two kinds of stars in the night sky, Nesharu had told Layka before. There were the stars that shimmered and which all moved together on the same path. Then there were the wanderers, the stars that glowed steadily, which traveled as they pleased to and fro across the sky, sometimes even turning around and going backward.

"I have seen the wanderers moving nearer to one another," Nesharu said. "Sometimes they dance away for a time, but then they turn and move toward each other again, always closer than before. It all began when the red moon appeared in the sky."

The man shook his head. "It is no moon. It is a planet, a wanderer, but one from a far-distant place. When it was brought here—when it was made to suddenly appear in the sky you see—

the movements of the other wanderers were disrupted. But now a harmonic is beginning to emerge: a new pattern. Very soon now, the others will fall into line behind the red planet. When they do, they will push it even closer to this world."

"I do not understand. What does this mean?"

"The shadows are only able to cross over into this land when the red wanderer draws close." He brought his fists together. "Since it appeared, the wanderer's gyrations have, several times, brought it just near enough for a few of the shadows to make the leap. But when the wanderers all stand as one, the red planet will come much closer, and few will become many. Already it is beginning to happen."

"So it is from the red moon they come," Nesharu said softly, nodding as she stroked her chin.

"Yes, and when more of them come, in a dark flood, they will destroy everything in this land—all its plants, all its animals, all its people."

Nesharu tilted her head to study the tall man. "You know much of them, stranger. How?"

"I know because that is what they did to my own land."

Nesharu drew in a breath, but before she could speak there was a sudden motion at the mouth of the cave. Like a spirit, the pale woman appeared in the opening. She must have gone outside without anyone noticing and now had reappeared.

"They are coming," she said to her companion. "A great many from the north. And their masters are with them."

Layka felt a pain in her chest, and she thought of the band of people they had met, the ones who had been journeying northward to find shelter.

"How do you know this?" Nesharu said, scowling at the pale woman.

"She can sense them," the tall man said, then he stood. "It was what she was made for. Come, we must leave this place. We are not safe here."

Frightened murmurs ran through the people.

"If they are coming, then we should stay in the cave," Tennek said. "We can defend ourselves here."

The white-faced woman glared at him. "Your spear cannot stop them from entering this cave. You could better hold back a river with a twig. Besides, for all you know, one of them is already in here."

The people cast wide-eyed looks at one another. Tennek gripped his spear and said nothing.

"No, the gray ones are not here, not yet," Nesharu said, her words sharp. "I know the eyes of my own people."

"Then get them out of here while you still can," the tall man said.

Nesharu gazed at him a moment, then she rose and leaned upon her walking stick. Without a word, she passed through the mouth of the cave, and the rest of the people followed.

The queer storm had passed as suddenly as it came, and remnants of clouds scudded across the night sky. The red moon loomed large above, and as Layka looked up she saw the orange, blue, and yellow dots of some of the other wanderers hovering close to the edge of the crimson circle, like insects drawn to some livid bloom.

Now that they were outside, the surging sound of the forest was louder. The storm was over, and the wind had died away. All the same, in the red light, the trees continued to sway back and forth. Layka shut her eyes, and the voices of the trees grew clearer.

Something is wrong. The light has changed. The ground trembles. . . .

"There, we have left our cave," Nesharu said.

Layka opened her eyes. Nesharu stood before the stranger, glaring at him as if he were not half again taller than she. "Now where should we go?"

"Look," the man said and pointed at the edge of the forest.

Nesharu did nothing to conceal her scorn. "You know not what you speak, *laru telaka*," she said, using the words that meant *one who wears the wolf*. "Do you not see how they bend and sway? It is not the wind that causes them to do so! Something has disturbed them. Were we to attempt to enter the forest now, our intrusion would not be borne. They would lash out and slay us all."

"No, they won't," the man said. "Not if someone calls out to them and tells them not to. It is the nature of the trees to defend themselves against threat and peril, and they have sensed that a great wrong has entered into the world. Only they do not understand what it is—they do not know its source. They must be told what it is that threatens this land. They need to be taught who their enemy is—that it is the shadows they must fight now."

Tennek spat on the ground. "You are a fool. We cannot talk to trees."

"No, we can't, not you or I," the *laru telaka* said. "Nor can any man, as far as I know. But there are others who might be able to. Aren't there?" Now he cast a look at Nesharu.

For a long moment her wrinkled face was thoughtful. "It is so," she said at last. "If a woman is very strong in the *wayru,* it is possible for her to hear the voices of the trees, and even to speak to them in turn. So it has always been, since the first people."

The others gasped as they stared at her.

"That is why you would watch us when we would hunt in the edges of the forest in winter," Tennek said, wonder on his brown face. "You were asking the trees not to harm us."

Nesharu gave her head a firm shake. "No, I was only watching them, for I could tell the difference between a branch moving in the wind, and when it was moving of itself."

"Then you cannot communicate with the trees?" the tall man said.

"Ulanni, who taught me of the *wayru,* could speak with them. I saw her do it. And when I was younger, I sometimes thought I could understand a little of what they were saying as well. Only now . . ." Her thin shoulders moved in a sigh. "Now I am old, and I hear only the rustling of leaves."

The man frowned. "Then our hope grows weak. But what of the woman who will be the next among you to practice the *wayru?* You must have chosen one to teach your ways before you pass."

Nesharu said nothing, but her gaze flicked toward Layka.

Layka felt a pang in her stomach. She had always enjoyed the things they talked of when they walked together, the ways of stars and animals and plants, but she had never guessed that there had been more to it—that all the while Nesharu was teaching her of the *wayru*. Now, looking at the older woman's expression, there could be no doubting it.

The tall man stood before Layka and laid large hands on her shoulders.

"What is your name?"

"Layka," she said, barely above a whisper.

"Listen to the trees," he said. "Listen hard, and tell me if you can hear their voices. Do you understand what the forest is saying?"

Scared, Layka could only gape at him.

"It is all right, child," Nesharu said gently behind her. "Answer him."

At last, Layka managed to nod. "They are frightened. And angry, too. They know something is happening, something bad. They want to fight against it, to protect themselves, but they don't know what it is."

"Then you will be the one to tell them," the man said, smiling down at her with white teeth as he squeezed her shoulders. "You will teach the trees that it is the shadows that must be fought."

Layka felt a warmth rush through her, and even had the crimson light of the moon not bathed her, still her cheeks would have showed red.

"Come," the man said, taking her arm. "There is no time."

The pale woman was already leading the way to the forest. The man walked after her, and the rest of the people followed. As they went, Layka fell in beside Nesharu, who leaned heavily on her staff, walking as quickly as her thin legs allowed.

"Nesharu, I don't know what to do," she whispered as loud as she dared. "I don't know the *wayru*."

"Yes, you do, Layka. I have not yet shown you all that I know, but I have taught you much. And even if I had taught you nothing, it does not matter. You can hear the voices of the trees. You can speak to them, just as the *laru telaka* says."

Layka swallowed hard. "Have you always known I could hear them?"

"I wondered. I watched you when you were younger, in springtime as we left the cave, or in autumn when we returned. I saw the way you looked at the trees, and I thought that perhaps you could hear them." Now she gave Layka a gap-toothed smile. "And I am not surprised. You are strong in the *wayru*—even stronger than Ulanni before me was. That is one thing I do know."

Despite the stone of fear in her stomach, Layka felt an excitement as well. She would not have to string shells in a necklace to make herself pretty. If she became a wise woman, she could choose any man she wished—or choose none at all, like Nesharu. No one told a wise woman what to do.

Then her excitement ebbed, and fear crested again as someone let out a cry. She looked back over her shoulder, and it seemed to her that the night had grown thicker to the north. There was a sharp line upon the land marking the border where the light of the red moon and the stars ceased to fall. Beyond was only blackness.

She thought perhaps it was the shadow of a cloud, but when she looked up she saw that the sky was clear. Then she looked back down, and the line was closer than a moment ago. Even as she watched, it moved past the rocky slope of the cave, flowing over the land like a black tide.

"Run!" the tall stranger called out, but there was no need. The people were already fleeing toward the forest.

"They are coming too quickly," the pale woman said, seeming to appear out of the night before Layka.

"I will do what I can to slow them," the tall man replied. "Guard Layka. She must reach the forest."

The woman nodded, her black eyes glinting in the red light. "Come with me," she said, seizing Layka's hand.

Layka gasped, for the woman's hand was as hard as polished

antler. But there was no resisting her pull, and Layka staggered after her, struggling to keep up.

After a moment, Layka managed to cast a look over her shoulder. The rest of the people were just behind her. Tennek and another young hunter were helping Nesharu, half-carrying the old woman between them as they ran. Behind them, the *laru telaka* had come to a halt. His back was to the people, and his hands were raised above him. He was shouting something in a strange language so sharp and harsh that it cut at Layka's ears.

She was forced to look ahead as the pale woman jerked her arm painfully, pulling her up an embankment. When Layka managed to look over her shoulder again, wonder and dread filled her. The tall man's hands blazed with red light, and a gap had opened in the ground before him. Quickly, the gap grew wider, its edges glittering red, creating an expanding emptiness like a coal burning a hole in the hide wall of a hut.

Only the rift in the ground wasn't empty, Layka realized. Instead, she could see stars within it, as well as the purple crescent of an unfamiliar moon. It was like a black lake reflecting some sky other than the one above them. The dark flood pouring across the land reached the edge of the chasm, then broke apart. Layka thought she saw a few black droplets spill into the void, but most flowed to either side, then began to pass around it. The rift had slowed the shadows, but it had not stopped them.

Another painful jerk on Layka's arm heaved her to the top of the embankment. Gray trunks stood in a line before her. They were nearly to the forest. Then, even as they crossed the last few paces, she saw a flutter of darkness to her left.

By the time Layka realized what was happening, the pale woman was already in motion. Like some strange white cat, she leaped past Layka and fell into a crouch. Three black tendrils slithered toward her across the ground like thick snakes.

One of the dark tendrils lifted itself up from the ground, rapidly expanding into a new shape. Multiple arms uncoiled from an amorphous body, making Layka think of an octopus she had once seen stranded in a tide pool. Only each of these arms ended in seven sharp claws. A maw split open to reveal a mouth full of jagged teeth. They gleamed in the light of the red moon as if they had already tasted blood.

The thing lunged, and Layka felt a scream rise in her throat. At the same time the pale woman sprang forward. Somehow she spun between the arms, avoiding them as they writhed and coiled, then slipped behind the dark form and circled a white arm around it, just below its widening gullet. Her own mouth opened in what seemed an expression of delight as she gave a brutal twist.

There was an awful cry like none ever made by animal or person—a keening that stabbed at Layka's skull. Then the sound was cut short as the thing's mouth snapped shut. It did not fall, but rather seemed to pour onto the ground, glistening there like a dark puddle.

"Go on!" spoke a deep voice.

Layka looked up to see the tall stranger beside her.

"Get to the trees. She will take care of the other two."

She started to turn, to look again at the *sar valak,* but the man laid a hand against her back, propelling her before him. She ran the last few steps, and then she was at the ragged line of trees that marked the beginning of the great forest. Such was her speed that she was unable to stop in time, and she stumbled forward. Her arms went out before her, and her hands slapped against rough bark.

Layka had seen the forest before, had gathered fallen wood near its fringes, but she had never been this close, had never touched one of the trees. The roar of the waving branches surrounded her, buoying her as if she were adrift in a green sea. Only she wasn't afraid. Instead, a fierce joy rushed through her.

Yes, she could hear their voices amid the roar, could understand their words. Only it was more than that. She could feel what they felt, just as she knew they could feel *her.* Branches bent down, surrounding her, and leaves brushed against her arms, her face. A strength coursed through her, as if she had sent her own roots deep into the ground. Layka tightened her arms around the trunk of the tree.

They knew something was wrong. The sunlight did not come when it should. Their leaves withered in the too-long days and froze in the cold of nights that did not end when they should have. The way of all things had been changed, they could feel it, but they did not know why.

Creatures came toward them upon two legs—the stronger, hairier ones who sometimes carried sharp stones which bit into bark and pith. Were they the ones who had brought about these changes? If so, the trees would rend them into pieces. . . .

"No, they are not the ones!" Layka cried out. She had almost become lost in the ocean of sound. Now she drew in a ragged breath, as if surfacing after long submersion. "Please, don't hurt them!"

The roar of the trees dulled a bit, and their branches drooped.

"Tell them it is the shadows they must fear!"

Layka looked back. The tall man stood a short distance away, his blue eyes intent upon her. Behind him, the people were coming up the slope, along with the pale woman. The three shadows were nowhere to be seen, but the rest of them had flowed around the rift in the ground. The first edges of the dark flood lapped at the foot of the embankment.

"Tell them it is the *gol-yagru* and their masters, the Ashen, who have brought this change upon the world. It is they whom the trees must fight."

Layka turned back, pressing her cheek against the rough bark. *The people will not harm you.* She thought rather than spoke the words. *They flee the shadows. It is the shadows that have changed the world—the gol-yagru and the Ashen. They come from the red moon. You must let the people pass. And you must stop the shadows.*

When she opened her eyes and looked up, she felt a cool wetness on her cheeks. She was weeping. Behind her, she heard the cries of her people. And the shadows came.

"Please!" Layka called out, raising her arms. "Please listen to me!"

And the forest did.

The trunks seemed to shift, opening a way like a mouth leading into a deep green cave. Crying out, the people fled within. Last of all came Nesharu, helped by Tennek and the other hunter. They stumbled into the gap in the trees.

Then a dark wave crashed up and over the top of the embankment. Wet arms uncoiled, and gullets widened. There was another being among them, tall and slender, the color of ashes. A mouth lined with countless pointed teeth grinned in its eyeless face. Layka screamed.

Suddenly the ground fell away from her. Confused, she looked down between her feet to see the shadows flow over the place where she had been standing a moment ago. Then she felt the green tendrils tighten around her waist—securely, but not so tight as to cause pain—as the branches bore her up to the tops of the trees.

From this vantage, all was clear. Dread gave way to fascination as Layka watched the first shadows reach the forest. Their glistening arms stretched out, probing for the people huddled behind the trunks.

The effort was futile. The reach of the trees was longer and swifter. Limbs whipped downward, seeming to grow as they did, striking the shadows and flinging them back. At the same time, roots burst upward from the soil, tangling around the dark forms.

More shadows came, and more, but the fury of the trees was ceaseless. Branches beat at the shadows until they began to fray like the edges of an old hide. Roots squeezed the shadows and pulled at them until they fell to pulp like rotted fruit. And all the while a great creaking and groaning and snapping filled the air.

Then another noise reached Layka's ears—the sound of strange, harsh words. She looked down and saw the pale woman moving in a swift circle, her arms and legs lashing out so quickly that they were difficult to see, destroying anything that drew close. A small island formed in the roiling black sea. The magician stood in its center, his hands afire.

As he chanted, the starry rift in the ground expanded behind the shadows, driving them toward the forest. Those that did not go forward were swallowed by the rift. Those that did were crushed and torn by the limbs and roots of the trees. Layka saw one of the slender gray beings fall into the gap, its mouth open in a soundless cry as it plummeted toward the stars below.

Then it was over. The magician lowered his arms, and the rift in the ground slammed shut. At the same time, the roar of the trees dwindled to a murmur. Of the shadows, there was no sign except for dark stains that seeped into the soil. The branches that held Layka curved downward. They set her upon the ground, then bent back up.

Before her, the magician leaned upon the arm of the pale woman. His face was drawn in a grimace, and the woman looked at him with an expression of worry. She said something that Layka could not hear.

"It is of no concern," he answered her. "I will soon have another better one to replace it." Then he raised his head and looked at Layka.

Now the grimace on his handsome face was replaced by a broad smile, and Layka felt a different kind of excitement in her chest.

"We did it," she said, rushing toward him. "The shadows are all gone."

"These ones at least. More will come—many more. But now these trees know to fight them when they do. You did well, Layka. Very well." He reached out and touched her cheek.

His hand was large, but its touch was surprisingly soft. After a moment, Layka ducked her head. "I must go to Nesharu," she said. "I must see if she and the others are well."

"No, there is one more thing we must do," he said, his voice stern. "Naiani—my White Thorn—will see that your people are safe. But you must come with me. Quickly, now."

He glanced at the pale woman. She met his gaze, then nodded and passed into the gap in the trees where the people had gone.

Layka wanted to follow after her, to see Nesharu and tell her what it was like to speak to the trees. Even now Layka could hear them, though their voices had settled into a whisper. They were pleased. Now they knew what it was they must do, what it was they must fight. No *gol-yagru*, no Ashen-thing, would ever be allowed to pass the edges of the forest. Layka could not help feeling pleasure herself as their satisfaction thrummed in her.

Then the magician took her hand, enfolding it within his own, and it was a different kind of pleasure that fluttered in her chest. How tall he was, and how brilliant his blue eyes.

"Come." He led her away from the trees, and she did not resist.

It was easy to find their way in the red moonlight. They hurried up the stony slope toward the mouth of the cave. As they entered, Layka detected a faint rotten scent on the air, probably from some animal that had perished in there during the years the people were away. The crimson stone still glowed within the fire ring, filling the cave with ruddy light.

The man glanced out the mouth of the cave, then turned toward her. "It might be good to wait until we fight off more of the Ashen, to be certain you are capable of bearing it." He shook his head. "But no, it has already taken me too much time to find you. I cannot wait any longer."

Layka didn't understand these words, but the idea that he had been searching for her gave her a thrill. As a wise woman, one strong in the *wayru*, it would be up to her to name the man who would be her mate.

"But I don't know your name yet," she said.

"I am called Myrrgon."

"Myrrgon," she repeated the strange name.

He lifted his hand, touching her cheek with a thumb. "You were very brave tonight, Layka," he said, his voice low. "But you will have to be braver still. This was but the first of them. Even now, as their world draws close, they are constructing more gates. This night will be long—longer than any you have ever known. But this will not end in a night, or even a year. You must keep teaching the trees to fight the shadows, just as you did."

This idea was terrifying. But then Layka thought of the way she had felt when she spoke with the trees, and she realized she was excited as well.

"Will you be with me?" she said.

"I will."

She pressed her own hand over his. "Then I am not afraid."

He smiled, his teeth white and straight. "Yes, I understand now how Gauldren did this."

Layka did not comprehend these words, but she quickly forgot them as he removed the gray wolf fur from his broad shoulders and spread it upon the floor of the cave. His bare chest gleamed in the crimson light. Having dwelled in a tiny hut with her parents all her life, it was no mystery to Layka what men and women did beneath the furs. Nor was she in any way afraid—though her heart had quickened all the same.

His hands were gentle as they stroked her hair, her throat, her shoulders. Then they became strong as they lowered her onto the wolf pelt. He laid himself down beside her. Their leathers had fallen aside, and she could see he was ready. As was she.

"Layka," he said, and her name seemed beautiful from his lips "Through you, I will truly live again."

Once again she did not understand his words, but it did not matter. All that mattered was his touch upon her body. His fingers roved over her breasts, her stomach, and below.

"There will be a pain," he murmured in her ear. "But only a little."

It was so. But it was a joy as well. Their limbs entwined around one another, like the coiling branches of trees. She cried out his name. And as their bodies became one, Layka knew that they were making a child this night.

That they were making a son.

CHAPTER TWO

IVY KNEW AT ONCE that something was terribly wrong.

She pushed herself up against the pillows, then groped a hand toward the nightstand, fumbling with the brass shield that covered the candle. The shield fell aside with a clatter, and a gold illumination welled forth.

At first she thought the commotion would wake Mr. Quent, but then the light burned away some of the fog in her brain and Ivy recalled that he was not in the city at present. He had gone to County Engeldon south of Invarel to meet with several of the inquirers and hear their reports regarding the state of the Wyrdwood in that part of Altania.

When Mr. Quent first made these arrangements, the intention was that Ivy would accompany him. She had not been out of the city since the events at the Evengrove several months ago, and a longing had been steadily growing in her to see clear skies and fields and—perhaps from a distance—feathery trees standing behind old stone walls.

There had been no opportunity for such a sojourn previously, as the destinations to which Mr. Quent's work took him were not usually the sort of places that one would go for a holiday. It was the matter of the Wyrdwood that occupied the inquirers, and—other than the Evengrove—the majority of the remaining stands of Old Trees were in the north and west of Altania. And these were precisely the parts of the country that were in the greatest upheaval at present. It was hardly safe enough for Mr. Quent to make the journey in the company of soldiers, let alone take his wife along with him.

Ivy did not know if it was strictly necessary for Mr. Quent to travel to County Engeldon, or if she had done a poor job of concealing her longing for a trip to the country. Either way, she had been delighted when Mr. Quent had proposed the excursion, and she had quickly agreed to the plan. Not only would it be an opportunity to see the countryside, but there was a chance they would be able to call on Mr. Rafferdy—or Lord Rafferdy, as he was now known to everyone else. His manor, Asterlane, was located in County Engeldon, and Ivy knew he went there when time allowed to make a survey of his estate—and, she presumed, to remove himself as far as possible from Assembly, where he sat in the Hall of Magnates. Given the grim affairs that consumed the nation at present, frequent respites from the workings of the government were likely a necessity.

Arrangements for the trip were soon made. Ivy wrote to Mr. Rafferdy, who replied that he would make it a point to be in Asterlane while they were in the vicinity. Mr. Quent agreed that this was excellent news, and a pleasant anxiousness filled Ivy as the day approached.

At the same time, however, a different sort of anxiousness arose. A regular event did not occur at its usual time. A quarter month passed, a half month and more, and still things did not proceed as expected. In addition, Ivy had begun to find it increasingly difficult to rise after sleep, and she was often gripped by a violent illness when she did.

By the time a doctor was summoned, few in the household had any doubt what the diagnosis would be—and indeed, his declaration that Ivy was now afflicted with a most tender and precarious condition was greeted with little surprise, though much interest. The doctor at once restricted her to the house and grounds for the majority of her time, with no more than one brief outing per day. And even that was to be discouraged, for she was to have only rest and quiet until she was well again.

A trip to the country, of course, was out of the question.

"He speaks as if I have contracted some grave malady!" Ivy had exclaimed after the doctor departed. "I am sure I am able to go to the country. Despite what some might say, it is all perfectly natural. It is not as if I am actually ill."

"I don't know, Ivy," Lily said as she played a mournful air on the pianoforte. "I thought you looked rather green this morning."

Ivy frowned at her youngest sister, though she could not deny she had felt rather poorly that morning.

Rose shook her head. "No, she's not just green anymore. There's a spark of gold to her now."

Ivy was curious at these words. It was not the first time her middle sister had mentioned seeing a light around Ivy, or around others. But before she could ask Rose about it, Mr. Quent said that he would stand by the doctor's prescription. Ivy would not accompany him to the country. Nor, by the look on his craggy visage, would he accept any argument on the matter.

"Do not be forlorn," he had said after her sisters departed the parlor. "Will not any disappointment you feel now be more than offset by the great happiness we will enjoy some months from now?"

Ivy could only concede it was true, and had kissed his bearded cheek. "But do not hold me so lightly," she admonished. "I have not become suddenly fragile. You will not break me!"

So encouraged, he enclosed her within his strong arms, and her disappointment was thus ameliorated.

A half month later, she was less sanguine when it came time for him to depart for the south. For his sake, though, she kept her expression brave.

"Be careful," she told him. "And do not feel you must interrupt your labors to return with great haste."

"On the contrary, I will be as brief as possible," he said, his brown eyes sober. "Indeed, I would not leave at all had Dr. Lawrent not recently arrived."

Dr. Lawrent was an acquaintance of his from County Westmorain, who had been a frequent visitor at Heathcrest Hall during the years when Mr. Quent resided there with the first Mrs. Quent. When Dr. Lawrent wrote that he was coming to the city to perform some work at the university, at Carwick College, Mr. Quent had invited him to take up residence at the house on Durrow Street during his tenure in the city.

"I am sure I will have no cause to disturb Dr. Lawrent and distract him from his research," she had said, "but he is very welcome here, and if it eases your mind, then I am doubly glad for his presence."

So Mr. Quent had departed again, and the quarter month that followed passed without incident—save for those that were reported in the broadsheets, which every day had another story of some violence perpetrated by rebels on the border with Torland, or up in Northaltia.

Yet distressing as these events were, they were far from Invarel. And while shortages of various goods had led to raised prices as well as tempers, the government had taken matters firmly in hand. Affairs in the city proceeded generally as they always had—as long as one made an exception for the many companies of soldiers that patrolled the streets, and which were gathered in great numbers around the Halls of Assembly and the Citadel.

Having a guest each evening at the supper table was not only diverting, but helped Ivy to bear Mr. Quent's absence—especially as Dr. Lawrent was able to provide interesting conversation regarding his work at the university. His research concerned the methods by which traits might be inherited between generations of animals, and Ivy was always eager to listen to him describe his theories. Though, given Lily's frequent sighs or Rose's yawns, Ivy was perhaps alone in this. What was more, Dr. Lawrent had been able to concoct a restorative for Ivy that did much to alleviate the sickness she felt upon rising. Save for the lack of Mr. Quent's company, the time passed in a pleasantly unremarkable manner.

Until she began having the dream.

It had started several nights ago, when she woke in the middle of an umbral from a dream that was unusually vivid. Yet even as she attempted to recollect the events of the dream it seemed to break apart, like a tattered letter that fell to pieces even as one tried to unfold it. She thought she remembered looking for shells along the seashore, and then huddling in some cold, dark place. That was all.

The next lumenal turned out to be long—not that this was a fact which any almanac had predicted. The new planet, Cerephus, had fundamentally altered the movements of the celestial spheres. As a result, the once infallible timetables in the almanac were now all in error—unlike the old rosewood clock on the mantelpiece in the library, which somehow kept perfect time no matter how wildly variable the umbrals and lumenals were.

In the light of that long day, Ivy quickly forgot about the peculiar dream. Fifteen hours later, when it became obvious that weariness would overcome them long before the sun set, they shut the curtains to make the house dark. This caused it to become hot and stuffy as well, but Ivy laid down, eventually falling into a fitful sleep.

And the dream came again. When she woke, a cool night had finally fallen, and she remembered more than she had the last time. She had been with other people who wore not silks and satins, but garb made of animal skins, walking across the land away from the shore. She remembered looking up at the sky and seeing the red spot of Cerephus. Only it was larger than she had ever seen it—a crimson circle as big as the moon.

Each time Ivy slept over those next lumenals and umbrals, she found herself caught in the same dream. And each time she recollected more and more upon waking. While she did not remember everything, what she did recall was peculiarly clear, as if she had really been present. She remembered the soft feel of the doeskin she wore, the smoothness of the shells in her hand. The dark space she and the others huddled inside was a cave. They had gone there to flee from something.

Only from what? Ivy couldn't remember, except that it was something terrible. And even as her recollections of the dream grew more detailed, so too a sense of foreboding grew within her. What was the source of her apprehension, she could not say, but it seemed to draw ever closer. Now, as the light of the candle sent the shadows scurrying to the corners of the bedchamber, a veil of dread draped itself over Ivy. Something awful was going to happen.

Or had it already?

She thought back, trying to recall the dream. It had progressed further this time—or perhaps it was simply that she had remembered more of it. She recalled the face of a woman, preternaturally white, and a man with blue eyes who wore a silver fur. And she remembered the way a darkness closed in around them like a black flood.

Only suddenly the darkness was gone, and she was back in the cave with the blue-eyed man. Something had happened there, something that mattered for some reason. It was important that she didn't forget it. Only . . . what was it? Ivy tried to will her sleep-muddled brain to think. A memory began to come back to her, a memory of joyousness and of—

—pain. Violent pain coursed through Ivy, piercing deep. Shocked by the suddenness and severity of the spasm, her back arched away from the pillows and she let out a cry. At the same moment, the door of her bedchamber flew open.

"Great Gods, Ivy, what's going on?" Lily exclaimed. She stood in the open doorway in her night robe, the pretty oval of her face lit by the wavering candle in her hand. "I heard you give a great shout. I wasn't sleeping, as I'm reading a very horrid book, but I'm sure the noise would have woken me even if I had been asleep."

The pain fogged Ivy's brain. Lily's bedchamber was at the opposite end of the corridor from Ivy and Mr. Quent's. "How did you get here so quickly?"

"It wasn't so very quick," Lily said. "It took me a minute to put on my robe. But you gave another shout just as I reached your door. What is it? Were you reading a particularly horrid scene yourself?"

Ivy held a hand to her brow; it was damp with perspiration. "It was . . . I was having a dream."

"A nightmare is more like it," Lily said, and frowned. "But I say, you look very queer. Are you all right?"

Ivy shook her head. "I don't know. I woke up and—" She grimaced as another spasm convulsed her.

Now Lily's expression grew worried. She hurried across the room and set down her candle on the nightstand. "What is it, Ivy?"

Ivy drew a tight breath. "I think something's wrong."

"It's your light," spoke a soft voice.

They both looked up to see Rose in the doorway, clad in a pink robe. Her soft brown eyes were wide.

"Her light?" Lily said. "What in the world are you talking about, Rose? There are only the candles."

Foreboding filled Ivy anew. Pushing herself up in bed, she threw back the covers. And all three of them stared at the dark spot that was slowly spreading across the white fabric of her nightgown.

"There was a spark of gold in your light before," Rose said, her voice barely a whisper. "Only now it's green again. Just green."

Ivy felt a terrible wrenching inside. She let out a gasp, then looked at their youngest sister.

"Lily, go find Mrs. Seenly. Tell her to bring Dr. Lawrent at once."

IT WAS LATE in the long afternoon, and little beams of sunlight darted among the leaves of the ash tree outside the window to dapple the room when Dr. Lawrent came once more to see how his patient was faring.

"I am sorry to have to disturb you yet again, Lady Quent," he said as Mrs. Seenly let him in. "However, as I mentioned earlier, in cases such as this it is important to make sure the loss of blood does not resume."

"Of course," Ivy said, pushing herself up against the pillows. "You must not be concerned, Dr. Lawrent."

"On the contrary, it is my business to be concerned. And I will be so until it is clear that you are perfectly well."

Dr. Lawrent was somewhat older than Mr. Quent. He was a

small, neatly kept man with a pointed silver beard and clear gray eyes. These now peered at Ivy over a pair of spectacles that were perched improbably on the end of his nose.

"I will leave you to speak privately," Mrs. Seenly said. Usually the housekeeper's ruddy face was open and cheerful, but today it was drawn in tight lines.

The door shut, leaving Ivy and the doctor alone. Her sisters had sat with her through the night and for much of that day, valiantly stifling their yawns toward the end. At last Ivy had convinced them to go to their rooms, and she hoped they were still asleep.

"How are you feeling?" Dr. Lawrent asked.

It seemed impossible, but physically Ivy felt much improved. The pain she had suffered last night was gone. She felt tired, but that was all. And the pain was not the only thing that had vanished. The sense of foreboding that had haunted her over the past few days had departed as well. What weighed upon her now was not a dread of some vague and awful thing. Rather, it was an all too comprehensible sorrow.

"I am well," she said. "There have been no more—that is, the discomfort is gone entirely."

He reached out his hands, then hesitated. "May I?"

She nodded, and with gentle motions he laid aside the clean white coverlet and placed his hands on her robe. He probed with precise, gentle motions, then withdrew his hands and replaced the coverlet.

"I believe the spasms have indeed ceased," he said, leaning back. "We must remain vigilant these next few days, of course. But seeing how rapidly you have progressed, I predict that you will make a swift recovery."

Tears stung her eyes. It seemed wrong that she should suffer so few consequences from what had occurred. How resilient was the body, to return to its prior form so quickly! Yet the mind was formed of a less pliable substance. The emptiness in her thoughts would not be so easily filled. Instead there was a hollowness among them—a place she had reserved for future joys which now would never arrive.

"That is good news, Dr. Lawrent" was all she could manage.

He laid his hand over hers on the coverlet and gave it a fatherly pat. Then, as was his habit, he gazed at her past the rims of his spectacles. In fact, so seldom did he actually look through the lenses that she had begun to think he wore the spectacles not out of any need, but simply so he could peer over them for effect.

"I know it can provide you little comfort now, Lady Quent, but you can have every reason to expect to be a mother in the future. You are very young and in excellent health."

She gave a hesitant nod. "But is it not possible that, under similar circumstances, a similar result may occur?"

"There is always a possibility. Nature is far from perfect in its workings, but it makes up for this with a remarkable persistence. And sometimes it can astonish us. Your own mother, Mrs. Lockwell, is proof of that. I examined her myself once, and I was quite convinced she would never be able to realize her wish to have another child after her first was taken from her. So I was very glad when you were brought into the household. Then, hardly a year later, your sister Roslend is born, and Liliauda two years after that. It was as if a capability that had lain dormant within Mrs. Lockwell was suddenly awakened by having a child about." He paused for a moment. "Or more specifically, by having *you* about."

Ivy sat up a little more in bed. What did Dr. Lawrent mean? She had always supposed it was simply due to luck that her mother finally had another child of her own. But what if there was a reason for it, a cause? Ivy thought of the little hawthorn and chestnut trees in the garden. Her father had planted the seeds after gleaning them from the edges of the Wyrdwood, but they had not sprouted and grown—not until Ivy came to the house. Perhaps her presence here had influenced another sort of seed to take root and grow as well, and Rose and Lily were the result.

But if that was so, then why had Ivy herself not been able to nurture the life that had been growing within her?

"So you see, you have no cause to abandon hope," Dr. Lawrent went on. "Occurrences such as this are actually quite common. And in this particular case, I suppose it was even to be ex—"

Abruptly he shook his head and looked away. Ivy wished he had not curtailed his speech. His words had enflamed the inquisitive spark that was a constant part of her being. Even now, when her heart felt broken, her mind continued along its usual course of curiosity.

"What were you going to say, Dr. Lawrent? Does it have something to do with your research?"

He looked back at her, his gray eyes startled. "I can't imagine you want to discuss my research right now, Lady Quent."

On the contrary, she had been confined to her bed all day, with nothing to do for endless hours but contemplate what she had lost. Right then, she wished for any sort of distraction.

"Please, I would very much like to know," she said earnestly. "You said nature continues to try when it does not at first find success. Does that relate to your work at the university? I can see how it might affect the manner in which traits are passed from a creature to its offspring."

He raised an eyebrow. "Sir Quent informed me that you possessed a scientific mind, and I see that he was right. That is an astute observation, Lady Quent. Yes, the persistence of nature indeed plays a part—though not so much in the manner in which these traits are inherited by offspring, but rather with the overall effect they can have over time."

Now that Dr. Lawrent was speaking of his work, his worries about disturbing her seemed to ease, and he went on with greater enthusiasm. While the exact mechanisms by which certain characteristics were passed from one generation to the next were not understood, he explained, what was known was the particulate properties of such traits, and how a characteristic could be passed from one parent wholly, and without dilution.

"For example, a white cat and a black cat do not necessarily produce gray kittens," he said. "Rather, their offspring may be entirely black or entirely white themselves."

As if sensing the topic of conversation, Miss Mew padded into the room. Evidently, Mrs. Seenly had not latched the door, and the little tortoiseshell cat had pushed it open with her nose. She hopped up onto the windowsill to look outside.

"That's all very interesting," Ivy said, and meant it, "but I'm not certain I see what that has to do with the persistence of nature."

"Why, it has everything to do with it! Because of the particulate nature of inheritance, a unique characteristic which arises by chance in a parent may be passed to its offspring. Thus, over time, a number of variants can accumulate in a population. And naturalists have observed, those species which display the most variation in form and shape are also those which are best able to survive disruption in the environment in which they live."

Ivy began to think she understood. "It's like drawing cards from a deck. The more cards you are able to draw, the better chance you have of finding one to help you win the current hand."

"Precisely! With a wide variety of types, it is more likely that—if some tragedy befalls, or the world about them changes—there will be at least some individuals able to survive under the new conditions. So, through this inherited variability, a species' chances of enduring are improved."

This idea was fascinating, but Ivy felt she was still missing something. "Yet why do such important variations arise in the first place? If they arise by chance, it seems they are as likely to have a negative effect upon the creature who gains them, or no effect at all. After all, it is just as probable that I will draw a card that doesn't help my hand a bit."

"Your mind is quick to seize upon the heart of a matter, Lady Quent," he said with an approving nod. "A variation that curtails a creature's ability to thrive and reach maturity has little chance of being passed on to its offspring. However, those variations that confer neither harm nor benefit can easily linger within a population. And if circumstances were to suddenly change"—he gave a shrug and smiled—"well, you never know when that card you had tucked in the corner of your hand suddenly trumps all others."

Ivy felt a familiar, pleasant humming as her mind worked

through these ideas. It was a curious but compelling notion that a creature might have heretofore unobserved features or abilities that remained hidden as they were passed from generation to generation, awaiting only the right event that would allow them to manifest themselves in some efficacious way.

By the window, Miss Mew began to lick at a paw, and at the same time another thought occurred to Ivy.

"What of those traits which can only be passed to some offspring?" she said. "Or more particularly, those traits that can only be passed to a male or female? I read once that tortoiseshell cats, like Miss Mew, are all girls."

Dr. Lawrent smiled at the little cat, who had turned her head at the sound of her name. "Another interesting question, Lady Quent. As I said, the mechanism by which traits are inherited is particulate, and it seems that some of these particles can be passed only to female offspring, while others go only to males. But as for the reason . . . I fear I do not know. Perhaps my research will someday give us a better understanding."

Ivy nodded, watching as Miss Mew resumed licking her paw, only it was not the color of cats that she was thinking of. Rather, it was magick. Only men could be magicians. And like Mr. Rafferdy, they were all of them thought to be descendants of one of the seven Old Houses.

Similarly, only women were ever witches, and it was a thing that seemed to run mother to daughter. The woman who bore Ivy—Merriel Addysen—was a descendant of Rowan Addysen, as were Halley Samonds and the first Mrs. Quent. And all of them had been witches. Did that mean magick and witchcraft were simply types of traits, like the color of fur? And if so, when and how had these traits arisen?

Before she could think of how to frame such a question, Dr. Lawrent rose from the chair. "We can speak again later, Lady Quent. For now, you should try to get some more rest."

The afternoon light that filtered into the room had turned a deeper gold. The long day was at last drawing on. And now that their scientific discussion had come to an end, Ivy found her spirits dimming in kind.

"Dr. Lawrent."

He paused by the door, his hand on the eagle-clawed knob.

Rather than look at him, she turned her head to gaze out the window at the waving branches of the ash tree. "It was a boy, was it not?"

The breath he drew was audible. "It was exceedingly small, Lady Quent. There had not been much time for it to form properly."

"But it was a boy," she said, now turning her head to look at him.

For a long moment he was motionless, then he nodded.

"I believe you are aware that I am a great-granddaughter of Rowan Addysen," she said.

"Yes, so Sir Quent told me. Though I confess, I would only have had to look at you, and to be told your origins are from County Westmorain, to know it for a fact. The first Mrs. Quent shared a similar heritage, and your features have much in common with hers."

So Ivy had been told. "You must have known her," she said.

He responded slowly, as if taking care in his answer. "Yes, I did. I saw her on several occasions when visiting Heathcrest Hall."

"And she was very much like me?"

Now he gave a soft laugh. "Like you? No, not at all. She had green eyes and fair hair, as you do, Lady Quent. But she was taller. And while you have a calm and serious intellect, I would say Gennivel's proclivities lay more in the direction of parties and dances and other such amusements. This is not to say she was frivolous, for she was also very accomplished in artistic endeavors, such as painting and music."

"So I was not like her after all," Ivy breathed, more to herself.

Dr. Lawrent gave her a solemn look over the wire rims of his spectacles. "If you have ever thought Sir Quent married you because you reminded him of her, then I think you are mistaken.

Rather, it was only when he met you that I think he was finally able to cease dwelling upon the past."

Ivy appreciated these words. It was reassuring to know that she was in fact different from the first Mrs. Quent. Yet there was still one characteristic that Ivy and Gennivel had in common—one which all witches shared. But how much did Dr. Lawrent know about that?

"I've heard it said in the county that there aren't many sons in the Addysen line," Ivy said.

He nodded. "I am given to understand there have only ever been a few male children born into that family. And they are often—"

He cut his words short, but Ivy knew what he meant. They were often similar to Mr. Samonds, the farrier in Cairnbridge. And while he was kind and handsome, he was not likely ever to marry or have a child himself. A pretty lady would never strike his affections that way.

"That is," the doctor went on after clearing his throat, "there seems to be a strong proclivity for women of that particular lineage to bear daughters rather than sons."

Ivy suffered a deep ache—though it was not the spasms returning. "Thank you, Doctor," she said quietly.

"Of course, Lady Quent. Please let me know if you have any need of me." Then he turned and left the room, shutting the door behind him.

Alone, Ivy leaned back against the pillows and watched the shadows of the branches weave upon the far wall. But if there was any meaning in the pattern made by the branches, it was beyond her understanding.

CHAPTER THREE

NOW WAS HIS MOMENT. Rafferdy gave his wig a quick tug to make certain it was set firmly upon his head. Then, before anyone else could claim the floor, he rose from his seat on one of the frontmost benches.

The High Speaker's gavel came down with a loud clatter. "The Hall recognizes Lord Rafferdy!"

Now that the floor was his, Rafferdy moved to take it as if he were in no great hurry, strolling to the front of the Hall of Magnates. Once there, he took the time to flick a wrinkle from his elegant robe of black crepe, plucked a stray thread from the sleeve, then proceeded to make a thorough examination of the state of his fingernails.

Sighs and mutters of impatience ran around the benches, but still Rafferdy kept his attention fixed on his fingernails. The Hall was hot and stifling, for the lumenal had been exceedingly long—more than twenty-five hours at that point, and it was not over yet. Anticipating this, Rafferdy had dressed very lightly beneath his robe, and he had directed his man to sprinkle a large quantity of powder inside his wig to prevent any rivulets of perspiration that might otherwise trickle down his brow. As a result, while many of the lords were boiling in their robes and dabbing at red faces with damp handkerchiefs, Rafferdy at the least appeared cool.

He waited for the sounds in the Hall to rise into a cacophony of cane thumping and calls of *Get on with it, sir!* All at once, as if suddenly recalling where he stood, Rafferdy looked up.

"Gentlemen, it has been proposed and seconded that we begin debate upon the Act of Due Loyalty and Proper Regard for Our Glorious Nation of Altania."

Rafferdy pitched his voice in a lower range than was natural for him, keeping his shoulders back and the muscles of his midsection taut. As a result, his voice sounded relaxed and unstrained, yet it carried easily throughout the Hall. It was a trick his friend Eldyn Garritt had showed him the last time they met at tavern, after Rafferdy mentioned that his voice had been getting hoarse from speaking loud enough to be heard at Assembly.

How Garritt himself had come to learn this trick, and why a clerk might have any need to project his voice, were questions that had only occurred to Rafferdy after the fact. Then again, he had gotten the impression from the fashionable coat Garritt wore that he was no longer working as a scrivener and had found other, more lucrative, business. Rafferdy would be sure to ask him about it when they next met, and to thank him for the advice.

Now, as he spoke, the noise in the Hall subsided, and magnates leaned forward on the benches. As Rafferdy had discovered, if you made men wait to hear you speak, they were more likely to listen when you finally did.

"It occurs to me," he went on, "that there is no one better suited to tell us more about this act than the one who proposed we debate it. To that end, Lord Davarry, perhaps you would enlighten us regarding the particular benefits that would arise from this proposal were it made law."

The subject of this address was just retaking his seat, having been as slow to depart the floor as Rafferdy was to take it. So addressed, Davarry had a right to speak on the issue, and he appeared more than eager to make his appeal on someone else's time rather than his own. He rose at once from his seat among the other members of the Magisters party.

"Opening the matter for debate was merely a formality required by the protocols of the Hall, Lord Rafferdy. I should hardly think it requires any debate at all."

Lord Davarry was neither very tall nor very handsome, two features which cast him in stark contrast to the prior leader of the Magisters. All the same, his blue eyes reflected a keen intelligence that Rafferdy had witnessed in effect more than once on the floor of the Hall of Magnates. An altercation with Lord Davarry was not something to be engaged in lightly.

And Rafferdy was about to provoke one.

"Yet to cast our votes in good conscience, we must hear both the arguments for and against an act." Rafferdy spoke in a tone that implied this was the most obvious thing.

"Of course," Davarry agreed, even as he made a slight motion with a gloved hand as if to cast the idea aside. "In this case, though, I believe no rational mind could possibly conceive of an argument against the act. That it should be considered a crime for anyone to make public speeches, or authorize words to be printed, that cast our nation in an ill light, and thus undermine the authority of our government, is self-evident."

"It is?" Rafferdy said, raising an eyebrow.

"Indeed," Davarry went on indulgently. "As I am sure all present are aware, our nation is beset by enemies all around. They seek constantly to find a chink in our walls, to discover a way to attack us from within, and there are no better weapons they can use to this end than words. A bullet can fell a man, but words might accomplish something far worse. That is, they might arouse his sympathies and turn his mind to traitorous thoughts. You might as well pick up a gun and go fight for those rebels in Torland, who seek to make a beachhead upon our shores for Huntley Morden, as make public criticisms of Altania's government or sovereign Crown."

Rafferdy affected a confounded look. "Forgive me, Lord Davarry, but I have become confused. You see, I thought it has long been the purpose of the Hall of Magnates to offer public criticisms of the Crown. And as for not criticizing the remainder of the government—gentlemen, I remind you that we are the government. And I do not think I should be hauled off to the prisons below Barrowgate for observing how crookedly other lords might wear their wigs or noting how foolishly they bet their money while gambling with dice among the back benches. Rather, I consider insulting my fellow magnates to be a God-granted right, and one that cannot be revoked."

Laughter erupted around the Hall, along with several calls of *Hear! Hear!* Lord Davarry frowned, perhaps rethinking his eagerness to engage in debate on someone else's time.

"Besides," Rafferdy went on as the laughter died down but before Davarry could have a chance to go on the offensive himself, "isn't this matter already addressed in the Rules of Citizenship?"

Rafferdy gestured toward the sheet of paper posted on the wall behind him, which provided exhaustive direction for the correct behavior of proper citizens of the country. It was the same notice posted in every public shop and tavern and market square in the city. Indeed, so abundant were the printed notices throughout Invarel that people had begun to take them for use as kindling to start fires and to paste upon their walls to stop drafts—two habits which had recently been addressed by Rule Forty-Six: *No one shall make use of these printed Rules for any purpose other than posting in public for the education of the people.*

"I believe the Rules already clearly state that it is prohibited to speak about the Crown in an unfavorable manner," Rafferdy continued.

"Yes, that's so," Davarry replied slowly, as if reluctant to offer any sort of agreement. "Yet as I am sure all present know, the Rules of Citizenship are maintained by the Gray Conclave, under the authority of the Crown itself. And while the Crown may issue rules to clarify the enforcement of the laws of the nation, it cannot enact laws itself. That is a right reserved solely for Assembly under the Great Charter."

"For which we all thank our forebears for their wisdom," Rafferdy interjected. "But if the Gray Conclave already has the power to regulate the speaking habits of the public in an effort to enforce our existing laws, then what need have we of new laws? It seems a dreadful waste of paper, which I do not need to tell you is getting scarce and expensive these days."

Davarry's expression darkened, and in his narrowed eyes Rafferdy noted the first glimmerings of contempt.

"Yes, the Gray Conclave has the authority to investigate those who bring suspicion upon themselves with their speech," Davarry said, enunciating each word carefully. "And those investigated have sometimes been found to have engaged in treasonous activities, and so are sent to the gallows. But just as often no evidence of a crime is found, and the perpetrator is released. So they are free to roam the city again and speak ill of our nation."

"But shouldn't they be released if they haven't committed a crime?"

"That is precisely the point," Davarry said. "Speaking out against the Crown in a seditious manner should be considered a crime of High Treason in and of itself, regardless of what other treasonous activities might have been engaged in. Yet only Assembly can make the law to add such a crime to the rolls."

Rafferdy snapped his fingers. "I see! Very well, then, I propose an amendment to the act in question."

"An amendment?" Davarry said, clearly surprised. "For what end?"

"For funds enough to pay for a very large quantity of rope."

Now Davarry's surprise became a scowl. "That seems exceedingly frivolous. What could a quantity of rope be required for?"

"To fashion all the nooses that will be needed for all the necks here in the Hall of Magnates, of course," Rafferdy said pleasantly. "For which of us hasn't at some point spoken ill words about the actions of the Crown—statements which have all been clearly set down in the records of this very Hall? If those who criticize the government of Altania are all to be hung, Lord Davarry, then we will all of us here need to have our collars fitted for longer necks."

Again laughter went around the Hall, only there was a nervousness to the sound of it this time, and it died out quickly. No one was entirely certain whether Rafferdy was making a jest or not.

Davarry's face reddened a shade, perhaps realizing that he had allowed himself to be goaded into a misstep. "That is a poor joke, my lord. I speak of men who would diminish the authority of the Crown by their speech. What we discuss here in the Hall of Magnates is hardly the same thing!"

"Isn't it?" Rafferdy said, and now his voice and his expression were utterly serious. He looked not at his opponent, but rather out across the Hall. Lords shuffled on the benches as his gaze swept over them. "For I wonder, what is the difference between a lord who speaks out against a particular law and another man? If the only difference is a fine coat and wig . . . well, a lord looks much like any man when dressed in sackcloth and a noose."

Davarry appeared ready to issue a hot rejoinder to this, but he was perhaps saved from further damaging his cause by the loud noise of the High Speaker's gavel banging against the podium.

"The lord's time is expired!" the High Speaker called out. "The lord will remove himself from the floor and take his seat!"

With a bow, Rafferdy did.

"I say, that was really splendid!" Coulten whispered as Rafferdy returned to his seat.

"I'm not certain Lord Davarry would agree with you," Rafferdy whispered back, doing his best not to grin as he cast a glance in Davarry's direction.

That Davarry would see such an expression was assured. The place where the Magisters sat was not far away, for over the last few months Coulten and Rafferdy, along with some of the other younger lords, had migrated from the back of the Hall toward the front. They had taken to calling themselves the New Wigs, as they had all recently adopted Rafferdy's habit of wearing a wig to Assembly—though these were not to be confused with the matted mop-ends worn by old country lords. Rather, their wigs were simple yet elegantly styled affairs, and they had a silvery color to them, as opposed to the blue tint favored by the Magisters.

Speaking of whom, the Magisters were all of them glaring in Rafferdy's direction—something which gave him great delight.

"I almost couldn't believe it when Davarry snapped at the bait you'd thrown out," Coulten said under his breath as, at the front of the Hall, the Grand Usher began to drone on about some matter of protocol. "But he did, and now everyone's neck is itching as they imagine what a rope feels like. I don't suppose anyone will want to debate the act now."

Rafferdy sighed, his delight receding a bit. "Oh, they will eventually. Davarry won't let it go, and a lord is bound to forget about his neck if his arm is wrenched hard enough. But this will at least delay things. If nothing else, I've given them doubts about granting Lord Valhaine and his Gray Conclave any more authority than they already have."

"I should hope so," Coulten said. His nod was emphasized by the pillar of his wig, which had been constructed to dramatic proportions to contain the tall head of hair concealed beneath. "The Gray Conclave has too much prerogative as it is. Besides, I don't understand why Davarry should want to support Lord Valhaine. After all, it was on Valhaine's order that all secret magickal societies were banned. And we all know Davarry wears a House ring under his gloves like most of the Magisters."

Rafferdy's gaze shifted a few degrees, and now it was not at Davarry he gazed, but rather at a pale-haired man who sat just behind him. Even seated, the other lord was tall, though his shoulders were somewhat hunched inside the heavy, thickly ruffled black robe he wore despite the sweltering heat in the Hall. Unlike all the other Magisters, he did not wear gloves. Instead, his hands were bare except for, on the right, a ring set with red gems, which even at that moment he was turning around and around on his finger. Other than Rafferdy, he was the only man in the Hall who wore a House ring openly.

"Poor old Farrolbrook," Coulten murmured in Rafferdy's ear, having noticed the object of his attention. "I'm surprised the Magisters still let him sit with them. Though I suppose it would be an embarrassment for them to cast out one of their own, especially the man who had once been their leader. *They* could never publicly admit to a mistake. And I suppose he doesn't seem quite as mad as he did a few months ago. At least these days he has the sense to sit there and say nothing."

It seemed impossible, as Coulten's whisper had been very low, but just then Lord Farrolbrook looked up and turned his head in their direction, as if he had heard his name uttered. His blue eyes seemed overly bright, but they were otherwise clear.

Suddenly, the High Speaker's hammer clattered down three times, signaling the end of the session.

"Thank goodness, I thought this would never end," Coulten said, leaping to his feet, a hand on his wig to keep it steady. "Come on, Rafferdy, let's get to the Silver Branch before all the benches are gone."

"That's a capital idea," Rafferdy said, rising. "My throat is wretchedly dry after all that speaking. I am sure I will expire if I don't have a whiskey soon."

"Well, we can't have that," Coulten said cheerfully. "For if you expire, how can I win back the twenty gold regals I lost to you last night?"

And he seized Rafferdy's arm, towing him from the Hall.

THE TWO FOUND THEMSELVES in a great crush upon leaving, as the Hall of Citizens was letting out at the same time. Also, there was a sizable throng of people on Marble Street, as was usually the case these days. The people gathered near the foot of the steps that swept down from Assembly. The majority of them were ill clad and poorly washed, and they shouted and shook their fists as the members of Assembly came down the steps.

The particulars of their declarations were lost amid the cacophony of calls and yells, but from what snippets could be understood, their complaints mostly pertained to the exorbitant cost of food and candles, or the lack of decent work for men seeking employment in the city. Easier to make out were the insults, though the presence of a line of stern-faced soldiers made certain it was only words that were hurled toward those departing Assembly, and nothing more substantial.

Rafferdy and Coulten jostled their way down the steps, then climbed into one of the waiting carriages as the redcrests brandished rifles fitted with bayonets and kept the crowd at bay.

"They seem to grow more numerous and indignant each day," Coulten said as the driver shut the door. He took off his wig, which otherwise would have scraped the ceiling, and dabbed at his brow with a handkerchief. The carriage was like an oven inside, for the lumenal continued to stretch on. "I wonder why they keep letting such people into the city."

"They're fleeing the troubles in the Outlands," Rafferdy said, gazing out the window as the carriage started to roll down the street. "Where else can they go?"

"To Torland, I suppose."

Rafferdy gave him a sharp look. "And be conscripted to fight for Huntley Morden?"

"Better than to fight for him here, I should say."

Rafferdy looked again out the carriage window and noticed, for the first time, how a few of the men in the crowd wore green ribbons tied around the white sleeves of their shirts. The Morden crest, of course, was a green hawk set against a white field.

He shook his head. "I would think they risk attracting the notice of the Gray Conclave by wearing an infamous symbol so openly."

"That's a curious thing to hear coming from you, Rafferdy." Coulten gestured to the House ring in plain sight on Rafferdy's right hand. In contrast, Coulten's hands were covered by kidskin gloves.

Rafferdy looked at the blue stone set into his House ring. What did it matter if he wore it openly? Had he not already attracted the attention of Lady Shayde? And there was no one more prominent in the Gray Conclave than her—barring her master, Lord Valhaine, himself. No, there was no use covering it up now; it would only make him seem as if he had something to hide.

Which, of course, he did.

Rafferdy tightened his right hand into a fist, then pounded on the roof of the carriage. "Faster, man!" he cried out. "We are dying for whiskey in here!"

Fortunately, it was not far down Marble Street to the Silver Branch, and once free of the crowd before Assembly, the carriage proceeded swiftly to its destination. Rafferdy and Coulten disembarked and, passing the pair of black-liveried guards that stood at either side of the door, entered the tavern which for more than two hundred years had been frequented by members of Assembly following a session.

And it seemed half of Assembly was already here. Rafferdy surveyed the scene, searching for a space. The heavy beams overhead were stained from years of tobacco smoke, and the eponymous branch hung from the centermost beam. It was more of a club than a branch, really: a heavy scepter gilded in silver, which long ago had been granted as a symbol of honor to the man who, it was deemed, had won an important debate in Assembly.

These days the branch was bolted to the beam, having too often in the past become an all too real weapon—one which was used to crack skulls when arguments from Assembly were rekindled and made hotter by drink.

"Over there," Coulten said, pointing.

Several members of the New Wigs sat at the end of one of the tables, though like Rafferdy and Coulten they had removed their headpieces now that they were outside the Hall of Magnates. The young men waved and gestured to a pair of spaces they had reserved. Rafferdy waved back, and he and Coulten proceeded through the crowded tavern to join their companions.

They managed to catch a harried barkeep as he passed, seizing the bottle and cups from the tray he was carrying. The man began to protest that these were intended for the lords at another table, but his complaints were silenced by a half regal Coulten tossed on the tray, and so cups were filled and passed all around.

Rafferdy took a drink of his whiskey, then nearly choked upon it as he was subjected to a number of claps on the back. The other young men grinned, congratulating him on his work at Assembly that day. A few of them went so far as to propose they stand up on the table, wrench the silver branch from its the beam, and present it to Rafferdy as a tribute for putting Lord Davarry in his place.

To Rafferdy's relief, this stunt was not attempted. They returned to their seats, and soon the conversation turned to other topics—

namely, who owed whom from last night's game of dice. Rafferdy was allowed to drink his whiskey in peace, and he gave a sigh as he took a sip of the sweet, smoky liquid.

"Speaking of gambling, I'd wager we're not the only ones who believe you bested Davarry today," Coulten said, leaning to speak in Rafferdy's ear so he could be heard over the din in the tavern. "Though I'd say some would just as soon strike you with the branch as hand it to you."

Trying not to make a scene of it, Rafferdy glanced over the rim of his cup. After a moment he saw them: a group of younger Magisters, still in their bluish wigs, casting sour looks in his direction.

"Maybe they don't like the taste of their punch," Rafferdy said.

"Oh, they have a bad taste in their mouths, all right," Coulten said cheerfully. "You made their leader look a fool—though he certainly lent you some help in that regard."

Rafferdy raised his glass. "To Lord Davarry," he said, and drank.

Coulten drank in turn. "I still don't know why Davarry is so keen on that dreadful act," he said, setting down his empty cup. "When Rothard was king, all the Magisters did was work against him. But now that the king is deceased, they're all for shoring up royal authority." He scratched his head, causing the mass of his hair to rise higher yet. "It hardly makes sense. Why are they for the Crown all of a sudden? After all, it's not as if they'll let the princess put it on her head."

Coulten's nature was so naturally cheerful and guileless that Rafferdy sometimes forgot that he could often be clever. His companion had raised a valid question. Previously, the only party in the House of Magnates that had supported the ultimate authority of the Crown was the Stouts. In contrast, the Magisters had always argued for the primacy of Assembly's power.

Then two things had happened.

The first item was the dissolution of the Stouts. The violent murder of their leader, Lord Bastellon, followed shortly by the death of King Rothard, had dealt a similarly fatal blow to the Stouts. While it might have been expected they would rally together in their support of Princess Layle, this had not been the case. King Rothard's writ of succession had never been ratified, casting the entire matter of royal authority under a cloud of uncertainty.

A strong leader might have been able to galvanize the Stouts, but there was no one with Bastellon's weight (at least not figuratively) to take his place. With neither a leader to guide them nor a crowned monarch to rally around, the party quickly unraveled. Some of its members left to join other parties, while a number retired from Assembly altogether, for the Stouts had always contained a disproportionate number of elderly lords.

With the Stouts out of the way, it appeared there would be nothing to stop the Hall of Magnates, led by the Magisters, from asserting the authority of Assembly over that of the Crown. That was, until another event occurred—namely the death of Lord Mertrand.

Whether Rafferdy and Coulten had perhaps had something to do with this, Rafferdy was still not entirely certain. Following Lord Eubrey's death, Rafferdy and Coulten had quietly and anonymously spread rumors among the young men in the Hall of Magnates regarding Lord Mertrand and the occult order to which he belonged, the High Order of the Golden Door.

They did not reveal the horrible details they had learned: how Mertrand had recruited young men descended from the seven Old Houses and delivered them to the magician Mr. Gambrel (known to most as Lord Crayford), and how by means of awful magicks Gambrel turned them into gray men—lifeless shells that no longer housed a man's soul but rather daemonic entities. All they did was say they had heard whispers that Mertrand had used some young men for ill purposes, and that he was to be avoided at all costs.

Rafferdy did not know if these rumors had helped to bring suspicion upon Lord Mertrand. Regardless, it was soon reported in the broadsheets that he had been linked to the death of Lord Bastellon, and though he professed his innocence, he was to be tried by the Gray Conclave. Then, before the trial could commence, Mertrand was found dead in his house in the New Quarter. Or rather, some parts of him had been found, for his demise had reportedly been of a ghastly nature. The stories in the broadsheets claimed that he had been killed by an accident involving some magickal experiment.

Rafferdy guessed the broadsheets were right on one account: it was certainly magick that had caused Mertrand's death. That it was an accident was something Rafferdy considered far less likely. Mertrand could not have been the only lord involved in delivering young men to Mr. Gambrel for his awful purposes. Gambrel had promised Mertrand knowledge and power in exchange for having suitable young magicians brought to him, and no doubt there were other lords who had been similarly tempted by such a bargain. Fearing the suspicion Mertrand might cast their way, they had instead done away with him.

That was Rafferdy's conjecture on the matter, at least. But whatever the cause of Mertrand's death, it had left the Magisters without a leader. Lord Farrolbrook could no longer fulfill that role—that was obvious to all in the Hall of Magnates, given his increasingly erratic behavior. Thus it seemed the party would be thrown into disarray like the Stouts.

And then Lord Davarry stepped in.

This had astonished many in Assembly. Davarry was the lord of a prosperous but, it was said, unremarkable estate in eastern Altania. He was a member of the Magisters, but no one could recall any debate or the passage of any act or law in which he had been instrumental. Indeed, few could think of a time when they had seen him take the floor to speak.

But that was exactly what he did shortly after Mertrand's death. While he had seldom spoken prior to that, he must have observed things closely, for it soon became clear he was a genius at maneuvering among the labyrinthine rules and protocols of the Hall of Magnates. Indeed, he often found a way to bend them to his purpose. Thus, while the public face of their leadership had changed, the ability of the Magisters to form and direct debate in the Hall was as strong as ever.

Yet the direction of their arguments *had* changed since Lord Davarry ascended to the head of the party. As Coulten had observed, the Magisters had increasingly become proponents of royal authority. Under Lord Mertrand, they had refused to approve King Rothard's writ of succession that declared the princess as his true heir. Some had gone so far as to suggest it was dangerous in times such as these—when witches in the West Country had been known to induce the Wyrdwood to rise up—to have a woman sitting on the throne. But now, whenever Lord Valhaine requested more authority or broader reach for the Gray Conclave, all in the name of Princess Layle, the Magisters were first and loudest to support it.

What had caused the Magisters to change their views? Was it the princess herself? This seemed unlikely. After all, it was not as if the Magisters were clamoring to crown her. While the members of the Hall of Citizens and the majority of the people in the city were eager to have the princess formally take the throne, the Magisters seemed more than content to wait.

Of course, there had been little opportunity for a coronation as of yet. First, there had been the requisite period of mourning following King Rothard's death. And since then, the government had been faced with matters of more immediate need. Besides, Princess Layle was already the legal ruler of Altania. By law, she had become so the moment her father passed.

Yet she could not be crowned queen until the succession was formally acknowledged and ratified by both Halls of Assembly. The Hall of Citizens had already done so, but not the Hall of Magnates. And for all their recent support for royal authority, the Magisters had yet to allow the matter of formal succession to be brought to a debate.

But why was that the case?

Before he could think more on the matter, Coulten leaned over and brought his mouth close to Rafferdy's ear.

"It's almost time," he whispered.

Idly, as if he were merely bored, Rafferdy turned his head, surveying the tavern over the edge of his cup. Here and there he caught another's gaze, and each time he gave the slightest fraction of a nod. The others returned the gesture in a similar fashion.

Many of them were lords of middle years, and some even older. A few weren't lords at all, but instead were doctors or barristers who were members of the Hall of Citizens. Only two or three were younger lords like Coulten and Rafferdy, and none of the others were members of the New Wigs.

Which was precisely the point. Now that magickal societies were proscribed by the Gray Conclave, it would not do to be seen congregating in a public fashion in Assembly or anywhere else. The New Wigs were all good men, but other than Rafferdy and Coulten, they were none of them practicing magicians.

Coulten rose from the table and wandered off, as if in search of a pot to relieve himself in. Over the next quarter hour, around the tavern, the others with whom Rafferdy had traded nods rose and departed in a likewise manner. Finally, Rafferdy himself rose from the bench. Engaged in a heated discussion about current politics, the other New Wigs did not notice as he left the table and made his way to the back of the crowded room.

He came to an open doorway that led to a corridor. Nailed to the wall next to the opening was one of the numerous copies of the Rules of Citizenship posted around the tavern. Evidently Lord Valhaine believed that members of Assembly were in particular need of admonishment regarding the proper way to conduct themselves. Rafferdy ran his eyes down the lengthy list. There it was, toward the bottom.

RULE FORTY-SEVEN. No good citizen of Altania shall become a member of any secret order, society, or organization dedicated to the practice of magick, occult matters, or the study of the arcane; for magick, comprising the abilities to open locks and reveal private knowledge without due authorization, poses a grave threat to the security of the nation as well as the proper functioning of the government. Anyone found to be violating this rule will be imprisoned while they are investigated for Treason against Altania; for while magick is not a crime in and of itself, it can have little other purpose than to be an agent for committing nefarious acts.

Earlier that year, the last time Rafferdy saw his father alive, the elder man had warned that a time of great suspicion was coming. How much sooner it had arrived than Rafferdy had thought! After the attack on the Ministry of Printing, and the deaths of Lord Bastellon and Lord Mertrand—incidents which had all clearly involved the arcane—Lord Valhaine had all the evidence he needed to support his ban upon magickal orders. No one had dared to question it, not even the Magisters.

Rafferdy cast a glance over his shoulder, looking to see if any eyes had followed his progress. Then he passed through the doorway. He followed the corridor to its end, ascended two flights of stairs, and made his way down a passage, counting doors as he went. They never met in the same place twice, and so the only guidance he had were the instructions that had appeared of their own volition in the journal, bound in black leather, that he kept locked in the desk in his study.

Upon reaching the fifth door on the left, Rafferdy stopped. He whispered a word of magick, and for a brief moment a blue rune flickered into being on the wood of the door. Just as quickly, it vanished. Rafferdy lifted his cane and gave three light taps on the door.

The door opened. Rafferdy stepped in, and the door was quickly shut behind him. Eight other men stood in the room, Coulten among them. Their number had been chosen carefully, for nine was a numeral well known to have certain properties and benefits with regard to magick.

A circle had been drawn on the floor of the room using a thin silver cord. Small silver disks, each marked with a rune, had been placed around the perimeter of the circle. Careful not to disturb them, Rafferdy stepped into the circle of silence to join the other men. As long as they remained within its bounds, no one would be able to hear their words, even if they stood right outside the door of the room.

Rafferdy raised his right hand, and the others followed suit. None of them wore gloves now, and the gems on their House rings sparked with the arcane energy summoned by the circle: red and purple, green and blue.

Coulten gave Rafferdy a grin. Rafferdy could not help smiling in return, only then his expression grew serious.

"The Fellowship of the Silver Circle will now convene," he intoned in a low voice.

"The Circle will not be broken," the others chanted in reply.

And the magicians proceeded with their illicit meeting.

CHAPTER FOUR

"**I**T'S OUT!" Riethe fairly bellowed as he burst into the dim interior of the Theater of the Moon. "It's come out, and I've got a copy!"

Onstage, the illusionists stopped in the middle of the scene they had been rehearsing. They looked up at the commotion at the back of the theater. At the same time, a winged horse and several clouds unceremoniously winked out of existence. Riethe came barreling down the aisle between the rows of shabby seats and mounted the stage with an athletic leap. The strapping young illusionist was waving a folded broadsheet before him.

"You're late to rehearsal, Riethe," Master Tallyroth said, leaning on his cane. His powdered face was drawn in a frown, but his tone was more bemused than irritated. "I presume, as usual, you have some excuse."

"So I do, Master Tallyroth," Riethe said with a grin. "You see, I knew it would be published this afternoon. And here it is, the latest edition of *The Swift Arrow*—still damp off the presses, mind you, so be careful as you handle it. I bought it just a minute ago from a boy out on Durrow Street. You owe me a penny, Eldyn, though I'm sure you can afford it now. Look."

He unfolded the broadsheet. Everyone gathered close, and expressions of amazement were uttered all around.

"I can hardly stop looking at it," Hugoth said, plucking at the whiskers on his chin as he peered at the broadsheet. He was the eldest illusionist at the theater, aside from Master Tallyroth, and the only one at present who wore a beard. "No painting or illusion is as clear as that. I feel as if I'm right there, watching it myself."

"I suppose the reproduction of the scene is very fine," Merrick said. He was a tall, thin young man with a beaklike nose.

The diminutive illusionist next to him wrinkled his own nose in a scowl. "You make it sound like a cup of wine you were just able to get down once you held your breath."

"That is not what I meant, Mauress."

Merrick was the only one who ever used Mauress's proper name, and then only when he was perturbed with him. Otherwise they all just called him Mouse because of his small size and the way his nose twitched when he was excited or agitated—which was his general state.

"I only meant the details are exceedingly small," Merrick went on.

Mouse shook his head. "Small? That's just like you to belittle something you couldn't have done yourself. I'd like to see you try to make an impression, and then we can all tell you how *fine* we think it—"

"Mouse," Eldyn said as he stepped forward, his tone gentle but warning, "Merrick is entitled to his own opinion."

"I was only trying to comment on the exceeding number of tiny details that serve to enhance the effect of the scene," Merrick said, looking at Eldyn. "There is a remarkable subtlety to it."

"And we all know that subtlety is something which is utterly lost on Mouse," Riethe said, looping an arm around Mouse and picking him up off the stage despite the smaller man's protests.

At last Riethe set the other illusionist back down. Mouse's nose twitched furiously, and he looked ready to give a hot rejoinder, but at that point Master Tallyroth stepped forward, leaning heavily upon his cane, and gave Mouse a sharp look. The master illusionist of the Theater of the Moon didn't conjure phantasms himself anymore, due to the effects of the mordoth that afflicted him, but he still had one remarkable power none of them could match—he could make Mouse be quiet.

"May I see?" Tallyroth gestured toward the broadsheet, and Riethe turned it around so he might look at it.

"Well," he said after a long moment. "That is without doubt one of the best impressions I have ever beheld, Mr. Garritt. Oh, I have seen others that achieved a similar level of clarity—perhaps even greater. But it is the composition of the scene, the way it is framed, and the choice you made regarding which subject to place in the foreground, that I think make it superior. Had I not already known, I would still have recognized it as your work. It has your characteristic sensibility."

Eldyn hesitated, almost afraid to see for himself. Then he took the broadsheet from Riethe, and for the first time gazed upon an engraving that had sprung from his own thoughts printed in crisp black and white on the front page of a newspaper.

He could not help being astonished himself. Perren had pulled a hasty print from the copper plate, but the print had been blurry and smeared, made with too much ink. Nor had there been time to make a better copy, for time was of the essence. No broadsheet would pay for an impression of a scene if they were not the first to have one; it was exclusive images that helped to sell newspapers.

After Perren wiped the plate clean, they had hurried to Coronet Street, to the office of *The Swift Arrow*. Eldyn might have been inclined to go to another broadsheet first, for he still recalled the cruel and mocking stories *The Swift Arrow* had printed some months ago, at the time when illusionists were being murdered. But Perren explained that a new publisher had taken over the broadsheet not long after that, one who was very keen on impressions. And indeed, the last time Eldyn happened to glance at a copy of *The Swift Arrow*, he had thought the stories to be sensationalistic, but not nearly so lurid and dreadful as before.

They had soon reached the office of the broadsheet, and there they met with one of the editors, whom Perren had sold impressions to in the past, and handed over the plate and the smeared print. The man discarded the print without looking at it, then took up a magnifying glass and used it to pore over the engraving plate. All the while, Eldyn had hardly been able to draw a breath.

At last the editor set down the magnifying glass. Without speaking a word, he opened a box, took out some coins, and counted three gold regals into Eldyn's hand. Eldyn had stared at them in wonder. Just as he stared now at the image on the front page of the broadsheet. He had known the detail would be better when printed on a real printing press by men who knew their craft. But even though he had created the impression, he had had no true idea how it would really look, or how closely it would match the scene he had envisioned in his head.

As it turned out, it was nearly perfect. The spires of Assembly rose up sharply against the clouded sky. Members of the Hall of Magnates and the Hall of Citizens rushed down the steps, their robes rendered so clearly the garments almost seemed to flutter. To the right, a line of grim-faced soldiers leveled their bayonets against a throng of people who shouted and shook their fists at the men who were departing Assembly. Everything Eldyn had pictured in his mind as he held the engraving plate in Perren's room above the Theater of Mirrors was there—the ribbing on the red plume that rose from a soldier's helmet, and the chunk of bread one woman gripped in her hand, as if she did not know whether to eat it or throw it.

If that was all the scene was, it would have been dramatic enough, he supposed, and might still have warranted publication. Yet for all its vividness, the altercation before the steps of Assembly was the background of the image. Large in the foreground was the thing that had caught Eldyn's eye as he walked down Marble Street that day, and which had made him want to try making an impression.

It was a dove, its eyes shut in death, lying atop the low wall that bordered the foot of the steps.

Eldyn's eyes moved to the headline above the impression. Is ALTANIA ALREADY AT WAR? it read in large type. It was a provocative statement, no doubt formulated to sell copies of the broadsheet. And it didn't exactly capture what Eldyn had been thinking when he envisioned the scene. The point wasn't that people were fighting with one another. Rather, it was the notion that something beautiful had perished in plain view when no one was paying attention.

Yet despite the choice of headline, Eldyn could not really be displeased by the quality of the printing—or the jingle of the extra coins in his pocket—for it was the culmination of several months of work.

It had all begun one night when he and the other players from the theater had gone to the Red Jester following a performance. This was a very familiar (if not very reputable) tavern just off Durrow Street. As he walked from the bar with a pot of punch for him and his companions, Eldyn had passed by a bespectacled young man who sat alone at a table, looking at a picture printed on the front page of a broadsheet. It was a particularly good impression—one that depicted a riot before a candlemaker's shop that had taken place the day before.

Eldyn had paused and leaned over to make a remark about the high quality of the impression. To his surprise the young man thanked him for this praise. A bit of polite inquiry ensued, and though the object of these questions was clearly bashful, Eldyn did not let up. Thus it was soon revealed that the other young man was in fact the originator of the impression; he had made it himself and sold the plate to the broadsheet.

Fascinated, Eldyn began to ask the other illusionist how impressions were fashioned, as he had always wondered. Only by then his companions were baying for their punch. Riethe had even conjured a dog's nose and floppy ears for himself as he howled. Eldyn knew he could not linger.

Unexpectedly his disappointment became delight as the young man offered to meet with him the following day, if he wished, so they might continue their discussion of impressions. Elydn had gladly accepted. Then, taking his leave, he hurried over to his friends. By then all of them had ears and noses in imitation of Riethe, and were barking like fools. After a few rounds of punch, Eldyn joined them.

The next afternoon he returned to the Red Jester, when the tavern was quieter and he was more sober. Upon entering, he saw the bespectacled young illusionist sitting at the same table as last night. Eldyn went to him at once and thanked him for coming.

"I'm Eldyn Garritt, by the way," he said, holding out his hand. "From the Theater of the Moon."

The other young man hesitated a moment, pushing his wire-rimmed spectacles up his nose, then reached out to clasp Eldyn's hand. "I know. I've seen your performance several times. You probably haven't seen me, though. I'm Perren Fynch, from the Theater of Mirrors."

Eldyn could only confess he hadn't seen the illusion play at that particular house for some time. Luckily, it didn't seem to matter. While Perren seemed to possess a rather quiet and reserved nature, all that changed as soon as Eldyn began questioning him about the methods by which impressions were made. He was soon chattering away as Eldyn listened in fascination.

And somehow, by their second cup of punch, he had gotten Perren to agree to teach him how to make impressions.

Of course, this was all easier said over cups of punch in a tavern than it was actually put into deed. The old illusionist who had taught Perren how to make impressions had claimed that only a few Siltheri possessed the requisite skill. And of those, only a few were willing to put in the many hours of effort it took to hone the craft to any sort of usable point. Eldyn, however, was determined to give it his best.

After all, he had the time.

Gone were the days when Eldyn was attempting to juggle two vocations at once. Since leaving Graychurch, he had not sought out another clerking position. Nor were familial or fraternal duties a distraction. His sister, Sashie, was not consigned to his care anymore, having been accepted into a nunnery in County Caerdun in the south, and his friend Rafferdy was too occupied with affairs at Assembly to have time to meet very often.

As for that most affectionate sort of relationship—there was no time lost on that account either. Not that Eldyn wouldn't have given up all his time in the world, and gladly, just to be able to look into Dercy's sea green eyes once again. Not a lumenal passed, no matter how brief, that he did not spend hours of it thinking about Dercy, recalling all their moments together. And not an umbral fell that did not find him awake at some point, touching the cold, empty space in the bed beside him, and wishing Dercy were there to fill it.

Throughout these last months, Eldyn had received but a single letter from Dercy, and this had contained but a few lines stating that he had arrived in the country safely and was staying at the house of his cousin, who was vicar in a small parish. That was all.

More than once, Eldyn had been tempted to buy a seat on the post and travel to the country. Only he knew he could not. After all, there was nothing he could do that might heal Dercy. In one violent, rending act, Archdeacon Lemarck had stolen more than half a lifetime of light from Dercy—afflicting him with the mordoth in the process. After those awful events, he had traveled to his cousin's house to convalesce.

Only it wasn't simply for the purpose of recuperation that Dercy had departed the city. Given how little light he had left, he could not ever risk crafting illusions again. Which meant he had to get away from Durrow Street, and from anything that might tempt him to make illusions.

Or from anyone. That included his friends at the Theater of the Moon. And that included Eldyn as well. It was vital that Dercy conserve his light, and being around other illusionists could only entice him to do the opposite—at least until such a time came when he had truly learned to set such temptations aside. Which meant that the only thing Eldyn could do to help Dercy was to wait for him.

And Eldyn *would* wait for him, no matter how long it took.

So it was, when he was not at the theater, there was nothing to distract Eldyn from dedicating himself to the study of making impressions. As it turned out, it was a good thing he had such a surplus of time. Eldyn quickly realized he was going to need it. Fortunately, he had an exceedingly patient teacher in Perren.

Indeed, so generously did Perren give of his time—in exchange for nothing save the punch or whiskey, which Eldyn always bought—that Eldyn often marveled at the entire situation. When he considered it, he could only suppose Perren was passing along the kindness that had been done to him by the illusionist who taught him to craft impressions. Or perhaps it was Eldyn's own diligence which inspired him. Besides, it was not as if they did not find amusement in their lessons, which often ended only when they were both of them too merry from drink to either teach or be taught.

During those first few lessons, Eldyn simply watched. From what he had heard before, he had believed that, when making an impression, an illusionist's thoughts somehow directly affected the surface of the engraving plate which he held in his hands.

He was entirely mistaken.

Instead, Perren would begin by heating a waxen substance— one that had particular properties—in a small pot over a flame. Then he would use a boar bristle brush to carefully apply a thin coating of the substance to the polished surface of a copper plate. It was called impression rosin, and it was this material, Perren explained, that actually responded to what the illusionist envisioned in his mind.

If done properly, it all happened very quickly. Afterward, the plate was submerged in a bath of mordant. The acidic mordant etched the copper plate anywhere the coating of rosin had been pushed aside from the surface by the force of the illusionist's thoughts. Then the plate was rinsed and the rosin stripped away, leaving it ready to be rolled with ink and pressed against paper to make a print.

"It's just like shaping the light with your thoughts," Eldyn had said after that first time he watched Perren at his craft.

"It is, with one important difference," Perren said.

"What's that?"

"When you craft an illusion, you can conjure anything you can imagine. But you can only make an impression of something you've witnessed yourself. And it has to be exactly as you saw it. If you try to alter even one small detail, the whole impression will fail."

Eldyn was astonished by this, but intrigued as well. "But why? Why can't you just make up a scene in an impression?"

"It's a property of the impression rosin," Perren explained. "It will only let you tell the truth."

Maybe that was why making impressions was so difficult, Eldyn thought. It was easy to envision a scene. But it was devilishly hard to envision it *truly*—as he discovered the first time he attempted to make an impression. He did this using a scratch plate—one that was too damaged to be used for printing—as engraving plates were costly. He shut his eyes and concentrated with all his might, seemingly to no effect. Only then, just as he was about to give up, he thought he saw the faintest glimmer of green light against his eyelids. At the same time he had the sensation of something shifting or giving way.

When he opened his eyes, he saw two things. The first was Perren's grin, his blue eyes bright behind his wire-rimmed spectacles. The other was a small but distinct smudge in the rosin that covered the plate.

Though small, it was a beginning, and it gave him hope. After that, it was really nothing more than a matter of long hours of practice, learning to touch the rosin with his thoughts and shape it just as he had previously learned to touch and shape light. As for what the rosin exactly was, and what was contained in it, Perren could not say. In the entire city, there were only three illusionists who made impression rosin, and all of them were reluctant to share the secret of its formula.

All Eldyn knew was that when he shaped the rosin with his thoughts, he would always see a green light against his eyelids. And the better he got at shaping it, the brighter the light grew.

There was much more to it than just affecting the rosin that coated the engraving plate, of course. Indeed, that was the simplest part. Much harder was learning to see in an entirely different way—to see the truth. Eldyn had always thought he was an observant person, but he quickly learned how wrong he had been when Perren set down a dozen playing cards face up on a table, then quickly turned them over and asked Eldyn to tell him the number of pips on each one.

That first time, Eldyn got hardly any of them right. But the more he practiced, the more he got. Soon he could recall the face value and position of a dozen cards that had been flipped over, then twenty-four, and then thirty-six. He and Perren would walk around the city, and suddenly Perren would stop him, tell him to shut his eyes, and order him to describe everything around them in minutest detail.

After two months of preparation and practice, Perren finally let him try his skills on a real engraving plate, not a scrap. After three months, they finally submitted a plate to the bath of mordant to etch it, then made a print. The result was so blurry as to be incomprehensible, but Eldyn used some of his wages from the theater to buy more plates and impression rosin (and more whiskey and punch for Perren and himself) and kept trying.

Then, just yesterday, he had at last created an impression that was good enough to have a chance at being printed in a broadsheet. Perren had known it the moment he took the plate from Eldyn, or so he said—even before they etched it in mordant and ran off that hasty print. They had left Perren's room above the Theater of Mirrors and rushed across the Old City to the offices of *The Swift Arrow* on Coronet Street.

And now, here before him, was the result.

"Well, I am sure we will have more time later to look at Mr. Garritt's fine work," Master Tallyroth said. "However, there is to be a performance tonight—providing this awful lumenal ever sees fit to end. Yet I can only assume it will at some point, and I remain unconvinced that everyone fully comprehends the new staging. Let us proceed through it once more." He thumped his cane against the stage. "Take your places, gentlemen!"

The master illusionist of the Theater of the Moon was a frail man with a powdered face, dressed in a ruffled coat of black velvet, but he might have been a general on the battlefield for the way the illusionists responded to this order. The players sprang into motion, hurrying across the stage to take up their positions. Not wanting to be last, Eldyn hastily set the broadsheet down and found his mark.

"And begin!" Master Tallyroth called out.

At once, the stage was transformed into a cloudscape beneath a brilliant blue sky. With a thought, Eldyn shaped the dusty light into the pearlescent form of a winged horse, galloping among the clouds. This time the horse was not riderless, for Riethe was here to complete the phantasm. He made a gesture with his fingers, and suddenly a maiden rode upon the back of the horse. She was clad in a flowing gold gown with a laurel wreath upon her brow and a blazing torch in her hand.

The clouds parted, and the maiden swooped down on the winged horse. Below her, rows of stiff figures marched across the stage. They were conjured only as faceless, shadowy outlines—for artistic effect, and also because it would have been too difficult to conjure them all in detail. Moving among the soldiers were several illusionists, clad in black themselves in order to blend in. They carried banners on poles: green hawks fluttering against a white background.

As the maiden raised her torch, beams of gold light radiated from it toward the army below. Each time one of the gold rays struck a shadowy figure, it raised its arms as if in agony, then vanished. In moments the army was destroyed, and the banners clattered to the stage. The horse and the golden maiden flew back up, disappearing into the clouds.

That was Eldyn's cue. He ceased the illusion of the horse, as it was now out of sight, then conjured a silvery aura around himself and stepped onto the stage, moving stealthily and casting looks as he went. When he reached center stage, he made a play of noticing one of the fallen banners and picked up a corner of the cloth.

He laughed, then let the cloth fall and hurried the rest of the way across the stage.

Tallyroth banged his cane again. The clouds dissipated, and the players all returned to gather around him to hear his pronouncement.

"Well," the master illusionist said, the corner of his mouth turning up just a fraction, "perhaps you grasp the new staging, after all."

Riethe grinned. "Of course we do, now that I'm here."

This resulted in several groans, and someone resummoned one of the clouds over Riethe's head, only now it was dark, and bolts of lightning stabbed down at the big illusionist's skull. He made a pantomime as if he had been struck a blow, clapping a hand to his brow and staggering about as the groans became laughter. That was Riethe—an enormous idiot, but hard not to like.

"Go on, then," Master Tallyroth declared. "Go get some rest before the performance tonight—whenever tonight shall be."

So directed, the illusionists all bounded from the stage like boys released from study by their schoolmaster, and Eldyn with them.

THE SUN LURCHED to the horizon, and night fell at last. The theaters opened their doors, and lights were conjured and tossed into the sky to signal to the city that the houses of illusion on Durrow Street were ready for business. By the time the curtain rose, the theater was only half full, but that was better than some nights. And there was hope the next night would be better, for the audience heartily applauded and stamped their boots at the newly added scene. Eldyn could only be glad for this, even if he could not say he cared much for the scene himself.

It was expertly designed, of course, as were all of Master Tallyroth's scenes. The problem was that it had little to do with the rest of the illusion play. It was the charter of the Theater of the Moon, granted by the Guild of Illusionists, to tell the story of the Sun

King and the Moon Prince—how the former ever pursues the latter, but can never really catch him. For even when it seems the silvery youth is captured at last, and the Sun burns him to a cinder,
the Moon is reborn to grow and shine forth once again.

Despite this deviation from the usual theme of the illusion play,
Master Tallyroth had little choice in the matter—not if the theater
was to remain in business.

Was it really just a few months ago that the receipt box had
been overflowing after each night's performance? It seemed so
long since that time. Their play had become a sensation on Durrow Street, and its notoriety was only increased by the series of
performances they gave that led to the downfall of the Archdeacon
of Graychurch—after exposing him as an illusionist who had used
his abilities to drive the Archbishop of Invarel mad.

Only then King Rothard died, succumbing to his long illness,
and the city entered the required period of mourning. By law during this time, displays of public merriment were halted, and so all
of the theaters on Durrow Street were forced to shut their doors,
going dark for two months. By the time the period of mourning
was over, only half of the theaters that had shut their doors could
open them again. Things had already been difficult on Durrow
Street prior to the king's death, and many of the theaters did not
have funds enough to survive so long a closure.

The Theater of the Moon was one of the luckier houses, for
Madame Richelour had reserved much of the earnings from their
success, and so it endured. But things hardly improved once the
theaters opened again. When people were worried about having
coins enough for bread and candles, they tended to spare few of
them for more frivolous expenses such as seeing an illusion play.

Of course, there were still plenty of people in Altania who had
great amounts of money to spend. After all, if certain broadsheets
were to be believed, it was the fact that so few possessed so much,
while so many had so little, that provided the tinder the rebels
were trying to spark into a fire. That disparity seemed to increase
daily in Invarel as more folk fled the troubles in the Outlands and
came to the city carrying what little they possessed on their backs

and in their pockets. At the same time, a number of lords, baronets, and well-to-do gentry had departed the city, making for their estates in the east and south of the country to remove themselves as far as possible.

Of those moneyed individuals who remained, fewer were willing to venture down to Durrow Street. Every day the newspapers printed stories of robberies of the most violent sort that occurred in the Old City. Thus it was, even with only half the number of theaters as there had been, they were making less than half of what they had before.

The only sort of audience they could really count on attracting to the theater these days were soldiers, for the number of them stationed in the city had greatly increased. This might have been a boon, as the redcrests were paid regularly and, when off duty, had little to do for amusement, most of them being young, unattached, and away from home.

Unfortunately, there were only two sorts of illusion plays that generally appealed to soldiers, these being burlesques or patriotic displays. Or better yet, a combination of both—for a buxom wench who waved the national banner before gustily offering herself up to an entire company of soldiers was a sight that always seemed to win approval.

Yet popular as such things might be, a scene like that would never be found at the Theater of the Moon. Madame Richelour refused to have a burlesque on her stage. Still, some concession to popular sentiment had to be made—hence the addition of the new scene with the golden maiden. Gold was one of the three colors of the national banner (the others being blue and green), and with her laurel crown and the winged horse, the maiden was intended to evoke a goddess of ancient Tharos. This in turn was meant to bring the princess, Layle Arringhart, to mind, as tradition held that the Arringhart line was descended from the emperors of Tharos.

In all, it was far from a ribald farce such as soldiers might find at another theater, but the maiden was made to be very pretty, and the audience, composed largely of soldiers, cheered when she used her blazing torch to smite down the shadowy army. That the army was meant to represent the rebel forces of Huntley Morden could not be made more plain given the banner they carried, which bore the green Morden hawk.

It was all dreadfully obvious, and not particularly artistic. But it was spectacle, and they executed it well. Based on the vigorous applause, their audience tomorrow would likely be bigger than tonight's, and for their efforts Madame Richelour rewarded the players with a few extra coins. Not so many as she might have given them in the past, but more than enough for them to get sufficiently drunk. This was a task the illusionists undertook at once, and they proceeded from the theater directly to the Red Jester. Soon the tavern's dank interior was made light by their laughter as well as the phantasms they spontaneously conjured.

Eldyn was already on his second cup of punch before he realized Perren was there at the tavern. Perren was a somewhat roundish young man with a habit of wearing rumpled clothes of the blandest colors, and the soft outlines in which he was drawn tended to cause him to fade into whatever was around him. This was in fact a good trait for an illusionist, for he would never distract from his illusions, though it sometimes made him difficult to spot in the smoky interior of a tavern.

But there he was, sitting in the corner by himself, looking at a broadsheet. This behavior in no way surprised Eldyn. If he did not know Perren was an illusionist, he would have taken him for a lawyer or a clerk. Then again, as Eldyn had been a clerk himself once, he felt a common bond with Perren. Not all illusionists could be so brash and flamboyant as Riethe—thank the light.

Taking up a second cup of punch, Eldyn headed to the corner where the other young man sat alone.

"Perren, why didn't you say you were here?"

"I was just . . . that is, you looked like you were occupied."

"Nonsense. I could never be too busy for you—especially tonight."

Perren smiled at this, but he quickly ducked his head, and

Eldyn could only marvel. He had never met so shrinking a fellow as Perren. They had known each other for months now, and had spent hours together working on impressions. There was hardly cause to be bashful.

Well, Eldyn knew how to get Perren in a bolder mood. He sat across from him and slid the extra cup of punch across the table. It was a good thing he had brought it over, for Perren seemed in great need of it. He took up the cup and, in several gulps, drained it. Eldyn took a sip from his own cup.

"We did it, Perren," he said, feeling exceedingly pleased. He tapped the broadsheet on the table. It was that day's copy of *The Swift Arrow*, with Eldyn's impression on the front page.

Perren shook his head. "You mean *you* did it."

"Yes, I suppose so, but I certainly couldn't have done it without you. You taught me everything, and for that I owe you."

Perren suddenly sat up straight, blinking behind his spectacles. "You owe me?"

Eldyn nodded. "More than I can express. I don't know how I'm ever going to be able to repay you for all that you've done for me, but I'll try my best to find a way. Anything I can do for you, I will. Perhaps refilling these will be a good start."

He picked up their cups to take them to the bar, but Perren laid a hand on his arm, stopping him.

"Yes," Perren said, his voice going low. "You do owe me."

Eldyn smiled. "No need to worry. As I said, anything you want. Which means this round is on—"

His words were cut short as Perren leaned across the table, still gripping his arm, and kissed him.

The empty cups clattered to the table, and Eldyn felt a flicker of light passing between him and Perren, as always happened when two illusionists kissed. In that instant he understood why Perren had been so generous with his time in teaching him to make impressions. How had he not realized it before? He should have seen it months ago. Only he had been so caught up in being a student that he had failed to study the teacher.

Gently, but with force enough that there could be no doubt that it was intentional, Eldyn pushed Perren's hand from his arm. Knocked off balance, Perren fell back onto the bench. He fumbled with his spectacles, straightening them on his face. Behind the lenses, his eyes were bright with pain and confusion.

"But I thought . . . you said that you owed me, that you'd do anything that I wanted."

Eldyn sighed, knowing he was in part to blame for what had happened. "I do owe you, Perren. And I would do anything to repay you—anything that a good friend would do."

"A friend?" Perren shook his head. "Is it because of how I look? I know you're handsomer than me, Eldyn. But you're more handsome than everyone. And I thought that, once you saw all that I could give you, you would have to give me something in kind."

Eldyn felt a pang in his chest. Even if he was looking for a companion of that sort, Perren would never have caught his eye. It wasn't just that he was pasty and dressed poorly; rather, it was his self-consciousness and his awkward attempts at conversation that kept him from being noteworthy in that regard. Besides, Eldyn wasn't looking for such a companion. How could he give his light to another man knowing that so much of it had been given to him by Dercy?

He couldn't.

"It's not how you look, Perren," he said, his throat tight. "It's because of me. I'm not . . . that is, I can't give that to another right now."

"Oh, I see now," Perren said, looking up. His round face, usually so soft, suddenly had a hardness to it, and his eyes had narrowed behind his crooked spectacles. "You can prevail upon another to teach you everything he knows. You can use him to get what you want, and you can take and take from him. But you can't be bothered to give one whit back, can you?"

The anger in these words astonished Eldyn. He had never heard Perren speak with such vehemence.

"That's not true, Perren," he said, unable to keep the shock from his voice. "I do want to give something back to you. I want to repay you for what you've done."

"Don't bother," Perren snapped, rising to his feet. He tugged on his rumpled coat, though this only made it sit more unevenly on his round shoulders. "I don't need your money. I can make plenty on my own. And don't think you can use my contacts at *The Swift Arrow* to sell your impressions. I'll tell them you can't be trusted to offer exclusive rights. After all, you played me false, so why wouldn't you sell your impressions to another broadsheet behind their backs?"

Eldyn was so shocked by these statements that at first he was struck speechless. By the time he found his voice, and called out to Perren, the other young man was already at the tavern door. Then he was gone.

"What was that all about, Eldyn?"

He turned to see Riethe before him. The big illusionist had a quizzical look on his face.

Eldyn drew a breath—then let it go. What use was there in explaining what had happened? It was done, and it could not be undone.

"It was nothing," he said.

"Well, come on, then. We haven't even spent half of the coin Madame Richelour gave us."

"Wait just a moment," Eldyn said. He turned back and took up the broadsheet from the table where Perren had left it and tucked it inside his coat. "There, I'm ready."

"You'd better be," Riethe said with a grin.

And he hooked his arm around Eldyn's, hauling him back across the tavern to the other illusionists.

CHAPTER FIVE

———————— ❧ ————————

JVY TOUCHED the Wyrdwood box, and the tendrils of wood
on its lid uncoiled like a nest of tiny brown serpents wriggling
away from one another. So often had she done this that she hardly
thought anything of it, or stopped to consider how remarkable it
was. Instead, she lifted the lid of the box and took out a book
bound in black leather.

Fondly, she brushed a hand across the cover of the book. Her
father had used its pages to keep a journal, and in it he had written down various entries regarding his magickal research and the
practices of the occult order to which he belonged. Such was the
nature of the enchantment he had placed upon the journal that an
entry appeared upon its pages only when certain celestial objects
were arranged in the heavens as they had been at the time when
her father penned the words; otherwise, the pages of the journal
appeared blank.

It was very much in keeping with her father's character to make
a mystery of it all. He had always liked to give her clever little ciphers and riddles when she was a girl, and she had liked equally
to solve them. In this case, though, the purpose of the puzzle had
been more than mere amusement. Rather, Mr. Lockwell had used
the enchantment and the Wyrdwood box as safeguards to keep
the thoughts and musings in the journal secret from the other
magicians in the Vigilant Order of the Silver Eye.

It was well that he had done so. As she had learned from some
of her father's later entries in the journal, one of his compatriots,
Mr. Gambrel, had betrayed the order and stolen the key to the
magickal door Tyberion in hopes of unlocking dread powers beyond. Ivy could only assume he had been helped in the matter by

Mr. Bennick, who had previously demonstrated his own duplicitous nature.

Years ago, Mr. Bennick and Ivy's father, Mr. Lockwell, had both
belonged to the Vigilant Order of the Silver Eye. Only then, driven
by a desire for power, some of the magicians formulated a plan to
seize the eponymous artifact which the order had been established
to protect. At the last, Mr. Lockwell managed to cast a spell to shut
the house on Durrow Street and safeguard the Eye of Ran-Yahgren.
But so much of himself was expended in working the enchantment that his mind was shattered, and his sanity lost.

That had occurred more than ten years ago. Then, just last
year, magicians from the Vigilant Order of the Silver Eye once
again sought to gain the artifact. Together, Ivy and Mr. Rafferdy
had looked for a way to gain entry to the house, so they could
renew the binding on the Eye before the magicians might seize it.
Only, as it turned out, that had been Mr. Bennick's plan all along.
Ivy's cousin Mr. Wyble unwittingly revealed how it was due to Mr.
Bennick's machinations that Ivy and Mr. Rafferdy had been introduced to each other. What was more, it was Mr. Bennick who had
helped Ivy to solve her father's riddles, and who had induced Mr.
Rafferdy to learn magick. The former magician had been manipu-
lating them both from the very start.

As if all this was not damning enough, Mr. Bennick had confessed that day at Durrow Street. He had admitted to using Ivy and
Rafferdy as a means to open the door to the house on Durrow
Street. Which meant that Mr. Quent's suspicions, expressed in a
letter to Ivy, could only be correct—it was Mr. Bennick who had
tried to take the Eye ten years ago. And he was helping the other
magicians to make another attempt.

Why he was doing it, Mr. Bennick did not say that day, for Ivy
had not given him the chance. But what other reason could there
have been? He had lost his magickal ability, presumably when it
was taken from him by the other magicians of the order after he
failed to gain the Eye the first time. Obviously he had hoped he
could win back their favor—and the return of his magickal
powers—by helping them gain entry to the house.

Fortunately, due to Mr. Rafferdy's magick, and a bit of ingenuity (and witchcraft) on Ivy's part, the magicians were thwarted, and the binding on the Eye was renewed. At present it remained locked in her father's hidden study two floors above her, while Mr. Bennick had fled to Torland and had not been heard from since.

As for Mr. Gambrel—or Lord Crayford, as he had been more recently known—Ivy had seen to it he could cause no more mischief. After he passed through the door Tyberion to the ancient way station on the moon of the same name, she had locked it behind him and removed the key. Shortly after, she had commanded the door to be plastered over. Because Mr. Rafferdy had ruined the only other working gate that led from the way station on Tyberion, Mr. Gambrel was trapped in that distant and desolate place— forever, she supposed, if he even still lived. Sometimes, as she passed through the gallery on the second floor of the house, she would go to the southern wall and lay an ear against the smooth, painted plaster.

But she never heard anything save for the sound of her own breath.

Now, in the library on the first floor of the house, Ivy opened her father's journal on the reading table before her, and just as she had every lumenal and umbral since first discovering the journal's secret, she carefully turned its pages one by one.

All of them were blank.

Ivy sighed and shut the journal again. Though she had continued her habit of checking the book once each day and night, it had been many months since she had found an entry on one of its pages. The last time had been the night of the party for her sisters, presenting them to society. Just before the party, Ivy had discovered the entry in which her father wrote how it was Gambrel who had stolen the key to Tyberion, and that he must never be allowed to pass through the door.

Since then, though Ivy diligently maintained her practice of examining the journal, she had never found any more of Mr. Lockwell's distinctive, spindly script. She supposed it was possible that her father had never written anything else after that last entry.

Yet, as the lengths of the umbrals and lumenals became increasingly unpredictable, Ivy began to suspect there was a different reason why she had not discovered anything more.

It was the nature of the journal's magick that an entry appeared only when particular stars and planets were aligned as they were when her father had penned it. Now the movements of the celestial spheres had been drastically altered by the appearance of the red planet, Cerephus. As a result, the heavens could never be arranged as they had been when her father had filled the journal's pages some ten years ago.

Which meant that the trick that had once protected the book's secrets now made it impossible that they would ever appear again.

Ivy placed the journal back in the Wyrdwood box, nestling it carefully alongside two small pieces of wood. One was carved like a faceted gem, the other in the shape of a leaf: the keys to the doors Tyberion and Arantus.

"If only I knew the key to unlock your words from these pages, Father," she said softly. "There has to be a way to undo the enchantment you placed on the journal."

Discovering it, though, was another matter. On one of the rare occasions when Mr. Rafferdy had been able to take time from his duties in Assembly to pay Ivy a visit, she had shown him the journal. He had examined the book for a long while, from time to time speaking words of magick over it, but in the end he had been confounded.

"It's not any usual incantation of concealment that your father bound this with," Mr. Rafferdy had said, handing the journal back to her. "Rather, I would say it was something very unusual and clever. Unfortunately, if we do not know what spell was used, there is no way to reverse it."

As Ivy knew few other magicians, that was that.

She shut the lid of the Wyrdwood box, and the tendrils of wood braided themselves together, locking it again. As they did, a feeling of heaviness came over her.

Not that this was unexpected; Dr. Lawrent had warned her that she would likely experience some degree of melancholia over these next days as she continued her recovery. Only it was not just her recent ordeal—or her dread of telling Mr. Quent about it when he returned from the country—that had made her spirits so low.

The lumenal prior, she had gone to the Madderly-Stoneworth Hostel for the Deranged to visit her father, as she did every quarter month. The wardens at Madstone's had continued to treat her father's illness using an electrical condenser. Every few days, a metal band was placed upon his forehead and attached to the device to apply a series of mild electrical shocks in hopes of stimulating the functioning of his brain.

At first Ivy had been horrified to learn what was being done to her father. However, soon after the treatment was begun, her father's condition had started to improve. He was calmer, his eyes were clearer, and he could more ably feed and dress himself. What was more, for the first time since Mr. Wyble had committed him to Madstone's, her father had begun to speak. Of course it was only a few words, or more rarely an entire sentence, but all the same this had given Ivy great hope.

Then, as the months passed, that hope began to diminish. On her visits to the hostel, Mr. Lockwell continued to speak intelligible words with regularity, and sometimes his eyes seemed to focus on her, as if he recognized her, but never anything more.

For so long, Ivy had sought a way to return her father to his senses. She had reasoned that if it was magick that caused his illness, then it was magick that would cure it. But women could not work magick, no matter how much they wanted to, and she had never found a magician who could help him. Then the wardens at Madstone's began the treatments, and she had started to let herself believe that it was another sort of power—the forces of electricity and science—which would restore her father's mind.

Only months of the treatments had not cured him, and now Ivy doubted they ever would. She had read of experiments in which electrical charges were applied to the limbs of dead creatures, and their muscles were made to flex and move as if alive. But they weren't alive, not really. And while the electrical treatments caused her father to speak and to look at her with what seemed awareness, Ivy was convinced now that these were merely thoughtless reflexes—trace impulses of what had once resided within him, jolted into being by the shocks. When he uttered words, Mr. Lockwell was no more speaking to her than the cadaver of a frog, connected to wires, was jumping to catch a fly when it twitched on a laboratory table.

Just as no electrical charge could bring life to a dead creature, it could not restore to her father the thing that was missing from him—that peculiar, rational essence that had once made him himself. In the end, Mr. Lockwell's mind no more resided in his body than it did in the journal in the Wyrdwood box. Both might offer fond echoes of the man he had once been. But they were neither of them *him*.

Ivy sighed and returned the Wyrdwood box to the drawer in the writing table. She rose, thinking she might go outside. Dr. Lawrent had said it was acceptable for her to venture on brief walks; and being among the small chestnuts and hawthorns in the garden always lifted her spirits.

As she started from the library, the old rosewood clock on the mantel let out a chime. Ivy paused to look at the clock. It was a beautiful device, its glossy wood inlaid with darker pieces shaped like moons and planets. The clock had three large faces, and on the rightmost of these a black disk moved a fraction so that it now covered exactly half of the gold disk below.

Ivy glanced out the library window and inferred from the short length of the shadows that the sun was directly overhead. The timetables in the almanac were no longer any use in predicting the lengths of lumenals and umbrals. Yet somehow, despite the disruption in the heavens, her father's old clock always predicted the start and end of each lumenal, and the timing of the four farthings of the day, with infallible precision.

By what inner workings this was achieved, Ivy could not say. All the same, somehow the clock was able to account for the changes Cerephus had wrought on the workings of the celestial spheres. It was a feat the members of the Royal Society of Astrographers had yet to duplicate themselves.

Despite her low spirits, Ivy could not help a smile as the clock let out a final chime, marking the start of the third farthing of the day.

Suddenly another chime seemed to sound in her ears, though this one was not emitted by the rosewood clock. Instead, it was the tone of a realization. Just like the clock's unknown maker, who had designed its workings to account for the effects of Cerephus, Ivy's father had been aware of the crimson planet long before it appeared in the sky. Which meant he had to have known that, one day, the movements of the heavens would become severely disrupted by the planet's approach.

So then why had he based the journal's enchantment on the workings of the celestial spheres?

LESS THAN AN HOUR LATER, Ivy retreated back into the coolness of the house. It had been too hot for a walk in the garden. Everything withered in the white light, and the chestnuts and hawthorns had been able to do little to thwart the rays of the sun that beat down from overhead.

Despite the heat of the lumenal, it was not overly warm in the house. Whether it was due to the peculiar nature of the stones from which the house had been built—some of which she knew to have magickal properties—or if it was simply that the walls were so thick, Ivy did not know. All the same, the house always seemed to retain some of the coolness of night, even on the longest days.

Feeling less torpid now that she was indoors, Ivy passed through the large front hall to the parlor where she and her sisters liked to sit on warm afternoons. A wisteria grew over the north-facing window, and the room was filled with a gentle green light.

As Ivy entered, a wooden eye that was set into the mantelpiece above the fireplace blinked open. It rolled around to gaze at her for a moment, then the lid closed with a faint click. Neither of her sisters seemed to take notice of this activity. They were all of them well used to the arcane eyes which kept watch throughout their father's house.

Lily was sitting at the pianoforte. It was one of three such instruments throughout the house, all purchased by Mr. Quent. This had seemed a great extravagance to Ivy, for she was sure Lily could make do with one.

"It is true *she* might make do," Mr. Quent had replied, "but I cannot, for I like to hear her play no matter where I am in the house."

Lily was not playing at the moment, however. Instead, as had been increasingly the case over these past several months, she was using a charcoal pencil to scribble upon the pages of a large folio that lay open atop the pianoforte. Whatever she was working on, she was going about it with great zeal, and a small crease was evident between the dark lines of her eyebrows. Rose was being similarly industrious, sewing the sleeve on a white shirt. Miss Mew sat on the sofa beside her, tail wrapped around her paws, her yellow eyes watching the needle go to and fro.

"I see that Miss Mew is making certain you don't miss a stitch," Ivy said.

Rose smiled up at her. "I am sure she will bat at my hand if I do."

Even if the cat were capable of noticing such an omission, Ivy doubted she would have any need for action. Rose never missed a stitch, as far as Ivy could tell, and it seemed every day she finished another shirt for the poor basket. Recently, Ivy had told her not to overtire herself with her diligent efforts, and to occupy herself on occasion with a more frivolous activity. But Rose had only shaken her head.

"The newspapers say there are more poor people in the city all the time," she had said. "So that means I need to sew more shirts."

Ivy had not been able to argue with that logic.

Now, as Miss Mew watched, Rose resumed her sewing, while Lily continued to apply the charcoal pencil to the pages of the folio with great speed and purpose.

A few times, after Lily first began such undertakings, Ivy had asked her what she was working on in the folio. Ivy had not meant to pry; she was only curious. Yet on each occasion, Lily slammed the folio shut and proclaimed it was nothing. Before long, Ivy gave up asking altogether. Though she could not help remaining a little curious about what her sister was so intent upon, and she hoped one day Lily would show them what it was.

For now, Ivy went to the bookcase on the opposite wall and ran her fingers along the spines of the volumes that filled the shelves. She hadn't finished the latest treatise concerning the study of electrical forces which she had started to read the other day, but after her walk in the heat outside her mind was too dull for such a subject. Nor did any of the other books concerning science or the occult appeal to her. What use was there in reading them anymore if there was nothing in their pages that could help her father?

Just then Ivy noticed a small book bound in red cloth that had been carelessly tossed on top of a row of books about astrography. She picked it up. The title on the spine read, in gilded letters, *The Towers of Ardaunto.* It must have been one of Lily's romances. On a sudden whim, Ivy took up the book. Perhaps it was time for her to follow the advice she had given Rose, and to pursue a more frivolous pastime for a while.

Ivy sat in a chair with the book while Lily sketched and Rose continued to sew. So familiar was the scene that, were it not for the grand size of the house around them, they might have been back in their little parlor on Whitward Street. It occurred to Ivy that, no matter how altered their situation had become, in many ways it was not so very different.

For a brief while, that had not been the case. After the party for her sisters, Lily and Rose had received more invitations to dances and dinners than could possibly be accepted—though Lily had certainly made a go of it. Seeing her sisters so happily engaged had given Ivy great joy herself. It seemed to her that Lily was benefiting from the influence of young women with refined manners; at the very least, she had given up speaking like a sea captain. And it was heartening to see Rose out in the world, being in the presence of others—if not always managing to find words to speak to them.

Then the bells rang out over the city, and with their tolling everything had changed. Upon King Rothard's death, all of Altania entered into a period of mourning. Parties and balls and any grand affairs were suspended by royal decree, and so Lily and Rose were deprived of the society to which they had only just been introduced.

After two months, the formal time of mourning came to an end. Usually, a great celebration would immediately follow as a new monarch was crowned. Only for reasons that might be evident to Assembly, but which Ivy could not fathom, Princess Layle was yet to have her coronation.

What was more, in the interim, the situation in the country had become exceedingly grim. Candles and all manner of goods grew rare while the sight of destitute and desperate people on the streets became common. The royal army was in great need of rations and supplies; and while before it might be seen as an indicator of station to throw a lavish affair, nowadays it was just as likely to be considered distasteful, or even unpatriotic. So it was that, while it was no longer against any edict to hold parties and balls, it was no longer very propitious to do so.

As a result, Ivy and her sisters had lived quietly and modestly these last months. Rose and Lily had attended a few teas or luncheons at the houses of young ladies whose acquaintance they had made. But soon even these small affairs ceased to occur as a growing number of prominent families removed themselves from the city and went to their lodges and manors in the south and east part of the country to escape the growing troubles.

Of late, Mr. Quent, Ivy, and her sisters had had only themselves for society, supplemented by an occasional and welcome visit from Mr. Rafferdy, or somewhat more frequently from Mr. and Mrs. Baydon. And of course, they were always invited at Lady Marsdel's. So far, her ladyship had hewed firmly to her position that they must not abandon Invarel for the country.

"If we let the fear of hooligans drive us from our own city, then it will be to concede them victory before the war has even begun," she had declared one evening at supper. "We are Altanians. We must not abandon our principles, but rather stand bravely before any adversity."

Ivy had raised her glass to that. While they did not have a great deal of society these days, she could make no complaint about the quality of what they had.

That Rose made no mention of the lack of parties and dinners and balls was expected. But to Ivy's surprise, Lily hardly remarked about the topic either. At last Ivy grew so perplexed by this behavior that she brought up the topic herself one afternoon as they took tea.

"Why should I care if we are not being invited to any balls?" Lily had replied with a shrug. "I have no want for society or ways to occupy myself. Besides, I cannot see that there is any point in going to a party now when all the bravest and handsomest men have already gone off to become officers in the army."

Ivy was at once surprised and pleased to hear her youngest sister utter a statement which seemed based on rationality. It was perhaps an exaggeration that there were no men of quality remaining in the city, but it was also a fact that the possibility of conflict had caused many young men from better families to buy commissions in the army—either out of a sense of duty to the nation, or from a desire to seek their fortunes in war.

All in all, Ivy could only be happy with how Lily and Rose were bearing up under the current circumstances. Still, she could hope for matters to improve. It was not fair that her sisters had been deprived of the benefits of wider society so soon after being introduced to it.

At the moment, though, Rose was contentedly sewing, and Lily was absorbed with whatever it was she was setting down in the folio, so Ivy opened the book she had found on the shelf. She turned to the first chapter and saw at once that, as she had suspected, it was a romantic novel. Ivy had never heard of the author, who, according to the brief paragraph following the frontispiece, was the son of a noble family from the Principalities, these being the wealthy city-states on the northern edge of the Murgh Empire.

Ivy doubted the veracity of the biography. More than likely the author was an Altanian schoolteacher who sought to lend an air of mystery to the novel by claiming a foreign background. That said, there was indeed an exotic flavor to the writing, which was of surprisingly good quality, and Ivy quickly found herself captivated by the story of a handsome but lowly young man, a gondolier in the ancient canal city of Ardaunto, and the beautiful daughter of a wealthy merchant whom he admired from afar.

Of course, circumstance promptly conspired to acquaint the two, and a romance was quickly kindled between them. Yet after that, the story did not immediately fall into the expected pattern. The young woman was not locked in her chamber by her angry father to await rescue by the young man who had conveniently discovered he was in fact the son of a nobleman.

Rather, there was a melancholy air about the young woman, for she seemed resigned to some unknown destiny. Curious what her fate might be, and if she could be saved from it, the young gondolier began to secretly pursue her father, despite the grave risk to himself should he be discovered. Then one night, as he followed the merchant to an abandoned tower, he discovered that his beloved's father was a magician. . . .

"Is something wrong, Ivy?" Lily said, looking up with a frown.

Ivy realized she must have let out a gasp at the revelation in the book that the merchant was in fact a magician. It was silly, of course, but she had gotten caught up in the story. She shook her head but lacked the voice to speak, as if she had just awakened from some sort of spell.

Lily's expression became one of concern. She set down her charcoal pencil and hurried over to Ivy.

"You're very hot," Lily said as she seized her hand. "And your face is flushed. I think we'd better call for the doctor. Rose, go see if Dr. Lawrent is in his room."

"No, I'm very well," Ivy at last managed to say. "The day is a bit warm, that's all. It gets so stifling on long afternoons."

Except the dim air of the parlor was still cool.

Rose was standing now, Miss Mew in her arms, her brown eyes wide. "Are you very sure you're well, Ivy?"

Ivy smiled for Rose's sake. "Yes, I'm sure. I want only to sit here a little while longer and finish the page I am on. I'm enjoying this novel of yours very much, Lily. But I don't think I've seen you reading it. Is it one you purchased recently?"

Lily's frown returned. "I haven't bought any novels lately."

"But I'm sure it must be one of your books. It's a romance."

Ivy held up the book so Lily could look at it, but her youngest sister shook her head.

"I've never seen that book in my life."

"Are you certain?"

"I'm sure I'd know if it was mine! Besides, I'm far too busy to read novels. I don't have time for frivolous diversions like you do, Ivy."

With that, Lily took up her folio and departed the parlor.

Ivy put a hand to her temple, for her head had begun to ache. No matter how the book had come into the house, she had been reading it longer than she had meant to. Through the screen of wisteria that covered the window, she could see that the shadows outside had grown long. The lumenal was at last drawing toward a close.

It was past time to give Mrs. Seenly instructions for supper. Ivy rose from the chair, then set down the book. Oddly, she felt a reluctance as she did so. An urge came over her to sit and read more about the young gondolier and the merchant's daughter and the labyrinthine canals of Ardaunto.

Now she was indeed being frivolous! She started toward the parlor door, then turned to look at Rose.

"I'm sorry to leave you all by yourself, dearest," she said. "I don't know where Lily's gone to."

Rose smiled at her from the sofa. "Don't worry, Ivy. I won't be alone."

Ivy returned the expression. No doubt Miss Mew would keep

Rose company until supper. Though now that she noticed it, the tortoiseshell cat was not on Rose's lap, or anywhere in view.

Well, most likely she was under the sofa, waiting for Rose to dangle a bit of thread to entice her to leap out. Ivy left the parlor and made her way toward the kitchen, wondering what Mrs. Seenly had managed to find for their supper, and hoping there had been something good at the butcher's, as they still had their guest, Dr. Lawrent.

IVY GAVE A great yawn as she climbed the steps toward the third floor. Despite the length of the lumenal, she had not taken a rest during the day. What was more, they had been longer at the supper table than she had expected, listening as Dr. Lawrent described some of his research, which he had recently been writing about in a scientific paper.

The research concerned a certain species of moth native to County Dorn, which Dr. Lawrent had learned, by looking at older samples preserved in the Royal Altanian Museum, had once possessed white wings. Yet it was the case that, over time, the color of the moth's wings had darkened, and nowadays they were a smoky gray. Over that same period of time, the practice of burning coal to fuel industry had greatly increased in that part of the country, and the soot blackened the bark of the trees where the moths tended to alight and roost.

In the paper, Dr. Lawrent intended to propose the theory that the birds which preyed upon the moths were able to easily see and catch the white moths against the dark trees. But darker moths would have a better chance of blending in with the bark and escaping notice, and so would survive to pass their coloring on to their offspring. Thus the entire population of moths over time had gone from white to gray.

The topic was fascinating—to Ivy at least, if not her sisters—and she had asked Dr. Lawrent a number of questions about the paper, which he had been happy to expound upon.

Now, though, she was more than ready to return to her own roost. Only, as she reached the second landing, it occurred to her that she had not yet looked through her father's journal. Ivy hesitated, a hand on the railing. It had been months since she had discovered an entry in the journal. Besides, if the umbral was as long as the lumenal had been, she would have plenty of time to look at the journal when she woke.

Except there was no guarantee that would be the case. And even if it was unlikely, due to the alterations of the heavens, that another entry would ever appear in the journal, it was a hope she was not yet ready to abandon. It would feel too much like she was betraying her father if she did.

Ivy sighed, then turned and went back downstairs.

The library was dark, so she took a candle from the front hall with her. As she entered the room, the wooden eye set into the lintel above the door watched her with (at least she fancied) an approving look. She set the candle on the writing table, opened the drawer, and took out the Wyrdwood box.

As she did, the old rosewood clock on the mantel let out a chime, already marking the end of the first span of the umbral. So it was not to be a long night after all, but rather a short one. Which meant it was well that she was checking the journal now.

Ivy opened the Wyrdwood box, took out the familiar book, and began to turn through it. She went at a fairly rapid pace, giving each page no more than a cursory glance. The night was already a third over, and she wanted there to be at least some of it remaining by the time she got to bed. She cracked a yawn, turning another page.

The flat white expanse on the desk before her suddenly grew dark, like the wings of the moths in Dr. Lawrent's scientific paper.

The candle flame flickered, disturbed by the breath that escaped Ivy's lips. She hesitated, then brushed her fingers over the page, as if to touch the words to make sure they were really there. So astonished was she that, for a minute, she did not even read the entry; she only stared at it.

At last the words became more than shapes, resolving themselves into things of meaning. As she read them, a strange feeling came over Ivy, a kind of gentle yet ominous sensation of floating, as if she were drifting in a gondola down a darkened canal toward some destination she could not see.

My dearest Ivy, the entry in the journal began. *It is about time. If you can read this, then it means you must begin to gather the others. I don't know where they will be by now, but you must seek them out. Bennick, Mundy, and Larken may all yet be here in Invarel. At least I hope that they are, for it will make your task easier. As for Fintaur, I believe you will find his whereabouts in the city of Ardaunto, across the sea. . . .*

Her heart beating rapidly, Ivy read the rest of the page. Then she took a pen and a sheet of paper from the desk to transcribe the entry. The umbral would be brief, and she knew by the time the sun rose her father's words would be gone from the page.

Just as she knew that she had not a hope of sleeping that night.

CHAPTER SIX

𝕿HEIR MEETING PLACE this time was in a room beneath a pewtersmith's shop on Coronet Street.

The smith was the cousin of one of their number and so could be trusted. All the same, a heavy black cloth draped the door, blocking even the smallest chink, and no sound could pass beyond the line made by the silver cord that lay on the floor, encircling the edges of the room. They had not told the smith why they were gathering there. Which meant that, if he was questioned, he could in all honesty tell an agent of the Gray Conclave that he had no knowledge of magicians beneath his shop—a fact which would protect him as much as it did *them*.

"The Fellowship of the Silver Circle will now convene."

It was Coulten who spoke the words this time. By design, their little order had no leader, no magus. Meetings were called by anyone who felt there was need and had arranged for a suitable place, and they were brought to order by the last to arrive.

"The Circle will not be broken." The other eight men gave the customary reply.

And that was that for arcane ceremony.

"Well, what is it, Canderhow?" Rafferdy said at once, looking across the circle at the subject of his address. "This had better be worth our while. I was planning on spending a pleasant evening at my club before I opened my book and saw your notice had appeared."

Canderhow was a plump man slightly older than Rafferdy and Coulten, being about thirty, and seemed far too mild of speech and accommodating of behavior to be a highly successful barrister—though in fact he was one. It was Canderhow's cousin who was the pewtersmith, and it was his request for a meeting which had appeared in all of their black books at the very moment he wrote it down in his own.

"I'm very sorry to have come between you and your enjoyable evening," Canderhow said in his characteristically sympathetic tone.

"Don't you dare apologize to him," Coulten said with a laugh. "I assure you, he never does anything at his club except drink brandy, take tobacco, and pretend to be interested in a broadsheet. I'm sure such pursuits are nowhere so important as anything we might do here."

"Indeed, they are of no importance at all," Rafferdy said, scowling at his friend, "which is precisely why they are so important to me. When all of life becomes crowded with profound and weighty matters, making time to engage in trivial things becomes an even greater priority."

Canderhow bowed in his direction. "You argue the point cogently, and I concede that you are likely right, Rafferdy."

While Canderhow was a barrister, and not even a baronet let alone a magnate, he did not say *Lord* before Rafferdy's name. No titles or honorifics were allowed within the circle. Whatever the nine of them were outside its bounds, within they were all of them equals.

"It is, in the end, the smallest delights which impart to us the greatest satisfaction," Canderhow went on. "But for us to enjoy the littler pleasures in life, ofttimes the larger problems must first be solved."

"In that case," Trefnell said, "if we are quite done with the matter of apologizing for disturbing everyone's supper, perhaps you can tell us your reason for calling a meeting, Canderhow. I presume it regards a matter of some urgency, as it was done with little notice. Though I am pleased to see everyone was able to attend."

For his part, Rafferdy was not so much pleased by this fact as he was relieved by it. The circle of silence would be at its most powerful if the number within it was no more and no less than nine.

Canderhow gave a half bow. "I hoped, once you heard the news, you would forgive me for providing so little warning."

"And I had hoped we were finished with apologies," Trefnell said, raising a shaggy gray eyebrow.

Trefnell had once been a headmaster at a school for boys, and he possessed an uncanny ability to speak in a tone that was at once kindly and formidable. Rafferdy found it difficult not to immediately leap to attention when the older man spoke, harkening back to his own years at boarding school—a time during which he had earned the ire of his headmaster on more than one occasion.

"Yes, of course, I'm sor—" Canderhow shook his head. "I mean, yes, I'm quite finished."

"Then go on."

Canderhow did so, and the news was not good. Like Trefnell and a few other members of their little order, Canderhow occupied a seat in the Hall of Citizens, and he had a great many connections there. Through some of these, he had heard whispers that a crucial vote was to come up during the next session of Assembly.

Specifically, an act was going to be put before both Halls at precisely the same time—a measure that would call for the immediate reduction of all stands of Wyrdwood within thirty miles of Invarel (with the exception of the Evengrove) to no more than five acres in extent. If the vote carried in both the Hall of Citizens and the Hall of Magnates, then the act would immediately become law, and all throughout central Altania groves of Old Forest that were deemed too large would be cut back to the proscribed size.

"Five acres?" Coulten said. "I confess, I have no idea how much that is, but it doesn't sound very large."

"That's because it isn't," Wolsted replied in his typically brusque fashion. He was a red-faced man who sat in the Hall of Magnates and had once been a member of the Stouts. "I am well used to walking about the lands of my estate, and I can tell you that you could stroll all the way around a five-acre grove in ten minutes, going at an easy pace."

"Precisely how many stands of Wyrdwood in the vicinity of the city do you think exceed that size?" Canderhow asked, as always attempting to apprise himself of the facts.

"I would say at least a dozen of them," Wolsted said, a grim look on his weathered face.

Coulten shook his head, causing his tall crown of hair to bow and sway. "But if that many groves are cut back, won't it only cause more of them to rise up and strike out? If their wish is to protect Altania from the Wyrdwood, it hardly makes sense to provoke it."

"On the contrary, it would make perfect sense to the Magisters, who are no doubt behind all this," Rafferdy said. "And I am sure their intent is anything but the protection of Altania."

"What do you mean?" Coulten said with a frown.

Rafferdy gave a sigh. Coulten was clever, but he had a tendency to ask for explanations rather than think things through on his own, even when he was perfectly capable of doing so.

"How many Risings have there been of late?"

Coulten cocked his head. "Very few. In fact, I should say there have been none at all. Despite the loss of the lord inquirer, the other inquirers have been doing their work well."

"Indeed. Too well, I suspect some think. Due to the efforts of the inquirers, the Wyrdwood has not been antagonized, and so there have been no Risings. Which is why, in Assembly, there has been little impetus behind any calls for the Wyrdwood's destruction of late. Yet given what happened, there are bound to be many who feel a reduction in the size of those groves closest to the city is a prudent measure. Indeed, so reasonable will the idea seem that most will find it difficult to oppose."

"But it is anything but prudent or reasonable!" Coulten exclaimed. "We saw that ourselves at the Evengrove, Rafferdy. If the groves are cut back, they will surely lash out at those who do the deed."

Rafferdy gave him a pointed look. "Precisely."

For a moment Coulten's expression was one of puzzlement, but then he blinked. "The Magisters want the groves to rise up. They want to make people afraid again."

Rafferdy nodded. "There have been too many other things for people to worry about of late—the cost of goods, brigands and rebels on the roads, and the rumors that Huntley Morden is planning to sail a fleet of ships from the Principalities to Torland. No one is thinking about the Old Trees. Which means, if the Magisters are going to get an act through Assembly calling for the eradication of the Wyrdwood, they're going to have to make people afraid of it again. Once people are rioting in the streets, calling for either the Halls of Assembly or the Wyrdwood to be burned— well, I suppose you can guess which of the two the Magnates and the Citizens would choose."

"I suppose I can at that," Coulten said with a sigh. "But are you certain the Magisters are behind it?"

"Of course they're behind it," Rafferdy said. "Or rather, the High Order of the Golden Door are behind it. I'm surprised I should even need to state it, Coulten. You know their proclivities."

After the rumors he and Coulten had spread in Assembly that Lord Mertrand was to be avoided at all cost, Rafferdy had thought the High Order of the Golden Door would disband. Only then Mertrand was murdered, and soon after the order was revived. As far as anyone knew, nearly every Magister now belonged to the High Order of the Golden Door.

"Yes, I know their proclivities quite well," Coulten replied darkly. "But it is baffling nonetheless. After all, the act to reduce the Wyrdwood is to be proposed in the Hall of Citizens as well."

It was Canderhow who answered him. "I fear the Magisters have more than a few allies there. Now that the Magisters have suddenly become fervent supporters of royal power, many of the Citizens are following their lead."

"Well," Coulten said, "now that we know they're planning a vote on the Wyrdwood, what do we do about it?"

Eight pairs of eyes turned toward Trefnell.

While the Fellowship of the Silver Circle had no magus, Trefnell was closer to being its leader than anyone else, and they all looked to the former headmaster before making any sort of decision. It was Wolsted who had discreetly approached Rafferdy and Coulten one day at the Silver Branch and spoken to them about joining the Fellowship, having observed their actions in Assembly as well as the House rings upon their hands. Yet it was very clear at their first meeting that, had Trefnell not approved of them, they would not have been admitted to the circle.

Fortunately, after no small amount of questioning—and a demonstration of their ability to read and invoke several magickal runes—Trefnell had shaken both their hands and welcomed them into the order. With the addition of Coulten and Rafferdy, the fellowship of nine was complete. Five of their number belonged to the Hall of Magnates, and the remainder to the Hall of Citizens. The purpose of the fellowship, Trefnell had told them during that first meeting, was to do all they could to make certain that Assembly passed no act or made no law that might cause harm to the Wyrdwood. And they had all of them together sworn an oath binding them to this aim.

Rafferdy had never been much for making pledges. After all, promises could become quite inconvenient when one had a sudden wish to change one's mind. All the same, he had few misgivings in swearing this particular oath. He would never forget entering the Evengrove with Mrs. Quent and traveling to the ancient pyramid in its center—the tomb of a powerful Ashen entity which was hidden within, and its vile powers contained by, the Old Trees. Rafferdy was in general a man happily free of convictions, but there were two notions to which, after that night, he now hewed with great faith. The first was that the Wyrdwood must never be harmed. And the second was that, in all of Altania, there was no woman more intelligent, more brave, and more beautiful than Mrs. Quent.

While it was not Trefnell who had founded the Fellowship of the Silver Circle, it was he who had quickly turned it to its present purpose upon joining the order. "It is no coincidence that, after so long, the Risings have begun again even as Cerephus approaches in the heavens," he had said quietly to Rafferdy after that first meeting. "We all of us in the circle know that the Wyrdwood has the power to thwart the magicks of the Ashen. But only you and I have seen it with our own eyes."

It was half a year ago when Trefnell had witnessed the abilities of the Wyrdwood for himself. A member of the arcane order he had belonged to at the time had been made into a gray man—his body hollowed out to a shell and his organs, along with his soul, replaced by a daemon.

After Trefnell, in the course of his research, stumbled upon this awful fact, his former compatriot pursued him, intending to murder him to conceal the secret. In desperation, Trefnell had fled to the country and there went to a small stand of Wyrdwood—for in his reading he had encountered a few hints of the ability of the Old Trees to resist daemons.

And that night, by the stone wall at the edge of the Wyrdwood, he had discovered it was true. He had watched as the branches of the trees lashed out, snatching his former compatriot up from the ground and rending the daemon into pieces that dissolved away into a gray sludge.

After hearing this harrowing tale, Rafferdy had related something of his own experiences at the Evengrove, how he had observed the trees stand in resistance to the magicks of the Ashen—

though he had given no details that might have indicated the presence or identity of Mrs. Quent, or even the true nature of what they had found there.

Despite Rafferdy's vagueness, Trefnell had been excited to learn of these additional facts, which added weight to his belief that the Wyrdwood had some important role in what was to come. For none of them had any doubt that the Ashen would continue to seek a way into the world.

"It seems the hour we have been preparing for has come," Trefnell said as the other magicians looked to him. "We must find a way to prevent the measure calling for the reduction of the Wyrdwood from being enacted. And I fear it is not enough to vote against it and hope others do the same. For should the act carry while we were in the negative, it would surely direct attention toward all of us."

Trefnell did not need to explain further. Lady Shayde continued to observe Assembly on a regular basis, and if she did not come, then Moorkirk—that hulk of a man who served her—came instead.

"Then we are bound to fail," Wolsted said, his ruddy face going grim. "If we do not vote against the measure ourselves, then we can hardly expect that others will do so."

"What if nobody were to vote on it?" Rafferdy said, an idea forming in his mind.

"I don't follow you, Rafferdy. If we speak nay to the motion to bring the act to the floor, or to the motion to end debate and call for a vote upon the act, we will draw as much attention to ourselves as if we opposed it outright. In any case, we cannot succeed."

"So it would seem," Rafferdy said. "Unless, of course, it is impossible for a vote to be called at all."

Canderhow stroked his jowled chin. "But that would only happen if a quorum was not present. And if word gets out that there is to be an important vote—which the Magisters will make sure happens just in time, mind you—then we cannot expect many will stay away from Assembly."

"Can't we?" Rafferdy said, arching an eyebrow for effect. "And what if some number of magnates found themselves otherwise . . . engaged?"

The others stared at him. Then, as he explained his idea further, he saw looks of understanding go around the circle—followed by grins.

All at once those grins ceased as there came three loud thumps on the ceiling above. These were followed, after a pause, by three more. Despite the protections of the circle of silence, they all held their breath and uttered no word. There was only one reason for the signal from above.

There were either soldiers in the pewtersmith's shop or suspected agents of the Gray Conclave.

For several tense moments they continued to stand within the circle, making no sound. Trefnell pointed at the door of the room, then clasped his hands together. The message was clear: *have your spells of binding at the ready.*

While Rafferdy had practiced his binding enchantments a number of times, so that the harsh words of magick came easily off his tongue, he had never used the spell on a living being. Nor did he ever have wish to do so. All the same, he tightened his grip on the ivory handle of his cane.

Suddenly there came two thumps from above, followed by two more. So loud was the noise that Rafferdy jumped in his boots, though he quickly let out a breath of relief.

"Whoever was here, they've left now," Canderhow said, dabbing at the beads of moisture on his brow with a handkerchief.

"Then I suggest we do the same," Trefnell said. He gave a nod in Rafferdy's direction. "I believe we all know what we are to do in advance of the next session of Assembly."

With that, the circle was broken and the cloth pulled away from the door. By ones and twos they went up and out into the night, allowing a few minutes to elapse between their departures from the pewtersmith's shop so as not to draw attention.

"I do hope you know what you're doing," Coulten said as he and Rafferdy walked down Coronet Street.

"What a peculiar thing to say," Rafferdy replied cheerfully. "Of course I don't know what I'm doing. You know I prefer to invent things as I go."

COUGHS SOUNDED about the Hall of Magnates, along with a constant rustling as lords and viscounts, earls and dukes fanned themselves with a folded broadsheet—always *The Comet* or *The Messenger,* of course, never *The Fox* or *The Swift Arrow.* Though it was still morning, the day was already sweltering, for the umbral had been exceedingly brief.

Another round of throat clearing echoed up toward the domed ceiling. Everywhere magnates turned their heads to look about them, as if expecting some event to occur. Despite this, the High Speaker's gavel lay still upon the podium, and the floor at the center of the Hall remained empty.

Across the aisle from where the New Wigs were situated, Lord Davarry sat alone upon a bench. Several rows of benches behind him were similarly empty. While he sat stonily, gazing forward without expression, it was plain to all that his agitation was growing. His cheeks were red, and his bluish wig had steadily crept forward on his head over the past half an hour as he repeatedly clamped his jaw.

There was a loud noise at the back of the Hall. Davarry leaped to his feet and turned to look toward the large gilded doors. But it was only an usher who, having grown dull with the heat and quiet, had leaned against one of the doors, causing it to slam shut. The young man gave a sheepish look, then hastily pulled the door back open, for the doors were not to be shut until Assembly was called to order by the High Speaker.

And that could not occur until a quorum—two thirds of their total number—was present.

Davarry glared at the usher, then sat back down on the empty bench.

"Were you waiting for something, Lord Davarry?" Rafferdy said, rising to his feet. He spoke as if merely making idle conversation—though his volume was more than enough to carry throughout the stifled Hall.

Now it was at Rafferdy that Davarry's glare was directed. "And what might you presume the answer to be, Lord Rafferdy?" He gestured to the empty benches around him.

"Ah," Rafferdy said, as if just noticing the empty seats. "It appears that you have misplaced your party, Lord Davarry."

"So it would seem."

A bout of nervous laughter went around the Hall at this, though it was not so much directed at Davarry as at the absurd situation. Rafferdy had to grant the other lord his due. Davarry was not one to be made a fool even when caught in foolish circumstances.

"Curiously, I find that I am in a similar plight," Rafferdy said, gesturing to the empty seats to either side of him, which were usually occupied by the other New Wigs.

This won him a suspicious look from the elder lord. "Yes, it is highly curious, Lord Rafferdy."

"Well, perhaps we can amuse ourselves while we wait for them to appear," Rafferdy said pleasantly.

"How so?"

The noise of coughing and the rustling of broadsheets in the Hall was suddenly much reduced.

"Well, we might discuss ways in which some of the difficulties that beset our nation could be confronted."

"You know we cannot conduct business in the Hall without a quorum!"

Rafferdy acknowledged this truth with a bow. "You are right, of course. Yet if the lords on the back benches are free to play at dice, then I am sure we up front may amuse ourselves by making conversation. I cannot think the High Speaker's rules would forbid us passing the time in such a fashion."

The High Speaker was, in fact, presently snoring as he leaned on an elbow propped upon his podium.

"Perhaps there is no rule against it," Davarry conceded. "But neither is there a point to it. After all, nothing we say will be entered into the record of the Hall's business."

"Again, you are right. Yet it might help us to organize our thoughts, so that once the session does come to order, we can conclude our business more expeditiously in whatever time remains." Rafferdy hesitated for the slightest moment. "Unless you do not think there is any need to conserve time, and that there is no great amount of work for us to do."

A man with as keen a mind as Davarry's could only know when he was being baited. But Rafferdy also knew that this same intelligence can also lead a man to abandon caution, presuming he can best his opponent at the other's game. As the saying went, a clever mouse always thinks he can nick the cheese without springing the trap.

Rafferdy was about to find out if that adage was true.

"Of course there is a great amount of work for this body to perform!" Davarry said, addressing not Rafferdy, but the rest of the Hall. "Anyone who believes otherwise, who feels there is no need for us to take decisive action, puts our nation in grave peril. We must not dither and falter as we so often do. We must refrain from paying sole consideration to politics and how this or that might benefit our own positions, and instead we must do all that we can to strengthen our nation and protect it from all threats."

This resulted in several calls of *Hear! Hear!* about the Hall, which after a few moments were timidly joined by others.

Rafferdy turned to look in the direction of some of these latecoming affirmations. "Indeed, Lord Davarry, no one in these times wishes to be seen as tolerant or coddling of any person or notion which might be perceived as a detriment to our nation. In fact, I am sure it is impossible for a man to dislike or dread such things too much! He could vocalize his detestation with great frequency and volume, could beat his breast and shake a damning fist at any who might offer the slightest disagreement, and still I'm sure it would not be deemed too much by some."

Davarry hesitated, as if uncertain precisely how to respond to this. "For anything which would weaken the sovereign crown of Altania, no revulsion can be too much," Davarry said at last.

"Altania above all else?"

"Indeed, above all!"

Rafferdy nodded. "Well, then we are in agreement. Yet perhaps I have found a topic for us to converse upon, for I find myself puzzled by one matter. Perhaps you can enlighten me."

"I might shine a light in a darkened room, Lord Rafferdy. Whether the light reveals the room to be full or empty is not under my control."

This resulted in a roar of laughter all around. Rafferdy gave a bow to conceal his smile.

"Then tell me this, Lord Davarry," he said, rising again. "You say we must seek to bolster the Crown, and I think all present would agree. But I cannot help wondering—would the Crown not be more easily bolstered if it were firmly situated upon someone's head?"

Murmurs ran about the Hall at this. At the podium, the High Speaker opened his eyes.

Davarry glared at Rafferdy. He could have disengaged then. As he had said, none of this mattered. But while Davarry disliked appearing a fool, he disliked even more to appear as if he was not up to a challenge. At least, that was what Rafferdy was counting upon.

"I presume it is the princess's head you refer to," Davarry said.

Rafferdy shrugged. "Unless there is another you think the crown belongs on."

"That would be treason, Lord Rafferdy," the other lord said darkly. "The crown of Altania can never be, *must* never be, worn on another's head."

There was something peculiar about this statement. The words which were omitted from it seemed to impart as much meaning as the words that were included.

"If that is the case, then when will it be placed upon Princess Layle's?"

"Such a public spectacle as a royal coronation is hardly prudent at the moment. I can think of no event which would attract so many hooligans and troublemakers. They must not be given a stage upon which to perform their mischief and so advertise themselves."

"Very well, then let it be done in private."

"That is not what is prescribed in the Great Charter!"

Rafferdy affected a bemused expression. "So a coronation must be public, and yet no one can be allowed to attend. Given these requirements, I find it a wonder Altania has ever had a ruler at all."

This time the laughter in the Hall belonged to Rafferdy, as did Davarry's scowl.

"You make it sound as if we have the benefit of no authority, Lord Rafferdy, when you know very well that is not the case. Lord Valhaine labors tirelessly to ensure order in the name of Her Highness. Just as we must labor ourselves to do the same. So let us set aside these idle discussions, and instead pursue subjects of real weight."

"Such as?"

"Such as the poor state of the exchequer! Or the proper deployment of the army, or the matter of the Wyrdwood, or—"

Rafferdy didn't hesitate. This was the moment he had been waiting for—indeed, whose occurrence he had been trying all this while to provoke—and so he seized it.

"The Wyrdwood?" he interrupted in a loud voice. "Really, Lord Davarry, you aren't still concerned by a few collections of ragged old trees? I thought we were to discuss true threats against our nation, not imagined ones."

"Imagined?" Lord Davarry sputtered. "God on High, man, the recent Risings have hardly been a fantasy. The Old Trees have lashed out. Men have been throttled to death by root and branch."

"True, but only those who have been dull enough to venture near the groves," Rafferdy said, making his voice crisp. "In which case the Risings have only served to benefit us by removing the most imbecilic individuals from the population and thereby increasing its general intelligence."

Lord Davarry gave his wig a tug. "You are very flippant, sir. I wonder if you would speak that way to the widow of one of the soldiers who perished at the Evengrove."

"No, for a soldier is not subject to his own stupidity but rather to that of his commanders." Rafferdy raised a finger, as if an idea had just occurred to him. "But speaking of soldiers, I wonder, Lord Davarry, if you have never considered that the Wyrdwood serves a similar purpose as they do? That it is perhaps for this very purpose that groves of the Old Trees have so long been preserved in Altania."

"What purpose are you referring to?"

"The purpose of defense, of course."

Lord Davarry's blue eyes narrowed, and he stood silently for a long moment. "Defense?" he said at last. "And what could the Wyrdwood possibly defend us against?"

"Against those who would invade our nation," Rafferdy said with perfect seriousness.

A silence descended over the Hall. A vibration could be felt upon the stifling air, like the beating of a great heart. All turned their eyes toward Lord Davarry, awaiting his reply.

Before he could speak, the noise of many footsteps echoed up to the marble dome. All turned to look as a group of twenty or so young lords in silver-tinted wigs appeared at the doors of the Hall.

"Well, look now, here is the remainder of my party," Rafferdy said, as if pleasantly surprised. "I'm sure the Grand Usher will correct me if I am in error, but I believe we might now have just enough to make a quorum and come to order."

And the trap was sprung.

Led by Coulten, the New Wigs proceeded down the aisle to occupy the benches around Rafferdy. The Grand Usher made his count, then announced they indeed had a quorum, with a slight surplus. The High Speaker brought down his gavel, and the Hall of Magnates came to order.

A few small matters of business were brought up, discussed, and voted upon, but nothing of great import. All the while Lord Davarry sat stock-still amidst the empty benches that were usually occupied by the Magisters. He did not dare bring up any measure about the Wyrdwood now, for fear it would not have the votes to carry.

Rafferdy had to give Lord Davarry credit, for he kept his face forward, and never once looked back at the gilded doors, which were shut now that the Hall was in session. But though he said nothing, once again his wig inched forward on his scalp as he clamped his jaw over and over. He had been caught in the snare, and he had not a crumb of cheese to show for it.

Soon the business of the Hall was concluded, and the High Speaker's gavel came down to end the session. Nor did this happen a moment too soon, for even as the doors opened and magnates began to stream from the Hall, a large number of men in elegant black robes and bluish wigs forced their way down the aisles.

It was the remainder of the Magisters.

Several of them reached Davarry, gesturing with great agitation as they spoke to him in voices too low to be heard. Rafferdy saw Davarry's cheeks darken to an even deeper shade of red. All at once he shouted out to the High Speaker to bring the Hall back to order, but it was too late for that. Half the lords had already departed by now, off to the Silver Branch or elsewhere to get their dinner. It was over.

"Great Gods, but that was entertaining," Coulten murmured, leaning his head close to Rafferdy's. "Your scheme worked perfectly."

Rafferdy could only concede that this was the case. "Did any of the New Wigs ask how we knew what was going to happen?"

"Of course they did. They're clever lads. I told them that we had heard a rumor that the Magisters were going to be delayed, and that we could have an impact on the proceedings if we timed our entrance carefully. They were more than happy to go along with the game, and they're delighted it worked."

So it had. The Magisters all milled about Lord Davarry now, looking in their black robes like so many angry crows.

Yet even as he watched this satisfying scene, Rafferdy's amusement faded. "They will not fall for that trick again."

"I suppose not," Coulten murmured. "But it really was brilliant. I wish I could have been a fly on the wall."

So did Rafferdy. He could imagine all the Magisters entering the dank warehouse down in Waterside, believing from the notice which had appeared in their black books that they were attending a hastily called meeting of their arcane order. Only their magus never arrived. And then, when they attempted to depart, they found the doors had been locked by magick, preventing them from getting out.

"Really," Coulten went on, "they must all be dreadful magicians if it took them all that time to figure out they were duped and to break the spells on the doors."

Not so dreadful as Rafferdy had hoped. Despite the strength of the bindings he and the other members of the Fellowship had placed on the doors of the old warehouse by the river, the Magisters had freed themselves and arrived at Assembly more quickly than he had expected. A few minutes sooner, and the Hall would still have been in session, and they might have been able to bring the plan for reducing the size of the Wyrdwood to a vote.

Of course, the whole scheme would have fallen apart if Lord Davarry had simply opened his own black book to see the meeting notice. As the leader of the Magisters—and presumably the magus of the Golden Door—he would have known at once that the message was false, for it came not from him. But if he *was* magus, and thus the one who called all the meetings, why would Davarry bother to open his own black book unless it was for the purpose of writing a message? He wouldn't. Or at least, that was what Rafferdy had reasoned. And it appeared he had been right.

"I say," Coulten said quietly as they left the benches, "you never did tell us how it was you got the notice for the meeting to appear in their black books. That was some trick. However did you manage it?"

"I have my methods."

"Come now, Rafferdy, don't be so secretive. I think you can tell me of all people."

Rafferdy's smile returned. "And so I will, but not quite yet. Now let's get to the Silver Branch. I am in severe need of a drink."

They proceeded from the Hall of Magnates with the other New Wigs. The Hall of Citizens was also just letting out of session, resulting in much crowding and jostling, and Rafferdy found himself separated from Coulten. All around, men were talking in loud voices, and it was quickly clear from bits of conversation Rafferdy overheard that the measure to reduce the Wyrdwood had not been brought up for a vote in that Hall either.

So Canderhow had been right. He had predicted that those in the Hall of Citizens who were in league with the Magisters would not dare to bring up the matter for a vote on their own, preferring instead to follow the lead of their more powerful allies.

Across the loggia, he saw the bulky figure of Canderhow departing the Hall of Citizens. Trefnell came a little ways behind him. Rafferdy met the older man's eyes for a brief moment, then quickly turned away before anyone might notice the exchange. Just then Coulten hurried up to him, a broadsheet in hand. He seemed to have something to say, but before he could get it out, a group of young lords in rich black robes and bluish wigs appeared before them.

"You think yourself very bold and clever, don't you, Lord Rafferdy?" one of them said, his tone sneering.

Rafferdy didn't know his name, only that he was one of the Magisters, and that he bore an uncanny resemblance to a bulldog, having a snubbed nose and sagging jowls that were accentuated by his glowering expression.

"I'm sure I don't know what you mean," Rafferdy replied pleasantly, though his fingers tightened around the ivory handle of his cane.

"On the contrary, I believe you know precisely what I mean. You fancy yourself a powerful magician. You believe that you and the rest of your arcane order can work spells as you please, without any sort of consequence, and you make no effort to hide the fact. Rather, you advertise it."

He made a gesture toward the House ring on Rafferdy's right hand.

Despite the spark of alarm he felt, Rafferdy gave an indifferent shrug. "It is a ring such as we all have, nothing more. I simply choose to display what everyone already knows is there. I can hardly think it of any note. As for working spells—I am sure you know as well as I that belonging to any sort of occult order is against the Rules of Citizenship."

Suddenly the other young man's face drew back in a loose-fleshed grin. "Oh, it's against the Rules for *you*, all right. But not everyone suffers under that same proscription now. Which means you might discover that you are not so clever as you think, Lord Rafferdy, and that what you consider to be boldness is in fact folly. Until later."

These last words were accompanied by a stiff bow. As one, the group of Magisters turned with a flourish of their black robes and proceeded away across the loggia.

Rafferdy frowned after them. "What do they mean, not everyone suffers under the same proscription now?" he muttered.

"I think it has to do with this," Coulten said in a low voice, and he held up the broadsheet he had been carrying. "Look here."

Rafferdy did, and the spark of alarm in his chest began to smolder and burn.

OFFICIAL ARCANE ORDER GIVEN CHARTER
BY LORD VALHAINE

The High Order of the Golden Door is now the sole order of magicians authorized by the Crown. The order has been commissioned to study occult matters and to make recommendations on all topics regarding magick to the government. At the same time, all other orders and clubs devoted to the practice of magick continue to be proscribed. In addition, as it is a place infamous for training magicians out of sight of the watchful eye of the Crown, the doors of Gauldren's College have been closed immediately and indefinitely.

Any sense of victory Rafferdy had enjoyed now vanished. "So the Magisters are no longer working for Lord Valhaine in secret. Their allegiance is out in the open."

Coulten nodded. "And it's more than that, Rafferdy. We're not the only magicians who have continued to meet under the assumption that the Gray Conclave wasn't making too great an effort to root out magickal orders, given that the Magisters all belong to one themselves. But now that the High Order of the Golden Door is officially sanctioned by the Crown . . ."

"It means the Black Dog is free to start sniffing around in search of other occult societies," Rafferdy said grimly.

Even as he spoke, he was aware of a dark figure emerging from behind a column at the far end of the loggia. She moved stiffly, so that he could almost hear the crackle of her black gown, and even though a veil draped down from her hat to conceal her face, he could imagine black eyes watching him.

Rafferdy felt the hairs on his neck prickle. He suddenly had no desire to have an encounter with Lady Shayde—the chief agent of the Gray Conclave and the Black Dog himself, Lord Valhaine. He stuck his right hand in his coat pocket, concealing his ring, and took up his cane in the left.

"Come on, Coulten, I need that drink more than ever. To the Silver Branch!"

CHAPTER SEVEN

JT WAS HOURS into the umbral, but though she was in her bed, Ivy was anything but asleep. She leaned against the headboard, her knees raised up under the bedcovers and a book bound in red leather perched atop them. A single candle burned low on the nightstand, casting a dim gold light on the open pages before her.

She could only suppose she looked very much like Lily often did, reading a romance in bed when she should be sleeping. But it was not a desire to know how the dilemma of the two lovers would be resolved that compelled Ivy to continue on. Rather, she was hoping to find an answer.

That was not to say she did not care for the story in *The Towers of Ardaunto*. The later chapters had proven every bit as compelling as the first few, if not more so. At times she would find herself turning the pages at a rapid pace to learn what happened next to the young gondolier and the magician's daughter, only to force herself to go back and make certain she had read every word, so as not to miss some subtle hint or vital clue.

It is about time, her father had written in the entry that had so unexpectedly appeared in the journal the previous umbral. More than once she had heard him mutter those same words when visiting him in his room at Madstone's. On the first such occasion, he had arranged twelve apple seeds in a perfect line on a plate while she was looking away. Could it be a coincidence that those same words had now appeared in the journal?

No, logic dictated otherwise. Just that afternoon, she had read in *The Comet* about a scientific paper that had lately been presented before the Royal Society of Astrographers. The authors of the paper theorized that, due to the disruptions of Cerephus, the celestial spheres that contained the eleven other planets were beginning to move with a peculiar consonance. If these patterns persisted, it would result in a Grand Conjunction—a configuration of the planets such that all twelve were arranged in a single row, one behind the other.

Previously, a Grand Conjunction had always been regarded as an impossibility, a thing that occurred only in myths and stories. But due to the effects of Cerephus, it was now an utter certainty. When exactly this event would occur, the authors of the paper were not entirely certain, for they were still refining their calculations. And as for what such a heavenly arrangement would mean—that was something no astrographer had yet predicted.

The candle flame wavered as Ivy turned another page. She was nearly to the end of the novel now. The handsome gondolier had at last managed to gain entry into the magician's tower. In this he was aided by a mysterious crone who had approached him one night. The old woman had bid him to sail across the sea to Altania and retrieve fallen branches from the edge of a particular grove of trees which she described.

After much peril—in the form of brigands and storms at sea— the young gondolier completed this task and returned to the canal city of Ardaunto. The crone set the twigs at the foot of the tower and commanded them to grow. To the gondolier's surprise they did so, stretching and twining up the wall of the spire like living things. Using them as a ladder, he was able to scale the wall of the tower, and so came to its highest chamber.

There, much to his horror, he discovered his beloved bound within a circle of candles and runes, the subject of some awful ceremony that was about to occur. He went to her and freed her from the ropes, but to his shock she would not leave with him through the window. Rather, she intended to submit herself willingly to the spells of her father and the other magicians of his order. It was, she said, for the good of all the world.

But is it for the good of you? he had asked her. *And for us?*

She had only shaken her head, tears in her eyes, and at last he understood the air of melancholy he had always sensed about her. Just then there were sounds outside the chamber door. She pleaded with him to leave, telling him he would perish if he stayed. As the door opened, he fled back out the window, but he did not climb down the tower. Instead, he clung to the braided vines and peered unseen through the window.

With horror he watched the scene unfold in the chamber. Nine men in black robes entered through the door. One of them was the father of his beloved. The magicians formed a circle about her, and they proceeded to work a terrible enchantment. The young gondolier wanted to leap into the chamber to put a stop to it, but words of magick slithered through the window, seeming to coil around him, binding him so that he could not move. The nine men closed in around the maiden, so that she was lost from view. Their chanting rose to a crescendo.

All at once came a terrible scream, followed by a long minute of silence. Then it was over. One by one, the magicians departed the room, until only the maiden and her father were left. He reached down a hand and helped his daughter to stand.

She did so with strange, stiff motions, and the gondolier's heart froze in his breast. Her skin, previously the lustrous color of almonds, was now pale as powder, and her hair and eyes were no longer a rich brown, but rather black as onyx. For a moment she stared down at her hands, then she looked up at her father, and her blue-black lips curved in a smile. At this, the gondolier was at last freed of the enchantment. With a cry he leaped through the window into the room and—

Ivy turned the page to read what happened next, then stared in puzzlement. There were no more pages following the one she had just read, only the back cover of the book. Yet how could that be? The story was far from finished, and she wanted to know what happened when the young gondolier entered the room at the top of the tower. Ivy lifted the book and opened it wider to examine the binding.

Close to the spine, between the last page she had read and the back cover of the book, were a number of sharp edges. The final pages had been removed from the book—not torn, but rather carefully cut out with a sharp knife or razor. But why, and by whom?

She thought she could guess the answer to the second of those questions. Who was more likely to have excised the pages from the novel than the very person who had delivered it to the house? Earlier that day, Ivy had spoken with Mrs. Seenly, asking if she had seen the red-covered book before. The housekeeper had nodded, and she described how she had discovered the book on the front step of the house a few days ago. Thinking Lily had left it there, she had taken the book to the parlor and set it upon the shelf where she knew it would be seen.

"I did not put it in among any of the other books, ma'am," Mrs. Seenly had said in her lilting Torland accent, "for I know how you like to keep all of the volumes in the house in a particular order, and I thought you would know best where it belonged. Was that right of me, ma'am?"

Ivy had thanked her and assured her she had done the correct thing.

That had solved the mystery of how the book had come to the house. As for the matter of who had left it on the step, there could be only one possibility. Mrs. Baydon sometimes brought books to share, but she always delivered them in person, as she had a great like for describing the best parts of a story before one had a chance to read them oneself. Which meant there was no one else it could have been except for *him*.

Ivy set down the book, slipped from the bed, and went to the window. There was no moon, but Cerephus pulsed in the heavens, casting a crimson aura over the city. By that livid illumination, she perceived that the garden below was empty save for the spindly figures of the hawthorn and chestnut trees.

The man in the black mask had not appeared to her in many months. All the same, she knew he was out there watching, and she had no doubt that he had been here very recently. Who else could have left a book on the doorstep—one that was entitled *The Towers of Ardaunto*—mere days before the entry appeared in her father's journal?

Bennick, Mundy, and Larken may all yet be here in Invarel, her father had written. *As for Fintaur, I believe you will find his whereabouts in the city of Ardaunto, across the sea. . . .*

Somehow the man in the mask knew about the journal, just as he had known about the magickal doors in the gallery and the Eye of Ran-Yahgren in her father's hidden study upstairs. But how was he aware of so many of her father's secrets? Not for the first time, she wondered if he had been a member of Mr. Lockwell's arcane society, the Vigilant Order of the Silver Eye.

As before, she dismissed the idea. In his letter to her, the one she found inside the celestial globe, her father had written that he did not know who the man in the mask was, but that she was to trust him. Besides, Ivy had never gotten the impression that the man in black was of an age with Mr. Lockwell. In fact, that last time he appeared at the house, the night she went through the door Arantus to the Evengrove, his mask had been askew, as if he had donned it in a great hurry, and a few locks of longish hair had protruded from the side. These had not been the coarse gray strands of an elderly man, but rather a pale and youthful gold.

Now that Ivy considered it, that fact was puzzling. For if the man in the mask had been coming to her father for years, how could he be young rather than old? Well, no matter who the man in black was, and whatever his nature, she was certain that once again he was trying to guide her.

Or to manipulate her . . .

No, she would not believe that. While she had previously doubted his motives, in the end he had only ever aided her. Just as she was sure he had done by leaving the book on the doorstep. Her father had written that Fintaur was somewhere in the city of Ardaunto. Which meant there had to be some clue in the red-covered novel that would help her discover where he was.

Only if that was the case, why had the man in the mask removed the final pages from the book?

Ivy could only suppose there was some reason why he did not want her to read the end of the book, at least not yet. And as puzzling as all of this was, it was surpassed by the mystery of her father's intentions. Why did he want her to seek out the other members of the Vigilant Order of the Silver Eye, the ones whom he had once trusted most, and why now?

Ivy didn't know, for he had not given a reason in the brief entry that had manifested last night. Yet there was one thing of which she was certain: this was the real purpose of her father's journal. All of the other entries that had appeared, everything else he had written, it had all simply been to serve as a kind of lesson—a way to teach her how the magick of the journal functioned. And now, at last, she understood.

Up until now, she had believed that the enchantment was such that an entry would appear only when the heavens were arranged just as they had been when her father penned the words. Now she knew that was not precisely the case. Rather, an entry would appear when certain celestial objects were arranged in a particular way. This prescribed arrangement *might* be the same as on the day the entry was written, but not *necessarily* so. It could instead represent some other, future configuration of planets and stars.

The entries that had appeared in the journal so far had been jumbled in their order because Mr. Lockwell had indeed linked them to the configuration of the heavens at the time they were written. Just as the approach of Cerephus had made gibberish of the timetables in the almanac, so, too, it had disarranged the entries in the journal, placing them out of order. But the latest entry, the one from last night, had appeared exactly when her father had wanted it to—she was sure of it.

Ivy lifted her gaze from the garden and looked up at the night sky. Somehow, just like the old rosewood clock, Mr. Lockwell had known that the approach of Cerephus would alter the motions of the other planets. He must have used his celestial globe, fitted with the twelfth orb—the one she had found in his magick cabinet at Heathcrest Hall—to calculate how the heavens would be arranged on dates yet to come. Thus he was able to place an enchantment upon certain entries in the journal so that they would appear at specific points in the future.

Like last night.

It is about time, he had written in the journal. But time for what? For the Grand Conjunction to occur, perhaps. Only then what would happen?

"Maybe the others will know," she murmured to the ghostly reflection that gazed back from the windowpane, an excitement growing within her. "Maybe that's why Father wants you to find them."

Of course, she could not very well sail to the Principalities, to the city of Ardaunto, to try to locate Mr. Fintaur. Nor did she dare seek out Mr. Bennick. As for Mr. Larken, he might be in the city, but Ivy had no idea where. However, there was one of her father's former compatriots whom she did know how to find.

Ivy drew the curtains over the window, then returned to bed.

When it was daylight again, she would proceed to Greenly Circle. She would seek out the dim side lane and the crowded shop with grimy windows and a faded silver eye painted on the sign above the door.

And there, she would pay the toadish Mr. Mundy a visit.

BY THE TIME IVY WOKE, the morning was already well under way and passing swiftly.

"Why didn't you wake me earlier?" Ivy said as Mrs. Seenly entered the room with a fresh pitcher of water for the basin.

"Do forgive me, ma'am, but the day caught us all by surprise. The umbral ended with hardly a moment's notice, and the next thing we knew the sun was leaping into the sky as if something gave it a fright. Nor do I think it will be very long until it departs again. I wouldn't be surprised if the lumenal was no more than four hours today."

Ivy realized she had been peevish to be so critical of Mrs. Seenly. The housekeeper's silver-and-copper hair was not drawn into as neat a knot as usual, and she had spoken rather breathlessly. No doubt she had been rushing as quickly as possible to ready the household for the day. Not that it seemed worth it. Four hours! Ivy could not recall there ever being a lumenal of such a short duration. At this rate it would practically be afternoon by the time they finished breakfast. Which meant, unfortunately, there was no possibility that she could go to Mr. Mundy's shop.

It was not that she thought the shop would be closed once the sun set. With the lumenal being so brief, most businesses in the city would have little choice but to light lamps and candles and continue conducting commerce. Yet Greenly Circle, where the shop was located, was a less than reputable part of the Old City. While it was not completely untoward for her to visit there during daylight hours, especially if Lawden drove her, being there after nightfall was not something she would consider. Propriety aside, it could not be deemed safe for a woman of any means to be in such a place after darkness fell, even in the company of a manser-vant, given the number of desperate people who had entered the city of late.

All this meant there was no point in hurrying now. She would simply have to hope the umbral was as short as the lumenal, so that she might get to Mr. Mundy's shop as soon as possible.

She smiled at Mrs. Seenly to let the housekeeper know she was in no way upset. "I fear I am a bit out of sorts to discover I had woken up not early but late. I'm sure tea will help matters."

Mrs. Seenly appeared greatly relieved. "Of course, ma'am. I'll have it waiting for you downstairs."

Ivy poured water in the basin to freshen her face, then pro-ceeded to ready herself for the day—and night—to come. As she was not going out, she gave her hair only the most perfunctory brushing, then put on a high-waisted dress of pale yellow lawn that was more notable for being comfortable than either fashion-able or flattering.

For a moment she paused, examining herself in the mirror. Her figure was as small and slight as ever. Ivy laid a hand upon her stomach, but there was not the least amount of swelling, and nor would there be, at least not for now. She suffered a sharp pang, but it had nothing to do with any physical malady. Dr. Lawrent had pronounced her completely recovered. And while illness might afflict the spirit or mind even as it did the body, Ivy could not claim she was really unwell.

True, she still felt a lingering sorrow, but that could only be expected after what had happened. And there were moments when a dread gripped her as she considered the news she would have to tell Mr. Quent upon his return. But the feeling of foreboding—the sensation of some awful, imminent thing—had not returned since her condition had changed. She had not even had the peculiarly vivid dream again, the one in which she col-lected shells on the beach, or hid with other people in a cave.

Indeed, with all that had happened, she had all but forgotten about the dream until that moment. It had been especially clear that last time. But now, with the light of morning pouring through the window, it was hard to recollect such ephemeral visions, and presently she began to suffer a keen craving for tea. Given the oddness of the umbrals and lumenals of late, she could hardly remember when she had taken any last. She made only the most cursory effort to thrust a few pins in her hair to keep it out of her face, then departed her bedchamber and went downstairs.

She crossed the large expanse of the front hall, making for the small dining room off the east end. When Mr. Quent was away, the sisters had a habit of taking breakfast and tea in the parlor, but as they still had Dr. Lawrent in the house, that would not do.

Yet as Ivy passed near the door to the parlor, she heard the sound of a voice speaking within. Had Mrs. Seenly, in her haste at the sudden morning, forgotten about Dr. Lawrent and defaulted to the habit of bringing tea to the parlor?

Ivy approached the parlor door, which stood ajar. By the sound, it was Rose who was speaking. Ivy could not make out what her sister was saying, but she seemed to be uncharacteristically loquacious, chattering away in a light tone. It was hardly usual for Rose to speak so with anyone outside their family, but Ivy had a difficult time believing Lily was already up and dressed. Had Rose finally grown accustomed to Dr. Lawrent and engaged him in conversation? Thinking this must be the case, Ivy opened the door and entered the parlor.

Rose turned away from the fireplace. There was, Ivy saw, no one else in the room, not even Miss Mew.

"Hello, Ivy," Rose said cheerfully, moving to embrace her elder sister.

Ivy could only smile and return the embrace. Rose's affections were like a bouquet of flowers; one could only be delighted to receive them, even if one did not know exactly what occasion they were for.

"Good morning, dearest," Ivy said as they parted. "You are in very good spirits today."

"I'm just glad we're all of us here together, at last."

As so often was the case, Ivy didn't quite know what to make of Rose's words. After all, they had dwelled in the house for well over half a year now. Besides, Mr. Quent was not home at present.

Despite her puzzlement, Ivy only said, "I am glad we are here as well."

Rose smiled, then moved back to the fireplace. On the mantelpiece, one of the carved eyes rolled in its socket to peer at her for a moment, then at Ivy. As if satisfied by what it saw, its wooden lid drooped shut.

"Were you reading aloud from something?" Ivy asked.

Rose shook her head, running a hand along the mantelpiece. "No, I wasn't reading anything."

"It's just that I heard you speaking a moment ago, when I was out in the hall. I thought you were talking to someone, but there's no one else here."

Rose appeared suddenly startled. She took a quick step away from the fireplace and clasped her hands together. This behavior renewed Ivy's puzzlement.

"I didn't mean to pry, Rose. If you were simply speaking to yourself, there is hardly anything wrong with that. I do the same very often!"

"But I wasn't talking to myself," Rose said, looking up.

Now Ivy felt a growing sense of alarm. Her eyes went to the window, but she could see nothing through the screen of wisteria that covered the glass panes. Despite her sudden concern, she kept her voice light. "Then who were you speaking to, dearest?"

Rose hesitated. "I don't think you would believe me."

Ivy did not always understand her next youngest sister, but to deliberately tell a mistruth was not a capability that Rose possessed. And while Ivy did not want to press, a worry had begun to grow in her: a fear that the man in black had appeared to Rose.

"Of course I would believe you," Ivy said seriously.

Rose bit her lower lip. "I was speaking to Father," she said at last.

Her voice was so soft that Ivy wasn't quite certain she had heard correctly. "To *our* father, you mean?"

Rose nodded.

Ivy moved to her. "But there is nothing wrong with that. I often speak to him myself as I go about the house or put away books."

Rose's eyes went wide. "You do? And he answers you, too?"

"Answers me?" Ivy could not help a small sigh. "No, of course he does not answer. How can he when he is not here?"

Rose shook her head. "But that's not true. He *is* here." She laid a hand upon the mantelpiece.

Now Ivy's concern was of a different sort. She kept her voice gentle, but made it somewhat stern as well. "Rose, you know that is not the case. Our father is at Madstone's, where he is receiving treatments for his illness. If it gives you comfort to speak aloud to him, and to think of him answering you, that is very well. But you know it isn't right to speak about things that you imagine as if they are fact."

"But it's not imagined!" Rose said, her voice rising and her agitation evident. "I had forgotten how bright and blue he used to be before he got ill—just like Mr. Rafferdy, only softer and a bit more silvery around the edges. It's been so long since I've seen Father like that, but I see that same blue light there now." She pointed at the mantelpiece. "And I've seen it by the stairs, and in the library, and in a dozen other places. Father isn't at Madstone's at all. He's here right now—here in this house."

Ivy was at a loss for words. It was not the first time she had heard Rose mention seeing a color around someone. She had always thought it to be one of Rose's peculiarities, that she liked to assign colors to people and things she cared for. But what if that wasn't the case? Now that Ivy considered it, there was a pattern to Rose's statements. She had said their father and Mr. Rafferdy were both blue—and both were magicians. And the night of Ivy's loss, Rose had said Ivy's color had changed, and that the spark of gold within the green had vanished. She had been right, hadn't she? Ivy had indeed lost the spark of life that had been growing in her.

Before Ivy could consider the matter further, Mrs. Seenly appeared in the door of the parlor.

"What is it?" Ivy said, startled, for the housekeeper was red-cheeked and appeared to have arrived in a great hurry.

"Pardon me, ma'am, but I knew you'd want to be told at once that he is come."

"You mean Dr. Lawrent has come down for breakfast?"

Mrs. Seenly shook her head. "No, ma'am, I mean the master—he has returned from his trip. I just saw him myself!"

In an instant, all other thoughts fled from Ivy's mind. A feeling passed through her, one so severe that she suffered it almost as a kind of pain, though she knew it was joy.

"Where is he?"

"I saw him out in the front garden. He had just come through the gate and was speaking to Dr. Lawrent, who had gone out for a stroll before breakfast."

"I'll go to him at once. Please set another place at the table, Mrs. Seenly. He is bound to be hungry and weary after traveling through the night."

As Ivy returned to the front hall, her heartbeat quickened. For a half month, she had wanted nothing more than to have Mr. Quent back. But now that he was here, she almost found she could not bear to face him. What would he think of her? She placed a hand on her stomach, then willed herself to look out a window.

Mr. Quent was indeed in the front garden, speaking with Dr. Lawrent. Both men wore somber expressions, and she supposed she could guess what news was passing between them.

Ivy sighed. She could only be relieved that she would not have to be the one to tell him what had occurred; she was not certain she would have been able to form the words herself. Yet that did not mean it would be an easy thing to come before him. Slowly, as if each step were taken through a thick mire, she moved to the door and went outside.

Mr. Quent saw her before she had passed the pair of stone lions that flanked the front steps, and he went to her at once. His riding coat and boots were thick with dust, and his curly brown hair was tousled. He looked like some wild being just emerged from the moors; and with his deep chest and the thicket of a beard, Ivy could only think that when the soldiers of the Tharosian empire first landed on the shores of Altania, it was men like this they found waiting for them, bronze swords in their hands.

Yet his demeanor was anything but warlike. Perhaps aware of Dr. Lawrent's presence, Mr. Quent did not enfold her in his arms in an embrace. But he took her hand, kissing it, and when he looked up his brown eyes gazed upon her with an expression as intimate as any caress.

"I should have been here sooner," he said, his voice so low she felt it rumble within her. It was a comforting sensation.

"You are here now," she said, holding his hand tightly, and then found herself unable to speak anything more.

"I believe I'll go indoors now," Dr. Lawrent said, ascending the front steps. "But it's very fine out. The two of you may wish to stay outside and enjoy the morning while you can, for it looks to be going swiftly." His gray eyes were thoughtful behind his spectacles.

Ivy gave the small silver-haired man a grateful smile, and Mr. Quent shook his hand.

"Thank you again, Dr. Lawrent."

"Of course, of course," the doctor said, and went into the house.

"The doctor is right," Mr. Quent said when they were alone. "I think we should stay out awhile."

He offered her his arm, and she wrapped her own around it tightly, as if she could borrow some of its great reserves of strength for her own. They walked through the garden, not speaking for the moment, content to simply be in each other's company again. But presently the compulsion to speak overwhelmed Ivy's trepidation.

"Forgive me," she gasped as they stepped beneath the arching limbs of a plane tree.

He disengaged her arm from his and turned to face her. "Forgive you, Ivoleyn? And for what awful deed should I forgive you? For bringing light into my life when I had heretofore dwelled in shadows? For giving me a reason to return home each time that I go away? Or is it for helping me remember how to laugh and breathe and feel the racing of my heart like a living man rather than a being of clay?" He laid his hands upon her shoulders. "Are these the things that I should forgive you for?"

She shook her head, and the dappled light beneath the tree turned to stars as moisture welled forth in her eyes.

"You have never done me any wrong that must be forgiven, Ivoleyn. Rather, it is I who owe you a debt—you who have given to me so generously, and have asked for so very little in return."

"But I would have given you more!" She at last managed to speak through her anguish. "I would have given you a son."

"A son?" he said, and he could not help but appear astonished. Then he looked away, and she could see his throat move as he swallowed. Nor could his beard entirely disguise the trembling of his lip.

"Didn't Dr. Lawrent tell you that as well? No, I see that he did not, and I suppose it is only right that he left it for me to give you that particular news." She turned away from him, unable to endure the lines of sorrow written upon his face. "Now do you see why I must ask you to forgive me, Alasdare? I know you can only have hoped to have a son."

For several moments the silence was broken solely by the whisper of the leaves above. Then she heard his footsteps behind her, and felt the warmth of his breath upon the nape of her neck.

"A son?" His voice was very low. "No, Ivoleyn, when I wed you, it was not out of any hope that we would ever have a son."

Now it was Ivy who was astonished. Did not every man hope for a son to succeed him? Only then she thought of her conversation with Dr. Lawrent the day after the spark within her was extinguished.

I've heard it said in the county that there aren't many sons in the Addysen line, she had said.

I am given to understand there have only ever been a few male children born into that family, the kindly doctor had replied.

A strange sort of calmness filled her, and a clarity of thought. "So you knew," she said now, turning around and looking up at Mr. Quent. "You knew, given my nature, that I was unlikely to ever bear you a son. And that even if I did, he would be . . ."

"That he would be like Mr. Samonds, you mean?"

Ivy could only nod, a tightness in her throat. Mr. Samonds was the farrier in Cairnbridge, the village near Heathcrest Hall, and like Ivy he was a great-grandchild of Rowan Addysen—one of the scant number of sons ever born into that line. It was his sister, Halley Samonds, who had vanished into the stand of Wyrdwood east of Heathcrest.

Mr. Quent took her hands, enfolding them easily within his own. "Know that I would have given him all of my love and attention no matter what, for he would have been our own. If society might have sometimes made his existence more difficult, or caused him to think poorly of himself, then I would have done even more to forge an easier path for him, and make him know how highly he was regarded and wanted."

An ache surrounded Ivy's heart, for she could almost picture him now: a boy with Mr. Quent's tousled brown hair and her own green eyes. It was only when she felt the warmth of tears flowing down her cheeks that she understood she was weeping. Mr. Quent was weeping as well, his usually stoic features arranged in grief. His thick arms went around her—not in an attempt to grant comfort this time, but rather seeking it. She clasped him tightly in return.

Though she might have expected otherwise, it was Ivy who first ceased to produce tears. Then, in time, he followed suit, and they moved apart.

"Not all men would think the same on the matter as you," she said after they had been silent for a while. "Many men would not be so accepting of such a son as we might have."

His thick shoulders heaved with a sigh. "Many men do not know what an inquirer knows. Society has not generally taken a kindly view of witches, either. But Lord Rafferdy long believed that they would play some important purpose in the scheme of things. And have you not proven him right with your actions? Given that, I can only believe the same is true for the sons of witches as well—that they have some vital role in all of this. What that might be, I cannot say. Perhaps it is simply to bring more beauty into the world. If so, then that is no small thing."

Ivy thought of the illusionists she had once seen working their craft at a party at Lady Crayford's. Though some considered it scandalous to have any sort of contact with Siltheri, Ivy had detected nothing inherently unwholesome in the visions they had conjured. True, they might as easily concoct lurid or violent scenes as beautiful ones. Yet that was merely the same choice that all people had—man or woman, magician, illusionist, or witch—the choice to live their life for good or ill.

"Thank you," she said at last.

Now it was a quizzical look that he gave her. "For what?"

"For always choosing to be good."

This time it was she who threw her arms around him, leaning her cheek against his chest. He enclosed her in his arms, holding her tightly.

"No, it is I who must thank *you*—you, who have let me know happiness one last time, when I believed I never would again."

Despite the warmth of his embrace, and the comfort she felt enclosed within the strong circle of his arms, a note of alarm entered into Ivy's thoughts. The words he had chosen seemed odd to her for some reason.

She pulled away enough to look up at his face. "But I am sure we will have much more happiness in the future! Even if we are never blessed with a son, can we not at least hope for a daughter?"

"Of course we can," he said, and brushed a lock of hair from her face.

She nodded, but she could not help a sigh. "A daughter would be a great joy, but she would not be able to inherit your title. There will be no one to carry it onward, I fear."

For a moment he looked away, as if he saw something in the

distance. Then his gaze returned to her, and he smiled. "As the title has been so recently granted, that can hardly be of much concern. But come—if I am to be the lord of this manor for the present, then I must have my lady beside me as I enter."

Gladly she acquiesced to the will of the master of the house, and together they went up the walk and passed within.

CHAPTER EIGHT

ELDYN STEPPED through the door, its square glass panes fogged with steam, and into the warm interior of the coffeehouse.

The establishment was crowded despite the fact that it was pitch-black outside the windows; or rather, it was crowded *because* of it. The umbral had persisted for close to twenty hours now, and there was no sign of an end. The city was glazed over with frost, and there were more than a few people in want of a hot cup to warm the blood and open the eyes. It was time for everyone to make a day of it, whether the sun would show itself or not.

At last Eldyn found a corner at the end of a table where he could crowd in. He called for a pot of coffee, and when this was brought he pressed his fingers against it to thaw them. It had been foolish to walk so far in the cold and dark, but he had wanted to get a copy of *The Swift Arrow* as soon as it was off the presses, and that meant going all the way across the Old City to the broadsheet's offices on Coronet Street.

He could have afforded a hack cab, given the regals he had just earned, but none could be found for hire, as carriages were always greatly in demand during long umbrals. So he had gone on foot through the streets of the Old City, keeping the shadows close about him any time he drew near a group of men who huddled around an open fire, wrapped in rags and old blankets. If someone were to slit his throat to take his coat and boots, it wouldn't be the first time it had happened of late.

The bales from the printer arrived at the offices of *The Swift Arrow* just after he did, and he paid a penny to get a copy off the top of the stack. By then he was shivering, and his fingers were too numb to turn the pages of the broadsheet. Seeing the sign advertising the coffeehouse across the street, he had hurried to it.

Now Eldyn tipped the pot to fill his cup. The coffee was too scalding to drink, so he poured some onto his saucer. He let it cool, looking around him as he did. The establishment reminded him a little of Mrs. Haddon's, for the tables were well worn and the air was thick with steam and the burnt caramel smells of tobacco and roasted coffee.

There was no more to be made of the comparison, though. This place was far from Covenant Cross, and the men who filled it were by appearances an older and coarser lot than the young men who attended the various colleges at the university. Nor did they engage in animated conversations about politics. Instead they quietly hunched over their cups. The various copies of the Rules of Citizenship posted around the room were all crisp and unmolested.

At last Eldyn's coffee had cooled and his fingers had warmed to a sufficient point that he was able to tip his saucer over his cup and take a long, satisfying drink. At once, a pleasant tingling coursed through him. He took another sip, then set down the cup and removed the broadsheet he had bought from his coat.

The story at the top of the front page discussed reports of a violent earthquake that had struck on the southern continent, on the edge of the Murgh Empire. According to the article, an entire city had been thrown down in rubble, and countless souls had perished in the devastation. As shocking as this news was, Eldyn's attention barely lingered upon the story. Instead, it was the headline just below that caught his gaze.

SEE AN ASTOUNDING IMPRESSION OF HER MAJESTY, it read. And just below it, in a slightly smaller typeface, *You Will Feel as if You Are Standing Before the Princess Yourself!*

While sometimes broadsheets put impressions on the front page to attract attention, it was the custom to print the most exclusive images on the second page, so that no one might sneak a look atop the stack without paying a penny first. His fingers trembling—with excitement now rather than cold—Eldyn turned the page.

And there was Layle Arringhart, gazing up at him.

He had worried that ink and paper would not be able to reproduce all of the details he had attempted to capture in the impression, but he need not have worried, for the quality of the printing was superior. He could easily make out each of the tiny pearls on the bodice of her gown and the facets of the large emerald that dangled at her throat. Fine lines were visible around her eyes, a reminder that she was not really so young anymore, though she remained a pretty woman.

In the impression, the princess was just stepping through an arched opening in a stone wall, a pensive expression on her face, as a pair of soldiers followed behind her. Several grave markers could just be glimpsed through the opening, and the branches of a gnarled hawthorn tree drooped over the wall from above. It was an exquisite scene, and Eldyn had been more than a little lucky to see it.

He had gone to Duskfellow's graveyard yesterday in hopes of catching a glimpse of Princess Layle. The moon was full, and as it was the third Brightday since the interment of King Rothard, Eldyn reasoned there was a chance the princess would be there. It was the general custom to visit the grave of a near relative three months after burial, and as far as Eldyn knew, the king's remains had yet to be removed to the family crypt at Arringhart Castle, in the south of Altania.

There had been few public sightings of the princess ever since the king's funeral, out of concerns for the safety of the royal person, and Eldyn reasoned there was enough speculation as to her present state that an impression of her, if such could be produced, would be of interest to a broadsheet. Layle had always been more popular than her father; and even those who did not care to see the crown go to another Arringhart could only be curious to see how she was bearing up since Rothard's death. Therefore, shortly after dawn, Eldyn proceeded through the Old City to Duskfellow's.

And promptly discovered he was not the only one who had concluded that the princess would be there. A great crowd of people gathered around the iron gates of the graveyard. Among them, Eldyn saw at least three illusionists whom he knew to be makers of impressions. He made an attempt to work his way up through the crowd to get within view of the cemetery gate, but after receiving more than a few angry glares, and an equal number of sharp elbows to the ribs, he abandoned the idea.

Defeated, Eldyn turned and walked down the street, the graveyard's high wall to his left. If only there was a way to peer through it! But it was without chink or crack, and there were enough redcrests about that he did not think it prudent to try to scale the stones. He would just have to find something else to make an impression of.

Though what that would be, he did not know; and if he did not sell an impression soon, he would not be able to even attempt making any more. His savings were gone, for he had used the entire sum to pay for Sashie's entry into the nunnery, and his wages from the theater, given how modest they were of late, were only enough to buy clothes and whiskey and the necessities of life.

As for the money from the impression he had sold with Perren's help, he had used it all to buy more impression rosin, mordant, and engraving plates. Unfortunately, he had gone through nearly all of it making impressions of scenes that had either not turned out or, if they did, had not been good enough to sell to a newspaper. He could only suppose Perren would be happy to hear that he had failed without the other young man's guidance; though thankfully he had not encountered Perren since their argument.

Consumed by these gloomy thoughts, Eldyn rounded a corner in the graveyard wall—and not twenty feet before him a pair of redcrests appeared through a small gate. They wore gold sashes over the blue coats: emblems that were worn only by members of the royal guard.

Two more men, also wearing gold sashes, stepped through the gate. Eldyn knew he couldn't hesitate. Though it was against every instinct to race *toward* a group of soldiers, he did so, gathering the shadows around him as he went. It was broad daylight, but given the shade cast by several old hawthorn trees, it was enough that the soldiers did not immediately see him.

By the time they did notice him there, a woman wearing a gown of dove-gray silk beaded with pearls was already stepping through the gate not a dozen paces away. Eldyn heard angry voices and felt strong hands grip his arms, but he ignored them. Instead he kept his gaze fixed on the princess, noting every detail of her face, her hair, her dress.

His boot heels scraped against the cobbles as he was uncere-moniously dragged away, but still he did not blink or turn his gaze, instead affixing every aspect of the scene in his mind.

At last he was flung down to the street in the mouth of a filthy alleyway. He scraped his knuckles as he tumbled to the cobbles. The soldiers shouted at him, saying he would be arrested and taken to Barrowgate if he ever attempted to approach Her Majesty again. Eldyn hardly heard them or felt the burning in his hands. He shut his eyes, envisioning what he had seen, fixing it in his mind. As soon as the soldiers left him, he leaped to his feet and was racing across the Old City, back to the theater.

Eldyn dashed up the stairs to his room above the theater, not stopping to speak to any of the other players who greeted him. Once in his room he shut the door and went to the table. Quickly yet carefully, he painted an engraving plate with a thin coating of impression rosin. Then he gripped the plate in both hands and shut his eyes, envisioning the shimmer of each tiny pearl, the glint of the rings upon her fingers, and the way the little lace coif had laid upon her gold hair as lightly as a spiderweb upon a marigold.

With all the force of his will, he directed these thoughts upon the engraving plate.

And saw green.

It was done in an instant. Without even looking at the plate, he put it in the mordant bath, counting the time aloud so that it would be etched neither a moment too short nor too long. Once it was finished, he took out the plate, washed it in water, and wiped it clean. Only then did he let himself examine it in the sunlight that fell through the window, and his heart gave a leap, for he was certain the impression was good.

Knowing time was of great importance, he raced down the stairs and departed the theater as swiftly as he had come, much to the bemusement of Riethe and Mouse and the others. He went directly to the offices of *The Fox*, having decided previously that was where he would attempt to sell his work. But once there he discovered, to his dismay, that the editor had just purchased an impression of the princess at Duskfellow's.

Evidently one of the other illusionists had managed to get a look at Her Majesty as well, and the paper had bought it. Cursing his poor timing, Eldyn went back out onto the street and tried to decide where to go next. The offices of both *The Comet* and *The Messenger* were in Gauldren's Heights, which was all the way on the other side of the Old City. If another illusionist had gotten a scene with the princess, Eldyn couldn't hope to beat him there. That left only *The Swift Arrow*.

Eldyn was reluctant to go to that broadsheet after what Perren had said. But their office was near to that of *The Fox*, and with no other choice, Eldyn tucked the engraving plate into his coat and hurried to Coronet Street.

His fears quickly proved unfounded. Either Perren had not made good on his threat to speak ill of Eldyn, or business trumped all other concerns. Once Eldyn told the publisher what he had, the man was eager to see it. He took the engraving plate from Eldyn and, as he had that time before, examined it with a magnifying lens.

He pored over the plate for a long time—so long that Eldyn

began to dread that there was something amiss with it. At last the man set it down, then opened a box and drew out five gold regals, which he set on the counter and pushed toward Eldyn.

Five regals! That was nearly twice what he had been paid before. Eldyn was hardly able to take up the coins for the way his hands trembled.

"You will bring me any further impressions you make that are of similar quality," the publisher had said, not speaking it as a question.

Eldyn had managed some reply, then had departed the office. And if it hadn't been for the heavy jingle of gold in his pocket, he hardly would have believed what had just happened. Later that lumenal, he had been absolutely worthless at rehearsal. When night fell, he barely slept a wink, and he had gladly risen in the cold, dark middle of the long umbral, anxious to see his work as soon as it was printed.

Now here it was before him.

The impression had turned out better than he had hoped. Everything he had seen was there in ink, along with some things he must have seen but had not really been sensible to at the time. For it was not simply an expression of sorrow on her face, he thought now, but a kind of resolution as well; and the way the hawthorn branch bowed into view from above made it seem almost as if it were bending toward her, as if to comfort her in its embrace. In all, it made him feel not just sympathy for the subject of the scene, but also a curiosity as to what she was going to do next.

Eldyn picked up his cup and took another drink of his coffee. He wondered if Perren would see the impression in *The Swift Arrow*, and if he would know it for Eldyn's work. If so, it could not make him think any more kindly of Eldyn, given that it had appeared in the very broadsheet to which Perren sold his own work.

Well, what was done could not be undone. Besides, he had just as much right to sell impressions to *The Swift Arrow* as Perren did, and he hoped this one would not be the last. It would be good to earn some extra coin to replenish his savings.

Except what was he saving for? Sashie was no longer his responsibility. As for himself, what need did he have for money other than to buy a new coat or a pot of punch? Once he had hoped to earn back the family fortune, and then he had labored to earn enough money to enter the Church. But he had since abandoned both of those notions.

His gaze went back to the broadsheet. Just below the impression of the princess was a large advertisement concerning a venture to the New Lands that was being readied. Seeing this provided a rueful reminder of how he had once given a hundred regals to Mr. Sarvinge and Mr. Grealing, thinking he was investing in a trading company, only to discover they were nothing but a pair of swindlers who had absconded with his funds.

This advertisement did not concern a trading company, though. Rather, it described a colony that was to be established on the mainland of the new continent. That this was a perilous venture, there could be no doubt, given what had happened at Marlstown around the time Eldyn was born. All of the colonists had vanished, and their fate had never been learned.

Yet the plantations on Aratuga and the other islands were exceedingly profitable, producing great quantities of sugar and rum, so it was only a matter of time before an attempt to found another colony on the continent was made. And if the advertisement was to be believed, this venture was to be far larger and better equipped than the Marlstown expedition.

Despite the awful stories about Marlstown, Eldyn had no doubt that many people would readily join this new venture. When things were so dreary and desperate in Altania, leaving its shores and traveling to the New Lands was a compelling notion. The threat of unknown adversities posed little deterrence when there were so many familiar troubles here at home. Eldyn could almost picture himself standing at the prow of a ship, a fresh wind upon his face as he glimpsed a green line on the horizon for the first time.

Yet that was just as much a fancy as winning back the Garritt family fortune or entering the Church. Those who went to the New Lands weren't likely to win a fortune, but they were sure to find burdensome labor as they attempted to carve a homestead from desolate landscapes ruled by cruel elements. Eldyn was no more a farmer or colonist than he was a magnate or priest. He was an illusionist now—one of the Siltheri, the Concealed Ones. That was all.

And when, after years of performing upon the stage, he had used up too much of his light, so that to craft any more illusions could only afflict him with the mordoth, the Gray Wasting, then what would he do? He would certainly have no children to look after him. So if he had no savings to live upon then, how would he live at all?

There was only one answer to that question. He would simply have to make certain he *did* have sufficient savings when that time came. Which meant he had better get to selling more impressions now. He finished his coffee, took up his broadsheet, and rose from the table.

"Hello, friend, is that space free?" someone said behind him. "It seems everything in Altania is scarce these days, including places to sit."

Eldyn turned to tell the other man that the space at the table was indeed available, but then felt a sudden astonishment at the sight of the tall, gangly young man before him.

"Orris Jaimsley!" he exclaimed.

The other's eyes went wide for a moment, then a bent grin appeared upon his homely face. "Great Gods, Eldyn Garritt! I never imagined I'd run into you in a place like this. I thought you had given up habituating coffeehouses. I can't recall the last time we saw you at Mrs. Haddon's."

"I suppose I did fall out of the habit," Eldyn confessed.

"No doubt there was too much talk of revolution for your taste," Jaimsley said with a laugh. "You always were the proper, upstanding member of society."

This caused Eldyn to grin himself. Back when he had attended St. Berndyn's College, he had frequently gone to Mrs. Haddon's coffeehouse with his fellow students. There, Curren Talinger had often spoken hotly against the government, and Dalby Warrett would attempt to douse the flames of his ire even as Jaimsley fanned them.

Not that Jaimsley had ever really seemed to share Talinger's opinions regarding the wickedness of the government; rather, Jaimsley had always been the prankish sort, and at St. Berndyn's he had ever liked to incite others to commit mischief as he watched in glee.

Of course, while Talinger had often spoken of revolt, he had never done anything more rebellious than tear down a copy of the Rules of Citizenship. All the while, unknown to the others, Eldyn had been engaged in business with true rebels, carrying secret missives for supporters of Huntley Morden—work in which he had engaged to repay a debt to the highwayman Westen Darendal. Eldyn wondered if Jaimsley would still think him to be proper and upstanding if he knew the truth of what Eldyn had been doing back then, or if he had an idea what Eldyn did for a living now.

"I just came in to get a cup against the cold," Eldyn said. "But how are you doing? And what of Talinger and Warrett? I went by Mrs. Haddon's some months ago to see if I might find you there, but the place was closed by order of the Gray Conclave."

Jaimsley's grin vanished. "Ill news, that. Though I can't say any of us were surprised, once we learned the truth of it."

"You mean you know why her establishment was closed?"

"You hadn't heard, then? But I suppose that's to be expected—no one wanted to act as if they knew what had been going on, for fear they might be considered an accomplice."

Eldyn frowned. "An accomplice to what?"

Just then another man got up from the table, clearing a second spot. Jaimsley took Eldyn's arm, pulling him down, and the two of them sat.

"There was more to good old Mrs. Haddon than any of us knew," Jaimsley said in a low voice, leaning his head close to Eldyn's. "You see, it wasn't only barrels of coffee beans that came into her shop. She was receiving kegs of black powder that were smuggled out of the royal army's own stores by Morden sympathizers. When the Gray Conclave finally learned what she was up to, they discovered heaps of the stuff right in the basement of her shop—enough to blow up an entire fort, or so I hear."

Eldyn felt the hair on his arms raise up. To think, all the while they were sitting there drinking coffee, there was a large store of gunpowder just beneath them! How many times had a bit of burning tobacco fallen from someone's pipe to the floorboards? He shuddered to even consider it.

"Was it these same men Mrs. Haddon was working with who blew up the Cenotaph?"

Half a year ago, a monument commemorating the war that established the rule of the Arringhart kings was blown up, and dozens of people were killed in the tumult.

Jaimsley shook his head. "No, it wasn't her band of men. They were shipping all the gunpowder to Torland. But the attack on the Cenotaph was made to look like Morden men did it, no doubt in an attempt to turn sentiment against the rebels."

"Then I wonder who really committed the deed."

"I can't say. For my money, I bet it was the same magicians who blew up the Ministry of Printing. I imagine they wanted it to look like rebels had attacked the Ministry as well, but one of them got caught. Good thing there was an illusionist there to get a picture of him, so everyone knew it was magicians behind it, and not Morden men."

Eldyn could not help feeling a note of pride. By their nature, impressions could not be false—which meant they could reveal the truth of a situation that might otherwise have gone unknown. Perhaps there were other reasons to make impressions than simply gaining some coin.

"But what's become of Mrs. Haddon?"

Jaimsley's expression grew uncharacteristically somber. "She's in Barrowgate now. The men she was working with have already been hung. She's told the barristers she didn't know what was inside the kegs she was storing beneath her shop, but I don't think anyone really believes that. I imagine it's only a matter of time before she goes to the gallows as well."

The coffee he had drunk now burned in Eldyn's stomach. Mrs.

Haddon was a frowsy, cheerful woman of middle years who had only ever been kind to him and the other young men who came into the coffeehouse. To think of her dangling from a rope beneath the gallows was terrible.

"God's mercy," he managed to say at last. "Is there nothing that can be done for her?"

"Oh, there's one thing that can be done," Jaimsley said, his voice falling to a whisper. "We can toss every magnate in Assembly out on the street where they can lie with the rest of the horse dung. And we can win ourselves a new king while we're at it."

This statement shocked Eldyn. Being a Torlander, Talinger had often professed his admiration for Huntley Morden, but Jaimsley had never followed suit. Rather, he had once told Eldyn that it was the people themselves who should rule Altania, not a monarch.

"I thought you didn't care for having a king," Eldyn said.

Jaimsley's brow crinkled above his large beak of a nose. "No, I can't say I care for kings. If the notion of monarchs could be dispensed with, then I'd be the first to do so. And maybe in some far-off time we'll be able to have a nation where the citizens lead themselves. But as for now—well, you know what people are like."

Yes, he did. He recalled the hanging his father had taken him to watch when he was a boy, and more lately the execution of Westen Darendal, which he had gone to see. Both times the people in attendance had gladly howled for the death of someone they didn't know, and who had caused them no harm. But it wasn't the men being hung whom they were angry at, whose death they wanted; rather, it was all that they represented.

"I think the people are afraid," Eldyn said. "They're afraid of what might be coming, and they're looking for someone to tell them what to do. I almost don't think they care who it is, just so long as it's someone who can tell them which direction to go."

Jaimsley nodded. "A drowning man will tend to grasp at any rope, no matter who throws it to him. The way things are proceeding in this nation, it's assured *someone* is going to seize the reins."

Eldyn's hand went to the broadsheet tucked in his coat. "But then why shouldn't it be the princess? I can hardly think Huntley Morden's claim to the crown is really any better than Layle's. His ancestry goes back to Torland and from there to the Northern Realms, but it's said the Arringharts were descended of ancient Tharos."

Jaimsley snorted. "That's hardly anything special. I'm sure Emperor Veradian's soldiers got a great lot of bastards on the women of this island once their ships landed on its shores. You and I can probably both count some lustful Tharosian infantryman as a progenitor."

Eldyn supposed that was not far from true, at least in the southern and central parts of Altania. From what he recalled of the lectures in history he had attended at St. Berndyn's, the armies of Tharos had never gotten all the way to the far western and northern parts of the island.

Perhaps that explained why the Outlands had always been somewhat less civilized than the rest of Altania. Unlike the Arringharts, the Mabingorian kings had hailed from the seafaring kingdoms across the frigid northern ocean. A thousand years ago, when the forces of Tharos retreated from the island, the men of the north took the opportunity to seize control. They came in dragon-prow ships, armed with ax and fire. They drove the last of the Tharosians from these shores, and they claimed a right to the crown of Altania based upon a common lineage with the original inhabitants of the island.

Three hundred years ago, when the last of the Mabingorian kings died without an heir, a war for the crown ensued among the House of Rothdale, the House of Morden, and the House of Arringhart. It was a long and violent conflict, but in the end it was Hathard Arringhart who claimed victory, and he was crowned King of Altania.

The Rothdale line was all but obliterated during the Three Corners War—as the battle for the crown came to be known—but some few of the Mordens endured in the West Country, in Torland. There, old hatreds stewed and simmered beneath the heavy lid of Altanian rule. Then, some seventy years ago, they bubbled up again with new heat. Bandley Morden took up the hawk banner and marched out of Torland with five thousand men at his back and his eye on the throne.

A few early victories lent heart to Bandley Morden and his followers, but the rebellion was short-lived. A number of earls and dukes who had intimated they would support a Morden gambit instead backed the king, and Bandley Morden found himself pushed back to the sea. Then, at the battle of Selburn Howe, with the help of shadows and other magicks conjured by the great magician Slade Vordigan, the Old Usurper was driven entirely from the shores of Altania. He fled across the sea to the Principalities, and no Morden had set foot on Altanian soil since.

Thus the Arringharts continued to rule. Yet some wounds never really healed, and over the years Torland remained a place of frequent troubles and unrest. Now it was rumored that Huntley Morden, the grandson of Bandley Morden, was preparing to sail from the Principalities, bringing with him a ship full of guns to arm the people of Torland and lead them to battle. Indeed, it was hardly considered a rumor these days, and it seemed only a matter of time until a ship flying the green hawk was sighted off the western shore.

"But do you really think it would make things any better if Morden were king?" Eldyn said—softly, in case there were any agents of the Gray Conclave in earshot. He did not want to get taken to Barrowgate himself. "It seems that to install him as such could only cost a great amount of blood. Is he truly worth such a dreadful price?"

Jaimsley gave a shrug. "Who can say if he's worth it? I'm not sure any man merits such a price. Though I've heard it said Morden is an honorable sort, and that he holds great affection for the people of Altania despite living all his life in exile. That said, for my part, I don't think King Rothard was a villain, or even most of the lords in the Hall of Magnates. They're weak, to be sure, and selfish and shortsighted, but not really more than most men. It might be better, and engender far less strife, if we could repair our nation rather than knock it down wholesale. But I don't think that's possible anymore."

These words sent a feeling of dread through Eldyn, but he suffered a peculiar excitement as well. "So you think revolution is coming?"

"No, I think it's already begun. The wheels are turning even now."

Eldyn could only be astonished. "You seem as if you know something."

Jaimsley was silent for a long moment, as if making a decision. When at last he did speak, it was without any of his characteristic drollery.

"As I said, the wheels are turning, and they will not cease until our present government is ground to dust beneath them. Altania will be broken, and if we want to have any say in how it will be built anew from the ruins, then we must put ourselves on the side of the victor. That's the only way we'll have a chance of making sure that whatever government comes to be, it's better for the people than what we have now."

"But what if you throw your lot in with Morden and it's the princess who wins?"

Jaimsley sighed and shook his head. "I can't say who will come out on top, but one thing I do know is that it won't be the princess. She's a pawn in all of this, nothing more. Why do you think they haven't let her put on her father's crown? Do you really think it's simply out of worry for the safety of the royal person at a coronation?"

Eldyn thought of the expression he had seen on Layle's face outside Duskfellow's. It had been a look of sorrow. And of resignation.

"So you think it's Morden who's going to win?"

"I can't say who will win. There are a great number of forces at work, some I'm sure we can't even see yet. But for my part, I hope it's Morden who prevails. I'd rather not have a king at all, but if that can't be, then I'd rather have a decent monarch than a tyrant of a far worse sort."

Eldyn frowned. What sort of tyrant did he mean? Before he could ask, Jaimsley rose to his feet.

"I'm afraid I've got to go."

"But you haven't had any coffee," Eldyn said, standing as well.

Now Jaimsley's crooked grin returned. "Talking with you has enlivened me more than a cup could, Garritt. It's truly good to have seen you. And in any case, I was planning to be quick about my business here."

Together, the two men left the coffeehouse and went out onto the street.

"So where are you off to in such a hurry, if I might ask?" Eldyn said.

"I've got to go meet up with Talinger and Warrett," Jaimsley replied, his breath making a fog on the air.

"For a lecture at the college, you mean?"

He shook his head. "There aren't going to be any lectures at St. Berndyn's today, or any of the other colleges at the university. I just got wind of it last night—the students are all going on a march to protest the closing of Gauldren's College."

Eldyn had read about it in *The Fox* the other day: how the Gray Conclave had locked the doors of Gauldren's College because the professors there were teaching on the subject of magick.

"But I always thought you considered the men at Gauldren's to be a lot of stuck-up prigs," Eldyn said.

Jaimsley laughed, his homely face lighting up. "That's because they *are* stuck-up prigs! But I'll still defend their right to study what and how they please. If the government can shut down one college because they don't like what's being taught there, then they can do it to any other. It could be St. Berndyn's next. So Talinger and Warrett and I are going to march with the men of the other colleges around Covenant Cross. We'll let the Black Dog know what we think of his policy."

Eldyn could only be impressed, but he wondered if it was wise to taunt Lord Valhaine and the Gray Conclave so openly, or to flout the Rules of Citizenship, which prohibited such gatherings. Then again, it would hardly be the first time students had gone on a march for some cause, though usually it was to protest the high cost of whiskey or the like.

"Well, I'm sure you'll be a merry band," Eldyn said.

"We'd be merrier with more. Care to join us, Garritt?"

For a moment Eldyn was tempted. It would be good to see Curren Talinger and Dalby Warrett again. He missed his days at university, and it would be good to feel he was part of it again, if just for a little while. That said, he was not certain he wished to risk attracting the notice of any soldiers or an agent of the Gray Conclave. Jaimsley may have spoken about rebels, but Eldyn had actually worked for them once, and he wished to take no chances. Besides, he had to return to the theater soon for a rehearsal. Maybe Jaimsley was right, and a great upheaval was coming; but in the meantime, the daily habits of life must proceed.

"Thanks, but I've got someplace to be myself," Eldyn said, then laughed. "Besides, I don't think I'm the revolutionary sort."

Jaimsley met his gaze, then nodded. "All right, then. But we can always use another trustworthy man, Garritt. If you ever find you've changed your mind about what sort of fellow you are, come and look me up. You can find me at the dormitories off Butcher's Slip."

Jaimsley gripped his hand and shook it. Eldyn warmly returned the gesture. Then, with a final good-bye, Jaimsley hurried up the street and was gone. Eldyn turned and went in the opposite direction, making toward Durrow Street. As he did, the sky above began to fade from black to gray. The long umbral was finally coming to an end.

As for how long the coming day would be, there was no way to know.

CHAPTER NINE

——————— ❧ ———————

MUCH TO IVY'S DISMAY, Dr. Lawrent left them soon after Mr. Quent's return.

There were two causes for the doctor's departure. First, his work at Carwick College had been disrupted by recent events at the university. One of the colleges, Gauldren's, had been closed by the Gray Conclave on the grounds that it was teaching principles of magick. That particular topic was now the sole purview of the High Order of the Golden Door, which had been granted a charter by Lord Valhaine to advise the Crown on occult matters. All other arcane societies or organizations devoted to the study or practice of magick were proscribed by law.

Angered by the closing of a college's doors by the government, and as a demonstration of their fraternity with the men of Gauldren's, the students of all the other colleges had ceased attending lectures. Instead, they had taken to loitering about the university, blocking anyone from entering the buildings, and several times had taken to marching about Covenant Cross to make a protest. On each occasion the students had been dispersed by redcrests, but each time when they returned it was in greater numbers.

Had it been only these events, Dr. Lawrent might have remained in the city for a time, waiting for tempers to cool as they always must, and for the disruptions at the university to come to an end. However, news had come out of the West Country that was greatly troubling.

Affairs along the border with Torland had grown so violent it was feared that the Crown's soldiers would be forced to abandon their outposts there, lest they be burned within them, and fall back to fortresses closer to Invarel. Which meant there would be nothing to stop bands of rebels from spilling into the westernmost counties of Altania and moving about freely.

If this were to occur, well-to-do families who were known to be loyal to the Crown would no longer be safe in the West Country. Therefore, Dr. Lawrent was returning to County Westmorain with all possible haste to remove Mrs. Lawrent from their home there, as well as their daughter, who was a widow and dwelled with them along with her several children. Dr. Lawrent's intention was to take them to the south of Altania, far from the troubles, to live with Mrs. Lawrent's sister. If by then affairs at the university had gone back to their usual state, he would consider returning to the city—but only if it could be assured his family would be safe in the south.

It was deep in the middle of a long umbral when Dr. Lawrent departed. He was to go as a passenger with the post, that being the safest way to travel these days, for it was always accompanied by a guard of soldiers. While it might have been more pleasant to have remained in their beds, the post always kept to its timetables whether it was dark or light, and so they went out into the cold and dark to bid the doctor farewell.

"I wish you could have stayed longer," Ivy told him as he took her hands in his.

"As do I," the doctor replied, "but present affairs demand otherwise. Like the moths of County Dorn, we must all adapt to our new circumstances, lest the birds spy us and pluck us up."

Ivy laughed at this. "I will endeavor to find a way to use some heretofore unknown trait in my possession to help me avoid them."

One last time, he peered at her over the rims of his spectacles. "Yes, I imagine that you will, Lady Quent."

Ivy didn't know how to respond to this. Then Dr. Lawrent was shaking Mr. Quent's hand and bidding good-bye to Lily and Rose. Moments later he was in the waiting carriage, a lantern hanging from the driver's bench, and away into the night. Ivy took Mr.

Quent's arm, walking back through the gate and up the walk to the house while Lily and Rose hurried ahead, eager to retreat from the chilly air.

As they entered the house, Ivy thought of Dr. Lawrent's reason for returning to County Westmorain, and she thought also of the others whom she knew there.

"What is it, Ivoleyn?"

She must have sighed without realizing it. Mr. Quent shut the door behind them and regarded her, concern in his brown eyes.

"I was just thinking of Mr. Samonds, and of Miss Samonds," she said. "I worry they will . . . that is, I do not think that they have any close family outside of County Westmorain with whom they might live."

"Ah," he said with a deep exhalation, and he reached for her hands, folding them inside his own. In public he made a habit of keeping his left hand in his coat pocket to hide the fact that it was bereft of its last two digits, but he had long since ceased making any attempt to conceal his old injury from Ivy or her sisters.

"It is kind of you to be concerned for the Samondses," he said. "Yet I do not think you should worry for them too much. Most people in County Westmorain would not have to search through many cousins to find one across the border in Torland. While those who hail from the east, and who have known ties to the Crown—like Dr. Lawrent—might have cause for concern, I do not think Mr. Samonds and his aunt have any great need to fear. If rebels from Torland were to cross the border, they would be bent on marching as swiftly as they could toward Invarel. I doubt they would remain in Westmorain for long. But let us hope it will not come to that. The army has not abandoned the border yet, and they will likely never do so."

As always, her husband spoke with much wisdom, and Ivy was reassured by his words. Only then she thought of what he had said about those who had known ties to the Crown.

"The Samondses may be well, but we would not be able to say the same if we were to return, would we? We cannot go back to Heathcrest Hall."

He hesitated, then shook his head. "No, Ivoleyn. I do not think that would be wise, at least not at present. I hope circumstances will change and allow us to return there one day, but for now it is best if we remain here in the city."

Ivy could not help feeling a sadness at this response. Of late, she had found herself thinking of Heathcrest Hall often. The city seemed increasingly confining, and a desire had grown within her to see the wildness of the moors and fells around Heathcrest once again.

Well, there was no use in fretting about it. Nor would it be anything other than churlish of her to complain about their present circumstance. They were perfectly safe here in the city, and had nothing to be concerned about, unlike Dr. Lawrent.

She smiled and kissed Mr. Quent's cheek to assure him she was well. After that, having various missives from other inquirers he needed to read and respond to, he retreated to his study. Ivy had her own work she wished to see to, but so far there had been no opportunity. Both of the lumenals since Mr. Quent's return had been brief, and she had not had an opportunity to travel to Mr. Mundy's shop off Greenly Circle.

Supposing she might as well make herself useful in the interim, Ivy carried a lamp into the parlor, intending to work on the household ledger. More than once, Mr. Quent had told her she did not need to maintain the ledger herself, for his bank employed clerks who could manage such things. All the same, Ivy had been reluctant to give up the responsibility. Just because they did not want for money did not mean they should be frivolous with it, and tallying the expenses of the household helped her to keep a good sense of the cost of everything—a number which was steadily rising these days.

The parlor was empty, and every bit as cold as the little parlor at Whitward Street used to be during long umbrals. Ivy rang for a maid to come stoke the fire. But as one did not immediately appear, she went to the fireplace and stirred it up herself, adding several pieces of coal. Once the fire was blazing nicely, she went to the table where she kept the ledger.

She found this in a chaotic state, being littered with books and newspapers and sheets of music all left there in great disarray—by Lily, no doubt. With a sigh, she began pushing these aside in search of the ledger. At last her hands seized upon a large volume, and she pulled it out from the heap. Her grip upon it proved faulty, though, and the heavy book slipped from her grasp. As it did, it fell open upon the table.

It was not, she saw at once, the ledger.

Rather than rows of expenditures, the exposed pages were filled with drawings done in charcoal. On one side was what appeared to be a scene from a play. Beneath the ornate curve of a proscenium arch, figures rendered in elegant lines moved upon a stage made to look like a forest. On the facing page were a number of small portraits and vignettes that could only be details of the figures on the stage. They showed young men with antlers sprouting from their brows or rising from the forms of horses in the guise of centaurs. The drawings were all extremely well done, having a remarkable verisimilitude, while at the same time retaining a freeness that allowed them to suggest and imply as well as to depict.

Fascinated, Ivy turned through the pages. They were all filled with drawings depicting dramatic and mythical scenes, along with numerous illustrations that showed particular bits of staging or scene dress, or players in their costumes. As she looked through the folio, Ivy noticed that many of the young men were depicted in a similar fashion, with fine, classical features as well as long dark hair and dark eyes. Amazed as Ivy was at the beauty of the drawings, a concern began to grow in her. These particular portraits were, she thought, very familiar seeming.

Footsteps sounded from behind her. The maid must finally have come.

"It's all right," Ivy said, turning another page. "I stoked the fire myself."

"Ivy! What are you doing?"

Startled, Ivy let the page fall and turned around. Lily stood in the door of the parlor, her brown eyes wide. A sudden shame filled Ivy. She had been so fascinated by the drawings that she had not stopped to consider what she was doing. Now she was mortified by her behavior.

"Lily," she said with a gasp. "It wasn't my intention . . . that is, I was looking for the ledger. Only I came upon this by mistake."

All color drained from Lily's face, and she spoke in a voice barely above a whisper. "You were looking through my folio. I never thought *you* would do such a thing, Ivy."

Ivy suffered a severe pang. "I'm so sorry. It fell open by accident when I pulled it out from the other papers."

"By accident? Really, Ivy, if you're going to snoop through my things, at least have the courage to tell the truth of it! It only makes it worse that you speak a falsehood about it."

Ivy was so astonished by this accusation that she could not find the words to defend herself; though she supposed the case against her did appear very bad. Lily hurried up to the table and slammed the folio shut.

"I'm sorry," Ivy said again. "I didn't mean to—"

"Don't even," Lily said, glaring at her through narrowed eyes. With a rough swipe of her hand, she brushed the tears from her cheek, then took up the folio and rushed from the parlor.

Ivy could only stare after her. Despite the fire crackling on the hearth, she felt miserably cold. To have violated her sister's privacy like that was awful. Yes, it had been an accident that the folio had come open, but Ivy had chosen to turn through its pages. There was no excuse for it.

And yet, now that she had, she could not say that there had been no benefit to her transgression. This was not a justification for what Ivy had done, but now that she had seen the drawings, she could not pretend she did not know what they portended. Ivy thought again of the many vignettes of the one particular player— the handsome one with long, dark hair—and she supposed she knew now why Lily had expressed so little desire to go to parties and dances where she might meet eligible partners. There was only one young man who engaged her fancies.

Ivy wasn't certain what to do with this knowledge. She would have to speak to Mr. Quent about it. And eventually she would have to speak to Lily as well—though likely she would have to wait until some time passed before Lily would speak to *her.* In the meantime, she might as well work on the ledger. She went to the fireplace for a minute to warm her hands, and then with much less anticipation than before, she searched for the ledger under the papers on the table. Finding it, she started on her task.

H̲ER FINGERS ACHED from the chill and from the many lines she had filled with ink by the time Mr. Quent came into the parlor. He encouraged her to set down her pen and then took up her right hand.

"But it's nearly frozen!" he exclaimed. He rubbed her hand gently, and blew upon it, until at last it began to grow warm. "Well, are we paupers yet?"

"No, but candles have become more expensive than ever," Ivy said as she turned back to the table and looked at the figures in the ledger. "Do you see? We are spending nearly as much on them in a month as I used to spend on the whole of our household at Whitward Street."

He came in close behind her and laid his hands upon her shoulders. "You know we have no need to worry over the expense, Ivoleyn."

"But what of all those who are less fortunate than we? It seems there have been more long umbrals of late, and I read in the broadsheets that some astrographers believe even longer spans of darkness are to come. I fear that soon people won't be able to afford candles at all. But how can they read or cook or go about their business without any light to see by?"

"There will be candles for them—some at least."

She shut the ledger and regarded him. "How so?"

"The Crown has been, for at least two years now, buying candles and lamp oil and keeping them in large stores. If the long umbrals continue, the government will begin delivering rations out of these stores to the people—not in large quantities, but enough to keep at least a little light in their houses. It is seen as an important measure to maintain order in the realm and to ensure commerce continues. For without any light, havoc would ensue."

Ivy was pleased to learn this, but puzzled as well. "I am glad for this news, yet I can only wonder why the government has for so long been buying up candles." Even as she said this, she realized the truth of it. "But they've known all this while, haven't they? The government has known that the lengths of lumenals and umbrals would become unpredictable, and that longer and longer umbrals would come."

"Known?" He stroked his beard. "No, it has not been known. But suspected, yes, by some at least."

"By the inquirers, you mean?"

"Yes, by the inquirers. Or rather, by Lord Rafferdy. I am not certain how he apprehended what he did, though he hinted to me once that it was from Earl Rylend that some of this knowledge came."

Ivy considered this in light of her own knowledge. Earl Rylend had possessed a deep interest in magick, and he and Lord Rafferdy had been close companions in their youth. It was Rylend who had led the elder Rafferdy, along with Lord Marsdel, into the cave in the far south of the Empire where they had discovered the Eye of Ran-Yahgren, the artifact which acted as a sort of window that looked upon the surface of the planet Cerephus.

"Earl Rylend must have known about Cerephus, just as my father did, and how it would affect the lengths of days and nights."

Mr. Quent nodded. "I must suppose that is the case. When he first asked me to become an inquirer, Lord Rafferdy told me that he believed a darkness was coming."

"You mean like the one the broadsheets say is coming—a greatnight that will go on and on, longer than any other ever before?"

"Yes, a darkness like that. But more than that, I think. Several times over the years, Lord Rafferdy spoke to me of a darkness that would descend upon the world, and I do not think he meant sim-

ply an umbral of exceptional duration. He said also that the Wyrdwood had some role to play in all of these happenings, and that
was why he accepted the post as lord inquirer." He regarded her,
his brown eyes solemn beneath a furrowed brow. "Discerning
things as we do now, I can only believe he understood much."

Ivy had to think that was indeed the case—that Lord Rafferdy
had been aware of Cerephus and how it would seek to draw near
to Altania, like a ship with red sails making for the green shore
ahead. Whether he had known of the shadowed beings who journeyed upon that vessel, she did not know, but certainly Lord Rafferdy had known a dark time was coming.

Just as he had known that the Wyrdwood, as well as those who
could hear its call and shape its actions, might have a role to play
when that darkness came. He had to have believed that, for else
why would he have worked through the Inquiry to guard and
keep watch over the Wyrdwood, as well as the witches who were
called to it?

She did not need to speak these things to Mr. Quent. It was
clear from his expression that his understanding was one with her
own.

"Lord Rafferdy was very wise," she said. "And the work of the
Inquiry is more important than ever."

Mr. Quent's rounded shoulders seemed to slump a bit, as if a
weight rested upon them. "So it is. And it is for that reason only
that I am willing to go subject myself to the scrutiny of Assembly."

Ivy felt a sudden anticipation, though whether it was of something good or ill she could not say. She rose from her chair. "What
do you mean?"

"Just a short while ago I learned that, as we have long suspected might be the case, Lord Valhaine has nominated me for the
post of lord inquirer. As a result, I am to be called before the Hall
of Magnates to testify, so that my suitability for the position can be
judged."

"Your suitability?" Ivy exclaimed. "But who could possibly be
more suited to be lord inquirer than yourself? Nor can I imagine

that Lord Rafferdy would have wished for anyone but yourself to succeed him. I am certain it is merely a formality."

Mr. Quent nodded. "It is a formality, yes, but one that cannot be escaped. It is the purview of the Crown to arrange special commissions at its will—commissions such as the Inquiry or the Gray Conclave. But it is also the right of the Hall of Magnates, as set down in the Grand Charter, to advise the Crown in such matters, and to give its approval of them."

"But how can they withhold their consent?" Ivy said. "They cannot possibly do so, not when the nation is in such great need."

"It is not the matter of their consent that worries me, but rather that of their questions." His voice went suddenly low, as if someone might be listening to them. "It is as I told you before—there are those within the government who would not condone the way I conducted matters in Torland last year."

Ivy shivered as a chill crept along her skin; the fire had burned down on the hearth and was in want of more coal.

Last year, Mr. Quent had gone to Torland and had succeeded in stopping the Risings by capturing the witch who had been aiding the rebels there. Only then he had let her go when she agreed to cease inciting the Wyrdwood. It had been the quickest and surest way to bring an end to the Risings and to prevent further deaths. But it was possible some might not view it that way, that they would instead accuse him of making a bargain with the enemy.

Some time after the Risings, Lady Shayde had gone to Torland to investigate for herself what had taken place there. Though the matter of the Wyrdwood—and thus the matter of witches—was under the purview of the Inquiry, the Gray Conclave was ever interested in the topic, and Lady Shayde was one of its chief agents. It was the purpose of the Gray Conclave to seek out all threats to the sovereignty and safety of the Crown, and it no doubt perceived such a peril in the Wyrdwood.

Only Mr. Quent had hastened to Torland ahead of Lady Shayde to put matters in order. Which meant she could not know what had occurred there. Besides, the White Lady served at the pleasure of Lord Valhaine, and it was Valhaine who had nominated Mr. Quent for the post of lord inquirer.

"I am sure the magnates will have few questions for you," she said, making her voice light. "They no doubt have many other matters to concern them. And Lord Valhaine would not have nominated you if he had thought there was any concern about undue scrutiny."

He did not utter an agreement with this logic, but nor did he refute it.

"How long will it be until you must testify before Assembly?"

"A half month, though I would rather it was not so soon. I will need to prepare myself, and I have much work to see to as it is."

Despite the seriousness of the matter, Ivy could only laugh. "But I am astonished by you, Mr. Quent!"

The creases on his forehead deepened again, though with a more quizzical expression this time. "How so?"

She brushed a curl of brown hair away from that furrowed brow. "I am sure another man would be eager to prove himself worthy of such a post, and would have at the ready many reasons why he was deserving of it. Especially knowing that another title, one even higher yet, might well be bestowed upon him if he were to win the appointment. Yet you want only to do your work, and seek no such accolades."

"I have no need of accolades or titles, Mrs. Quent," he said, pulling her toward him. "I have all that I need in you."

Ivy could not help but be pleased with this answer. All the same, she affected a disinterested tone. "That is your belief, perhaps. But that you will receive such things as you wish from me is not *confirmed*, Mr. Quent. I will need to interview you myself."

His coarse beard parted as he grinned, and he looked, as he sometimes did, like some wild faun out of Tharosian myth. "Oh? And for what position shall I be interviewed?"

"Allow me to explain it to you."

She stood upon her toes to kiss him—and then those same toes quickly left the floor as he swept her up in his embrace.

———

$\mathcal{S}$HORTLY AFTER DAWN CAME, Ivy departed the house on Durrow Street in the cabriolet.

Lawden had put up the calash top, for the morning was dim. A rain drizzled down from clouds that were so low they touched the heights of the Crag, and the Citadel was all but lost among sheaths of gray. All the same, the streets were busy with carriages and carts, and people on horseback or on foot. The umbral had again been long, and no matter the damp or chill, people were eager to get out and conduct their business while they might.

Ivy had business to conduct herself, for she at last had an opportunity to go to Mr. Mundy's shop. She had checked her father's journal diligently each umbral and lumenal these last days, but no further entries had appeared to explain why he wanted her to seek out his former compatriots from the Vigilant Order of the Silver Eye. Yet she had to believe Mr. Mundy would be able to offer some clue regarding the matter.

Provided he would let her into his shop. The toadish little man had been anything but cordial to her the last time she had encountered him. But at the time she had not known he had once been a friend of her father's, and likewise he had not known she was Mr. Lockwell's daughter. Thus she had every hope that things would be more amicable this time.

As Lawden navigated the cabriolet through the cramped streets of the Old City, Ivy turned her attention to the folded note on her lap. It had arrived at the house just as she was going out the door. Usually she would have left any correspondence to read upon her return, but seeing the bold and attractive, though somewhat careless, penmanship with which the address was written, she had taken it from Mrs. Seenly.

Opening it now, she saw that it was indeed from Mr. Rafferdy, as she had expected. It was very brief, as was his typical style.

My dear Mrs. Quent, it began. This was in accord with their prior agreement to continue addressing each other as Mr. or Mrs. rather than Lord or Lady. *I have just been commanded to present myself at Lady Marsdel's when evening falls today—whenever that might happen to be. As I am far down on the list of her ladyship's favor, I am sure that those who are higher upon it must also be summoned. Thus consider yourself fairly warned! I hope this notice will allow you to avoid this doom, as I myself have not.*

The note was signed simply *R.*

Ivy smiled as she folded the note again. She had learned that Mr. Rafferdy seldom asked in a plain way for anything he wanted. Rather, he would pretend not to wish for a thing, preferring it to be spontaneously offered to him instead. In this case, it was clear he was letting her know that he would be at Lady Marsdel's in hopes she would be tempted to go herself.

Which, of course, she was. It had been some time since she had gone to her ladyship's, for with Mr. Quent away it had been her duty to entertain their guest. But with Dr. Lawrent now departed, and Mr. Quent returned to the city, there was no reason she could not go. If Mr. Rafferdy was unable to avoid this doom, then as a friend it was her duty to join him in it.

The cabriolet jostled to a halt. Ivy looked out and saw they were on the edge of Greenly Circle. A moment later Lawden appeared at the door.

"Forgive me, my lady," the driver said in his characteristically soft voice, "but I don't know that I can maneuver the carriage any farther. I fear that if I do, I will never extract it again."

Ivy suspected he was right. Greenly Circle was thronged with people who were making their way among various stalls and carts. There was barely room enough to walk, let alone drive.

She told Lawden that she could go on foot the remainder of the way. His hesitation to agree to this was evident upon his homely face, but she assured him that she would be very well. After all, it was daylight, and there were many people about.

Lawden gave a reluctant nod, then opened the door of the cabriolet. Ivy instructed him to wait where she might easily see him, then made her way along the periphery of Greenly Circle. Even keeping to the edges of the broad circle, she was forced to wend her way among knots of people gathered before various stalls offering apples or eggs or candles. Though from what Ivy could tell, most of the vendors seemed to have more customers than they did goods to sell, and she was witness to more than a few angry exchanges and shaken fists as she passed.

Ivy did not linger, and she soon found herself starting down the lane on which Mr. Mundy's shop lay. At once sooty buildings closed in above, shutting out the greater part of the light that seeped from the dull sky. The bustle of Greenly Circle became a muffled drone behind her, and the sound of her footsteps skittered ahead along the narrow way, which was barren of people. Suddenly Ivy felt less certain that it had been a good choice to leave Lawden and the cabriolet behind.

Well, she was here now, and not far ahead she glimpsed a sign above a door. The light was just sufficient that she could make out the faded silver outline of a staring eye painted upon the sign. Lifting the hem of her gown off the cobbles, she hurried toward it.

Yet when she reached the door, Ivy found herself reluctant to push it open. She stepped to one side and peered through the windows of the shop, but they were even grimier than the last time she had been there, so that she could glimpse only a few indistinct shapes through them.

She went back to the door, its blue paint flaking as if it were afflicted with some scabrous malady. What would she say to Mr. Mundy? Should she tell him how she had learned her father wanted her to seek out his old friends from the Vigilant Order of the Silver Eye? That might not be wise, given that Mr. Lockwell had intended the journal for her and no other.

She would not tell Mr. Mundy everything right off, Ivy decided. It would be best simply to say that she knew the time had come to make contact with her father's former compatriots, and then see what Mr. Mundy volunteered on his own. Resolved, she gripped the doorknob and pushed.

The door did not budge. Ivy tried again, giving it all her strength, but still the door did not open, nor would the knob turn.

Ivy stared stupidly at the door. So intent had she been on finding an opportunity to go to Mr. Mundy's magick shop that she had never considered he would not be there when she did! And it seemed peculiar that his shop was closed after the long umbral. Though now that she considered it, what with the practice of magick now being regulated by the Gray Conclave, perhaps it was not so unexpected after all.

Hoping he was perhaps within, even if the shop was closed, Ivy knocked upon the door. She waited, then knocked again, harder this time. However, the door remained shut, and she heard no sound behind nor saw any glimmer of light through the dirty windowpanes.

At last she was forced to surrender. If Mr. Mundy was in his shop, he was not answering. Yet she had the feeling that he was not there. Now that she noticed it, there was a large drift of refuse piled before the door—old leaves and crumpled pages from broadsheets matted together by rain. It gave the feeling that no one had opened the door for some time. Perhaps Mr. Mundy had left the city, as so many others had.

In which case, she had little more knowledge of his whereabouts than she did that of Fintaur or Larken. The gloom that filled the lane now settled into Ivy's chest, as if she had been breathing it in all this while. It was time to return to the cabriolet; Lawden would be wondering where she was.

She turned back down the lane and emerged once more into Greenly Circle. The traffic was so thick that there was no going against it to return by the route she had come, and instead she was forced to move with it, though this meant going the long way around. Even this was no easy feat, and when a lorry suddenly rattled past her, she was forced to press herself against the window of a bookshop to avoid being trampled.

The lorry hurtled by, and with a relieved breath Ivy stepped back from the window. Beyond the glass was a table stacked with a number of volumes; and being a person who was ever devoted to books, she could not help glancing at them, reading the spines and covers.

All at once a gasp escaped her, and the large eyes of her reflected self stared back at her from the window glass. A moment later she was at the door of the shop, pushing it open.

The place was a labyrinth of dark wood shelves that were crowded, though in neat and orderly fashion, with all manner of books. The air had a bluish tint to it, colored by a beautiful transom of stained glass above the door, which bore the design of a winged lion standing rampant against an azure background.

A peculiar sensation of familiarity came over Ivy, as if this was not the first time she had been to this place. Yet she was sure she had never bought anything in this store before, and she supposed it was simply the dusty odor of books—a thing so well-known and comforting to her, and which hung thickly upon the air of the shop—that made it seem so familiar.

Wending her way around a tall shelf, Ivy came to the table situated before the shop's window and she picked up the book she had seen through the glass. She ran a finger over the gilt words on the red cover. They read, *The Towers of Ardaunto,* and beneath that in smaller type, *By an Anonymous Prince of the Fabled City of Canals.* She opened the book near the end and saw at once that the final chapters, which had been excised from the book she had at the house, were present in this copy.

"Can I assist you in some way, madam?" spoke a voice behind her.

Startled, Ivy shut the book and turned to see a man before her. She supposed he was the bookseller, for he had a rather bookish appearance himself. His eyes were small and squinting, and his shoulders were hunched within a suit that was, like his store, at once neatly kept and somewhat dusty. His white hair was carefully parted to either side of his crown like the open pages of a book.

"I saw this in the front window," she said. "Is it for sale?"

He peered at the book in her hands, then frowned. "But that's not right at all."

"You mean it isn't for sale?" Ivy said, tightening her fingers around the book. That she could possibly leave the shop without it in her possession was unthinkable.

The bookseller gave her a reassuring smile. "No, of course it's for sale, as are all of my books. It's just that the table in the window is not its usual place, and I'm sure it wasn't there a little while ago." He stroked his chin with a hand. "I suppose it must have been that peculiar fellow who was just in here. Other than you and him, I haven't had another customer this morning. I fear no one wants for books when they're fighting over candles."

A thought occurred to Ivy, one that made her heart leap. "Was your other customer today dressed in a strange black costume?"

The other shook his head. "A black costume? No, he wore a blue coat, one that was very rich, by its look. It wasn't his dress that was odd, but his behavior, for he wouldn't speak a word to me. Instead he kept wandering about my shop, so that I began to fear he was intent on pinching something. Then, when I turned around for a moment, he was gone."

Ivy considered these words. She had wondered if it was the man in the black mask who had left the book in a place she might see it. But if it was, then he had not been dressed in his usual garb.

Well, no matter who it was who had placed the book on the table, he was gone now, and Ivy was eager to take it home. She asked the bookseller the price, then opened her purse to draw out a silver half regal.

"Do you mind if I inquire how you became interested in this particular book, madam?" he asked as he accepted the money. "Is it the title that caught your interest?"

Ivy hesitated, wanting neither to tell a falsehood nor speak too much. "I was reading another copy, but the last pages were missing from it."

"How dreadful! Printers cannot be trusted these days. But you must have liked the book then, to want to read it all the way through."

"Yes, I do like it," she said, more quickly this time, for it was the truth.

His smile returned, broader than before. "Very good, I'm glad to hear it. I like this one very much myself."

Ivy nodded absently, hardly hearing him. Now that the book was hers, she wanted nothing more than to read the last chapters.

She bid the bookseller farewell, then went out the door. And even as she walked through the crowds of Greenly Circle, she opened the book and began to read.

CHAPTER TEN

———— ❧ ————

IT WAS THE FIRST long lumenal in a quarter month, and Halworth Gardens was busy with people who had come out for a stroll in the bright sun. Rafferdy walked along a path, past scarlet geraniums and yellow hibiscus, swinging his ivory-handled cane as he went and tipping his hat to any pretty young ladies who smiled at him.

There were no small number of these, for he was smartly dressed in a new green coat that was cut tightly to his figure in the latest mode. Yet while Rafferdy in no way minded this attention, neither did he stop to speak to any who offered it to him. There was only one lady he would have wished to walk with in the gardens, but she was not here. Besides, it was not for an idle stroll that he had come to this place.

Rafferdy cast a glance behind him, making certain no one was paying him any heed, then turned onto a narrow side path that wound away to a quiet grotto. There, a man sat on a marble bench beneath the braided canopy of a wisteria tree. He was dressed in a dark blue coat that was overly ornate and heavy for a stroll in a garden on a warm day.

The man on the bench did not look up as Rafferdy approached. Instead, his attention was fixed on the small sketchbook open on his knee. He tucked a stray lock of long, pale hair behind an ear, then made a scribble on the page with a charcoal pencil.

Again Rafferdy looked over his shoulder, making certain he had not been followed, then sat upon the bench.

"Good day, Lord Rafferdy," the fair-haired man said without looking up. He made several more marks upon the page. The ring on his right hand flashed red as it caught a stray sunbeam.

"Hello, Lord Farrolbrook," Rafferdy said in a voice so low that someone a dozen feet away would have heard only bright birdsong and the murmurings of the wisteria tree. "I am glad that you were able to come today."

The other man gave a small shrug. "I have little else to occupy me of late. So it all went as you had hoped, I heard."

Rafferdy could not help a grin. "Yes, quite as I hoped. Lord Davarry found himself very much alone, and the measure to reduce the size of the Wyrdwood was not brought up for a vote."

"I am not surprised that was the case. It was a clever scheme."

"No matter how clever, it could never have succeeded without your assistance. But you were not there to witness its fruition yourself."

Farrolbrook reached into his coat pocket and drew out a small pocketknife. He unfolded it and began whittling the end of the pencil. "I thought it best not to be seen that day. I did not want anyone to have cause to think of me. Not that any of the other Magisters suspect me of duplicitous behavior. Why should they? I am sure they think me quite impotent these days. And indeed, without your aid, I could not have worked even so small a spell as it takes to write a message in my black book."

Rafferdy did not doubt this. Farrolbrook had hardly been able to utter the words of magick that day in the dim parlor of his house in the New Quarter. Rafferdy had been forced to sound out the runes one by one for him. But at last, after great effort, the deed was done. Farrolbrook had inscribed the message in the small book, bound in black leather. At the same moment, the message had appeared in the black books possessed by every other member of the High Order of the Golden Door. Thus it was, rather than going to Assembly to vote on the matter of the Wyrdwood, every magician in the order had gone to a warehouse down in Waterside, thinking they had been summoned to a secret meeting by Lord Davarry. All except for Davarry himself, who—being the one who normally called meetings—had not been bothering to regularly check his own black book.

Rafferdy imagined that would change henceforth. The Magisters knew now there was a traitor in their midst, but they couldn't know who. It was the magick of the books that what was written in one was written in all of them, but there was no way to know in which book the message had originated. And as Farrolbrook had said, no one was likely to suspect him, given how poor he was at magick.

Indeed, so feeble was his ability to work spells these days that it was remarkable he remained in the High Order of the Golden Door at all. Perhaps some of the Magisters still held him in regard for the service he had rendered unto the order in the past—or more precisely for the way the order had made use of him. Or perhaps it was simply that he had become so low as to be beneath their notice.

Whatever the reason, it was fortuitous that Farrolbrook was still a member of the Golden Door. And it was for that very reason Rafferdy had sought him out again two months ago.

It was not long after Rafferdy and Coulten had joined the Fellowship of the Silver Circle that Rafferdy conceived the notion to speak to Farrolbrook. The idea was perhaps more mad than clever. After all, the purpose of the Fellowship—to prevent the passage in Assembly of any measures against the Wyrdwood—was directly at odds with that of the High Order of the Golden Door, to which many Magisters belonged, and Farrolbrook was the former leader of the Magisters.

Yet Rafferdy was sure that if the Fellowship was going to counter the maneuverings of the Magisters in Assembly, they were going to need a greater comprehension of the working of the Golden Door. And who better to provide such than one of their own? Farrolbrook had already aided Rafferdy once before, on the day Rafferdy had pursued Coulten to Madiger's Wall. It was Farrolbrook who had revealed Mr. Gambrel's plan to break open the tomb of the Broken God—and to sacrifice Coulten in the process.

Rafferdy had never been one to overthink things. Like a necktie or a bouquet of flowers, an idea was best if one did not fuss with it too much. Thus he did not bother debating the matter, and one afternoon directed his driver to take him to Farrolbrook's large, gaudy house in the New Quarter.

On his one prior visit to that abode, Rafferdy had found the servants disagreeable and fearful of guests while the master of the house had shut himself in a darkened parlor greatly in need of cleaning. Expecting the same or worse this time, he was surprised to discover a new set of servants who were both efficient and courteous, and he was shown to a bright, airy room where Lord Farrolbrook received him in the most friendly manner.

Rafferdy could only express his surprise at such a welcome.

"And why should I not welcome you?" Farrolbrook had said that day. "I have a great deficit of company, for no one else ever comes to visit me. And as they say, a pauper cannot be particular. Now, I suppose you've come to learn about the Magisters. Would you care for tea?"

Rafferdy could only nod as he accepted a cup. And so began their regular meetings.

That there remained something wrong with Lord Farrolbrook, there could be no doubt. Rafferdy did not know exactly what malady had caused him to fall from his position as leader of the Magisters. From what Coulten had said, Farrolbrook had begun to dress and act strangely following the death of his father the previous year. Perhaps this loss, compounded with the pressures of leading the Magisters—in appearance, at least, if not in fact—had caused the onset of his erratic behavior.

Fortunately, Farrolbrook was far more lucid that day in the parlor than on the first occasion Rafferdy had gone to him, and his condition seemed to improve each subsequent time they met. True, there were limits to these improvements. The other day, Rafferdy had observed the way Farrolbrook's brow beaded up with sweat, and how his hands trembled as he held his black book, laboring to inscribe the message in it with Rafferdy's assistance.

Then again, his hands seemed very steady now as he worked the pocketknife upon the pencil to sharpen it. Both the blade and his House ring flashed in the dappled sunlight as he worked, and Rafferdy found himself wondering if the other man was indeed so entirely impotent.

Evidently satisfied by the sharpness of the pencil, Farrolbrook put away the knife and resumed drawing in his sketchbook.

"If I may say so, you seem very well today," Rafferdy said.

Farrolbrook worked the pencil in bold strokes upon the page. "As I said before, I have learned it is best not to try to resist or struggle when the spells come upon me."

"Yes, you did say that, though you never mentioned how you discovered the fact."

"It was in a letter from my late father. I discovered it a few months ago among his things, and it contained a large amount of advice on the topic."

"The topic of your illness, you mean?"

"Yes. Though I was not aware of it, it seems he long suffered from the very same malady that has now afflicted me."

Rafferdy was intrigued by this news. The elder Lord Farrolbrook must have known, or at least suspected, that his son would contract this same illness. "And in his letter, did your father impart to you knowledge of what this peculiar malady is?"

"No, I fear not," Farrolbrook said. "While he offered much advice for managing the condition and ameliorating its effects, he seemed to understand its nature and origins no more than I do. I suppose eventually it will take its toll upon me as it did him."

That it was already taking a toll was apparent. Despite his general improvement, there was still an impression of illness about Lord Farrolbrook. His complexion was pale and slightly jaundiced, and though it was obvious he kept his person clean, still Rafferdy often noticed that there was a faint but unpleasant odor about him—a cloying scent, like that of fruit that had been left in a bowl too long.

Farrolbrook shifted his grip on his pencil, and for the first time Rafferdy noticed a small blemish on the back of his hand—a suppurating wound or a moist sore. As if aware of Rafferdy's gaze, the other man suddenly set down his pencil and book on the bench.

"I'm glad you could come today," Rafferdy blurted out to mask the awkward moment. "I wanted to thank you again, for inscribing the message in your black book."

The other man gazed at him with pale blue eyes. "And is that the only thing you came for today?"

Farrolbrook might have been infirm and a poor magician, but he was not so dull of wits as Rafferdy had once believed. It was quite the opposite, for his perception in this matter was keen.

"No, it's not. There's something else I was hoping you'd do."

Rafferdy explained his intention, and Farrolbrook raised a golden eyebrow in response.

"Are you certain that's a good idea, Lord Rafferdy? What will the other members of your order think?"

"I'm sure they'll all come around. Once their hearts begin to beat again, that is."

Farrolbrook gave him a wan smile. "Very well, if you think it would be of use."

Rafferdy still didn't understand why Farrolbrook was helping him. Perhaps it was to have some revenge against the order that had so callously used and abandoned him. Or perhaps it was for some other reason. Either way, Rafferdy would take such aid as he could garner.

"Yes, I do think it would be useful."

"Very well, then." Farrolbrook took up a cane that leaned against the bench and, with its benefit, rose to his feet. "I will not bother to say farewell, as I will see you soon enough. And I believe I may have something important to tell you then. I will soon know for certain."

He gave a nod, then moved away down the path. Such was his slow pace, and the frilled, outmoded nature of his dark blue coat, that but for his gold hair he could have been mistaken for an elderly lord out for a toddle.

It was only after he was out of sight that Rafferdy realized Farrolbrook had left his sketchbook on the bench, still open to the page he had been drawing upon. Well, Rafferdy would have a chance to return it to him soon. He took up the book.

As he did, a shiver passed through him despite the warmness of the air. The open pages of the sketchbook were filled with a profusion of dark, crooked lines—a mirror to the braided branches of the wisteria tree that hung over the bench. Only the drawing was anything but an idyllic garden scene. Rather, the branches seemed to writhe and pulse across the pages, pushing in from the edges toward the center. There, a small figure rendered all in black stood alone within the small circle of white, its hands thrown up as if in one last gesture to hold back the encroachment of the black tangle.

A compulsion came over Rafferdy, to turn the pages and see what other visions were contained within the sketchbook. Instead, he snapped the book shut, tucked it into his coat pocket, and departed the grotto. There was only one mystery he wished to consider at the moment.

And that was where to get a drink before going to supper at Lady Marsdel's that night.

E̶VENING TOOK the city unawares, as the sun made a series of sudden lurches into the west. So it was, pressed for time, that Rafferdy was forced to present himself at Lady Marsdel's abode on Fairhall Street without the prior benefit of a whiskey or two. His desire to dull his senses, however, was quickly removed when he entered the parlor. As if directed by some preternatural instinct, the first thing his gaze fell upon in that vast room was the very thing he had wanted to see most.

Mrs. Quent smiled at him from her position standing beside the pianoforte some distance away, where Mrs. Baydon sat at the bench, but said nothing; for of course it was not *her* parlor, and it was not she whom he must greet first.

"You appear to be having some difficulty in locating me, Lord Rafferdy," came Lady Marsdel's echoing tones from across the room. "Allow me to aid you, then—I am over here."

Rafferdy went past the pianoforte and approached Lady Marsdel. She sat in a large chair at the far end of the parlor, near the fireplace and the old stone sphinx—the one which Lord Marsdel had brought back after his time in the far south of the Empire. On a pillow on her lap was a bit of white fluff he presumed was either a dog or a ball of yarn her ladyship was attempting to untangle. He gave a smart bow. As he did, a growl emanated from within the ball of fluff.

A dog, then.

"Good evening, your ladyship," he said, rising. "And thank you for directing me. Such is the great size of your parlor that I have a tendency to get turned around in it."

"Your head is turned, I suppose, but I somehow doubt it is the size of my parlor that has done so," Lady Marsdel said, her eyes narrowing.

Before Rafferdy could consider what these words meant, Lord Baydon spoke up.

"You are just in time, Lord Rafferdy," Lady Marsdel's brother said, his voice thin and reedy but still containing its usual jovial tone. "My daughter-in-law was about to perform another song on the pianoforte."

Mr. Baydon gave the broadsheet he was reading a snap to remove a crease. "A song—is that what that last exercise was meant to be? I thought Mrs. Baydon was attempting to discover every out-of-tune key on the pianoforte, and having great luck at it."

"I believe it is your ears that are out of tune, Mr. Baydon," his wife said. She looked very pretty as she sat upright on the bench at the pianoforte, her golden hair falling in ringlets over her shoulders. She was wearing a blue gown that matched her eyes. "Perhaps you might have them adjusted the same way the strings of the pianoforte were done recently."

"I assure you, my ears are working very well," Mr. Baydon said.

Mrs. Baydon affected a pretty frown. "Well, either my playing or your hearing is off. We cannot both of us be right in the matter."

"Perhaps you can at that," Rafferdy said, moving to the pianoforte. "After all, given their remarkable size, it's quite possible that Mr. Baydon's ears perceive tones or vibrations that are beneath the notice of the rest of us—aside from her ladyship's dog, perhaps."

Mr. Baydon glowered over the top of his newspaper, while Mrs. Baydon let out a laugh.

"Yes, perhaps that's it, Mr. Rafferdy," she said brightly. "My husband is very handsome, of course, but he *does* have curiously large ears."

Being at once insulted and complimented by his wife, it was evident Mr. Baydon didn't know how to respond. Instead he raised his broadsheet once more and muttered something unintelligible behind it.

Mrs. Baydon smiled up at Rafferdy. "I'm so glad you were able to come tonight, as we have been greatly in need of amusement of late. We have been deprived of that which most delights us."

"So have I," Rafferdy said, though it was not at Mrs. Baydon that he looked. Instead, his gaze went beyond her, to Mrs. Quent.

She stood on the other side of the pianoforte, wearing a simple but very lovely gown of pale yellow that complemented her green eyes. Her hair, which was a lighter shade of gold than Mrs. Baydon's, was worn more loosely and naturally, in a way that suggested it had just been stirred by some passing zephyr. It could only make him think of when they were at the Evengrove, and the way the trees had lifted her up to their crowns and carried her away.

"And good evening to you as well, Lord Rafferdy," Mrs. Quent said, smiling at him.

He realized he had been staring, and he gave a quick bow to cover up the fact. "Good evening, Lady Quent. I trust your husband and sisters are well?"

"Yes, they are all well."

"And yourself?"

It seemed her smile faltered for just a moment. "Yes, I'm quite well, thank you."

A note of concern sounded within him, but before he could wonder what he perceived in her expression, Lady Marsdel was addressing him again.

"Come, Lord Rafferdy, sit beside me and allow Mrs. Baydon to finish her recital so that we may proceed to supper."

"Are we not awaiting any others?" Rafferdy said as he turned around, for their number was but six at present.

The coating of powder upon Lady Marsdel's face could not conceal the way her wrinkles deepened as she pursed her lips. "We are all for the evening. There is hardly anyone of worth left in the city to invite, for so many have gone to their estates in the south and east. We might have been more, for an invitation was extended to Lady Quent's people, but I have been informed that they declined to come."

"Sir Quent told me to extend his sincere regrets," Mrs. Quent said—a bit breathlessly, as if she felt real distress. "His work at the Citadel has detained him beyond his control. And as I mentioned, my sisters were greatly disappointed they could not attend, but they had previously accepted an engagement."

"One they might easily have broken, I am sure, to attend dinner at a lady's house."

"Unless, of course, they were invited to a countess's house," Rafferdy said with affected innocence. This won him both a glare and a growl from the direction of her ladyship, which let him know he had scored a point. "Besides, why should they come here? Wherever it was they were invited, they are far more likely to meet eligible men there than they would here."

"I am sure you are quite eligible, Lord Rafferdy. But perhaps you mean they would be more likely to meet *notable* men."

Rafferdy winced. Now it was Lady Marsdel who had scored a point. Rafferdy had recently heard whispers at Assembly that Sir Quent might be made into an earl if he was confirmed as lord inquirer; and if Rafferdy had heard such a rumor, then it was certain Lady Marsdel had as well. If it was indeed the case that Sir Quent would be raised up to an earl, then it was far from impossible to think the Miss Lockwells would each marry a lord, or even better.

Rafferdy shifted on the sofa, suddenly finding his seat uncomfortable. The thought that Lady Quent's sisters might soon be above him was not one he relished. But why was that the case? It was not as if he had an eye upon either of the Miss Lockwells.

"Please, Mrs. Baydon, play your song," he said through clenched teeth.

She did so, and any sour notes she might have struck were only echoed by the ones already sounding in his head.

At last Mrs. Baydon's exercises upon the pianoforte were concluded, and it was time to proceed to the dining room for supper. Despite the benefit of a cane, Lord Baydon struggled to rise from his chair next to the fireplace, and Rafferdy went to him to lend a hand.

Lord Baydon had been frequently ill over the last half year. What had at first seemed only to be a mere head cold had progressively worsened. As far as Rafferdy knew, the doctors had not determined the nature of the older lord's illness, though he suffered from a general weakness of the body, and he was prone to chills and spasms. As a result, he had been able to attend sessions of the Hall of Magnates only occasionally, and it had been far more than a month since Rafferdy had last seen him there.

"Thank you, my good sir," Lord Baydon said once he had gained his feet with Rafferdy's help. "I find I have more difficulty rising from a comfortable seat than a hard one these days."

"Then it is assured you will have no issue gaining your feet when next you come to the Hall of Magnates," Rafferdy said, "for you will find the benches just as uncomfortable to sit upon as ever."

Rafferdy paused, expecting the older lord to pronounce that he was certain he would be at Assembly during the very next session. It had ever been Lord Baydon's habit to adopt the best possible view, to constantly assume that good things would happen rather than ill.

Only this time Lord Baydon shook his head. "No, you will have to cast your votes without me, Lord Rafferdy. I do not think I will be going back to Assembly soon."

This response seemed greatly out of character, but Rafferdy attempted not to display his surprise. "I am sorry that you are still feeling so unwell. This illness has no doubt been a great bother to you."

"No, it is no bother," the older man said quietly, and blew a breath through his gray mustache. "Rather, it was the least I could do. I could not go with them, after all."

As he spoke, Lord Baydon looked not at Rafferdy, but rather at the sphinx that crouched next to the fireplace. The stone figure was a twin to the one that dwelled in the study at Asterlane; like Lord Marsdel, Rafferdy's father had brought it back from the south as a memento of his time in the Empire. Its stone surface was worn and pitted from eons spent beneath the sands of the southern Murgh Empire, but its eyes of lapis lazuli remained smooth and blue, gazing serenely forward as if they saw things in their eternal wisdom that mortal men could not.

If that were really the case, perhaps the sphinx would understand the riddle of Lord Baydon's words. What had he meant, that it was the least he could do? Before Rafferdy could ask, Lord Baydon looked away from the sphinx and said they should follow after the others.

Indeed, the rest of the party was just departing the parlor, so Rafferdy proffered his arm to his companion. They went slowly, for the older lord was out of breath after only a few steps. As long as Rafferdy had known him, Lord Baydon had been a very plump man, but now his suit hung on him somewhat loosely, and there was a hollowness to his cheeks.

By the time they reached the dining room, the others were already seated. Rafferdy helped Lord Baydon into his place, then took his own.

"I warn you, supper is bound to be very poor tonight," Lady Marsdel said as the first plates were brought. "I have directed my cook several times of late to produce better fare, but she has made no efforts in this regard."

"I imagine it is not for lack of effort," Mrs. Baydon said. "My own cook complains there is nothing good to be had in the city anymore. Is it not the same for you, Lady Quent?"

Mrs. Quent nodded. "The other day when I was out, I noted that the selection in the shops was very scant but that there was a surplus of people trying to purchase it."

Rafferdy could not help a smile. He doubted any other lord's wife would go to a shop to observe things directly for herself. Only Mrs. Quent.

"It is little hardship for us, but I worry about those who are poorer," she continued, "and if they will be able to buy enough to eat."

Mr. Baydon gave a snort. "Well, if not, then you can blame it on the hooligans in the Outlands. I'm sure they are waylaying all carts and wagons that are bound for Invarel and making off with the goods; for God knows they are too dull and lazy to grow anything fit for proper people to eat in Torland. Yet I wonder that the Crown's soldiers allow it."

"Perhaps they have other matters to concern themselves with," Rafferdy said.

"Well, I am sure some effort might be made to improve the situation," Lady Marsdel declaimed. "I would dismiss my cook if I thought there was a chance I wouldn't end up with someone even more dreadful. But that is hardly likely, for the best servants have all been taken away by the households that have left the city due to the troubles."

She took a spoonful of her soup, then waved a napkin at her bowl so that a servant hurried forward and whisked it away.

"I tell you," Lady Marsdel went on, "I have become greatly wearied by all this awful business. If it would confine itself to the West Country, I would care nothing about it, but when it causes us such misery here in the city, then it has become too much indeed."

"Hear! Hear!" Mr. Baydon said, then tucked into his own soup, seeming to have no concerns for its quality.

In fact, everything set before them seemed to Rafferdy to be quite good, though he supposed the variety was less than would have been found upon Lady Marsdel's table in the past. There were few exotic items or rare delicacies, but what was there was anything but poor. The soup was flavorful with fresh herbs, and the beef so tender it melted on the tongue. Rafferdy took a sip of his wine and found it to be an excellent vintage. If this was misery, he knew there were a great many people in the nation who would gladly wish themselves miserable.

Yet, as he set down his glass, he could only think that the present state of affairs in the nation had indeed weighed upon Lady Marsdel. Rafferdy had never before thought of her ladyship as in any way old. Mature and stately, yes; but she was far too vigorous and forceful a woman to be described by a word that implied frailty and weakness.

Only tonight her shoulders looked thin and curled inside the stiff shoulders of her russet dress, and the shadows in the dining room—more numerous than usual, for the number of candles was less—accentuated the sharpness of her cheeks and the thin bones of her hands. It might be ridiculous to think of a woman in a grand house dining on beef and wine to be miserable. Yet was not misery a relative state? It represented the difference between what one felt one *should* have and what one *did*. And that gap had grown for everyone in Altania over the course of these last months—the high as well as the low.

Rafferdy set down his wineglass. "I wonder," he said, "if the best goods and the best servants are to be found in the east, perhaps you should consider leaving the city and removing yourself to your manor at Farland Park. I imagine you would find the society of more families there—and so have a better chance of luring away a good cook."

He spoke these words lightly, but Lady Marsdel's reply was the opposite. "My father fought against Bandley Morden's soldiers," she said, letting her fork fall loudly against her plate. "Lord Marsdel's father did as well. They did not put up with this Morden mischief then, and I will not do so now. We will stand our ground, as all true patriots of Altania must!"

She spoke these words with force—though Rafferdy could not help noticing how her hand trembled as she took up her fork again. All the same, it was a pronouncement that could not be argued with. Rafferdy picked up his own fork, and they all resumed eating their supper with much grimness, as if it were their duty to their nation.

Once this was concluded, they returned to the vastness of the parlor. Lady Marsdel seemed to have no wish for conversation, and she asked Mrs. Baydon if she would play some more on the pianoforte. Both Mr. and Mrs. Baydon appeared pained at this suggestion, but after the display at the supper table, no one seemed to think it wise to deny her ladyship's wishes.

"You must consider it your obligation as a patriot," Rafferdy murmured in Mrs. Baydon's ear as he pulled out the bench for her.

She gave him a wan smile. "I suppose I must, at that."

Mrs. Baydon made a game attempt to play—and Mr. Baydon made a similar effort to conceal his criticisms behind his broadsheet. Lady Marsdel seemed intent upon listening to the music, while her brother dozed in a chair beside her. So it was that Rafferdy at last had an opportunity to speak to Mrs. Quent. The two of them sat on a sofa some distance away, and if they leaned their heads together, and spoke in low tones, no one might hear their voices over the music.

"It seems so long since we have seen one another," Mrs. Quent said first, apparently as eager to have a conversation as he was.

"Much too long, I would say, and for that I can only blame myself."

"I am sure your work at Assembly is far more important than coming to call at Durrow Street."

He shook his head solemnly. "On the contrary, nothing could be more important than calling on you, and your husband and sisters. Yet it is often the case that matters less important but more pressing distract us from the things that press less upon us but are far more important."

"If that is the case, then perhaps I should harry you more to come to visit us, so that you give the matter the proper urgency," she said, smiling.

Rafferdy laughed for what seemed the first time in days, though he kept the sound of it low. "I wish that you would."

"I will," she promised, and then her expression became serious. "But I would never wish to take you from your work at Assembly. In times such as these, I am sure it cannot be more vital."

"Nor would I want to distract your husband in any way, for his work is even more so. I have heard he has been nominated for the post of lord inquirer, and that he will soon come before the Hall of Magnates to testify ahead of his confirmation."

"I do hope you will not be too hard on him in your questioning, Mr. Rafferdy." She spoke this as a jest, though he thought he saw a hint of real worry in her expression. Nor could he say that such a reaction was entirely unfounded.

"I fear that Sir Quent must expect that some will indeed attempt to make the interview difficult for him, due to the nature of the post itself."

Now the concern was open upon her face. "He knows this. There are those in the government who do not see the work the inquirers do with the Wyrdwood in a favorable light."

Rafferdy could only be astonished by these words, for her understanding of matters was clearly deeper than he had thought. But now that he considered it, why shouldn't it be so? Given the work her husband had done for years, as well as her own nature, it was likely she knew far more about the matter of the Wyrdwood than Rafferdy did himself.

Yet there were things he knew that she could not. He hesitated for only a moment, then dismissed any uncertainty. There was no one in all of Altania he could trust more than Mrs. Quent.

"You are right," he said. "There are those in the government, within the very Hall in which I sit, who seek to do all they can to disrupt the work of the Inquiry—or even to undo it. But know also that there are others who do not intend to make this an easy task for them."

Her green eyes grew wide, and her voice dropped to a whisper. "What do you mean?"

"I have joined another arcane order," he said, whispering himself. "It is a small order, only nine in number, but our purpose is to prevent any law that might cause harm to the Wyrdwood from making its way through Assembly. Just recently, we were able to thwart an effort to pass an act calling for those stands of Old Trees nearest Invarel to be reduced in size."

Her voice quavered with what might have been dread or excitement, or perhaps both. "Then you performed a great good for the country, and surely prevented more Risings—and so more reprisals against the Wyrdwood. But I can only admit that I am astonished by this news. Isn't it more perilous than ever to belong to an arcane order, Mr. Rafferdy? All have been forbidden, save the one sanctioned by the Gray Conclave. I fear that you place yourself in grave danger with your actions."

Rather than any sort of alarm, her words filled him with a powerful satisfaction; and if he sat up straighter, and thrust his chest out a bit, it was not something he could help.

"There is danger in it, I concede. All the same, it must be done. There are those in the very order you mentioned—the one sponsored by the state—who seek to cause some of the smaller stands of Old Trees to rise up, so that people will then call for the destruction of all of them. Yet you and I know that must never happen. We have seen the way the Old Trees have the ability to fight against *them*."

He cast his eyes upward for a moment, as if they were outside and the red planet glowed in the sky above.

"The Ashen," she murmured, almost without sound. "These men who seek to harm the Wyrdwood . . . they are aligned with them somehow?"

"How can they not be?"

Before she could respond, it impinged upon him that the parlor had grown suddenly quiet. Mrs. Baydon had ceased her playing. Even as Rafferdy realized what this portended, there came a sharp *snap* that could only be the sound of Lady Marsdel's fan closing.

"Lord Rafferdy and Lady Quent, I observe that you are being very selfish in your conversation," her ladyship called out, and if her voice had sounded weary before, it in no way lacked force now. "Either attend to Mrs. Baydon's playing in a courteous fashion like we all are doing—or, if what you are saying is of such grave importance that it cannot wait, then do share your thoughts with the room."

There was no more opportunity for words, but the look he and Mrs. Quent exchanged was enough. She gave a small nod, her green eyes shining; and for his part, Rafferdy could not help being exceedingly pleased.

Together, they turned their attention to Mrs. Baydon.

CHAPTER ELEVEN

*D*ARKNESS PROWLED at the door of the library, kept at bay by the light of the several candles Ivy had lit. They were burning low now; it was past time to retire upstairs. All the same, she did not rise from her chair. It was not as if Mr. Quent was waiting for her, as he was once again late with his work at the Citadel.

Besides, she was nearly finished with the book.

Ivy turned another page of *The Towers of Ardaunto,* reading as quickly as she could by the dim gold light. She had not had time to finish the story on her return from the bookshop near Greenly Circle, for it had been difficult to read as the cabriolet jostled along the streets of the Old City. Even if she could have, there still wouldn't have been time, for there were more pages remaining than she had thought there would be. Whoever had excised the pages from the copy left on the doorstep (and who could it have been but the man in the black mask?), he had removed a number of them.

Once back at the house on Durrow Street, there had been no time to read more of the book, for she had found an invitation from Lady Marsdel waiting for her in the parlor. Evidently Mr. Rafferdy had written a note to her ladyship as well as to Ivy, and here was the result.

In the note, Lady Marsdel invited Ivy to dine at her abode that

THE MASTER OF HEATHCREST HALL 179

evening. She also urged Ivy to bring Mr. Quent and her sisters with her. But as it turned out, only a little while before, Lily and Rose had received an invitation to a dance at one of the few households that they were acquainted with and which remained in the city, and they had accepted.

Though her sisters leaned toward breaking the engagement, for the affair had been very suddenly and hastily arranged, Ivy told them they should never break a promise, even one just made. Besides, they would no doubt have much enjoyment at a dance.

"I'm sure Rose might, but I shan't," Lily said. "I only accepted the invitation for *her* sake."

Rose looked up from petting Miss Mew, who was curled up on the sofa beside her. "But I don't like to dance at all! You know that, Lily. I only said I would go because you were going. I'm sure I won't be able to move if someone asks me to be his partner. So you *must* dance, for both of us."

"I don't know," Lily said, and played a somber chord on the pianoforte. "It seems very ill of us to be making merry here in the city, when so many soldiers are going off to fight in the Outlands. I wish we could offer *them* some amusement, rather than simply amusing ourselves here."

Rose bit her lower lip. "I don't understand. I thought the soldiers were fighting to keep the rebels away from the city so we could all continue to live as we were. So how can they be offended if we do?"

Ivy could not help smiling. Once again, in her simple way, Rose had stated a truth that more complicated arguments could only fail to do.

"You're right, Rose," Ivy said, sitting beside her. Miss Mew let out a great yawn, and Ivy stroked the little tortoiseshell cat. "The soldiers must believe they have someplace good to come back to when their battles are done. We must do our best to show them that their efforts are for a purpose, and that they have preserved the spirit of our city and nation." Now she looked at Lily. "Besides, it is far from impossible that there will be some lieutenants or captains there, in the city on leave for a little while. In which case, you *can* provide them some amusement—by dancing with them."

Lily did not agree with this statement, but nor did she immediately counter it, and this gave Ivy some relief. She remained concerned by what she had seen in Lily's folio the other day—the many drawings of dramatic scenes upon a stage, and the handsome actors who all tended to have dark eyes and dark, flowing hair.

Previously, she had believed Lily had gotten over her infatuation with Mr. Garritt, as well as her fascination with illusion plays, but the sketches in the folio showed that was far from the case. Indeed, Lily had somehow conflated the two; though why that was so, Ivy could not guess.

Ivy had still not had an opportunity to discuss the matter with Mr. Quent. Then again, she had not seen Lily working in the folio since that day. Perhaps the discovery, though awkward and painful on both their parts, had made Lily reconsider the wisdom of her actions. At the very least, it was an encouraging sign that she was willing to go to the dance that evening, and Ivy could hope that some handsome young man of station might catch her eye and cause her to forget her other preoccupations.

Once it was resolved her sisters would attend the dance, Ivy might have had some time to read more of the book. Only a glance out the window showed that the day was suddenly failing, and then all of them were in a great rush to ready themselves for their evening engagements. As she dressed, Ivy hoped Mr. Quent would return from the Citadel so he could accompany her; but all that arrived was a note from him, stating that he would be very late, and that she should not wait for him.

Ivy's disappointment at Mr. Quent's absence, while not forgotten, was at least ameliorated by the party at Lady Marsdel's, which while small in size was of the best quality. (Though she was concerned to see Lord Baydon looking in such poor health, despite his usual good cheer.) She was particularly happy to encounter Mr. Rafferdy there, for it had been some time since she had seen him. .

And now she knew why, for he had joined up with another arcane society!

Ivy did not know whether to be thrilled at the idea or worried. Perhaps both reactions were justified. It was perilous indeed for him to be a member of an occult order. Unsanctioned societies were now expressly forbidden by the Gray Conclave, and to be caught as a member of one was a crime against the nation. Nor could Mr. Rafferdy expect that his status as a magnate would preserve him from a trial or conviction were his actions to be discovered. Just that morning, Ivy had read an article in *The Comet* concerning a lord who was found to have been sending missives, about the size and condition of ships in the royal navy, to the Principalities—where they were likely passed to agents of Huntley Morden. That the lord in question would hang for treason was almost certain; his title would not preserve him.

Yet despite this, Ivy felt an excitement at Mr. Rafferdy's news. What he was doing was perilous, but it was worthy as well. And while the Gray Conclave might brand it a crime, Ivy knew otherwise. No doubt most people who called for the destruction of the Wyrdwood did so out of simple fear. But what if there were those who knew what Ivy and Mr. Quent and Mr. Rafferdy did—how the Wyrdwood could fight against the power of the Ashen? If there was a magician in Assembly who was beholden to the Ashen, would he not seek to pass laws to have the Old Trees cut down and burned?

Ivy could only believe that was the case. Thus she was grateful that Mr. Rafferdy and his compatriots worked to prevent the passage of such laws. And she was astonished as well. She knew that Mr. Rafferdy was brave; she had witnessed that firsthand when they confronted the magicians of the Vigilant Order of the Silver Eye, and again at the tomb of the Broken God within the Evengrove.

Yet it was largely due to her actions that he had been placed in those situations, and she had to confess, she tended to think of Mr. Rafferdy as a man preoccupied with himself and his own people rather than society at large. She had not known he was capable of acting in such an entirely selfless manner—to willingly place himself in a position of harm for the sake, not of himself or someone he cared for, but of the country.

Well, she had misjudged him. And now that she knew what he was doing, Ivy could only feel an even greater pride and affection for him. She had an urge to tell Mr. Quent about it. At the same time, she was not certain this was wise. True, Mr. Quent was a defender of the Wyrdwood. Yet Mr. Quent was an agent of the government as well, and was often in communication with members of the Gray Conclave. Would he not be bound by oath and duty to report Mr. Rafferdy's doings—or be complicit in the crime if he did not?

If so, then it would be exceedingly wrong of Ivy to place him in such a position. She thought about the matter during the entire drive from Lady Marsdel's, and by the time the carriage reached Durrow Street she had come to a conclusion. While the idea of keeping a secret from Mr. Quent pained her, holding Mr. Rafferdy's confession in confidence was the only way she could protect both her husband and her friend. To do anything else would put both men at risk. Whatever distress keeping the secret might cause her, it was nothing to the anguish it might cause if she did not.

Resolved in the matter, Ivy entered the house on Durrow Street and discovered that neither her sisters nor Mr. Quent had returned. Which meant she at last had time to finish *The Towers of Ardaunto*.

Now, as the candles burned low in the library, Ivy turned the final few pages, at once fascinated and horrified by what she read. When she first found the book, she had thought it to be a romance: a fanciful tale of two lovers. How wrong she had been!

After witnessing the occult ceremony, the young gondolier had leaped into the room at the top of the tower. It had been his crazed thought to wrest his beloved free of her father. Yet before he could reach them, the merchant flung out a hand and shouted harsh words of magick. At once the gondolier became as a statue, unable to move or speak. He could only watch, mute and powerless, as the merchant led his daughter from the chamber.

As they went, she cast a look over her shoulder. Her face was as white and hard as porcelain, but in her now-black eyes he thought he could still see a glimmer of the same regret and sadness he had perceived in them that day they first met. Then she turned, and the two were gone.

Hours passed, and at last the gondolier could move again. He staggered down the steps of the tower. He found the door at the bottom open to the night, and there was no trace of his beloved or her father.

The pages that followed described the young man's effort to find his beloved, in hopes he could undo the transformation that had been wrought upon her by her father and the magicians. His search lasted many years, becoming an increasingly fevered hunt—one that took him deep into the Murgh Empire, across the ocean to the island of Aratuga, and to the frigid and desolate realms of the far north. Always he sought out and followed the trail of father and daughter, never ceasing no matter how scant the clues or how perilous the routes along which they pointed.

At last he came to Altania, following whispers and rumors to a half-ruined castle in the rocky northwest of the island. By then, he was much transformed himself. No longer was he a handsome young boat keeper from the canal city of Ardaunto. His travails had left him gaunt and scarred, and his obsession to find his beloved had descended into a form of madness.

He entered the keep and went down to the crypts below, to a vaulted sepulcher, and there he came upon a terrible scene. Thirteen men lay sprawled dead, their blood and mangled limbs obscuring the arcane lines and occult runes which had been drawn upon the stone floor. Among them he recognized the corpse of the merchant, his once dark hair now a stark white.

Then the gondolier heard a whisper of cloth behind him, and when he turned he saw her there—his beloved. Unlike him, she ap-

peared just as she had that night in the tower years ago: her skin a flawless white, her hair and eyes as black as polished onyx.

"I have found you at last!" he cried.

"So you have," she replied, her voice clear as the tone made by striking a crystal goblet with a knife.

"But what happened here?" he said, unable to keep his eyes from roving to the maimed and torn bodies of the magicians.

"They attempted to open a gate."

"To open a gate?"

"Yes." She stepped over one of the bodies with a murmur of black silk. "For long years they have sought to open a door, a way leading to great power. All my life my father labored toward this purpose. It is why he did everything. It is the reason I was born—and why this was done to me."

She lifted a black-gloved hand and touched her face, her dark hair. Anguish filled the gondolier, so that his knees buckled, and it was all he could do to keep his feet.

"But why?" he said, staggering a step closer to her. "Why did he need you to be a part of this awful endeavor?"

"It was my purpose to protect them, so that they might pass through the gateway unharmed. Their White Thorn, they called me."

His gaze flickered down to one of the twisted corpses. "But they were harmed after all."

She gave a small shrug. "And why should I have protected them? Why should they have been rewarded after what they made me into, after what they made me do?"

A moan escaped him, and he could only wonder what terrible deeds they had forced her to commit over the years, to temper her like a weapon for their intended use.

"Yet such was the enchantment they had placed upon me that I could not turn against them directly," she went on. "So all these years, I let them believe that I would do as they wanted, that I would use the unholy abilities they had granted me to protect them from what waited beyond the gate. And when at last they were able to open the doorway"—her dark lips curved in a smile—"I did not lift

a finger, save to protect myself, until they were all of them dead, and the gate was closed again."

It was an awful deed; he could not help shuddering in the damp air of the ancient castle. Yet what choice had she been given? She had simply done what she must to survive. Even as he considered this, a spark of joy that had lain dormant in his breast so long he had all but forgotten its existence now flared to life.

"Then you are free," he said, the joy blazing brighter within him, so that he forgot the chill, forgot his pain. "You are free of them!"

She curled a hand beneath her chin. "Free?" She spoke the word as if she did not truly understand its meaning.

"Yes, you are free, my love—free of their terrible designs for you. You do not have to run any longer. We can be together at last."

"Together," she murmured, and her black eyes seemed to soften with that same regret he had seen in them so long ago. Her hand slipped inside a fold of her gown, as if to press against her heart.

But she did not need to feel sorrow any longer! The spark of joy blazing in his heart filled him with renewed vigor, and he sprang across the room to her, enfolding her in his arms and holding her fiercely. Then, as he had wanted to for so many years, he bent his head and pressed his lips to hers.

Cold. Her lips were cold and hard as the stones of the castle as she kissed him in return. The coldness seemed to pierce him, sinking deep into flesh and bone. With a gasp, he stumbled back.

And only as they parted did he see the knife she held in her hand, stained with blood. Another spasm of pain passed through him, and the warm spark in his heart wavered and dimmed. He lifted a shaking hand, touching it to his chest. It came away as red and wet as the knife she held.

"Why?" He managed to croak the word.

"Because a thorn can only pierce when it is grasped," she said, and now there was no longer any regret in her black eyes. "My father and the others are ended. But nothing can unmake me what I am."

Tears flowed down his cheeks, as freely as the blood from his wound. "What will you do?"

"I will return to Ardaunto. The prince there has asked me to be his servant, and I have agreed. He can use a stiletto, he told me, one that is both sharp and easy to conceal. And that is what I will be—a knife in his hand, one to wield against any who would defy him."

The gondolier understood. It was not just her father and the magicians she had sought to free herself from, but from everything that might have tied her to her former life. Everything, and everyone.

His legs buckled, and he fell to his knees as his life ebbed in a warm flood from his body. He had never thought his journey would end like this. Now a great weariness fell heavily over him; he wanted only to rest. And he thought, if this was to be his end, then better it was by her hand than any other's. They were both of them passing away from their old lives now.

"I love you," he said, the words barely above a whisper as the last of his life faded.

She gazed at him, her face a white mask. "I do not love you, nor any thing. They took that ability from me that day in the tower."

"Then I will love for both of us," he said.

Or at least he tried, though he was not certain his lips made any sound. The floor tilted upward to meet with his cheek, and he heard a distant, echoing noise. Then a shadow fell upon him. He thought perhaps it was her bending over him, that the coolness he felt upon his cheek was not the stone floor, but the touch of her hand.

Then all became darkness, forevermore.

HER HAND TREMBLING, Ivy turned the page, but no more followed it, and this time she knew it was not because any had been cut from the book. This was truly the end of the story. Only what did any of it mean?

She set down the book and crossed her arms, shivering, for the fire had burned out on the hearth long ago. She could easily imagine why it had been published, for horrid books were popular these days; people took a great thrill in reading about terrible things.

But why had the man in the black mask—if it had indeed been he—left the book on the front step? And why had he excised the final chapters? Surely he had known she would eventually seek out a complete copy. In which case, why bother to cut out the last pages at all?

Besides, it was not as if they had offered any illumination. The story had been fascinating, to be sure, particularly the descriptions of the transformation the magicians had wrought upon the merchant's daughter. Ivy wondered what the magicians had sought through the gate, and how the young woman—the White Thorn—was to have protected them. The author had never really said, though for some reason it all felt vaguely familiar to her. . . .

But of course it was. Before she had ever opened this book, Ivy had already known the story of a young woman who, by the actions of a magician, was transformed into a preternatural creature with alabaster skin. It was the story of what Mr. Bennick had done to Ashaydea—how he had made her into the cold, pitiless being called Lady Shayde. No wonder Mr. Quent had warned Ivy in a letter about Mr. Bennick. Years ago, Ashaydea had been his childhood companion at Heathcrest Hall. Knowing what Mr. Bennick had done to her, Mr. Quent could only have been horrified when he learned the former magician had then approached Ivy.

Yet it appeared that Mr. Quent was not the only person familiar with Lady Shayde's origins. Surely the author of the book had known about her, and had used her as inspiration for his story. Or was it the other way around? Had Mr. Bennick read a copy of this book, and through it gotten the idea to research ancient magicks and learn to make a White Thorn for himself?

Ivy didn't know. But while the story had been fascinating, as far as she could tell it had contained no clues regarding the whereabouts of her father's old compatriot in magick Mr. Fintaur. So then why had the man in the mask left it for her in the first place?

Ivy went to the desk, took out the Wyrdwood box, and opened it with a touch. She picked up the sheet of paper on which she had transcribed the last entry to appear in her father's journal.

You must begin to gather the others, he had written, knowing the entry would appear only when Cerephus had drawn close. *As for Fintaur, I believe you will find his whereabouts in the city of Ardaunto, across the sea.* . . .

Mere days before this entry had appeared, a copy of *The Towers of Ardaunto* had arrived on her front step. It could not be chance. There had to be a clue somewhere in the book. Only she had been too dull—or too caught up in the story—to see it.

Which meant she would have to read the book again, more slowly this time. Only now she was far too tired for such an endeavor. She looked through the journal, but finding all of its pages to be blank, she locked it back inside the Wyrdwood box.

Then Ivy blew out the candles and went to bed.

$\mathcal{S}$HE WOKE TO FIND Mr. Quent snoring softly beside her. Ivy smiled and touched his bearded cheek, then slipped quietly from the bed.

Downstairs, she found Rose and Lily already at the breakfast table.

"I am surprised to find you awake so soon," Ivy said. "I would have thought you would still be sleeping."

Lily dropped several lumps of sugar into her teacup. "Sleeping? Why in the world should we still be sleeping?"

"Because, though it is very enjoyable, dancing can also be very tiring."

"And I am sure that is why we are awake already," Lily said, dipping a spoon into her teacup and stirring vigorously. "For there wasn't a bit of dancing to be had last night, as there was no one at all to dance with."

Rose set down her toast. "But there were several gentlemen there, Lily. I am sure they would have asked you to dance, but you always happened to turn and walk away at just the moment they approached."

Though it was clear Rose was trying to help, the look Lily gave her sister was anything but grateful. "Well, it's not my fault, for I didn't see them coming. And anyway, I am sure they wouldn't have asked *me* to dance, as they were all very old. Of course, if they had been soldiers, I would have danced with them no matter what. It would have been my duty to help lift their spirits while they were in the city on leave. But none of them were officers, and I had no desire at all to dance myself."

Ivy considered stating that it was curious Lily had known the age and civilian nature of the men who approached her when she had not ever seen them, but she let the remark pass. It was clear her hopes were misplaced, and that a dance populated by young men (she was sure they had not been old) had not caused Lily to forget her preoccupation with illusion plays, or her fascination with Mr. Garritt.

Ivy would have to bring up the matter with Mr. Quent. Perhaps he could speak to Lily and encourage her to pursue other interests; Lily adored him, and so might listen to him when she would not her older sister. But for now, Ivy let the topic drop, and instead mentioned that she would be going to Madstone's after breakfast, as it was visiting day.

"Can I come with you?" Lily said suddenly, setting down her teacup.

Ivy hesitated, then shook her head. "As we've discussed, I don't think that's a good idea, Lily."

"Why not? Why are you always able to go visit him and not us? I miss Father, too, you know. I should like to be able to speak to him sometime, and I'm sure Rose would, too. Wouldn't you, Rose?"

Rose smiled. "But I do—" Her expression faltered, and she looked to Ivy. "That is, I would like to speak with him as well."

"I will arrange for you both to visit Father, soon," Ivy said. "I promise."

And she would. It was not fair that Lily and Rose had been deprived of their father's company for so long. Yet Ivy did not know exactly how she would keep this promise. Though the room Mr. Lockwell was in now was pleasant enough, to reach it one must pass near to those parts of the hostel where the most severely mad and deranged were housed, and where their father had once been held. That her sisters must never glimpse that portion of the hostel—or hear the awful cries and keening that filled it—Ivy was resolved.

Well, she would find some way to keep her promise. It would be good for her sisters to see their father.

Or had Rose already seen him? No, that was not possible; Mr. Lockwell was at Madstone's. But perhaps she could glimpse some remnant of him—some echo of his power which yet lingered here. How else to explain the light Rose claimed to have seen about the house?

That Rose had indeed seen something, Ivy was increasingly convinced. After all, it was not in Rose's character to willingly speak a mistruth. Nor did she possess, as Lily did, a fanciful imagination which was capable of inventing such things. Yet if Rose could see some trace of her father in the house, what did it mean? Ivy didn't know, but she would be sure to bring it up with Mr. Quent, along with the matter of Lily's folio.

For now she finished her breakfast, then departed the house. Lawden had the cabriolet waiting, and he drove her to the very east end of the city, to the long, low building of drab stone which stood apart from all other structures at the crest of a long, low hill.

She was admitted through the iron gate, and one of the day wardens led her away from the cacophony of wails and screams to the quieter wing where her father resided. The warden unlocked the door with a heavy iron key. She had not seen him before, though he was generally indistinguishable from the other wardens given his gray smock and the impassive expression upon his soft, colorless face.

"Pull the cord at once if he should grow violent and attempt to harm you, Lady Quent," he said placidly.

Ivy had long ago given up responding to such statements as this. At least for a change he had gotten her name right. "Thank you" was all she said, and entered the room. There was a grinding noise as the lock turned behind her.

Across the room, a wispy crown of white hair rose above the back of a chair, like a puff of tobacco smoke exhaled by the chair's occupant. At once, all thoughts of the wardens and the hostel receded. Ivy crossed the room and came around the chair.

"Good morning, Father."

He did not speak, or even move. His blue eyes stared blankly at the iron-barred window. However, she saw the slight relaxation of his shoulders and a shallowing of the furrows upon his brow, which let her know he was, at least in some way, aware of her presence.

As always, an ache crept into her heart at the sight of him. It was good to see him, but how she wished he could see *her* as well, and know her for who she was. How she wanted to be able to speak to him, to tell him about all the things that had happened, and to ask for his counsel on all the things that were to come.

"I trust you have been well this past quarter month," she said, kneeling beside his chair. "Have you been watching the weather out the window? It's been very peculiar of late. The other night it was hot and stifling, even though it was a long umbral. And it seems every lumenal a wild storm blows through, which is then gone as suddenly as it comes."

Ivy stroked his hand as she spoke. It was limp under her own, but warm, and his face, though slack, had good color. His clothes were clean, if somewhat rumpled, and his cheeks had been shaved. In all, he looked well enough. His appearance would not alarm her sisters.

Yet he did not move in response to her touch, nor did he speak in answer to her words. She could only believe the electrical shocks had lost whatever potency they once had. The wardens must have come to similar conclusions, for it was evident they had not performed the treatment on him in some time. The metal band used to transmit the shocks to the brain always left red weals upon his brow. But other than the usual rows of wrinkles, the skin of his forehead was unblemished.

Or perhaps it was simply that the wardens had become bored, disappointed that the patient had not continued to make exciting progress that would lend credence to their novel theories, and so had abandoned him in favor of treating more promising cases. Ivy considered discussing it with them, then dismissed the idea. She doubted she could convince them to do anything they had not decided to do themselves. Besides, what use was there in putting her father through the ordeal of further treatment if it could not help him?

Instead, she straightened his collar and used her fingers to correct the errant coils of his white hair. As she did, she spoke to him of small matters—what further repairs had been undertaken on his old house, and how the garden was faring. All the while he remained motionless and silent, until Ivy could no longer maintain her cheerful tone, and she fell silent herself, lest she begin to weep.

"I wish you could speak to me, Father," she said at last, and she knelt again by his chair, taking his limp hand and looking up at him. "I wish you could tell me why you want me to find the other magicians from your order. I'm trying to, only I don't know where they are. Well, except for Mr. Mundy, but he wasn't at his shop the other day. And even if he was, I don't know what I'm supposed to tell him or the others."

She thought he gave the faintest sigh, but that was it. Once again, Ivy recalled the time when he had arranged twelve apple seeds in a line on a plate, and he had uttered the words *It is about time*. Was that why he wanted her to find the others from his order now, because the twelve planets were beginning to align? If so, it was not here in this room that he would be able to tell her the reason for finding the other magicians of his order, but rather in his journal, if and when another entry appeared.

And even as she thought that, Ivy realized there was no use in keeping him at Madstone's anymore.

The idea came to her with a start, so that she gasped and stood. As she did, her father's hand slipped from hers and fell to his lap. It was strange—if she was truly abandoning hope that he could be cured of his malady here at the hostel, should she not feel despair rather than this sudden, fierce joy that now filled her?

Yet that was precisely what she felt at the thought of bringing

Mr. Lockwell home, to his house on Durrow Street, to be with his daughters and his old friend Mr. Quent. Nor was there anything to stop her from doing so. She still had the king's dispensation, granting her father release from Madstone's, locked safely in a drawer in the library. King Rothard might have passed, but royal authority was enduring, and unless the order was specifically rescinded by a new monarch, it remained valid. All she had to do was present the paper to the wardens, and they would have no choice but to release Mr. Lockwell from the hostel into her care. And then—

"I can bring you home, Father," she said, her elation rising further yet. "I can keep my promise to Lily and Rose, and you can be there with us, where you belong."

Perhaps it was selfish to feel this way, but she no longer cared. If reason and logic dictated that one did what one's heart wished for the most, then so be it. She threw her arms around his neck and kissed his cheek, and she did not care that he did not utter a sound or make a motion in response. To feel his warmth was enough.

Just then came a grinding sound as the lock turned. Ivy released her father and stepped toward the door as it opened.

"Visiting hours are over, Lady Quent," the warden said from the doorway. "I am sure you are relieved to depart."

No doubt he had mistaken the color in her cheeks for distress rather than excitement. Ivy didn't care; soon she would not have to speak to any of the dreadful wardens again. It was her impulse to tell the one before her now that she was removing her father from the hostel at once.

Only that would not do. She would have to present the king's order to take her father away. Besides, she had to make arrangements for him at the house, and prepare a room for him. And first of all, she should discuss the matter with Mr. Quent—though she had no doubt he would be as elated as she was at the prospect of having Mr. Lockwell back at the house.

And so they would, very soon. For now, she reluctantly allowed the warden to lead her from the room. Ivy cast one more fond glance at her father, who still gazed out the window at the gathering clouds.

The next time I come, it will be to take you home! she said silently, as if her father might somehow hear her.

Then the iron door shut with a *clang*.

CHAPTER TWELVE

LOUD WHISTLES and jeers filled the Theater of the Moon, drowning out the voices of the actors upon the stage.

Eldyn hesitated, waiting for the noise of the audience to die down, but the roar only continued. He repeated his line, speaking it at the top of his lungs. Only it was no use; his words didn't have a chance of carrying over all the shouting and catcalls. Then came a *crash* as a bottle flew from out of the darkness and smashed upon the stage.

Another bottle came hurtling after the first, and this one struck Hugoth on the side of the face, causing him to stagger back. A moment later, a red line appeared on his cheek, and a rivulet of blood snaked down to mingle with his crimson-dyed beard.

"Curtain!" Eldyn heard a voice calling from the wing nearest him. It was Master Tallyroth. "Draw the curtain, Riethe!"

Offstage to the right, Riethe leaped at the ropes and pulled hard, working them with his strong hands and arms. Moving so fast they conjured a wind, the red curtains sped shut across the proscenium arch. And not a moment too soon, for the thick cloth was momentarily dimpled as several more objects struck it.

At once Eldyn dashed across the stage to Hugoth. Mouse and Merrick, who had been conjuring an array of stars and comets in

the background, had already reached him, and they were steadying the older illusionist as he pressed a hand to his cheek.

"Hugoth, are you all right?" Eldyn said. The roar of the audience continued, but the curtain blocked some of the din, so that
he could actually hear himself speak. "How badly are you hurt?"

Hugoth grinned through his red beard. "I've had worse reviews
for a performance than that," he said as blood seeped between his
fingers. Together, they helped him to the wing and sat him down
on a box of props.

"Move your hand and let me see," Merrick said.

Hugoth did so, then winced as Merrick dabbed at the wound
with a handkerchief.

"It's not too long of a cut," the tall, thin illusionist said, his expression even more somber than usual. "But it's going to need a
stitch or two to keep it closed. And it's going to leave a scar."

"Luckily you're an ugly bastard, Hugoth," Mauress said cheerfully, "so it won't really matter."

"Mouse!" Eldyn said admonishingly, but Hugoth only laughed.

"You've heard the definition of an ugly Siltheri, haven't you,
Mouse?" he said. "It's any illusionist past his thirtieth birthday. So
you'll be joining me before too long."

Mouse giggled in response, and Eldyn was glad that Hugoth
was able to make light of the situation, for it meant he couldn't be
too badly hurt. Of course, Hugoth was not really old, nor was he
ugly. But youth and beauty were prized among the Siltheri, and as
a man of average looks and forty years, Hugoth was far from the
popular ideal on Durrow Street.

Not that any of them was very popular with the audience at the
moment. The cacophony had not ended on the other side of the
curtain; rather, it had only grown in volume and force. The house
was nearly full with soldiers from the royal army that night, and
they were now stamping their boots, so that the entire theater
groaned and shuddered.

"They're not leaving," Mouse said, peeking through the thin slit
at the edge of the curtain.

"I think we knew that already, Mouse," Riethe said. He rubbed his hands; they were bright red from pulling the rope so quickly. "And they're going to bring the whole place down around our ears if they keep that up. What do we do now?"

He looked to Tallyroth. The master illusionist's face was whiter than could be accounted for by a coating of powder alone. He shook his head as he gripped his cane.

"We must give them what they want," Madame Richelour said loudly as she hurried across the stage from the opposite side, the feathers sewn to the shoulders of her purple gown fluttering behind her like wings. "They have come here for one thing tonight— because the Theater of the Veils went dark and cannot give it to them. And so we must provide it instead."

Master Tallyroth gave her a startled look. "Are you certain, madam?"

She laid her hand atop his as it gripped the cane. "I know it is not what you wish. Nor do I wish it myself. But we have no choice. If we do not, they will ruin the place, and we do not have the funds to repair it. We will be bereft of any sort of livelihood."

The madam of the theater and the master illusionist gazed at each other for a long moment. To Eldyn, it seemed an unspoken message passed between them. Tallyroth briefly pressed his other hand on top of hers. Then he turned toward the illusionists who huddled in the wing.

"We will perform the scene with the torch maiden," he said.

"But that scene doesn't come until the second act," Merrick said.

Tallyroth thumped his cane on the stage. "Not tonight. We perform it now. Only let there be several maidens this time. What's more, you must make them all lively and buxom, and bare their breasts. Leave not one thing to the imagination."

They all stared at him.

"Are you sure?" Riethe said.

Tallyroth frowned at him. "Come now, Riethe, I'm sure a lewd scene is well within your capabilities. Quickly now, take your places."

He struck his cane against the stage again, and they all leaped to action. Even Hugoth.

"Are you well enough?" Eldyn said to him, concerned.

He nodded, holding the handkerchief against his cheek. "Conjuring the shadow army doesn't take any great skill, so Mouse and I can manage that."

"Hey!" Mouse exclaimed.

"You and Riethe and Merrick conjure the maidens," Hugoth went on, ignoring Mouse. "They need to look as fetching as possible, and you're the best three for the job. The rest can conjure horses, along with a fog to hide us all on the stage."

Eldyn nodded; it was a good plan. The illusionists all dashed back onto the stage. The curtain continued to ripple as it was struck by various objects on the other side, and the soldiers beyond stamped their boots, demanding to be entertained.

As he took his position, Eldyn cast a glance back at the wings. He could guess how difficult this was for Madame Richelour and Master Tallyroth. Both of them had always been against putting on this sort of burlesque at the theater, and instead insisted on only staging plays of artistic quality, even if it meant less take in the money box after each performance. But they both wore expressions of grim resolve now.

"Scene!" Tallyroth called out, and he and Madame Richelour worked the curtain ropes themselves. The noise of the audience rushed over the players as the folds of red cloth parted.

And the show went on.

IN ALL HIS TIME at the theater, Eldyn could not remember a performance that had felt as interminable as this one. For what seemed many hours (though was in fact a trifle less than one), he conjured a voluptuous maiden out of light and air and paraded her upon the stage as Riethe and Merrick worked the same trick beside him.

The soldiers applauded as the torch maidens first swooped down upon their winged horses, then let out cheers and whistles as an illusory breeze blew their hair back, revealing the pale, large, and improbably pert globes of their breasts. Riethe caused his maiden to rock back and forth lustily in the saddle as her horse galloped through the air, and given the positive reaction this won from the audience, Merrick and Eldyn hastily followed suit.

After that, the scene proceeded much as in previous performances, with the maidens defeating the shadow army meant to represent Huntley Morden's men. This evoked more cheers, but when it was finished, it was clear from their whoops and yells that the soldiers were far from sated.

Concealed in the gray fog that flooded the stage, Eldyn quickly whispered an idea to the others, and so the scene continued in an impromptu fashion. Their work done, the three maidens came to a forest fountain, and there they dipped themselves in the water to wash away the stains of battle. For a while they scrubbed one another, splashing as they did, and this bit of business proved popular with the audience.

Yet in time the soldiers grew restless again. There was a sound of shattering glass somewhere in the theater. Riethe hastily whispered another idea, and the scene took a more salacious turn as a trio of goat-legged satyrs crept from behind a tree and spied upon the maidens.

The satyrs wore dirty green coats, a clear signal to all that they were meant to represent Morden men. Their shaggy legs were trouserless. Thus the evidence of their lust was quickly apparent, and this was no less improbably proportioned than the feminine attributes of the maidens—a fact which caused howls of laughter from the soldiers in the audience.

The maidens looked up to see the satyrs. But by then the three goat-men had extinguished their torches, which they had left outside the fountain. Bereft of their powers, the maidens could do nothing as the satyrs picked them up and carried them off, no doubt to ravish them.

Before this could be achieved, however, three tall men in golden armor and blue cloaks appeared with swords in hand— gold and blue of course being two of the national colors of Altania.

With the maidens temporarily out of view, Eldyn, Riethe, and Merrick took over conjuring the satyrs, who engaged the warriors in a battle which spared no sight of blood or gore; and this display of violence met with as much approval from the audience as the sight of the maidens' nakedness.

At last, with the beasts slain, the golden soldiers sheathed their swords, and the maidens returned. They ran to the warriors, knelt at their feet, and clung to their legs, looking up in adoration. The men bent down to kiss them, a gesture which the maidens gustily returned. At this, a number of the real soldiers in the audience called out lewd comments and encouragements. It was clear they wished to see a consummation.

However, by then, all of the illusionists were spent. Eldyn's hands trembled as he kept weaving and shaping the light, concentrating with all his ability to prevent the phantasms from dissolving. He knew that, by now, he was drawing on some of his own light to achieve this, but he had no choice; weaving his own light required less focus and will, and it was the only way to keep the illusions from failing.

Yet even with the help of his own light, he was growing too exhausted to maintain such a high level of clarity and detail. Already the maiden's form was growing softer and more vague. The same was true for the other phantasms on the stage. Next to him, both Riethe and Merrick wore expressions of pain, their jaws clenched, a slick of sweat upon their brows. They were all of them about at an end.

The illusionists had no choice but to let the maidens and their rescuers sink down to the stage as the fog enveloped them—though by the rhythmic motions of their misty silhouettes, Eldyn hoped it was clear what act it was they were engaged in as they did, and that this would be enough to satisfy the soldiers in the audience.

Then, as the figures vanished into the fog, the curtains sped shut.

At once, all of the phantasms ceased existence. For a full minute the illusionists simply sat upon the stage, staring at one another, too fatigued to move or speak. Eldyn listened, waiting to hear the noise of shouts and jeers resume on the other side of the curtain, and for the red cloth to ripple as it was struck with empty bottles.

Instead came a low murmur of voices and the shuffling of boots. Mouse crawled across the stage and lifted the hem of the curtain to peer out.

"Thank God, they're leaving," he said, then flopped onto his back and let out a groan.

Eldyn sighed and mopped his brow with a hand. Either the play had finally sated the appetites of the soldiers—or it had whetted them enough that the men were off in search of real rather than illusory flesh to continue their entertainment. Either way, they were departing the theater. Which meant it was finally over.

"Good riddance," Merrick said, his arms around his knees as he sat on the stage. "To think, these are the men who are supposed to preserve our nation from hoodlums. How can they, when they act like hoodlums themselves?"

"I know their type," Riethe said as he gained his feet. "They're simple men, is all, many of them just off the farm, away from their mothers and in the city for the first time. It's their commanders you can blame. They set the example the men follow, and I spied more than a few coats with lieutenant's and captain's bars up in the boxes."

Riethe extended a hand down to Merrick and then to Eldyn, who gladly accepted it. Once standing, he went to the curtain and parted it a fraction to peer out. Mouse was right; the soldiers were leaving. Only a handful remained, snoring in their seats.

"It looks like there's a few drunks we'll have to clear out, but that's all."

Riethe nodded. "We'll toss them out in the gutter to sleep it off. And then I'll be ready to sleep myself."

Mouse gaped at him. "But you always want to go to tavern after a performance."

"Not tonight," Riethe said. "And thank God we're dark tomorrow. I don't think I can do this again any time soon." He held out his hands before him. The fingers of one were still a bit crooked from being broken last year, and both were visibly shaking.

"Well, you've earned your rest," Hugoth said, clapping the big young illusionist on the shoulder. "And Eldyn and Merrick as well. To conjure such a finely detailed phantasm for so long—now that's a feat."

Eldyn looked at Hugoth. The wound on his cheek was covered with a dark crust, but was still oozing.

"You were amazing, too," Eldyn said, and meant it. "And so was Mouse. I don't know how you found the wherewithal to conjure the golden soldiers right after the satyrs." He frowned as a thought occurred to him. "But who conjured the third?"

He, Merrick, and Riethe had been fashioning the maidens, and helped with the satyrs during the battle with the golden warriors. But other than Hugoth and Mouse, there was not another illusionist at the Theater of the Moon who could craft illusions of such complicated, humanistic figures. That was, no one except . . .

Eldyn turned to stare at the right wing of the stage. He was not the only one who had come to that conclusion, for the others did the same. Then as one they rushed to the shadows at the side of the stage. Merrick conjured a dim, wavering light, and Eldyn felt his heart stutter in his chest.

Master Tallyroth lay upon the floor, his cane fallen several feet from him. The master illusionist's mouth was open as he panted for shallow breaths, but his eyes were half shut. His thin fingers tapped out a faint, chaotic rhythm against the wooden planks of the stage.

"No," Mouse said, the words going hoarse. "He didn't . . . but he's not supposed to . . ."

He fell silent as Madame Richelour looked up at them. She knelt on the floor beside Master Tallyroth, the feathers sewn into her shoulders quivering as they betrayed her quiet sobs.

"Riethe," she said, tears making tracks through the thick coating of powder on her cheeks, "help me carry him upstairs."

———

ELDYN WOKE to hot sun on his face.

Groggily he sat up in his bed, pushing dark, damp coils of hair from his face. He had no idea how long he had been sleeping. Last night, it had taken him and the other illusionists hours to clean up the theater. Normally they would have gone to the Red Jester to drink and laugh after a performance. But by the time they finished hauling out the drunk soldiers, setting all the seats aright, sweeping up the broken bottles, and throwing sawdust in the corners where men had relieved themselves, the sky was growing light with a fast-coming dawn.

They had already been weary from their efforts on the stage. Now utterly exhausted, going to a tavern had been the last thing on their minds. Eldyn had stumbled up the steps to his room and flopped into bed. So weary had he been that he had forgotten to draw the shutters. Now the hot, white light of day spilled through, and the room was stifling.

Unsteadily, he got up from the bed, groaning as he did. His head ached as if from the worst hangover, though he hadn't drunk a drop last night. It was the aftereffects of conjuring so many illusions, he knew, and drawing upon his own light. It had left him hollow and shaky.

Well, coffee was cure for a hangover, so he could hope it would help this condition as well. He went to the window, squinting against the glare. Outside, the sun was high in the sky. The day was nearly half over; though whether the morning had been long or short was impossible to say. He drew the shutters, then put on his boots. There was no need to bother with anything else, for he had not taken his clothes off last night.

Downstairs, the rooms behind the theater were quiet. He went to the large room where they gathered before performances and to take meals, but there was no sign of the woman whom they hired to cook and bring in food for them. There were dirty dishes upon the table, though, and several coffeepots, but they were all empty. So he was one of the last to rise, then.

The others must be back abed, or out and about in the city, or perhaps already at the Red Jester by now. Eldyn almost considered going there to see if that was in fact the case, only it was not rum he needed, but coffee. And it looked like he would have to find it himself.

He headed to the rear entrance of the theater. As he passed the foot of the stairs, he thought about going up to the second floor, to Master Tallyroth's room, to see how he was doing.

Last night, just as they were finishing up their work to restore the theater to order, Merrick had come down to tell them how Master Tallyroth was faring. The good news was that Madame Richelour had gotten him to drink an elixir—one of her own fashioning, made with wine and honey and herbs. This had eased his pain and spasms, and he was sleeping now.

"And the bad news?" Riethe had said, setting down a bucket of sawdust and wiping his hands against his trousers.

Merrick's face was even longer than usual. "Crafting the phantasms has aggravated his mordoth. It appears to have undone all the progress he's made since he stopped working illusions, and he is more ill than ever."

This was bad news indeed, though not entirely unexpected.

"What now?" Riethe had asked, his face as gray as the sawdust in the bucket.

They all adored Tallyroth, but the big illusionist perhaps more than any of them. No one received more scolding from the master illusionist—or more fatherly affection—than Riethe, and no one did more for him in return. Riethe was always at some task or running some errand for the master. It would have been him up in Tallyroth's room at his bedside, except they all knew Merrick was the better choice, for he had spent three years apprenticing to a physician before becoming an illusionist.

"Won't he just get better again, if he stops conjuring phantasms like before?" Riethe said.

Merrick did not answer, but he didn't need to. Eldyn knew it wasn't that simple. Refraining from creating illusions had kept Tallyroth's mordoth from worsening, but it hadn't made it any better, either. After all, a man only had so much light in him. And given his weakened condition, there was only one way Tallyroth could have conjured the illusions that he had tonight—by drawing on his own inner light.

Which meant he now had less light than ever to sustain the force of his own life. It had been terribly foolish. And terribly brave. *Above all else, the show*—that was the motto of the Siltheri.

"I'm going to the Theater of the Doves," Merrick said at last. "The master illusionist there is an old friend of Tallyroth's, and I've heard he knows more about the mordoth than anyone on Durrow Street. He may have some advice about what we need to do."

Riethe laid one of his big hands on Merrick's thin, stooped shoulder. "Thank you."

Merrick gave a wordless nod, then was gone into the night. After that they finished their work in the theater, then went up to bed.

Now, Eldyn put his foot on the first step, thinking to go up to Master Tallyroth's room. Only that could serve no purpose other than to disturb him, and that was the last thing Eldyn wanted to do. Last night, Merrick had said Tallyroth needed sleep more than anything else. Besides, if there had been any great change in his condition, one of the others would have woken him. It was better to let him rest, and then talk to Merrick later.

Eldyn turned from the steps and headed out the back door of the theater into the alley beyond. It was time to find some coffee before his headache grew any worse.

There were several coffeehouses along Durrow Street, but Eldyn didn't patronize any of them. They were no more disreputable than the taverns on the street, but while strong rum might taste fine coming from a chipped or dirty cup, the same wasn't true for weak coffee. So despite the ache in his head, he walked some distance to a coffeehouse on King's Street. It was a small establishment and tended to be quiet—something which suited both his mood and his head.

He sat near the window, sipping from a hot cup. He had drunk no more than a quarter of it, though, when a flash of blue passed just on the other side of the window.

It was a soldier running along King's Street, his hand on the hilt of the saber that was belted alongside a pistol at his hip. Two more soldiers followed after him a second later, moving as swiftly as the first, the red plumes on their helmets whipping as they went.

Surprised, Eldyn stared out the window. Where were the soldiers going in such a hurry? He didn't know. But given the way they were running, and the hard looks on their faces, there must be some commotion there. Which meant maybe there was some scene worth making an impression of. He hadn't sold anything to the publisher of *The Swift Arrow* since the impression of the princess, and he could do with some coin if he wanted to buy more engraving plates and impression rosin.

Eldyn took one last swig of his coffee, then regretfully set the cup down. Well, if he sold another impression, he could afford many more cups. He tossed a coin on the table, then dashed out the door of the coffeehouse. Looking down the street, he glimpsed three flecks of red just a moment before they vanished around a corner.

If he didn't hurry, he was going to lose them. Eldyn broke into a run himself, weaving among horses, carts, and startled people who glared and shook their fists at him as he careened past, having just recovered from the abrupt passage of the soldiers.

He was panting for breath by the time he reached the intersection where the soldiers had turned. While performing at the theater was physically demanding, it did not exactly provide the sort of vigorous exercise that running for long periods required, and he was still weary from last night's exertions. All the same, he did not let up his pace as he turned the corner and ran down the broad avenue.

He had lost sight of the soldiers, but he quickly knew he was still going in the right direction when a big bay gelding nearly ran him down from behind. The rider wore a blue coat marked with the gold stripes of an officer, and he spurred the horse in a gallop down the street.

Eldyn ran after the horse. Now a low, roaring sound emanated from up ahead. It sounded almost like rushing water, though there was a rhythm to it he almost but didn't quite recognize. The street had suddenly become deserted, so that he no longer had to dodge and weave among carriages and passersby. All the same, he was forced to slow to a walk, for his lungs were afire and his side ached.

It was only then that he realized where he was. So intent had he been on following the soldiers that he hadn't looked up to see where it was they were leading him. Now he did. This was University Street, and in the distance rose the spires that surmounted the various colleges.

A dread welled up in Eldyn. He suddenly thought he knew where the soldiers were going. Despite the burning in his lungs, he lowered his head and broke back into a run. The street bent to the left, then ended on the edge of the open expanse of Covenant Cross.

Only the cobbled square was anything but open. Wooden crates, barrels, and loose timbers had been heaped into makeshift barricades. Some of them were on fire, and the air was hazed with the resulting smoke. The tolling of bells rang out, a counterpoint to the clatter of hooves and the rhythmic, roaring noise, which Eldyn now realized was chanting.

Feeling suddenly exposed, Eldyn shrank against the wall of a bookshop and, hardly thinking about it, brought in close what shadows could be found along the edges of the street. From that vantage, he could see a great portion of Covenant Cross.

There were dozens of young men in the center of the square—no, he amended, hundreds of them—hurling rocks and pieces of wood toward the soldiers and waving flags that bore the crests of various colleges. There were the seven rings of Gauldren's College, the crossed quills of Highhall, the crook and miter of Bishop's College, and even the gold chalice of Eldyn's old college, St. Berndyn's. As the flags waved to and fro, the young men shouted a slogan over and over, though Eldyn could not make out what it was for the way it echoed and reechoed about the cross.

The soldiers were gathered to Eldyn's right, on the east end of the square, out of range of anything the students might throw. There were at least thirty of them, and a good number more on horse, but they were still vastly outnumbered. What's more, the various barricades and obstacles prevented them from advancing in any sort of formation which might have afforded them some protection. Instead, to progress toward the center of the square, they would have to break up into smaller groups to pass around the heaps of wood and refuse.

Even as Eldyn watched, some soldiers went up to one of the barricades to begin dismantling it. At the same time, several of the university men rushed up and tossed burning brands onto the barricade. It quickly burst into flame, obviously having been primed with some form of fuel, and the soldiers were forced to retreat as the flames leaped up.

Eldyn regarded this scene in astonishment. He knew that students from the university had marched several times since Gauldren's College was shut down, and that some of the protests had been unruly in nature. But this wasn't merely a case of young men making impromptu mischief as an excuse to avoid attending lectures. Erecting the barricades must have taken a great amount of effort and coordination. Also, there was a fervor to the shouting of the students—an anger that was as palpably hot as the flames that rose up from the burning barricades. More missiles of stone and wood were launched in the direction of the soldiers.

A young man in a brown coat came running up University Street from the direction Eldyn had come, a broadsheet wadded up in his hand.

"Ho there!" Eldyn said, leaping out of the shadows and grabbing the other man's arm as he passed. "What's going on here?"

"What's it look like?" the other fellow replied in a voice that had a noticeable West Country inflection, and he gave a wide grin. "The university men are trying to get a rise out of the soldiers. And it looks like they're doing a right fine job of it."

Eldyn gaped at him. "But the soldiers have guns!"

"Aye, and we have rocks and torches," the other man said, his grin vanishing. "And there are more of us than them, so if they think we're afraid of their pistols, then they can think again. Besides, if we don't put up against them now, they'll just come for us later when we're not all banded together, and take us in ones and twos."

"You can't know that."

"Can't I? And why don't you just ask old Mrs. Haddon what she thinks about that?"

Eldyn shook his head. "What are you talking about? Mrs. Haddon is in Barrowgate."

"Not anymore she's not." He thrust the crumpled broadsheet against Eldyn's chest. "Here, read it for yourself. Then either come join us, or stay out of our way." And he ran into Covenant Cross, ducking around a barricade and vanishing through a cloud of smoke.

Eldyn pressed his back to the wall. He smoothed out the wrinkles from the newspaper. It took him a moment to find the article. Then he saw the small headline near the bottom of the first page, and as he read it he knew the reason why this demonstration was larger and angrier than the others.

COFFEEHOUSE PROPRIETRESS, TRAITOR TO HANG AT DAWN, read a dark line of print.

He wasn't certain when the sun had risen that morning, but it had to have been hours ago. Long enough for the awful deed to have been done. Long enough for news to spread, and for anger to grow.

A sick feeling came over Eldyn, and a sorrow with it, but it was not only for the sake of Mrs. Haddon. He felt it for all of them out in the square—the young men who had frequented her coffeehouse, whom she had doted on and mothered. She had paid for her actions against the Crown with her neck. How many here today in Covenant Cross would do so with their blood?

Even as he wondered this, there was a crackling noise like a load of copper kettles falling from a cart. Eldyn snapped his head up, then drew as many shadows about himself as he could grasp. Across the square, six soldiers pointed their smoking rifles into the air. The sudden volley had caused the university men to scurry back, and under that cover a number of soldiers ran forward to throw buckets of water on two of the barricades. Then they quickly scattered the steaming timbers.

By the time the students realized what was happening, it was too late. The soldiers marched forward double-time, and now they had enough room to fall into a proper formation, their rifles arranged in a precise double row, one held high and one low in alternation, and all of them fitted with bayonets. The soldiers were still greatly outnumbered, but if they were to advance toward the center of the square now, no one would be able to stand in their way, lest they be pierced by those sharp points.

A hush descended over the square. The students ceased chanting their slogans and crouched behind the remaining barricades; the soldiers stood stock-still. Even the flames flickered and sank down. All in the square seemed frozen; or rather, all was pulled taut as a cord under a great load, stretched to the very point where it must be released or break.

Eldyn held his breath, as if even the slightest motion might ruin the precarious balance. Surely the university men knew that they couldn't stand against the soldiers now. They had made their point; they had demonstrated their outrage for all in the city to see. But now they must fall back and give up their protest.

Then, at last, the students began to do just that. They crept away from the barricades and retreated west, toward the streets and alleys by which they could depart the square. They lowered their flags as they went; they were leaving. Eldyn breathed a sigh of—

The sharp report of breaking glass shattered the stillness. Had a bottle been thrown at the soldiers? Or had it simply fallen to the cobbles from some unstable perch atop a barricade? Eldyn didn't see. But it was in horror that he witnessed what occurred next.

Maybe the loud noise had sounded too close to gunfire. Maybe a splinter of glass had gone flying and struck one of the soldiers, making him think he'd been shot at. Or maybe the sound had simply startled him, causing his finger to jerk and pull a trigger it already rested too firmly against.

No matter the reason, the result was the same. There was a flash and a cloud of smoke near the center of the line of soldiers as one of the redcrests fired his rifle. Perhaps afraid they were under attack, or simply startled into action, another soldier in the line did the same, and another, until all of them fired their rifles in a terrible display of smoke and fire that filled the square with thunder.

As the noise and smoke dissipated, other sounds quickly rose within the walled confines of Covenant Cross: cries of dismay and of pain. Most of the students had been safe behind the cover of the barricades, but not all. In the center of the square, several young men staggered and limped, blood streaking their faces or oozing between hands clutched to their arms or chest. Nearby, two more men lay sprawled upon the ground, and these did not move; though even as Eldyn watched, crimson rivulets began to extend from beneath them, threading their way among the ridges and grooves of the cobbles like crimson serpents.

Quickly, the square was plunged into chaos. Many of the men who had been creeping to the west now ran pell-mell, fleeing down the side streets and alleys. But at least as many remained behind their barricades, and they launched a new volley of bottles, stones, and pieces of timber toward the soldiers, who were now at closer range.

The soldiers who had fired knelt and put the butts of their rifles against the ground to begin reloading them. At the same time, those soldiers who had been crouching low now stood and extended their rifles before them. One of them staggered back as a rock struck him on the forehead, causing a fount of blood to burst forth, but the others held their ground.

"No!" someone was shouting. "Get out of there! All of you, get out of there now!"

The ragged voice was, Eldyn realized, his own. He had stepped away from the wall and, madly, was waving his hands. But his shouts were lost as fifteen flashes of light simultaneously appeared, followed by fifteen peals of thunder. For a moment all was obscured by smoke, then the fog swirled and broke apart to reveal several more forms lying crumpled on the cobblestones.

Men were yelling and screaming and fleeing in all directions now. A large number of them were running straight toward Eldyn. If he didn't move, in a few moments he would be trampled.

Only he didn't move, not right away. Instead he stared, eyes wide and unblinking, as he fixed the awful scene in his mind—the smoke, the sprawled bodies, the glittering lattice of blood in the cracks of the cobbles. Then another volley of rifle fire rang out, the sound of it causing him to flinch, shutting his eyes in reflex.

And by the time he opened them again, Eldyn was running with the other men down the street.

CHAPTER THIRTEEN

IVY MOVED DOWN the grand staircase to the front hall, a robe over her nightgown and a wavering candle in her hand. As she reached the bottom, the light gleamed off the mosaic that covered the floor of the hall, like torchlight from a ship on the ocean, revealing the dim shapes of fish and dolphins just beneath the surface.

She sailed across the hall herself, her robe fluttering like a silent sail behind her. A light at the north end of the hall guided her. She approached it, then peered through into the room beyond.

From the door, Ivy watched as Mr. Quent worked at the writing table in his study. Furrows creased his brow as he concentrated upon several sheafs of paper before him, and he scratched his thick brown beard absently as he read. He wore only a linen shirt, for it was one of those peculiar umbrals again—warm and stifling despite its length.

In all, Mr. Quent looked more like a huntsman making an inventory of his lord's hounds and horses than an official high in the government—one who might very well be made into a lord himself in the coming days. Not that Ivy minded to see him dressed in such a manner, as the powerful shape of his arms and chest was more easily discerned for the light cloth of the shirt. Even in the act of reading, and pausing now and then to write down some note, he was vigorous. He gripped the pen with what she imagined was the same firmness as he might a skinning knife.

She must have made some small noise, for he suddenly looked up from his papers.

"What are you doing awake, Ivoleyn?" he said in a low voice.

"I might ask the same of you," she said, crossing the threshold of his study. "It is very late, yet you are still working."

He gave a sigh. "And I fear I will be a little while longer."

"Are those reports from other inquirers?" Ivy never pried into the particulars of his work; she knew secrecy was crucial to the operations of the Inquiry. All the same, she could not help but be curious regarding the work that so often engrossed her husband.

He raised an eyebrow as he regarded her, then nodded. "At present there are a great number of inquirers out of the city performing investigations. They all submit a report each quarter month, or more often as needed. And each of their missives must be responded to." His beard could not conceal the grimace that shaped his mouth. "In great detail."

Despite the seriousness of the matters before him, Ivy could not help a fond smile. She had no doubt he would much prefer to be one of the inquirers trekking about the country, observing the Wyrdwood or pursuing rumors of a Rising, rather than the one back in the city reading reports of investigations conducted by others.

Yet if he was to be lord inquirer, the latter would be more often the case. He would need to remain here in Invarel, directing and digesting the work of the inquirers rather than performing such work himself. And while it might not be what he wished to do, she knew that he would perform his duties well. Mr. Quent would always do what was required of him to serve the good of Altania.

Besides, while he might prefer to be out in the country working as an inquirer, Ivy was glad that accepting the post as lord inquirer would force him to remain in the city most of the time—even if it meant he would often be up late working. That this was a selfish thought, she conceded; but as her own wishes in this case were well aligned with the needs of Altania, she did not suffer any guilt over it.

"I'm sorry if I have kept you awake waiting for me, Ivoleyn. I will be done soon. I only have one more report to respond to tonight."

"I was quite awake as it was," she said truthfully. "The night is too warm to sleep. I think I'll go read for a while."

Ivy departed his study, so as not to delay the completion of his work with her interference, and carried her candle to the library. She lit a lamp, then sat and took up a small book bound in crimson leather—the copy of *The Towers of Ardaunto* that she had bought at the bookshop off Greenly Circle.

She had begun reading it again in hopes of seeing some clue she had previously missed. After all, it was hardly practical for her to set off on a ship to the Principalities—a fact of which both her father and the man in the black mask had to be aware. Which meant there must be something in the book, some hint that would tell her how she could make contact with Mr. Fintaur in the city of Ardaunto.

So far, she had found nothing that she had not noticed before. All the same, the story was just as striking as it had been the first time she read it, perhaps even more so. She could only shudder as the young gondolier's love for the magician's daughter blossomed and grew, knowing what it was she was fated to become.

Ivy turned a page, the sound of it loud in the hush of the library. The only other noise was the faint whir that emanated from the rosewood clock on the mantel. She glanced up at it. On the right-hand face, a thick crescent of the gold disk was yet visible behind the black, indicating the umbral was far from at its midpoint. And though she watched for what must have been several minutes, neither of the disks appeared to move. She would have thought the clock was broken if it wasn't for the sound of the mechanisms turning within. It was evidently going to be another very long night.

As she had so many times before, Ivy wondered how the old clock was able to predict what the almanacs and the astrographers no longer could: the length of the lumenals and umbrals. Somehow it was able to account for the influence of the planet Cerephus, and to compensate for its effects, just like her father's celestial globe. Not for the first time, she wished she could ask her father about both the globe and the clock—where they had come from, and how they were made.

That wasn't possible, of course. But while she could not benefit from her father's wisdom on this topic, they would all soon benefit from his presence. Upon returning from her last visit to Madstone's, Ivy had spoken to Mr. Quent about her wish to bring Mr. Lockwell home, and he had emphatically agreed.

He had spoken to Mr. Barbridge later that same day, to discuss plans with the builder, and already a suite of rooms was being prepared in advance of Mr. Lockwell's return. These were on the second floor, in a part of the south wing that was at once quiet and not too far removed from the busier parts of the house. They would comprise a bedchamber as well as a sunny parlor which could contain books and other such objects and instruments which might lend him comfort or occupy his hands when they became restless. As soon as the rooms were ready for him, they would bring Mr. Lockwell home from Madstone's.

Ivy could hardly wait for that day. She knew Rose would be overjoyed to hear the news that their father was coming home. So would Lily, of course. But whether Mr. Lockwell's homecoming would be enough to distract Lily's mind from other pursuits, Ivy was less certain. Earlier that day, she had finally had an opportunity to speak to Mr. Quent about the matter of Lily. Only he had been somewhat distracted by his work, and had not seemed to fully grasp the import of the matter.

"Were the drawings good?" he had asked to Ivy's surprise, after she finished describing what she had seen in Lily's folio.

"Yes, very good," she was forced to concede. "Though she has had no instruction in drawing, her talent at it is at least equal to her ability at the pianoforte."

Mr. Quent nodded. "Lily is possessed of an artistic and expressive nature. I am sure it cannot be a harm for her to indulge her fancies. Rather, I would think it is best for them to have an outlet so that . . . so that these urges do not manifest themselves in less constructive ways."

He absently touched the gold ring on his right hand as he said this—the wedding band he had put on the day they married—and only then did Ivy recall that the previous Mrs. Quent had been an artist. She had painted scenes of the stand of Wyrdwood near Heathcrest Hall before that fateful evening when she was called to it, and then fell to her death while attempting to scale the stone wall that bounded it.

Perhaps he wondered, if he had encouraged her painting more, whether she might not have been compelled to venture to the Wyrdwood. Ivy was not so certain of that, or of the notion that if they indulged Lily's drawings it would satisfy rather than inflame the impulses behind them. All the same, she let the matter pass for the moment. They could discuss it again at a time when he was less preoccupied by his work.

Feeling preoccupied herself, Ivy set down the book. There was no use in reading it if she was not of a mind to read it carefully; otherwise she could easily pass over a clue she had already overlooked the first time. Instead, she went to the desk, took out the Wyrdwood box, and undid the wooden braid that locked it shut.

She had already looked through the journal once that night, not long after sunset. Still, it could not do harm to check it again. It was a very long umbral, after all, and so it was conceivable that the stars and planets might have moved enough in the heavens to form a new alignment, and so cause an entry to appear.

Only, as she looked through it, she found that was not the case. When she reached the last page it was blank, like all the others. She picked up the journal to return it to its box, but just then a noise startled her: a distant clatter that ceased as abruptly as it began. Ivy set the journal down and left the library. She saw noth-

ing in the front hall, and so hurried to Mr. Quent's study to see if
he had heard it.

As she entered the study, she saw the source of the noise at
once. No longer did she fear some intruder in the house, and instead she smiled as she knelt to pick up the stopper from an ink
bottle that had rolled off the desk to the floor. Only the stillness of
the house had made it seem so loud; and indeed it had not been
so loud as to disturb Mr. Quent. He leaned forward upon the desk,
his cheek upon his arm, snoring softly.

It was far from the most comfortable bed, but she was reluctant
to wake him, for fear he would return to work. Instead she took
her shawl from her shoulders and draped it over his. Then she
lowered the wick on the lamp until it gave off only the faintest
light and withdrew from the study, closing the door soundlessly
behind her.

Ivy glided across the darkened hall and went back to the library. She had no wish to return upstairs to bed without Mr.
Quent. Besides, being startled by the sudden noise had made her
feel awake. She sat in the chair, picked up the small red book, and
continued reading as the rosewood clock hummed to itself upon
the mantel.

THIS TIME IT WAS a chiming noise that startled Ivy. She opened
her eyes and sat up in the chair. As she did, the small red book
tumbled from her lap to the floor.

The chime came again, then once more. It was the old rosewood clock, striking the end of the third span of the night. The
candle next to the chair had burned down and extinguished itself
in a lump of wax. All the same, she could see, for a faint gray light
passed through the windows. Dawn had come, though it seemed
more wan than it should have been. Even as she thought this, the
low sound of thunder rattled the windowpanes.

Ivy bent and picked up the book. She had stayed up for hours,
reading in the silence of the library, until once again she reached
the end of the book. She had found it just as fascinating and awful

as before, but no more illuminating. If the man in the black mask had left it on the doorstep because there was a clue within it, then she had been too dull to find it. Nor did she think another reading would reveal anything, for she had gone through it word by word. She would just have to hope the nameless stranger would observe her puzzlement and leave another hint for her.

In the meantime, she was in great want of tea and a hairbrush. She set down the book, then departed the library, smoothing gold tangles from her face as she crossed the front hall. Upon entering her husband's study, she saw that the papers had been cleared away from the desk and the chair was empty. The stopper was firmly set in the ink bottle.

Ivy went back out to the front hall and there found Mrs. Seenly, who informed her that Mr. Quent had departed for the Citadel before dawn. Though Ivy wished he had allowed himself to rest awhile longer, she was not surprised by this news. And she had her own tasks to see to that day—overseeing the preparations of her father's rooms chief among them. She started upstairs, only then it occurred to her that she had never put away her father's journal last night.

Not wanting to leave such an important thing lying about, especially when there were workmen in the house, Ivy returned to the library. The journal was where she had left it, lying open on the writing table. She picked it up, to return it to the Wyrdwood box—

—and gasped. Just as she was shutting the journal, a dark spot caught her eye. Hastily she opened the book again and saw that she was not mistaken. A word had appeared on the otherwise blank right-hand page. Then another word appeared beside it, and another.

My dearest Ivy, they read.

Carefully, as if her motions might disturb the enchantment, Ivy set the open journal on the desk. More words manifested themselves upon the page. They did so gradually, stroke by stroke, and sometimes with pauses between them. They were appearing precisely at the speed he had written them, she realized, and the pauses must represent when he had dipped his pen. For some reason the writing was somewhat fainter than usual, but still easily read.

Have you found any of the others yet? I fervently hope that you have. For if you are reading these words, it means that the wheels of the heavenly clock are continuing to turn, and time is already growing short. I know it is an awful burden to place upon you, my dear daughter, but it is imperative that you find them all. Everything you have done up to now has been a mere prelude to this. Now is the time when your actions will matter most.

Years ago, we each of us took a single piece of it for safekeeping— Bennick, Mundy, Fintaur, Gambrel, Larken, and myself. You see, it was far too dangerous for any one person to possess the whole. The risk would be too great if it were to fall into the hands of someone who would seek to use it for ill. Thus, upon my suggestion, we broke the keystone into six parts before any one of us had made a study of the entire thing, and we distributed the fragments among us, swearing to keep them secret and safe.

As it turned out, I was wiser in my suggestion than I could have guessed. Had the keystone remained whole, and had Gambrel ever seen the thing in its entirety, great harm might have been done. As it was, we gave him one of the fragments, not knowing him yet for the scoundrel he would turn out to be. That was a deed that could have ruined everything.

Thank goodness for Mr. Bennick! How I don't know, but he convinced Gambrel to show him his fragment of the keystone, and Bennick made a charcoal rubbing of the runes upon it. He should still have this copy in his possession. So it is that the runes on Gambrel's fragment are not lost to us, despite his duplicity. What I would have done without Mr. Bennick's cleverness and his loyalty, I do not know. I owe so much to him, and it is my hope that he is with you now, guiding and helping you.

Ivy could only wince as she read these words. Her father had discovered Mr. Gambrel's betrayal, but the truth of Mr. Bennick's nature had been hidden from him. Yet at the last, Mr. Bennick must have revealed his true intentions when he attempted to seize the Eye of Ran-Yahgren, and her father had been forced to use all of his magickal ability—indeed, to give up his very sanity—in order to bind and protect the artifact.

As for why he had worked to convince Gambrel to show him his fragment of the keystone, Ivy could guess the reason easily enough. Bennick had wanted to gain the whole of it for some awful purpose, and the traitorous Gambrel had been duped into revealing his portion—perhaps with promises from Bennick that he would involve Gambrel in whatever it was he was scheming. But what was the nature of the keystone? Where had it come from, and why was it so perilous that her father had broken it apart?

Ivy kept reading as spidery handwriting crept across the page.

I must trust that the others have remained true, and that they have kept their fragments hidden. That Mr. Bennick has done so is certain, and I am sure Fintaur and Larken have as well. I might have feared Mundy would misplace his in that pack rat's den of a shop that he keeps, if I did not know it to be impossible. Have you found his shop yet? I dread to tell you exactly how, for fear of who might be reading this in spite of all the protections I have placed upon it. But if you follow the gaze of the Silver Eye, you will surely come to him.

Larken you will find in good time. Of us all, he ever wore the crown of punctuality. I can think of at least a dozen and a half occasions when he scolded us for being late. As for Fintaur, as I mentioned before, you will find him residing under the aegis of the princes of the city of Ardaunto. Find them, along with Mundy, and bring their pieces of the keystone to Bennick. He will know what to do with them.

That is enough for now, my dearest. I will give you some time to seek out the others, but not too much. For if my calculations are correct, even as you read this, the Grand Conjunction fast approaches. Look for another note from me when the alignment begins. Until then, know that though I am not with you in body, my spirit resides with you there at my house on Durrow Street.

Ivy waited a minute, gazing at the page, but no more words appeared after these last; so she sat at the writing table, took out a pen and paper, and transcribed the entry. As she did, her mind hummed like the rosewood clock on the mantel.

At least she knew now for what reason her father wished her to find the others—to gain the pieces of this keystone. But what was this object and why was it important? And what did it have to do with the Grand Conjunction that he believed was coming? Ivy didn't know. Just as she still didn't know how to find Fintaur or Larken.

Or did she?

Her father had guarded the knowledge in the journal with Wyrdwood locks and magickal spells, and had obscured it with riddles, all to keep it safe from unwanted eyes. Yet at the same time he had also intended for her to discover and understand the wisdom imparted on its pages.

As a girl, Mr. Lockwell had often given her mysteries and enigmas to solve. Ivy supposed he had been training her for the very task before her now. While the puzzles he had posed to her back then had often been difficult, they had never been unfair or impossible to solve. She could not believe those in the journal were any different. Which meant he had to have given her enough information to decipher the riddles in the journal. She was just being too dull to understand them.

Ivy took a paper from the Wyrdwood box. It was the one on which she had transcribed the previous entry that had appeared in the journal. *As for Fintaur, I believe you will find his whereabouts in the city of Ardaunto,* her father had written. She had assumed that meant Fintaur was in that city, in the Principalities on the northern edges of the Murgh Empire.

Only her father couldn't possibly have expected her to board a ship and sail across the southern sea, not in such troubled times. Besides, as Ivy knew from past experience, it was important to read a riddle precisely. Her father had not said that Fintaur was *in* Ardaunto, only that she would discover his *whereabouts* there.

Propelled by a sudden excitement, Ivy rose and began looking through the shelves of books that lined the walls of the library. She ran her fingers over the spines, moving past volumes about the New Lands, the Northern Realms, the Murgh Empire. . . .

She halted, then pulled a book from the shelf. The title, written in florid gold script on the cover, read, *A History of the Principalities*. Not bothering with a chair, Ivy opened the book and began to read. The book was rather old, and was written in a style that was as florid as the script upon the cover. All the same, it was filled with many beautiful plates illustrating the fanciful costumes and ornate architecture of the various city-states that, centuries ago, had broken away from the Empire, and whose rulers had become fabulously wealthy through sea trade. She kept turning pages, looking over each one quickly—

"Oh!" Ivy said aloud, and took a step back from the shelf, the book still in her hands.

On the page before her was a beautifully wrought engraving of a shield. *The Royal Crest of the Princes of the City-State of Ardaunto,* read the caption below the illustration. But Ivy's eyes lingered on these words only for a moment before returning to the engraving. Drawn on the shield was the figure of a lion, standing rampant upon its hind legs. From the back of the lion sprouted a pair of eagle's wings, spreading out to either side.

Ivy shut the book and returned it to the shelf, though this action was difficult for the way her hands trembled. *As for Fintaur . . . you will find him residing under the aegis of the princes of the city of Ardaunto.*

Aegis. It was a word that meant auspices or protection.

Or shield.

Ivy knew now where she could find her father's old compatriot Mr. Fintaur. Indeed, she already *had* found him.

Quickly, she returned to the writing table and used a shaker to sprinkle sand over the sheet on which she had transcribed her father's words. She shook off the excess, made certain the ink was dry, and put the paper in the Wyrdwood box. She started to close the journal, to put it in the box as well, then gasped.

Even as they had appeared on the page, the spidery words were now vanishing one by one. Only it could not have been more than half an hour since they first appeared. Never had Ivy noticed one of her father's entries vanish so soon after transcribing it. Usually the writing was visible for hours.

But not this time. Even while she had been transcribing them, the words in the journal had been unusually faint—more gray than black—as if they had not fully appeared. Now, as Ivy watched, the last of them faded away. A dread came upon her. What if she had not happened to look at the journal when she did? She would never have seen this entry!

Only she *had* seen it, she reassured herself. All the same, something was happening to the enchantment of the journal— something that had made this entry appear more faintly and briefly than those before it. What if, as a result of this effect, there were other entries she had missed?

If that was the case, there was nothing she could do about it now. She could only check the journal more frequently in the future. But at present, her first concern was to go to Greenly Circle. Ivy put away the journal and box, then hurried from the library. Rain lashed against the windows of the front hall. She passed through and found Mrs. Seenly in the dining room, making the table ready for breakfast.

"Mrs. Seenly," Ivy said, a bit breathlessly, "please tell Lawden to ready the cabriolet."

The housekeeper could not conceal her astonishment. "You're going out, ma'am? But it's raining in sheets out there!"

"I'm sure he will put the top up. Tell him to be ready in a quarter hour." Without waiting for a reply, she left the room and swiftly ascended the stairs.

In her chamber she prepared herself to go out into the inclement weather, putting on a dress of brown velvet, a sturdy bonnet, and a woolen coat. All the while she thought of her last trip to Greenly Circle, and of the bookshop where she had purchased the complete copy of *The Towers of Ardaunto*. The shop had seemed peculiarly familiar to her, but she had been so intent upon the book she had seen in the front window that she had not really paid attention to anything else in the shop.

Except there had been one thing besides the book she had noticed. It was the intricate piece of stained glass above the door: a beautiful work that depicted a lion standing rampant against a blue background.

A lion with wings.

It was the crest of Ardaunto. The aegis. Which meant the hunched, white-haired proprietor from whom she had purchased the book was . . .

". . . Mr. Fintaur," she said aloud as she hastily fastened the buttons of her coat.

Now she knew why the bookshop had seemed familiar to her. She had always had a memory, from when she was a girl, of her father taking her into a bookstore. She remembered how she had breathed in the dusty air, as if she could somehow inhale the knowledge the books exuded, until she became light-headed and her father had been forced to take her outside. That the bookshop of her memory was the very one where she had bought *The Towers of Ardaunto,* she was certain.

Ivy almost laughed at herself, though if she had, it would have been a rueful sound. Here she had been wishing for another clue from the man in the black mask, when he had already led her right where she needed to go. He had left the book on the steps of the house knowing she would find it, knowing she would be curious as to why the last pages had been cut from it, and that when she saw the book in the window she could only enter the shop. All of which meant that if he was not the peculiar customer who had put the book in the shop window, then it had to have been some accomplice of his.

That was an interesting idea, to think the stranger in black was perhaps not working alone, but that was something she could consider while Lawden drove her to Greenly Circle. She fastened the last button of the coat, then hurried from her chamber.

The quarter hour had barely passed by the time she descended to the front hall. Mrs. Seenly met her at the foot of the staircase.

"Is the cabriolet ready?" Ivy asked.

Mrs. Seenly clasped her hands tightly before her waist. "You have a visitor, ma'am."

"A visitor?" Who would come to call so early in the lumenal, and when the weather outside was so foul?

She started to ask who it might be, but before she could do so movement caught her eye. Across the hall, a figure in a gown as black as a mourner's rose from a chair by the window. Her visage was pale and smooth in the gloom beneath the sharp brim of her hat, like the face of a porcelain doll. Yet unlike a doll, her lips and cheeks were not touched with pink, but rather with blue-black shadows. The woman approached, the crackling of her dress audible in the silence of the room.

"I will leave you with your guest, ma'am," Mrs. Seenly said, or rather gasped, and hurriedly departed from the hall as another roll of thunder rattled the windowpanes.

The noise seemed to rattle Ivy's nerves as well. She tried to gather her thoughts, to comprehend how and why this most unexpected visitor was here, but the other closed the distance before she could do so.

"Good morning, your ladyship."

The other woman did not make a curtsy, for she was a lady herself. Though what her precise rank was, or indeed if she had any title at all, Ivy had no idea. All she knew was what people called her guest.

"Lady Shayde." She managed to speak the words, though they were rather faint.

"I hope you will forgive me for calling upon you unannounced." Her voice was not harsh or piercing, but rather low, and with the slightest hint of an exotic accent. "I am sure it is impolite of me. Yet I come on an errand of some importance."

Ivy shook her head. "But Sir Quent is not here. He has gone up to the Citadel this morning."

"Yes, I know, Lady Quent. But it is not for your husband that I have come. Rather, I came to see you."

Ivy stared stupidly. Inside her heavy dress and coat, moisture trickled down her sides, yet she felt chilled. The wooden eye on the newel post regarded the visitor with curiosity, though it had sounded no alarm. All the same, something told Ivy that she was in peril.

"To see me?" Ivy said, and lifted a hand to the base of her throat, as if to press the words out. "You are of course very welcome. I know you are . . . that you have long been acquainted with my husband. But I hope you can understand my surprise, for I am sure any business you might need to conduct would be better accomplished if Sir Quent were present."

"On the contrary, Lady Quent, my business is something that can only be accomplished in the absence of Sir Quent. As you know, he has been nominated for a very important post in the government, and it is required that candidates for such high positions are scrupulously examined with regard to their abilities, their history—and of course their connections. So I am here at the command of Lord Valhaine."

Ivy's astonishment was redoubled. "But my husband has served the Crown for many years. I am sure Lord Valhaine knows him very well."

The other woman made a languid gesture with a white hand, as if to gently set aside these words. "That may be so. All the same, long-established rules cannot be dismissed simply because Lord Valhaine is familiar with the man who is nominated to be lord inquirer. Propriety would not be served if he were to forego the usual practices. Indeed, it might even undermine your husband's ability to perform in his post if it were perceived that he gained it, not because of his worth, but rather due to some form of partiality."

Ivy could concede that it was logical to investigate the history and connections of someone nominated to a government post, and to do so without exceptions. Not that she could imagine anyone would ever think Mr. Quent did not deserve to be lord inquirer. After all, it was public knowledge, reported in the broadsheets, that he had averted further Risings in Torland.

Then again, if the exact manner by which he had accomplished this was known, opinions of him might be altered. The wooden eye upon the newel post rolled in its socket, looking at Ivy, then back to Shayde.

Shayde's lips curved upward ever so slightly, though it was difficult to call the expression a smile. Rather, it seemed a consequence of a tightening of her smooth, pale visage. Ivy found herself thinking of the merchant's daughter in *The Towers of Ardaunto*, the White Thorn, and how she said she would be a stiletto in the prince's hand. Whose hand was it that wielded Lady Shayde? Lord Valhaine's, Ivy supposed.

"Besides," the other woman continued, "even if Lord Valhaine does know your husband, is it not the case that we can never really learn all there is to another? There is always more to know. For instance, I do not know *you*, Lady Quent. Shall we sit?"

She gestured to a pair of nearby chairs. Before Ivy even thought to do so, she realized she was moving toward them, as if there had been some unspoken command in the other's gaze or voice.

"Can I offer you tea?" Ivy said after she removed her coat and they were seated.

"Your housekeeper kindly offered, but I am quite well, thank you. Now, may I ask you a few questions?"

Ivy nodded, gripping the arms of the chair, and for the next quarter hour she answered queries posed by her unexpected guest. How long had she dwelled on Durrow Street? Where had she lived prior to that? What was her father's vocation, and the names of her sisters? And how long had it been since Mrs. Lockwell had passed away?

Many of the questions had an odd particularity to them. What was the name of the street where she had lived in Gauldren's Heights? How many floors had the house possessed? Did it have a garden?

These questions all seemed very innocuous to Ivy. Yet after a while, she began to discern a peculiar repetitiveness about them. She might never have noticed it, except that her father had taught her to always look for patterns and sequences in things, and she had just been looking for riddles in his journal. Yet once noticed, there was no mistaking it: Lady Shayde would pose the same question on several instances, but each time in a slightly different manner. Which church was nearest to their dwelling in Gauldren's Heights? How many flights of steps were in the house? What sort of flowers grew in the garden?

Ivy concentrated, always making sure to give an answer that would not contradict or depart from what she had said previously. She could only believe this interview was a mere formality. Why else would Lady Shayde ask her such superfluous questions? Even so, she did not want to say anything that might jeopardize Mr. Quent's confirmation as lord inquirer. It was far too vital to the nation that he take on those duties.

Yet surely Lady Shayde knew that. After all, it was her own master, Lord Valhaine, who had nominated Mr. Quent for the post. Ivy knew there was a long-standing tension between the Gray Conclave, which was headed by Lord Valhaine, and the Inquiry. Yet in the end, they all served the Crown and wished what was best for Altania. Lady Shayde was here because protocol required it, that was all.

Despite the nature of her guest, Ivy felt her dread recede. She answered more easily, and her hands no longer gripped the arms of the chair. Then, more quickly than she would have thought, it was done. Ivy had no idea if she had said anything at all useful, but Lady Shayde seemed pleased enough. Her lips curved upward again, and this time it seemed a true smile, for all that it put not a single crease in her white face.

"Thank you, Lady Quent," she said as they stood. "This has been very useful. And if I have a few more questions at some point, may I return?"

"Of course," Ivy said as they walked toward the door. Now that she was over her initial surprise, she found herself fascinated with her visitor. This was not only the famed White Lady, whose mere gaze was said to compel traitors to confess and reveal their secrets, and who had single-handedly sent dozens to the gallows. This was also Ashaydea, who years ago had been Mr. Quent's childhood companion at Heathcrest Hall.

Ivy thought back to the story Mr. Quent had once told her—how Ashaydea had been born in the Empire to an Altanian lord and a Murghese woman, and how Earl Rylend had brought her back to Heathcrest after one of his voyages to the south and had raised her like a daughter. The elder Mr. Quent was the earl's steward. Thus, the young Alasdare Quent had often been at Heathcrest, and he and Ashaydea had often been playmates.

Only then, as they grew toward adulthood, something had happened. Or more specifically, Mr. Bennick had happened. For some unknown purpose, Mr. Bennick had performed a magickal ceremony on Ashaydea, one that had transformed the almond-skinned young woman into a being with pale skin, black hair, and preternatural abilities—just like the merchant's daughter in *The Towers of Ardaunto*.

A sad and pitiful creature, Mr. Quent had once called her, when they saw her in the Citadel.

Yet Ivy could not say she felt pity for the woman walking beside her now. Lady Shayde moved languidly and gracefully, yet with a power and confidence that could not be mistaken. She was hard, to be sure, and cool. But that had to be expected in one who held such a position as she. Whatever intentions he had for her, Mr. Bennick had not been able to place her under his command. Like the White Thorn in the novel, in the end she was her own being and served whom she chose.

Again, Ivy was struck by the similarities between the novel and Lady Shayde's own story. Nor could this likeness be due to coincidence. Surely some of the other magicians in Mr. Bennick's order were aware of what he had attempted with Ashaydea. What if Mr. Fintaur was one of them? And what if he was not just the proprietor of the bookshop where Ivy had bought the book? She recalled what he had said that day as she held the book.

I like this one very much myself. . . .

A sudden crack of thunder shook the windowpanes.

"Is something wrong, Lady Quent?" Lady Shayde said in her melodious voice. "Your color has gone very white of a sudden."

Ivy was no longer so at ease as she had been a moment ago, but she managed what she hoped was a reassuring smile. "It's only the thunder. It startled me."

"It will be a violent storm," the other said, gazing out the window. Then she turned and regarded Ivy with her dark eyes. "By the way, I meant to ask you how Lord Rafferdy is faring of late. Is he well?"

Ivy blinked. "But surely you know he has passed away!"

"I meant the *present* Lord Rafferdy."

"Of course," Ivy said, wincing at her mistake. But she always thought of her friend as *Mister* rather than *Lord.* "You know him, then?"

"Yes, we have met. I was of course well-acquainted with his father. But I haven't had occasion to speak with Lord Rafferdy lately. I suppose he has been greatly occupied." She touched a gloved finger to her chin. "Let's see, how long is it that he has been pursuing the study of the arcane?"

Ivy opened her mouth to reply—then froze. How easily might she have stepped into the trap that had been cleverly laid for her. She had been put at ease and had been directed into a mode in which answering questions had become simple, even automatic.

He has been studying magick for more than a year.

The words had been on the tip of her tongue before she even realized it; she had almost uttered them. Only her shock at realizing the truth about Mr. Fintaur had jarred her from that malleable state.

She clenched her jaw until she was certain she could answer in a careful fashion. "I think very well of Lord Rafferdy, but I confess, I have never known him to apply himself to any course of study—except perhaps that of the latest fashions."

Once more Lady Shayde's blue-black lips curved upward. Like the first time, the expression was anything but a smile.

"Of course," she said. "Thank you for your time, Lady Quent. I will be sure to return if I have more questions."

Yes, I am sure you will, Ivy thought. But she said only, "Good day, Lady Shayde. I trust you will not be caught in the storm."

"I am certain I will not," the other replied.

As soon as the front door closed, Ivy clasped her arms around herself, shivering. How foolish she had been to let herself think this interview was simply a formality. It had been anything but.

Another peal of thunder shook the windows. Still shivering, Ivy went back across the front hall to retrieve her coat, and put it on.

CHAPTER FOURTEEN

$\mathcal{S}$HORTLY AFTER RISING, Rafferdy opened his black book and saw that a new message had manifested upon its pages. There was to be another meeting of the Fellowship of the Silver Circle that night.

The timing was excellent. He had just one arrangement to make. Still in his silk night robe, he sat at the writing table in his bedchamber and penned a note with a few brief instructions. He gave the note to his man, taking a cup of coffee in return, then proceeded to make himself ready for the day.

If it could be called such. For the lumenal that ensued was so gloomy that Rafferdy feared he would have no way to know when night was falling and the moon rising. For hours on end, raindrops pelted the windows, as if seeking to force their way inside. The sound made him think of angry voices shouting, so that he kept looking out the windows to see if there were crowds marching in the street.

It would not be the first time. Recently, in Covenant Cross, a riot had broken out among a large gathering of university students, and it had grown violent when the redcrests appeared. Whether it was the students who first threw stones or the soldiers who first fired their rifles depended upon which broadsheet one read. Either way, the result was the same: a number of young men, all of them students, had been shot dead.

Rafferdy had been astonished when he first heard the news from Mr. Baydon, while at Lady Marsdel's for dinner. It was one thing to hear of soldiers shooting rebels in the country; it was quite another to have those shots fired upon university men here in the city. For a moment, a terrible thought had come to Rafferdy: what if Eldyn Garritt had been there in Covenant Cross when the soldiers opened fire?

That was a baseless fear, however. Like Rafferdy, Garritt no longer attended lectures at the university. Which meant he could have had no cause to be there that day. All the same, Rafferdy had written him a note to make certain he was well. So far Rafferdy had not received a reply, although this couldn't really be a concern. Garritt was often very tardy in replying to letters of late. Why a man who was a scrivener all day long should find it so difficult to scratch out a few lines to a friend in the evening, Rafferdy did not know, but he would be sure to chastise Garritt the next time they met at tavern. In the meantime, all Rafferdy saw as he gazed out the window were sheets of rain lashing against the street.

At long last the storm subsided and the clouds broke apart, so that Rafferdy could see it was just afternoon. Which meant he still had many hours to waste before that night's meeting. And as there was no place where an hour could be more effortlessly wasted than his club, Rafferdy took up his hat and called for his driver.

He soon found himself seated in a comfortable leather chair in a richly appointed room whose windows were happily swaddled with heavy drapes. This was not a place one came to consider the outside world, unless it was through the refracting lens of a brandy glass or the pages of a broadsheet.

Rafferdy paged through one of these now, though he did not bother to read any of the awful articles. It was simply something to occupy his hands in between rolling tobacco papers or drinking tea or eating lamb curried with hot Murghese spices. All the while, the low sounds of conversation went on around him. He had no wish to join in any discussions himself, but it was pleasant to hear the drone of voices, for it allowed him to be alone without feeling in any way lonely.

Thinking it was time to take a brandy or perhaps smoke more tobacco, Rafferdy started to set down his broadsheet. Just then, something caught his ear. It was spoken no more loudly than anything else in the room, but it is an odd fact that certain words will leap at one out of a jumble of voices. Once such a thing is heard, the listener will naturally focus upon the conversation, and so hear everything that would have previously gone unnoticed.

In this instance, the word was *Quent.*

"And I see here in *The Comet* that he is to testify before the next session of Assembly," the speaker went on, a little ways off to Rafferdy's right. The voice had a clear, youthful tone to it. "I imagine that would be an amusing thing to witness."

"Indeed, I would be most amused to hear how he can justify being nominated for such a high post," replied another man—somewhat older, given the gravelly sound of his reply. Rafferdy could not see either of them, for he had lifted the broadsheet up, pretending to read as he listened.

"Well, they say he has given excellent service to the realm," the first speaker said.

This was answered with a snort. "So it is claimed. But that cannot change the fact that his station is not at all in keeping with such a position in the government."

"I understand he is a baronet."

"Yes, but one only recently made. Besides, even a baronet is too low to be lord inquirer. I do not know what Lord Valhaine was thinking."

"Perhaps he's thinking the post is not so important as it once was. After all, he has his magicians now to help him root out rebels and traitors. And as for the matter of the Wyrdwood . . ."

The speaker's voice grew low, so that Rafferdy was forced to strain to hear behind his broadsheet.

". . . I've heard that he's making it his own business to seek out witches. He's scheming some way, with the help of his magicians, to make it a simple matter to know if a woman is a witch or not. For he considers them to be the greatest of threats to the nation."

"Is that so?" There was an audible scowl in the older speaker's tone. "Even greater a threat than Huntley Morden's men?"

"I know, it seems improbable to me as well. It's not as if we have Old Trees here in the city. But that's what I've heard from a very reliable source. I will say, if the Black Dog wants to find a witch who threatens the nation, he may not have far to look."

"What do you mean?"

"Take up that copy of *The Swift Arrow* there, the one from today, and look at the second page."

"*The Swift Arrow*? Why would I ever look at that dreadful publication? Its editors are practically rebels themselves."

"No doubt," the younger speaker replied. "Still, they have been printing some remarkable impressions of late."

"Impressions? I hardly approve of those, either. Those degenerate illusionists make them, you know."

"Of course, they are the most reprehensible sort of men. But they have their uses. You should see for yourself."

Rafferdy glanced at the top of the page before him and was surprised to see that he was in fact holding a copy of *The Swift Arrow*. He had picked it up at random from the reading table. As quietly as he could, so as not to draw notice, he turned to the second page.

He had passed by it before, not looking at the pages as he idly leafed through them, but now that he saw it, Rafferdy had to agree the impression was striking. It showed a scene of Princess Layle departing St. Galmuth's cathedral, where she had gone to attend a service following the terrible events in Covenant Cross.

The illusionist who made the impression had caught it just as the princess reached the bottom of the cathedral steps. He had framed it cleverly, presenting the view from the side, so that the soldiers who no doubt walked before and behind her could not be seen. Rather, she seemed alone save for a stone saint in the background, gazing down with a sorrowful expression as if in sympathy, and a gnarled holly tree that bordered the steps, its ancient branches twisting around the edges of the scene.

"There, do you see?" said the younger speaker, his voice still low. "As I said, Lord Valhaine may not have to go far to find a sibyl of the wood, if that's what he seeks."

Even as he overheard these words, Rafferdy noticed how the twisted branches of the holly tree seemed to bend downward in the impression, as if reaching of their own volition to touch the woman passing below.

"What are you implying?" replied the older speaker.

"I'm implying nothing," said the other. "But it's said that the Arringharts trace their lineage back to the first kings of Altania—and the first queens. And everyone knows how it is said Queen Béanore vanished into the forest all those centuries ago, after the armies of Tharos defeated her at the last. She had a great *affinity* for the trees."

"I see," the older fellow said after a long pause. "I will hope you are not right, but if you are, we may indeed have need of a lord inquirer with a strong and capable hand."

This resulted in a laugh. "Well, I fear we shall not get one. Or didn't you know that Sir Quent is missing a good portion of one of his hands?"

"Of course, I've heard such. But as he is from the country, I always assumed it was a mishap with a thresher or some such."

"Oh no," the other said in a scandalous tone. "It's far worse than that. I've heard the truth of it—that he suffered the injury when he spent a night alone in the Wyrdwood."

"Spent a night in the Wyrdwood?" the older lord exclaimed, then lowered his voice again. "Then he is not just a country fool. He is a madman with an unhealthy fascination for the Old Trees. I wonder what Lord Valhaine can be up to in nominating him."

Rafferdy did not wait to hear any further speculation on the matter. He folded the broadsheet with a snap and stood abruptly. The two men who had been speaking looked up from the chairs where they sat a short distance away. They were, as he had suspected from their voices, two men of diverging years, though both were dressed in exceedingly fine clothes.

"I say, is something amiss, my good fellow?" the young one said, raising an eyebrow.

A great agitation filled Rafferdy. He could only think of how Sir Quent labored tirelessly to defend Altania with his efforts. Yet what was he working so hard to defend—men such as these? A loud voice began to speak, and only after a moment did Rafferdy realize it was his own.

"No, nothing is amiss," Rafferdy exclaimed. "Indeed, all can only be aright with the current state of affairs when the rich and idle are able to sit in leather chairs, drink brandy, and criticize the very men whose labors have ensured that they are free to do so."

The two men stared, clutching the arms of their chairs. Throughout the large room, heads turned as Rafferdy's voice rose in a thunderous oration.

"In fact, you can pay no higher honor to the men who have sacrificed themselves to safeguard Altania than to occupy yourselves here, reading newspapers, smoking tobacco, and belittling their bravery. For only in a free nation, one at the very pinnacle of civilization, and one so rigorously defended by good men, are sniveling cowards able to fashion such fine and comfortable lives for themselves. So by all means, mock those who give their efforts, their blood, and their very lives to protect us. By doing so, you give them the highest credit. You are reassuring them that they have made this nation safe for even its most useless citizens— namely men such as all of us at this club, and every other one like it in the city."

With that he raised his brandy glass in a toast, then downed the contents in a single quaff.

The room was utterly silent now, and every pair of eyes was fixed upon Rafferdy. His face felt hot, and he could tell that he was shaking. All the same, he carefully set down his glass, straightened his coat, and then slowly walked to the door. No one moved or spoke as he went, and a servant handed him his hat and cane with a white-faced expression.

As he departed through the door, Rafferdy heard a sudden hubbub of conversation erupt behind him within the club, cut short as the door shut firmly behind him. Cane in hand, he walked to the street, where his driver met him.

"You're leaving very soon, sir," his man said as he opened the door of the cabriolet. "Will you be coming back later?"

No, Rafferdy knew he would never be coming back. After that little speech, he would no longer be welcome at this club—or any other club in the city, once word got around. Not that it mattered. The idea of sitting in a richly appointed room with men such as these filled him with revulsion. Far better to meet Eldyn Garritt at some ramshackle tavern in the Old City. At least there, the thieves and swindlers didn't try to pretend they were anything but.

"I believe I will need to find other amusements from now on" was all he said.

The driver nodded and shut the door. Once back at his house, Rafferdy went to the parlor, and there took out a book of magickal runes and spells, studying it until the lumenal expired.

THIS TIME their meeting was at an inn situated just beyond the edges of the city, on the road to Hayrick Cross. A paleness upon the horizon hinted at the moon that had not yet risen. Rafferdy was early, but that was as he had planned it.

The inn would be empty of patrons, for they had paid the innkeeper a handsome sum to keep the establishment shut that night—and to keep his mouth shut as well. A man with a bald pate and pockmarked cheeks opened the door in answer to Rafferdy's knock, then peered out through narrowed eyes.

"There are two crows on the roof," Rafferdy said, speaking the prescribed phrase. It was somewhat absurd and rather overdramatic, but then that wasn't entirely a surprise, given that it was of Coulten's devising.

The innkeeper grunted, then opened the door. "One of your friends is already here, sir. He's been waiting in the front parlor for nearly an hour."

Rafferdy smiled as he entered the inn. He knew it could not be any of the other members of the Fellowship, for the meeting was not supposed to begin until after moonrise. Which meant the note he had written that morning had been received.

"Excellent," he said. "Please tell him to stay a while longer in the parlor. Wait until fifteen minutes after the last of the others has arrived, and then bring him upstairs."

The innkeeper scowled as he shut the door, but he nodded. "As you wish, sir."

Rafferdy was satisfied. He did not care if their coin bought the man's approval, only his cooperation and silence.

Not that, even if questioned by an agent of the Gray Conclave, the man would be able to reveal much. The inn was dim, with only a scant few candles burning, just as they had ordered it to be, and Rafferdy wore a hat that cast his face in shadow. The others would all do the same. The innkeeper did not know their names, and even if he wanted to, he would not be able to provide a description of anyone who came there that night.

Rafferdy proceeded to a private dining room upstairs—one that afforded a clear view of the road before the inn. He sipped a cup of thin wine the innkeeper brought him and waited for the moon to rise.

It did this soon enough, and by the time it was a short distance above the horizon, the meeting of the Fellowship of the Silver Circle had been called to order.

"I trust everyone took care they were not followed here," Trefnell said, his eyes glinting beneath shaggy gray eyebrows. "As you know, we must redouble all our efforts at secrecy."

Indeed, Rafferdy had observed that the former headmaster had taken great care in laying out the length of silver rope around the edges of the room as the circle of silence was conjured.

"I am sure everyone took the proper precautions, given the new state of affairs," Canderhow said, then his several chins bobbed as he swallowed. "Didn't they?"

Nods went all around the circle, and the plump barrister let out a relieved sigh.

"Very good," Trefnell said. "But do not let your guard down for an instant. We must be vigilant at all times. Previously, we could count on a certain lack of effort on the part of the government to seek out illicit magickal orders when so many lords belonged to such a society themselves. Now that the High Order of the Golden Door has been officially sanctioned, we can no longer expect such laxity on the part of the Gray Conclave. Rather, we must presume they will be vigorous in their efforts to uncover secret societies like our own. One misstep on our part, and we may all find ourselves in Barrowgate."

More than a few looks of unease went about the circle, but to their credit no one so much as suggested their meetings be discontinued. Rafferdy could only think that Trefnell had chosen the membership of the order well. Either that, or they were all of them fools, Rafferdy included.

"Well, at least some good came out of the announcement that the Golden Door has been granted authorized status," Rafferdy said pleasantly.

Coulten turned toward him with a confounded look. "Good God, how much of the innkeeper's awful wine did you consume, Rafferdy? How can there be anything good in the Gray Conclave giving special preference to the very magickal order that we know is scheming to have the Wyrdwood destroyed—a thing they can only be attempting because they are in league with the same awful characters who view the Old Trees as a threat?"

Rafferdy knew Coulten was right. There could be only one reason why the High Order of the Golden Door wished to have the Wyrdwood destroyed. It was the same reason why they had used occult rites to make young magicians into soulless vessels inhabited by daemons—to sow strife and disorder in the nation, to weaken its defenses, and to help prepare the way for the Ashen to enter into the world.

"There is something good in it," Rafferdy said, "because it tells us something about them."

"Such as?" Wolsted said. The former Stout wore a dubious look on his ruddy face.

"It tells us why they made it obvious that magick was involved in the attack upon the Ministry of Printing, as well as in the deaths of Lord Bastellon and Lord Mertrand," Rafferdy said. "The magicians of the Golden Door could easily have made all of these acts appear as if they had been perpetrated by rebels or traitors to the Crown, but instead they made the effects of magick plain for all to see."

Coulten sat in a rickety chair. "Yes, they did make it plain, but I can't fathom why."

"I believe I can," Trefnell said, looking at Rafferdy as he spoke. "They were manufacturing a reason for the government to outlaw all magickal orders, so that when the time came, theirs would become the only sanctioned arcane society."

Rafferdy took one of the cups of wine the innkeeper had left on the sideboard and handed it to Coulten. "Precisely. First they make all magicians appear to be the worst sort of villains. They get arcane orders banned, and even get Gauldren's College shut down. And then they offer themselves up to the Gray Conclave with promises to aid in ferreting out their own kind. There's no one better suited to catch one criminal than another, as the saying goes. I'm sure Lord Valhaine couldn't resist the idea of using magicians he thinks are loyal to the nation to root out those he fears are not."

"Only they're the ones who are up to mischief themselves!" Wolsted said, the old lord's expression even more dour than usual. "And now that the Black Dog's gone and given them a government warrant, it'll be all that much harder for anyone else to work against them."

"For us to work against them, you mean," Coulten said glumly. He took a long swig from the cup he held, then grimaced.

Trefnell fixed Coulten with a stern look—the same one he had no doubt given to errant students over the years. "It may make it harder for us, but it won't put a stop to us. We kept the act for the reduction of the Wyrdwood from winning passage in Assembly, and you can bet we'll thwart whatever devilry they scheme up next."

"I'm sure we will," Canderhow said, clasping his hands behind his back and pacing around the circle. "Yet you must admit, Trefnell, that the Golden Door has a great advantage now. We do not dare try to warn the Gray Conclave of their true nature, for doing so would only alert the government to our own activities. The magicians of the Golden Door can operate in the open, free to meet as they wish, while we must skulk about in the shadows. Nor can we expect they will fall for a trick such as Rafferdy devised the last time to keep them from voting. If we are going to continue to succeed at our purpose, we need some advantage of our own to counter theirs."

"Well argued, sir," Rafferdy said, then smiled. "Fortunately, I've brought just such an advantage with me tonight."

Much to his pleasure, the other eight men all looked at him with apparent surprise and interest.

"An advantage?" Coulten said after a moment. "Well, then, don't keep us on tenterhooks. What is it, Rafferdy?"

"Not what, Coulten, but rather *who*."

This won several frowns, but before anyone could speak, there came a rapping at the chamber door. The others' surprise was renewed as they all looked at the door.

"Ah," Rafferdy said nonchalantly, "that must be him now."

Coulten looked ready to blurt out a question, but Rafferdy went to the door, and in so doing stepped beyond the line made by the silver cord on the floor, breaking the circle of silence. Coulten snapped his mouth shut, and the room went quiet, save for the creak of hinges as Rafferdy opened the door. A tall figure dressed in a ruffled black coat entered the chamber. He removed his hat, releasing a cascade of pale hair.

Coulten leaped to his feet, though neither he nor the others spoke until the door was shut and Rafferdy stepped back over the silver cord.

"Him?" Coulten exclaimed when the circle of silence had been restored. "He's your great advantage?"

Rafferdy raised a finger. "Manners, Coulten. Allow me to present my guest. Lord Farrolbrook, this is the Fellowship of the Silver Circle. I believe you are already acquainted with more than a few of its number."

Farrolbrook nodded, his expression placid. "I am."

"This is outrageous, Rafferdy!" Wolsted said, his face assuming an even deeper shade of red. "We all agree that we must keep our actions secret from the magicians of the High Order of the Golden Door, then you let one step right into our meeting. And for what reason, I cannot presume. Why do you think *he* would ever help us?"

"Because he already has," Rafferdy said.

The others stared at him.

Rafferdy had expected this revelation would cause a strong re-action, and he could not say he did not enjoy being the cause of this little spectacle. All the same, it was best not to draw out the torment for the others. A few of them, like Wolsted, might be lia-ble to burst a blood vessel.

"How do you think it was," Rafferdy went on, "that I was able to make a message appear in the black books of all the members of the High Order of the Golden Door?"

Coulten scratched his head, driving his tall crown of hair to even greater heights. "I don't know. I just assumed you'd devised some clever trick that you'd reveal to us when you were ready to gloat over it."

"And so I am," Rafferdy said and gave a smug bow.

When he rose again, he saw Trefnell gazing at him. "I hope you know what you're doing, Rafferdy, for if you're wrong, then you've just signed nine arrest warrants—one for each of us. He may have helped you once. But if he's played traitor to his own order, what's to stop him from betraying us?"

"No, I didn't betray them," Farrolbrook said, his voice so soft they were all forced to lean in toward him to hear. "They betrayed themselves. They have given themselves to an awful cause. Some out of desire for how they might be rewarded if they do, and some out of fear for what reprisals they will suffer if they do not."

"And what about you?" Trefnell said slowly. "Why have you not given yourself to this same cause—to the cause of the Ashen?"

Farrolbrook did not look at the other men. Instead he gazed out the darkened window, into the night. "I'm not entirely sure. Perhaps they are wise to ally themselves with what is surely the greater power. Those who aid the Ashen are likely to soon rule over us all. I only know that it . . ." He rubbed one gloved hand with another. "It feels wrong to me, the idea of joining *them*. It induces a nausea in me, like the idea of willingly drinking a deadly poison in the misguided belief it will make one strong."

Wolsted gave a great snort into his handkerchief, then wadded it up as he glared at Rafferdy. "The rumors say that he lost his position as head of the Magisters party for being half mad. In which case I'd say the rumors are only half right. It seems to me that he cracked after they discarded him, and now he's grasping for revenge in any way he can."

"I don't blame you for thinking little of me," Farrolbrook said, looking at Wolsted and the others with what seemed a feverish light in his eyes. "After all, *they* do—the Magisters, and the High Order of the Golden Door. But what I've told you is the truth. There is much I don't comprehend. In fact, it seems these days there is less and less that I do. But I know that the members of my order must be prevented from doing what they are trying to do."

Rafferdy could not help shivering a little. That Farrolbrook was crazed was something he had considered himself. Yet there was a conviction to the way the fair-haired lord spoke that Rafferdy could not believe was feigned. Nor could he forget the paintings he had seen in Farrolbrook's parlor once—the brilliant landscapes marred by blotches of black paint—or the drawing of the twisted trees in his sketchbook.

Rafferdy had brought the sketchbook with him to the meeting. He took it out now, and handed it to Farrolbrook. As he did, he once again caught the faint, sweet odor of decay.

"And what is it they are trying to do now?" Rafferdy said. "You hinted at something the last time we met, but you did not say what it was."

"That was because I did not know, not for certain. But I do now."

"Well, if you've come all this way to tell us what it is, then out with it," Trefnell said. "Are they planning another vote on the Wyrdwood?"

Farrolbrook opened the book in his hands and flipped through its pages. He passed the sketch of the tangled branches, then opened to a stark drawing that depicted the silhouette of a man atop a high crag, raising his arms toward black clouds that billowed and roiled above.

"No, it is not to be a vote on the Wyrdwood," Farrolbrook said, touching a finger to the drawing. "Not this time. Rather, claiming it to be for the salvation of Altania, the Magisters are going to cast down the Crown. In its place, they will raise up a new ruler—not a monarch, but a Lord Guardian of the realm. He will be granted all powers that he deems necessary to assure the safety of the nation. His authority in all matters will be absolute, and his word will be no different than law."

"But that's madness!" Wolsted exclaimed, sputtering. "Why would they ever grant a single man such power over all things?"

"Because they hold power over him."

At last Rafferdy understood. "Lord Valhaine," he said, grimacing as the sour wine he had drunk curdled in his stomach. "That's who they're going to raise up as Lord Guardian. He is already under the influence of the High Order of the Golden Door, which is one and the same with the Magisters. If they control him, then they will control the nation."

Silence stifled the air of the chamber. The other men gazed uneasily at one another.

"But this plan has not yet come to fruition," Trefnell said at last. "Surely there is a way to put a stop to it."

"No," Farrolbrook said quietly. "You can't stop their plan."

"But why not?" Coulten said, his voice quavering.

Farrolbrook shut the sketchbook and looked up at them. "Because it has already been set in motion."

CHAPTER FIFTEEN

⁘HE UMBRAL had been swift and short, allowing the world little time to throw off the swelter of the previous day, and by midmorning the lumenal had already become hot and stifling.

Ivy had chosen the lightest gown she could that was still appropriate for the occasion—a dress of dove gray silk with lace at the neck and wrists—but even so she felt overly warm in the closed air inside the four-in-hand. She had bound her hair up beneath her hat, but stray curls kept finding their way free and clinging to her damp cheeks and neck.

In contrast, on the carriage's facing bench, Mr. Quent appeared to be quite cool despite his heavy suit of charcoal wool. Indeed, while Ivy felt flushed, her husband's usually weather-tanned face had a pale, even grayish look to it. It was, she supposed, a different sort of oppressiveness than the heat which he felt at the moment.

"How long do you think will be required to give your testimony?" she asked, even though she had asked this same question last night.

His answer was the same as well. "I cannot say. I hope it will not be very long, but it is entirely up to the members of the Hall of Magnates."

"I should think they would have a great deal of other business to attend to, and so would not seek to make this a protracted affair."

"So you might think," he replied. "But the minds of lords do not always function in the same manner as those of lesser men, nor do they always arrive at the same conclusions."

Despite the trepidation she presently suffered, Ivy smiled. "Is that so? Then I suppose I must prepare myself for a sudden change in your manner of thinking if you are confirmed for the post and made into a magnate. Though I do hope you will not rethink too many of your previous conclusions, as I have no wish to alter the curtains in the house or the style of my gowns."

"I cannot make promises about the curtains," he said gruffly. "What I preferred as a baronet I may find odious as a lord. But there is one matter on which I will never change my mind—that whatever dress you wear, Ivoleyn, it will be the most beautiful and fashionable gown in all the nation because it has the happy circumstance to adorn *you*."

Now Ivy felt a different sort of flush upon her cheeks. She reached across to take both of his hands—the one that was whole and the one that was not—in her own. "Now I truly wish that this testimony does not go on for long, so we might return home as quickly as possible."

At last a bit of color did appear on his cheeks, and a spark shone in his brown eyes. "Why, do you wish to interview me again, Lady Quent? I thought I answered your concerns very thoroughly on the last occasion."

She merely arched an eyebrow and smiled, while in return he let out a great laugh.

After that, the air seemed a bit less stifling as the carriage continued to slowly make its way down Marble Street. Ivy looked out the window, wondering if she could tell if the lumenal were to be long or not, for she had forgotten to look at the rosewood clock before leaving, to see how quickly the disks were turning. There was another reason to hope Mr. Quent's interview before Assembly did not require the whole of the day, as she had not yet been able to go back to Mr. Fintaur's bookshop in Greenly Circle.

She had wanted to go the lumenal before last, but Lawden had said the horses had become too rattled and spooked by the violent storm, and it would be too dangerous to attempt it. Besides, Ivy had been rattled herself by her conversation with Lady Shayde. By the time the storm and the agitation of her nerves subsided, Mr. Quent had returned home, and her priority then had been to tell him of Shayde's visit that day.

It had been some time since she had seen Mr. Quent angry, but he had been so then, looking much as he had during her first months at Heathcrest Hall, his eyebrows drawn down in a fierce glower.

"She has no right to come here," he had said, making his left hand into an imperfect fist and pounding it against the right. "She may ask me what she wants. She may make investigations into my doings as she wishes. But she does not have the right to approach you, Ivoleyn. She does not!"

It had taken Ivy some time to calm her husband. For several minutes he had continued to rail against Shayde, pacing back and forth across his study like a wolf defending his den. Finally Ivy had gotten him to sit and take a glass of whiskey, and with her fingers she had stroked his head, his neck, his broad, stooped shoulders. At last he had grown quiet, and had reached up to take her hand, pressing it against his cheek.

"Forgive me," he had said, his voice low and hoarse. "It is only that . . . I cannot trust Ashaydea. Or rather, I could trust Ashaydea, but not Shayde. She has a powerful intellect—she always did. But the threads of sympathy and morality, which bind most people to one another, have in her been irrevocably severed. Shayde thinks what she does is right, but in fact she is blind to what is right and what is wrong. She can no longer discern between the two, for in granting her other powers, Mr. Bennick took that ability from her. She believes Lord Valhaine is a good man, and so by her logic anything that he commands her to do must be for the good as well, and so she does it without question."

"But is Lord Valhaine not in fact a good man?" Ivy had said, startled by his words. "Surely he wants what is best for the nation."

Mr. Quent had nodded. "Yes, I believe that he does. But even good men may commit errors, Ivoleyn. And there is no one more perilous than a man who is so certain of his own benevolence, taking it as a matter of fact, that he never pauses to consider if his choices are in fact for the greater good."

This reply had fascinated Ivy. She had wanted to ask him more about Lord Valhaine, and about Lady Shayde. Or rather, about Ashaydea. What had she been like before Mr. Bennick had altered her? And how had Mr. Bennick worked this transformation? Had it been an occult ceremony such as she had read about in Mr. Fintaur's book, the one that had turned the merchant's daughter into a creature they called the White Thorn?

Only she had not wanted to agitate her husband further. Nor had there been time to go to Mr. Fintaur's shop after that, for the day was failing. There had been no opportunity either on the following lumenal, for they had been consumed with anticipation of today's events.

The four-in-hand came to a halt, and Mr. Quent helped Ivy out of the carriage. The white towers of Assembly soared above, and for a moment she felt dizzy, grasping Mr. Quent's arm to steady herself. There was a great roar of noise from all the people, but a wall of soldiers, standing shoulder to shoulder, kept the throngs of people at bay, so that Ivy and Mr. Quent were able to proceed up the steps unimpeded.

As they went, cheers and applause rang out. Many let out a call of "Sir Quent! Sir Quent!" And Ivy even heard a few instances of "Lord Quent! Lord Quent!" That her husband was still regarded as both a famous personage and a hero of the realm was evident.

Yet, as they went, Ivy heard jeers and whistles as well. And there was one voice, so shrill it rose above the others, that cried, "Witch lover!"

Ivy turned her head, to try to see who had shouted. As she did, she caught her foot on the edge of a step and would have stumbled, except Mr. Quent held her arm tightly, supporting her.

"Do not listen to them," he said in a low voice, only for her.

She kept her face turned forward, and at last they reached the top of the steps and passed through the gilded doors, into the Hall of Magnates. The din was hardly any less in here than upon the steps, for everywhere men in black robes, many of them wearing white wigs, were milling about and speaking with one another. Ivy looked around, wondering if she might catch sight of Mr. Rafferdy, but if he was here, she could not pick him out.

"These are the stairs to the upper gallery," Mr. Quent said, leaning his head toward hers. "Would you like me to accompany you to your seat?"

Ivy managed what she hoped was a brave smile. "I am sure I can find my way by myself.".

"I have no doubt of that, Ivoleyn. How often you have had to do for yourself without my help when I have abandoned you."

She laid a hand on his arm. "You have never abandoned me. Anytime you have been gone, it has only been because your work required it."

"Yes, it has been required. I have been so often at the Citadel of late because I know what it is they discuss there. And I have done my best to bend that conversation away from any direction which might lead to actions being taken against the Old Trees. The Wyrdwood must not be harmed, especially not now—that is something Lord Rafferdy believed, and I believe it as well."

Ivy looked up at him, meeting his somber eyes. "And I believe that your words are being heard at the Citadel. Why else would you have been nominated for this post?"

"We shall soon see," he said softly, more to himself than to her.

By then there were several lords pressing in toward them, and it was clear she could no longer keep Mr. Quent to herself. She wished him luck, and dared to give his cheek a fleeting kiss, before leaving him to the men who were to interview him.

Unaccompanied, Ivy made her way up the staircase to the gallery. She found that a seat had been reserved for her at the front of the balcony, which permitted a full view of the rostrum below. The chairs around her own were already occupied, and as soon as she was seated, she found herself returning the greetings and well wishes of many gentlemen and ladies whom she had never met. Her nervousness began to subside; it was clear that her husband still garnered much goodwill in the nation.

Then, just as Ivy's heart had begun to beat at a more usual pace, it quickened again as a figure came into view below. The woman might have been lost amid all the lords, for she was draped in black just like they were, but the sea of robes parted before her as she moved, then closed in behind her once she passed. From above, it looked like the pattern of ripples made by a black stone dropped into a pond.

Languidly, as if the opening of the session would naturally wait on her, Lady Shayde ascended to a seat on the rostrum, above and behind the High Speaker's podium. She arranged the stiff black folds of her gown, then lifted the veil from the brim of her hat, exposing the perfect whiteness of her visage. Her black eyes made a survey of the Hall, then turned up toward the gallery.

Ivy shrank away from the balcony, but not before she felt that cool gaze touch upon her. Several times in the days since Shayde's visit, Ivy had gone over the conversation in her mind, trying to remember if she had given away anything to the White Lady that she should not have.

Fortunately, Ivy had retained enough wits not to speak of Mr. Rafferdy's study of magick, or the fact that he had joined an arcane order. There was one thing, though, which Ivy had inadvertently confirmed: the fact that she and Mr. Rafferdy were indeed acquainted. But then, this was not something they had ever concealed, and was likely a matter of public knowledge.

Had that been Shayde's real purpose that day—not to learn about Mr. Quent, but rather to discover if Mr. Rafferdy was practicing magick? Shayde had to know he was a magician, for he never made a habit of concealing his House ring. And the practice of magick by anyone other than the High Order of the Golden Door was proscribed by the Gray Conclave. Perhaps she suspected Mr. Rafferdy was in violation of that edict.

Which, in fact, he was.

While Ivy had told Mr. Quent about Shayde's visit, she had not been able to tell him about the final question concerning Mr. Rafferdy. Ivy could not put Mr. Quent in the awful position of knowing that a close acquaintance of his was at odds with the law. Not that Ivy liked having to conceal something from her husband;

rather, it was a cause of constant distress for her. But she knew it was right. She could not place a further burden on him, not when he was so burdened already. At the same time, she must do nothing that might endanger the work of Mr. Rafferdy's order. For their goal was the very same as Mr. Quent's—to ensure that the Wyrdwood did not come to harm.

Ivy leaned back toward the balustrade again, and she risked a fleeting glance at Lady Shayde. The White Lady gazed placidly at the Hall now. Ivy supposed the magicians of the Golden Door had convinced the Gray Conclave that the Wyrdwood must be destroyed, that it was a threat to Altania. Did Lady Shayde know the truth about them—the true reason they wanted the Wyrdwood destroyed?

No, Ivy did not think so. She could only believe that Shayde's desire to defend Altania from its threats was genuine. But it was as Mr. Quent had said—she could not discern right from wrong. If only Ivy could tell her how she was in error, that she should not trust the magicians of the Golden Door! But to do so would require telling her how Ivy had come by this knowledge—and that would mean revealing that Mr. Rafferdy belonged to an illegal order.

Ivy knew what happened to those who committed crimes against the nation these days; she had seen stories in the broadsheets concerning the numbers that were sent to the gallows at Barrowgate each quarter month. No, she did not dare tell Lady Shayde what she knew.

Even as she thought this, a pair of familiar figures caught her eye. The two men were just taking their seats on one of the front benches. One of them wore an exceedingly tall wig. The other's was more understated, but he looked very well in a simple but elegant robe of black crepe.

The latter was Mr. Rafferdy, of course, in the company of Lord Coulten. Ivy was very happy to see him, and was grateful to know her husband would have at least one trusted friend in the audience. An impulse came upon her to raise a hand and wave in order

to catch Mr. Rafferdy's eye. Only doing so might catch Lady
Shayde's eye as well.

Ivy kept her hands firmly clasped on her lap. The High Speaker
banged his gavel, and the magnates took their places as the Hall
came to order. Some various pieces of business were conducted,
but in short order the Hall turned to the primary matter of the
day.

"Will Sir Alasdare Quent, if he is present, please come forward!" the High Speaker called out.

Mr. Quent rose from a seat on the side of the Hall. Because of
his forceful presence, Ivy always thought of her husband as being
larger than in fact he was. But though he possessed a powerful
build, he was not in any way a tall man. Now he looked suddenly
small as he made his way up to the rostrum by himself. All eyes
were upon him as he went—including Lady Shayde's.

"Sir Quent, you have been nominated for the post of lord inquirer," the High Speaker said. "It is the right of the Hall of Magnates to advise the Crown on such matters, and to provide its
consent. Toward that end, are you willing to answer any such
questions as the Hall may have of you?"

"I am," Mr. Quent said, his low voice rumbling throughout the
Hall.

"Very well, then be sworn in."

The Grand Usher brought forth a copy of the Testament, and
Mr. Quent laid a hand upon it as he gave an oath to speak only
truth, to the very best of his ability. This done, Mr. Quent took a
seat upon the rostrum, just below the podium, and without further ado, the interview began.

It was the right of any lord in the Hall to ask a question, and a
number proceeded to do so. Though what question they were asking was in general not easy to discern, for most lords seemed more
inclined to make a protracted statement than pose a query to the
subject on the rostrum.

Some expounded at length on the great importance of the post
of lord inquirer at a time when the nation faced many threats, in-

cluding Risings of the Wyrdwood. Others recounted the excellence of the late Lord Rafferdy's work as the leader of the Inquiry. And still other lords rose to praise Sir Quent's long history of experience as an inquirer himself, and to recount his achievements in putting a stop to the Risings last year in Torland. For his part, Mr. Quent was able to add little to these lengthy expositions, other than to give his agreement or thanks.

In all, it was less like an interview than a series of toasts and long-winded digressions at a dinner party. Ivy's nervousness receded. The Hall was overly warm due to the heat of the day, and as heads began to nod and drowse around her, Ivy found herself tempted to do the same.

"Thank you, Lord Stulwich," the High Speaker said as an elderly lord, who had asked questions in a quavering voice that no one in the Hall could comprehend, retook his seat. "Are there any more queries to be made?"

Other than a rustling of robes, a silence fell over the Hall of Magnates.

"If you have a question, stand and be recognized," the High Speaker called out, but no one responded.

Ivy's heart leaped. Was that all? If so, then she could not believe there was anything that could impede Mr. Quent's confirmation to the post. For nothing had come out in his testimony that reflected even the slightest bit poorly on her husband, save that it was clear he was a modest man.

But it indeed seemed to be over. The High Speaker reached for his gavel. "If there are no more questions, then this Hall will—"

"Actually, I do have one more thing to inquire of our subject," spoke a voice. "It is just a small matter, if he would be so kind as to indulge us with one more answer."

All heads turned toward a man who had risen from one of the front benches, opposite the Hall from where Mr. Rafferdy sat. The speaker had an unremarkable appearance, being of middle years and middle height, and not particularly thin or fat, or handsome or plain. He had a good speaking voice, though, and it carried throughout the Hall.

The High Speaker set down his gavel. "The Hall recognizes Lord Davarry. You may address the witness."

"Thank you," Lord Davarry said, and approached the rostrum.

Ivy dabbed at her damp cheeks with a handkerchief. She had hoped the interview was over, but she supposed she could endure one more question, if Mr. Quent could do so. She hardly paid attention to the lord's words as he went on. Only then she happened to glance down at Mr. Rafferdy, and she saw the way he sat stiffly on the edge of his bench, his eyes fixed on the questioner.

A note of alarm impinged upon the dullness in Ivy's brain. She looked again at the lord who was presently speaking, now paying attention to his words. As she did, her alarm rapidly grew.

". . . and I must congratulate you on your testimony so far," Lord Davarry was saying. "It is clear you are both very well-regarded in this Hall, Sir Quent, and very well-qualified for the post."

"Thank you," Mr. Quent replied, as he had many times already that day.

Lord Davarry nodded and smiled. He started to turn away from the rostrum, as if he were finished. Only then, abruptly, he turned on a heel and raised a finger.

"Oh, that's right, there was one thing I wished to ask you, Sir Quent, if you do not mind. It's something that concerns the Risings in Torland last year. You do recall them?"

Mr. Quent nodded. "Of course, very well."

"I am sure you do," Lord Davarry replied. "After all, you were very integral in bringing about their end, is that not so?"

"There were many who had a part in achieving that—in the Inquiry, the Gray Conclave, and the royal army."

Davarry waved a hand. "Yes, of course, I'm sure that's the case. I do not mean to deprive anyone of the credit they are due. But I think we can all agree that you had an *especial* importance in bringing about the end of the Risings. We all read the reports in the broadsheets, which described how you yourself were able to locate the sibyl who was in league with the rebels there, and who was inducing the Wyrdwood to rise up on their behalf."

Mr. Quent did not reply. It had not been a question, and all of this was a matter of public record.

Lord Davarry angled his body so that he was no longer looking just at Mr. Quent, but at the Hall as well. "There's just one thing I'm curious about, Sir Quent. The articles in the broadsheets were never clear on the specifics of how you managed to effect the capture of the witch. I can only imagine it was a difficult task to find her. How did you manage it?"

Ivy could see Mr. Quent draw a breath before he answered in his deep voice. "Over the years, the inquirers have accumulated a large body of knowledge concerning all the groves of Old Trees in the nation—their locations and dimensions, and the condition of the walls around them. By comparing observations of various stands of Wyrdwood to their known last descriptions, I was able to determine which groves had been recently disturbed, and so was able to infer her whereabouts."

"How dry and tedious you make it sound, Sir Quent!" Lord Davarry said with an indulgent laugh. "You would have us take you for a clerk poring through dusty records. But you are too humble. I am sure it was quite exciting to hunt down a witch hiding among the Old Trees and no doubt guarded by rebels. Even if you knew what grove she was hidden within, how was it you managed to approach her unmolested?"

Furrows appeared on Mr. Quent's brow. Again Ivy could observe the way he struggled to form a careful answer.

"I called out to her, and was able to convince her to come to the edge of the grove."

Lord Davarry held a hand to his chest in a gesture of shock. "You called out to her? And she came?"

"She did."

"Forgive my ignorance of such affairs, but I do not comprehend this. The witch was safe within the Wyrdwood. Why should she listen to you? Unless you threatened to burn down the grove, that is."

Mr. Quent shook his head. "No such threat was made. To harm

the Old Trees so directly could only have led to further Risings, as she would have been well aware."

"Then I am astonished, Sir Quent. While you have spoken very well here today, I do not discern any unusual power in your voice to induce or compel others to do your will. Or am I mistaken, and all of you have been convinced to vote aye on the matter of Sir Quent's nomination?"

He spoke this last to the Hall, and a round of nervous laughter rose up from the benches.

"But with all due gravity," Lord Davarry said, returning his attention to the witness, "how is it that you were able to formulate such a speech as would cause a witch to depart her only sanctuary?"

The laughter quickly succumbed to a taut silence. On the stand, Mr. Quent cleared his throat.

"I have known . . ." He clasped his right hand around his left. "That is, through my work, I am familiar with their ways and habits."

For a moment Lord Davarry said nothing. He merely gazed at the witness, a hand beneath his chin.

"Indeed, Sir Quent," he said at last, "is it not the case that you are, in fact, most intimately acquainted with witches?"

The sound of gasps was audible throughout the Hall. Ivy could not prevent herself from recoiling away from the edge of the balcony. She had never met this Lord Davarry. How was it possible that he knew? A dread came upon her, a certainty that all eyes in the Hall would turn up to look at the gallery where she sat.

Only that was not the case. Rather, all eyes were locked on the witness who sat upon the rostrum. And Ivy realized it was not to *her* that Lord Davarry had been referring. It was the witch in Torland. Her face hot, she leaned forward in her chair again.

"Please take your time answering the question, Sir Quent," Lord Davarry said pleasantly. "And I am sure I do not need to remind you that you are under oath."

Ivy held her breath. From her seat behind the High Speaker, Lady Shayde looked down with what appeared a keen interest.

"Over the years, in the course of my work, I have had occasion to interact with many suspected witches," Mr. Quent said at last.

"I am sure you have," Lord Davarry replied. "Tell me, what is your impression of them? How do you regard them?"

"I should say I regard them . . . with much sadness."

Lord Davarry had been pacing back and forth, but now suddenly stopped. "Sadness? You speak as if you have a great sympathy for them. But I am puzzled. For are not these sibyls a threat to our nation?"

Mr. Quent shifted in his chair. "It is not always by their choice that this is so."

"Not by their choice?" the questioner said, and now his voice rose, taking on an angry timbre. "What do you mean by that? Surely it was the choice of the witch in Torland to induce the Old Trees to lash out. Just as it was her choice to come to the edge of the Wyrdwood when you called to her. And speaking of the matter, what is the current status of the witch? Does she remain in custody of the state?"

Mr. Quent's cheeks were visibly flushed. It was from the heat in the Hall, no doubt, yet it had the effect of making him look nervous. "The law does not permit me to reveal the whereabouts of those detained by the Inquiry."

"And I am sure you are a man who understands the importance of obeying the law, Sir Quent, but that is not what I asked." Lord Davarry's voice rose, growing more forceful yet. "I did not ask where she was. I asked if she was in the custody of the state. Surely you can tell us *that*."

Mr. Quent drew in a breath. "No, she is no longer in the custody of the Crown."

More gasps and murmurs sounded throughout the Hall.

"No longer in the Crown's custody?" Lord Davarry shook his head. "But how can that be?"

"She was released."

"Released? But who would ever release her?"

Ivy clutched the edge of her chair, wishing in desperation he would not answer. But she knew he would, and so he did.

"I did. I released her."

"You released her?" Lord Davarry exclaimed, then resumed his pacing on the rostrum, rapidly now. "But this is very grave news, Sir Quent. This was the woman who caused the Wyrdwood to rise up in Torland, the sibyl who caused the deaths of countless men, and who aided the cause of rebels. And yet you let her go? Why—why would you do such a thing?"

Ivy shut her eyes, for they burned too fiercely to keep open. For a long moment there was no answer. Then at last Mr. Quent spoke; and though his voice had grown lower in volume even as his questioner's had increased, still his every word reached the farthest benches.

"Because I gave her my word."

A terrible silence ensued. The very air in the Hall seemed to strain, as if anxious to carry what words would be spoken next. Ivy opened her eyes. On the rostrum, Mr. Quent seemed to have shrunk in his chair; his shoulders were rounded, his face gray. Lord Davarry looked down at him with an expression that bespoke not shock but triumph.

"You gave her your word?" he said at last. "So you are saying that you struck a deal with the witch—that you bargained with a known criminal and traitor to the realm. Do you deny this fact, Sir Quent? And may I remind you once more, you are under oath."

Mr. Quent looked up, and though his face remained pale, there was a firm set to his jaw. "I did what was best for Altania."

"That was not my question!" Lord Davarry declaimed. "Speak the truth, Sir Quent—did you bargain with a witch?"

For a moment, Mr. Quent seemed frozen in his chair. Then his brown eyes turned, looking up toward the gallery. Toward Ivy. For a moment, their gazes met. And in his, Ivy saw a grim resolution.

No! she wanted to cry out, but she could not draw a breath.

"I made an agreement with her," Mr. Quent said, "that if the Risings ceased—if she could bring about their immediate end—that I would not hinder her from leaving the grove of Old Trees I found her in. She upheld her end of the matter. And so I did mine."

Lord Davarry gave a satisfied nod, then he turned to face the High Speaker's podium. "You may release the witness," he said. "I have no further questions."

But his words, as well as the clatter of the High Speaker's gavel closing the session, could hardly be heard for the sudden tumult that erupted in the Hall. Everywhere lords were rising to their feet and speaking with one another. Many gazes turned toward Mr. Quent, but no one approached him as he departed the podium, save the ushers whose duty it was to accompany guests from the Hall. But even they seemed to keep their distance as Mr. Quent walked up the aisle toward the gilded doors.

"Traitor!" someone in the throng shouted.

But Mr. Quent did not pause in his step. He kept his head high as he went, his expression solemn.

Ivy lurched up from her chair, and she noticed that no one seemed interested in speaking with her now. Instead, the other observers all hurried from the gallery. Ivy gripped the balustrade, for fear she might tumble over it, and looked down to see if she could glimpse Mr. Rafferdy. That he would not look at her husband with the same shock or scorn as others now did, she was certain.

But she could not pick him out in the chaos of black robes. Nor did she see Lady Shayde anywhere. Only various lords milling about, and her husband departing stiffly through the open doors.

Ivy went to the stairs, and this time she was not distressed when others drew away from her, but rather glad, for she was able to hurry down the stairs, and so meet her husband. She went to him, and put her arm through his. To her astonishment, she could feel him trembling.

"I am sorry, Ivoleyn," he said, his voice gruff, so that only she might hear.

Somehow, his anguish had the effect of strengthening her. Her mind grew clear, and she tightened her grip upon him, steadying him. It was time to leave this place.

"Do not be sorry, Alasdare," she said. "You must never be sorry for what you did."

"No, it is for what will come that I am sorry."

It seemed he wanted to say more, but if so he could not find the words. Ivy took her husband's arm, leading the way from the Hall of Magnates. And there was more than one person who, upon feeling the gaze of her green eyes, hurriedly stepped out of their way.

CHAPTER SIXTEEN

E LDYN HURRIED through the streets of the Old City. The afternoon had been brilliant and warm when he left, but then the sun took a sudden lurch to the west, and now the daylight was faltering. He considered turning around and heading back to the theater, for there was to be a performance at moonrise that evening. But he was nearly to Coronet Street; he might as well finish what he had set out to do.

He walked the last few blocks at a brisk clip, and soon reached the office of *The Swift Arrow*. Fresh bales of newspapers had just been delivered from the printing house, and were being offloaded from a wagon even as he arrived. Eldyn could have simply waited for a boy to come down Durrow Street hawking broadsheets, but he was anxious to see the latest impression he had sold. It was, he had thought when he created it, particularly vivid.

Eldyn paid his penny and got one of the first copies off the stack. He walked a short ways away, then leaned against the wall of the building and unfolded the broadsheet. They had printed the impression on the front page this time, for such a macabre image could only cause people to be curious about the article that accompanied it.

Even in the fading daylight, each detail was rendered so crisply that the objects depicted in the impression seemed to float above the surface of the page at varying distances, imparting a sensation of depth. The scene showed the gallows in the desolate square before Barrowgate. Three empty nooses hung from the gibbet, while atop perched the black silhouette of a crow, as if waiting patiently for the ropes to be put to use.

This alone might have made for an interesting image, but it was the figure in the foreground that had caught Eldyn's eye that day, and which had altered the perspective of the scene. A young boy, perhaps six or seven, knelt on the cobbles before the gallows, his hair a tousled mop, and his bare knees dirty. He was playing with a bundle of sticks. Was he making an innocent game of them—or was he building his own miniature gibbet?

Eldyn couldn't say. Yet it was that very question the scene begged, and which made it so interesting. Living in such times, witnessing such things, could any child remain innocent? Certainly the hanging Eldyn's father had taken him to see as a child had affected him deeply. He supposed it was the memory of that day that had caused him to stop when he saw the boy playing before the gallows.

The resulting impression was not so sensational and violent as the one he had made of the terrible events at Covenant Cross last quarter month. Nor did it involve a famous personage, like the images he had crafted of Princess Layle departing the graveyard or, more recently, walking down the steps of the cathedral. Yet he had thought this one was perhaps his best work yet.

The editor of *The Swift Arrow* had agreed when Eldyn handed him the engraving plate.

"Our circulation has increased measurably of late," he had said as he counted out several gold regals. "I trust you will not consider selling your work to any other publication, Mr. Garritt."

Eldyn had assured him he would not, then pocketed the coins. There was a part of him that could not help feeling it was wrong to profit from such awful events. Yet it was important for people to know what had really happened that day.

While illusionists could create anything they wished out of light, it was not so with impressions. As Perren had said, an illu-

sionist could only make an impression of something he had actually witnessed himself. Nor was this simply because the mind
could not invent things in sufficient detail; after all, Eldyn could
create very detailed figures upon the stage. Rather, it was the impression rosin itself. Somehow it knew whether the image it was
being shaped into was true or not.

Eldyn had learned this for himself recently. In his room above
the theater, he had coated a plate with rosin, then had held it in
both hands as he pictured Dercy's face. He had concentrated with
all his might, imagining every line, every familiar angle. Why
shouldn't it work? he had reasoned. After all, he had gazed upon
that face many times.

But when the green flash happened, it was dim. Then, after he
coated the plate with ink and pressed it against a piece of paper,
the resulting image was blurred and indistinct. He could make out
only the barest shadow of a face in the smudges of ink. It wasn't
enough to simply imagine how Dercy looked. He would have had
to call to mind a specific scene with Dercy in it, one that had happened just recently. Which meant it was impossible Eldyn could
make an impression of him now.

As painful as this realization was, it was because impressions
could only be true that they could also sell broadsheets and command high prices. The impression Eldyn had made of the scene in
Covenant Cross was remarkable not just for its clarity, but because
it proved beyond doubt that the university men had not been
rushing forward to attack the soldiers, as some early reports had
claimed, but rather had been falling back when the redcrests fired
upon them.

Which meant, by selling his impressions to the broadsheets, he
wasn't just making a profit from awful happenings. He was doing
something of worth. At least, that was what he told himself. Yet
there were times when he could not help thinking that he should
be putting his abilities to a different use. Though what that might
be, he could not say.

The shadows along the street were lengthening; it was time to get back to the theater. Eldyn folded the broadsheet as he stepped into the street.

And just as quickly stepped back. He raised the broadsheet before his face. He considered gathering the thickening shadows, wrapping them around himself, but resisted the urge. After all, another illusionist would be liable to notice the trick.

Cautiously, Eldyn peered around the edge of his broadsheet. A plump, bespectacled young man was walking from the door of *The Swift Arrow*. He held a small, square bundle wrapped in paper, and there was a sour expression on his round face.

Eldyn quickly ducked back behind the newspaper before Perren could see him. An encounter with the other young man was the last thing he wished—not now, after his impression had just been published, and when it was clear Perren had failed to sell his own. For what else could the square bundle in his hand be, or the cause of the dyspeptic look on his face?

It was uncharitable of him, especially after the way Perren had helped him, but Eldyn couldn't help feeling a small note of satisfaction. After all, it had not been out of kindness that Perren had taught him to make impressions. Rather, he had expected payment in the form of Eldyn's romantic affections. And when these were not received in due, he had revealed his to be a mean and petty nature.

Perren had said he would tell the editors of *The Swift Arrow* not to buy Eldyn's impressions. But it appeared it was Perren's impressions they were refusing to buy instead. Behind the broadsheet, Eldyn smiled. Then, as his gaze took in the words before him, his smile went flat. He had given little thought to the article that the editors would print as an accompaniment to his latest impression. As he scanned the words, a weight descended in his stomach, as if he had swallowed cold lead.

THE GALLOWS GAME, read the title under Eldyn's impression, and the article continued below.

Who shall be the next to meet an untimely end upon the gibbet before Barrowgate? Predicting this is a grisly game, no doubt, but one

*sure to provide amusement all the same, such as that being found by
the young boy in this striking scene. There is, we are sure, no short-
age of suitable necks to choose from these days, but one in particular
comes immediately to mind.*

*Last year, the people of Torland were subjected to the horror of
the first Risings of the Wyrdwood in centuries. In an awful spectacle
that hardly seems possible, numerous men lost their lives—beaten
and strangled to death by the branches and roots of Old Trees under
the influence of a witch. Now, in shocking testimony before the Hall
of Magnates, elucidated by the clever questioning of Lord Davarry,
a terrible truth has been revealed.*

*Previously, like so many others, we regarded Sir Alasdare Quent,
of County Westmorain and late of East Durrow Street, as a true
champion of the realm for his actions in putting down the Risings in
Torland. Now, by his own astonishing admission under oath, we
have learned how he was able to work this feat. It was through col-
lusion with the very witch who caused the Risings that he was able
to effect their end.*

*One can only wonder, if this heinous conspiracy could so swiftly
and abruptly bring about an end to the Risings, might it not also
have been the source of its sudden inception? We have all heard of
depraved men who have set a house on fire so they can be the first
to it with a bucket of water and present themselves as a savior.*

*There can be no doubt that Sir Quent has benefited greatly from
his reputation as the one who ended the Risings. He was granted one
title, and had hopes of another being bestowed upon him. But this
then begs the question: did Sir Quent secretly induce the witch to
make the Old Trees lash out so that he could then publicly manufacture an end to the Risings, and so be proclaimed by all as a hero?*

*We do not know the answer to this question. But if that in fact
turns out to be the case, then Mr. Quent—forgive us, Sir Quent—is
no hero at all, but rather the most monstrous sort of villain. And so
we will have a winner in the gallows game. . . .*

Eldyn could barely make out the final lines of the article, for
the daylight had gone to ash. All the same, their meaning regis-

tered clearly. Trembling, he lowered the newspaper, no longer thinking about Perren.

Could the story be true? He knew the broadsheets had a penchant for publishing inflammatory pieces in order to win readers. And it seemed impossible that a man as solid and patriotic as Sir Quent would aid and abet an enemy of the realm, and a known witch.

Or was it? Archdeacon Lemarck had been blinding illusionists and torturing them in an attempt to create witch-hounds—men who would be able to know when a sibyl was brought before them by detecting the telltale light around her. Eldyn recalled the glow he had seen around Lady Quent at the party for the Miss Lockwells. It had been as green as leaves in sunlight, and as bright and shimmering as any light woven by illusionists.

Illusionists. Siltheri. Sons of witches . . .

The broadsheet slipped from Eldyn's hands and fell in the gutter. The twilight was thickening, and there was no sign of Perren. He hurried along the street; it was time to get back to the theater.

"THERE YOU ARE, ELDYN!" Riethe exclaimed with a relieved expression as Eldyn stepped from the wings onto the stage. "We looked upstairs to see if you were asleep, and then we went to the Red Jester, but you weren't there either. Where in the Abyss were you hiding?"

"I was just . . . I went out for a walk," Eldyn said. And it was the truth, if only a part of it.

"Out for a walk?" Mouse echoed, and his nose crinkled in a scowl. "Have you lost your wits, Eldyn? We can't go on without you. And in case you hadn't noticed, it's not exactly safe out there on the streets. Or have you forgotten what happened in Covenant Cross?"

No, he had not forgotten. Rather, the details of that day—the puffs of black smoke, the mad scramble of men, the blood pooling on the cobblestones—were indelibly etched upon his brain, as if by mordant upon an engraving plate. Only he had not told the other illusionists about the impression he had made of that awful scene; he had not wanted them to be worried for him after the fact.

Nor did Eldyn care to discuss the latest impression he had sold, not after reading the article that had accompanied it in *The Swift Arrow*. It was awful to think that an impression he had fashioned might be used to turn people's opinions against Lady Quent's husband. It seemed impossible that Sir Quent would really be convicted of such a dreadful crime. But if somehow he was, what would become of Lady Quent and her sisters?

He would have to ask Rafferdy about it the next time they met for a drink; surely he would know the truth of it all. Though, even as he thought this, it occurred to Eldyn that he hadn't been back to his former residence near the cathedral in over a half month. He had an arrangement with the new occupant of the rooms, who would collect any correspondence that came for Eldyn, for he couldn't very well give Rafferdy his present address.

Periodically, Eldyn would go back to the apartment to retrieve any notes or letters that came for him, giving the man who now lived there a few coins for his trouble. But it had been some time since Eldyn had had a chance to go back to the old monastery. It was possible there was a note from Rafferdy already waiting for him.

Well, Eldyn would go back there as soon as he could. At the moment, he had other matters to concern him.

"I'm sorry I worried you all, Mouse," he said. "But you know, it's not exactly safe here in the theater either."

Mouse sighed but didn't disagree. How could he? A thick pink scar was still clearly visible along the edge of Hugoth's cheekbone.

"Let's just get our costumes on," Mouse said.

They did so. Though as it turned out, they need hardly have bothered. They opened the doors of the theater and sent up the shaft of illusory light that signaled there was to be a performance. Only, by the time the moon rose into the sky, there were no more than a dozen stragglers in the audience—mostly drunks who had stumbled in from nearby taverns.

There was not a single soldier among them. Either the red-crests had gone to another illusion play that night, or their duties prevented them from seeking out entertainments that evening. Had the illusionists known there would be no soldiers attending, they would have let the theater stand dark and gotten some much-needed rest instead.

Only there was never any predicting when the soldiers would decide to show up all in a group, and if they had found the doors of the theater closed, they would have broken them down. So Madame Richelour had had no choice but to open the doors, and now the players had no choice but to put on a show for the few men who had paid their coin to enter.

Just because the show had to go on, though, didn't mean it had to be a very good one, or very long. The illusionists moved through the scenes quickly, in the most perfunctory fashion, and in general they relied on the physical sets and costumes, dressing these with only a minimal sheen of illusion.

After less than an hour, the curtain whisked shut. The men in the audience grumbled their complaints, or let out slurred curses, but all the same they got up and stumbled out of the theater. As soon as they were gone, Riethe shut the doors and locked them against any latecomers seeking entrance. Then Madame Richelour opened up the receipt box. But the take was so pitiful that none of them would have any of it from her.

"Looks like there won't be any punch for us tonight," Mouse said wistfully.

Perhaps if they had ventured to another part of the city, they might have found a tavern where they could pass off a penny disguised to look like a gold regal. But it was too dangerous to venture far afield at night, and all the barkeeps along Durrow Street were well aware of the abilities of illusionists, and knew to bite a coin before accepting it. Even so, Mouse and the others would get their punch.

"Don't be so glum," Eldyn said. "You can each buy a pot on me."

"Really?" Mouse said, his eyes lighting up. "Then let's get going!"

"Hold a moment," Riethe said, clamping his hands on the small man's shoulders. "Eldyn, that's good of you. God knows, the only way to get Mouse to shut up is to get him so drunk he can't speak. But don't you need that money to buy more things to make impressions?"

"I have plenty of materials," Eldyn said. Which was in fact the case, given his recent sale.

Though he supposed it would be the last sale as well. He did not see how he could sell any more impressions to *The Swift Arrow,* not after the awful way his latest image had been used. That meant he didn't need his coin for engraving plates or impression rosin anymore. In which case, they might as well spend it on punch.

"Go on and get started," he said, taking a gold regal and flipping it toward Mouse. "I'll be along with more in a little while. I just want to go up and pay Master Tallyroth a visit."

Mouse gripped the coin. "All right, but be swift about it. This won't last us very long."

"Mouse!" Riethe growled.

But the little man had wriggled from his grip and was heading to the back of the theater. The others followed after.

"Here's another regal," Eldyn said, pressing a coin into Riethe's big hand. "Don't let Mouse go through it too quickly."

"If he gulps too much, I'll throttle his neck to keep him from swallowing," Riethe said with a grin. "And don't hurry on our account. Master Tallyroth will be happy to see you. He was asking about you when I was sitting with him earlier."

"How was he?"

Riethe's grin vanished. "Go on up" was all he said, then he followed the other illusionists out the back of the theater.

Eldyn gripped the banister for a moment, then ascended the stairs. The night Master Tallyroth had collapsed after conjuring illusions, they had carried him up to the little parlor just above the theater, for it was the nearest room. He had remained there in the days since, as the parlor was bright and sunny; and if they propped him up on the chaise, he could see the length of Durrow Street out the window—a sight which always seemed to cheer him.

Upon reaching the parlor, Eldyn lifted a hand to knock, then halted. The door was ajar, and through the opening he caught a glimpse of a scene that he was certain was not intended to be performed for others.

Madame Richelour sat next to the chaise which now served as Master Tallyroth's bed. The chaise was arranged to face the window and was laden with pillows, so that Eldyn could only see the back of it and not its occupant. Madame Richelour leaned forward in her chair, moving her arm in a gentle manner that suggested some tender action. Caressing a hand, perhaps, or smoothing hair back from a pale brow.

As always, her face was heavily adorned with rouge and powder, though no cosmetics could conceal the deep lines of weariness that marred her visage. All the same, her expression was not one of anguish. Rather, her crimson lips curved in a smile, and the light in her eyes was not a product of sorrow.

Eldyn wondered how long she had loved Master Tallyroth. Had it been since after he came to the Theater of the Moon? Or was it because she could not marry him that she had married the theater instead, to find a way to be near to him? No matter the case, it was clear he loved her as well. Not in any sort of carnal manner, of course. He was Siltheri, after all, and he had taken many other illusionists for lovers over the years.

Yet in the end he had always come back to the theater, and back to Madame Richelour. Theirs was a singular relationship. It was not a marriage; it could not be, given his nature. Yet it was far more than friendship. Nor did it matter what their relationship was called, or what others might think of it. They were as close as two people could be in this world.

Silently, Eldyn stepped back from the door. He waited several moments, then approached again, being sure to make more noise this time, and then knocked. The door opened, revealing Madame Richelour. She smiled at the sight of him.

"He's been waiting for you."

Eldyn could only nod. She gave his cheek a fond pat, then departed with a rustling of silk and velvet.

"Is that you, Mr. Garritt?" came a reedy voice from the chaise.

Eldyn drew in a breath, then made his voice as lively as he could. "Yes, it's me, Master Tallyroth." He went over to the chair and sat. And even though the sight that greeted him broke his heart anew, still Eldyn kept a smile fixed upon his face.

The master illusionist of the Theater of the Moon lay on the chaise, swaddled thickly in blankets, for it was difficult for him to stay warm. His cane leaned nearby, as if he might have need of it, but that was as much an illusion as any phantasm that had appeared on the stage that night. His dark hair was elegantly combed, and his face was shaven and powdered, but that could not disguise the hollowness of his cheeks, or the livid bruises beneath his cloudy eyes.

Over these last days, Merrick had gone several times to the Theater of the Doves. The master illusionist there had been able to impart some useful advice about what tinctures and decoctions were best for quieting spasms or easing breathing in one afflicted with the mordoth. But other than making Master Tallyroth comfortable, there was little that these could do. If he retained a great enough portion of light to sustain the workings of life, then he would endure. And if he did not . . .

"How was the performance tonight?" Master Tallyroth said, turning his head on the pillow to look at Eldyn. "Was there a very large audience? Though I don't suppose there was, for I think I would have heard them."

Eldyn shook his head. "No, the soldiers didn't come tonight. We had barely a dozen in the house. They had all paid for their admission, though, so the performance went on as planned."

"Above all, the play," Tallyroth said, his voice faint but approving.

Eldyn winced a bit. "Well, we didn't strictly give it our all."

A frown creased the powder on the master illusionist's face. "An illusionist should always do his very best, Mr. Garritt, if not out of regard for the audience, then out of respect for the craft."

"I'm sorry, Master Tallyroth. You're right, of course. But we thought . . . we are just rather tired after the last few performances."

"That is understandable, Mr. Garritt. The additions necessary to please the soldiers have made the show very demanding, to be sure. But that simply means you must allow yourself enough time between performances to rest and recover." He studied Eldyn for a moment. "Your light does seem a bit dimmer than usual. Have you been making more impressions lately?"

"A few," Eldyn admitted.

"Well, that is part of the problem. You must be very careful not to create too many impressions, Mr. Garritt. Instead, make them only sparingly. They are wondrous—perhaps the grandest sort of illusion a Siltheri can fashion. But they are costly as well."

Eldyn shook his head. "Costly? What do you mean?"

"When you make an impression, you are not shaping light, Mr. Garritt. You are shaping a physical thing—the impression rosin upon the plate. Yet like any illusion, light is still required to work the craft. Which means the only light you can use when you make an impression is your own."

Eldyn could only stare. He had never considered that he was using light to work the impressions; he was always so caught up in the act of making them that he didn't think about it. But even as Tallyroth spoke, Eldyn knew it was true—that the green flash he saw in the moment he made an impression was a bit of his own light being expended.

It was something of a horrifying realization. How much of his light had he used up? Not very much, he had to think, for he was not suffering from any adverse effects, other than being a bit tired. Besides, it didn't matter anymore, for he had no desire to sell anything else to *The Swift Arrow*.

"I don't think I'll be making any more impressions for a while, Master Tallyroth."

"That is good, Mr. Garritt. Promise me that you will only make another impression if it is for something truly worthwhile."

"I promise."

This response seemed to please the master illusionist, though he made no reply. Instead he exhaled, and his gaze went back to the window. Outside, the moon rose over Durrow Street. The two men were silent for a time, content to watch that silvery glow bathe the darkened theaters along the street.

"And how is Mr. Fanewerthy?"

Eldyn sat up in the chair, lifting his head as he did. He was so weary he must have nodded off for a moment. Or more than a moment, for the moon was gone from view. Now the only light visible through the window was the red ember of the new planet, pulsing against the black sky.

"I'm sorry," Eldyn said. "What was that?"

"What is keeping him so long?" Master Tallyroth said, his reedy voice faint but peevish. "He hasn't come to visit me all day."

Eldyn shook his head. "Who hasn't come to visit you?"

"Who do you think? I mean Dercy, of course! That rascal."

A pang stabbed at Eldyn's heart. It wasn't just that he missed Dercy. It was also the fact that Master Tallyroth had forgotten he was gone. Nor was this the first time that had happened.

"Dercy isn't in the city," he said gently. "He left for the country months ago, to try to get better. You remember that, don't you?"

The master illusionist stared blankly for a moment, confusion in his clouded eyes. Then his sunken chest rattled with a sudden breath.

"Yes, Mr. Fanewerthy has left us," he said, the words no more than a whisper. "He is gone, I do remember."

Eldyn rose from the chair. "I think I need to go get some of that rest you prescribed for me earlier. You should do the same."

Master Tallyroth nodded; words seemed beyond him now. Eldyn smoothed his covers, then bent to kiss his brow. When he rose again, the older man's eyes were closed. Quietly, so as not to wake him, Eldyn went to the oil lamp to turn down the wick. Master Tallyroth needed to sleep. That was the only thing that would help him now.

Except that wasn't true. There was one other thing that could be done for him—something that could help with the mordoth that afflicted him.

There is only one way to reverse the effects of the Gray Wasting, the master illusionist at the Theater of the Doves had said to Merrick. *You can press your lips to his, and grant him some of your own light. It is not any sort of permanent cure, mind you. Each dose of light he receives will sustain him for but a finite time before it fades. Yet if those who love him wish it, then in this way they can help him to endure. . . .*

Merrick had repeated these words to Eldyn, Hugoth, and Riethe late one night. Though Riethe had expressed his doubts.

"No, it's true," Merrick had said. "We all know that a little bit of light passes between Siltheri each time they touch. And the more intimate the touch, the more the light."

Hugoth had given a grim laugh. "I'd have thought that was something you were well aware of, Riethe, given what a strumpet you are. It's a wonder you don't have the mordoth yourself. Then again, I've found it's always the big, strapping lads who want to be on the receiving side of things!"

Riethe had begun a red-faced rejoinder, but Eldyn had intervened. Then Merrick had asked him what he thought.

Eldyn knew Merrick was right, that it was indeed possible. After all, that was the reason Dercy was ill. First he had given Eldyn some of his light. Then Lemarck had stolen more of it—a great quantity. Eldyn would never forget how the archdeacon's skin had glowed with a golden radiance as Dercy's own went ashen. And he would never forget Dercy's screams as his light was drained from him.

Only this wouldn't be the same. It would be their choice to do it. And they would only give a little bit, just enough to sustain him until he could regain his strength.

Except Master Tallyroth would never take it from them. Eldyn knew it. All the same, they went to speak with Madame Richelour. But as soon as Merrick started to say what they were thinking, she waved a hand to silence him, rings flashing and bracelets jangling.

"You say this out of love for him, I know," she said. "But I also know that the very idea would cause him pain. He would never accept such a thing, not from young men whom he loves as his sons."

Merrick shook his head. "But he needs—"

"He needs to know his boys are well, and that the play goes on each time the theater doors open. That is what will sustain him, if—"

Her words fell short, and when she spoke again it was to dismiss them from her chamber. But Eldyn knew what she had been about to say. *That is what will sustain him, if he is sustained at all.*

After that, none of them brought up the idea again.

Now, upon the chaise, Master Tallyroth drew slow, rattling breaths. Eldyn turned down the wick on the oil lamp a little further, so the light would not wake him. Only he fumbled the knob, going too far. The wick sank into the lamp, and the flame was snuffed out.

IT WAS JUST AFTER SUNRISE when Eldyn awoke. He had no idea if the umbral had been short or long, or how many hours he had slept.

Not many, he thought as he went downstairs, for the theater was quiet. He supposed he should go back to bed. Only his sleep had been restless, filled with ill dreams. In them, he kept looking up at the sky as the new red planet grew larger and larger. Only then it wasn't a planet anymore. Rather, it was a great eye, rimmed with flame, peering down at him from the heavens, and beneath its fiery gaze his soul shriveled and blackened.

It was a duplicate of the vision Archdeacon Lemarck had once forced upon him. He still dreamed about it from time to time. And even though he knew it had only been an illusion, and that Lemarck had perished after expending all of his light while shut in a dark prison, still the image filled Eldyn with dread.

And shouldn't it? Lemarck might be dead, but what of the ancient god he had claimed to serve? Ul'zulgul, he had called this being. Afterward, Eldyn had told himself that it was all just another phantasm, an invention of the madness that had possessed

Lemarck. Only what if it wasn't just an invention? What if Lemarck really had seen something through that window he found deep beneath Graychurch, and some eldritch power really had spoken to him?

But Lemarck was gone, and there was no point in thinking about it. Eldyn was shaken by the bad dreams, that was all. He just needed some coffee to properly wake up. Unfortunately, once again, there was no sign of the woman who cooked for them. So Eldyn went back upstairs to retrieve his coat, then left the theater in search of a hot cup.

He made his way down Durrow Street toward his usual coffeehouse. After no more than a minute, a boy with a dirt-smudged face ran up to him, holding several rumpled broadsheets that looked as if they had been plucked from the gutter.

"Today's edition of *The Swift Arrow,* sir," the boy said. "Same news as what will cost you a penny elsewhere, just a half penny here."

Eldyn supposed the papers were from a bundle that had fallen off the back of a lorry and had broken apart on the street. Yet he had no interest in broadsheets, no matter the price—especially *The Swift Arrow.* He started to brush past the boy. Only then the picture on the front page caught his eye. It was his own impression, the one he had made after the terrible events at Covenant Cross.

"Are you sure those papers are from today?" he said with a frown. "From last quarter month, more likely."

"Not on your life, sir! It's today's, sure as we stand here. Have a look yourself at the date."

He thrust the newspaper up at Eldyn. The boy was right; it was indeed today's edition. Not that this was entirely surprising. It was common for broadsheets to reprint an impression several times, given how much they cost to acquire, and how popular they were. But why reprint this one, with its awful scene? Then he saw the headline beneath the impression, and he understood the reason.

COVENANT CROSS MASSACRE NOT FORGOTTEN, it read. And beneath that, *Names of Those Slain Are Revealed by a Secret Patriot.*

A jolt far stronger than any provided by coffee surged through Eldyn's brain. He snatched the paper from the boy's hand.

"Hey now, that'll be a half penny!"

Eldyn groped in his coat pocket, found a two-penny silver, and flipped it at the boy.

"Sorry, sir, no change!" the boy cried, snatching the coin out of the air and dashing down the street.

If he feared pursuit, he needn't have bothered. Eldyn stepped to the side of the street, reading the story on the front page as he went.

Up until now the government has refused to publish a list of the men who lost their lives in the confrontation at Covenant Cross last quarter month. Nor has the Citadel even stated the number of men who died that day, shot down by the government's own soldiers. Perhaps it was the government's belief that, if it does not acknowledge that awful deed, we will all forget it. But we will always remember. And now we can remember as well the names of those who fell that day, wrongly and cruelly struck down in their youth. For the list that the Citadel has tried to keep secret has now come into our possession, thanks to one who will remain unnamed but who is a true patriot of Altania. The roll of names is longer than we all have feared, and you will find it printed within these pages. . . .

Eldyn opened the broadsheet, looking for the list. And there it was, printed in large type on the centermost page. Quickly he read through the list top to bottom, looking for the name he feared might be upon it.

The wheels are turning, Orris Jaimsley had said that day Eldyn had run into him at the coffeehouse on Coronet Street. *And they will not cease until our present government is ground to dust beneath them. . . .*

In the days since witnessing the massacre in Covenant Cross, it had been Eldyn's fear that Orris Jaimsley had been there, marching with the other young men. After all, Eldyn had seen the flag for St. Berndyn's among those of the other colleges in the square, and

Jaimsley had seemed intent on the idea that the government was bound to fall.

Yet as Eldyn ran a finger over the list, which was ordered by surname, the entries went from *D. Hennifree* to *M. Lindrew,* skipping the place where *O. Jaimsley* might fit. His name was not there. Eldyn started to draw a relieved breath—

—then the air passed out of him again in a gasp, as if he had been struck in the chest. Again he read the two names at the very bottom of the list, though it was difficult for the way his eyes blurred.

C. Talinger, read the one. And below that, *D. Warrett.*

As people and horses moved past him on the street, Eldyn stared at the broadsheet, as if the letters on the page would at any moment rearrange themselves into a more comprehensible order. Only the black ink they were printed in was as indelible as blood.

Eldyn knew they had gone once to march with Jaimsley in Covenant Cross. But that had been before the demonstrations had taken a violent turn. Back when they used to meet at Mrs. Haddon's, Warrett's phlegmatic demeanor had always countered and cooled Talinger's West Country temper. Eldyn was sure they would have had the sense not to be there in the square when the soldiers opened fire.

But Eldyn had been there, hadn't he? And he had made an impression of the scene, of the blood flowing on the cobblestones, not knowing that some of it belonged to two men who had been his friends.

Two men who were now dead.

Eldyn lowered the broadsheet, crumpling it in his hands as he did. He staggered to an alcove by a doorway, then slumped within it and wept. As he did, shadows crept from nearby corners and crevices, gathering about him, as if to comfort him like a soft, dark blanket.

A sound jarred Eldyn from his grief: the noise of marching boots. He shrank back against the doorway, pulling the shadows closer, as a small band of men wearing red-plumed hats marched along the street in close formation. The sun glinted off the brass buttons on their blue coats, and off the barrels of the rifles on their backs.

He wondered if some of them had been there that day at Covenant Cross, if they had fired those rifles. Perhaps some of them had been the ones who had hauled Mrs. Haddon to Barrowgate. Or maybe a few had been there in the audience that night at the Theater of the Moon, threatening to tear the place down if they were not entertained, until Master Tallyroth joined in the play to appease them, and in the act expended himself until he was nearly dead.

The redcrests had sworn an oath to protect the people of Altania. But who would protect the people against *them*? Certainly not the government, for that was whom the soldiers served.

At least, not *this* government.

The soldiers passed by, and Eldyn staggered from the alcove onto the street. He looked down at his hands. Though stained black with ink from the broadsheet, they remained delicate and smooth. His father had always mocked him for the fine appearance of his hands.

A woman would be pleased to have such hands as yours, Vandimeer Garritt would say with a laugh if he was in a good mood. *Be careful not to tear a fingernail, now.*

Despite his father's words, Eldyn was not afraid to put up a struggle. He had shown that when he brought about the demise of the highwayman Westen Darendal, and when he confronted Archdeacon Lemarck beneath the chapel in High Holy. Eldyn was no soldier, he knew that.

But there were other ways to fight a war than with guns.

He was already walking past carriages and horses and people before he even realized where he was going. Moving at a quick march, he made his way along University Street, then turned down a narrow lane, coming to a set of stone stairs between two buildings. BUTCHER'S SLIP, read the metal plaque on the arch above the stairs.

The stairs ended in a small close. The buildings leaned inward as they rose up all around, so that only a dim light filtered down

into the little courtyard. On the far side was a door set into a wall
lined with many small windows. Eldyn hesitated, but only for a
moment. Then he went up to the door and knocked loudly.

The door opened. On the other side was a long corridor
blocked by two men about his own age. Both of them were tall,
with thick necks and meaty forearms.

"What do you want?" one of them growled.

"My name is Eldyn Garritt."

"And?"

"I'm here to see Orris Jaimsley. I think he's staying in the dormitories. He told me to come see him if . . ." He drew in a breath.
"That is, he said you could always use another trustworthy man."

The two gazed at him with narrowed eyes, as if taking his measure, then they looked at each other. Eldyn willed himself not to
slink away and pull the shadows around him.

Finally the young man who had spoken nodded.

"If Jaimsley told you to come see him, then you should see
him."

The door opened wider, and Eldyn stepped through.

CHAPTER SEVENTEEN

IT WAS THE MIDDLE of a long lumenal, and Ivy and Mr.
Quent sat together in the garden on the side of the house, on a
blanket spread out in the dappled shade beneath the tall plane
trees.

Surprisingly, it had been his idea to leave their dwelling and go
outside for a while. She would have been quite content to spend
the remainder of the day in bed, encircled in his arms, engaging in
those same tender activities with which they had whiled away the
morning. But then he had risen, and he had suggested they go out.

Nor could she disagree with the notion once she looked out the window.

It was a perfect day to be outdoors. There had been so much queer weather of late—days that were too stifling, or that were violent with storms. But today, at this moment, it was beautiful. The arching branches of the plane trees swayed languidly in a breeze that was perfectly warm, and their leaves imparted a green tincture to the gold light that filtered from above. Ivy breathed in, finding the light and air to be every bit as heady as the cool wine which Mrs. Seenly had brought out to them on a tray.

Ivy wondered if her sisters would spy them through a window and come out to join them, but so far they had not. Rose's had never been a gregarious personality, and she had been particularly withdrawn of late. Recent events had affected her—had affected all of them. Ivy had banished all broadsheets from the house, but that did not mean her sisters were entirely ignorant of what had occurred when Mr. Quent appeared before Assembly. They had both asked questions, and some news did not need to be printed upon a page in order to travel. Ivy had overheard a few of the servants whispering—though after she informed Mrs. Seenly, this behavior quickly stopped.

As for Lily, she had been astonishingly well-behaved over the last quarter month. Ivy had not seen her once with her folio, and so could begin to hope Lily had given up her fascination with illusion plays. What was more, Ivy could not recall a single outburst or argument, or any kind of peevish behavior—even when such might have been justified.

While invitations to dinners and parties had become infrequent in recent months, due to the number of families who had departed the city, now such notes and letters ceased entirely. And even if people did return to Invarel at some point, invitations for the Miss Lockwells—or for Ivy—were unlikely to resume. Newspapers might have been banished from the house, but they were plentiful about the city. At this point there could be no one with any sort of connection who was not aware of the accusation that had been leveled against Mr. Quent.

The fact that this charge had not been proven was incidental. Ivy could not forget how the merest intimation of treason had required Mr. Rafferdy to break off his engagement with Miss Everaud. She had been forced to flee the country with her father, Lord Everaud, who according to whispers had been sending funds to the Principalities for the purpose of helping Huntley Morden to raise a fleet of ships.

Lord Davarry had made no such accusation of treason against Mr. Quent. But meeting with a witch, one who was known to have aided Torland rebels, was more than enough to cause people to abruptly and irrevocably break off all association. Not so very long ago, at the party for Lily and Rose, Lady Crayford had told Ivy that she was bound to rise higher yet in society. How things had been altered in the few months since then! Ivy knew that, if she were to arrange another party now, no one but themselves would come.

As for Lady Crayford, fortune had progressed in a far more awful manner. After Lord Crayford—or rather, Mr. Gambrel—was implicated in the affair of the archbishop's madness, Lady Crayford had fled the city to their manor in the east. While being cast from society's highest circles was no doubt a stinging punishment for her, this had been superseded by a more terrible and final judgment. Lady Marsdel had only lately learned that, some time ago, the country manor of the Crayfords had been consumed in a fire. So quick and violent had been the flames that the entire house had burned to the ground before any of its denizens could escape.

When Lady Marsdel had imparted this news in a recent letter, Ivy felt both shock and sorrow. Lady Crayford had betrayed her, and had used her in the most reprehensible manner, but still Ivy would not have wished such a dreadful fate upon her. Ivy shuddered when she thought of it—of the pain and fear Lady Crayford must have suffered in the end.

FOR IVY'S PART, she could hardly claim what had happened was any sort of punishment for *her.* True, she was not invited to parties anymore, but nor was she in any way abandoned. In addition to notes from Lady Marsdel, she had received a visit from Mrs. Baydon, assuring Ivy of her continued affection and regard. And while she had not heard from him, she was certain that Mr. Rafferdy would still condescend to associate with them. After all, he had had prior dealings with a witch himself—namely Ivy.

Still, there was no pretending that they were not in general cut off from society in the city. Yet despite this, Lily had seemed unperturbed these last days. Ivy would have thought her to be distraught at the sudden severing of their connections, and this was one occasion on which Ivy would not have begrudged her an outburst of tears.

Instead, Lily had seemed content to read books or help Rose sew shirts for the poor basket. When she played the pianoforte, she chose lighter and more melodious pieces than the ominous compositions she used to favor. Ivy was confounded by Lily's unexpectedly good behavior, but she could hardly complain about it.

"Can I pour you some more wine, Ivoleyn?"

She turned her gaze from the branches above to her husband on the blanket beside her, and she smiled.

"Perhaps a little," she said. "Though it feels indulgent to have more than one glass in the middle of the day."

"As you are in general very poor at indulging yourself, I think we should seize upon this opportunity."

He spoke this so seriously that she could only laugh, and she willingly held out her glass so he could fill it from the bottle. He filled his own, and they reclined upon the blanket as they sipped the pale yellow wine.

Now it was not the branches she watched, but her husband. Despite the events of these last days, he looked very well. It was too warm for a coat, and his cream-colored shirt was rolled up at the cuffs and opened at the throat. His beard was newly trimmed, and the muted, dappled light beneath the trees softened the rugged lines of his face.

It was curious. She had noted how Mr. Rafferdy had grown more handsome even as he had become more serious, but for Mr. Quent it was the opposite. He seemed calm and at ease now, and this had a decidedly positive effect upon his appearance. Coils of brown hair tumbled over his brow, and a few similarly colored tufts peeked out from the open collar of his shirt. She could only smile at him, her Tharosian faun, out amid the green.

"What are you looking at?" he said. "You have a peculiar gleam in your eyes."

"I was simply admiring the view," she said teasingly.

Mr. Quent gave her a scowl, but it was an expression of humor rather than vexation, and he went back to drinking his wine.

Ivy smiled, for it was good to see him away from his study. He had continued to work diligently over these last days, reading and writing answers to numerous missives from other inquirers, and poring over maps and reports. But at no point since his testimony had he gone up to the Citadel.

That he would never succeed Lord Rafferdy and be confirmed as lord inquirer was so assured that they had hardly bothered to speak of it. Ivy could not claim she wasn't saddened by this fact, though it was not for herself that she felt sorrow. Rather, it was for him. He had not craved the acclaim he had previously gotten, and neither did he deserve the scorn he was receiving now. She knew he wanted only to do his work to the best of his ability. So she was saddened for Altania as well, that it should be deprived of the benefit of his efforts.

And as for the witches he might have found and aided in his efforts to prevent Risings—Ivy felt not sorrow but dread. For who should discover them now? Lady Shayde and the Gray Conclave? Or would young women instead hear the call of the Wyrdwood, and scale its walls and venture into its depths, losing themselves amid its green tangles. . . .

No, she would not think that. There were yet other inquirers carrying on Lord Rafferdy's work. And for her part, despite all these concerns, Ivy could not say that she missed the letters and invitations, or the comings and goings in the household. Rather, it was pleasant for things to be so quiet and peaceful, and to have Mr. Quent here at home with them. It was strange, but in a way she could not recall a time when she had been so content.

She noticed that he had set down his glass on the tray, and was rubbing two fingers against his temple.

"You have a headache again," she said.

"It will pass."

He had been having frequent headaches since the day following his appearance before Assembly. Not that this was surprising, given the concerns that must weigh upon his mind.

"Come," she said, in a tone that brooked no argument, and she took his shoulders, leaning him back until his head rested upon her lap. She smoothed back his brown curls, and with gentle motions stroked his forehead. He shut his eyes and let out a breath, and soon the lines upon his brow lessened in depth—though they did not fade altogether. They were ever present, as they had been since she first met him.

How deep the lines upon his forehead had been that day! He had returned to Heathcrest Hall to find his young wards, Clarette and Chambley, all in a commotion, and he had been obviously displeased with the efforts of his new governess—that was, with Ivy. She had quailed at his grim expression and solemn demeanor. Though somehow she had found the courage to keep from retreating in the face of his ire.

What would she have thought that day, if she had known that in the future he would be lying peacefully with his head upon her lap? At the time, she would never have been able to imagine it. But both of them were greatly altered since those first days at Heathcrest.

"I wonder how Clarette and Chambley are," she mused aloud.

"I am sure they are well. Last we had a letter, they had gone with their aunt and uncle to the east, far from the troubles."

Ivy was sure that was the case. All the same, it was hard not to wonder about them. For so many months at Heathcrest Hall, the two had been her only real companions.

"Do you remember the day the children knocked over the stuffed fox in the front hall at Heathcrest?" she said as she stroked his brow. "I was trying to put the stuffing back into it, hoping I could do so before you saw what had happened. But then there you were, standing over us, so that we were all of us in a great terror, I no less than the two of them."

"Was I really so frightening as that?" he said, his voice a growl, though there was a hint of a smile at the corners of his lips.

"You were very stern," she said with a laugh.

"Well, it was the first fox I ever hunted with my father. I was quite attached to it."

"It is peculiar that, after shooting the creature once, you should then be so concerned about another hole in its side."

"If you cannot understand that, then you have much yet to learn about the nature and behavior of men. I suggest you consult a book on the topic, as is your habit."

She gave a plaintive sigh. "I am not sure there is a book that reveals such mysteries as those. I fear I will dwell in ignorance without instruction."

"Very well, then I shall take you on a hunting party in the country as soon as it is convenient."

He spoke these words in jest, but all the same a sudden, wild feeling came over Ivy. At that instant, she no longer wished to be sitting in a neatly tended garden, but rather riding across moors of heather and gorse at the foot of rocky fells.

And why shouldn't she? It was impossible Mr. Quent would become lord inquirer now; there was no need for him to remain close to the Citadel. Nor was there anything preventing them from removing her father from Madstone's at any time. She had been waiting for his rooms here at the house to be finished, which they nearly were. But there were plenty of rooms at Heathcrest Hall, all simply waiting to have the sheets pulled off the furniture and the windows opened and a fire lit in the grate.

As for Lily and Rose—there was nothing for them in the city either, not now; they would find no suitable society here. But what about at Cairnbridge? Would they not be welcomed there? Surely all in County Westmorain would be glad to have people at Heathcrest Hall once more. Ivy knew Rose would like both Mr. Samonds and his aunt; theirs were gentle spirits, like her own.

And Lily could throw balls that everyone in the county would want to attend.

No, there was no reason for them to stay here in the city anymore. . . .

"What is it, Ivoleyn?"

Ivy realized she had ceased her ministrations upon his brow, and that she had sat up very straight. He must have noticed this change, for he sat up himself, his brown eyes curious as he looked at her.

"Is something wrong, Ivoleyn?"

She shook her head. "No, I am well. It's just what you said a moment ago, it made me think about . . . That is, why don't we go? Why don't we go to the country?"

"Now, you mean?"

"Not just now. For always."

He stared a moment, then his eyes opened more widely and his lips parted as he let out a breath. She was not certain if his expression was one of astonishment or joy. But either way, as he was mute, she kept speaking, her cheeks glowing as she did.

"Let's leave the city. Let's leave at once and go back to the country. We can all live at Heathcrest Hall—Lily and Rose and my father, and you and I. Everyone in Cairnbridge would be happy to have us back—or at least many would, I am sure of it. And there is more than enough room for us all at your manor. So we would not want for either space or society." She reached out and took his hands in her own. "We could not want for anything, not if we were all of us there together."

He was quiet for a long moment, his gaze going past her, as if he gazed at some far-off place. At last he looked at her again.

"I will not become a lord, Ivoleyn. It may be that I will no longer even be a baronet, or that—" He shook his head. "Things may not be what you think they will be."

She tightened her grip on his hands. "I have no care about that. It was neither Sir Quent nor Lord Quent that I married. Rather, I married Mr. Quent, the master of Heathcrest Hall. And if I were to dwell there with him again, then I could never wish for anything more."

"On the contrary, I fear you may wish you had never married me at all," he said, his voice going low. "You may wish that you had married Mr. Rafferdy instead."

She stared at him, astonished. "Mr. Rafferdy?"

"Or Lord Rafferdy, I should say. For he is a magnate now—something I will never be myself."

"But I care nothing about that!"

"No, I suppose you do not. Yet it is true that you did care about *him,* didn't you? Lily once told me that you had hoped for a proposal from him, before you ever received my letter inviting you to Heathcrest Hall."

Ivy suffered a pang of anguish. That had been thoughtless of Lily to say such a thing. It could only cause harm, and it was of no consequence anymore. How could it be? After all, the past could not be altered. . . .

"Did you love him very much, then?" Mr. Quent said, his brown eyes intent upon her.

That Ivy could lie to him when he gazed at her like that was impossible. "Yes, I did," she said, then shook her head a little. "Or rather, I believed at the time that I did. He was tall and charming and witty, of course. But it was more than that. He was so far removed from the small, plain circle of my world—from all the troubles and worries in it. Mr. Rafferdy seemed to fly above it all as easily as an exotic bird might fly above the rooftops of some damp and dreary city. I could only find that captivating. And yet . . ."

"Yet what?"

She thought of how to explain it. "A bird is a wonderful creature. I might look up at it, and long to fly away with it." She shrugged. "But I am not a bird myself. Rather, I am a thing quite firmly fastened to the ground. Regarding it all now, I know that my affections for Mr. Rafferdy, though strongly felt at the time, were based upon fancy and whim. It was only when I met you that I realized what I really wanted for myself, and the traits that I truly admired: bravery, strength of character, and a selfless and unwavering resolve to always do what is right and good. Charm and wit can be delightful, but in the end they are too easily paired with vanity and callowness."

"And you believe Mr. Rafferdy possesses these latter traits?"

She opened her mouth to reply, but her thoughts, so clear a moment ago, were suddenly confused. Was Mr. Rafferdy vain and callow? Perhaps he had been once. But now? She could hardly call him such things, not after his actions at the Evengrove, or in Assembly. Yet he still tended to indulge himself with fine clothes and fancy canes, and he continued to make a habit of speaking in a silly fashion about serious things.

"No," she said slowly. "He is not those things, at least not anymore."

"Then you hold him in high esteem?"

"Yes, I do," she said, only realizing how true it was as she spoke the words. She thought of how brave Mr. Rafferdy had been to face the magicians of the Silver Eye with her, how strong he had been to resist the dreadful magicks at the tomb of the Broken God, and how he was presently risking his life to safeguard the Wyrdwood from the machinations of politicians. "In the very highest esteem."

Ivy realized Mr. Quent was studying her, his eyes intent upon her face. At last he gave a slow nod, and she wondered what it was he had seen. She could feel her cheeks glowing, and the beating of her heart seemed fluttery and uneven. But this agitation was useless. It was not simply that the past could not be altered; it was that, even if she could do so, she would not.

Her thoughts grew calm, and she tangled her ten fingers among his eight. "What has gone before this moment does not matter," she said. "All that matters is what comes after it. Let us go to Heathcrest Hall. We will be happy there, I know it."

He was silent for a moment, and it seemed he gazed past her, into the distance. "Maybe it will be so," he said softly, as one might speak a prayer. "Maybe it will be allowed, for us to go back."

Ivy did not understand—who was to allow it but themselves?

But before she could say more, his gaze returned to her, and crinkles appeared beside his eyes as he smiled.

"No matter what is to come after, the first thing I must do following this moment is to write a bit more. I should return to my study for a while, if that's well with you."

Ivy felt a brief disappointment that their peaceful afternoon in the garden was at an end. But it was no matter. After all, they would have countless more such days together in the country.

"As the master pleases," she said, giving him an impish smile.

Though she had meant it as a jest, his own smile receded into his beard. "My Ivy," he said at last, his voice a low thrum.

He caught her in an embrace, bringing her to him and encircling her with his strong arms as he kissed her, and Ivy returned these affections with all of her own strength. Then he rose and went back into the house, leaving her alone beneath the swaying trees.

A SHORT WHILE LATER, Ivy returned to the house as well, for the lovely weather had at last been marred by a cloud that came through, and which then proceeded to rain upon the city. It was no more than a halting drizzle—just enough to make the air sticky and uncomfortable.

Ivy walked past the door to Mr. Quent's study, but it was shut. He must still be at his work, so she proceeded to the library to see to a task herself. She took out the Wyrdwood box and her father's journal, then turned through the pages to see if any more words had manifested. None had.

She took out the sheet on which she had transcribed the last entry that had appeared in the journal. *As for Fintaur,* she read the words again, *you will find him residing under the aegis of the princes of the city of Ardaunto.*

Ivy still had not returned to Mr. Fintaur's bookshop. The events following Mr. Quent's testimony before Assembly had precluded doing so, for she had not wanted to be far from her husband in his time of need. Yet he had seemed well today, even happy, and now he was engaged in his study. If not now, then when? If they would indeed be leaving the city soon, she would not have many more opportunities.

Ivy glanced at the clock. The gold disk was turning slowly on the right-hand face; the afternoon was clearly going to be a long one. Which meant she had time. She could go to Greenly Circle now, and tell Mr. Fintaur of what she had learned in her father's journal. He could speak to the others. No doubt he knew Mr. Mundy, given the close proximity of their shops. And she imagined he knew how to find Mr. Larken as well.

Ivy returned the sheet of paper to the Wyrdwood box—then drew it back out as a thought occurred to her. She understood the riddle her father had written in the journal about Mr. Fintaur. And the line about Mr. Mundy was easy enough to comprehend.

If you follow the gaze of the Silver Eye, you will surely come to him.

There was a silver eye painted on the sign above Mr. Mundy's magick shop, of course. But what about Mr. Larken's whereabouts? Again Ivy read the words her father had written.

Larken you will find in good time. Of us all, he ever wore the crown of punctuality. I can think of at least a dozen and a half occasions when he scolded us for being late.

It had to be another riddle, like the others in the journal, and like so many that Mr. Lockwell had posed to her when Ivy was a girl. As she read the words they seemed to tease her, tempting her with a secret truth even as they remained just beyond understanding. She set her fingers against her temples and leaned over the paper, concentrating on the words, trying to see through them to the real meaning beyond.

"I know you can solve it, Ivoleyn." She heard the familiar sound of her father's voice.

"But I don't see the answer," she murmured in reply, as she had so many times as a girl.

"It's right there before you," Mr. Lockwell said. "Remember, the most obvious meaning is not the only one. You must search for other meanings, ones that lie beneath the surface. Look deeper, and you will see them. . . ."

And Ivy's eyes grew wide. Yes, she did see the deeper meaning. And she realized that, just like Mr. Fintaur, she had been close to Mr. Larken on a prior occasion without even realizing it.

"Well done, Ivoleyn," her father said, as he had so many times before.

And the clock on the mantel let out a chime.

With a gasp, Ivy turned to look at the old rosewood clock. She half-expected to see her father standing behind her, encouraging her to solve the cipher as he had so many times when she was young. Only he was not there.

But of course he wasn't. He was still at Madstone's. Nor had he spoken to her like that since she was twelve years old, before he lost his mind while binding the protections around the Eye of Ran-Yahgren. She had simply recalled the sound of his voice, and the things he used to say while she was solving a puzzle, that was all.

Except it hadn't seemed like her father's voice had been a memory in her mind. It was as if she had really heard his voice, here in the room, just like the chiming of the clock.

No, that was impossible. Just as it was impossible the clock had chimed. It was not the top of the hour, and it was past the start of the third farthing of the day. All the same, Ivy went to the fireplace, looking at the old clock on the mantel. She could hear the soft whir of its inner workings, and a steady ticktock as it kept time.

Carefully, Ivy turned the clock around, then she opened the door in the back. There was a small brass plaque on the inside of the door, but it was too tarnished to read what was etched upon it. She breathed on the plaque, and polished it with the edge of her sleeve. Then she turned the clock so that the brass plate caught the light coming through the window.

D. F. Larken, Clockmaker, read the fine words engraved on the plaque. *No. 18 Coronet St., Invarel.*

Ivy stared, dumbfounded. Now that she understood the riddle, it was obvious. She had indeed found Larken in good time—inside the beautiful old clock. And the references to the crown, and the number of scoldings he had given, were obvious as well. A coronet was a type of crown, and a dozen and a half was the same number as eighteen.

A shroud of riddle obscured by magick and shut in a locked Wyrdwood box—why had her father gone to such lengths to conceal the knowledge in the journal? What was this keystone?

She didn't know, but she was going to find out.

Carefully, Ivy shut the door on the back of the clock. There was at least one thing she understood now, and that was how the rosewood clock was able to keep time even when the almanacs no longer could. After all, the mechanics of Mr. Lockwell's celestial sphere had been able to accommodate the addition of the twelfth planet. Why shouldn't a clock made by Mr. Larken be able to do the same?

A thrill came over Ivy. Perhaps she would go see not only Mr. Fintaur that afternoon, but Mr. Larken as well. After all, she knew where he was. She had been to No. 18 Coronet Street once before, when she brought in the old rosewood clock, thinking it broken. Only this time, she would not settle for speaking with an apprentice. She would speak to the master clockmaker himself.

An excitement rose within Ivy at the idea of speaking with her father's old compatriots. They would know why the keystone was important; they would understand what it was her father wanted them to do. And with her duty in the matter discharged, she could have no reservations about leaving the city. Her heart quickening, Ivy turned from the fireplace.

And halted.

The tall silhouette of a man stood outside one of the library windows. Despite the warmth of the day, he was dressed as always in heavy, frilled garb of black.

It is too late, he said, and this time the words indeed sounded in Ivy's mind. *You have delayed too long. He has returned.*

She could not move, could not breathe.

"What do you mean?" she said, or at least, she tried to. "Who has returned?"

Look.

As if compelled by a will not her own, her head bent and her gaze went to the low table by the sofa. Despite the fact that she had banished them from the house—and the fact that she was certain there had not been one there a short while ago—a broadsheet lay open on the table. Like a puppet, impelled to movement by another's thoughts and actions, she moved toward the table, then looked downward.

BOOKSHOP PROPRIETOR FOUND MURDERED, read the headline on the open page. *Perpetrator Unknown in Violent Slaying Near Greenly Circle.*

A coldness came over Ivy, and at last she was able to make a sound: a low moan. Suddenly freed of the force that bound her, she took a lurching step forward, nearly falling onto the table before catching herself. She drew in a shuddering breath, then looked up.

There was nothing outside the window save the little chestnut and hawthorn trees in the garden.

A QUARTER HOUR LATER, Ivy sat inside a hack cab as it jostled through the streets of the Old City. She had not asked Mrs. Seenly to have Lawden ready the cabriolet; there had been no time. Instead she had dashed through the front gate onto Durrow Street, and had waved down the first available carriage for hire.

It was only as the hack cab started into motion that she realized she had rushed out of the house without telling anyone what had happened or where she was going. Not her sisters or Mrs. Seenly. Not even Mr. Quent, who had still been shut in his study. After seeing the man in the black mask, her mind had been consumed

by a singular thought: she must warn Mr. Larken that he was in
dire peril.

That was, if he had not already met the same fate as Mr. Fintaur.

For a moment she considered returning to the house to tell Mr.
Quent what had happened. But by then the hack cab was already
proceeding down the street at a full clip. Ivy had waited too long
to return to Mr. Fintaur's shop, and now she would never have an
opportunity to talk to him. She could not risk the same occurring
with Mr. Larken.

As the carriage continued along, Ivy looked down at the broadsheet on her lap, for she had brought it with her. According to the
story, the incident at the bookshop off Greenly Circle had occurred
the prior lumenal, and several gruesome details were given.

> *great quantity of blood . . . the proprietor was discovered on the*
> *floor of . . . but with no sign that the lock on the door had been*
> *forced . . . and a report, unconfirmed, that the flesh of his chest had*
> *been flayed apart and dressed in the most careful fashion, like the*
> *carcass of a deer after it is shot. . . .*

Ivy folded up the broadsheet, unable to read anymore.

"Poor Mr. Fintaur," she whispered, and her eyes stung with
tears. How she would have liked to talk to him, to come to know
him, and to ask him about his memories of her father. Now she
never would. Someone had made certain of that. But who had
done this thing?

Except she already knew the answer to that.

He has returned, the man in black had said. But the magician
Mr. Gambrel had been locked beyond the door Tyberion, forever
trapped inside the way station on a moon circling the planet Dalatair. There was only one other man Ivy knew of who would resort
to such awful means to gain Mr. Fintaur's fragment of the keystone.

And Torland was not nearly so far away as Dalatair's moons.

The hack cab came to a sudden halt with a clatter of hooves. A moment later the driver was at the door.

"I'm sorry, ma'am, but there's some commotion blocking the street. Would you like me to go around by another way?"

A fear gripped Ivy. She fumbled with the door, thrusting it open, and was out and down to the street before the driver could so much as move to help her.

"Are you well, ma'am?"

With numb fingers, she found a few coins in the pocket of her gown and pushed them into the man's hand. Then, without waiting for a reply, she hurried past him down Coronet Street. The driver was right; there was indeed some sort of disturbance. Carriages and wagons were all at a standstill, and people were pressing forward between them, as if trying to get a view of something.

Ivy wormed her way among the people, relying on her diminutive size when her strength was not enough to force her way through a gap. Abruptly she burst through the front edge of the crowd—and she could not clamp a hand to her mouth quickly enough to stifle a choking cry.

Three soldiers in blue coats stood in front of the open door of a shop. With their stern looks, as well as the rifles fitted with bayonets which they gripped, the redcrests had managed to keep a large half circle before the shop free of onlookers. Behind them, dozens of clocks kept time in the shop's window, pendulums swinging and hands turning. The number 18 was chiseled into the stone above the door.

The soldiers made an effort to stand close to one another, blocking the crowd's view of the doorway. But they could not conceal the stream of crimson that had flooded over the threshold to cascade down the front steps. Then another soldier emerged from the shop, his face gray. As the other men parted to let him pass, Ivy caught a fleeting glimpse through the doorway. A form lay upon the floor, limbs splayed out at unnatural angles like the legs of an insect pinned inside a naturalist's shadow box.

"Good God!" someone shouted. "They opened him up and gutted him like a pig!"

Gasps and cries rose from the crowd. The soldiers returned to their positions, closing off the view through the doorway. It didn't matter; Ivy had seen more than enough.

A sickness rose up in her, and a dizziness swam inside her head. People were continuing to push their way forward to gain a look at the scene, and she ceased resisting their pressure. Ivy fell back, and in moments found herself on the ragged edge of the throng. She turned around, wondering if the driver of the hack cab had waited for her. As she did, a man in a dark coat caught her eye.

It was not the driver.

He was walking down Coronet Street, away from the clock-maker's shop: a tall, gaunt man dressed in a charcoal-colored suit, a broad-brimmed hat on his head. As he walked, he cast a furtive glance over his shoulder, back in the direction of the shop, and suddenly Ivy felt as if it were her own blood draining into the street. For in that moment she saw the man's face beneath the brim of the hat. It was long and sallow, with narrow eyes set deep above a sharp blade of a nose. Then he turned and hastened away down the street, passing around a corner.

With that, Mr. Bennick was lost from view.

For a moment, Ivy was gripped by a paralysis. She felt she should run after him in pursuit, or shout out for the soldiers. Only it was no use; he was gone. Nor could it have done any good. It was not as if Mr. Bennick would have kept a bloodied knife about him or any such obvious evidence of his crime. He was far too clever for that. Calling for the redcrests was more likely to hinder her than it was *him*.

Besides, she was too late; he had gotten what he had come for, and now he was gone.

Only he had not gotten everything he wanted yet, had he? There were two more fragments of the keystone in the city—presuming Mr. Mundy had not already met a similar fate as Mr.

Fintaur and Mr. Larken. The man in the mask had been right; she had indeed delayed too long. Only she had never imagined Mr. Bennick would dare to show himself again, not after the way he had been defeated in his attempt to gain the Eye of Ran-Yahgren.

But she should have known the temptation of power would be too great, that it would eventually induce him to return. Mr. Bennick had been deprived of his magick. How this had been done, she did not know. She had thought it was his own order of magicians that had taken his power from him, though Mr. Gambrel had claimed that was not the case.

Well, no matter how it had happened, Ivy had no doubt that he sought a way to gain his power back. Could this keystone be part of that plan? Whatever the keystone was, it was clear he wanted all the pieces for himself.

Ivy turned around, searching, but there was no sign of another hack cab for hire. Yet perhaps a carriage was not the quickest way to where she needed to go next. Across the street, between two buildings, was the start of a stairway. If she recalled correctly, that was Market Stair, which led down from Coronet Street to Greenly Circle.

Without stopping to consider the wisdom of trying to beat a murderer to what might be his next destination, Ivy crossed the street and started down the stone steps. The narrow stair twisted back and forth as it descended among buildings that leaned back into the steep incline. More than once, in her haste, she nearly lost her footing on the steps, which were worn smooth from centuries of passing feet.

At last the stair let out into a dim lane. To the left, the lane opened up into a large space filled with horses, people, and market stalls. But it was not to Greenly Circle that she needed to go. Instead, she turned to the right, moving farther down the grimy lane.

Ivy was not certain she knew how to find it coming from this direction. A fear of more mundane origin began to rise in her—that even by daylight it was not prudent for a woman to be wandering along these dim, labyrinthine streets alone. Then, just

when she was thinking she should go back toward the bustle of
Greenly Circle, she saw a sign hanging above a door a short way
ahead. The silver eye painted on the sign seemed to shimmer in
the gloom, almost as if it were winking at her.

Quickly, she closed the last distance to Mr. Mundy's shop. Like
the prior time she was here, the door was shut and the windows
to either side were so hazed with dust that she could not see
through them. Nor did any light shine from within. Perhaps Mr.
Mundy had feared Mr. Bennick was going to return, and so had
fled. Perhaps he was long gone from the city.

Or perhaps the shop was dark because Mr. Bennick had already been here.

Ivy realized she was trembling. She took a breath to steady
herself, bracing for what she might see. Gripping the cold handle
of the door, she pushed—

—and the door swung inward, moving so rapidly that the handle was violently ripped out of her grasp.

"Oh!" she cried out, recoiling back a step.

"Ah!" exclaimed the small, toadish man on the other side of the
threshold as he did the same.

It took both of them a moment to recover from their shock, but
Ivy was a bit swifter.

"Mr. Mundy!" she gasped. "I've come to warn you. I believe
you are in grave danger."

Even as she said this, she cast a furtive glance over her shoulder, fearing the sight of a tall, gaunt figure striding toward them
down the lane.

"Who are you?" Mundy said, peering at her with his bulbous
eyes, the one more prominent than the other. "Wait now, I know
you. You've been in my shop before. You're Lockwell's child—the
foundling he took in."

This astonished Ivy. Those times she had been to Mr. Mundy's
shop, she had not thought he had known her. Only he had. He
must have known what it was she was up to at the time but had
said nothing. Yet why?

There was no time to worry about that now.

"You must go, Mr. Mundy," she said. "You must leave the city at once."

He scowled, and his jowls puffed up. "And what do you think I was doing before you decided to block my way? I knew he would come back. 'Mark my words,' I told Fintaur and Larken. 'I don't care how he was banished, you'll not keep the likes of him away.' Both of them scoffed at me. They said it was impossible now." He shook his head. "But I was right. Just as I feared, he has returned."

"Yes, I know," Ivy said breathlessly. "I saw him, just now."

Mr. Mundy let out a croaking sound, and he looked past her, his face going mushroom pale and his eyes bulging even farther from their sockets. "You saw him? Blood of the Magnons, then he is near."

"Yes," Ivy said. "He was coming from Mr. Larken's shop. And I fear that Mr. Larken is . . ."

"Murdered?" Mundy finished, looking up at her.

Ivy forced herself to swallow, then nodded.

With a shaking hand, Mundy wiped a dank strand of black hair from his brow. "After what happened to Fintaur yesterday, I thought he would have the sense to stay away from his shop. But Larken was ever the punctual follower of routines. I suppose he didn't even think about what he was doing, but rather followed his usual scheme like clockwork. Damn the old fool."

"But you returned to your shop as well," Ivy said. "You were gone when last I came here. I knocked, but you didn't answer. Only now you've come back."

He let out a gurgling laugh. "What makes you think I was gone?"

"You mean you were here that day?" Ivy gasped, and now she supposed it was her own eyes that were bulging in their sockets. "You were here, but you hid from me?"

"Don't be so presumptuous. I wasn't hiding from *you* in particular. I was hiding from everyone. I wanted everyone to think I'd left the city. Fintaur was the only one who knew I was still here. And if he and Larken had been wise, they would have done the same."

"But now you are leaving."

"Yes, and I won't be coming back."

With that he stepped onto the street, shutting and locking the door behind him.

"Wait," Ivy said, reaching for him. But when he glared at her, she withdrew her hand. "Why did he kill Mr. Fintaur and Mr. Larken? Was it for their pieces of the keystone?"

His squinted at her. "How do you know about that?"

"From my father."

"Lockwell! You mean he's spoken to you about that?"

Ivy shook her head. "No, I read it in his . . . that is, in something he left for me years ago. I'm sure you know that he has been deprived of his intellect."

"Yes, yes," he said, waving a hand dismissively. "I know all that. You needn't educate me about history that I witnessed myself. I was there when Lockwell forfeited his mind to strengthen the binding on the—" Abruptly, he clamped his jaw shut.

"On the Eye of Ran-Yahgren," Ivy said.

He raised an eyebrow. "Oh, you know about *that*, do you? Very well, then, yes—he gave up his intellect to bind it against the others."

Ivy sighed. "I know. His mind is lost."

"Lost?" He let out a snort. "Nonsense, Lockwell's mind is not lost. On the contrary, we all know precisely where it is located."

Ivy stared at the little man, trying to comprehend what he had said. "But have you not seen him since then? Surely you have seen for yourself how . . . that my father does not possess his faculties."

"Of course he doesn't!" Mundy said with some amount of spittle. "As we have discussed, he gave up his mind to strengthen the bindings on his old house, to channel and direct the house's innate magicks. And there his mind remains in residence, functioning exactly as he intended."

"It remains there?" Ivy was forced to reach out and press a hand to the wall to keep from stumbling. "You mean his intellect still resides in the house on Durrow Street?"

"Yes, just as it has ever since he worked the enchantment. And might I say, *your* intellect is not particularly strong if you have only just realized it."

For a moment, all the fear and dread of the last hour vanished, and a wonder filled Ivy. It wasn't just her father's magick that was in the house. Rather, *he* was there, dwelling with them, protecting them . . .

. . . speaking to them?

Know that though I am not with you in body, he had written in his journal, *my spirit resides with you there at my house on Durrow Street.*

He had told her the truth himself, only she had not understood! And so had Rose. Ivy had scolded Rose for claiming to speak with their father. But Ivy had been wrong to do so. She knew Rose was sensitive to emanations of magick and other energies. What else could explain the way she claimed to see light around certain people? Besides, had not Ivy heard Mr. Lockwell's voice herself?

Yes, she had. And she would apologize to Rose, and ask her about what their father had said to her. Perhaps he was trying to tell them something. Perhaps he was trying to explain how—

"How to reunite his mind and his body," Ivy said aloud.

Mr. Mundy frowned. "What's that? Reunite Lockwell's mind and body?" He rubbed his beard-stubbled jowls. "Oh, it's possible, of course. Indeed, it would be fairly elementary. You would need to bring him to the location where his mind resides, remove the binding upon the house, and then work it anew upon his physical being."

"Then you mean you can do it?" Ivy gasped. "You can restore my father's mind to him?"

"Of course not!" Mundy snapped. "Or rather, I might be able to do so, though I am not the magician I was. But either way, I shall not. Once he told us what he intended to do, Lockwell made us all swear an oath upon many runes that we would never seek to undo it. For if we did, then the Eye would be unguarded, and his efforts would be for naught."

"Please," she said, her joy turning to anguish. "If you will not do it, can you at the least tell me how?"

"Tell you how?" he said, then made a gurgling noise deep in his throat that was not quite a laugh. "I can think of no greater waste of time than trying to explain a matter of magick to a woman. And time is something I have none of at the moment. I have already tarried too long. Good-bye!"

Ivy was too astonished to move or speak as the toadish little man moved past her at a quick waddle.

"And you'd best be careful," he called over his shoulder. "Now that he's back, he'll come for Lockwell's piece of the keystone as well."

Then he turned a corner, and Mr. Mundy was gone.

For some time, Ivy could only stare down the narrow street. So difficult was it to comprehend all that had occurred in such a short span of time, that she hardly had any thought at all. Her mind was as dim and empty as the lane before her, as if she was the one bereft of intellect.

Then, all at once, a jolt of fear started the wheels and cogs in her head turning again.

He'll come for Lockwell's piece. . . .

Ivy did not know where her father had concealed his fragment of the keystone. But it had to be hidden somewhere in the house on Durrow Street. Which meant *he* might already be there to fetch it. A horror came over Ivy as she pictured a scene of Lily answering a knock at the front door, and opening it to reveal Mr. Bennick on the other side. Just like Mr. Mundy, she had tarried too long.

Ivy turned and dashed down the lane. She passed by the foot of Market Stair. It would take too long to climb back up, and she was more likely to find a carriage for hire in Greenly Circle.

Or at least, so she had thought. But as she left the mouth of the lane, she found the broad expanse of Greenly Circle all in upheaval. Men were running to and fro, shouting as they went. Merchants were shutting up their stalls even as people pressed forward, trying to seize food and goods from them—though whether to buy these things or simply to take them, Ivy could hardly tell. Hooves clattered and horses let out shrill neighs as men whipped them, trying to maneuver them through the confusion.

It was as if everything had gone suddenly mad—as if all those polite rules which allowed strangers to cooperate and dwell in harmony among one another had abruptly been suspended, and now it was each for their own. She looked up and saw the dim spot of the red planet, like a blemish of disease upon the sky. Was this some new effect of its approach? Had it disrupted the workings of society even as it had the mechanics of the heavens?

"He's landed!" a man shouted. "The Hawk has landed!"

A horse galloped past, its hooves striking sparks from the cobbles as it passed mere inches from her. A new fear came upon Ivy, and it had nothing to do with magicians or planets. Rather, she dreaded she would be trampled by a carriage or crushed against a wall by a crowd of people.

At random, she ducked down another lane to escape the tumult. A few men came running from the opposite direction, but they paid her no heed. One of them was letting out loud whoops, like an aboriginal from the New Lands, and he waved a green handkerchief as he ran past.

Ivy picked up the hem of her dress and ran herself. She began to think that perhaps she knew what was happening, that this commotion had nothing to do with the red planet, and everything to do with a green banner. If she was right, then it was more urgent than ever that she return to the house. Making her best guess at the direction to go, for she had little knowledge of these streets, she turned to the right, then made a left down a curving lane, followed by another right.

Her sense of direction was better than she had presumed, or perhaps she was simply lucky. Either way, she now found herself on Durrow Street, at a point just east of Béanore's Fountain. She looked back and saw more people milling about, and there was a column of smoke rising from the vicinity of the fountain.

A trio of redcrests marched past her at double time, heading in that direction. Ivy recalled what had happened the last time a band of soldiers had confronted a group of young men. She did not want to be near if another such skirmish occurred.

She kept moving along Durrow Street, though this was not easily done. People, horses, and carriages were going every way imaginable—though it seemed a larger number were going in the opposite direction she was, toward Greenly Circle.

Just ahead, several young men were marching along the street, linked arm in arm and shouting a slogan she could not make out amid all the noise. Something about *crown* or *down,* or perhaps it was both. With no way to get past them, Ivy tried to cross the street to be out of their path. Only before she could get halfway across, she was brought up short by a soldier that cantered by on horse. Ivy veered away to avoid being trampled, only she lost her balance as she did, lurching into the middle of the street. She looked up, and her eyes went wide. A black cabriolet bore down on her at full speed. There was nowhere to turn, and no time to get out of the carriage's path.

Ivy shut her eyes and screamed.

The rattle of wheels and the clatter of hooves was so loud that, even when it ceased, Ivy could hardly hear for the way her ears rang. Only after a moment did she realize that she had not been crushed beneath the carriage, and that someone was shouting—shouting at *her.*

"Mrs. Quent!" a man's voice called out. "Mrs. Quent, over here—you must hurry!"

Ivy opened her eyes, then gasped. The cabriolet had come to a halt just before her, the horse still stamping and straining at the bit. A calash top was drawn over the carriage, but a man leaned out the side and was gesturing to her. She saw a spark of blue on his hand.

"Mr. Rafferdy!" she cried out in great relief.

Then, heeding nothing else around her, she dashed forward to the cabriolet. Mr. Rafferdy leaped out and helped her into the vehicle. Quickly he followed after, then shut the door and cracked a whip.

It seemed impossible they should be able to navigate through the chaos, but the cabriolet was small and nimble, and Mr. Rafferdy's driving was expert. With clucks and calls and precise flicks of the reins, he directed the horse through every available gap and opening.

Once they were a little farther from the fountain, the throngs on the street began to thin and dwindle. A short ways more, and Durrow Street was all but empty of people, as if everyone who was inclined to go somewhere already had—and everyone else was shut indoors.

"Mrs. Quent, are you well?" Mr. Rafferdy said as soon as driving did not require his full attention. She was not immediately able to answer, and he gave her a concerned look. "Have you been hurt?"

"No," she managed to say. "But, Mr. Rafferdy, how did you find me? And what is happening in the city?"

Except she already knew. Hawks coming to land, and crowns and green banners.

"I was driving from my abode in Warwent Square to your house," he said, his expression grim. "Only then all this madness broke out, and I got caught in the snarl on the street."

"It's Huntley Morden," she said, hardly believing the words as she spoke them. It seemed no less a fairy tale come to life than seeing the Wyrdwood rise up. "His ships have landed, haven't they?"

He nodded. "The news has just come out of the West Country. A soldier brought me a message from the Citadel. I think messages were sent to all the members of the Hall of Magnates. But if it was their intention to give the lords a head start, then it is not much of one, for it didn't take long for word to get out to the public at large. As you have seen firsthand."

His words were astonishing, yet it struck her that there was something more, something that he had not told her.

"But is that why you were driving to my house?" she said. "To tell us about Huntley Morden? I would have thought, if a soldier was dispatched to inform you, one would be similarly sent to my husband with the news."

Mr. Rafferdy's expression became, if possible, even more somber. His hands were tight upon the reins. "No, I don't believe it is for the purpose of bringing news that soldiers will be dispatched to your house."

A moment ago she had felt relief in the safety of the cabriolet. Now fear seized her again, and a feeling came over her that they were not driving away from danger, but rather toward it.

"What is it, Mr. Rafferdy?" She reached over and gripped his arm. "Please, tell me why you were coming to my house!"

"I thought we would have more time," he said, his voice marked by anguish. "Or at least, I hoped we would. I and the other members of my order have just recently learned that Lord Valhaine has been anticipating this moment—that he has long been laying preparations in its advance."

Ivy shook her head. "Lord Valhaine? What preparations do you mean—those to fight a war against Huntley Morden?"

"Yes, but more than that. He means to use this moment to his great advantage."

"What advantage?"

Mr. Rafferdy turned to look at her, his face pale. "It is not for fear of Princess Layle's safety that Valhaine has refused to allow her coronation to proceed. Rather, he will use Huntley Morden's landing upon the shores of Altania as an excuse to shut her away, claiming a woman cannot be called upon to rule in a time of war. He will attempt to seize rule for himself—and I fear there may be nothing that can be done to stop him."

Ivy could scarcely believe what she had just heard. She would have thought it an example of Mr. Rafferdy's peculiar wit, if his expression was not so grim. "But that can only be the most heinous crime. Surely others will prevent him from doing such a thing!"

He shook his head. "No, they won't. You see, it won't be a crime—not if he can have the laws of the nation changed in order to support it. What's more, he will move swiftly against anyone in a position of trust or authority who he suspects might provide any opposition to his plan. Indeed, he moves so already."

Even as he said this, Ivy understood why Mr. Rafferdy had been driving to Durrow Street.

"My husband," she said, but could speak no more.

"I fear so," Rafferdy said. "Lord Valhaine intends to dismantle the Inquiry. In his view—or in the view of the magicians who advise him, for I don't believe there is any difference—the Wyrdwood is a thing that can only aid the rebels. That's why he's been seeking to eliminate it, but the Inquiry has stood against him up until now."

Ivy gripped the edge of the seat. She had believed, despite the disagreements between the Gray Conclave and the Inquiry, that Lord Valhaine trusted her husband, and that was why he had nominated Mr. Quent to be lord inquirer. Only it was the opposite! Valhaine had known exactly what would occur when her husband was made to testify before Assembly. Mr. Quent had been cast not as a hero to the nation, but as a traitor.

And Valhaine would make an example of him.

"Please, Mr. Rafferdy," she said, though it was hard to speak for the way her throat was constricted. "Drive quickly."

Mr. Rafferdy did so, cracking the whip, and the cabriolet careened along Durrow Street. Any other time, Ivy would have been in mortal fear of the speed at which they went, but now she leaned forward on the bench, as if she could urge the carriage to go faster yet.

It seemed an agonizing length of time, but in fact it was just minutes later when Mr. Rafferdy brought the carriage to a halt before the front gate of the house. The street was devoid of people, and the garden beyond appeared tranquil. A hope rose within Ivy. The news about Huntley Morden had only just reached the city. Lord Valhaine would move swiftly, no doubt, but it would take him some time to act. And because of Mr. Rafferdy's most courageous and loyal aid, they had been warned of the Black Dog's true intent. She and Mr. Quent would depart the city at once, her sisters and father with them; they would return to the country.

Ivy was out of the carriage before Mr. Rafferdy could come around to assist her. She pushed through the gate and ran up the front steps. Yes, they would go far from the city, and far from the Gray Conclave. They would leave at once, and would stop to pack nothing. It did not matter what they left behind. They would have one another, and that was all they needed. Her heart racing, she burst through the door of the house.

Her footsteps echoed in the vast emptiness of the front hall, a noise so jarring it caused her to stop. Then another noise registered upon her ears: the sound of sobbing.

Ivy turned. Near the open door of Mr. Quent's study, Rose and Lily sat together on a sofa. They were holding on to one another, while Mrs. Seenly stood a few paces away. Lily's face was white, her brown eyes unblinking, while Rose wept openly and bitterly.

Slowly, Ivy approached her sisters. Dimly, she was aware that Mr. Rafferdy came with her, though it was hard to really see anything. It seemed so dark in the house, and everything had a vague and blurred appearance, as if seen through a mist.

At last she reached the sofa where her sisters sat. Ivy looked at Mrs. Seenly, but the housekeeper appeared stricken and did not speak. Beyond her, through the open door of the study, Ivy saw loose sheafs of papers scattered all around. The chair by the table was tipped over, and a bottle of ink had fallen to the floor.

"Lily," Ivy said, her voice low, "what has happened?"

Her youngest sister only shook her head.

"Lily," Ivy said, more sternly now, "where is Mr. Quent?"

It was Rose who answered. "The soldiers took him!" she blurted between sobs. "They took him away, just like Father!"

Then Lily was weeping, too, holding on to Rose, while Mrs. Seenly slumped and covered her face with her hands. The tiled floor seemed to ripple and flow, as if the mosaic was not merely a picture of a seascape, but rather surged under the influence of a tide. It was only as she felt Mr. Rafferdy catch her that Ivy understood she was in fact falling.

He was able to ease her to the floor as all strength ebbed from her. It seemed he was saying something, but Ivy could not hear what it was, and she could not raise her head to look at him. Instead, her gaze went through the open door of the study, to the fallen ink bottle. The ink had gushed out of it in a black flood.

Only in the dimness, to Ivy, it looked like blood.

BOOK TWO

The White Thorn

CHAPTER EIGHTEEN

"I AM MUCH RELIEVED that you are leaving the city for Farland Park, your ladyship," Rafferdy said.

On the sofa, Lady Marsdel snapped her fan shut so suddenly that the little dog curled up beside her gave a yip. "I have no doubt you are relieved, Mr. Rafferdy," she said, looking up at him through narrowed eyes. "Indeed, I am sure you are quite pleased to be excused from ever presenting yourself for dinner, or meeting your other obligations to this household."

"But Mr. Rafferdy can come visit us in Farland Park, of course," Lord Baydon said, his voice faint but still retaining its characteristic cheerfulness. "It is not so very far from Asterlane, after all."

Rafferdy turned toward Lady Marsdel's brother. He sat in a chair by a sunny window in the parlor, wrapped in a woolen blanket. Given the thickness and bulk of the blanket, it might have been easy to think the elder lord was as plump as ever. But the hollowness of his cheeks, and the sharpness of his brow and jaw, belied the illusion.

"I'm afraid I won't be going to Asterlane, your lordship," Rafferdy said. "At least, not any time soon."

Lord Baydon's gray mustache drooped in a frown, and a trembling hand emerged from folds of wool. "But I don't see why not. I suppose Assembly has much business to discuss, what with all the bother out west. But surely they can make do without a lord or two. After all, I shall not be there."

Rafferdy exchanged a look with Lady Marsdel. Her expression was grave now. She spread her fan open again; it was decorated in the latest motif, with a stylized pattern suggesting the tangled branches of a tree.

"It is because you are going that I must not," Rafferdy said, turning back toward Lord Baydon. "After all, we cannot deprive Assembly of both of its very finest lords."

Lord Baydon let out a wheezing laugh. "I suppose we can't at that. They need at least one clever head present. But perhaps I should direct my son to remain in the city so he can occupy my seat. He is not as clever as you or I, Mr. Rafferdy, but he is very adamant in his opinions, and I think that should count for something."

Across the parlor, Mr. Baydon lowered his broadsheet to reveal a frowning countenance. He looked ready to make a reply to his father's statement, but Lady Marsdel spoke first.

"No, Mr. Baydon is coming with us," she said with a tone of finality. "We must have a man at the house in Farland Park—that is, one who is not infirm. I will not have us be unprotected."

Mrs. Baydon raised an eyebrow as she regarded her husband. "You do know how to shoot a pistol?"

"Of course I know how to shoot a pistol!" Mr. Baydon said indignantly.

His wife laid a hand on his arm. "I do not doubt your capabilities, darling. Like her ladyship, I am quite content to depend on your protections while we are in the country."

Mr. Baydon gave a satisfied nod, as if sufficiently vindicated, and raised his broadsheet again.

"It's just that I have not observed you to have the steadiest hand," Mrs. Baydon said, and sipped her tea.

There was an audible groan from behind the broadsheet, but no other reply followed, and this time the newspaper remained in place.

While the other occupants of the parlor took in either news, tea, or sun, Mr. Rafferdy went to Lady Marsdel and sat on the sofa next to her. He eyed the little white dog situated between them warily. Only then, to his surprise, the dog rose, turned around, and laid back down with his head resting upon Rafferdy's thigh.

"I am astonished," he said. "I expect to be nipped, and instead receive affection."

"As is your habit, Mr. Rafferdy," Lady Marsdel said. "Ever you retreat from others rather than risk discovering they hold you in poor esteem. Yet by that, you also fail to learn how often you are adored. When a man chooses to risk himself, Mr. Rafferdy, he may indeed have his fingers nipped. But he may reap great rewards as well."

The little dog looked up at him with warm brown eyes. Rafferdy found himself smiling, and he scratched the dog's head, an act resulting in much tail wagging.

"I believe you are right, your ladyship," he said.

"Of course I am, Mr. Rafferdy. I am older and wiser than you, and you must always take my advice." She let out a sigh. "My brother's words, however, you should not heed."

Rafferdy's smile faded, though he did not cease petting the dog.

"Lord Baydon's mind wanders much of late," Lady Marsdel went on, her voice low now, and only for him. "He has heard the news of Sir Quent, but he fails to grasp the meaning of it, and what it bodes for Lady Quent. He cannot see why we do not all go to the country together."

Rafferdy only nodded. There was no need to speak, for Lady Marsdel knew what Rafferdy did—that if he were to leave the city, and go to Asterlane or Farland Park, Mrs. Quent and her sisters would be utterly abandoned. It was to her ladyship's great credit that she had refused to break off association with Mrs. Quent, though most others surely would.

"The Marsdels do not forsake their people in times of need" was all Lady Marsdel had said on the matter the day the news arrived at Fairhall Street, and that was that.

Rafferdy cast a glance back to Lord Baydon, who now dozed in his chair by the window. "What do the doctors say about him?" he said softly, turning back toward Lady Marsdel.

The lines beside her mouth deepened. "Nothing of use. They

say his condition worsens, as if we cannot all observe that for our-selves. I hope the air at Farland Park will benefit him, and improve his health. But then, I hoped the same for Lord Marsdel years ago."

The dog let out a little whine as Rafferdy withdrew his hand and sat up straighter. "What do you mean?"

"The malady that afflicts him is very like that which took my husband years ago."

This statement shocked Rafferdy. The progression of Lord Bay-don's illness indeed seemed familiar. Only it was not Lady Mars-del's late husband who came to mind. Rather, it was his own father. It had been just like this for Lord Rafferdy. He had begun to waste away, growing ever weaker and more gaunt despite all the efforts of his physicians.

And then death came.

The dog squirmed and gave another little whine. Rafferdy re-sumed petting its head.

"Is it still your plan to leave tomorrow?" he said. "I hope you will not delay. I have heard reports that Huntley Morden's forces are already marching eastward from Torland. Though I am sure it is impossible that his army would ever reach Invarel."

"Nothing is impossible, Mr. Rafferdy. Besides, the war need not reach the city for it to have an effect upon us, or to deprive us of one of our own. I fear that if things begin to go ill, an order of conscription will come down from the Citadel, compelling all able young men to join the army in defense of Altania." Her gaze trav-eled across the parlor, toward where Mr. and Mrs. Baydon sat. "Do keep this between us, Mr. Rafferdy, but while I love my nephew, I do not think he is very well suited for making war."

Rafferdy could not help a grim laugh. "I wonder who can really be suited for such a thing?"

Lady Marsdel turned her gaze on him now. "I believe you would do very well as an officer, Mr. Rafferdy. You lack discipline, of course, which would be a hindrance. But my brother is right— you are clever. And more importantly, you have an exceedingly high opinion of your own worth, and from this a strong sense of self-preservation naturally follows. There can be no characteristics more suitable for a military man, I think."

Rafferdy would have thought he was the victim of wry mockery, were her expression not so solemn.

"What of bravery?" he said. "And loyalty to one's companions? Are those not the most important characteristics for a soldier to possess?"

"I believe you demonstrated a more than ample supply of those particular qualities, Mr. Rafferdy, when you made it clear you would not abandon Lady Quent."

For a moment, Rafferdy could only stare. "You have not abandoned her either," he said at last.

"No, but I am a woman, Mr. Rafferdy. And even were I younger, I could not join you on the battlefield no matter what qualities I possessed. A woman must fight in her own manner."

Rafferdy found himself thinking of how Mrs. Quent had prevented the magicians of her father's order from gaining the Eye of Ran-Yahgren, or how she had compelled the trees to carry her and Rafferdy through the Evengrove. Yes, a woman could be as brave as a man, or even braver still. And there were other ways to fight than with a rifle and bayonet.

"I will do all I can to protect my own, Mr. Rafferdy," Lady Marsdel went on. "I know you will do the same. Now, return my dog to me, for I will require him in Farland Park."

Rafferdy realized that the dog had crawled entirely onto his lap and curled up. "I have no doubt he is both loyal and brave," he said, "and will snap at the shin of any rebel that might try to approach you."

Gently, he handed the little creature back to its owner. Then he started to rise from the sofa. Only before he could, Lady Marsdel leaned over to give his cheek a firm kiss.

"We shall miss you very much, Mr. Rafferdy. I hope we will not be parted for long."

He found he could only nod. Once again, Rafferdy had received warm affection when he had expected something colder and sterner. Perhaps, he thought, he should cease being so astonished.

It was time for Rafferdy to depart. The denizens of Lady Marsdel's household needed to make their final preparations for the trip to Farland Park in the east. And Rafferdy had his own tasks to see to.

He bowed to Lady Marsdel and wished her farewell, then went to say good-bye to the others.

"I trust you will work in Assembly to do what is best for the nation," Mr. Baydon said, rising to his feet.

And what was best for the nation? No doubt Mr. Baydon had firm ideas on this matter. But for his part, Rafferdy did not know anymore. There was only one thing he was certain of—that what Assembly was about to do was for anything but the good of Altania.

All he said was "I will, sir." And he shook Mr. Baydon's hand.

"Do not worry after us, Mr. Rafferdy," Mrs. Baydon said. "We will want greatly for your company, but will otherwise be well. But you must take good care of yourself while we are gone. And of Lady Quent."

He nodded. "Be assured I will try my best."

"I know you will," she said, and then her blue eyes became very bright. "Oh, Mr. Rafferdy, I'm so frightened for her. For all of us."

And she threw her arms around him, holding him tightly. Her husband gave her a startled look, but Rafferdy could not say he was surprised by this reaction. Mrs. Quent was very dear to her.

"Don't worry, Mrs. Baydon," he said quietly in her ear and patted her shoulder. "I cannot yet see how all the pieces will fit, but as you know, every puzzle works out in the end."

She stepped back from him, and though there were tears in her eyes, she smiled up at him. "You're right, of course. They always do."

He kissed her hand, and she his cheek. After that, there was only one more farewell to make. While the others busied themselves with plans for tomorrow's departure, Rafferdy went to the chair by the window.

"Oh, good morning, Mr. Rafferdy," Lord Baydon said, looking up. Despite the sunlight, his blue eyes were dim, like the sky as twilight draws near. "But aren't you supposed to be at Assembly voting on some important measure or another?"

"The Hall of Magnates is not in session today," Rafferdy said. "It will convene tomorrow."

"Excellent! I trust you'll come to agreement on what to do about this villain Bandley Morden."

Rafferdy knelt beside the chair. "You mean Huntley Morden. It's the Old Usurper's grandson who has landed in the west."

For a moment the elder lord's eyes were hazed, but then he nodded. "Of course, Huntley Morden. That's what I meant."

"I hope to be able to visit you soon, Lord Baydon. In the meantime, I am sorry you are being bothered by your health."

"It is no bother," the older lord said, his voice rasping but resolute. "Rather, it was the least I could do. After all, I was too frail as a lad to go into the army and join them on their adventures. But life is peculiar, isn't it? For I became more hale, and they grew weak. So it only seemed right that I should help them, when I could not do so earlier, and share the burden with them."

Rafferdy frowned, trying to comprehend this utterance. Was Lord Baydon's mind wandering, as his sister had said it often did? The older man's hand twitched upon his lap, and Rafferdy realized there was a piece of paper there, tucked in the folds of the blanket. He reached out and took it.

It was an impression—the very same one that Rafferdy and Mrs. Quent had previously discovered in Lord Marsdel's library. The picture showed three young men wearing the coats of Altanian army officers, but with turbans on their heads, standing before bending date trees and a sea of sand. It was Earl Rylend, Lord Marsdel, and Lord Rafferdy. They were the three Lords of Am-Anaru who, along with Sir Quent's father, had gone into a cave deep in the desert and discovered the Eye of Ran-Yahgren within. And they had found something else there as well: a malady—or perhaps a curse—that struck them all down in time.

A chill came over Rafferdy, and a fascination as well. "What do you mean, Lord Baydon? How did you share the burden with them?"

The elder lord's face had gone slack, and he seemed to look past Rafferdy. "The onyx box," he said faintly. "Lord Marsdel said the three of them had each taken a bit from themselves and put it inside the box. And all I had to do was open it. I was very hearty, he said. It would cost me but a few years, and would grant them all many. And I had seen what became of Rylend's steward. Poor Mr. Quent! What a dreadful end. So how could I not help them? I opened the box, and gladly. How like an adventurer I felt! Like one of their little band, boldly venturing into the desert. Like . . ."

He gave a rattling sigh and fell silent.

Now it was with a horror that Rafferdy gazed at the elder man. The impression slipped from his fingers and fell onto Lord Baydon's hand. The elder lord gave a start and blinked.

"What is it, Mr. Rafferdy? Was there something you wanted to say?"

Rafferdy drew in a breath. "I just wanted to say good-bye, Lord Baydon."

A smile crossed his thin face. "Well, no need for such formalities, Mr. Rafferdy. You can always call on us again tomorrow."

Rafferdy made no reply. He simply squeezed the elder man's hand. Then he rose and exited the parlor. In the past, he had attempted to go as long as possible between visits to Lady Marsdel's. Yet as he departed the house on Fairhall Street, he found himself wishing he could indeed call again the lumenal next. Only no one would be here if he did.

Besides, he had other affairs to attend to tomorrow. And if he was right about what was to happen, then he hoped her ladyship would depart early in the morning, and drive with all possible haste.

―――

THE NIGHT WAS LONG, and the morning broke sluggishly over the city, as if reluctant to cast its light in witness upon what this day was to bring.

For his part, Rafferdy was anything but sluggish, but was rather filled with a peculiar energy. He rose in the dark, dressed by lamplight, and took a breakfast of only coffee, being in need of no further sustenance. By the time the sun heaved itself over the shoulder of the Crag, he was already in his cabriolet as his man drove him through the Old City.

Three lumenals ago, these streets had all been in turmoil as he drove to Mrs. Quent's house. Now they were orderly, even quiet. A few people moved about on their business—as did what seemed a nearly equal number of soldiers in blue coats.

When the news of Huntley Morden's ships landing in the west reached Invarel, a great tumult had ensued. Some people had cried out in glee, many others in dread, and thieves and hooligans took it as a holiday. Things were quickly brought to order, though, as a great number of redcrests marched down from the Citadel and throughout the city. Crowds were dispersed, fires snuffed out, and any belligerents who resisted the soldiers were hauled off to Barrowgate.

If prior to all this some had called the Crown foolish for withdrawing so many soldiers from the Outlands in recent months and recalling them to the city, they now praised it as wisdom. A few skirmishes occurred, but all were quickly resolved in favor of the soldiers, and by the following lumenal order had been restored.

In fact, the city seemed almost tranquil now. That it had lost a sizable fraction of its population in the last few lumenals was certain, as, like Lady Marsdel and the Baydons, many families that had resisted departing for their estates in the east did so now. At the same time, most of the young men who had run about waving green banners and shouting "The Hawk" three days ago had since left the city themselves. Only it was not to the east they fled, but rather to the west.

For the last two days, a calm had ruled in the city, but it was an uneasy sort of peace. The princess had yet to make any appearance or statement, which was a matter of much talk and speculation. All waited, wondering what news would come next out of the West Country—or down from the Citadel.

A bit of news Rafferdy was waiting on himself was word from Eldyn Garritt. He had dispatched another note, but again no reply had come back. As a result, Rafferdy's concern had increased. If he did not get a reply soon, he would have to seek out Garritt in person to assure that he was well. How he would have liked to be sitting in a tavern with his friend, sharing a pot of punch! At the moment, though, other business required him.

The cabriolet came to a halt. Rafferdy opened the door and climbed out. Members of both Halls were already ascending the marble steps before Assembly. Rafferdy followed suit, moving more quickly than most, though he could not say this was from any eagerness. Rather, if an awful thing must happen, it was best to get on with it.

As he went, he could not help thinking about Lord Baydon. Until yesterday, Rafferdy had continued to hope that the elder lord would again be able to accompany him to Assembly someday. Now, after what Rafferdy had learned yesterday, he feared that would never happen.

What had Lord Marsdel done to Lord Baydon? But it was all too clear, Rafferdy supposed. *The three of them had each taken a bit from themselves and put it inside. . . .*

Rafferdy could only wonder if Earl Rylend and Lord Rafferdy had been aware of what magick Lord Marsdel planned to work with the onyx box—how he intended to take most awful advantage of his cheerful and good-natured brother-in-law. Had Rafferdy's own father been complicit in this dreadful plan to cheat the curse of Am-Anaru, extending their own lives at the expense of another's?

Rafferdy wanted to believe that his father would not willingly and knowingly commit such an abhorrent act. Yet who was to say that even a good man might not rationalize such a deed in order to preserve his life, telling himself it was for the sake of his wife and infant son? A man could justify the most heinous of deeds if he convinced himself it was for the greater good. Were they not about to witness that very thing this morning?

He reached the top of the steps and at once found his arm seized by Coulten, who had been lying in wait for him. The other young man pulled him aside, into the shadow of a marble column.

"Great Gods, there you are, Rafferdy." Coulten's hair seemed to have reached even greater heights than usual, as if driven upward by the force of his anxiety. He dropped his voice to a conspiratorial volume. "So then, what is your plan?"

"Plan? I have no plan."

"This is not the time for quips and cracks, Rafferdy. You have been very close since the last meeting of our little band, but I know you—you always have some clever scheme. So out with it. What are we going to do?"

"There is nothing we can do," Rafferdy said gravely, keeping his voice low. "You heard what Farrolbrook said as well as I did."

Coulten pulled his gloves tighter over his fingers and wrists. "So that's it, then? We just let it happen?"

"We have no choice but to let it happen." Rafferdy leaned in closer, whispering now. "As soon as Assembly convenes this morning, Lord Davarry is going to introduce a measure that will appoint Valhaine as Lord Guardian of Altania. The measure will command him to act as the steward and protector of the nation for the duration of the present crisis. It is a duty he is sure not to decline, and the measure will grant him any and all powers necessary to act out this role."

Coulten frowned. "I know all that—as you said, I was there when Farrolbrook gave us the news."

"Then I shouldn't have to say anything more. But I can see by your look that I do." Rafferdy laid a hand on the other man's arm, pulling him in nearer yet so no one could possibly overhear. "Think it through, Coulten. Lord Davarry's measure is bound to also introduce a new host of laws—measures even more strict and terrible than those proposed in the Act of Due Loyalty. To criticize or speak out against the government in the most timid manner will be a crime punishable by imprisonment. To take the least action that might be construed as an attempt to weaken or threaten the nation will be a capital offense. Nor will you have the luxury of facing your accuser before a judge. Allegations will be made anonymously, testimony spoken against you by any official of the state will be taken as fact, and judgment will be swift, merciless, and final."

Coulten's face blanched. "But surely we can vote against Davarry's measure. It won't become law if it doesn't pass both Halls."

"You're still not thinking," Rafferdy said, thumping his index finger against Coulten's brow. "We can't know how many votes he has. Nobody can. So what if we vote against it, only then it passes? And what if the measure contains a stipulation that causes it to be retroactive in nature, so that the laws apply not only to deeds going forward, but to any committed since the commencement of this crisis?"

Coulten started to shake his head—then ceased this action abruptly as his jaw fell open. "But that would mean, if Davarry's measure is supposed to strengthen the nation, then anyone who stands against it can be accused of weakening Altania."

"Now you're thinking," Rafferdy said with a grim nod. "To have voted against the measure will be deemed a crime by the measure itself. Any lord or citizen who is on record as having called out a nay will be accused of treason. And since no one can be sure ahead of time that the measure won't pass, only a madman would vote against it. Thus, in a single act, Valhaine will begin a reign more absolute than any king's. For anyone who does not support his authority will become a criminal by definition, and will be hauled off to Barrowgate and summarily hanged."

Coulten put a hand to his brow, pressing the place where Rafferdy had thumped it. "I know the Black Dog is rabid in his desire to protect Altania from its enemies, but I can hardly believe this. Whatever he is, Valhaine has always been loyal to the Crown."

"Has he? Surely you've heard the rumors going about the city that Princess Layle is a witch—or at least that she has the capacity to become one, given her supposed descent from Queen Béanore. And who do you suppose has been spreading these rumors?"

"The Gray Conclave?"

"Well, it certainly wasn't the inquirers," Rafferdy said with a snort. "More likely it's the Magisters. But whoever is to blame, Lord Valhaine will use these pernicious rumors as an excuse to confine Layle to her chambers. He'll say it is for her own good, that she must be protected from the unwholesome influence of the Wyrdwood. But it will be no different than a prison; she will be able to do nothing against him."

Coulten slumped against the column. "Good God, then we're done for. Everything we've accomplished up to now has been for nothing. The magicians of the High Order of the Golden Door will have the confidence of the most powerful man in all of Altania. And if they are beholden to the Ashen, then he will be as well—whether knowingly or not—and they will do away with the Wyrdwood at once. We have lost, Rafferdy."

"Today, yes," Rafferdy said, then he tightened his grip on Coulten's arm. "But this is only one battle. A consequential one, yes, but far from the last. Valhaine will have much to occupy him in the coming days. He can hardly send his men dashing about the nation to burn down the Old Trees as they please—not when most stands of Wyrdwood are in the West Country, and it's from the west that Huntley Morden marches. That means we still have time. And if we are careful here this morning, then we can remain free to work against him another day."

"And how can we do this?" Coulten's tone was skeptical, but he stood up straight, and a bit of color had returned to his cheeks.

"Come, I'll show you."

Still holding on to Coulten's arm, Rafferdy pulled the other young man along the colonnade and through the gilded doors into the Hall of Magnates, which was rapidly filling. They took their places on the bench alongside the rest of the New Wigs. The other young men all looked at Rafferdy, as if to see what he was going to do, but his own gaze traveled across the Hall.

The members of the Magisters party already occupied the front benches opposite where the New Wigs sat. They all of them sat serenely, as if this were just another session of Assembly. All, that was, save for one. Farrolbrook hunched upon their periphery. It was difficult to see what he was doing, but Rafferdy guessed he was drawing something in his sketchbook. Now and then there was a crimson flash as the ring on Farrolbrook's hand entered a shaft of light falling from the slits in the dome above.

Other sparks of red and purple and green caught Rafferdy's eye as well. No longer were he and Farrolbrook the only men in the Hall who had foregone gloves. The Magisters all wore their magicians' rings openly now, just like the smug expressions on their faces.

Rafferdy twisted his own ring around on his finger. Damn the Magisters! This was why they had been so eager to support the Crown in recent months but not the princess; they would have their own monarch, in fact if not in title. Already they had employed him to hunt down any magicians who might oppose them. Now they would use him to wage a war—not upon Huntley Morden, but upon the Wyrdwood.

And upon those who might call out to it.

I've heard that he's making it his own business to seek out witches. So said the man Rafferdy had overheard at his club, referring to Valhaine. *He's scheming some way, with the help of his magicians, to make it a simple matter to know if a woman is a witch or not. For he considers them to be the greatest of threats to the nation. . . .*

Now it was not Rafferdy's ring that was twisting, but rather his stomach. What if Valhaine really was creating some manner of witch-hunter? And what if one were to come before Mrs. Quent?

But that was speculation. How could Valhaine even manage such a thing? All the same, that Mrs. Quent must depart the city as soon as possible was a certainty. She was in grave peril as long as she remained in Invarel. It would be best if she departed for the east at once; she could go to Farland Park with Lady Marsdel. Yet Rafferdy knew it was useless to urge her to flee. She would never leave the city, not while her husband was being held in prison.

The only person in Altania who might have a chance of convincing her to go was Sir Quent himself.

Which meant Rafferdy had to find a way to get into Barrowgate to see him. Only how? For the last three lumenals, Rafferdy had racked his brain to think of a way he could aid Sir Quent, but so far he had conceived of nothing. Sir Quent had been arrested on suspicion of treason for his acts in Torland. By vouching for him, Rafferdy would achieve nothing save to incriminate himself, and he could hardly be a help if he was in prison. There had to be some other way to get into Barrowgate to see him. But how?

A loud noise jarred Rafferdy out of his thoughts. The High Speaker had struck the podium with his gavel. At once a solemn hush fell over the Hall. Only the Magisters knew for certain what was about to happen, but it was clear that everyone knew something momentous was about to occur.

Above and behind the High Speaker, Lady Shayde sat in her now customary seat. She was gowned in black as always, and the veil that draped from the brim of her hat concealed the upper portion of her face. All Rafferdy could see were her white hands, a white chin, and the blue-black curve of her lips.

Again the High Speaker banged his gavel. "The Hall is called to order!"

A silence ensued, broken only by the rustling of robes and a periodic cough. Heads turned as lords looked around in anticipation, but no one rose up to speak. A wild hope flared in Rafferdy. Perhaps something had happened, something that had caused them to abandon their plan. Perhaps they feared they did not have enough support after—

"The Hall recognizes Lord Davarry!" the High Speaker called out.

Rafferdy's hope vanished, a spark snuffed out before it might kindle. The leader of the Magisters walked deliberately to the rostrum, then turned to address the Hall.

"The time has come," Davarry said, and his voice did not carry through the Hall so much as it smothered all other sounds. "The time we have long feared. The Usurper's forces have landed on

Altanian soil. They march even now from the West Country. It is a time most dire, but we need not fear for our sovereignty, not if we have among us just such a leader as these times demand."

"Where is the princess?" someone called out. Rafferdy couldn't see who, and he hoped Davarry couldn't either. It was a brave act, and dreadfully foolish.

"Her Highness is safe in the Citadel," Lord Davarry said. "Though it is not her that I speak of today. The rebels have shown their willingness to use the Wyrdwood to achieve their ends. So all must agree that a woman cannot be asked to lead us under present circumstances. Especially a woman of a *particular* nature."

The pressure of the air in the Hall seemed to change as all drew in a breath at once.

"But we are blessed in our hour of need to have another who is able to take up the charge Her Highness cannot. Indeed, the ship of Altania might have already foundered but for his guidance these last months. And he will navigate us to calm waters again, if we but grant him the powers he requires to do so. I speak, of course, of Lord Valhaine. It is he who can—and who must—lead our nation."

"As king, you mean?" someone else called out.

Lord Davarray raised a hand. "That would be treason," he said, as if scandalized by the notion. That the shouter had been planted, Rafferdy was certain.

"The crown of Altania can never, *must* never, be worn on a head other than that of its rightful heir," Davarry went on. "But if we are deprived of a royal monarch who is able to lead us, that does not mean we must founder without a strong and wise hand to guide us in this most fateful of hours. If we cannot have a king, then let us have a Lord Guardian instead—one who will lead us to victory."

Even as Davarry spoke, Rafferdy let his gaze rove over the Hall. Here and there he met another's gaze—Wolsted, and the other magnates who were part of the Fellowship of the Silver Circle. Each time he gave a grim nod, and each time it was answered in kind. Then he leaned his head toward Coulten's and whispered,

"Whatever he calls for, vote aye. No matter what it is, no matter how terrible, you must vote aye."

Upon the rostrum, Lord Davarry spread his arms wide. "I propose that Lord Valhaine this day be raised to the position of Lord Guardian of the realm, Protector of Altania, with all powers pursuant and necessary to fulfill the duties of this position!"

And Rafferdy was one of the first in the Hall to leap to his feet and call out in affirmation.

CHAPTER NINETEEN

ELDYN SHRANK within the shadow of a doorway at the bottom of Wickery Street, listening for the sound of boots against cobblestones. His hand was tucked inside his coat, and he gripped the leather tube concealed there. If a soldier were to accost him, he knew exactly what to do—how to squeeze the tube, breaking the vial of ink within, and thus destroying the message on the paper that was wrapped around the vial.

After all, this was not the first time he had been a courier of illicit messages in the dark of an umbral.

Previously, he had performed this sort of night work under duress, in an effort to pay off a debt of a hundred regals and to protect his sister from the rapacious actions of the highwayman Westen Darendal. Westen had styled himself as a rebel against the Crown, but in fact he had been nothing more than a self-aggrandizing brigand. He had cared nothing for aiding the people of Altania, and only for furthering his own fortune and fame. Nor was he alone in that. Many a man liked to think he was a rebel when in truth he was merely a thief, and as likely to steal from innocents as from the government.

But there were good men who had joined the rebellion, Eldyn

knew that now—men who were risking their lives while trying to free the people of Altania from tyranny and oppression by aiding the cause of Huntley Morden. Men like Orris Jaimsley. And this time, Eldyn had not been blackmailed into carrying secret messages. It was his choice.

As it turned out, though, his prior experience was useful. The day he had gone to the dormitories off Butcher's Slip, Jaimsley had been astonished to see him, but pleased as well, laughing as they clasped hands. Then both of them had become grim as Jaimsley confirmed the awful news Eldyn had read in *The Swift Arrow*— how both Curren Talinger and Dalby Warrett had been among those shot dead in the recent confrontation between students and soldiers in Covenant Cross.

Yet after a round of whiskey, and a toast to their companions, their sorrow was replaced by a solemn resolve. Eldyn had pledged his help to the cause of the revolution, and Jaimsley had gladly accepted it.

"We can use as many pairs of loyal eyes as we can get in the city," Jaimsley had said. "We need men—and women, for that matter—who can keep watch on the comings and goings of soldiers in every part of Invarel: where they routinely patrol, in what numbers, and how often."

Eldyn had felt a note of disappointment at this. He could understand how such information might be valuable, but he had rather hoped he might do something else for the revolution— something more *glamorous,* for want of a better word. He had said as much to Jaimsley, asking if perhaps they had need of a courier for carrying messages, but the homely young man had shaken his head.

"That's good of you to volunteer for such a duty, Garritt. And I do not doubt your ability or your bravery. But it takes a certain nerve to keep one's wits and stay composed when accosted by a soldier while carrying a message. Perhaps after you have had more experience . . ."

"But I do have experience," Eldyn had said, and he had gone on to explain the work he had done previously as a courier.

It was no discredit to Jaimsley that he had appeared a bit in-credulous. But Eldyn had described the particulars of his prior work, and with the details that he was able to put forth—the form the messages took, and how they were exchanged—Jaimsley could only concede the truth of it all. What was more, another of the young men in the room at the time recalled being present on one of those occasions when Eldyn went to an address to pick up a message. He recognized Eldyn's face and could vouch for his story.

Presented with such facts, Jaimsley could only agree Eldyn in-deed had the requisite experience. And so, that very night, Eldyn began his work carrying messages in the name of Huntley Morden and the revolution.

Now, within the shadow of the doorway, Eldyn's ears pricked up at the sound of approaching footfalls. He recognized the crisp cadence and the bright click of steel toes against stone.

It was the Lowgate patrol. The patrol operated in shifts of four hours. Six soldiers would spend the entirety of the shift patrolling along Wickery Street, which here ran parallel to the high stone wall on the edge of the Old City. The soldiers would march from the Lowgate up Wickery Street half a furlong, then back to the Lowgate, then down Wickery Street a similar distance, and finally back to Lowgate once more to resume the pattern. In all, the entire route took the soldiers five minutes.

After four hours, there was a changing of the shift at the station beside the Lowgate as fresh soldiers relieved the prior patrol. This process required five minutes. As a result, once every four hours, the length of time in between the patrol's successive appearances at the lowest point of Wickery Street was not five minutes but rather ten.

And ten minutes was just enough time for what Eldyn needed to do.

The sounds of marching boots grew louder, echoing down the street. There was a slight pause, then the footsteps started up again, only this time they were retreating. Eldyn waited just a few heartbeats more.

Then it was time.

He left the protection of the doorway, beginning the count under his breath as he did. "One, two, three . . ."

Like a watchful eye, the red planet glared in the sky above. Eldyn paid its gaze no heed as he hurried along the narrow lane, keeping to the edges. After a few dozen paces, the lane ran into Wickery Street. Eldyn cast a quick glance to his left. The sound of boots was louder now, but still receding, and the soldiers were not in view; they had already gone around a bend in the street as they marched up toward the Lowgate.

Eldyn turned right and moved swiftly and silently down Wickery Street, still counting as he went. "Nineteen, twenty, twenty-one . . ."

His count was at the rate of once every two seconds, or thirty per minute. Which meant he had to be finished with his task and off Wickery Street by the time he reached three hundred.

He had spent a good while practicing with Jaimsley, making certain he had the cadence exact, for there was no room for error. Perhaps it was from all his time carefully scribing columns of numbers, or from precisely timing cues onstage at the theater, but whatever the reason, Eldyn was a quick study. Even when Jaimsley timed him with a clock, Eldyn's count was never off by more than a fraction.

"Thirty-nine, forty . . . ," Eldyn breathed, and then he was at the bottom of Wickery Street, precisely on schedule.

While the most ancient parts of Invarel were enclosed by a wall, this was not the case for the entirety of the city. Soldiers were stationed at all the main ways that led in and out of the New Quarter, Gauldren's Heights, Lowpark, and Waterside, but the edges of these districts were porous, bounded by lower walls, hedges, and embankments, or in some places by nothing at all. If a man was watchful, and knew the routes, it was simple enough to hop a garden fence or drop from a rooftop and be out of the city with no one the wiser.

The same could not be said for the Old City. In centuries past, the Mabingorian kings had erected a stout wall around what, at the time, had been the whole of Invarel: namely those parts that now represented the Old City, Marble Street, and the Crag upon which the Citadel stood. The wall was high and not easily scaled, and attempting to do so would put one in plain view. What was more, there were only a limited number of passages through the wall: the Morrowgate, the Hillgate, the Barrowgate, the Lowgate, and a few other gates and arches.

There had always been soldiers standing guard at each of the passages in the wall, but ever since Huntley Morden's landing, these posts had all been trebled in size. Also, while in the past the soldiers had been somewhat lax in their attitude, the guards were now vigilant and alert, and additional soldiers patrolled the vicinity of each gate. Which meant there was no way a man might pass in or out of the Old City without putting himself under the scrutiny of Lord Valhaine's redcrests.

But for something smaller than a man—a thin leather tube, for example—there was yet a way. It was vital that those loyal to the revolution have a way to pass information about the doings of the government to their compatriots outside the city, so that these missives might eventually find their way to Huntley Morden himself.

Missives like the one tucked inside Eldyn's coat.

The wall of the Old City loomed above Eldyn like a flat wall of shadow. In most places, buildings abutted the base of the wall, but there was one small section here at the foot of Wickery Street where this was not the case. Instead, there was a gap to allow water that ran down the street to flow into a small culvert in the base of the wall, for otherwise the street would have flooded when it rained.

Eldyn cast a glance over his shoulder, making certain no one was in view, then he squatted down and crept into the culvert.

A thin rivulet of water ran down the bottom of the drain, but luckily there had not been a storm recently. All the same, the stone beneath Eldyn's boots was slick, and he used his hands to steady himself against the curved sides of the drain as he went. He had to move in a severe crouch, or else he would scrape his head against the ceiling. All of this made for slow going. Even so, the starlight quickly vanished and the darkness closed in around him, so that in moments it was pitch-black.

Jaimsley had warned him the drain would be very cramped and dark. For Eldyn, though, this was the easiest part of his task. He had spent many hours as a boy hidden away in some small, confined place, surrounded by shadows as he hid from his father. The darkness was not oppressive to him, but rather a comfort.

His heart quickened with alarm only once, when he heard a skittering noise behind him. He paused for a few moments and listened, wondering if someone had followed him into the drain. But the sound did not come again, and he imagined it was just a bit of stone falling from the crumbling walls of the drain, stirred loose by his passage.

Not daring to delay his count any further, Eldyn pressed on. "One hundred thirty-six, one hundred thirty-seven . . ."

Then he sensed a change in the air, and he detected a rusty scent. Eldyn reached out, and his fingers found rough metal bars. He had reached his goal, and only a few counts late. Nor was that a concern, as he could easily make up the time by keeping the exchange swift.

Eldyn sidled up closer to the iron bars. They were spaced closely together, forming a grate across the whole of the drain. The bars were anchored deeply in the stone of the wall, and they were so thick that any attempt to hew at them would require an enormous effort, and would cause a great deal of noise to come echoing out of the culvert, thus assuring any such activity would be noticed.

All the same, the bars had to have gaps large enough to let rainwater pass, and that meant other things could be passed between them as well. Eldyn drew the leather tube from his coat.

"Hello," he whispered softly.

The sound dwindled into the sound of trickling water. There was no answer.

"Hello there," he called out again, then paused to listen. Still there was no reply. All the while, he kept the count going in his mind. *One hundred fifty-four, one hundred fifty-five . . .*

Now fear did begin to well up within Eldyn. There was no answer from his counterpart on the other side. If he did not arrive by the time the count reached one hundred sixty-five, Eldyn would have no choice but to turn back.

Just as the count reached that very number, there was a scuffling on the other side of the grate.

"I'm sorry I'm late. The guards were off their pace tonight."

There was no time to talk about it. "What's the password?"

The phrase differed with each exchange. It was written upon one message, and then had to be provided in order to receive the next. What's more, the password was written in a code which required a key to solve—a key which only the most loyal members of the cause possessed.

"Thimble Lark Whiskey Bridle Seven-Two-Nine-Nine-Five."

Those were the right words and numbers, in the right order. Jaimsley had given them to Eldyn earlier that night.

"Here," Eldyn said and passed the leather tube between the bars of the grate. Despite his desire to hurry, he did this slowly, careful not to squeeze it in the process, lest the vial of ink within rupture. The tube was pulled from his fingers, then another replaced it. Eldyn drew it through the bars, then hastily tucked it into his coat.

"Good luck, brother," came the whisper from beyond.

"You as well, friend," Eldyn said, already backing away from the grate. *One hundred eighty-five, one hundred eighty-six,* he counted in his mind. He was twenty counts behind now, but if he hurried, and did not worry so much about the noise that resulted, he should be able to make it up.

At least, he had to hope he would. For while the guards did not do so every time, it was known that the patrol, upon reaching the bottom of Wickery Street, sometimes had a habit of holding a lantern up to the mouth of the culvert and peering within.

Hunched over double, Eldyn sidled along the tunnel, moving

as quickly as he could, hoping the scrape of his boots was not being magnified as it issued from the culvert. *Two hundred forty-two, two hundred forty—*

Something warm and heavy dropped onto the back of Eldyn's neck, and a jolt of terror went through him, so that he let out a cry. It felt like a hand falling onto him from behind. Only it was impossible that someone could be behind him in the drain.

Possible or not, something sharp as a knife was slicing at the flesh of Eldyn's neck. He lurched forward, and the weight rolled off his shoulder. There was a splashing of water, followed by the same skittering noise he had heard before. It was risky, perhaps even foolish, but Eldyn dared to conjure a tiny illusory light. He turned and looked behind him.

Two red sparks glittered in the darkness of the drain.

Eldyn let the light grow a little brighter, and now the wan illumination revealed an enormous rat. The rodent reared up on its hind legs, baring long yellow teeth, and hissed like a cat. Then it turned and scuttled back down the culvert in the direction of the grate. Eldyn reached back to touch the back of his neck, then winced. He drew his hand back and stared; his fingers were stained with blood. The damnable thing had bitten him.

Yet he would be in for a worse fate than that if the soldiers caught him. His dread was renewed. How long had he been delayed fending off the rat? Ten counts, no more, he guessed. And what had the count been before the thing attacked him? Yes, it had been two hundred twenty-two, he was sure of it.

Panting as he resumed the count, Eldyn made like the rat and crawled forward along the drain. A wan glow appeared ahead, and he let the illusory light perish. Using his hands as much as his feet, he propelled himself the last of the distance.

Just inside the mouth of the culvert, he paused to listen and heard the echo of boots. The guards were approaching, but had they come around the corner into view of the culvert yet? Perhaps he should risk hiding in the tunnel. Only what if they paused to shine their lantern inside? He could draw the shadows around him, but they might grow suspicious if the light of their lamps did not carry. What if they were to thrust a bayonet inside to see what was blocking the way?

"Two hundred eighty-six," he whispered, "two hundred eighty-seven."

No, he did not dare remain inside the drain. He still had enough time. Gripping the edges of the culvert, Eldyn pulled himself out and then staggered onto the bottom of Wickery Street—

—just as the first of six soldiers marched around a corner of a building and into view. Eldyn could only stare. The affair with the rat had caused him to miscount. He did not have enough time. Rather, he was utterly out of it.

"Hold!" one of the two leading soldiers called out. He raised the lantern he carried and peered toward the mouth of the culvert. "Who's there?"

"What are you looking at?" said the redcrest behind him.

"I thought I saw something move."

The other soldier took a step forward and looked around. "Have you been at the rum again? You know what the captain says about having a nip before duty."

"I haven't been at the rum! I saw something move, I'm sure of it. It might be a rebel sneaking about."

"Aye, and look—there it is!" exclaimed his compatriot, gesturing with his rifle.

Beside the drain, swaddled within the cocoon of shadows he had hastily woven around himself, Eldyn froze. The bayonet fixed upon the end of the rifle was pointed directly at him. Despite his shroud, the soldiers had seen him. He reached into his coat, wrapped his fingers around the leather tube, and began to squeeze. Only just then something wriggled out of the mouth of the culvert to scuttle along the base of the wall.

It was the rat that had bitten Eldyn—or another one just as fat.

Guffaws of laughter rose from the men. "There's your rebel. Go on then, arrest him!"

"Oh, shut your trap," the other replied. "At least I'm keeping an eye open, unlike you louts. Now come on."

The patrol turned about, then marched back up Wickery Street and out of view. Eldyn let out a breath as the shadows fell away. His fingers gripped the leather tube so tightly it was difficult to unclench them.

He forced them to do so, then made like the rat and scurried away down the lane.

A QUARTER HOUR LATER, Eldyn descended the steps of Butcher's Slip. Two tall, thick-necked fellows stood by the dormitory door. They leaned against the wall with arms crossed, as if merely loitering about, though Eldyn knew they would leap into action in a moment and block the way if someone they did not know attempted to enter.

One of them gave Eldyn a nod. He returned the gesture, then headed into the dormitory. At the end of the long corridor, he found Orris Jaimsley in a room with two others. Knowing them all to be in Jaimsley's confidence, he reached into his coat and took out the leather tube.

"I don't know if it's angels that watch over you or daemons," Jaimsley said with a laugh as he reached across the table where he sat and took the tube. "Either way, there's none better at giving the redcrests the slip. You get by them every time. How do you do it?"

Now that the ordeal was over, Eldyn's prior alarm vanished, and he could not help feeling an immense satisfaction. "I'm just lucky, I suppose."

"Oh, I have a feeling it's more than mere luck that helps you escape the notice of the soldiers."

Now Eldyn's dread suddenly returned. He felt a compulsion to glance down and see if some of the shadows still clung to him, but he did not dare. "What do you mean?" he said carefully.

"I mean," Jaimsley replied with a crooked grin, "that you are far too modest, Garritt. It's not luck that gets you past the soldiers. It's cleverness and skill. Your feet are nimble, and so are your wits. I should have seen at once that you were suited for this sort of work."

Eldyn let out a breath, his pleasure returning. "I'm just glad I can be of help to Somebody."

Jaimsley did not open the leather tube, but instead put it in a drawer. "And if we all can serve his cause as well as you, then I'm sure Somebody will soon be here in Invarel to thank us all himself."

"And to buy us a drink!" one of the other young men said. He had a boyish face and sandy hair.

"Indeed, he'll owe us that much," Jaimsley said. "But in the meantime, we'll have to manage on our own. I do think this occasion calls for a drink. Can you aid us, Brackton?"

The sandy-haired fellow took a bottle and a cup out of a cupboard. He filled the cup, and they passed it around. The whiskey was fiery, but Eldyn took a big swallow anyway, and felt his nerves settle a bit.

"Good man," Jaimsley said, handing the cup back to Brackton. Then he smiled and gave a wink. "Now, I think you and Miggs here have some business to attend to, am I right?"

Evidently they did, for the two departed at once, leaving Jaimsley and Eldyn alone. Now it was Eldyn's turn to be impressed. Jaimsley wasn't much to look at: skinny, already balding, and possessed of a nose that was as large and bent as were his teeth. All the same, he had been the most popular man at St. Berndyn's College, and it seemed nothing had changed in the interim.

"All you ever have to do is grin," Eldyn said with a laugh, "and everyone readily commits to whatever bit of mischief you're scheming. They all happily follow your lead and do as you say."

Jaimsley did not return Eldyn's laughter. Instead, he looked down at his hands. "Talinger and Warrett didn't do as I said."

"Perhaps," Eldyn replied, his voice solemn. "But they did follow your lead, didn't they?"

"I told them to stay away from Covenant Cross that day, that I had a feeling things were going to take a bad turn. Only they just couldn't listen, damn them. No, they had to go there."

"Because *you* were going there. As I said, they were following your lead, just like we all do. Besides, I'm sure Talinger was determined to face off against the soldiers, what with that hot Torlander blood of his."

"No, it wasn't Talinger who was the instigator," Jaimsley said, looking up with blue eyes. "I think, if it had been just him, he would have listened to me. It was Warrett who was bent on going that day, and once it was clear he was, Talinger wouldn't be left behind. When the redcrests showed up, I told them to keep behind the crates. But then the soldiers fired the first shots, and a man from Highhall went down. When that happened, Warrett ran out from behind the barricade."

Furrows appeared on Jaimsley's brow. "It was the strangest thing. You know Warrett—there was no one as mild, or as bland, I might say. But at that moment there was a look on his face, a fury such as I've never seen before. I suppose anger can stir even the dullest man into passion. He ran straight for the soldiers even as they were reloading their rifles, as if to tear them apart with his bare hands. Talinger ran after him, brave idiot that he was, calling out and trying to stop him. Then the soldiers fired, and I saw both of them fall not ten feet away from me. Warrett's face was half gone, and Talinger had a hole in his chest you could have put a fist through. God, but it was an awful sight."

He drew in a breath and fell silent. Eldyn felt a chill creep up his neck. It seemed impossible that a man usually so placid as Dalby Warrett could be moved to such a violent fervor. In a way, it terrified Eldyn to consider it. How many other men who had heretofore seemed dull and ordinary would now be stirred into action of the most extreme sort? And how many of them would lose their lives like Warrett and Talinger? Again Eldyn saw the flashes of light, the clouds of smoke, and the bodies crumpling to the ground.

"I saw the blood on the cobbles," Eldyn said softly, "but I had no idea it was theirs."

Jaimsley looked up, his frown deepening. "Were you there, Garritt? If so, you never told me."

"I mean I saw it in the impression, that's all," Eldyn said hastily. "The one that was published in *The Swift Arrow*."

"Of course," Jaimsley said. "I'm not sure what I've ever thought of that sort, though I suppose it was nothing kindly. But if I met the illusionist who made that, I'd shake his hand. That picture brought more than a few lads who were sitting on the wall over to our side of things. It's one thing to read about something, but to see the soldiers standing there over the corpses—well, it made more than a few realize they couldn't just stand on the side anymore. They had to join the fight."

Eldyn stared, trying to think what to say.

"Well, go get some rest, Garritt," Jaimsley said first. "You've earned it. I have no idea if tomorrow is to be a short or long lumenal. I suppose only God knows these days, if even he really does. But either way, I'm sure I'll have more work for you once it gets dark."

"Get some rest yourself," Eldyn said.

Jaimsley nodded, but then he began looking over the maps and letters on the table, and Eldyn doubted that he would. Leaving his friend to his work, Eldyn headed out of the dormitory. A different pair of men stood by the door. One touched a finger to his brow in salute, a gesture which Eldyn returned, though he felt a bit peculiar doing so. It was not as if he was a soldier.

Except he supposed that he was, even if it was messages he carried rather than a rifle. Important information could turn a battle, just like a well-aimed shot. Besides, if he was caught in his night work, he would be hung just like any rebel who wielded a gun.

Eldyn climbed the steps of Butcher's Slip, then pulled the shadows around himself as he walked down University Street. He might not be carrying secret messages at present, but he still had no wish to be accosted by soldiers and questioned as to why he was out at this hour. No doubt he could have found a place to flop down at the dormitory, but despite the late hour and the swig of whiskey he felt peculiarly awake. He was tempted to stop at a tavern to see if another drink or two might rectify the problem.

Only the taverns would all be closed by now. By order from the Citadel, all drinking houses were to close four hours after dark, no matter how long the umbral might be.

It was just as well. He should get back to the theater. Riethe had been sitting with Master Tallyroth when Eldyn left, and though the bighearted oaf would never admit it, Riethe was sure to need a break by now. They had all taken turns staying with Tallyroth lately, for his breathing had grown labored. Often he needed help sitting up on the chaise so that he could get air in and out of his lungs.

Just as Eldyn turned onto Durrow Street, a pale glow appeared in the east. The sky hardly had time to linger upon gray before it was painted with pink light. Just like that, the night changed to dawn, as quick as it might onstage during an illusion play.

Eldyn went around the back of the theater, said good morning to one of the large fellows they had hired to watch the door, then went upstairs. It was not Riethe who was with Tallyroth, but rather Hugoth.

"I sent Riethe to bed a few minutes ago," Hugoth said. "I was afraid he'd nod off and fall out of his chair."

"That was good of you," Eldyn said. "It would be like Riethe to land on his face and break his nose."

"Not that it could make him any homelier," Hugoth said with a grin. "But I wouldn't want the clatter to wake Master Tallyroth."

Eldyn's gaze went to the chaise. The master illusionist reclined upon a heap of fringed and embroidered pillows, his thin form covered with numerous blankets. His eyes were shut.

"How is he?" Eldyn said quietly.

"Resting. His breathing has been a little easier tonight. I don't know what Madame Richelour put in the last potion she gave him, but it seems to be working. I think he's been dreaming about conjuring illusions. His hands keep moving beneath the covers."

Eldyn could only smile. "He's probably directing us in a bit of new staging. Would you like me to sit with him for a while?"

"No, I'm fine. You go get some rest, Eldyn. Who knows how long the day will be? And we have a performance tonight." The older illusionist sighed. "Or rather, we might have one."

Hugoth didn't have to explain further. The Citadel had already limited the times when taverns could stay open, and coffeehouses as well. No doubt they were seen as likely incubators for the seeds of revolution, or places where illicit thoughts might flourish. Many felt it was only a matter of time until Lord Valhaine shut them down completely. And if the taverns were shut down, could the theaters be far behind?

So far, though, no such order had come down. Not that it would matter if business continued to dwindle as it had these last days. Ever since the news of Huntley Morden's landing, the soldiers in the city had been too busy to attend illusion plays. If the ticket receipts didn't improve soon, the theater would have to shut its doors no matter what the Citadel might order. Already several more theaters on Durrow Street had gone dark. Less than half the number of houses were open compared even to just a few months ago.

Hugoth returned to the chair to sit next to Master Tallyroth. Eldyn left them and went up to his little room on the topmost floor. The excitement of the night's work had finally faded, leaving him weary at last. As he opened the door of his room, he could not help for just a moment picturing Dercy lying on the bed. No matter how tired Eldyn might be, anytime he saw that sight he had been filled with renewed energy.

But the room was empty, and chilly from the night. Eldyn took off his boots and laid on the bed, alone. He shivered, but before he could bother to pull the covers up, he was asleep.

WARM SUNLIGHT was streaming through the window by the time Eldyn woke. He put on his boots and went to the sideboard. There he poured some water from a clay pitcher into the basin and splashed it against his face. After that, he surveyed his appearance in the small silver mirror on the wall. How long he had been asleep, he did not know, but by the state of his hair, it had been some time.

He dampened his fingers and used them to comb the tangles from his dark hair, which was getting long again, then bound it behind his neck with a ribbon. This done, he went to the window and looked out. People and horses and carts moved on the street below, and with all the bustle it might have been any normal day in the city. Except that, upon second glance, a large number of the people going to and fro were not merchants or washerwomen or boys selling broadsheets, but were in fact soldiers, the morning light glinting off their brass buttons and the bayonets on their rifles.

Eldyn's skull throbbed, none too gently reminding him that he was overdue for a cup of coffee. A glance at the sky above the rooftops confirmed his hope that, however long it had been, the morning was not over. That was well, for by Lord Valhaine's order all coffeehouses were forced to close their doors as soon as the sun reached the zenith. Which meant, on short lumenals, people had to be quick to take a cup. And if Eldyn was quick now, he might yet get a cup himself.

The theater was quiet as he went downstairs. Everyone must have been out and about already. Though a peek through the door of the parlor on the second floor confirmed that Madame Richelour was sitting with Master Tallyroth. Having no wish to disturb them, Eldyn proceeded to the first floor, and as it was daytime he departed by the front door. He turned to start down Durrow Street, eager for a hot cup—

—then stopped short, gaping at the man in front of him. The other was tall, of an age with Eldyn, and if not precisely handsome, was all the same very pleasing to look at in his fashionable gray suit.

Except Eldyn was anything but pleased to see him at this moment.

"Garritt!" the other man said at the same time as Eldyn exclaimed, "Rafferdy!"

For a long moment both of them stared at each other. The sunlight was hot, and Eldyn felt sweat trickle down his sides.

It was Rafferdy who managed to speak first. "I have been greatly worried about you, Garritt. You haven't replied to any of my notes lately. I went to your address near the cathedral, only the landlady said you no longer live there, and nor had you been by in some time to retrieve your letters."

"But how did you find me here?" Eldyn said, rather breathlessly.

Now Rafferdy frowned. "Good God, Garritt, you hardly sound happy that I have done so! And here I was worried you had been shot dead in some riot. But then your landlady's son told me that he had followed you one day after you picked up your letters."

"He spied on me?"

"Yes, he is apparently an enterprising lad. No doubt he thought the information might be of value someday. And so it was, for I had to give him half a regal to get it. At first, when my driver pulled up to the address, I thought I'd been swindled out of my coin. Only I see the boy was right after all, for here you are." He glanced up at the sign over the door of the theater, then raised an eyebrow. "But why *are* you here, Garritt? I would hardly expect to find such a diffident soul as yours strolling on such an unwholesome avenue as this."

A sharp edge of fear cut through Eldyn. But then it passed and was replaced by a resignation. Indeed, it was even a peculiar kind of relief he felt, such as a murderer who has been on the run for years must feel when he is at last apprehended. For so long he had dreaded this moment, but now that it had come, it could no longer be avoided. There was no use in dissembling or lying to his friend anymore.

"I live here," Eldyn said.

Rafferdy leaned upon his cane, as if caught off balance. "What do you mean you live here? This is a playhouse, Garritt. I don't understand."

"Then let me show you."

Eldyn lifted his hands, holding the palms together like a little stage, and looked down at them. There was so much light all around that it took hardly any effort. A golden dove with ruby eyes manifested on Eldyn's hand, and he could not help smiling a little as it did, for it was beautiful. The dove flicked metallic feathers and opened a jeweled beak. Then, all at once, it spread its gleaming wings and flew up to the sky.

Eldyn let the phantasm dissipate, but he did not lift his gaze from his now-empty hands.

"I'm sorry," he said quietly. "It was wrong to hide this from you for so long. But I could never bring myself to tell you. Only now you know the truth. I'm sorry, Rafferdy. You must be repulsed."

He waited for his friend to reply. Only they wouldn't be friends, not anymore. There would be words of anger, of scorn and disgust, and after that the two of them would never see each other again.

Only when Rafferdy at last replied, it was not with words at all, but rather with laughter.

Unable to believe his ears, Eldyn at last looked up. But sure enough, Rafferdy was gripping the handle of his cane and laughing heartily, as if he had just heard the most amusing joke. Then he leaned forward, his eyes gleaming with curiosity.

"Show me that again, Garritt!" he said.

CHAPTER TWENTY

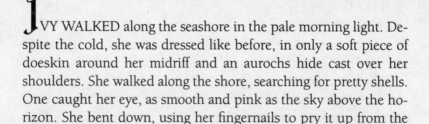

IVY WALKED along the seashore in the pale morning light. Despite the cold, she was dressed like before, in only a soft piece of doeskin around her midriff and an aurochs hide cast over her shoulders. She walked along the shore, searching for pretty shells. One caught her eye, as smooth and pink as the sky above the horizon. She bent down, using her fingernails to pry it up from the half-frozen sand. . . .

No, this wasn't right. This wasn't where she was supposed to be. Ivy struggled, willing herself to be elsewhere.

And then she was. It was night now, and she huddled with her people in the darkness of the cave. She pressed close to them for warmth, breathing in the familiar, comforting scent of their bodies. From outside came a sound like the murmur of waves upon the shore. Only the people were many days of walking from the sea now, and the noise was that of the trees of the great forest, heaving to and fro in the wind.

Suddenly a hot spark of light appeared at the mouth of the cave. At first she wondered if it was the new red star shining through the opening. Only then a man and a woman stepped into the cave, and the light was coming from what looked to be a glowing coal in his hand. Yet it was brighter than a coal, and he held it against his flesh as if it were cool as stone.

The light illuminated the strange pair. The woman wore black leathers that clung to her like a second skin, while her own skin was as pale as bone. The man was tall and handsome, a silver wolf pelt draping his broad shoulders. His sharp blue gaze roved over the people, then fell upon Ivy.

A terror came over her. *No!* she tried to call out to the people. *Do not let him in! Do not follow him!*

But she could make no sound. The man and woman came farther into the cave. Ivy recoiled against the stone wall, but there was no way out. Her lips opened in a silent moan of fear. She knew the man, she knew what he wanted and what he would do. And she already knew his—

"Ivy!"

Something shook her back and forth. She imagined black branches reaching down, coiling around her, and lifting her up.

"Ivy, wake up! You're having a horrid dream again."

She opened her eyes and saw, not a tangle of trees, but rather orderly rows of books upon shelves. She was not in a cave or by a forest, but rather in the library. Floating above her like a worried moon was the oval of Lily's face. As if to be certain, she gave Ivy's shoulder one more robust shake.

"I'm awake," Ivy said hastily, hoping to avert any further assaults.

A bit dizzily, she sat up on the sofa. As she did, a book tumbled to the floor. It was the copy of *The Towers of Ardaunto* she had bought from Mr. Fintaur's shop. She had been reading the book once again to see if there were any further clues to be found within its pages—any hints about the keystone or what its purpose was. Only she must have fallen asleep, and the shocking nature of the events in the book had inspired similarly awful dreams.

"Who is Mr. Murgen?" Lily said.

Ivy pressed her fingers to her temple, for it was throbbing. "I do not know anyone by that name. Why do you ask?"

Lily picked up the fallen book and sat beside Ivy on the sofa. "You called out the name just a moment ago, in your sleep. Murgen, you said. I thought it must be someone named Mr. Murgen that you were dreaming of."

Ivy grimaced as she rubbed her temple. She was certain she wasn't acquainted with anyone by the name of—

A sudden breath rushed into her. Yes, she could still recall bits of the dream: the crimson glow from a gem in his hand, the wolf pelt across his broad shoulders. His name was not Mr. Murgen, but rather—

"Myrrgon," she murmured.

"Yes, that's the name," Lily said. "So you do remember, then. But who is he? I'm sure I haven't met him."

"No, you haven't, and nor have I. He's a magician. Or rather, he was long ago. He established one of the seven Old Houses of magick, or so it is said."

Lily frowned. "Well, that's a queer thing to dream about."

Yes, Ivy thought, *it is.*

"You're not thinking about trying to work magick again, are you, Ivy?" Lily thumbed through the pages of the red book.

"No, I'm not."

"Good, because as I'm sure you'll recall you had no talent for it. And besides, it's all forbidden now anyway, even for men if you're not doing magick for the government—and I do not think we will be doing anything for *them*. Do you mind if I borrow this?" She shut the book.

Ivy had found no further clues in the book's pages last night. It had already told her all it could. "Not at all," she said. "Though I will warn you, it contains many horrid scenes."

"Excellent," Lily said with a grim satisfaction. "If it is very horrid, then perhaps everything else won't seem so dreadful in comparison. There's tea in the parlor." She gave Ivy's cheek a kiss, then departed the library.

Ivy supposed a cup of tea might help ease the aching in her head, but she did not get up at once. For after she drank a cup of tea and readied herself for the day, what would come next? Lily had woken her from a nightmare, but what Ivy had awakened to was hardly any less awful. Mr. Quent had been arrested under suspicion of treason. The soldiers had hauled him away to the prisons at Barrowgate. And just yesterday she had been informed that he was to be formally charged with illegally freeing a witch from official custody before she could be tried for treason. This had not previously been a crime, but now by an act of Assembly it was so, as were many other actions deemed to be harmful to the nation.

"But he cannot be charged with a crime when it was not a crime at the time to do such a thing!" Ivy had exclaimed yesterday at the Citadel, speaking with the magistrate who had informed her of the news. She was no expert in law, but there were several volumes on the subject in her father's library, which she had perused over the years.

"In fact, he can be," the magistrate had replied in a disinterested tone, as if they were discussing some arcane and mildly interesting legal theory rather than a man's fate. "The Measure Against Treasonous Activities makes it very clear that one may be charged for any harm caused to Altania, in either the present or the past, or even one intended to be committed in the future."

"But if that is the case, then it is a crime to simply think of something which might cause harm to the nation!" Ivy had exclaimed.

The magistrate had peered at her down the length of his nose. "Have you had thoughts about harming Altania, Lady Quent?"

Ivy had stared at him in horror. She had gone to the Citadel to make a petition to be able to see her husband, but the magistrate had denied it based on the grounds that he was now awaiting trial. Sir Quent could not be seen by anyone not involved in trying his case, she had been informed, lest they affect his testimony or collude with him to alter it. She had intended to argue the decision, but after the magistrate's statement, she had wanted only to be gone from the place. So she had fled.

The days since had been filled with an anguish so severe she suffered it as a kind of tearing pain in her body and her brain, as if some vital part of her had been ripped away. This she experienced in alternation with long periods of numbness during which she felt nothing at all. At such times, it was as if she were enveloped in a thick gray fog that obscured and muted all things, and which imparted such a listlessness that she could hardly move.

The only time she was not afflicted by one or the other sensation was when she was able to concentrate upon the needs of her sisters, which would momentarily outweigh her own. To console and soothe them helped to soothe her as well, though it was Rose who was more often in need of such attention. Often the smallest thing—a cup clattering against a saucer, or a tangled thread when she was trying to sew—would cause her to burst into tears.

Lily, in contrast, had been astonishingly brave. She had wept the day the soldiers took Mr. Quent, but since then Ivy had not once seen her indulge in any kind of outburst. Instead, though she was solemn, even grim, Lily seemed peculiarly calm. If she had a fear of what was to become of them, she was not revealing it to her sisters. The only real change Ivy had noticed in her was that she had taken to drawing in her folio again, spending hours at it in the parlor or in her room.

What sort of drawings Lily was filling its pages with, and if they were similar to before or something entirely different, Ivy did not know. Nor did she seek to find out. Whatever Lily was drawing, if it gave her solace, Ivy would not discourage it—just as she had made no comment that Rose was allowing Miss Mew to sleep on her bed. They all must take what little comfort they could find these days.

As for Ivy, her only source of comfort other than her sisters was found in the presence of Mr. Rafferdy. He had stayed as long as he could that awful day after bringing her to the house, until his duties forced him to depart. Since then, he had come to call several times, and on each occasion his presence had been like a beam of light breaking through clouds. It had reminded her that, even if she could not escape the storm lashing about her, at least there was something beyond it, some brightness yet left in the world.

At least for now, that was. During one of his recent visits, Ivy had shown him the copy she had made of the most recent entry that had appeared in her father's journal. Also, she had told him about the grim sight she had witnessed at Mr. Larken's shop, and how she had seen Mr. Bennick there. It was not that she hoped he could tell her what to do; it was more that the knowledge of it all was too much for her to bear alone. He had listened to all solemnly, and when she was done was silent for a time.

"Why do you think your father intended to wait until the Grand Conjunction began to reveal another entry in the journal?" he asked at last.

"I'm not certain," she had replied.

Or was that so? She thought of the poem her father had left for her, hidden in the endpapers of a book. *When twelve who wander stand as one, through the door the dark will come. . . .*

"I think something's going to happen when all the planets are aligned with Cerephus," she said. "Something that has to do with the Ashen."

"Perhaps that's the moment they're waiting for," he had said quietly. "From what I've learned in my studies, a conjunction is considered a time of great power and consequence with regard to magick. Perhaps that's when the Ashen will seek to enter into our world."

Ivy had shuddered, for at that very moment a sudden dusk had fallen outside the window. They had ceased their discussion on the topic then, but they had discussed it several times since. Also, Mr. Rafferdy told her that he had brought it up with the members of his arcane order, to see if they might be able to learn more about what might occur during the Grand Conjunction, though so far they had not.

Mr. Rafferdy's exceeding kindness in frequently visiting her—and the hazard he took in doing so—was not lost upon her. Nor was he the only one who had refused to abandon her. Both Lady Marsdel and Mrs. Baydon had come to assure Ivy of their continued affection and allegiance. This show had moved Ivy so deeply she had hardly been able to utter her appreciation; but a touch of Lady Marsdel's warm, dry hand and a kiss from Mrs. Baydon told her that she was understood.

But now Lady Marsdel and Mrs. Baydon had departed the city, along with Mr. Baydon and Lord Baydon. And other than Mr. Rafferdy, no one came to call. Not so long ago, lords and viscountesses had accepted invitations to the house on Durrow Street. Now, not even the butcher or candle seller would pay a call to the house, and Mrs. Seenly was forced to send one of the servants out for such things, or go herself.

Despite this isolation, Ivy could only feel a relief when a day passed with no caller appearing at the gate. For there was one visitor whose coming she greatly dreaded. Yet so far Mr. Bennick had not appeared at the door. But was it not only a matter of time before he did so? He had murdered Mr. Fintaur and Mr. Larken for their pieces of the keystone, and Mr. Mundy would no doubt have met a similar fate had he not hidden himself and then fled.

Why Mr. Bennick had not yet come for the piece of the keystone belonging to her father, Ivy could not guess. Perhaps he had not found a way to breach the house's defenses. And Ivy would certainly not invite him in! Nor would her sisters or any of the staff, for Ivy had instructed them all to let in no visitor other than Mr. Rafferdy.

All the same, each time she looked out the window, she dreaded to see the tall figure of Mr. Bennick striding up the walk. It was for this reason, along with the general state of upheaval to the household, that she had not yet gone to Madstone's to retrieve her father. He could only be safer there, locked behind the iron door of his room within the thick stone walls of the hostel.

If only they could flee the city themselves, as Mr. Mundy had done! More than once Ivy had considered the thought, but each time she rejected it. How could she leave Invarel when Mr. Quent remained imprisoned? She would leave the city with him or not at all. Besides, it was not as if they could return to Heathcrest Hall now. By all reports, Huntley Morden's troops were marching from the west, gathering supporters and fighting any resistance. The rebels could be approaching Cairnbridge at this very moment.

No, they could not go into the west. But they could go east. It seemed inconceivable that Huntley Morden should ever press so far as to come near Invarel. Surely the Altanian army would stop him. But what if they did not? If there was even a small chance the rebels could reach the city, then Ivy must take action to be certain her sisters were as far away from harm as possible. She was only waiting for Lady Marsdel and the Baydons to be settled in the east country. Once a little time had passed, Ivy intended to write to Lady Marsdel and ask if Lily and Rose might be sent to stay with her ladyship at Farland Park. Ivy had no doubt Lady Marsdel would consent, and so Lily and Rose could be sent out of harm's way.

As for Ivy herself, she would remain in the city to watch over her father, and to do anything she could to aid in her husband's case.

Yet Huntley Morden was not the only danger. Again she wondered what she would do if Mr. Bennick were to come to the house. It occurred to her that she might be better able to protect the keystone if she knew what it was or where Mr. Lockwell's fragment of it was hidden. Only she had no knowledge on either account.

She went to the desk, took out the journal, and turned through its pages. But just like the last time she had looked, all of them were blank, devoid of any of her father's wisdom. How she wished she could speak to him, to ask him what she should do about Mr. Bennick and the keystone.

But couldn't she? Mr. Mundy had revealed to her the truth of what her father had done to strengthen the house's magickal defenses in order to protect the Eye of Ran-Yahgren. She had always believed he had sacrificed his mind to work the spell. And so he had, but that was only half of the enchantment, for his mind had not been lost in the act. Rather, his intellect had been transferred from his body into the structure of the house itself, as if to grant the inanimate thing a will and thus bolster its ability to defend itself against intruders. And if Mr. Mundy was right, which she believed he was, his intellect resided here still. After all, had not her father told her the very same thing?

Know that though I am not with you in body, my spirit resides with you there at my house on Durrow Street. That was what he had written in his last entry in the journal. He had been trying to tell her.

Ivy shut the journal and laid her hand upon the leather cover, as if it were a kind of Testament. "Father," she whispered.

It felt odd to address him as if he were there. But he *was* there in the house, she was sure of it.

"Father, can you hear me?" she said, a little louder now. "I don't know what I am to do. Mr. Quent has been taken from us. We are alone without him. And I'm afraid that Mr. Bennick will take advantage of our situation, and that he will show himself at the door."

She tilted her head, listening, but the library was still and silent. Dust motes wafted upon the air, glowing like tiny stars and planets in the shaft of light that fell through the window.

"Please, Father," she said, her voice rising. "If you can hear me, let me know. I need your wisdom now more than ever. Please let me know that you're here with us."

And a voice said, "Ivy?"

It was not a man's voice, but rather the soft voice of a young woman. Ivy put a hand to her throat and turned around.

"Rose!" she gasped, then forced herself to take a breath. "I didn't hear you come. You startled me."

Her next youngest sister stood in the door of the library in a pink dress, her brown eyes wide. She took a step into the room. "Was he speaking to you just now? Father, I mean. Did you hear him?"

Ivy stared at her. "No, I didn't hear anyone. Only you."

"But you wanted to hear him," Rose said quietly, and took another step into the room. "You were trying to talk to him. You know Father is here in the house, don't you?"

Ivy hesitated, then at last she nodded. "You told me so, Rose. Only I didn't believe you. I even scolded you for telling me. I'm so sorry—you must be very angry with me."

Rose rushed forward, closing the last of the distance between them, and threw her arms around Ivy. "You mustn't be sorry, Ivy! I know it was hard to believe. But you know now, and I'm so glad. I know you've missed him terribly, only you don't have to anymore. He's here with us, just like when we were little. Has he spoken to you at all yet?"

Ivy started to shake her head, only then she thought of the other day, and how it seemed her father had been speaking to her when she was looking at the rosewood clock and trying to solve the riddle about Mr. Larken. Ivy had told herself she had simply imagined it.

But she hadn't.

"Well, if you haven't heard him yet, I'm sure you will soon," Rose said gaily. "He told me that he's very proud of you, and of everything you've done, but that you're going to have to be extra brave for what's ahead. Do you know what he meant by that? I don't always understand what he tells me. But we can talk about it later. Come, let's go to the dining room before Lily drinks all the tea."

It was the first time Ivy had seen her sister happy since the day the soldiers came for Mr. Quent, and she could not resist as Rose took her hand, clasping it tightly, and led her from the library.

———

THEY WERE toward the end of taking their breakfast when Mrs. Seenly entered the dining room and informed Ivy that Mr. Rafferdy had come to call. Ivy's teacup struck the saucer with a clatter and she leaped to her feet. She was hardly in a fit state to be seen, having slept in the library. But there was nothing she could do about it now except smooth her hair and dress without the benefit of a mirror, pinch her cheeks, and go out to see him.

She found him in the front hall, examining the Dratham crest above the fireplace. He turned as she approached.

"Mrs. Quent, you look well this morning."

Ivy nearly laughed at the absurdity of this statement. After all that had happened lately—and after half an umbral sleeping upon a sofa in her dress—she was certain she looked anything but *well*. She would have thought he was being wry with her if his expression was not so solemn. Instead, she supposed he was simply being a gentleman.

As for him, *he* looked very well. He wore a dark suit cut in an elegant style. His hair, which he usually kept short and neat, had been allowed to grow untended for some time, but this slight dishevelment made for an appealing contrast to his tailored coat and ivory-handled cane. A man, if made too perfectly, did not appear manly. Rather, to look his part, he required some imperfection or roughened edge.

"Mr. Rafferdy, it is so good to see you," she said, and no words could have been truer. She reached out a hand, and he took it in his own.

"But you are wearing gloves!" she said, surprised at the fact. "I thought you had given up the fashion."

"I'm afraid it is one that has lately been forced upon me again," he said as he withdrew his right hand, which was encased in gray kidskin. "To flaunt a House ring is a sure way to attract unwanted notice. Only the members of the High Order of the Golden Door wear their rings openly these days."

Despite the gravity of this statement, she again felt an absurd sort of levity rise up within her. "I do not know what shocks me more, Mr. Rafferdy—the idea that the magicians who seek to deliver Altania to the Ashen can move about openly while those who would guard the nation must go in secret, or the knowledge that attracting notice is now a thing you wish to avoid. Both are astonishing facts."

A wry crease appeared beside his mouth, putting a crack in his solemn veneer. "Perhaps they are at that. Though I'm sure the one is of far more import than the other."

"Is it? I'm not so certain, Mr. Rafferdy. The world is changing at an awful pace, and there are numerous things to dread at present. Armies that march across the land, or shadows that seek to slip through doors. Yet most of all, I dread that it is we ourselves who are changing, that no matter what happens—no matter if things are resolved in the way we hope for most—we will never be the same again."

At some point as she spoke her mirth had vanished, as had his smile.

"Perhaps we won't be the same," he said quietly, "but that does not mean we will be left in ruins. Events are bound to alter us, Mrs. Quent. Indeed, I am sure they already have altered both of us. Nor do I think it has necessarily been for the worse."

He took the glove from his right hand, and the gem of his House ring threw off blue sparks in the sunlight streaming through the windows.

"I was furious when Mr. Bennick sent me this ring, tricking me into putting it on. I loathed it for the fact that I would never be able to take it off so long as I lived. Yet now, even if it were possible to take off this ring, I would not do so. I have become . . . accustomed to its weight upon my finger."

He put his glove back on and regarded her.

"What of you, Mrs. Quent? Would you undo all of the things that have altered *you*?"

Her gaze went past him to the windows, and to the straggly

hawthorn and chestnut trees in the garden. She thought of the way they had once heard her commands and obeyed her, just as the trees of the Evengrove had listened to her. Would she go back to the way she had been before, if she could, to being ignorant of what she was able to do?

At last she returned her gaze to Mr. Rafferdy and shook her head.

"No, I did not think so," he said slowly, then suddenly his smile returned. "Besides, Mrs. Quent, did it never occur to you that we are not changing at all—that rather, we are simply becoming more ourselves?"

Now Ivy was astonished anew by him. Mr. Rafferdy had ever possessed a clever mind and a cutting wit. But when had he become so entirely rational as well? Only perhaps it was like his talent for magick. The ring on his finger had changed him no more than the touch of Wyrdwood had her; these things had simply revealed what had always resided within them.

"Thank you, Mr. Rafferdy," she said.

He made a bow, then gave a speculative look as he rose. "You know, if you really wish to thank me for anything I might have done, you could offer me a cup of coffee. It is horridly early."

"Yes, it is!" She could not help touching her hair. "In fact, I wonder that you are out and about at such an hour."

"Do not worry, Mrs. Quent. The desire to rise early is not another novel change that has come upon me. Rather, I have an appointment at the Citadel. But it is important that I speak to you before I go to it. May we talk?"

They went into the parlor off the front hall, and Ivy called to Mrs. Seenly for a pot of coffee. Once this was delivered, Ivy shut the door, then took a chair opposite his.

"Ah, this is excellent," Rafferdy said, sipping his cup. "My man does not make coffee such as this."

"We are lucky to have Mrs. Seenly," Ivy said.

Indeed, they were very lucky. Mrs. Seenly was from Torland. She might have fled the city once news of Huntley Morden's landing reached them, for fear of reprisals against those of West Country heritage. But she had not. Even Mr. Quent's situation had not deterred her, and she remained steadfast in her service to the family.

Mr. Rafferdy balanced his cup on his knee. "And how are Miss Lockwell and Miss Lily faring?"

"They have both been brave, and are bearing up. Though as you might imagine, Rose has been the most agitated by it. She has been very distraught since they . . . ever since that day. Except her mood was improved this morning when—" She hesitated.

Mr. Rafferdy raised an eyebrow. "When what?"

Ivy drew in a breath, then she told Mr. Rafferdy about how Rose had claimed to have been speaking to their father. Without pausing, she explained what Mr. Mundy had revealed: how by means of the enchantment Mr. Lockwell had worked all those years ago, his spirit now resided in the house, at least in some form.

"So Mr. Lockwell really is here," he said, his expression one of amazement. "But I wonder at this especial sensitivity that Rose possesses, and that allows her to hear him when others do not."

"I do not know," Ivy said. "Rose has always been . . . peculiar in some ways. It is often my feeling that she does not perceive the world around in quite the same manner that most of us do. For one thing, she often claims to see colors around people."

He took another sip of coffee. "Colors?"

"Yes, like a light or a glow."

"And does she see these colors around all people?"

"She has claimed to see a green light around me at times. And a blue light around you, similar to what she says she also used to see around our father."

"So she does not see light around just anyone," Mr. Rafferdy said, balancing his coffee cup on his knee again. "But rather, around witches and magicians."

He spoke these last words quietly. The carved eye on the mantel blinked open with a soft click and turned around in its socket.

Slowly, Ivy nodded. "Yes," she said. "I believe that is the case."

"And what of your other sister? Does she see colors or hear your father's voice?"

"No, I do not believe so. Lily is sensitive in her way, but her sensitivities lie in another direction."

"Which is?"

Ivy hesitated. It did not seem quite right to air private facts about Lily—especially habits and interests which might be considered improper or even scandalous by some. But then, Ivy had no one to discuss such matters with now that she was deprived of Mr. Quent. Besides, there was no one closer to their little family than Mr. Rafferdy. If he could not be held in confidence about such matters, who could be?

Resolved, she described for Mr. Rafferdy Lily's long-standing interest in illusion plays, as well as her recent artistic efforts in her folio. Ivy did not know if Lily was drawing scenes from plays again, or poses of men who looked very much like Mr. Garritt, though she strongly suspected it.

By the time she finished explaining all this, Mr. Rafferdy was staring at her. Slowly, he set down his empty cup. A worry came over Ivy that she had gone too far, that she had described something which should have remained exclusive to the family.

"You say she draws scenes of illusion plays, and that some of the men upon the stage look like Mr. Garritt?"

She nodded.

"How can that be?" he said musingly, though it seemed he spoke this more to himself than to Ivy.

"Please, Mr. Rafferdy," she said. "I ask that you say nothing of it to anyone. I know there are many other things for people to worry about these days, but I think it would be best if Lily's fascinations were not publicly known."

"Of course," he replied, now directing his words to her. "But I may have something more to say to you on this subject later. Right now, I do not think I am at liberty to do so. Nor do I have time in any case, for I must depart soon, and I have yet to tell you why I've come—other than seeking a cup of coffee, that is."

Ivy could hardly imagine what he meant by all this. Then, as he continued to speak, she quickly forgot about Lily's folio.

"I believe there is a way I can arrange for you to see your husband," he said, leaning forward in his chair. "Fortunately, Sir Quent has not been charged with any sort of usual crime, but rather with an act of High Treason."

"I can hardly see how that is fortunate!" she gasped, gripping the arms of her own chair.

He grimaced. "Forgive me. That was an exceedingly poor choice of words. What I mean is, we can use this fact to our advantage. Common misdeeds are tried by magistrates, while most crimes against Altania are brought before the special courts of the Gray Conclave. But High Treason is exceptional, for such cases must be tried before the Hall of Magnates."

Her heart made a great leap in her chest. "Then you can vote to acquit him!"

"Remember, Mrs. Quent," he said soberly, "mine is but one vote out of many. And these days, there are few in Assembly who are willing to cast a vote against the Gray Conclave or Lord Valhaine, for fear they will be the next taken to prison. But I have learned that, as a member of Assembly, I have the right to question the accused in preparation for the hearings."

Her excitement was tempered by his words, but only a little. "Then you can go to Mr. Quent at Barrowgate, and for that I would be very grateful. He can only be in great need of the sight of a familiar and compassionate face. But . . . what of me?"

"I will bring you with me. If anyone questions why, I will say simply that your presence is required for my investigation, and then they cannot deny your passage. It is my right to question him as I see fit. But—"

"What is it?"

He met her gaze. "To see him, we must venture into the prisons beneath Barrowgate. I do not believe it will be . . . pleasant for you, Mrs. Quent. You must know that it will mean not only witnessing terrible sights, but also seeing your husband amid them. Are you willing to tread in such a place?"

She thought of the first time she had gone to visit her father at

Madstone's—how hands had reached for her through iron bars, and the cries of the demented had sounded all around. It had been an awful scene, but it had not deterred her. Nor would this.

"I would bear anything to see him," she said.

He nodded and leaned back. "That is what I thought you would say. I only wanted to make sure of it before I arranged the meeting."

"When will it be?"

"As soon as possible," he said, standing. "I fear the Gray Conclave may seek to move quickly upon his case."

Ivy was afflicted by many feelings at that moment. Horror, at the thought of her husband locked in the bowels of Barrowgate alongside thieves and murderers. Dread, at what might occur when he was brought once again before Assembly. But most of all, at that moment, she was overwhelmed with a profound gratitude. That Mr. Rafferdy should risk himself in such a dire manner in order to help her—it was hardly comprehensible.

"Oh, Mr. Rafferdy," she said. She leaped to her feet and threw her arms around him.

Only a few days ago, she had told Mr. Quent that her one-time hope to marry Mr. Rafferdy had been based on fancy and nothing more. But if she had known then, upon first meeting Mr. Rafferdy, that he was capable of such courage, such selflessness—

But there was no point to this. No matter what she thought of him *then,* he could not have married one of her station. And no matter what she thought of him *now,* it could not alter their present positions, or the relationship between them. Yet her thoughts were suddenly confused. It should all be so clear, but somehow everything was muddled. Ivy did not know what to think as she held on to him; she only knew that she had no wish to release him.

Then, gradually, she was aware that his body had gone rigid. At last he gave her shoulder an awkward pat. Hastily, Ivy released him and stepped back. How awful of her, to have placed him in such an uncomfortable position! She worked to compose herself, so that she could express herself in a more appropriate manner.

"Thank you, Mr. Rafferdy," she said, more calmly now. "For everything that you have done for us."

"Of course," he replied.

She would have said more, but he seemed suddenly to be in a hurry to go. They departed the parlor and proceeded to the door of the house.

"Good-bye, Mr. Rafferdy," she said.

"I will let you know at once when the meeting is arranged." He took his cane and hat from Mrs. Seenly and started through the door. Then he paused and looked back. "Until then, please be careful, Mrs. Quent. Do not go out of the house if you do not absolutely need to. And I would also say, do not venture near any trees when in public."

Ivy stared at him. What did he mean by these statements? Before she could ask, he put on his hat, walked down the path, and departed through the gate.

CHAPTER TWENTY-ONE

J T WAS LATER in the afternoon when Ivy understood what Mr. Rafferdy had been speaking of as he left.

After Mr. Quent's appearance before Assembly, she had banished all newspapers from the house, and this order had been reiterated after his arrest. Ivy had no desire to see what false and awful things were being written about her husband, nor did she want Lily or Rose to see them. Thus it was that she was surprised, upon going into the library, that she once again saw a broadsheet lying open upon her writing table.

It was her intention to snatch up the newspaper without looking at it, throw it at once into the fireplace, and tell one of the servants to burn it. Only as she drew close to the table her gaze roved to the top of the broadsheet, as if doing so against her will, and read the large words printed there. A horror came over her as she did.

INQUIRY DISSOLVED, read the headline. And, *Gray Conclave to Direct Effort to Locate Witches.*

She did not want to read the article beneath, but she could not stop herself from doing so. Quickly she learned that Lord Valhaine had declared that the Inquiry was without a leader and now dwelled under a cloud of suspicion due to the illegal actions of at least one, if not additional, inquirers. As a result, the Inquiry could no longer be effective in disposing of its charge—namely, to seek out those who would instigate Risings of the Wyrdwood and stop them before they might succeed—and so it had been disbanded. Effective at once, the Gray Conclave was assuming all responsibilities previously given to the Inquiry. Its agents were even now beginning a search for all purported witches throughout Altania.

> *Under the Inquiry, a sibyl was tolerated to go free if she had no record of inciting the Wyrdwood. But it seems to us that a person who nurtures private malice against Altania in his heart is no less a traitor than one who publicly speaks against the government in order to undermine its authority. They are both a pernicious weed that must be uprooted, even if only the one has so far gone to seed.*
>
> *Similarly, a reasonable mind must conclude that any woman who has the capacity to commune with the Wyrdwood must be considered a threat to the nation, whether she has ever been near to an Old Tree or not. For if she ever does go near a grove of Wyrdwood, how can she be trusted not to fall under the corruptive influence of the trees and do their bidding?*
>
> *What's more, while in the past there might have been no simple way to determine if a woman had such proclivities, we are given to understand that this has now changed, and that the government is even now devising a method by which any woman who is a witch might be immediately revealed as such, and will no longer—*

Here the article was interrupted with a note indicating it continued within. Ivy started to reach for the newspaper, though whether to crumple it up or to turn the page, she was not certain. At that moment, the curtains billowed as a sudden wind blew into the library. The broadsheet fluttered in the gale, then was swept off the table to the floor.

Ivy gasped, as if freed from some coercive spell. She hurried to the window, where the curtains were now snapping like whips. Someone, one of the servants she supposed, had opened the window and forgot to shut it. Now, by the tendrils of cloud writhing across the sky, a storm was coming. Ivy gripped the window, pulling it shut.

The curtains went limp. She went back to the table, bent down, and picked up the paper. This time she did not read it, but rather took it to the fireplace and put it on the grate. She took a lamp that had been left burning on the mantel, removed the shield, and turned up the wick, then used it to light a splinter of wood, which she laid against the paper on the grate.

Flames licked the edge of the broadsheet, then leaped up hotly as the newspaper blackened and curled in on itself.

Ivy stood up, then gripped the mantelpiece, for she was trembling. To think, she had once believed Lord Valhaine had the nation's best interests, and therefore her husband's, in mind! Now his purposes were rendered as clearly as the words printed in ink upon the broadsheet, and they were every bit as black. He had nominated Mr. Quent to lead the Inquiry knowing well how his interview before Assembly would bring up the matter of his actions in Torland; indeed, he had likely been in league with Lord Davarry to assure that they would be, and that Mr. Quent would be discredited. But his true purpose had been to discredit the Inquiry itself—to deprive it of its leader, cast it under a cloud of suspicion, and ultimately bring about its ruin.

She could only rue that she had been entirely oblivious to these machinations. If she had been able to anticipate what would happen, she could have warned Mr. Quent not to accept the nomination for lord inquirer.

Yet if he had not done so, she had no doubt there would be another inquirer locked beneath Barrowgate at present, and either way the Inquiry would stand discredited. Now it had ceased to exist, and the Gray Conclave at last had the authority it had so long craved—to seek out witches and dispose of them as it would.

Ivy could not help wondering if there always had been those within the Gray Conclave, magicians in league with the Ashen, who knew all along of the threat the Wyrdwood posed to the Ashen, and so sought a way to destroy it. Or was it the case, in the beginning at least, that the Gray Conclave had simply viewed witches as being of possible use in a rebellion, and as such posing a threat to the government?

Well, whatever the purposes of the Gray Conclave had been previously, now that Lord Valhaine was under the sway of the magicians of the High Order of the Golden Door, there could be no doubt as to its purpose. It would do all in its power to bring about the end of the Wyrdwood.

As well as any who might call out to it.

A shiver so strong it was more like a convulsion passed through Ivy. She dreaded to consider what agents of the Gray Conclave would do to any woman who fell into their custody whom they suspected of being a witch. But what had the article in the broadsheet meant, regarding this method they had devised to discover women who had the capacity for being a witch? Perhaps she should not have lit the broadsheet on fire. Ivy supposed she could venture out to get another. . . .

No, she would not leave the house. Instead, she would ask Mr. Rafferdy about it when he came next. Given his warning to her, he must have some idea what the government intended. She shivered again and moved closer to the fireplace. On the grate, the newspaper gave a hiss like a dying breath as it burned.

𝔗HE LUMENAL was not long, but such was Ivy's agitation that it seemed nearly a greatday. She could not concentrate upon any task, be it reading, or composing a letter to Mrs. Baydon, or aiding

Rose with her sewing. Instead, her eyes went continually to the old rosewood clock, whose faces hardly seemed to turn no matter how long she looked at them.

At last a sullen dusk began to gather, and it was then that a messenger came to the gate. Mrs. Seenly immediately brought the letter to Ivy in the parlor; it was from Mr. Rafferdy.

She opened it at once, and a thrill ran through her. His request to see Mr. Quent had been granted! He had been given permission to interview the prisoner at his leisure.

All the same, I believe it is best that we not delay, Mr. Rafferdy wrote. *It is my hope the umbral will not be a long one, but whatever its length, look for me not very far into the morning. I will bring my carriage to retrieve you, and then we can go to Barrowgate together.*

Ivy's heart soared. Ever since that awful day, she had only wanted to be able to see her husband, and now Mr. Rafferdy had managed it. Her only complaint was that they could not go to him at once. But they would see Mr. Quent soon enough.

How they would manage to effect his release from prison, Ivy still did not know. She had attempted to retain a lawyer, but so far all of her inquiries to various firms had gone unanswered. On her own, she had pored through books of law in her father's library, but so far she had seen nothing that might help them. Of course, the law books were all old, and Lord Valhaine was rewriting the laws of Altania upon a daily basis. Yet she would not abandon hope. After all, she had previously despaired of being able to see her husband, and now she was to do so in the morning.

Such was her excitement, Ivy thought rest would be impossible. But that night she slept soundly, even dreamlessly. She had left the curtains open on purpose, and she woke as soon as a coral glow illuminated the window glass. By the time dawn came, she was already dressed, taking a cup of tea in the parlor downstairs.

She was only halfway finished with it when there came the clatter of the brass knocker on the front door. Mr. Rafferdy was early indeed! Ivy put down the teacup and, before any of the servants could do so, hurried to the front door herself and opened it.

"Oh," she gasped.

She could not move; she felt made of stone, like the lions to either side of the door. Across the threshold, Lady Shayde's dark lips curved up into that expression which was not a smile.

"You appear surprised, Lady Quent. Were you expecting another, perhaps?"

The question was posed pleasantly, but Ivy knew there was peril in answering it. She did so carefully.

"No, I was not expecting anyone to call today." She willed herself to keep her eyes upon the white face of her unexpected guest, and not to look toward the street to see if Mr. Rafferdy had arrived. "As you can imagine, I have very few callers of late."

"Yet you have some still, I presume?"

As the question was posed in a rhetorical fashion, Ivy chose prudence and did not answer.

"Well, if it is the case that you are not expecting any other society this morning, would it be agreeable if I were to enter and speak with you, Lady Quent? It will not take long. I only wish to add a little to our conversation from the other day, and to pose a few more questions."

Ivy hesitated, trying to decide what to say. Above the plane trees, the sky was continuing to brighten. Mr. Rafferdy might arrive at any time.

"You seem uncertain, Lady Quent. There isn't someone in the house whom you do not wish me to see, is there? Or perhaps you have some reason to try to avoid answering further questions?"

Now an element of anger entered into Ivy's fear, transmuting it into something harder and stronger.

"No, not at all." Ivy smiled herself, and the expression was every bit as warm as Lady Shayde's was cold. "I would enjoy speaking with you. Please, come in."

Now it was her guest who seemed surprised. She hesitated for a moment, and Ivy could not help feeling a note of satisfaction. She gestured for the other woman to enter. Lady Shayde crossed the threshold, her black gown making a crinkling sound, dry as paper.

As the other woman passed her, Ivy glanced at the sky, which had turned a clear blue. She had to hope Mr. Rafferdy would not come too soon. Yet if he did, she supposed it would not be a catastrophe. After all, Lady Shayde knew they were acquainted. All the same, Ivy did not want Mr. Rafferdy to be discredited by any present association with the Quent household; it was best if it was thought he had broken off the acquaintance. Nor did she wish to subject him to any undue scrutiny by Lady Shayde—especially not when he belonged to an illegal order of magicians.

Ivy led the way into the parlor. Mrs. Seenly was just setting down a fresh pot of tea and an extra teacup, no doubt anticipating a guest after the knock at the door. But like Ivy, this was clearly not the guest she had expected. The housekeeper set the pot down with a clatter, then fled without a word.

Lady Shayde seemed unperturbed, as if this was all very usual. Ivy poured tea for both of them, and managed to spill only a little.

"Would you care to sit?" she said, holding out a cup and saucer.

Lady Shayde took them, then set them down. "Tell me, Lady Quent, how is Mr. Rafferdy of late?"

"I fear I do not know," Ivy said. "I have not seen him in some time. I am not certain if he even remains in the city, or if he has gone to his home in the country."

She was surprised how easily the lie came to her, and how natural it sounded. Ivy had never thought she would be so glib at formulating mistruths. But then, as she well knew, desperation had a way of awakening previously unknown talents.

Before her guest could speak, Ivy went on, hoping to direct the subject away from Mr. Rafferdy. "You used to live in the country yourself, didn't you? At Heathcrest Hall, I believe. Do you ever miss it?"

The white oval of Lady Shayde's face was motionless save for one of her eyebrows, and this arched upward a fraction. Ivy supposed the White Lady was accustomed to being the one posing the questions rather than having them posed to her.

"No, I do not miss it."

"You mean to say that you never think of your time there?" Ivy said lightly, or so she hoped. "I was not there nearly so long as you—only a matter of months—but I find that Heathcrest Hall, and the moorland around it, are often on my mind."

"I said I did not miss Heathcrest, Lady Quent. I did not say that I never thought of it."

The words were sharp, neatly snipping the thread of conversation, and ensuring it could not be further unwound. Ivy labored in her thoughts, trying to think of something else to ask.

She was too slow about it.

"Now, Lady Quent, as you are unfamiliar with Mr. Rafferdy's present state, perhaps you can answer for yourself. How have you been faring these last days?"

Ivy's face stung as if it had been struck. She hastily set down her cup, lest she drop it. Then, to her shock, she found herself speaking. The words seemed to fling themselves out of her, and Ivy felt as if she were a bystander who could only watch a scene rather than affect it.

"Is this why you have come?" Ivy observed herself saying. Her voice no longer contained any pretense of warmth or civility. "To mock me, and to gloat over my present situation? I have been deprived of my husband. He is in prison, and his future and my own are utterly unknown, and perhaps beyond hope. Tell me Lady Shayde, how would *you* fare if that which you adored above all else was suddenly seized from you and you were left only with dread?"

For a moment Lady Shayde was utterly still, and her face appeared not only hard, but brittle as well, like tempered steel cooled too quickly. Ivy could almost believe her words had somehow had an effect upon the other woman. Only the moment passed, and Lady Shayde's face was smooth and flawless once again.

"You mistake me for one who can apprehend such things as adoration or dread, Lady Quent. It is a mistake people commonly make, for they want to assume, even given the peculiarities of my appearance, that I am more like them than not." She moved to the pianoforte and laid a gloved hand upon it. "But as they always discover, they are wrong in this. I assure you that I am no more capable of such sensibilities than is the wood encasing this instrument. It might vibrate with the music played upon the keys, but that does not mean it can perceive any feeling or passion that might be expressed in the music. That is why Lord Valhaine chose me for my position." She ran a finger over the glossy wood of the pianoforte, tracing an unknown design. "He knew that no sensibilities or sympathies would ever keep me from fulfilling my purpose, and doing what must be done for Altania."

Despite her fear, Ivy found this speech fascinating. She could only think of the merchant's daughter in *The Towers of Ardaunto*. Nor could Ivy believe that the similarities between Lady Shayde and the character in the book were simply a coincidence. After all, Mr. Fintaur must have known Ashaydea from the times he had been to Heathcrest in the company of Mr. Lockwell. And he must have seen what Mr. Bennick made her into. . . .

"So do you understand now, Lady Quent, that I have not come to mock you, or take any sort of pleasure in your misfortune?"

There was a certainty in the voice, one so cool and inexorable that Ivy found herself nodding without even thinking to.

She forced herself to be still. "If that is so, that you cannot feel such things, then why ask me what you did? Surely logic would have sufficed in the absence of empathy."

"So it did, but I wanted to confirm what I had concluded, that you must miss your husband, and would go to great lengths to have him returned to you. What I am to say would have no purpose if you had wished him to be gone, as some wives might wish of their husbands. But I see now that I was right, and this is not the case."

"I do miss him," Ivy said, not wanting to, but unable to keep the faint words from escaping her aching throat.

"Yes, you do. We both know it now. And what if I were to say that you might have him returned to you?" Lady Shayde took a step closer, her black dress whispering, as if echoing each of her words. "What if I told you there was something you could do—

something that would not be a great effort on your part, but which would be for the good of Altania? And more than that, it would assure your husband's release from prison as well. Would you not leap at the chance to do such a thing?"

Ivy opened her mouth, though what she was going to say, she did not know. She hoped it was to ask what thing this was. She feared it was to simply cry out the word *Yes!* Before she could utter anything, though, a figure in pink appeared in the doorway of the parlor. In a motion as quick and supple as that of a serpent, Lady Shayde turned to face the door.

"Oh!" Rose exclaimed, her brown eyes growing large. She clutched a large book to the bodice of her pale pink gown.

Ivy took a hurried step forward. "Rose," she said when she could draw a breath. "Can you not see I have a guest? You should not interrupt us."

"You need not admonish her on my behalf," Lady Shayde said, and now there was a sound almost like a cat's purr in her voice. "I presume she had no idea we were here. After all, I arrived without notice."

Rose nodded, still gazing at Lady Shayde. "I'm sorry, I didn't know anyone was in the parlor. I only wanted to come in before Lily noticed and put this . . . that is, I wanted to put something back on the pianoforte."

"The book, you mean?" Shayde said languidly. "But did your sister not know you had it? Here, give it to me and I will put it back for you."

And just like that, Rose handed over the book. How simply had Shayde convinced another to comply and give up what had previously been held close. Ivy could only imagine the White Lady was skilled indeed at extracting secrets from others. And now she held Lily's folio.

"Rose," Ivy said gently yet firmly, "you may go now."

Rose did not move, though Ivy could see her trembling. She was like a little bird faced with a cat, too frightened to fly. Lady Shayde set the book on the pianoforte, then opened it and turned slowly through the pages.

"These illustrations are done with great skill," she said. "Did your younger sister draw all these?"

Ivy willed Rose not to speak, to turn and go at once.

"Yes, Lily made them," Rose said, clutching her hands together. "I know it was wrong to take it. But she leaves it out sometimes, and at night when no one else is up I like to look at the pictures."

"Of course," Shayde said, turning another page. "What harm could there be in merely looking at pictures? You were not ruining the book in any way, were you?"

Rose took a step forward. "No, I would never! The pictures are so beautiful. They remind me of the time we read from the old Tharosian play with Mr. Garritt and Mr. Rafferdy, in the parlor on Whitward Street. It was the most marvelous day. I remember how handsome they were, and how solemn as they read from the play—well, Mr. Garritt at least. And I remember the way the colors grew brighter around them both even as they read."

Lady Shayde shut the book and turned back toward Rose.

"The colors?" she said, and though her voice remained calm and low, interest sparked in her dark eyes. "What colors do you mean, Miss Lockwell?"

Now Rose shrank back a step under that gaze. "I mean, the colors of the light all around them."

"Rose!" Ivy said, sternly now. "Leave us at once."

"You say you saw a light around them?" Lady Shayde advanced on Rose. "Do you often see light around people?"

Rose looked at Ivy, then back at Lady Shayde. "No. I mean, that is, not often."

"But you do see it around some people. And for such people, the light is there each time you encounter them. Perhaps a little brighter or dimmer, but always there."

"Yes."

"And what of me? Do you see a light around me?"

Rose shook her head.

"But you do see something, don't you?" Shayde took another step closer. She was within arm's reach of Rose now. "Tell me, what do you see around me, Miss Lockwell?"

"A cloak of shadow," Rose said in a very small voice. "Like a cloud over the moon that drains away all the light. It's—"

Rose's words were lost in a sob. She picked up the hem of her pink dress, then turned and fled from the parlor, her footsteps echoing away in the front hall.

"Remarkable," Lady Shayde said quietly, gazing through the door.

Ivy dared to approach her. "Please forgive my sister's interruption. You must think nothing of her utterances. Rose is very sweet, but she is simple in some ways, and often says peculiar things."

"No, the things she said are not peculiar at all." Lady Shayde turned to regard Ivy. "I know from our prior discussions that your father was a doctor, and I believe you have inherited some of his interest in the sciences, is that right?"

Ivy could only nod.

"Then I will share something with you, Lady Quent, that I think you will find fascinating. Not long ago, during an investigation of a peculiar occurrence in High Holy, the Gray Conclave came into possession of a man. He was a wretched and broken thing. He had been deliberately blinded, and even allowing for the fact that he had recently suffered a violent blow to the head, it was clear his mind was utterly ruined. Yet, in questioning him to see if he knew anything of the fire at the old chapel in High Holy, something very interesting became apparent."

"What was it?" Ivy said, curious despite herself.

"Despite the fact that he had lost his eyes, he seemed to be able to see a few certain people as they approached him in his cell. In time, we learned it was because he could detect a light around them."

Ivy's heart stuttered in its rhythm, then started up again, more quickly than before. "A light?"

"Yes, but given that the man had no eyes, it could not have been any sort of usual light. And we noticed that the individuals that he saw the light around were all members of the High Order of the Golden Door. That is, they were all magicians. So we made more experiments, and brought more people to see the blinded man. And do you know what we discovered?"

Ivy could only shake her head.

"We learned that it was not only magicians that the prisoner could see a light around, but illusionists as well. Now, I am sure you know what many believe about the Siltheri—that they are the sons of witches. In fact, they would be witches themselves had they been born female rather than male, and this is said to account for both their abilities and their perverse tastes." Her black dress made a crackling noise as she shrugged. "I care little about such things as that. What interested me was this question—if the man could see a light around illusionists, could he perhaps detect it around witches as well?"

A terror came over Ivy. "Can he?"

Shayde returned to the pianoforte. "We do not know, Lady Quent. The Inquiry always kept any witches they discovered a secret from the Gray Conclave. Then, recently, the prisoner fell deeper into his madness, and finally was found choked to death on his own tongue." She pressed the lowest keys on the pianoforte, striking a deep, thrumming chord.

Despite that ominous note, Ivy felt a keen relief. Whoever this man was, he had perished, and his ability with him. Only then Shayde went on, and Ivy's relief quickly became a horror again.

"It seemed we would never be able to understand the prisoner's ability. But then two things happened. First, as you know, the Inquiry was ended. And then we discovered, in the course of our investigations, that there were others like the prisoner."

Ivy gasped. "Others who had been blinded?"

"No. While we believe the prisoner's eyes were taken from him to increase his sensitivity, we have found that the ability to detect a light around someone occurs quite naturally in people, if rarely. Yet there is one thing we have discovered that increases its likelihood of occurring. Do you know what that characteristic might be, Lady Quent?"

Ivy felt made of clay. It was hard to move. At last she shook her head.

"I am surprised a clever mind such as yours cannot guess at this commonality, Lady Quent. We have only ever found a few individuals with this ability, but all of them have been either the sisters of illusionists, or they have been illusionists themselves. That is, they are all of them the offspring of witches. And now, quite by chance, I discover that your own sister appears likely to have this very same proclivity."

Ivy knew she was in grave peril, and Rose as well. She made herself speak as calmly as she could. "I'm afraid you can make no examination of Mrs. Lockwell, as she has passed away."

"Yes, I know that. But while Mrs. Lockwell was Miss Lockwell's mother, she was not yours, was she, Lady Quent? I understand your mother was childless for many years of marriage. Only then you were brought into the house as a small child, and hardly a year later your sister Rose was born. It seems very curious, doesn't it?"

Again Ivy thought of the hawthorn and chestnut trees in the garden. Her father had written how the seeds he took from the Wyrdwood had failed to sprout—that was, until he brought Ivy into the house. Not long after that, Mrs. Lockwell, who after losing her infant son had been unable to bear another child, suddenly conceived a daughter. So Rose was not the child of a witch. But was it because of the presence and influence of a witch—because of Ivy herself—that Rose had been born at all? If so, that might explain Rose's ability to see light around others.

Yet, despite these thoughts, all Ivy said was "I don't know what you're talking about."

"Don't you?" Lady Shayde closed the cover over the keyboard. "Very well then, Lady Quent, let us put scientific discussions aside and turn to practical matters. As I said before, there is something you can do—a thing which would be for the good of Altania. And were you to do this, I think it would be possible for you to make a plea of leniency on behalf of your husband. He would still be stripped of his post, and of his title as well. After all, there must be some penalty for the crime he committed. But a display of patriotism on the part of his wife would help the Gray Conclave to believe that he had only ever had the good of Altania in mind, despite his flawed actions, and so he would be released."

As Lady Shayde spoke, an eagerness arose in Ivy, a willingness to do anything it would take to assure her husband's release. She cared nothing for posts or titles. She wanted Mr. Quent returned to her, that was all.

"What is this thing?" she said, cautiously.

Then Shayde spoke, and Ivy knew that she was not being rescued from the steel jaws of a trap that had closed around her. Rather, she was being asked what limb she would prefer to sever in order to free herself from the snare. Her horror was too great to be felt anymore. Numbly, she listened as Lady Shayde described the proposal.

It would, in all, take no great effort on Ivy's part. As she must be aware, Lady Shayde explained, all magickal orders were forbidden except for the High Order of the Golden Door. Magicians possessed abilities that could be of great advantage to Altania. Yet they could not be trusted to operate according to their own devices, not when magick was a thing that could be used to open doors and undo locks, uncovering things which must, for the good of the nation, remain protected.

That was why Lord Valhaine had commissioned an official order of magicians, one that could be watched and controlled. But it was known that there were still other arcane societies in existence, ones operating in secret, and with purposes that were opposed to those of the government. While Huntley Morden might assail the nation from its shores, these magicians were working to sabotage Altania from within. Lord Valhaine wanted an end put to all of them.

And this was how Lady Quent could prove her loyalty to the nation.

"We are aware that Lord Rafferdy continues to visit you with some regularity," Lady Shayde concluded. "You need not appear surprised. The Gray Conclave makes many observations in the city, and as a result we know many things. All that is important is that you continue to encourage Lord Rafferdy to call upon you as often as he can. Remain in his confidence, and listen to all that he says. Then, each time after he leaves, simply compose a report that recounts everything that he has said. You need not try to discern what is important and what is not. We will do that. Rather, just write down everything he relates to you, however small or insignificant it might seem."

Ivy's legs could no longer bear her weight, and she found herself sinking down into a chair.

"Do you see how little a thing it is I ask of you, Lady Quent? It would be like dashing off a brief note to a friend, describing your conversations with Lord Rafferdy. That's all."

The parlor seemed to tilt at a dizzy angle, as if some titan from Tharosian mythology had lifted up a corner of the house.

"And what if I were to refuse?"

Lady Shayde moved around the pianoforte to Lily's folio. She opened it once more and turned through the pages.

"Sir Quent will soon be brought again before Assembly, this time to be tried for the crime he is accused of. What do you think would happen if, during the trial, it was revealed that a sister of his wife had an unhealthy interest in illusionists, and another sister possessed an ability known to be associated with illusionists and witches? What if it was also revealed that this wife of Sir Quent maintained a close acquaintance with a man publicly known to wear the House ring of a magician? I do not think it would bode well for his defense if such things were made known." She closed the book again and looked at Ivy. "Do you, Lady Quent?"

Ivy was shaking now, and could do nothing to conceal it. She felt ill, as if gripped by a fever. "Do you hate him, then?" she said at last.

"Hate him?" Lady Shayde folded her gloved hands before her. "No, I do not hate Sir Quent."

"Then why? Why are you doing this to him?"

The other woman's face was as cool and hard as porcelain. "I do not hate him, but neither do I love him. As I said before, Lady Quent, I suffer no such sensibilities. I only do what must be done for Altania."

"Are you certain of that? Is it really for Altania that you do these things, or is it simply for him—for Lord Valhaine?" Despite her trembling, and the weakness that gripped her, there was a sudden sharpness to Ivy's voice. "You are like a knife in his hand, Ashaydea. You cut in whatever direction he wields you and assume it is what is most right. But what if it isn't? What does a knife do, Lady Shayde, when it discovers the hand that holds it is in fact that of a murderer or a madman?"

Once again, for a brief moment, it was as if fine cracks appeared upon the smooth surface of Lady Shayde's face, and it grew paler yet.

Then the moment passed. "Will you aid me as I have requested or not, Lady Quent?"

Ivy made no answer.

Lady Shayde moved toward the chair where Ivy sat. "I am puzzled, Lady Quent. Of these two men, do you not love your husband the best?"

"You answer your own question. He is my husband."

"Then you will do as I ask of you?"

Ivy looked down at her hands. Every instinct in her strained to say yes. She wanted Mr. Quent returned to her, more than anything in the world.

Yet it was not simply a matter of whom she loved best. Even if she could somehow endure betraying a dear friend in the suggested manner, a thing she knew she could not bear, what if Mr. Quent were to learn how she had achieved his freedom? How could he not recoil from her in loathing? For she would have revealed herself as the most maleficent deceiver, one who would betray a man to certain death in order to gain what she most craved and desired. And so she would not lose one of the two men she held most dear in all the world, but rather both of them.

And it was even more than that. Lady Shayde said what she did was for the good of Altania, only it was not. Ivy knew her husband, and she knew there was one thing he would want her to do above all—to do what the Inquiry had always striven to do, to protect the Wyrdwood. And that was why Mr. Rafferdy needed to remain in Assembly, along with the other members of his arcane order.

A peculiar kind of calmness came over Ivy. She was still trembling, but the feeling of illness and fever had passed. She looked up.

"No," she said, quietly and simply. And again, "No."

For a long moment Lady Shayde looked down upon her. Yet there must have been some hardness in Ivy's own countenance, for the other woman gave no argument to this reply.

At last she said, "I would feel pity for you, Lady Quent, if I could. I will not come to you again as an agent of Lord Valhaine. Good-bye."

There was a stiff crackling of cloth, followed by silence. But Ivy did not see the other depart. Instead, her face was in her hands as she wept.

CHAPTER TWENTY-TWO

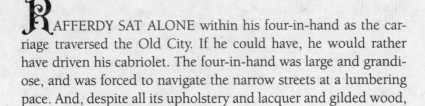

RAFFERDY SAT ALONE within his four-in-hand as the carriage traversed the Old City. If he could have, he would rather have driven his cabriolet. The four-in-hand was large and grandiose, and was forced to navigate the narrow streets at a lumbering pace. And, despite all its upholstery and lacquer and gilded wood, it was anything but comfortable.

Yet it was appearances that mattered today, not comfort. Rafferdy had chosen to take the four-in-hand for the same reason he had put on a formal suit of rich black wool that was far too heavy for the rapidly warming morning. Namely, he needed to appear in every way a lord—a magnate of stature, one whose demands must not be questioned.

He leaned back against the overstuffed seat and took an object from his pocket. It was a small gem or crystal, pale in color, and with a cloudy interior. Trefnell had given it to him last night, along with another that was its twin in every way. This was after Rafferdy had risked going to Trefnell's house and explained why he had come. At the time, Rafferdy hadn't been certain there even was a magick that could do what he wanted; though he had reasoned that if anyone knew, it would be Trefnell.

He was right. After Rafferdy described what he hoped to accomplish, the former schoolmaster had gone into his study, then soon emerged again with the two matching gems, one in each hand.

"I came upon them many years ago in the Principalities," he had said. "The gems are quite old. Their enchantment is such that they are bound. That is, light that enters into one is reflected in the facets of the other."

"So, they're like our black books."

"Not quite. Our books have a sympathetic resonance that links them. But these gems are more like two halves of the same magickal door, though their power is somewhat limited. To activate a gem, one simply taps it three times in quick succession. What light reaches it for the next several minutes will be absorbed into it, and then it will go dark. Then, if one similarly taps the paired gem at a later time, it will emit all of the light gathered by the first."

"Fascinating," Rafferdy had said, accepting the two gems.

"Careful!" Trefnell had cautioned him. "Do not let the gems come in contact with each other. It is best if you keep them well apart."

"Why is that?"

"As I said, they are like two halves of the same magickal gate. And if you should happen to accidentally tap them three times while they are in contact with each other . . ." Trefnell raised a shaggy eyebrow. "Well, I believe you know what happens if a gate is ever made to open upon itself."

Yes, Rafferdy did. Or at least, he had read many warnings about what would happen. Over the years, more than one magician had accidentally demonstrated the perils of creating a magickal gate or doorway such that its entrance was in the same location as its exit. In this case, anything that entered the gate would, at the same time, be leaving it—and also entering it again. This circle could not be broken, and it would repeat itself an unfathomable number of times in an instant. The arcane energy would rapidly build upon itself—doubling, quadrupling, and so on—until an irrevocable instability resulted, violently ripping apart the gate. Along with the unfortunate magician, if he happened to be anywhere near it.

Of course, the paired gems were small, and their enchantment limited. All the same, Rafferdy had used great care as he placed the gems into opposite pockets of his coat. Then he quickly departed Trefnell's house before anyone might notice he was there. It was the habit of the members of the Silver Circle not to be seen speaking with one another if possible, lest anyone become aware of their connections.

Now, Rafferdy held the small gem up to the circular window in the carriage door. Like its twin, which was now locked in a drawer at his house in Warwent Square, the gem was cut and polished. Only it seemed not to reflect the sunlight that fell upon it, but rather to absorb it into its center. He peered closer at the gem, and after a moment he almost thought he could detect a movement in its cloudy depths, like mists swirling. . . .

With a clattering of hooves, the carriage came to a halt. Rafferdy looked up from the gem. Outside, beyond an iron fence, was a large, handsome house built of reddish stone. He was there.

Usually he looked forward to seeing Mrs. Quent under any circumstance, but Rafferdy could not help suffering a trepidation on this particular occasion. He had found a way to get Mrs. Quent into Barrowgate, presuming everything went as he intended. Yet, so far, he had conceived of no way to get Mr. Quent out of that same place. He had some ideas, of course, but they were no more than half-formed notions. And while he knew Mrs. Quent would never directly place such a demand on him, still he would see it in her eyes: a hope that he would be able to effect her husband's release.

Well, he would not stop trying to find a way. And no matter how it would happen, the first step was to see Sir Quent, to assure that he was well, and to get his thoughts regarding the ideas Rafferdy was considering. Once Sir Quent had helped him choose the most likely path of success, Rafferdy would do everything in his power to follow it.

At this thought, he could not help letting out a rueful laugh. It was not lost on Rafferdy that he was subjecting himself to dire risk in order to save the very man who possessed the one thing Rafferdy had ever really wanted—namely, Mrs. Ivoleyn Lockwell Quent. It was a paradoxical thought, that he should now be helping his rival at possible cost to himself!

Except Rafferdy would have done it no matter his history with Mrs. Quent, for he both liked and respected Sir Quent. What was more, Rafferdy knew how important an ally he was of Altania and the Wyrdwood. It was for the good of the country that Sir Quent be freed. Yet as true as all of these things were, none of them were the real reason he was trying to help free Sir Quent. Rafferdy knew himself, and he knew why he was really doing this. It was for Mrs. Quent, and for her alone.

The carriage door opened. "We have arrived, sir," the driver said.

Rafferdy climbed out of the carriage and tucked the gem into the pocket of his coat. He made his way up the walk, past the stone lions, and rapped on the door with the ivory handle of his cane. The housekeeper promptly answered and showed him in. She was more tight-lipped than usual, but given present circumstances, that could hardly be considered a surprise.

He waited but a moment in the front hall before a pretty figure in a yellow dress entered from the parlor. Only it was not Mrs. Quent, but rather the youngest Miss Lockwell.

"Good morning, Miss Lily," he said with a bow.

She looked up, as if she had not realized he was there. "Hello, Lord Rafferdy." She was holding a large book in her hand.

He waited for some bit of silly chatter from her, but when it did not ensue, he said, "Is Lady Quent about?"

"My sister? She's upstairs at the moment. I'm sure she'll be down very soon. She was delayed by another caller who just left."

Another caller? Rafferdy could not guess who would have come to pay her a visit now that Lady Marsdel and Mrs. Baydon were no longer in the city, nor did Lily say. Indeed, she seemed preoccupied with something, and was already drifting toward the stairs. Rafferdy found this strange, as he was used to being plied with annoying and unwanted questions by Lily, yet she seemed to have no interest in him at all.

"I will be sure to tell Mr. Garritt hello for you the next time I see him."

It was the first thing he could think of to get her attention. Indeed it worked, for she turned from the staircase, her brown eyes a bit wider now in her oval face.

"Mr. Garritt? Do you mean you've seen him lately?"

"Yes I have, very recently. It was at a . . ." He hesitated, realizing he had not selected this topic with much forethought. It would hardly be appropriate to say where it was that he had met Garritt. "It was the other day," he finished awkwardly.

She took a step toward him, holding the large book close to her. "And how did he look? Was he well?"

Rafferdy tried to decide how to answer this question for her. In fact, he was still trying to answer it for himself. To find Garritt coming out of a theater on Durrow Street had been both astonishing and puzzling. Rafferdy would never have expected to encounter such a fine and diffident soul in such an unwholesome and disreputable place.

Then the illusion of a golden bird had appeared on Garritt's hand, and suddenly it had made sense. Not simply his presence there, but everything in their entire history—from Garritt's confounding interest in poetry and plays to his equally confounding disinterest in pretty girls.

Rafferdy could not claim this revelation had not shocked him; it had, for it was something that had never occurred to him. All the same, when the bird fluffed up its impossible gold feathers and then, on Garritt's cue, flew up into the air and vanished, he had been utterly fascinated and delighted. Rafferdy was not a person who could ever remain in a state of surprise or disbelief for very long. He was too much enamored of novelty for that. In the same way he had quickly recovered from his astonishment at discovering Mrs. Quent's nature at the Wyrdwood, so he all but immediately found himself wanting to learn more about Garritt's abilities.

With this idea in mind, he seized Garritt's hand and fairly dragged him into the dim interior of the nearest tavern. Despite his startling disclosure, he was clearly still the same old Garritt, for he at once assumed the most glum and morose demeanor, hanging his head over his cup.

"You can only despise me now that you know what I am," he had said. "You have brought me here to rebuke me for deceiving you for so long, and I cannot blame you for it."

"Good God, Garritt!" Rafferdy had exclaimed with a great laugh. "If I wished to chastise you, I would hardly be buying you a cup of punch! Now tell me, what can you do? Do you simply have an interest in that theater, or have you been performing on the stage there yourself? I rather think it's the latter, as you've hinted previously that you have some business that is going well for you."

Garritt had looked up and, by his slack expression, was incredulous at these words. But Rafferdy reiterated them, and coaxed him further, and bought him more punch, and at last Garritt was induced to reveal all. Indeed, once the tale began to flow out of him, it could hardly be stopped. A dam that has long held back a reservoir does not bear up long once a chink is opened in it; instead, a flood gushes out, washing the barrier away, and so it was with Garritt.

Rafferdy learned about the things Garritt could do, how he shaped light and performed in illusion plays at the theater, and even how he had learned to make impressions, several of which he had sold to the broadsheets. For all his newfound forthcomingness, though, there was one thing Garritt did not reveal, at least not directly.

Yet it is the case that sometimes the pauses and the spaces and silences between words carry as much meaning as what is spoken. There was a young man Garritt alluded to several times. Rafferdy got the impression he was gone now, but it was clear this other young man was sorely missed. Only once did Garritt speak his name, *Dercy*, but this was done with a tone of such tender sadness that there could be no doubting how the two of them had been related—and not through the fraternal camaraderie felt by two members of the same venture.

After these revelations, many men might have recoiled and withdrawn, but not Rafferdy. On the contrary, he felt only a greater affinity to his friend. Previously, Garritt had seemed so wholesome and chaste as to be almost exasperatingly decent. But in truth, he was as marvelously imperfect as any man fashioned of flesh, blood, and bone. To learn it was a relief!

At last the pot of punch was done, and Garritt heaved a great sigh, his shoulders moving as if relieved of a dreadful weight.

"I don't know how to thank you, Rafferdy," he said. "To have you still sitting here with me, after all I've said—it's remarkable. I'm sorry to have kept this all a secret from you for so long."

Rafferdy was usually not one to offer apologies, but this was not a usual occasion. "No, it is I who am sorry, Garritt. I have always treated you as if you were some marble icon of a saint—a thing too pure and unblemished to harbor indecent thoughts like the rest of us. It was terribly unfair to impose such a constraint upon you. When I gave you no room to commit even little sins, how could you have revealed what some would hold to be a great one?"

"And don't *you* hold it as such?"

Though it was rare for Rafferdy to be at a loss for words, he was then—but only for a moment.

"I know that's what we're told to believe. But then again, lately I have learned that a great many things people believe about this world and its denizens are in fact utter rubbish. Given my knowledge of you, Garritt, I'm forced to relegate such beliefs to the same category. I cannot accept that being an illusionist makes a man innately wicked—not when I know without doubt that *you* are inherently good."

And with that, it was done. Garritt had business to attend to, and so did Rafferdy. They rose from the table, went outside, and shook hands, friends still and for always.

"I haven't told you everything, you know," Garritt had said then, rather wistfully.

"No, I'm sure you haven't," Rafferdy replied. "But then again, neither have I."

Garritt had gaped at him, but Rafferdy only winked, then swung his cane and started off down Durrow Street. That they would speak again soon, he was sure. And maybe then it would be time for Rafferdy to reveal a few of his own secrets. That he could trust Garritt with them, he was sure; they were both of them outside the bounds of society now.

"Lord Rafferdy?" Lily said, and took another step toward him. "I asked you if Mr. Garritt was well."

He blinked, realizing he had been silent as he decided what to say. Only why shouldn't he answer with the truth?

"Yes, he's very well," Rafferdy said, and smiled.

Lily smiled herself now. "I'm very glad to hear it. I wonder—that is, do you think he will ever come to call on us again?"

"I do not know," Rafferdy said, again being truthful.

"I don't think that he will," Lily said, and she tightened her arms around the large leather-covered book. "I think that, if we ever wish to see him again, we'll have to go look for him ourselves."

Rafferdy's smile dwindled at this response. Previously, Mrs. Quent had told him about Lily's drawings and their subject matter. Before he could think of what to say, though, a small yet elegant figure descended the stairs.

"Good-bye, Lord Rafferdy," Lily said, then turned and bounded up the staircase even as Mrs. Quent reached the bottom.

She was lovely in a dress the gray-green color of heather, and several stray locks of gold hair fell upon her shoulders like shafts of sun upon a moor. Yet she looked exceedingly pale, and when he took her hand in greeting he felt it quiver, curling within his own like some tiny, frightened creature seeking refuge. He would have thought the idea of seeing her husband would fill her with excitement more than dread.

"Are you well, Mrs. Quent? Perhaps we should wait for a moment before we go."

But she said, or rather gasped, "Lady Shayde was here."

So that was who had come to call at the house. Now he understood the reason for her trembling.

Rafferdy kept his grip on her hand, holding her steady. "What did she say to you?"

Mrs. Quent looked away. "Awful things."

"I fear that can be no surprise. Did she come hoping to learn something? Something about your husband?"

"No. Or rather, not anything regarding Mr. Quent."

Rafferdy shivered himself, despite his heavy wool suit. "But she did come seeking knowledge of someone."

Mrs. Quent looked back at him again, and now he no longer held her hand, but rather she gripped his, tightly.

"Lady Shayde knows, Mr. Rafferdy. Or at least, she strongly suspects that you are involved in"—she leaned in close, and the wooden eye upon the newel post turned in its socket, as if interested in what she would say—"she knows that you are involved with an arcane order that threatens the government."

The reaction this evoked in Rafferdy surprised him. He knew he should dread the fact that Lady Shayde held him in suspicion. Yet instead he felt a peculiar sort of pride and satisfaction. In a way, to be deemed a possible threat to the government was a noteworthy accomplishment. Besides, he had long known that Lady Shayde suspected him of working magick.

"I am sorry to have put you in such a dreadful position, Mrs. Quent," he said. "But in a way, this is excellent news."

"Excellent news! How so?"

"It means, for all her suspicions, Lady Shayde has no proof of anything our order has done. If she had, she would move against me herself, rather than try to prize secrets from you."

Mrs. Quent hesitated, then nodded. "I think that must be so. Nor did I tell her anything that might have helped her."

"For that, I thank you."

It seemed she wanted to say something, but after a long moment it was only a sigh that escaped her.

"Shall we go then?" he said.

And they did.

BARROWGATE was situated on the northwestern edge of the Old City, and the drive there seemed inordinately long. Not only was the four-in-hand forced to proceed slowly, the streets were also thick with royal soldiers in their blue coats and red-crested helmets.

Except the redcrests weren't truly royal soldiers anymore. Princess Layle was shut away somewhere in the Citadel, and no one had seen her in nearly a half month. The army was under the command of the Lord Guardian of the nation; they were Valhaine's soldiers now.

Often the soldiers would stop a cart or carriage at random to question the occupants or examine any goods contained therein. Several times the four-in-hand was blocked from progressing along a narrow street as the soldiers made an examination of some other vehicle just ahead. Yet they never stopped Rafferdy's carriage. Such a grand and gilded coach could only belong to an important lord. At least, that is what Rafferdy had hoped they would think. Whether this was the case, or it was merely chance, they at last reached Barrowgate unhindered.

Barrowgate itself was no more than a low, nondescript door set into the wall that ringed the Old City. During the time of the first Mabingorian kings, when Altania was afflicted by bloody civil wars and subjected to invasions from the Murgh Empire, it was the passage by which the vast number of prisoners who were executed or otherwise perished in jail were taken out of the city to be heaped in unmarked graves.

These days it was not empty fields that lay beyond the wall, but rather the district of Lowpark, for Invarel had grown much since then, and the door was now used by people moving between the different parts of the city. But after all these years, some things about the Barrowgate had not changed. There was still a prison beside the door, and its walls of black stone were still devoid of any windows, so that neither light nor hope could enter into the dungeons below. As always, a gibbet stood in the square before those black walls. And those who met their end upon a rope were still taken through the door in the wall, to be buried on unhallowed ground outside the city.

The carriage came to a halt. The broad square before Barrowgate was empty now; the gallows stood unused, for the moment at least.

"Would you like to wait here in the carriage?" he said to Mrs. Quent, who sat on the bench opposite him. "I can go in to make sure he is . . . that all is ready for our audience."

His fear was that Sir Quent would be in a physical state that might be shocking for her to witness, and he wanted to have a chance to correct that, if possible, before she saw him.

"Thank you, Mr. Rafferdy, but I will go with you." Though her face was pale, there was no quaver to her voice.

The driver opened the door. Rafferdy exited, then took her hand to help her from the carriage. Together, they approached the soldiers standing before the prison. Rafferdy exchanged a few words with a stern-faced captain. His coming was expected; a soldier was ordered to take them to see the lieutenant inside the prison. They entered the hulking stone building, and it was like stepping from lumenal into the depths of an umbral. Oil lamps lined the halls, casting a wan and sputtering light.

"It is cold in here," Mrs. Quent murmured, tightening her hold on his arm as they followed the soldier.

Mr. Rafferdy had previously thought the wool suit too hot, but now he was glad for it, for the thick stone walls radiated a chill. Mrs. Quent wore only her light gown of gray-green.

"Stay close to me," he said, and it was not only her shivering that was on his mind as he said this. Rafferdy had noticed the looks some of the soldiers had given her as they entered; he imagined many of them had not been close to a pretty lady in some time. While he feared no untoward action on their part, still he did not want her subjected to such gazes.

They were soon brought to the office of the lieutenant. He was a smallish fellow of middle years who was easier to picture as a bank clerk than a military man and a superintendent at a notorious prison. The papers on his desk were organized into neat regiments, and he had a habit of frequently using his handkerchief to wipe his hands after touching almost any object.

Rafferdy explained his purpose in coming, and the lieutenant quickly retrieved a paper from within one of the stacks.

"I have the letter from the Citadel, and everything appears to be in order," he said, his eyes on the paper rather than Rafferdy. "Corporal Lewell here will escort you to a chamber where you can wait while the prisoner is prepared. Once he is ready, you can interview him however you will, your lordship."

Rafferdy felt Mrs. Quent stiffen beside him. He imagined she did not care for the idea of the prisoner being *prepared* any more than he did.

"Thank you, Lieutenant" was all Rafferdy said.

The lieutenant nodded absently. He made some marks upon the paper and placed it on a different stack, then took out his handkerchief and wiped his hands.

Rafferdy waited for some comment regarding the presence of Mrs. Quent, but none came. Perhaps a woman was beneath the lieutenant's notice. Or more likely, the orders from the Citadel had contained no proscription against the interviewer being accompanied, and so it was not a thing of note. It was clear all that mattered to the lieutenant was being able to properly marshal his papers upon his desk, and he proceeded to do this now, as if the visitors were no longer there.

"Follow me, sir," the corporal said.

He led them through more dark hallways and down a stairway, and the air grew colder yet. Finally they were shown into a small room furnished with only a single wooden bench.

"Please wait here," the soldier instructed. He used a large key to lock the door by which they had entered the room. Then he went to another door in the opposite wall of the chamber. This door was made of metal rather than wood. He exited through it, and again they heard a lock turning. They were, for the moment, prisoners themselves.

"I hope it will not take them long to bring Sir Quent to us," Rafferdy said, then winced at the way his voice echoed in the bare room.

"I do not care how long it takes," Mrs. Quent said.

Rafferdy only nodded. Even if speaking was not so disconcerting in this echoing space, still he would not have known what to say. He was bracing himself for the sight of Sir Quent just as much as she was.

"I was ill, you know," she said softly, breaking the long silence.

He looked at her beside him on the bench, startled by this.

"Ill?" he said at last. "When?"

"A few months ago, the last time my husband was out of the city," she said. "It was not yet public knowledge, but we were all of us in the household expecting a happy occasion, one that is often anticipated a year or so after marriage. Only I had . . . that was, a misfortune occurred, and after that our hopes were let go. It was not to be."

Now he could only stare at her. If any confusion as to the meaning of her words remained, it was dispelled as her hand crept to the waist of her gown, as if to touch something that was no longer there.

Rafferdy found himself in shock for a moment. To think of Mrs. Quent as a mother was—well, he did not know what it was he thought, but all the same it left him unsettled. Yet that was a vain and inconsiderate notion, and it was quickly dismissed and replaced by real concern. To have Sir Quent taken from her was a grave sorrow, but it had not been her first of late.

"I am very sorry," he said quietly.

"It was to have been a boy. But I am . . . that is, I think you must understand, Mr. Rafferdy, that it is not likely I will ever be mother to a son. And if by some chance I ever were, then he would almost certainly be . . ."

He would be like Eldyn Garritt, Rafferdy wanted to say. *And that is far from a terrible thing.*

But that was not his news to impart, so he remained silent.

"As grieved as I was by what happened, I was comforted by the belief that we would still have a child someday, a bright little daughter to delight us both." Now she looked, not at Rafferdy, but at the iron door in the opposite wall. "But I must wonder if that will really happen, if I will ever in my life know the joy of being a mother."

Rafferdy wanted to speak, but to say what? How could he assure her that she could anticipate such a happy future when he still had no idea how to free Sir Quent from this place? Yet why were they here at all, if they did not have some hope?

"I do not know what will come to be," he said at last. "But I do believe that there is yet joy in your future. I cannot say I have ever believed much in my life, but I do believe that."

Still she kept her gaze fixed on the door, but her hand slipped from her gown and found his where it rested on the bench, gripping it tightly. He hesitated for only a moment, then he clasped that small hand in return, and he could not help noticing how fine and light it was.

With a clanking of metal, the door in the far wall opened. Rafferdy rose to his feet, as did Mrs. Quent beside him. Then Corporal Lewell stepped through the door.

"The prisoner is ready to be interviewed, sir."

Rafferdy turned to Mrs. Quent. "Let me go first. Then when all is ready, I will call for you."

He did not know if it was the graveness of his voice, or if it was that she understood his concern, but this time she did not insist on going with him, and only nodded. Rafferdy gave her a look he hoped was reassuring, then he went to the door and stepped through.

The slab of iron shut with a clanging behind him.

As it was his desire to speak to Sir Quent in private, Rafferdy was relieved to see the corporal had not followed him through. What was more, his relief was compounded as soon as he set eyes upon Sir Quent himself.

They had placed him in a chair which was bolted into the floor, and had bound his wrists and ankles to it with manacles. This was a hard sight to bear, but it was ameliorated by Sir Quent's appearance. He looked pallid, as was to be expected from a deprivation of sunlight, and his hair and beard had been allowed to grow to a rather wild state. But other than these things, he appeared well. His face was clean, as were the gray shirt and breeches they had clothed him in. True, he seemed somewhat thinner than before, but he was in no way emaciated, and in the light of the oil lamps mounted on the wall his eyes were bright and clear.

"Great Gods, sir," Rafferdy found himself saying as he rushed forward, "but it is good to see you."

That tangled beard split in a broad grin. "I can claim the same with regard to you, Lord Rafferdy. I was told only that a magnate wished to interview me, so you can imagine I was looking forward to the occasion with little relish, even though I was glad enough for a chance to leave my prison and move a bit. But to see it is you who have come . . ." Now that grin faltered, and his eyes grew brighter yet. "I am grateful beyond words. But please, can you tell me, how is Lady Quent?"

That Sir Quent's initial concern was not for the fact of his own imprisonment, but rather for the state of his wife, was no surprise to Rafferdy. Another chair had been arranged some distance from Sir Quent's. Rafferdy dragged it closer and sat.

"She is grievously distressed, as you can imagine, and so are her sisters. Yet she bears it all with remarkable fortitude and composure, as you can also imagine." Despite the grim environs, he could not help smiling. "But you will be able to see for yourself, for she is here, just beyond that door."

Sir Quent's expression was one of great bewilderment, as if he hardly comprehended what Rafferdy had said. Then, gradually, a look of wonder crept across his visage.

"Ivoleyn is here." He spoke lowly. "I had not believed such a thing possible. I had resigned myself to it. But now . . . is it so? Will I truly be able to see her once again?"

Rafferdy laid a hand on his shackled arm. "Yes. I had only wanted to make certain that . . ."

"That my appearance was not too shocking," he replied, meeting Rafferdy's gaze. "Yes, that was good thinking. But for all that I am rarely let out of the little chamber I am imprisoned in, and there are few comforts to be had within it, my treatment here has not been overly cruel. Therefore I trust I am not too dreadful to behold."

"Not at all," Rafferdy said. "You look remarkably well. I will go fetch your wife at once." He started to rise from the chair.

"Wait for a moment, Lord Rafferdy."

These words were spoken in a deep and solemn rumble. Rafferdy hardly knew what to think of them. Sir Quent's lovely and utterly remarkable wife was just beyond that iron door. That he should seek to delay his reunion with her was inconceivable.

"Was there not something else you and I needed to discuss before I see Ivoleyn?" Sir Quent said.

Yes, there was. Rafferdy had become so caught up in the idea of reuniting Mrs. Quent with her husband that he had forgotten what other business they needed to conduct. Slowly, he sat back in the chair.

"I have some thoughts on the matter of your situation," he said, with urgency now. "I would call them notions, really, for they are not well formed and are based on conjecture. You are more familiar with the methods of the Citadel than I, and I can only guess at the workings of the Gray Conclave. But I have some abilities I can bring to bear in Assembly. We have not yet foregone all of our old rules! Some due must be paid to them for Lord Valhaine's authority to have any semblance of credibility. If I describe my thoughts to you, then you can add your insight to them, and so we might form them into a plan to effect your acquittal before the Hall of Magnates."

Rafferdy leaned forward in the chair, eager to explain the obscure rules he had discovered and the procedural gambits they might permit, but before he could do so, Sir Quent shook his head.

"No, Lord Rafferdy, that is not what I meant. You and I could easily discuss such matters on our own. But even if there was any use to such an exercise, that cannot be why you brought *her* here."

No, it wasn't.

"It is dangerous for Lady Quent to remain in the city at present," Rafferdy said, getting right to the point. "It is no longer a rumor that the Black Dog has formulated a method of detecting whether a woman is a witch or not, but rather a fact."

Sir Quent's face blanched another degree, but all the same he nodded. "I have suspected for some time that Lord Valhaine sought such a thing. He has increasingly spoken of the Wyrdwood as a grave threat to Altania."

"I believe in that he is only echoing the opinions of his magicians," Rafferdy said. "The High Order of the Golden Door are surely in league with those who dread the Wyrdwood and what it might do."

Sir Quent nodded. "I believe you are correct, Lord Rafferdy. And you are correct as well that my wife is in peril so long as she remains in Invarel. You no doubt wish for her to go to the east, to stay with Lady Marsdel I presume, if her ladyship has retreated there by now. But Ivoleyn will never consent to leave the city while I am imprisoned here. And so you brought her to me, so that I could convince her to depart the city."

"Yes," Rafferdy said plainly.

Sir Quent gave a firm nod. "Good man. And yet . . . you must know that peril could easily follow Lady Quent into the east, or anywhere she might go—at least so long as she bears that name."

Rafferdy did not understand; or rather, perhaps he did not wish to. "What do you mean?"

Sir Quent let out a deep breath. "You know what will become of her as the wife of a confirmed traitor to the nation. If I face trial, and if I am convicted of this crime, then everything that is mine—every coin and inch of land—will be stripped away and returned to the government. She will be left with nothing. She and her sisters will be deprived entirely of support."

"Lady Quent can want for neither thing so long as she has friends such as Lady Marsdel and myself."

"But she will be deprived of these as well! To shun her will be required by law. To aid her or take her in will be to bring the wrath of the government upon you. Could you allow such a thing to happen to Lady Marsdel?"

No, he could not, Rafferdy knew. "But still I would help her."

"Yes, I know you would, Lord Rafferdy. Or that you would try. But could you bear up to the scrutiny on the part of the government that such an act would surely bring upon you?" His gaze went to Rafferdy's right hand, to the ring they both knew lay concealed beneath the kidskin glove. "You are the son of the former lord inquirer and a known magician. What would happen once you provide aid to the wife of a convicted traitor? How much more suspicion need be cast upon you before you find yourself situated just as I am now? Not much, I would think."

Rafferdy wanted to counter these words, but before he could think how, Sir Quent went on.

"You know that I am right in this. To help her after I am convicted would only assure your own doom. And so she would have no one at all in the world to protect her. She would be utterly alone and in ruins. That is something I will not allow." He clenched his hands within the manacles, and his voice grew so low it was as if he were speaking to someone other than Rafferdy. "I failed to protect Gennivel, to keep her safe when it was my duty. I will not fail to do the same for Ivoleyn."

Rafferdy did not even attempt a response to this. He knew the story of the first Mrs. Quent, and how she had died years ago trying to climb the wall of a stand of Wyrdwood.

"You must work to get Ivoleyn out of the city at once, Lord Rafferdy," Sir Quent went on, addressing him now. "I will do my best to convince her to leave. Yet, in the end . . ." A visible shudder passed through him. "In the end, I believe there is one thing only that will release her and permit her to go."

Rafferdy stared, a creeping feeling progressing up his neck. "What do you mean?"

The other man looked down for a moment, as if to gather his thoughts. Or perhaps his courage. Then, at last, he raised his head.

"Tell me, Lord Rafferdy, what are your feelings for Ivoleyn? Are they similar to what you might feel for a friend, such as Mrs. Baydon? Or are they perhaps something more than that?"

Rafferdy leaped from his chair, and his face stung as if he had been struck a blow. "She is your wife, sir!" he exclaimed.

"A fact of which I am well aware. And if you think I do not treasure her as jealously as any king ever did a jeweled treasure . . . but no, I see that you do know this. All the same, if your feelings for her are something other than what you would profess publicly, or might even admit in private, then I wish you would speak them to me now."

Rafferdy might almost have thought he was being mocked or tormented except for the solemn light in the other man's brown eyes. Still he said, "Even if it were true, why would I ever confess to such a thing as that?"

"Because it would give me assurance that she will be cared for. In the times that come, she will have great need of something more than an acquaintance or friend can give. But I will not be able to provide that for her. I appreciate your efforts on my behalf, Lord Rafferdy, and I do not doubt your cleverness. But be assured that any scheme you might try in the name of freeing me will prove futile. I know Lord Valhaine well. The Black Dog does not bite without sinking in his teeth."

With a look and a flick of his finger, he silenced Rafferdy's retort.

"It is a fact, Lord Rafferdy. There is nothing that can be done for it. If I am brought to trial before the Hall of Magnates, I will be convicted. And as I told you, I cannot permit that. Above all else, I cannot let Ivoleyn become the wife of a confirmed traitor to the realm."

"But then what can you do?" Rafferdy managed to say at last.

"Do not worry, Lord Rafferdy. Lord Valhaine has always thought me stolid and dull, but I am not without my own ability to scheme. There is yet one thing I may do."

"And what is that?"

"You need not know the particulars. Suffice it to say I have a favor I can call in—an old debt, if you will. So that is resolved. But one thing is not—you have yet to answer my question."

Rafferdy wanted to believe he had no idea what sort of debt Sir Quent intended to collect, and how he planned to avert his conviction before the Hall of Magnates. Only that wasn't so; he did have an idea, a most terrible idea. And knowing that, how could he answer with anything but the truth? Throughout his life, Rafferdy had always been quick with a glib falsehood if it suited his purposes. But he could not lie to Sir Quent—not here and not now.

"Ivoleyn is the most beautiful and remarkable woman in all of Altania," he said, his throat so tight the words inflicted a pain upon him, but he forged on all the same. "I admire and love her to the fullest extent I am capable. I have ever since meeting her, though I was too stupid to understand at first what it was I felt. And once I did, I was too cowardly to make a stand for it."

Rafferdy's hands made themselves into fists at his sides—then he forced them to unclench. If Sir Quent could bear his fate resolutely, then at the least Rafferdy must bear this.

"So you see, even if she had never made your acquaintance, Sir Quent, still I would not have won her for myself. I know what I am. I may be clever, as you say, and I will allow that of late I have done some things which have been of use. But I can assure you that this Lord Rafferdy is no more worthy of Lady Quent than Mr. Rafferdy ever was of Miss Lockwell."

Rafferdy thought he should say more, but he could not think of what. He supposed he should have been aghast to have made such a confession, but he was not. Sometimes a truth is so precious that it cannot be disowned, no matter the consequence.

For a long minute, both men were silent. At last Sir Quent nodded.

"Get her away from the city, Lord Rafferdy," he said at last. "Do whatever you must to accomplish it. Promise me you will do this."

A feeling came over Rafferdy then which surprised him. It was not sorrow, or regret, or any sort of dread. Rather, it was a determination that was so grim as to be peculiarly satisfying.

"I will," he said. "I swear it."

Both men gazed at each other and saw that it was settled. There was only one thing left to do. Rafferdy withdrew the small, colorless gem from his coat pocket. Quickly, he explained its use. Then he knelt and slipped it into Sir Quent's boot.

"Keep it hidden," he said, rising. "And if you should determine there is some other way to proceed, use it as I have described to send a message, and I will do what I can to come to you again."

"I may use it," the other man said, "but there is no other way."

Rafferdy bowed, not wanting Sir Quent to see the anguish upon his face, then he turned and went to the iron door.

"And, Dashton," Sir Quent said behind him.

Rafferdy paused, his hand upon the door.

"Make yourself worthy."

Rafferdy squared his shoulders and arranged his face into a solemn but calm expression. Then he opened the door and went to inform Lady Quent that her husband was ready to see her.

CHAPTER TWENTY-THREE

———————

$\mathfrak{T}$HE IRON DOOR shut behind Ivy with a knell that made her recall the thunder rolling across the moors around Heathcrest Hall.

She was aware of the figure of a man sitting in the center of the dim, windowless chamber, but she could not bring herself to look at him directly. It occurred to her that she should have gone to him at once, and flung herself down to put her head upon his knees, but she did not. Or rather, she could not, for a terror gripped her.

"It is all right, Ivoleyn," said a low, familiar voice. "You need not fear what you see when you look at me. I am well."

Slowly, through great force of will, Ivy turned her head and lifted her eyes. At last her gaze reached him, and what she saw filled her not with dread or sorrow, but with a sudden and piercing joy. Now she did rush forward, and knelt down on the cold floor before him. For a while they only looked at each other. No other sort of exchange was necessary. Eventually he let out a sigh, and she reached up to touch his face with both hands.

"Your beard is like a thicket of brambles!"

It was a silly thing to say, not in any way appropriate for the situation. Yet it caused him to laugh, and she would have laughed herself, if she had not already been weeping.

At last she withdrew a hand to wipe her cheeks. "You are too thin," she said. "And your face is pale. It is so dark in this place."

"Not anymore," he murmured, looking down at her. "Now it is exceedingly bright."

"You sound like Rose," she said, "seeing lights around me."

"But I do see a light around you, Ivoleyn. I always have."

She looked up at him, and his brown eyes shone, so that she almost could believe they did behold an illumination besides that of the smoking, sputtering oil lamps.

Ivy rose then, and proceeded to make an examination of him with light touches. She brushed her fingers over the familiar landscape of his shoulders, across the rugged crags of his face, and through his hair, which had grown into a long and tangled thatch like his beard.

"Are you satisfied I am well?" he rumbled at last.

"No, I am satisfied you are my husband. It might have been anyone beneath such a disheveled exterior."

Again he laughed, and this time she was able to echo him, if briefly. But quickly she grew solemn again.

"Dearest, what must we do?" she said softly, urgently. "What must we accomplish to have you released from this place?"

"I have already discussed such matters with Lord Rafferdy," he said in a low rumble. "There is nothing more that needs to be arranged on that account right now. The soldier will return for me soon. I would rather spend what time we have left in better ways. Learning how you have been, for one thing."

Ivy could not say she was entirely satisfied with this request. She wanted to know, without delay, how they were to effect his release. Yet she could not deny his request, not in his current state. Besides, she could ask Mr. Rafferdy later about what he and Mr. Quent had discussed.

"Now, bring that other chair close," he said. "Sit, and take my hands in yours, and tell me everything that has happened since I saw you last."

Ivy obeyed, sitting and twining her fingers with his, braiding them together like twigs of Wyrdwood. At first he gazed at her lovingly as she spoke, but his expression soon became one of growing concern. Ivy had not intended to burden him with the grim details of all that had happened, but once she began speaking about them, she found she could not stop.

Hardly pausing for a breath, she told him how they had been cut off from society, but that her sisters were bearing it well, and that Lady Marsdel and the Baydons had not abandoned her; only now they were gone from the city. Then she spoke of more troubling matters: the manner in which Mr. Fintaur and Mr. Larken were murdered, her conversation with Mr. Mundy, and her visit from Lady Shayde.

It was as she described this last happening that his expression grew especially grim. At last she was finished with her bleak litany. She wished she could have brought him news to lift his spirits in that awful place. But that she could have kept anything from him was, she knew now, impossible.

"So Ashaydea came to you again," he said, the furrows on his brow deepening. "And she offered to aid my cause if you would help her injure Lord Rafferdy's."

"But I could not," she said, and now she hung her head, suddenly unable to look at him.

"No, Ivoleyn, do not have any regrets. Your choice was the right one. To betray Lord Rafferdy for our gain would have been an abominable crime, one for which you would never have forgiven yourself. Besides, I can assure you that, even if you had held true to your end of the bargain, Lady Shayde would not have done the same. To release me, she would have had to undo the very laws which grant her master his power. She could no sooner do that than a knife could, of its own will, turn itself on its wielder. In the end, she would have betrayed you."

"Just as she betrayed you!" Ivy cried, her voice rising with anguish. "How can she see you come to this? Does she care nothing for your common history, for the years you spent together?"

He stroked her hand with his thumb. "No, Ivoleyn, there is no use in feeling anger for Ashaydea. She cannot be anything other than what she has been made into. Better that you should pity her than hate her."

"Why?" Ivy said, looking upon his face again. "Why should I not despise her?"

He gave a great sigh. "It would take a long time to explain, more time than I fear we have. But you spoke of our common history, and you should know that, while what happened to her that

day at the circle of stones near Heathcrest was Mr. Bennick's doing,
I cannot claim that I had no part in it. All of us in Earl Rylend's
household did."

As he spoke, some of Ivy's anguish was replaced by curiosity.
She remembered the old elf circle near Heathcrest Hall, and the
way the great stones appeared as if they had been cracked and
burned. What had happened all those years ago, when Ashaydea
was a ward of Earl Rylend, and Mr. Quent was the son of the earl's
steward? That the two had been close friends once, Ivy was certain. Only then Mr. Bennick had come to tutor the earl's son, and
everything was altered.

Yet as curious as she was, her husband was right. This time was
too precious to waste it upon discussions of Lady Shayde. Instead
she asked him about his treatment in the prison, which though
hard and oppressive, was not unbearable. He in turn inquired
after her sisters, and she spoke more of what she had learned of
Rose's ability to see light around certain people. This both fascinated and worried him, and he told her to keep her sister away
from any others that might be curious about this peculiar talent—a
matter upon which she agreed. When both of them were satisfied,
he glanced at the door opposite the one through which Ivy had
entered the chamber, but still the soldier had not come back for
him.

"I wonder," he said, "if Lord Valhaine has taken any actions
against the Wyrdwood yet. I did not have a chance to ask Lord
Rafferdy about it."

"I do not believe so," she said. "Or at least, no actions that have
been made public."

Ivy thought of the door Arantus in the upstairs gallery at the
house on Durrow Street. It occurred to her that she could unlock
it, step through, and look through the other portals that still
opened onto stands of Wyrdwood to see if they had been disturbed. Though she could not help thinking, if they had in fact
been attacked, somehow she would know it.

"But would it not be folly for him to do so?" she went on.

"Surely Lord Valhaine knows the reason why the Wyrdwood has been left all these years, and what would happen if it were attacked. No doubt you have told him that the more it is harmed, the more it will rise up and fight back."

"Yes, so I have told him, many times. I told him what my own father told me long ago, that the only way to win against the Old Trees is to lose something to them. But I fear that, in his heart, Valhaine has never really believed me. He was never a man who could accept any sort of defeat. And now he is greatly influenced by the magicians of the Golden Door."

"What of this?" she said, gently touching his left hand, and the thick scar where the last two fingers should have been. "Doesn't he believe this?"

He let out a low grunt. "He thinks it only a sign of my folly and an unnatural fascination with the Old Trees. Valhaine does not know the particulars of what happened."

"Neither do I," she murmured, stroking his wounded hand. "You told me it happened when you spent a greatnight in the Wyrdwood. But you've never told me what took place that night."

"No," he said gruffly, "I have not."

"But why?"

"I do not know. It was not something I had a wish to conceal from you, but nor was it something I have ever been eager to relate. Perhaps it is simply because, when I am with you, it is not the past and its hard lessons that I care to dwell on."

Still the soldier had not yet come. Ivy tightened her own fingers around the three that remained on his left hand. "Please," she said, gazing into his brown eyes. He looked away from her, and for a moment he was silent, so that she thought he would not speak at all.

Only then he did.

"My father gave me a small pocketknife the day I turned twelve," he said, then smiled fondly. "I do not have the knife anymore, but I can still picture it clearly. The blade was on a hinge, so that it could be folded inside the haft, which was inlaid with ivory he had brought from the Murgh Empire. It was exceedingly fine and was exceedingly sharp as well. As you might imagine, there was not a boy in the West Country who was prouder of a knife, and I used it to whittle many a stick and skin many a rabbit."

Ivy smiled herself at this image of her husband, not as the hale and powerful man she had always known, but as a boy of twelve, hunting for rabbits among the gorse upon the moors.

"Not long after my birthday came the start of the new year," he went on, his voice louder now. "It was still the custom then in the country, on the first umbral of the year, to beat the bounds of the village."

She shook her head. "Beat the bounds?"

"A bit of West Country superstition. Mrs. Seenly would know what I speak of. Beating the bounds is a tradition in which all the men would march about the edges of the village, banging pots and hammers or the like in order to make the greatest racket possible. The idea of old, I suppose, was to scare off any ghosts or spirits that might have slipped through the crack between the old year and the new. Of late, it was more an excuse for a noisy revel. But as I was twelve, I was now old enough to go with the men as they beat the bounds, and I was very excited to do it."

Fascinated, Ivy listened as he described that night more than thirty years ago. It seemed she was no longer in a dank chamber beneath Barrowgate, but there on the West Country moors, as people reveled in the village of Cairnbridge and bonfires leaped up toward the black sky.

At that time, the elder Mr. Quent had been the steward of Earl Rylend for many years, and the Quents dwelled in Burndale Lodge, in the hollow of the slope beneath Heathcrest Hall. Despite his service to the earl, Mr. Quent had not forgotten his ties to Cairnbridge. While the people of the manor did not participate in such quaint folk customs as First Umbral, Mr. Quent never failed to attend—his duties allowing, of course. So that year, young Alasdare Quent and his father rode down from Burndale Lodge to the village to join in.

The elder Mr. Quent was not game for beating the bounds of the village himself. By then, he was already under the grip of the illness which, though they did not know it then, was afflicted upon him by the curse of Am-Anaru. But the illness was not so severe then, causing only a bit of weakness and palsy, and he was happy to find a chair and a cup of wine near the bonfire. He gave his son permission to go with the other men on their rounds, and young Alasdare eagerly ran off to join them, the ivory-handled knife tucked in his pocket, just in case.

As it happened, the first umbral of the year was also a great-night, and so it was that the band of village men, having plenty of time and ale as well, roved far and wide around Cairnbridge, over heath and stream and dale, lighting the way with torches and lan-terns. Alasdare had little issue keeping up with them, as he was not drinking the ale himself, and he banged on his pot with great enthusiasm all the way.

In the course of their rounds, they did not come upon any ghosts or spirits. But there are other sorts of shadows that slink about on a greatnight. So it was, plunging down a slope and through a hedge, the group suddenly came upon a man leading five horses down a bridle path. The man wore a kilt of ragged plaid above scuffed boots, and a sword hung at his side in a worn scabbard. That he was a Torlander was as obvious from his kilt as the *hoo-thar-nows* he spoke to the horses to keep them from rearing up at the sudden noise of the men breaking through the hedge.

Back then, the hills between County Westmorain and Torland were thick with bandits and brigands. Many of them were sup-porters of the Old Usurper who had been driven there by the king's soldiers years ago, and now they made their living by creep-ing out of the Grimwolds on long nights to pilfer cattle and horses on either side of the border.

No doubt the fellow had presumed the folk of the village would all be keeping close to the fires and the ale casks that night, and that they would not be roving so far afield. Yet if he had thought the revelry would provide cover for his mischief, he was mistaken. Now he had been caught leading five horses that were known to be the property of Handon Arrent—for Arrent was there in the party, and he recognized the horses at once as his own.

The village men shouted at the thief and made a grab for him. But the Torlander whipped the horses with a stick, sending them galloping at the men, forcing them to scatter. The villagers quickly calmed the horses and rounded them up, but in the interim the thief had turned and fled into the night.

The men quickly broke up into two groups to pursue him. One struck off for the river, in case he had used a coracle to make a crossing, and the others headed for the road to Low Sorrell, as that was the quickest route out of the county. There was only one other direction he might have gone from that place: over the hill north of Cairnbridge to strike out cross-country. But that would take him closer to the village, and treading the sides of the hill would have put him in plain view to all eyes, for the moon was rising by then, and no one thought he would be so foolish as that. With their plan formed, the men gave chase.

"And did you go with them?"

Mr. Quent shook his head. "No, Handon Arrent told me this was no longer a merry jaunt, and that I was to head back to the village. Then they left me there on the bridle path as they headed off into the night."

Ivy met his gaze. "But you didn't go back."

Again he smiled. "No, I did not. I had the notion that if I were the one to find the thief, then I would make my father very proud of me. At that age, there was nothing else in all the world that I wanted."

"And did you find the thief?" Ivy asked, though she thought she already knew the answer.

"Yes, I did," he said, his smile vanishing. Then he finished the story.

Young Alasdare knew he couldn't follow the village men, for if he caught up to them, they would only send him home. While the others had dismissed the idea that the thief would go over the hill,

Alasdare wasn't so certain the Torlander wouldn't make a go of it. If he were a thief, he reasoned, he would head in the direction everyone least expected.

So it was that Alasdare plunged back through the hedge and headed back the way they had come, climbing stiles and scrambling over stone walls. He ran as fast as he could, not stopping when he barked his shins on stones or nettles stung his hands. Soon he reached the hill that stood north of the village and started up the slope.

Whether his reasoning was right, or it was simply luck, he had gone halfway up the slope when, above him, he glimpsed a man in a dirty kilt pacing before a stone wall. Beyond the wall rose a tangle of black branches.

Alasdare understood the man's hesitation, for the thief was in a quandary. The crown of the hill was covered with a stand of Wyrdwood. The thief could circle around to either side of the hill, but the sides were bare of all but heather and grass, and the moon was bright above. What was more, numerous red sparks of light moved all around the base of the hill. They were torches and lanterns, for more men had been enlisted in the search. All that one of them had to do was look up at the hill, and if the thief was there, exposed on the slope, they would see him.

So the Torlander dared not go around, but he could not go down either, for that way lay the village, and Alasdare could hear the church bell tolling an alarm. There was only one other way the man might go—over the wall.

Yet it was clear he was loath to do so, and nor could Alasdare blame him. For as long as he could remember, his father had warned him never to venture into a stand of Wyrdwood. Of course, he knew of a few boys who had done so upon a dare. But even then, for all their boasting, they had done nothing more than to creep a few feet into the eaves of a grove of Old Trees before turning back, and then only in the middle of a long lumenal.

Now it was a greatnight, and the branches of the trees hung over the wall like hands withered by fire.

Alasdare thought for certain the thief would attempt to go

around the side of the hill, clinging to the shadows by the wall in the hope he would escape notice. Only then the fellow looked up, and he let out a cry of surprise to see Alasdare standing there below him in plain view, lantern in hand.

That a brawny and coarse-faced man should have been afraid of a boy—one who was short for his twelve years—was astonishing. But perhaps the Torlander assumed that the appearance of Alasdare meant the men were just behind. If so, the fear of being captured evidently outweighed any other, for at once the Torlander scrambled up the stone wall, using the overhanging branches to pull himself up and over. In a moment he was gone, vanished into the Wyrdwood.

"I should have gone back to the village," Mr. Quent said. "I should have told my father what I had seen. But I was taken with the idea of catching the Torlander—though I confess I had little idea what I would do when I did. And so I climbed up the wall after him."

Even though she had fully expected this, based upon her knowledge of his history, still Ivy let out a gasp.

"You went into the Wyrdwood," she murmured.

"Yes," he said, though he did not seem proud of it. "In my eagerness, all of my father's warnings were forgotten. I scaled the wall quickly enough, being a nimble climber, then dropped to the dry leaves on the other side. Then, following the Torlander, I went deeper into the stand of trees."

Now he looked away from her, into the darkness that filled the chamber, as if gazing into that shadowy grove once more.

"Even if I wished to, I could scarcely recount for you what took place after that. I could see little in the gloom, for I had left my lantern, being unable to carry it as I climbed the wall. And if there are words capable of describing such sounds as I heard, I do not know what they are. But as I went into the Wyrdwood, the air was filled with a terrible creaking and groaning, and the trees thrashed as if stirred by a fierce wind, though I was sure the night had been clear and calm.

"Before long, I forgot any desire to find the thief, and I wanted nothing but to make my way back to the wall. But I could not find it. On my way into the grove, I had followed what seemed to be a little path, one that shone faintly in the glimmers of the moon that fell through the branches above. But when I tried to retrace it, the path seemed to bend around, leading deeper in the grove. It was as if the trees had somehow shifted. Soon I was certain I had gone around in a giant circle.

"I began to feel a great fear then. I tried to call out, but the air stifled my voice so that it did not carry. Indeed, I felt an over-whelming surety that my presence in the wood was unwanted. An urge came upon me to run through the grove in any direction. It did not matter which way—to stand still was unbearable. But at that very moment, I saw him in a wild flicker of moonlight: the Torlander. Just past him, between the tossing branches, I glimpsed a rough expanse of gray. It was the wall. He must have seen it as well, for he let out a shout and ran toward it. But then . . ."

He shook his head, and for a minute he was silent. When at last he spoke again, his voice was very low.

"I could see little, for even as the thief moved the forest grew suddenly thick, as if the trees crowded around him. I saw him draw his sword and try to hack at the branches. But this only seemed to make the trees bend and lash all the more vigorously. After that I could not see him through the branches. But the sounds—what I heard froze my blood. There was a grinding, and a noise like the snapping of dry twigs. I heard him cry out again, and then his cries ceased in a most unnatural manner.

"Still the trees tossed and bent, as if whipped by a wind I could not feel myself. I caught another glimpse of the wall, not twenty yards away through the trees. My every desire was to run for it, but I knew I dared not, that if I ran, if I fought against them in any way, then the trees would close around me just as they had around the Torlander. So instead I huddled in a hollow at the foot of an old oak, pressing myself against the rough bark of the great trunk, trying to make myself as still and small as the least bit of fungus or mold that clung to it. I shut my eyes and did not move. And in that way, I spent the remainder of the greatnight in the Wyrdwood.

"It seemed an eon. Indeed, I know now it was nearly twenty hours that I crouched against the tree without motion. After a time I felt a pain in my hand, one that grew worse by the hours, but still I did not dare to move. Only when, at last, I detected a light warmer and brighter than moonlight on my face did I open my eyes. Little dapples of sunlight fell upon the mold of the forest floor. Morning had come.

"There was not a breath of wind, and all the grove was still. My father had always said it was at night the Old Trees woke, especially on a greatnight, and that by day they drowsed. Recalling this, I thought to leave the hollow where I had crouched. But as I tried to move, I found that my left hand was caught fast in a crack in the tree. The bark had curled and folded around my fingers during the night, clasping them fast, and no amount of tugging would free them. I cried out, hoping my father might hear me, for certainly he was searching for me. But the listless air in the wood muffled my shouts, so that they did not carry. Nor would my father ever think I would be so foolish as to venture into the Wyrdwood. I would have to find my own way out.

"With my free hand, I took out my ivory-handled pocketknife. I thought to use the blade to pry free my hand. But, even as I set it against the bark, a shudder passed through the tree, and I thought I heard, or felt rather, a groan emanate from it. I recalled the way the Torlander had swung his sword at the branches—just before I heard him scream. And I recalled as well, from looking at the almanac previously, that the day was to be a short one.

"There was nothing that could have compelled me to endure remaining in the wood for another hour, let alone another night. And so, to free myself, I turned my knife upon that which I knew could be safely cut without invoking any retribution from the trees."

"No!" Ivy gasped, propelled up from the chair by a horror, as if she were witnessing the scene. "Not upon yourself!"

But she knew the truth of it. She had always believed it was the Old Trees that had taken his fingers. But they hadn't; he had surrendered them willingly. And so he had lived.

He turned his left hand in the manacle and traced the thumb over the thick scar on the side. "Once I was over the wall, I found one of the men who was out looking for me, and he took me to my father in the village. I told him what I had done, how I had followed the thief, and where I had been. He looked at my hand, then wrapped his handkerchief around it and drove me home. He did not rebuke me for failing to heed his warnings about the Wyrdwood—not then or ever afterward. I lay in a fever for some days, and when I was well again, he did not speak of that day. Nor did he ever."

At last he fell silent.

"And what of the Torlander?" Ivy asked, sinking back into the chair.

"The thief was never seen again. But some years later, a shepherd told a tale of finding a rusted sword on the slope near the Wyrdwood, as if something had heaved it over the wall."

She reached out and took his hand again, the maimed one. Then, helplessly, she began to weep.

"Do not cry, Ivoleyn," he said in a gruff tone. "It was all long ago, and I survived, as you know."

"But it was so awful!" she exclaimed, still unable to stop the flood of tears.

"No, not really so awful as that," he said. "A little cut, and it was quickly done. And given my state at the time, I hardly felt a thing. Besides, I was lucky. I have seen the Wyrdwood do far worse. As have you."

She could only think of Gennivel Quent, how she had tried to scale the wall of the Wyrdwood—and had tumbled to her death.

"You must hate it so," she said, her sobs easing at last. "The Wyrdwood."

"Hate it? No, I do not hate the Wyrdwood. You must know that." Now it was he who gripped her hands, straining against the manacles to do so. "But it is older than mankind, and cares little for it, I think. What I learned that day, and have learned over again in my work as an inquirer, is that the Wyrdwood is not a thing to be hated or feared, but rather respected. And I learned something else as well."

"What was it?" she said, when he failed to go on.

He hesitated, as if thinking of how to answer. Or rather, she had the sudden, peculiar impression that he knew what he wanted to say, but that he was gathering the courage to speak it.

Mr. Quent tightened his hold upon her hands. "I learned that sometimes you must be willing to lose something precious to you in order to escape, and to endure—that no matter how unthinkable it might seem to make such a sacrifice, all the same it must be done so that you may persist."

The spheres of light cast by the oil lamps seemed to shrink in on themselves, and the darkness of the cell pressed in around Ivy.

"What do you mean?" she said, or rather whispered.

His brown eyes were somber, but bright as well with love and adoration. He opened his mouth to speak something. Only at that moment the far door of the chamber was flung open, and Corporal Lewell strode in.

"New orders have arrived from the Citadel," he announced sternly. "Only members of the Hall of Magnates are to be allowed to interview the prisoner. You must leave at once, madam."

No! Ivy wanted to cry out, only her throat was so constricted she could make no sound.

Mr. Quent leaned forward as far as his bonds would allow him. "Kiss me, dearest," he murmured.

And such was his tone, and the light in his eyes, that she obeyed him, thinking not of the corporal's watchful eyes. Undeterred by the coarseness of his beard, she pressed her lips to his. How long they remained so connected, she did not know; she was utterly subsumed within that embrace.

Only then it was broken as he was roughly forced back in his chair by the corporal's hands upon his shoulders.

"You must leave at once, madam," he said and came around to take her arm, treating her no more gently than he had Mr. Quent.

Ivy ignored the pain in her arm and gazed at her husband. "Alasdare . . ."

"Good-bye, Ivoleyn," he said, his brown eyes calm as he gazed up at her.

Then the soldier hauled her bodily from the room, and the iron door shut with a final clap of thunder.

CHAPTER TWENTY-FOUR

J T WAS SEVERAL HOURS into an odd lumenal, during which the sun did not rise into the sky so much as it skimmed just above the horizon, when a soldier arrived at the Theater of the Moon. He knocked loudly upon the door with the hilt of his sword as several of the illusionists rushed downstairs, hoping to stop the racket before it disturbed Master Tallyroth.

It was Riethe who reached the door first and flung it open.

"The play does not begin until after night falls, whenever that might happen to be," the big illusionist said brashly. Then, upon eyeing the other man up and down, his tone grew more accommodating. "Though if you wished to come in for a private performance . . ."

The soldier, who cut a smart figure in his blue uniform, took a step back as his face blanched. He held a letter before him as if it were a stout shield rather than a folded piece of paper.

"I have a missive from the Citadel for the owner of the playhouse."

By now several of the others had gathered behind Riethe, including Eldyn, Merrick, and Mouse. All of them gaped at this news. Riethe started to reach for the letter.

"I'll take that," Madame Richelour said as she glided past the young men and plucked the letter from the soldier's hand.

"Are you the owner of this establishment, ma'am?"

"I am, so you may consider your duty discharged, young man. You may depart now."

The soldier did so, and eagerly, turning on a heel and marching double-time down the street. Riethe gave a wistful sigh, then shut and bolted the door.

"What do you think it is?" Mouse said. The small man crowded in close to Madame Richelour, trying to get a look at the letter.

"What would you suppose it is?" Merrick said sharply, his face even longer than usual. "What order would arrive from the Citadel, unless it was an edict ordering that the theater be shut down?"

Merrick tended to be overly gloomy, but in this case Eldyn found himself agreeing with the other illusionist's prediction. Given the ever more restrictive rules that had been imposed upon taverns and coffeehouses, it was only a matter of time before the theaters were addressed as another sort of place where undesirable ideas might be fomented. Silently, they all watched as Madame Richelour broke the waxen seal on the letter and unfolded it. The paper wavered, betraying the shaking of her hands.

"Well," Mouse exclaimed, impatience driving his voice up a register, "is it an order shutting down the theater?"

Madame Richelour lowered the paper and, despite the vivid makeup she wore, her face seemed wan and faded. "No, not our theater."

"Then what is it?" Riethe said when she did not continue.

Gently, Merrick removed the letter from her hand and held it up to read it. "It is as Madame Richelour says, our theater is not being closed," he said, though despite this fact, his voice grew even more morose. "But there is now a general prohibition against the performing of illusion plays in the city."

Riethe swore. "Well, a lot of good it does for us to keep the theater open if we can't perform plays."

"But we will be performing," Merrick said glumly. "The stirring and patriotic nature of our recent plays has been noted. As a result, along with several other theaters on the street, we have been commanded to perform six times each quarter month for the benefit of the Altanian army, 'to provide the soldiers with lively diversions and amusements suitable for defenders of Altania, to help relieve their cares and to inspire them in their service to the nation.' For our work, the state will compensate the theater in the sum of twenty regals a week."

"Twenty regals!" Mouse exclaimed, practically hopping into the air. "They might as well turn their rifles on us and rob us. Even on a bad week we make twice that much. There's no way we should take that deal."

"It is not a deal we may choose to take or not," Madame Richelour said, gazing at the shut door. "If the order is not complied with, the government will shut the theater down and seize the premises."

Merrick gave a grim nod. "That's what the letter says. We don't have a choice, not unless we all want to be out on the street. Or worse. I've heard the government is sending out gangs of soldiers to pluck up men loitering about and conscript them into the army."

This thought filled Eldyn with a queasiness, but he could hardly believe it. "They might send the soldiers to see our plays, but surely the Altanian army has no place in it for illusionists."

"Maybe not when the nation is at peace," Riethe said, crossing his arms over his broad chest. "But during war . . . they'll be plenty happy to give any one of us a gun and send us up to the front lines. Better a Siltheri provide fodder for cannons instead of some red-blooded Altanian man."

Eldyn had to concede there was a ring of truth to Riethe's words. Yet it was not the illusionists at the theater whom Eldyn was most worried about. They were young, and they could use their talents to escape notice and survive. But where would Madame Richelour go if she lost the theater? And what would become of Master Tallyroth?

Madame Richelour started for the stairs, her red velvet dress sighing.

"What are we to do, madam?" Riethe called after her.

"I must go see to Tallyroth," she replied over her shoulder. "I suggest you all ready yourselves for tonight's performance for the soldiers."

Then she started up the stairs and was gone.

Eldyn exchanged looks with the other young men. "Come on," he said, sighing himself. "We'd better go over the staging and make sure everything is suitably 'stirring and patriotic.'"

Mouse looked ready to make some smart reply, but Riethe gave him a preemptive crack on the crown of his head, and together they went to round up the others for a rehearsal.

IT WAS FIVE HOURS into the umbral when Eldyn slipped out the back door of the theater, fashioned a cloak of shadows around himself, and made his way along the alley.

He had been afraid it might be difficult to get away from the theater without the others noticing, but circumstances had served to aid him. The soldiers had been so unruly as they filed into the theater that the start of the play had been delayed. Only when a captain shouted orders and threatened to put anyone who wasn't in his seat in the stocks instead did the men become orderly enough for the play to commence.

Even so, there were still plenty of whistles, jeers, and crude heckling as the performance began. Yet it was a credit to the players that none of them were so rattled as to miss a cue or flub a phantasm; and it was a credit to their staging that the jeers and shouts that were at first intended for the players soon became directed at the characters and events in the play. By the end, the soldiers cheered as the heroic warriors conquered the shadow army with the aid of the golden maidens on their winged mounts—and then conquered the maidens in turn.

By the time the players made it to the Red Jester, there was barely half an hour left to quaff a cup of punch before the tavern was forced to close under the new rules. Not that it mattered.

None of the players felt very cheerful after the performance, despite its success, for the next umbral would only bring a new batch of soldiers. They returned to the theater and retired to their rooms, except for Mouse, who went to sit with Tallyroth.

As a result, Eldyn was able to slip downstairs without being seen. Which was well, as he had no time to explain himself to any who might ask where he was going. He had to hurry if he was going to get to the dormitory by the appointed time, for he was to carry a message that night.

It struck Eldyn as somewhat absurd that, only a few hours after using illusions to entertain soldiers, he was now likely to use them again to work treason under their noses. Though hopefully he would not make a mistake in his counting tonight and have such a need.

By the time he reached the top of Butcher's Slip, the moon was rising over the city. The red planet had risen as well, and its light stained the sickle moon like blood upon a blade. Eldyn descended the steps, nodded to the two men outside the door, then went into the dormitory to find Jaimsley.

He did find him, and in a state of much agitation.

"You won't be carrying any messages tonight, Garritt," Jaimsley said, pacing about the little room, an uncharacteristically grim expression upon his homely face. "And likely not the next night, or the night after that."

"What's happened?" Eldyn said, still breathing hard from his rapid pace.

"One of our lads made it back into the Old City just before nightfall. The guards at the Lowgate stopped him, of course, but he didn't have anything on him, so they had no choice but to let him go. He got here just a little while ago, and I'm glad he did, for he brought some ill news."

Eldyn listened with growing dismay as Jaimsley described what had happened. One of their messages, smuggled out of the city through the drain at the foot of Wickery Street, had been intercepted. The man carrying it had been waylaid unexpectedly by a band of soldiers marching on the road in the dark. Suspicious, the soldiers had stopped him, and then discovered the leather message tube upon his person.

Reading the paper contained within, they knew him at once for a traitor. They tried to bind him to bring him to the city, but he fought to get away. In the struggle, a butt of a rifle was brought down against his head. The blow was meant to subdue him, but dashed in his skull instead, killing him. All of these happenings were known from a clerk working at the Citadel who was one of their own, and who had read the report.

"But why didn't the courier break the vial of ink inside the message tube?" Eldyn asked, horrified by this account. He wondered if the man was one he himself had handed a message through the grate.

"He did," Jaimsley said. "But it didn't work, or at least not well enough. From what our man in the Citadel learned, the ink didn't have time to spread over the whole of the message. Enough of it was still readable to incriminate the courier, and to alert the government that messages bound for Huntley Morden's troops are being passed out of Invarel. Not that this can entirely be a surprise to them. Yet you can wager they'll be more vigilant than ever now about searching any man they catch heading away from the city."

Eldyn swallowed, feeling ill. "Then what are we to do?"

"I haven't hit upon that yet," Jaimsley said, creases marking the high slope of his forehead. "But until we can find some way to make sure our messages can't be read if they're intercepted, we'll have to stop smuggling them out of the city."

"But then how will we inform Somebody about the state of affairs in the city? Surely it's even more vital the farther east he marches."

"Yes, it is. But having our messages caught is worse than not sending them at all. We just can't risk it, not until we find a better way. You might as well go back home and get some rest. You look tired anyway."

Eldyn had to admit he was tired after the performance, but all the same he had no wish to go to his bed, for he knew he would not be able to sleep. Instead, a jittery sort of energy filled him. He had come there that night to work for the rebellion, and he was not willing to simply give up. There had to be some better way to get messages to Huntley Morden's forces.

Then he looked down at his hands, and he knew what it was.

"What is it, Garritt?"

Eldyn raised his head. Jaimsley was looking at him.

"I have an idea," Eldyn said, and even as he realized what he was going to do, a cloud of butterflies fluttered up into his chest.

"Well, what is it, then?" Jaimsley said, a light in his small blue eyes.

"I can't tell you," Eldyn replied. "It's something I have to show you."

Then, without another word, he dashed back down the corridor and out into the night.

J T TOOK A LITTLE MORE than an hour to return to the theater, gather the things he needed, then make his way back to the dormitory. By the time he descended the steps of Butcher's Slip, the sky was already fading from black to gray; it was going to be a short umbral.

He found Jaimsley still awake. Indeed, he was poring over maps of the city in the company of Brackton and Miggs.

"Brackton here is helping me see if there's a better route for getting messages outside the Old City," Jaimsley said, "one that might make it less likely for our men on the other side of the walls to run into soldiers."

"What about me?" Miggs said with a scowl. He was a rough-looking young man with thick eyebrows and a black shadow of stubble on his cheeks. "Aren't I helping?"

"You couldn't read a map any better than you could read a poem written on your backside," the sandy-haired Brackton said, a grin on his youthful face. "Your task is to keep our whiskey glasses full—and you're doing a right poor job of it, I'd say."

Miggs scowled, but he grabbed the bottle and splashed whiskey into the three cups on the table.

"Pour one for Garritt, too, for he looks like he could use a drink," Jaimsley said, lifting his gaze from the maps. "What's going on, Garritt? You ran off in quite a hurry earlier."

Eldyn took one of the whiskey glasses and downed its contents in a single gulp, then he held it out for more. He could scarcely believe what he was going to do. But it was for the revolution, he had told himself repeatedly on his way here. And if it meant that another man didn't perish from having his skull dashed in by the butt of a rifle, then it was worth whatever discomfort it might cause Eldyn himself.

"I know how we can get messages out of the city," he said, setting a cloth sack on the table.

"It's not getting a message out that's the problem, Garritt," Jaimsley said, lowering his whiskey glass. "It's what happens if the man carrying it is caught and the message is read."

"But they won't know how to read this message," Eldyn said. "In fact, they won't even know it's a message at all."

The others watched with curious intent as Eldyn drew several objects from the sack: a thin metal plate, a bottle of ink, and two more vials of fluid—one thick and cloudy, the other thin and yellowish.

Jaimsley rubbed his chin. "What is all this, Garritt? Some sort of chemical experiment?"

"You'll see." Either it was the whiskey, or perhaps the certainty that this was what had to be done, but Eldyn felt steadier now. "Jaimsley, write out a message on a piece of paper while I get things ready. It doesn't matter what the message says. It's just to show you what I can do."

Jaimsley's expression was full of questions, but he did as Eldyn said, taking pen and paper and writing down some words. While he did this, Eldyn readied things, borrowing a flat pewter platter and a ceramic washbasin from the sideboard. By the time Jaimsley finished composing the message, all was ready. Eldyn picked up the parchment—then raised an eyebrow.

"A rude verse?"

Jaimsley shrugged his thin shoulders. "It was all I could come up with in a pinch."

Despite the churning in his stomach, Eldyn laughed. "Good old Jaimsley."

Then he got to work. He opened the vial of thick, cloudy fluid, poured a small amount of it on the metal plate, then used a brush to spread it into an even layer. Next he took up the paper on which Jaimsley had written the verse. He stared at it, committing not just the words to mind, but the shape and arrangement of them upon the paper.

At last he was ready. He set down the paper, then took up the metal plate again, holding it in both hands with the coated side away from him.

"What is all this?" Brackton said, but Jaimsley punched his arm, silencing him.

Eldyn drew a breath, then shut his eyes. He pictured the paper he had memorized, envisioning every curve and line of ink. Then the image in his mind vanished in a bright green flash.

He opened his eyes. It was finished.

"Now what?" Jaimsley said, somewhat skeptically.

"Now we get to see what I've done."

Eldyn set the plate in the basin and emptied the vial of yellowish fluid over it. He counted to the requisite number, then used a cloth to pick up the plate by a corner and poured water from the pitcher, rinsing it off. Next he used the cloth to wipe away the residue of the thicker substance and polish the plate to a shine. Finally, he painted a thin layer of ink on the pewter platter, then pressed the metal plate against it.

Now came the final step.

"Give me a fresh sheet of paper, Jaimsley," Eldyn said.

Jaimsley did. Eldyn laid the paper on the table and pressed the ink-covered side of the metal plate against it. Then, carefully, he lifted the plate away.

The other three men stared at the paper. Printed upon it in black ink was a nearly perfect replica of the verse Jaimsley had written. Comparing them side by side, there were slight differences in the shape of a letter here or there, but still there was no mistaking it for a close facsimile of the original.

"Good God," Jaimsley said, his blue eyes gone wide, "it's an impression, isn't it?"

Eldyn nodded. He was aware of the astonished looks of the other two men, but he kept his gaze on Jaimsley as he spoke.

"Not many people know how impressions are made. A soldier isn't likely to recognize the engraving plate for what it is. And the impression rosin is clear once it dries. There's no way to see the impression unless you put the plate in a mordant bath for just the right amount of time and then make a print from it. What's more, you have to be timely about it. After a few hours, the volatiles in the rosin begin to evaporate, and before long the impression is gone altogether."

Jaimsley picked up the engraving plate by the edges, turning it this way and that in the light. "Even if one of our men were caught leaving the city with this, the soldiers wouldn't know what it was he was carrying. And even then they couldn't read it, which means they'd have no cause to delay the courier. Then, once he's safely away from the city, a print of the message could be made from the impression to take to our forces in the west."

"Exactly," Eldyn said. "And once they're done with the plate, they can break it or use another round of mordant to etch away the impression."

"But wait now," Brackton said. "How did you do this, Garritt? I thought illusionists were the only ones who could make impressions."

"They are," Miggs said, his thick eyebrows drawn down in a sneer. "And it turns out Garritt here is one of them—a dirty, mincing illusionist."

Miggs's eyes were narrowed into a glare, and Brackton wore an expression of shock on his boyish face. Eldyn felt his own face glowing, and he started to retreat. But Jaimsley reached out and laid a hand on his arm, stopping him. Then he turned to regard Miggs.

"The rebellion needs heroes, not prats with horseshit between the ears," he said in a low voice. "Garritt has shown which one he is time and again. I wonder, which are you, Miggs? I know what opinion Huntley Morden will have of the man who devised a way to smuggle vital messages out of the city. It's time you decided what opinion Morden will have of *you*."

Miggs met Jaimsley's look for a moment, then lowered his gaze. At last he looked up again, and his expression was sheepish now. "Sorry, Garritt. It's just . . . I'm not used to that sort of thing. It might take me a bit, all right? But Jaimsley's right—I'm not going to speak against anything that could help the revolution, and it's clear what you can do has its uses."

"Uses indeed," Jaimsley said, winking at Eldyn. "I think we know now how Garritt was so good at always giving the soldiers the slip."

He laughed, and so did Brackton and Miggs. With that, the tension in the room dissolved. The other two men departed, having some mischief to work, leaving Eldyn and Jaimsley in the room.

Jaimsley refilled two of the whiskey glasses and handed one to Eldyn.

"I'm sorry if I surprised you," Eldyn said.

"And I'm sorry in turn, for I wasn't surprised at all," Jaimsley replied with a crooked grin.

Eldyn gaped at him.

"Come now, Garritt. It was obvious to me the first time we ever met Curren Talinger. As usual, he had drawn in all the prettiest lasses in the room to him, and we were cursing his handsome face. Except when the girls saw you and your even handsomer face, they all started batting their eyelashes in your direction. Only you were entirely oblivious. You ignored every one of the lasses, and all your attention was on Talinger. I'm not sure you even realized it. Nor did anyone else, I suppose. But I did."

Eldyn could only believe it was true; he recalled how fascinated he had been with Talinger when they all first met the striking Torlander, at a party near the university. He had hardly even known why at the time, though he did now. As did Jaimsley, it seemed.

"Illusions do not appear to fool you, Jaimsley," Eldyn said ruefully.

The other young man laughed. "When you look like I do, you tend to see the plain truth of things. Luckily, I have my charm to make up for my face."

He clinked his glass against Eldyn's, and they both quaffed the contents. Jaimsley's expression grew serious then.

"It was you who made the impression of the shootings at Covenant Cross, wasn't it, Garritt?"

After a moment's hesitation, Eldyn nodded.

Jaimsley set down his empty glass. "That was good work. Like I said before, that picture won over a lot of lads to our side. They couldn't just stand by, not after they saw for themselves what had happened."

Eldyn couldn't answer for the lump in his throat. He should have been glad the men who died that day hadn't done so in vain, that they had helped to bring others to the cause of the revolution. But all he could think of were Dalby Warrett and, especially, Curren Talinger. It didn't matter how handsome or dashing Talinger had been. None of that mattered to a bullet.

"Well, you look weary," Jaimsley said. "You should go get some rest. I have it on good authority that tomorrow is to be an important day, and you'll have work to do when we set your plan into action." Again a grin crept across his homely face. "Indeed, I'm already thinking of other ways we can put this ability of yours to good use."

ELDYN CONSIDERED heading back to the theater, but the sky was already fading to gray outside, and he didn't want to show up at the theater just before dawn. Better for the others to think he had gone out early, and not that he had stayed out all night, for otherwise they would ply him with questions about where he had been. So he caught a little sleep on a free cot at the dormitory, then made his way back to the theater an hour after sunrise.

He sweated in his coat as he went, for despite the early hour it was already hot. The sun seemed too large and red in the sky, staring down on the city like a glaring eye.

It was just as he turned onto Durrow Street that he was nearly trampled by several horses. He did not see them at first, for sweat had gotten into his eyes. But he heard the loud commotion of their hooves bearing down on him and managed to leap aside. He blinked, clearing his vision in time to see a band of cavalry soldiers thunder past, scattering people and carts like chaff before a wind.

The soldiers were riding east, toward the Citadel.

Eldyn resumed his course down the street, but he had hardly gone a dozen steps before he was forced to leap into a doorway as more redcrests rode by, followed by a whole troop on foot, marching in swift formation. Nor were the soldiers the only ones in motion. As he continued on his way, he noticed that people were going to and fro in a great hurry, and many shops that should have been just opening for business were instead closing their doors and shutting their windows.

The coffeehouse where Eldyn sometimes got a cup was still open for business, though. Indeed, it was overflowing with men, so that Eldyn had no hope of getting in.

"What's going on?" he asked one of the men milling outside the door of the coffeehouse.

"Huntley Morden's army has been spotted east of Baringsbridge," the man fairly shouted. He was a corpulent fellow, and his face and bulbous nose were flushed and ruddy.

"Baringsbridge!" Eldyn exclaimed himself.

Baringsbridge was a large town situated on the River Telfayn. The Telfayn was generally considered the border between the

West Country and the more civilized heartlands of Altania, and Baringsbridge was no more than two hundred miles from Invarel.

"But how is that possible?"

"I'm sure the Black Dog's asking himself the very same thing," the other man replied, and his harsh bark of laughter made his allegiances more certain. "Two full regiments of the Altanian army were supposedly defending the bridge and watching the banks. Only there's a great number of trees that crowd along the far side, and some are saying that Morden's forces crept down to the river under the cover of the trees, then made the crossing on rafts."

"But it hardly seems probable they could have reached the east side of the river unseen," Eldyn said.

The man gave a sly nod. "So it does. But folk are saying a queer fog rolled out of the trees on the far side to give the rebels cover, and so Valhaine's forces were taken by surprise. They were outnumbered, too, for the rest of the battalion had been sent south on rumors Morden was intending to make a landing near Point Caravel. I'm guessing that was all a ruse, though, to draw Valhaine away from Baringsbridge."

"If so, it sounds as if it worked."

The man gave a snort. "So it does. Given how outnumbered they were, the Altanians had to fall back or be overrun by the Torlanders. Now Morden's men are on this side of the Telfayn. It means the West Country is entirely lost. It's only a matter of time before he marches on Invarel now."

Eldyn suffered a terror at this idea. Or was it excitement? Jaimsley had said today was going to be an important day; he must have known something was brewing.

"But now what will we do?" he said aloud, and though he had not meant it as a question for the other man, the fellow answered anyway.

"Who's to say? But you can bet the Black Dog will be clamping his jaw down on the city tighter than ever now."

Yes, he would.

"Damn it, can't a man get in this place to get a cup?" the red-faced fellow growled, then tried to use his bulk to force his way into the coffeehouse.

Eldyn continued down the street, wending his way through the throng of people. Where any of them thought they were going, he didn't know. It was not likely the soldiers were letting people in or out of the city, not with news like this. Perhaps, he thought, they merely wanted to be out of their houses, to feel that they were part of such consequential events.

"Mr. Garritt!"

Eldyn was nearly to the door of the theater when he heard, over the clatter of hooves and wheels and boots, someone calling out his name. Was it Madame Richelour? It was a woman's voice. Only it was higher-pitched than hers, and it came not from the direction of the theater, but from behind him. He turned around.

And stared at a dark-haired young woman in an ivory dress bedecked with ribbons as pink as her lips and cheeks.

"Miss Lockwell?" he said, dumbfounded.

"Mr. Garritt, it is you after all!" Lily cried, closing the last distance to him. "I've been running after you for what seems a mile! I was beginning to think my eyes were playing tricks on me."

So did he. "But what are you doing here?"

"Looking for you, of course. Only I thought I would never find you. I went all along the street, showing people the picture I made."

She waved a piece of paper for emphasis. In a brief flutter, he saw it bore a skillfully done drawing of a young man with dark hair and eyes. It was a face he recognized well from looking in the mirror.

"I was sure someone here had to know you. But everyone was utterly awful and would hardly even speak to me. I was in a great despair. Only then I turned and was sure that I saw you walking up ahead, so I hurried after. And now I see that I wasn't mistaken."

She was beaming now, her eyes very bright, though with what emotion he could not say.

"Oh, Mr. Garritt!" she exclaimed, and then flung her arms

around him in the most familiar manner. "I am very glad to see you."

And Eldyn was so astonished that he could do nothing but return the unexpected embrace.

CHAPTER TWENTY-FIVE

J VY WOKE in a tangle of bedclothes.

She sat up in bed, pushing damp curls of hair from her face. Hot light spilled through the window, for she had forgotten to draw the curtains before going to bed, and the room was sweltering.

Perhaps it was the feverish heat that had induced the nightmares she had been lost in. What they had involved, she was not certain, for already the phantasms were evaporating in the searing light. It seemed to her that she had been caught among a web of black branches that coiled around her body. But it was just the sheets and blankets that were twisted around her. Nor did she have need to sleep to become caught in nightmares. For now that she was awake, she found herself in what seemed another awful dream.

Only it wasn't a dream, was it? For it was morning, and she was fully, terribly awake. Ivy threaded her hand through the tangled bedclothes, groping among them. But the other side of the bed was empty, just as it had been when she laid down.

With some effort, she extracted herself from the bed, then went to the window, blinking against the harsh light. The bulbous orb of the sun hung low in the sky like an overripe fruit. She had never seen it so large or so crimson before. The trees in the garden drooped beneath its fiery glare.

Ivy pulled the curtains shut, then went to the bureau to splash water on her face and make herself ready for the day. Yet for what exactly was she readying herself? Yesterday afternoon, after driving her back from Barrowgate, Mr. Rafferdy had deposited her at the front gate of the house. She had been so entirely numb that she had not been able to thank him for what he had done for her, or even to say good-bye to him. Instead, she had gone through the gate and stumbled up the walk. But she had not entered the house. Instead, she had stood there how long she knew not, staring at the door, gripped by a paralysis and unable to enter.

She might have been there still when night fell had Mrs. Seenly not opened the door, having seen her through a window. The housekeeper brought her in, leading her like a small child, and took her to the parlor and brought her a cup of tea.

This revived Ivy sufficiently that she had been able to speak in a somewhat coherent fashion when her sisters came in, asking about her ordeal. Ivy had attempted to describe things in a fashion that would not seem entirely bleak, but evidently she failed, for Rose burst into tears.

Seeing her sister in such need lent Ivy a strength she had not thought she possessed, and she had tried to reassure Rose. But it seemed Miss Mew was the only one who could comfort her, and taking up the cat in her arms, Rose fled the parlor. In contrast to their middle sister, Lily shed no tears and seemed oddly composed, though her round face was uncharacteristically solemn. She had taken Ivy's hand in her own, clasping it tight.

"I'm frightened, Lily," Ivy had whispered then. It seemed improper to confess such a thing to her youngest sister, but she could not help herself. "I'm so terribly frightened, and I don't know what to do."

"But you will," Lily had said, and squeezed her hand. "You always know what to do, Ivy. That's what makes you so marvelous, and it's why we all love you so much. You'll find a way to take care of Rose, and Father, too, because you must."

Ivy had nodded, though she didn't know how she would achieve such a thing, or how she would manage to do anything but collapse to the floor and never rise up again.

"What of you, dearest?" she had managed to say at last, brushing a dark lock of hair from the pretty oval of Lily's face.

A small, serious line appeared between Lily's dark brows. "Oh, you do not need to have a concern for me, Ivy. I will be very well, I assure you."

And with that she had departed the parlor.

Had she had more presence of mind at the time, Ivy might have thought these words peculiar. But she had been too exhausted to think of anything. Her sisters both retired to their rooms without taking supper, and Ivy did the same. Once she had rested, she would know what to do, just like Lily said. At least, that was what she had told herself.

Only now it was morning, and she felt no less heavy and tired than yesterday. Rather, she felt heavier than ever, for now that she was finally able to think, she could at last consider what it was Mr. Quent had said just before the soldier removed her from the chamber. What had he been trying to tell her in those last moments, after he told her the story of his youth and his night in the Wyrdwood?

Sometimes you must be willing to lose something precious to you in order to escape, he had said, *and to endure. . . .*

A knock came at the door, and Ivy let out a gasp. She hastily dried her face, then turned around.

"Come in," she called.

The door opened, and Mrs. Seenly entered bearing a tray of tea. Despite the heat of the morning, Ivy gladly accepted a cup in trembling hands and took a sip.

"Will you be going up to Madstone's today, ma'am?" Mrs. Seenly said. "Or will you be staying at home again?"

Ivy stared for a moment, then at last comprehended the question. Of course—the quarter month had fled by, and it was visiting day at Madstone's again. She had foregone the previous visit, much as it had caused her regret not to see her father. Yet she had not wanted to be away from the house, not when she knew Mr. Bennick had returned to the city.

So far he had not presented himself, but no doubt he was scheming for the right moment. He had murdered Mr. Larken and Mr. Fintaur for their fragments of the keystone, and it was only a matter of time before he came in search of the piece belonging to her father. So she had remained at the house, for fear that he would approach Lily or Rose if she was away. It was only the great importance of going to see Mr. Quent yesterday that had caused her to leave the house for a while. She dared not risk it again.

"No, I do not think I will be going to Madstone's," she answered at last.

Again, this gave her a regret, but she knew it was the right choice. Her father was safe behind the locked gates and iron doors of the hostel. It was better that she stay here at the house, in the event Mr. Bennick chose today to show himself.

"As you wish, ma'am," Mrs. Seenly said. "I will see that breakfast is set out. Though I fear it will be very poor. I do not think there is a fresh egg or pint of milk to be had in the city that has not gone to the soldiers!"

A short while later, Ivy descended to the second floor. She wore her lightest dress of green lawn and had put up her hair, but still she felt hot, for the air in the house was stuffy and close. She went into the dining room off the large gallery and found Rose there, twirling a spoon in her teacup. Despite the sickness in her heart, she attempted a smile for her sister's sake.

"Good morning, dearest," Ivy said, sitting at the table, but Rose did not look up from her cup. "Have you seen Lily?" Ivy tried again.

Rose shook her head. "Her door was closed when I passed her room." She continued to stir her tea.

"Well, I'll go see if she is awake," Ivy said, rising again. "She should not still be sleeping in this heat. It will give her a headache."

Ivy was glad to have any excuse to think of someone other than herself at the moment. She left the dining room and passed through the great space of the second-floor gallery toward the stairs. As she did, a flutter of motion caught her eyes. She glanced to her left—

—then halted. Across the gallery, sunlight fell upon the door Arantus, illuminating the glossy wooden leaves that covered its ornate surface. Its twin, the door Tyberion, was concealed beneath wood and plaster in the opposite wall, but Ivy had left Arantus uncovered. She had no fear someone might try to open it, for she kept the key locked in the Wyrdwood box in the library. Besides, it was beautiful, and it always gave her pleasure to look at it, for it reminded her of the Evengrove.

Only it was not a pleasure she felt now as she gazed at the door. The leaves carved upon it trembled and shook as if they felt the force of a gale. Even as she watched, wooden tendrils spread outward from the door, coiling up the walls and creeping across the floor of the gallery, as if the door itself was taking root and growing. It was impossible, of course.

But then, she always saw impossible things when *he* was near.

Her heart beating rapidly, Ivy hurried to one of the windows. She looked down into the garden, and there he was, standing near the little grove of hawthorn and chestnut trees. His black mask was turned up toward the windows. Its mouth was twisted in a grimace. At first she thought perhaps it was an expression of anger, only then she heard his voice in her mind, and she knew what the look upon the mask really was.

It was anguish.

Your father is not safe, the masked man's words came to her by some unknown means. *You must go to him.*

A fresh terror came over Ivy. Though she still did not know his purposes, she knew the man in the strange black garb had never lied to her. She had to go to her father at once.

"But what if Mr. Bennick comes for the fragment?" she managed to speak aloud.

You are not so clever as you believe. His harsh words sounded in her mind. *You have made assumptions that are profoundly in error. Matters are not as you think.*

Ivy shook her head. "Then help me to understand."

There is no time to explain things if you do not already understand. You must go to your father. Now!

These last words were a growl of anger so fierce she half-believed she really heard them with her ears. Then, with what seemed a rather unnecessary flourish of his frilled black cape, he turned and prowled across the garden, disappearing from view.

Ivy stared through the glass for a moment, then she turned and ran downstairs, finding Mrs. Seenly in the front hall.

"What is it, ma'am?" the housekeeper asked, looking up from her dusting.

"Tell Lawden to ready the carriage," Ivy said, breathlessly. "I am going to Madstone's after all today, and at once."

Ivy HARDLY SAT upon the bench of the cabriolet. Rather, she gripped the edge with white hands, and her arms were so straight and rigid that she was all but suspended by them above the surface of the bench. While sometimes she heard the cadence of marching boots above the noise of hooves and wheels, she saw nothing of the scenes that passed outside the carriage; it was all a blur. Instead, her vision was turned inward as her mind raced from one terror to the next. She did not know whom to fear for most, her husband or her father. That one faced dire peril knowingly, while the other could only be oblivious, made no difference in the end.

At last the carriage came to a halt. Lawden exited, but before he could come around to help her, Ivy was out and down to the street.

"Wait for me," she said to the driver, then hurried to the gate before the hostel.

It was shut, but she gripped the thick iron bars and called out, and at last one of the day wardens shuffled into view. His hair and face were both the same colorless gray as his smock.

"Can I help you?" he said.

"It is visiting day," she said in exasperation, for why else would she have come. "I am here to see my father."

"Are you certain?" the warden said.

Ivy had to take a breath and will herself not to scream at him. "Yes, of course I am certain."

"It is just that we have few visitors these days, what with the state of affairs in the country." He took out a ring of large keys and unlocked the gate. "Not that we care for such things, mind you. We are concerned only for the health and well-being of our charges within these walls. But I only wanted to make certain you had not arrived here looking for a crust of bread to be given out or some such thing."

Ivy stared. Her driver had brought her in a glossy cabriolet drawn by a sleek chestnut horse. Besides, surely he recognized her, for she had seen this particular warden on many occasions.

Only it was clear he did not in fact recognize her, for as he opened the gate he said, "And who are you here to see?"

"Mr. Lockwell," she said.

He stared at her blankly.

Ivy sighed. "That is, number Twenty-Nine-Thirty-Seven."

"Ah!" he exclaimed, nodding. "And are you certain that is the correct patient?"

"Yes, I am quite certain."

"Very well, then, follow me."

They entered the hostel, and despite the awful cacophony of screams and moans and sobs that echoed off the hard walls, Ivy felt a great relief. The warden would not be taking her to her father if anything was amiss. The man in the mask must have warned her in time. Ivy followed after the day warden, making sure to keep as far away as possible from the iron bars of the cells to each side.

At last they reached the door that led to the quieter part of the hostel where the wardens dwelled, and where her father was also housed. The warden took out his ring of keys, then paused to look at her.

"You did say number Twenty-Nine-Thirty-Seven, didn't you?"

"I did."

"Are you certain?"

Again Ivy had to draw a breath. "I could not be more certain," she said through clenched teeth.

"Of course," he said with a nod. "It's just that our patients seldom get any visitors, let alone two in one day."

Now Ivy was certain that it was her own face that had gone gray. "What do you mean?"

"I mean that a visitor already came to see that particular patient today—just a short while ago, in fact."

Before she could react to this, he put a key to the lock. But at his touch the iron door swung inward. It was not locked or latched.

The gray of his face darkened a fraction. "Well, that is most peculiar. Our procedures here are very strict on the matter of locking doors."

Ivy reached out and gripped his arm. She must have done so tightly, for he let out a startled cry.

"Who was it?"

He shook his head, gaping at her.

"Who came to visit my father?" She tightened her grip on him, terror lending her unusual strength.

"You mean number Twenty-Nine-Thirty-Seven?" the warden squealed. "I do not know who he was. A friend or a relative, I assumed."

"What did he look like?"

"He was a tall fellow, I think. Yes, I can recall him now. Thin and rather sallow, with a long nose and very dark eyes."

Mr. Bennick. It could be no other, for that description fit the magician perfectly. Ivy let go of the warden and moved past him. She pushed the door open and started down the corridor.

"But you must wait for me!" the warden called out behind her. "That is the rule, I am quite certain!"

She ignored his cries and ran down the corridor, past rows of closed doors. Her heart pounded so fiercely in her chest that it caused her a pain, but she ignored it and ran on, until she reached the door that led to her father's room.

It was open. Ivy halted, and though she had been running a moment ago, now she could hardly bring herself to move slowly to the door and through. At last she did.

Too late she clapped her hand to her mouth to stifle a scream. Blood—there was blood everywhere. It spattered the ceiling, ran down the wall in dark rivulets, and pooled upon the floor. A man lay upon the floor, though he was hardly recognizable as such, for his body had been ravaged and dissevered in the most violent manner.

At first she thought it must be her father, torn apart like Mr. Larken. Then she saw the shredded remains of a gray smock that still clung to the corpse. The man was one of the wardens.

But then where was her father?

She looked up. The table had been overturned, and the books pulled from the shelves. But the winged, high-backed chair remained upright, facing the window as always.

Ivy entered the room, lifting the hem of her dress and carefully stepping around the pools of gore. She approached the back of the chair, dreading what she would see if she moved before it. But she must. Ivy drew a breath, then stepped around the chair.

It was empty.

Ivy stared, hardly knowing whether to feel relief or a new terror. Her father was not in the room. Which meant that Mr. Bennick had taken him. But to where, and for what purpose? Why had Mr. Bennick not simply murdered her father as he had done with Mr. Fintaur and Mr. Larken?

Perhaps, an awful thought came upon her, it was because he needed Mr. Lockwell to recover his piece of the fragment. Perhaps, in order to pass through the arcane defenses that protected the fragment, Mr. Bennick required the man who had first created them. And if the fragment was at the house . . .

"Rose," she whispered. "Lily."

Ivy turned and fled the room. The warden stood in the door,

his mouth agape and his face no longer gray, but white. Ivy paid him no heed. Instead she pushed by him and raced back down the corridor.

CHAPTER TWENTY-SIX

RAFFERDY PACED beneath the coiling branches of the wisteria tree, grateful for its shade. The morning was hot and oppressive, and he was sweating inside his linen coat.

He glanced along the path that led to the grotto, but it was still empty. Rafferdy frowned. Typically, he was the one who was late. It was not usual for Lord Farrolbrook to be delayed. Had something happened? If so, he had not been informed of it. Though it had seemed to him, on the way to Halworth Gardens, that there were more soldiers than usual on the streets, and that they had gone about with more than usual haste.

Well, there was nothing to do but wait. As he paced, he drew a small object from his coat pocket. It was a gem. Its polished facets glinted in the harsh morning light, but the gem's interior remained dim and cloudy.

Since yesterday, Rafferdy had made it a near constant habit to take out the gem and gaze into it. He had hardly slept last night, for it seemed every few minutes he would jerk awake and look at the gem. It was his hope that Mr. Quent would make use of the gem's twin, and employ it to send a signal that he had conceived of some way to effect his release. Only each time Rafferdy looked at it, the gem was dark.

Sighing, Rafferdy tucked the gem back into his pocket.

Despite the heat, he stepped away from the protective canopy of the wisteria to get a better look down the path. In the distance, between the trees, he could just glimpse the spires that surmounted the Halls of Assembly rising into the sky. They were tinged red in the livid glare of the morning sun, as if stained with blood.

That appearance was more than appropriate. How many lives had been ended, and how many more deaths would result, from the laws that had been enacted in the halls beneath those sharp spires of late? Assembly had declared so many actions to constitute treason against the nation that it might have been easier to simply list those few things that would *not* result in one being hung by the neck.

That Rafferdy had voted in favor of every one of these acts was a fact which caused him not inconsiderable horror. Nor was it any consolation that every other magnate and citizen had done so, and that all of these laws had passed through Assembly upon unanimous votes. How could they not, when every man on the benches knew that to cast a vote in opposition was a crime itself? They were all like puppets acting out a play, seeming to flail their arms of their own will, when in fact everything they did was determined by the tugs that the puppeteer made upon the strings.

Yet Lord Valhaine did not hold every string. Not yet. A few of those puppets still had a cord or two that was free. A shadow caught his eye. He looked up and saw a tall, fair-haired man striding along the path.

"You're late," he said when Farrolbrook reached him.

"I know, and I am sorry," the other lord said. His words were somewhat gasping, and the tangles in his long hair, as well as the general dishevelment of his attire, imparted a harried look. He wore an odd black cape that was too heavy and frilled for such a warm day.

"Well, what kept you?"

Farrolbrook dabbed at his brow with a lace-trimmed handkerchief. "I was . . ." He shook his head, and there was a vagueness in his eyes. "I suppose I don't know, exactly. But I'm here now. And I have news."

He drew closer to Rafferdy, and the perfume of the purple wisteria blossoms could not mask a distinctly putrid scent. Though some effort had been made to conceal them with powder, the blotches upon Farrolbrook's hands, neck, and face were visible in the glaring light. They were darkly livid with yellowish edges, like bruises. Whatever condition it was he had inherited from his father, it was worsening.

Despite the unpleasant odor, Rafferdy did not retreat or pull away. "What have you learned?"

"A message from the magus appeared in our black books," Farrolbrook said, his eyes becoming clearer and more focused. "It was a warning for us all to prepare ourselves."

Rafferdy was surprised. After the little trick he had previously arranged, he wouldn't have thought the magicians of the High Order of the Golden Door were still using the black books to send messages to one another. Perhaps they had purged any initiates or sages they suspected of duplicity, and had taken their magick books from them. Fortunately, they had not thought to take Farrolbrook's away. It appeared that, being beneath their contempt, he was yet beneath their suspicion.

"The magus warned you to prepare for what?"

"The Altanian army suffered a severe defeat by Morden's forces. The whole of the West Country is now considered lost. As a result, Lord Valhaine intends to tighten his hold upon Invarel. What's more, he is going to dissolve Assembly. In its place, he will assume the establishment of all law as Lord Guardian of the realm and commander of the army."

Rafferdy felt as if he had been struck across the cheek. Only it was not so much due to the actions that Valhaine was taking as it was the fact that he was doing all this in response to Morden's victory at Baringsbridge. So there really was a hope, then! Yet there was no use becoming too elated, for the news of Valhaine's plans was dire.

"He is going to close the city completely, isn't he?" Rafferdy said.

Farrolbrook nodded. "Yes, the gates will be sealed so that no one can enter or leave Invarel. It may happen as quickly as tomorrow. The city will be closed to protect its people against the advancing rebels."

"Or so Valhaine will claim," Rafferdy said darkly. "Though the city's people will not be wards of the state, but rather hostages should Morden ever make it this far. I am sure that many a rebel has a relative here in the city."

Farrolbrook reached up a gloved hand, touching one of the dangling wisteria blooms, as if fascinated by it. "I suppose you are right. At any rate, the magus was giving members of the order advance warning in case any of us might wish to depart ahead of the closure. Though, for his part, he stated that he and the sages will not be leaving Invarel."

So Lord Davarry was going to stay in the city—presuming that Davarry was in fact the magus of the High Order of the Golden Door. They all guessed that he was, but even Farrolbrook did not know for certain. It was the custom for the magus of an arcane society to always wear a heavy cowl to keep his identity a secret from all but the sages.

"Well, some of the magicians of the High Order of the Golden Door may be staying, but there is no point in any of us doing the same," Rafferdy said. "If Valhaine is to dissolve Assembly, there is nothing more we can achieve here in the city. Not that we have achieved much to date, save to bear witness to the awful things that Valhaine has wrought."

"That is not so," Farrolbrook said, releasing the wisteria bloom. "Your actions caused great delay to their plans before Valhaine seized power. And by then, Morden had landed and the rebels were on the march. The Wyrdwood might already be burned to ash if you had stood by and done nothing."

Rafferdy could not help thinking that perhaps there was some fragment of truth to this, and he stood up a bit straighter. "Well, if we hope to have any further influence upon matters, we must all of us get out of the city at once. I will send a message to the other members of the Silver Circle, telling them to depart Invarel at once."

"Yes, that is wise. You should all make haste to leave."

Rafferdy arched an eyebrow at the way this was phrased. "And what of you? Surely you are leaving as well, Farrolbrook."

The other man tilted his head, his gaze distant, as if he were listening to some far-off sound. "No, I must . . ." He shook his head and sighed. "That is, I am not yet certain what I will do."

This response concerned Rafferdy. What if the High Order of the Golden Door were to discover Farrolbrook's duplicity? There would be no one to aid him and no place for him to flee. Rafferdy considered making an argument to convince him to leave the city—then dismissed the notion. It was not his place to advise another man what to do. Especially when he could not truly know how Farrolbrook was suffering.

"Thank you," he said instead, and held out his hand. "I must say, you have been of great help in all this."

Farrolbrook hesitated, then extended a gloved hand. "You sound surprised."

Rafferdy could not help a grin. "That's because I am."

Farrolbrook smiled himself as they shook hands, though the expression changed after a moment to a grimace, and he pressed his hand to his chest, as if he felt some pain there.

"Good-bye, Lord Farrolbrook."

The other man nodded. "Do not sound so final, Rafferdy. You may yet see me again."

Rafferdy could not help gazing at the blotches and sores visible beneath the layer of powder on his face.

"I hope that is so," he said, and then he turned and walked along the path, leaving Lord Farrolbrook beneath the wisteria tree.

LESS THAN AN HOUR LATER, Rafferdy made ready to depart his home on Warwent Square. He had instructed his man to put a few clothes and a bottle of whiskey in the four-in-hand. Anything else he might have need of was already at Asterlane.

There was only one other item he needed to take. Rafferdy went to the writing table in the parlor, unlocked the drawer, and took out his black book. He opened it with a muttered spell, then turned to the first blank page and hastily penned a message.

Lord Valhaine is to declare martial law and close the city, he wrote. *You must all leave Invarel at once. Make for my estate in Asterlane, if you have no other place to go. I will meet with you there.*

He waited a minute for the ink to dry, then he shut the book, put it in his coat pocket, and departed the house. Whether he would ever see it again, he did not know.

"I will drive with all haste to Asterlane, sir," the driver said as he started to close the carriage door. "If the day is as long as it looks to be, we will arrive there before the umbral falls."

"Very good, but do not make for Asterlane yet," Rafferdy said. "There is one place in the city we must go first. Take me to the east end of Durrow Street, to Lady Quent's abode."

The driver nodded and closed the door. A moment later, the carriage started into motion. Rafferdy sat upon the edge of the seat. He did not know exactly what Sir Quent had said to his wife in the cell beneath Barrowgate, for she had been in no state to speak afterward. But it was his hope Sir Quent had been able to convince her to depart for the country. For if Valhaine closed the city, and then loosed his witch-hunters within the walls . . .

No, he would not consider such a possibility. He would urge Mrs. Quent and her sisters to leave for Asterlane with him and would not accept any refusal on the matter. Resolved, Rafferdy leaned back against the seat—

—then sat forward again with a start. He had felt a peculiar twitch within the folds of his coat, as if some living thing had crawled into a pocket and now sought an escape. Again he felt something give a slight jerk. He reached into his coat pocket and drew out an object.

It was the gem, the twin to the one he had given to Sir Quent.

While previously it had been dim and cloudy, now it emanated a bluish light, and it was hot even through his glove. The gem twitched again. He tightened his grip upon it, then brought it close to his face. The center of the gem was no longer clouded. Rather, it was utterly black, as if he were staring through a hole into a lightless space.

Abruptly the image of a hand filled the whole of the gem's interior, then quickly it shrank in size. Of course—the hand must have been holding the gem, which was why it had been dark. Only then the hand had placed the gem somewhere and had let go of it. Now that the hand had pulled back, Rafferdy could see its owner—or the owner's silhouette, at least, for the image remained dim. Still, Rafferdy did not need to see the other clearly to know who it was. The stoop of the thick shoulders and the outline of a shaggy beard were enough for that.

It was Sir Quent. He must have tapped the gem three times in quick succession, just as Rafferdy had instructed him, to invoke its enchantment. Had he done so in order to send Rafferdy a message? There was no way to speak through the gem, but surely using pantomime Sir Quent would be able to communicate some meaning. Perhaps he had rethought his situation, and there was some way after all to win his release. If that was the case, Rafferdy would send Mrs. Quent and her sisters to Asterlane and remain in the city. He would do so gladly, no matter the risk, if there was any chance of freeing Sir Quent.

Rafferdy brought the gem closer to his eye. By the perspective of the image within, it was his guess that the gem's twin had been stuck into a crack or crevice midway up a wall. He waited for Sir Quent to do something, to make some signal. . . .

Within the gem, the image of Sir Quent turned away, so that all Rafferdy could see was his broad back. This seemed odd, for how could Sir Quent send a message when facing away? Then the gem brightened as a figure carrying an oil lamp appeared beyond the bars of the cramped cell. The light illuminated Sir Quent's dirty white shirt and his shaggy hair, but the figure itself could not be seen as anything more than a slender shadow. Sir Quent clearly recognized the visitor, though, for he nodded and stepped away from the bars. The door opened, and the other entered the prison cell.

Rafferdy swore an oath, then clamped his jaw as if the people in the gem might hear him—though of course that was impossible. The woman holding the lamp was dressed all in black, so that her form merged with the darkness, and her white face seemed to float upon the air like the visage of a ghost. Again Sir Quent nodded, as if he had been expecting her. Lady Shayde glided farther into the cell, and the iron bars closed behind her.

Something that is horrible can also be fascinating, and so it was that Rafferdy could not look away from the scene in the gem. Lady Shayde moved in a slow circle around Sir Quent; or rather, she *prowled.* It appeared she was speaking something, though of course Rafferdy could not hear what it was. Yet by the smile upon her black lips, and the drooping curve of his shoulders, he thought he could surmise what it was. She was gloating in her triumph over him. For long years had the Gray Conclave been at odds with the Inquiry, but now Valhaine's victory over the inquirers was complete.

At least, that was what Rafferdy believed. Only then the scene in the gem changed, and he no longer knew what to think. By the movements of his hands and shoulders, Sir Quent spoke something, and Lady Shayde's expression was altered. She retreated from him, her arms folded tight over her black dress, her lips formed into a grim line.

Now it was Sir Quent who moved. He approached her, and with what could only be perceived as the gentlest motions, he reached out and touched that white face, tilting it upward to gaze at his own. For a long moment they gazed at one another. At last she gave a stiff nod, as if some agreement had been made between them.

Now such things occurred within the gem as to make the hair on the back of Rafferdy's neck stand on end. Deliberately, Sir Quent lowered himself onto one knee, and then to the other. He bowed his shaggy head, as if in prayer. Or in surrender. Lady Shayde gazed down at him, her face a white mask without expression. Then, like two black snakes, her arms lashed out, coiling around Sir Quent's head and turning it in a swift, violent motion halfway around upon his neck.

Sir Quent slumped limply to the floor and did not move.

"Great God, no!" Rafferdy cried aloud.

He gripped the gem in a white-knuckled hand. The scene within it could not be believed. Except Rafferdy knew the twin gems did not have the power to fabricate visions, only to take what light fell upon the one and pass it through the other. Which meant what he had witnessed had indeed just occurred. Impossible as it seemed, there was no denying it.

Sir Quent was dead, murdered by Lady Shayde.

Only then an even more terrible thought came upon Rafferdy. Had it truly been murder? *There is yet one thing I may do,* Sir Quent had said yesterday when Rafferdy spoke to him beneath Barrowgate. *I have a favor I can call in—an old debt if you will. . . .*

Though it hardly seemed possible, Rafferdy's horror increased. Within the gem, as if to confirm his dreadful conclusion, Lady Shayde knelt beside the body of Sir Quent. She turned him over, and brought his head around to stare lifelessly upward. Slowly, she brushed a pale hand over his worried brow and bearded cheeks.

Then she bent down and pressed her lips to his.

What he was witnessing now was beyond Rafferdy's comprehension. But he did understand that, somehow, this was the favor Sir Quent had referred to yesterday. This was how he had assured Mrs. Quent would never become the wife of a convicted traitor to the realm. Sir Quent would never face trial now, and so he could never be convicted. He had given everything, his very life, to preserve Mrs. Quent.

But that did not mean she was now safe.

No, it was quite the opposite. Within the gem, Lady Shayde rose to her feet. She turned from the body on the floor of the cell—then halted, her dark eyes narrowing. She took several steps, and suddenly her face waxed larger within the gem like a gibbous moon. That visage was without line or crease, as always, but the hard line of the mouth bespoke anger. A white hand appeared, consuming the whole of the scene.

The gem twitched in Rafferdy's hand, then went dark.

"Sir?"

Rafferdy blinked, then realized the driver was at the carriage door. He hadn't felt the vehicle come to a stop.

"I heard you call out, sir. Do you have new directions for me?"

Rafferdy turned the gem in his fingers. Its center was cloudy once more, but its work was done. Sir Quent had used it to send a message after all, and Rafferdy understood what it was. He slipped the gem into his pocket.

"No, continue on to Durrow Street," he said to the driver. "And for God's sake, be swift about it, man."

CHAPTER TWENTY-SEVEN

I VY LEANED FORWARD upon the bench of the cabriolet, as if she could will the carriage to go faster. There was some commotion in the streets—soldiers going this way and that, and people and horses crowding about—but Lawden expertly maneuvered around all such obstacles, guiding the cabriolet swiftly through the Old City.

Fleetingly, Ivy wondered at the cause of the turmoil, if it had something to do with the war. Only her brain could not retain its hold on such thoughts; for that organ was all in turmoil as well, filled with images of the dead warden, and the blood spattered around her father's room at Madstone's. Mr. Lockwell was gone; Mr. Bennick had stolen him away. But why? Why had Mr. Bennick simply not murdered him like Mr. Larken and Mr. Fintaur? And where had Mr. Bennick taken him?

To the house on Durrow Street. It was the only answer of which her fevered mind could conceive. Mr. Bennick needed Mr. Lockwell to gain his piece of the keystone, and so had taken him to Durrow Street to get it. *Hurry,* Ivy tried to tell Lawden, but her throat was so constricted she could not speak. Then, as the cabriolet clattered along the street, a familiar sight hove into view: a large house of red stone beyond a wrought-iron fence.

Ivy leaped out of the carriage before it had fully stopped moving. Either this action startled the horse, or something else had spooked it, for suddenly the beast let out a whinny and reared up, so that Lawden was forced to leap down himself and grapple for its bridle in an attempt to calm it. Ivy did not wait for him to do so; instead, she pushed through the gate and hurried up the walk to the front steps.

The stone lions to either side of the door yawned, baring white marble fangs, and shook their moss-stained manes. Ivy let out a cry, nearly falling as she stumbled back down the steps. Then, as comprehension came over her, she turned around. By then the man in the black mask was already stepping from among the little grove of stunted trees.

As he drew near, she saw that his state was similarly disheveled as that of the little hawthorns and chestnuts. The black costume was rumpled, the heavy black cape frayed on the edges. His mask was slightly askew, so that she could see a thin line of pallid skin and a few long strands of gold hair. It was strange that his hair should be that color and not gray, given that he had first appeared to her own father so many years ago. How could he endure so long without showing signs of age or decrepitude?

Except, it did not seem that he was in fact enduring. There was a weakness to his gait, like a limp or shuffle, and an unpleasant odor emanated from him. It was a sickly smell, like that produced by rot or disease. Despite this, she did not shrink away, but rather hurried to meet him on the path.

"Help me, please," she said. "Mr. Bennick murdered a warden and took my father from the hostel. I think Mr. Bennick is going to bring him here, to retrieve my father's part of the keystone."

"No, you are mistaken." His words were somewhat muffled, for they did not sound in her mind, but rather came through the onyx mask. "Bennick will not bring your father here. Lockwell's piece of the keystone is not in the house. Rather, it is with him, just as it has always been, and now the two of them are no longer in Invarel. Bennick has taken your father beyond the city walls."

Ivy's shock was so great she could hardly breathe. Yet by what means could her father's piece of the tablet be with him? She could not comprehend how that could be. All the same, there was one thing she did understand.

"We must go after him. Mr. Bennick will murder my father to gain his fragment of the keystone, just as he did Mr. Fintaur and Mr. Larken."

The mouth of the onyx mask twisted in a smirk. "As I said before, you are clever, but not always so clever as you think. It was not Bennick who took the lives of Fintaur and Larken, and so took their portions of the keystone. No, it was Gambrel."

Ivy gaped openly. Surely she had misheard him. "Mr. Gambrel? But it cannot have been Mr. Gambrel! We locked the door to Tyberion, and all the gates beyond it were destroyed. He was trapped there forever."

"Only a very few things are forever," the masked man said, gazing down at his black gloves. "The gates that were part of the ancient way station on Tyberion were all broken, it is true, but not all of them were entirely destroyed. And there is no man more resourceful than one who is desperate. Gambrel searched among the gates until he found one that yet retained a spark of magick. He reassembled its stones, and mixed his own blood with the dust of that forsaken place for mortar, and etched runes upon it."

Now he looked up, and his black mask was wrought into a queer expression, like a sort of admiration. "By the time bright threads of magick crackled over the stones, Gambrel was all but dead. He flung himself through the gate, and so he escaped the prison you made for him. Still, he would have perished then, but he had had the wits to direct the gate to a place where he knew he would find aid—that is, to his estate in the east of Altania. And there he did find one who preserved him."

A coldness came over Ivy. "Lady Crayford," she whispered.

The other nodded. "Yes, he went to his wife. And while she should have had the sense to flee at the sight of him, yet some tenderness for him must have remained in her heart. Or perhaps it was simply that she had nothing and no one left to her. Whatever the reason, she summoned doctors, and he was brought from the brink of death, and recovered his health. Then, as her reward, Gambrel murdered her, and the doctors as well. Then he burned the servants in the house, for no one was to know of his return."

Ivy was trembling now, and an ill feeling writhed within her. So the fire that had consumed the Crayford manor had not been an accident. Instead, Gambrel had set it deliberately. Lady Crayford had attached herself to Gambrel in order to rise higher in society. But in the end, she had been cast down to her death.

"Where is he?" Ivy said when she was at last able to speak. "Where is Mr. Gambrel now?"

"He is here in Invarel. He has been for some time, for he is the magus of the High Order of the Golden Door. He became magus after Lord Mertrand was murdered—an act which Gambrel no doubt played a role in."

Ivy did not think she could be further astonished, yet she was. "The Golden Door! But they are Lord Valhaine's own magicians."

Again a smile twisted the mouth of the mask. "Yes, they are. Or perhaps I should say, he is their Lord Guardian now."

"But how?" she said, struggling to understand. "Gambrel—that is, Lord Crayford—was implicated in that affair with the archdeacon. Had he not vanished, he would have been arrested."

"Yes, and he was indeed arrested upon his return to Invarel. Using his connections within the High Order of the Golden Door, Gambrel gained an audience with Lord Valhaine. He turned himself in to the Gray Conclave, and let himself be put in shackles and taken to a cell beneath the Citadel. Had he been wise, Lord Valhaine would have thrown away the key, or better, walled up the door. But instead, thinking to learn more about the forces that threaten Altania, he went down to the cell on several occasions to speak to Gambrel, and to question him.

"That was a grave error, as it did not take long before Valhaine was seduced and corrupted by Gambrel's words. First Gambrel revealed to him the full horror of the Ashen, and the destruction they would unleash upon all the world. Then he convinced Valhaine that, if Altania was to ally itself with the Ashen, this nation would be preserved in favor of all others."

"But that is a lie!" Ivy cried. "The Ashen will destroy everything."

"Yes, they will," the masked man said, and then his voice grew low. "They cannot create, they cannot preserve. They can only devour. All the same, they need agents among mankind to help prepare the way for them to enter the world. Just as they will need men to serve them after they come to dominate all things—men who can lead and command the various governments of the world in a manner that suits the purposes of the Ashen. It is the potential of holding such positions of great power that entices men like Gambrel to ally themselves with the Ashen. And it is the knowledge of the destruction that the Ashen will bring, and the desperation to avoid it no matter the cost, that drives men such as Valhaine mad. It convinces them to do anything in order to avert the coming horror—and blinds them to the horrors they end up committing themselves in their efforts to do so."

These words were fraught with an inevitable and terrible sort of logic, and Ivy could only believe what the masked man spoke was truth. "But why didn't you tell me all of this sooner?" she said, her voice cracking with despair. "If we had known Mr. Gambrel had returned, my husband could have warned Lord Valhaine not to listen to him."

"Could he have? That presumes Sir Quent's ability to persuade would have exceeded Gambrel's—a thing which I doubt. But even if that were the case, I could not have told you any sooner, for I did not know the truth myself, not until earlier this very day. Despite what you might think, I am not always able to move freely where I would or choose in what place I will be. It has ever been that I must wait, and seize what opportunities I can. But at last I was able to speak to Lord Davarry, and in questioning him I learned the truth."

Now the onyx mask twisted into a sardonic expression. "Indeed, it was simple once I finally found myself alone with him, for as it turns out he is not much of a magician. All this while, he has been Gambrel's puppet, acting as if he led the Magisters and the High Order of the Golden Door while in secret it was Gambrel who worked the strings. It was not easy to get close to Davarry in private, for Gambrel was keeping him close. But this form I am able to don from time to time is one the magicians of the Golden Door have little fear of. And today, Gambrel has been preoccupied by other matters. Thus I was at last able to get to Davarry alone and in secret. I bent his will to mine, and so learned all I have told you now."

This fascinated Ivy. She had always assumed the man in the mask knew all—that he appeared precisely when he wished and revealed precisely what he wanted, deliberately withholding greater truths from her for some unknown reason. Yet it seemed that was not so, that there was in fact some limitation upon how he could move about and apprehend things. But what was it? What did he mean by the words, *this form I am able to don from time to time*? She wanted to ask more questions. . . .

Only what did it matter? Lord Valhaine was the most powerful man in Altania—and he was now under the command of Mr. Gambrel.

"There is nothing we can do," she murmured, a heaviness descending upon her. "It is all hopeless."

"No," the other said, and now his mask was formed into a stern expression. "Until the planets all stand in a line in the Grand

Conjunction, and a ceaseless night falls, there is yet hope. But if there is to be any hope at all, then you must leave the city at once."

"Leave the city? But why?"

"Gambrel knows the truth of your nature, that you are in fact a sibyl, and thus Valhaine knows as well. They will seek to do away with you. They fear all women such as yourself—women with the power to command the Wyrdwood. Just as they feared your husband for his work with the Inquiry to preserve the Old Trees."

Ivy took a staggering step backward, as if the ground had pitched violently beneath her feet. She felt a sharp pain and then a sudden emptiness, just as she had the night she woke to bloody sheets and the cold knowledge her body no longer harbored a life within it. How she wanted to believe she did not understand the masked man's words! But instead, a most awful clarity came over her.

"You said they *feared* my husband," she said, or rather gasped. "Yet what I think you mean is, they fear him no longer."

He made no reply, but his silence was answer enough. Ivy pressed one hand to her head and another to her heart, as if to somehow dampen the searing lines of pain that passed back and forth rapidly between those two poles. But it was no use.

It is done, she thought. *It is all at an end, and there is no purpose in anything. I shall fall to the ground and never rise again.*

No, this is all far from done, the masked man said, and this time his voice sounded in her mind. *If it were truly over, then they would not have taken your husband away, nor would they be coming for you now. Rather, it is precisely because all is so precarious, because everything yet hangs in the balance, that they seek a way to control things.*

A gloved finger touched her chin, tilting it up. The onyx mask was stern, even hard, but she could see a glint through the mask's eyeholes. The real eyes beyond were blue, she thought, and not without sympathy.

You can yet alter the balance, he said. *But to do that, you must not allow yourself to be apprehended. You must go immediately. As must I.*

And with a flourish of his tattered cape, he turned and started down the path in his limping gait.

"Wait!" she cried out. "Don't leave!"

I have already stayed too long, came his reply. *This form grows weak, and were it to perish, then I would perish with it.*

"But I don't understand," she called after him. "Where can I possibly go?"

Listen to your father. He will tell you what to do.

Then he passed through the iron gate and was gone.

How long Ivy stared after him, she did not know. She could not think, could not move. It was as though, with his departure, she had gone back to lifeless stone like the lions beside the front steps. At last came the sound of the door opening behind her, followed by a voice.

"Lady Quent, there you are! You should come in. You have a visitor waiting for you."

Terror broke her paralysis. She turned to see Mrs. Seenly in the front doorway. A visitor? Had Valhaine already sent men from the Citadel to take her away and hang her as a witch?

No, given the lack of alarm in Mrs. Seenly's expression, it could be no such thing. Ivy's only want was to enter the house, to shut herself in her chamber, and weep. But first she must make this visitor depart. In the most detached manner, as if she were operating a puppet rather than her own body, she directed her limbs to move, to carry her up the steps, through the door, and into the front hall.

A handsome young man in a well-tailored gray coat rose from a bench by a window. He had long brown hair and soft brown eyes.

"Lady Quent, I am glad you are here," he said, and bowed.

Ivy was too numb, and too astonished, to do anything save to utter the obvious. "Mr. Garritt!"

He took a step toward her, an earnest expression upon his handsome face. "Forgive me for coming unannounced, but there is something important I must tell you—though I think you will not like to hear it."

Ivy could only stare, wondering what other terrible news was to be revealed to her this day. Between her father and her husband, had she not already been presented with enough?

"It involves your youngest sister," Mr. Garritt went on rapidly. "Miss Lily, that is. She has gone to one of the theaters at Durrow Street."

Previously, this revelation would have been serious news indeed, but it seemed of little consequence now. Yet it did serve to pierce the dull haze that shrouded Ivy's mind. She ached to grieve, but just as when her mother passed, she had to maintain her composure for the sake of Lily and Rose. All that mattered now was to collect her sisters and leave the city.

"Thank you, Mr. Garritt," she said. "You can be assured that I will admonish Lily for what she has done. It was thoughtless and foolish of her. But for the moment, I must speak with her and Rose about another matter, if you will forgive me."

He shook his head. "But that's just it, you *can't* speak to her. That is, unless you go to the Theater of the Moon on Durrow Street. I tried to convince Lily to return here with me, but she refused. She says she will not leave the theater unless we throw her upon the street, and Madame Richelour—that is the lady who owns the theater—has said she will allow no such thing. It seems she has developed an immediate fondness for your sister."

Ivy's mind had suffered too many shocks today; she could scarcely comprehend what she was hearing. And why was it from him that she was hearing it at all?

"But, Mr. Garritt," she said, "how can you know all this?"

He drew in a breath, as if gathering his resolve. "I know because . . . it is the fact that I am employed at the very theater I speak of, as an illusionist in their company of players. Lily had gone to the west end of Durrow Street and was showing people there a drawing of me. I came upon her just as she was approaching the Theater of the Moon, where they would certainly have recognized the drawing she had made. She insisted I take her within, and to remove her from the street I did so. It was my intention after that to accompany her home, but she was adamant that she would not leave."

Ivy was beyond astonishment. Not that she should be entirely surprised, she decided after a moment. She thought of the drawings she had discovered in Lily's folio—scenes of a handsome young man with dark hair and eyes, conjuring wonders upon a stage.

"Lily knew," she said softly. "Didn't she?"

A vivid blush colored his cheeks, and he hung his head. "Yes, I'm afraid she did. She saw us in . . . that is, she discovered it the night of the party for herself and the other Miss Lockwell."

A moment ago Ivy had felt so weak as to collapse to the ground, but now a sudden and fierce energy coursed through her. Mr. Quent and Mr. Lockwell were beyond her help now. But her sisters required her, and she would not fail them. She would retrieve Lily, and then with Rose they would leave the city at once. But first—

"You must take me to her, Mr. Garritt," she said, gripping his arm. "I will convince Lily to return home. She cannot refuse once I tell her that . . . once she knows what has happened. And then we must depart the city with all possible haste. Our very lives may depend upon it."

Motionless, Mr. Garritt stared at her hand upon his arm. Perhaps he was shocked that she had made no comment upon his personal revelation. And at another time, perhaps Ivy would have done so—though it would not have been to rebuke him, but only to gain some assurance that he was well and taking proper care of himself. Yet it was clear from his dress and manner that he was indeed quite well, aside from somewhat shadowed eyes and pinched cheeks that bespoke recent exertion. Besides, it was for Lily that Ivy's attention was required now.

"Please, Mr. Garritt," she said. "Take me to this theater where you perform."

He drew himself up, then met her gaze.

"Of course, Lady Quent, at once."

Together they started toward the door—then abruptly halted as a loud knock sounded against it. Indeed, so great was the force being applied from the other side that Ivy feared it was a band of soldiers attempting to strike it down. Then, before Ivy could tell her not to, Mrs. Seenly hurried forward and opened the door.

Mr. Rafferdy stepped into the front hall, holding a cane and clad in an elegant brown suit. Ivy was too greatly relieved at his appearance to suffer any further surprise. She left Mr. Garritt and hurried to meet him.

"Mrs. Seenly, please leave us, if you would," she said.

Mr. Rafferdy waited until the housekeeper had departed, then he spoke in a low voice, one that was for Ivy only.

"Mrs. Quent, I do not know how to impart to you what news I must." His face was a grayish hue, and he gripped his gloved hands one in the other. "Somehow I must find a way. But before I say anything else, you must prepare yourself and your sisters to depart the city at once. Do not think to take anything but yourselves, and perhaps a cape if a chill umbral should fall. I fear, even at this moment, soldiers might be marching here."

Despite his grim urgency, the sight of Mr. Rafferdy had the effect of steadying her further. Gladly she would direct her thoughts to the matter of Lily, or to the task of leaving the city, if it meant for a little while longer she could keep from considering that far greater cause for despair.

"I know," she said. "The soldiers are coming on Lord Valhaine's order to bear me away."

"You already know this?" he said, then his gaze went past her. "Great Gods, Garritt," he said, his voice rising even as his eyebrows did. "What are you doing here?"

Ivy laid a hand upon his arm. "He came here to tell me about my youngest sister. It seems that, propelled by her fascinations with plays, Lily has fled the house on a whim and has gone to—" Ivy hesitated, realizing she had been about to impart something that was not hers to reveal.

"She has come to the theater on Durrow Street where I am employed," Mr. Garritt said, taking a step toward them.

Mr. Rafferdy's gaze went from Ivy to Mr. Garritt, then returned to her again.

"Ah," he said.

By that one utterance, Ivy understood that he had already been privy to this bit of news about Mr. Garritt. Ivy was glad for it; that there should be such secrets between friends was untenable. Nor would she have any secrets with either of them now.

"I came here because Miss Lily refused to leave the theater," Mr. Garritt went on. "She claims she wants to design scenes for plays, and that nothing will stop her from doing it. She cares nothing for propriety."

"Or for good sense," Ivy said, and shut her eyes. "Lily—dear, strong-willed, foolish Lily. I should have known you would attempt something like this, and at the very worst time." She took in a breath and opened her eyes again. "Mr. Rafferdy, I have called upon you for your help so often, I hardly know how I can do so again. But I must, and Mr. Garritt's help as well. I need you to help get my sisters out of the city."

"And you yourself," Mr. Rafferdy said, his gaze fixed upon her.

She turned her head away. "I cannot claim to care what happens to myself now, save as it has a bearing upon my sisters."

Now it was he who put a hand on her arm. He bent his head toward hers. "Then you already know my other news as well, it seems."

Ivy was frozen for a moment, then at last nodded. "I have lost him," she said, almost in a kind of wonderment; only the words burned her throat as if she had drunk some caustic fluid. "My husband is gone. He is dead."

She heard Mr. Garritt's exclamation of dismay behind her. Slowly she looked up, and now a wonder did come over her. For while she had yet to shed a tear herself, one even now coursed its way down Mr. Rafferdy's cheek. In his brown eyes was a look of such anguish, and of such tenderness, that she had a sudden compulsion not to seek comfort for herself, but rather to comfort *him*. She touched his cheek, wiping away the dampness there.

He opened his mouth to speak.

Before he could, the clatter of hooves against cobbles emanated through the front door, which stood ajar. Mr. Rafferdy gave her a startled look, then he turned and went to the door.

"We are too late!" he exclaimed as he peered through the opening. "The soldiers have come already."

Ivy's heartbeat became a peculiar kind of flutter, and she felt suddenly light-headed, as if she might faint. Only she could not. What happened to her did not matter now, but Lily and Rose must be protected.

"Soldiers?" Mr. Garritt said, hurrying toward the two of them. "But what do you think they want?"

Ivy turned to regard him. Again she was resolved they would have no secrets between them, not now when they were all in peril.

"They seek to arrest me on account of being a witch—a sibyl of the Wyrdwood."

Mr. Garritt's mouth opened as his handsome face was wrought in an expression of astonishment. Only then he gave a slight nod, as if he had come to an understanding of something.

"Dercy was right," he murmured. "That's why I saw it around you. Why I can see it around you now—a green light."

"You can see a light around Ivy?" spoke a voice from the staircase. "But I can see a light around her, too!"

They all turned in renewed surprise. It was Rose who had spoken. She stood upon one of the lower steps, clad in her favorite pink gown, smiling down at Mr. Garritt.

Rose descended the last steps. "The light is green," she said, coming toward them. "But there is a dapple of gold to it as well, like leaves in the sun. I can see it even now. Can you?"

Mr. Garritt turned his soft brown gaze toward Ivy, then he nodded. "Yes, I can. It's very bright."

"You have a light, too, Mr. Garritt," Rose went on excitedly. "It's green also, but there's a bit of purple to it, like the air in the garden just as twilight begins to gather. And there's a light around Mr. Rafferdy as well. It's blue just like our father's light always was, but brighter, and there's a tinge of—"

"Rose," Ivy said sternly, interrupting her sister. "You must go upstairs. Now. It is very important."

Rose blinked and took a step backward, but she did not return to the stairs.

Mr. Rafferdy hurried back from the window he had been looking out. "They are outside the gate," he called back. "And I saw some of them moving along the line of the fence."

"What do we do?" Mr. Garritt replied.

Mr. Rafferdy shook his head. "I don't know. I imagine they are going all around the house. They'll be watching every egress. There is no way to escape them now."

"But there is a way," Rose said suddenly.

All of them gazed at her in renewed astonishment.

"That's why I came downstairs," Rose went on earnestly. "Father wanted me to tell you something, Ivy."

"Your father?" Mr. Rafferdy said. "But how—?"

Ivy stepped toward her sister. "You were talking to him again, weren't you, Rose?"

Her sister nodded solemnly.

"What did he want you to tell me?"

"He said that we have to go to Heathcrest Hall, that there's something you have to do there. And he said that it's very important that we leave at once by the very quickest way. Do you know what he meant?"

A cool shiver of realization passed through Ivy. Yes, she did know. *Listen to your father,* the man in the mask had said. *He will tell you what to do.*

And so he had.

"Rose is right," Ivy said quickly. "There is one other way we can leave here."

Mr. Garritt looked at her with puzzlement, but she saw a light of understanding glimmer in Mr. Rafferdy's eyes.

"Rose," Ivy said, looking at her sister, "go up to our rooms and fetch two capes—the ones we take with us on jaunts in the country. Get the capes, and then meet us in the gallery on the second floor, by the door with all the carved leaves upon it."

Rose's face had gone very white; she did not move.

"You must hurry, Rose," Ivy said, gently but with a firmness in her voice. "We are depending upon you."

Rose nodded, then turned and dashed back up the stairs.

"I know what you intend," Mr. Rafferdy said. "But what of your other sister? What of Lily? You know we cannot follow you that way to bring her to you."

Ivy suffered a pain deep in her breast. First her father, then Mr. Quent, and now Lily—one by one, she had been forced to abandon thoughts of helping each of them that day. Who else would she be made to abandon?

Not Rose. She would not relinquish Rose.

Ivy turned to face Mr. Garritt. "You must take care of Lily for me, Mr. Garritt. You must see that she remains safe at your theater. Tell no one who she really is. It is dreadful of me to ask it of you, yet all the same I must." She gripped his hand in her own. "Please, will you do this for me?"

His face was blank for a moment. What thoughts must be racing through his mind! But then he placed his other hand upon hers.

"I will keep her safe," he said solemnly. "I swear it."

Ivy felt her fear recede a fraction. To think that Lily was to be staying in a theater full of illusionists was now a matter to inspire relief! Yet all could be altered in a moment, and she knew Mr. Garritt would see to Lily's well-being—if anyone in the city could be well, with Huntley Morden marching toward Invarel.

"Thank you, Mr. Garritt," she breathed.

Mr. Rafferdy shut the door and locked it. "The soldiers are starting through the gate. What do we do?"

The three of them came together in the hall for a hurried congress.

"We must get upstairs without being seen," Ivy said. "Only there is something I need from the library first."

"Go retrieve this thing you need," Mr. Garritt said. "I can make certain they do not see us."

"How?" Mr. Rafferdy said, frowning.

Now the hint of a smile curved upon Mr. Garritt's lips. "They will see something entirely else, instead."

Ivy did not wait to find out what Mr. Garritt intended. She had to trust him, for they had but moments left. Lifting the hem of her gown, she raced across the front hall and entered the library. At once she went to the writing table, unlocked the drawer, and took out the Wyrdwood box. Even as she did, the old rosewood clock on the mantel let out a low chime.

She glanced at the clock. The day had been so hot and stifling that she had assumed it would be long. But on the right face of the clock, the gold disk was now nearly half-covered by the black. The umbral would fall soon.

Good. The trees were always more wakeful at night.

Holding the Wyrdwood box tight, Ivy returned to the front hall. She saw Mr. Garritt and Mr. Rafferdy standing within the curve formed by one half of the double staircase, behind a pair of chairs arranged opposite a long sofa. She hurried to join them.

As she did, there came a furious pounding upon the front door.

"Lie down here," Mr. Garritt said, taking her arm and guiding her to the sofa. "At all cost, you must not move."

Ivy did as he directed, laying her length upon the sofa. Then she opened her mouth to ask Mr. Garritt what he meant. Only at the moment, two things occurred.

The first thing was that the front door was suddenly flung open. A maid who had just entered the front hall in answer to the knocking gave a scream, then turned and fled as a half-dozen men in blue coats streamed into the house. They wore grim expressions upon their faces and sabers at their hips.

The second thing was that Mr. Rafferdy and Mr. Garritt no longer stood behind the chairs. Rather, in Mr. Rafferdy's place, was a tall grandfather clock of brown wood. Beneath its face was suspended a pendulum with an ivory weight that looked very like the head of Mr. Rafferdy's cane. Near the clock, instead of Mr. Garritt, there now posed a marble statue of some classical Tharosian hero or poet, clad not in a gray coat, but rather gray folds of stone. What was more, the air around them had thickened, darkening and obscuring the scene like a thick coat of varnish upon a painting.

One of the soldiers barked some order, and the men began to fan out through the length of the front hall. Some ducked into other rooms—the library, the parlor—then appeared again in the hall.

"She must be on one of the other floors," one of the soldiers said.

And the men moved toward the staircases.

A terror came over Ivy, for several of the soldiers were going to pass directly by the three of them. Her urge was to rise and flee. Instead she remembered Mr. Garritt's order, and she held her breath as she laid upon the sofa. Her only motion was to flick her gaze downward. What she saw was not the green fabric of her gown against the cushions, but rather a series of pillows and drapes that she knew were not really there. One of the pillows toward her feet was embroidered with the pink face of a cherub. She could only imagine her face had been made to appear its twin.

To Ivy's astonishment, the soldiers passed by the three of them without so much as a glance. Only then her surprise transmuted into a horror as the soldiers reached the foot of the stairs. Ivy had told Rose to go to the gallery on the second floor, to wait by the leaf-carved door. She would be standing in plain sight.

The soldiers started up the stairs.

Ivy nearly leaped up off the sofa, consumed with some half-mad thought to surrender herself to the soldiers so they would leave Rose alone. Only before she could do such a foolish thing, one of the men gave a shout.

"Look, out there!"

So startled was she that Ivy momentarily forgot Mr. Garritt's rule and lifted her head to look. Only it did not matter, for by then all the soldiers were running across the hall toward their companion who had called out. He pointed to one of the windows. Beyond the glass, Ivy saw something move: a lithe shadow. The dark figure flitted past the glass, too quickly to be seen clearly, then disappeared from view.

"She's gone to the garden!" one of the men exclaimed, and at once the soldiers ran to the door and exited.

The moment they were gone, the Tharosian statue sprang to life and went to Ivy. Only it was no longer a statue at all, but Mr. Garritt.

"That was a most excellent trick, Garritt," Mr. Rafferdy said, grinning as he lowered his cane and turned it upright. "But I fear it won't fool them for long."

"No, it won't," Mr. Garritt said, and he reached down a hand to help Ivy to her feet.

"How did you do that?" she breathed, all else forgotten in a moment of wonder.

He smiled a little. "It was a phantasm. But contrary to what Rafferdy here said, it was anything but excellently done. Rather it was hasty, and we lacked proper costumes, which was why we had to stay very still. Even so, if the men had looked directly at us for more than a few moments, they would have seen it."

"Only they didn't."

He nodded. "An eye will tend to behold what its owner expects to see. The soldiers would not presume anyone to have remained in the front hall when they barged in. So I allowed their eyes to glimpse the very things they anticipated instead—a room empty of all but furniture—and they accepted this sight willingly."

"I suppose they might have expected to see their quarry flee into the garden as well," Mr. Rafferdy said. "And so you created the phantasm outside the window."

Now Mr. Garritt frowned. "Perhaps they did expect such a thing. The soldiers certainly needed little convincing to go in pursuit of it. But it is not possible to create two illusions at such a distance from one another, or at least not for me. Perhaps some illusionists could do so, but I cannot."

"What are you saying?" Mr. Rafferdy said, scowling himself.

"I mean that I did not conjure the figure outside the window. Whatever the men saw beyond the glass, it was really there."

"But then who was it?"

Perhaps it had been the man in the black mask. Though even as Ivy thought this, she recalled that the shadow had not been nearly so tall as he. Then again, he could conjure illusions himself, though they were not entirely the same sort as Mr. Garritt's.

There was no time to consider it further. Whatever the figure outside the window had been, the soldiers would soon return to the house when they realized Ivy was not in the garden.

"We must hurry," Ivy said, starting up the stairs. "Rose will be waiting for us."

The two men followed after her.

Ivy expected to hear shouts and the sound of booted feet at any moment, but the only noises were those which their own feet made upon the stairs. Quickly they reached the top, then passed through an arch into the long space of the gallery. Rose stood at the far end, beside the door Arantus, a bundle of cloaks in her arms.

"What is it, Ivy?" Rose said as they reached her. Her eyes were wide. "I heard men shouting below."

"They were soldiers," Ivy said.

Rose hugged the cloaks tight to her. "You mean rebel soldiers?"

Ivy shook her head. "No, not rebels, but all the same we must not be seen by them."

"They are bad soldiers, then. Like the ones who took Mr. Quent."

"I do not think those men were truly bad, Rose. They were only doing as they were commanded by their officers, as are these men. Even so, we must leave here at once."

"Leave? To go to Heathcrest Hall, you mean?"

"Yes, just as Father said."

Rose gasped. "Oh, but I've always wanted to see Heathcrest, ever since reading your letters, Ivy. Are Mr. Rafferdy and Mr. Garritt coming with us?"

"No, Rose, they are not."

She bit her lip, looking crestfallen for a moment, but then she brightened. "But Mr. Quent will be coming, won't he? It's his house, so I am sure he will be joining you and Lily and me there."

Ivy drew a breath, knowing she did not have time to fully explain everything to her sister, and not certain she could do so even if she had hours rather than moments. "You will learn more when we arrive there, Rose. But Lily won't be coming with us. She is going to be staying in the city with Mr. Garritt for the time being."

Now Rose's look of wonder was replaced by one of confusion. "I don't understand. Why isn't Lily coming with us?"

Ivy sighed. "I am sorry, dearest. I know this is all very sudden, but there isn't time to explain right now. We must go at once. Nor are we going to Heathcrest by any usual means. What you are to see may frighten you, but I promise you that all will be well. I'll need you to be brave, though. And to shut your eyes when I tell you to, and not open them. Can you do that?"

Rose's eyes were very large at the moment, but she nodded.

"Have the soldiers returned yet?" Mr. Garritt said.

Mr. Rafferdy took a few steps toward the stairs and shook his head. "I don't hear them."

That struck Ivy as odd. It seemed to her the soldiers should have discovered she was not in the garden by now and returned to the house to look for her. Well, in any case, she would not delay. She lifted the box of Wyrdwood and touched its lid. The tendrils of wood, frozen and lifeless a moment ago, now untwined themselves from one another.

Ivy heard all three of the others draw in a breath.

"Oh!" Rose exclaimed. "It's the box made from the Old Trees."

Ivy looked up at her, startled. "How do you know that?"

"Father told me about it. Just like he told me about the doors here in the gallery, and how they open to other places."

Mr. Garritt was gazing at Rose with a puzzled expression, but Mr. Rafferdy nodded. "So Mr. Lockwell really is still here," he said, his voice low with wonder. "Or some part of him, at least."

Yes, her father was still here. And because of him, and because of Rose, there was yet hope. Ivy opened the lid of the box and took out the wooden key that was shaped like a leaf. She approached the door Arantus and searched for the place where there was a slight gap in the pattern of carved leaves.

There it was, near the center of the door. Ivy set the wooden leaf into the gap. It fit into place with a satisfying click. Ivy gripped the doorknob and took in a breath.

Then she opened the door.

A puff of air blew outward: cold, dry, and faintly metallic. It was old, this air—more ancient than any contained in a clay jar, still sealed with wax, that had been disinterred from a Tharosian ruin. All the same, it did no harm to them as they breathed it in. As Ivy had discovered previously, there was some manner of protection around the way station: a magick that protected it from the frigid aether that filled the void between the planets.

"By all the saints," Mr. Garritt said behind her, his voice somewhat faint, "what in Eternum is this place?"

"It is indeed celestial in nature," Ivy said, "but it is nothing to do with Eternum." She moved closer to the door. Beyond was the same featureless plain of gray-green dust she recalled. Stars blazed in the firmament, and a great lavender orb, skirted by a circle of sharp-edged rings, dominated a full quadrant of the black sky. "The planet you see above is Dalatair, and we are gazing at the surface of one of its moons, Arantus. Those heaps of stones you can spy in the distance are gates—doorways that open to other places. Places here in Altania."

"But that's impossible!"

"No, Garritt," Mr. Rafferdy said, clapping a hand on his shoulder. "It is magick."

Rose tightened her grip on the cloaks and lifted herself up onto her toes. "You did it, Ivy! You did magick after all, just like you tried to do that day in the parlor on Whitward Street."

Despite all that had happened, and all that must yet occur, Ivy could not help smiling a little at that memory, which now seemed so long ago. How silly she had been to think she could work magick. She knew now that she never would. But she had her own abilities.

"No, Rose, I did not make this. I only unlocked it. The door was created by a magician long ago, the one who built this house."

Mr. Rafferdy took Ivy's arm and drew her aside. "Are you certain about this?" he said, his voice low so Rose could not hear. "What if you become lost?"

"We won't," Ivy said. "When I was here before, I looked through many of the gates. Some of them still open into stands of Wyrdwood, and there was one that I am sure is the very grove near Heathcrest."

There was worry in his brown eyes, and his expression was grim, but he nodded. "All the same, you must be careful. Even if it is no issue to find the gate you seek, what lies beyond it I cannot say."

Nor could Ivy, but it was what she had to do. "I will be careful," she said. "But there is more you do not know, about my father."

"Mr. Lockwell? What is it?"

Quickly, keeping her voice to a whisper as he had done, she explained how Mr. Bennick had stolen her father from Madstone's; how he was seeking the fragments of some powerful artifact, a keystone; and how he could only be in league with Gambrel, who had returned, and was the true magus of the High Order of the Golden Door, rather than his puppet Lord Davarry.

For a moment Mr. Rafferdy was dumbstruck by these revelations. At last he nodded. "So Gambrel is back. I confess, things make more sense now that I am aware of this fact. It certainly goes a great distance toward explaining what became of Lord Mertrand, and how one so unremarkable as Lord Davarry could suddenly rise to a position of leadership."

Ivy laid a hand upon his arm. "You must be careful yourself, Mr. Rafferdy. I do not know what Gambrel schemes, but I know he will tolerate no magicians who are not in league with him."

He seemed to stiffen. What he was thinking, she did not know, but at last he nodded.

Mr. Garritt came to them then, after having been at the windows for a moment. "I still do not hear the soldiers below," he said. "And I do not see them out in the garden, either."

This puzzled Ivy, but all the same she would not delay further, for surely the men would return at any moment.

"You must both leave at once," she said. "And if you see any of the servants, tell them to flee. They already have their wages for the month."

Mr. Garritt gave a solemn nod. "Do not have any fear about us, Lady Quent. I can get Rafferdy and myself out of here unseen."

Ivy could only marvel at this. "Mr. Garritt, you are remarkable! You have helped us escape from soldiers with hardly the bat of an eye. I must believe you are used to this sort of thing."

For some reason, this caused him to blush, and he seemed bereft of any suitable reply.

It was Rafferdy who spoke instead. "There is one more thing." He removed something from his coat pocket. It was a dim gray gem. He spoke several words of magick over it, then pressed it into her hand.

"This has already expended itself once," he said quickly. "But I have cast an enchantment on it that should allow you to see an echo of the things that it revealed to me. When you are ready, tap it three times and gaze into it."

Ivy turned the gem around in her fingers. "But what is it?"

"It has to do with your husband, and with Lady Shayde. They were . . . but no, I cannot explain. It is best if you see it for yourself. Now go."

Ivy slipped the gem into the pocket of her dress, then took one of the cloaks from Rose and put it on while her sister did the same. Ivy clasped Rose's hand, and together they approached the door. As they reached the threshold, she cast a glance over her shoulder, at Mr. Rafferdy and Mr. Garritt standing beside each other. She could only think how fortunate she was to know two men who were so brave, so kind, and so true. Somehow, though it seemed impossible, she found herself smiling at them.

Then she turned to face the door, and squeezed Rose's hand. "Do not be afraid, dearest."

"I won't be afraid if I'm with you," Rose said, squeezing back.

Together, the sisters stepped through the door.

CHAPTER TWENTY-EIGHT

"**W**ELL," RAFFERDY SAID as he quietly shut the door, "she is gone, then."

"That place we saw through there," Eldyn said, his eyes fixed upon the leaf-carved surface of the door, "is it really on some moon? I suppose it looked strange enough to be such. In which case, I wonder if Mrs. Quent and her sister can really be safe there?"

Rafferdy turned away from the door. "Safe? No, they are anything but safe now. All the same, I have no doubt Mrs. Quent will make her way through and, with her sister, find Heathcrest Hall as she intends—even if I have no idea why she believes she must go there. But that she has a reason is certain. You must know, Garritt, you will not find any man possessed of a greater intellect or greater bravery than Mrs. Quent. She is a singular woman."

Eldyn regarded his friend thoughtfully. He had known Rafferdy long enough to know all of his moods or whims—or at least so he thought. But while he had seen Rafferdy disconsolate before, even despondent, he had never seen the sort of expression such as the other man wore upon his face now. It was not, Eldyn thought, precisely sadness. Rather, it was a kind of grim and determined resignation—the look of a man who has let some precious thing go of his own free will, and with no hope whatsoever that he should ever get it back again.

"You love her, don't you?" Eldyn said.

To his credit, Rafferdy neither hesitated nor demurred. "Yes, I do love her. I have done so from the time we met, though at first I was too engrossed in my own cleverness—or what I believed was cleverness—to comprehend it."

Leaning upon his cane, he moved toward one of the windows. "You see, Garritt, prior to then, I had only ever given a thought to what others thought of me. I never really considered what I thought of *them*. Not until it was too late, until she was forever beyond my reach, did I understand the truth of it. To think, had I not been such a blind and conceited dolt, she might have been married to me!"

He gripped the ivory handle of his cane, then turned back to regard Eldyn. "But no, even had I realized the truth in time, still she would never have consented to such a match. She has ever been too practical, and possessed of too much good sense, to make such a blunder as that."

Eldyn knew it was hardly an appropriate reaction given all that had happened, yet he found himself smiling. "Oh, I don't know. If you were overly conceited before, I think now you are perhaps overly critical of yourself. You sell yourself rather short, Rafferdy."

"Do I? You saw the sort of man she married, Garritt—a man of whom she has now been so wrongfully deprived. Who could ever be more exemplary, more worthy of such a wife, than he was?"

Eldyn's absurd smile vanished at once; all the same, he did not let the matter drop. "I mean no offense to Sir Quent, and if he is dead—which I can only believe, for I heard her speak it herself—then it is a most terrible thing. The void he leaves is not one that could ever be easily filled. Yet I would hazard to say, Rafferdy, that if any of us are allowed to continue on with our lives when all of this is done, that if she should choose to look, Mrs. Quent may one day find another, similarly exemplary man. I have to think, in times such as these, more than a few such men will be made by events, though they may have no inkling of it now."

Rafferdy bowed his head and was quiet for a long moment, as if thinking. Then all at once he tapped his cane upon the floor.

"Come, Garritt. Though I am puzzled by it, I see or hear no sign of the soldiers returning. But let us not give them a chance to do so."

He went to the door through which Mrs. Quent and her sister had gone and removed the leaf-shaped key. "I believe it might be best if you held on to this for safekeeping," he said, handing the key to Eldyn. Then he started for the stairs with great purpose. Eldyn pocketed the key and followed after.

As he did, he heard a noise behind him. Eldyn looked over his shoulder and saw a dark flicker of motion in the mouth of a corridor that led away from the gallery. The hair upon his neck stood up, and he recalled the shadowy figure they had glimpsed outside the window downstairs, the one that had lured the soldiers away. Only then a small form dashed out of the opening and darted across the gallery.

Eldyn gave a sigh. It was no mysterious interloper, but rather the small tortoiseshell cat that was a pet of the household. The poor creature must have been frightened by the commotion. He clucked his tongue and held out a hand, but the cat only hissed and ran under a chair.

Well, he supposed one of the servants would find it. Rafferdy had already started downstairs, and Eldyn hurried to catch up to him. The two men proceeded to the first floor. All was empty and silent. Cautiously, they made their way to the front door, which was yet open, and peered out. There was no one in the garden, or on the street beyond the gate. The soldiers had gone, though what had caused them to leave was beyond Eldyn's guess.

"I must return to the theater," Eldyn said to his friend. "I promised to look after Miss Lily, and I will do so as best I can until she might be reunited with her sisters. But what of you, Rafferdy? What will you do now?"

"Assembly is to be dissolved, and there is nothing else I can do here. I must leave the city straightaway, before Valhaine has it entirely shut. Though I confess, I am not certain what I will do after that. I suppose that I might . . ." His words trailed off, and he glanced away.

"You might what?"

He drew in a breath, then looked back at Eldyn.

"You will no doubt think it a foolish whim, but someone once told me I would make a good soldier, and I think I should like to go join up with the rebels. Though I do not know what I would do for them, or even how to find them. I suppose, even if I did, they would simply shoot me on sight."

Eldyn found himself grinning. "I suppose they would at that. Unless you knew the proper codes and passwords, of course."

"A fine suggestion," Rafferdy said with a scowl. "But how am I supposed to discover such—" All at once his jaw dropped. "Gods and daemons, you know these things yourself, don't you?"

"It is true," Eldyn said, lowering his voice even though the garden was desolate. "I have been working this last half month to help smuggle messages out of the city to Huntley Morden's army. I can take you to the fellow I work for. If I vouch for you, he will have no problem trusting you. He can tell you where to find Morden's men, and how best to approach them."

For a long moment Rafferdy stared at him, then all at once he gave a laugh. "I should think you were being facetious, Garritt, except I know such is impossible for one so irresistibly earnest as yourself. So it is I can only believe, remarkable as it seems, that you are indeed the most notorious sort of traitor and rebel."

Eldyn could not help feeling a note of pride at this. "Hardly notorious, I would say, but my talents have had their uses."

"I imagine they have at that," Rafferdy said, and raised an eyebrow. "Even after all these years, you are full of unexpected revelations, Garritt! I am very glad to have known you. Just as I am glad to know we will be fighting on the same side."

"As am I," Eldyn said wholeheartedly.

"Well, then, lead me onward." Rafferdy gestured with his cane toward the path before them. "To war," he said grimly, eagerly.

And Eldyn replied in kind, "To war."

BOOK THREE

Again, Heathcrest

CHAPTER TWENTY-NINE

THE PEOPLE HUDDLED in the cave and listened as the wind shook the branches of the trees outside.

Ivy groped around in the darkness. She knew this place; she had been here before, she was sure of it. Only her name wasn't Ivy or Ivoleyn. It was something else, something more lilting and musical in the way it was spoken. And the others crouching in the cave around her were not strangers; rather, they were the people of her tribe. She recognized their warm, familiar scent. It should have been a comfort to her.

Only there was another scent on the air as well, sharp and metallic. Like lightning. Or like fear.

Abruptly, a crimson glow appeared at the mouth of the cave. At first Ivy wondered if it was the new red moon shining through the opening in the cliff. Then she thought perhaps Tennek, who had been standing guard, had raised up a burning brand. But that was foolish, for what if the gray ones saw him? Tennek had seen them before. They looked like men, but their eyes were as dead as a shark's, and when cut their wounds seeped a thick, colorless fluid instead of blood. Did Tennek not recall how the gray men had nearly killed him that time? And what of the shadows with teeth—the things described by that other tribe they had encountered?

Only then Ivy recalled that they had not lit a fire in the cave from which her brother might have pulled a branch. And as the man and the woman stepped into the cave, she saw that it was from neither moon nor fire that the red light came.

The man was tall—taller than any of the men of her tribe—with eyes as blue as the sea. A wolf pelt was thrown across his broad shoulders, and though he looked different from the men of her tribe, with his square face and jutting nose, he was still pleasing to the eye. All the same, an unease filled her at the sight of him, a sense of foreboding. Nor was she reassured by the appearance of the one who accompanied him. The woman was clad in strange, supple skins that clung tightly to her body, and her face was as pale and smooth as the inside of an abalone shell.

Before Ivy could tell the others to be wary, Nesharu had risen and hobbled forward to meet the strangers. It was Nesharu who had taught Ivy about the *wayru*—that was, how to understand the rhythm and pattern of all things in the world. She was the oldest and wisest woman in the tribe, and therefore its leader. She exchanged words with the strangers, but Ivy did not hear what they said, for even though the trees were a good distance from the cave, the roaring of the wind in their branches filled her ears. It was a sound like many voices spoken in unison.

Something is wrong, the voices of the trees seemed to say. *The light has changed. The ground trembles. The rain is bitter. Something is wrong. . . .*

The red light brightened. Ivy jerked her head up and realized that Nesharu was inviting the strangers into the cave. The red glow came from a stone resting upon the palm of his hand. Ivy had never seen such a thing. Its light fell upon the people, staining them like blood.

All at once a dread came over Ivy—a feeling so powerful that a moan was forced from her. A red light. A man wearing the silver pelt of a wolf. A woman with skin as white and hard as quartz.

Yes, Ivy had seen all of these things before. She had seen them, and she knew what was going to happen next. The shadows would come—the shadows with teeth—and the people would flee from the cave. They would follow the tall man to the edge of the trees.

He would call upon the ground to swallow up the shadows while the woman struck at them and beat them back with arms that moved as swiftly as pale snakes. Together, they would protect Ivy from the shadows, and help her to get to the forest. Then Ivy would call to the trees, asking them to protect her and her people.

And the trees would listen. Through her, they would learn that the shadows were their foes, and the trees would never afterward forget this. Their trunks would bend, their branches would reach down, and they would lash out at the shadows, breaking them, beating them into dust. All of the people would be saved.

No, not all of them. Not her son . . .

Even as Ivy realized what was going to happen, it was already happening. The tall man took her by the hand and led her away from the people, back into the cave. She went willingly, her heart still beating rapidly from the feeling of the trees bending to her wishes, and from the sight of the stranger's strong limbs and handsome face.

He set down his glowing stone and came close to her. For a moment she caught a trace of an unpleasant smell, like dead fish washed up on the shore. But this was forgotten as he laid her down upon the floor of the cave and their clothing fell away.

Through you, I will truly live again, he said.

And he held her close as their bodies became one in a moment of pain and delight.

It was not until later, when her belly swelled and she gave birth, that she finally learned what he had meant by those words he spoke. For then, even as she held her newborn son for the first time, the tall man who had become her mate crumpled limply to the ground. His body, once strong but now feeble and covered with sores, became still and lifeless. And at the very same moment his final breath rattled from him, the infant in her arms opened his eyes.

They were blue, those eyes. And gazing into them, she realized that she recognized the spirit beyond them. So it was that she

knew the horrible truth, and understood at last how she had been
betrayed by the tall man with the wolf pelt on his shoulders. How
she had been betrayed by . . .

"MYRRGON," cried a voice.

Ivy sat up in the horsehair chair, pressing a hand against her
midriff as she did. The windows of the long front room of
Heathcrest Hall were all black, and they shook as a rain lashed
against them.

A light approached, and Ivy suffered a momentary terror as she
recalled the dream she had been caught in. Only the light was
gold, not crimson, and as it came near she saw its source.

"Rose," she said in relief.

Rose drew closer. She held a brass candleholder, and a flame
flickered atop the stump of wax. "Are you all right, Ivy? I heard
you call out something."

"I'm sorry if I frightened you, Rose. I was having a bad dream,
that's all."

Ivy thought back to the dream she had been caught in when
Rose woke her. It was the same, strangely vivid interlude that always began with her collecting shells along the shore of a sea. She
had had the dream a number of times back in Invarel. Then, oddly,
it had ceased after the night her body rejected the tiny life—the
son—that had been growing within her.

For a while she did not have the dream at all, or at least not that
she recalled. But then, after the soldiers took Mr. Quent away, the
dream had come to her again. And ever since their arrival at
Heathcrest Hall, she had had the dream with increasing frequency,
until now it came to her nearly every time she shut her eyes and
managed to fall sleep.

And each time, she remembered more of it upon waking.

Now, as she stared into the light of Rose's candle, Ivy began to
recollect the final moments of the dream. Leaving the cave with
the tall man. The moon waxing and waning in the sky as they trav-

eled the shadowed land. His large hand resting upon her belly as it swelled. And then he smiled as he said their son's name would be the same as his. That it would be—

"Myrrgon," she whispered.

"Yes, that's it," Rose said. "That's the word I heard you call out. What does it mean?"

That was a good question. Why was Ivy having a dream about a young woman who lived by the sea, and a man with the name of an ancient magician? And why was it coming more and more often? Again, she thought back to the dream. She could remember nearly all of it now—the people's flight from the sea, the cave, the man with blue eyes and the white-faced woman, the trees, and the shadows. It was only the very end of the dream that remained murky and indistinct. Her belly had swelled as a life grew within her. She had held a child in her arms. Only then something had happened.

Something awful.

Ivy's gaze went to an old stuffed wolf that was mounted upon a wooden stand nearby. Its glass eyes glinted, and in the flickering candlelight its gray fur rippled as if it was moving.

"I'm not sure what it means," Ivy murmured, more to herself than to Rose.

All the same, Rose seemed to accept this answer. "I found a box with some tea in the kitchen," she said, taking up the candle-holder as she stood. "It was in the corner of a cupboard. It's very old and dry. I could try to brew us a cup from it. I'm sure it's not any good, but I think at least it should remind us of tea."

Like the shadows before Rose's candle, the dream flitted away. Outside, the rain still beat at the windows, and a spasm passed through Ivy. Only it wasn't pain this time, it was simply a shiver, for she was cold.

"Yes," Ivy said, "I would like that."

And she went with Rose to the kitchen.

———

THE TEA was not so poor as they feared, for the leaves had been well-wrapped in a waxed cloth inside the box. Ivy wondered if it was Mrs. Darendal who had last used this tea. Had the house-keeper closed the box carefully, expecting to open it again soon? Or perhaps it had been the housemaid, Lanna, who had done so.

But neither of them had ever opened the box again. Mrs. Dar-endal's son, the highwayman Westen, had come to Heathcrest Hall intending to take Ivy away and so lure Mr. Quent into a fatal trap. Only Mr. Quent had arrived with soldiers, and they had shot Westen's compatriots while the highwayman fled. After that, Lanna had returned to her family in the village of Low Sorrell. And Mrs. Darendal had perished.

Ivy filled a kettle with water, then made a little fire in the stove. For this, she used some of the wood stacked beside the fireplace that dominated one end of the kitchen. That the cavernous fire-place had once been used to roast whole boars brought back by the earl's hunting parties, Ivy had no doubt.

Theirs was a decidedly smaller party; and once the tea was hot they took it to the parlor off the front hall. They had been spend-ing much of their time in the little room, for it was easy to keep warm. The last several lumenals had all been swift and fleeting, while the umbrals in between had each been longer than the last, and a perpetual chill had settled over the house.

As they sat by the fire and sipped tea, Ivy could only think of all the time she had spent in this room when she was a governess, tutoring Clarette and Chambley. Several volumes of the *Lex Alta-nia* still resided on the bookshelf in the corner. How many hours had they spent being entertained by those battered old books! She would observe as the children took turns reading passages from them, all the while keeping an eye on the parlor window, waiting for the gruff and forbidding master of the house to return.

Only he would never return again. Heathcrest Hall had no master now.

That the house remained itself was a wonder, she supposed. It had been raining and dark the night Ivy and Rose emerged from the little grove of shabby trees and stumbled across the moor. Ivy was still astonished at Rose's bravery throughout the entire ordeal. She had gone willingly through the door Arantus, and had followed Ivy across the dusty gray-green plain toward the stone arches that stood in the distance.

Ivy had searched among the gates—those that still stood—looking for ones that opened onto scenes of crooked trunks and straggling branches. And of these, there was one in particular she was searching for, one she was certain she would recognize. All the while, Rose had demonstrated no trepidation, and instead had been fascinated with the stars above them, and the great purple crescent of the planet Dalatair. It was as if she had already known such things lay beyond the door. Ivy could only wonder what else Rose had discussed with the spirit of their father.

At last Ivy had found the gate she recalled seeing on her previous visit to the way station. Though it was dark through the gate, and thus difficult to make out the scene, still there was a familiarity to the silhouettes of the trees beyond. That she was glimpsing the very grove that stood on the ridge just east of Heathcrest, she was certain.

When Ivy told Rose they must go through, and not to be afraid of the trees or of anything they might do, Rose had merely nodded. Hand in hand, the two had approached the gate. One moment they trod on gray dust, and the next old leaves crackled beneath their feet.

At once Ivy had felt the presence of the ancient trees. For a terrible few heartbeats there was a menace to the creaking and groaning of their branches as they shook under the force of a gale. Only then Ivy called out to the trees with her thoughts, and they listened and were soothed.

A path opened before them, and Ivy and Rose followed it to the high stone wall that surrounded the grove. Ivy had wondered how they might scale it; she did not want to alarm Rose by having the trees pluck them up off the ground. But there was no need, for a great crack had opened in the wall—a gap Ivy was certain had not been there when she dwelled at Heathcrest.

Whether the crack had been made from the outside, or from

within, Ivy did not know but it was just wide enough for Ivy and Rose to slip through. It was with some reluctance that Ivy left the grove, and she brushed her fingers over the rough trunks as she did, feeling the life, the power, flowing like sap within them.

I will come to you again, she thought.

Then the sisters left the wall behind and made their way down the slope, through the heather and gorse. The night was so dark that Ivy half-feared she would not know which way to go. But memory served where sight could not. Soon they left the one ridge behind and ascended up the side of another. Just as they reached the summit, a gust of wind tore through the clouds, and the moon sailed free of its shroud. In the silvery light, a familiar, blocky outline hove before them.

It was Heathcrest Hall. She had returned at last.

A joy had filled her, and seizing Rose's hand she had raced the last distance toward the house. Only as they approached, her joy was replaced by a sudden dread. On one side of the house, moonlight shone through empty windows, for the roof had fallen in, and the stones were stained black with soot. There had been a fire.

A fear came over Ivy that she had lost Heathcrest as well, but this fear was lessened as they drew closer to the house. The windows were all intact on the main part of the manor, and the walls unstained. It was evident the fire had been confined to the southern wing. Then the clouds closed over the moon, and rain began to fall again. Hurriedly, the sisters approached the house, eager for shelter.

It was only when they reached the house and found the front door locked that Ivy realized she should have expected this. Mr. Quent had closed up the house when they left for the city more than a year ago, and no one would have been in it since then.

Ivy had stared dumbly for a moment, but soon an idea occurred to her. She took the Wyrdwood box, which she had carried all this while, and held it near the door. As she concentrated, several tendrils of wood uncoiled themselves from the box. They probed the lock like tiny fingers, then slipped inside the keyhole.

Turn it, Ivy thought.

There was a click as the tumblers moved within the door. Ivy coaxed the little twigs out of the lock and back into place upon the Wyrdwood box. Then she pushed upon the door. It opened with a low sigh.

And that was how the lady of the house had returned.

That had been well over a half month ago. Or at least, Ivy guessed it had been that long, for it was hard to know precisely how much time had passed. Though she searched room after room, there did not seem to be a working clock anywhere in the house. She had found an almanac in the parlor, but it was from years ago, its pages cracked and yellowed. Besides, even a new almanac would have been no use. The lumenals and umbrals alternated in the most fragmented and jumbled fashion. Sometimes a day appeared hardly to be half done when the world suddenly seemed to tilt and the sun lurched toward the horizon. At other times it was as if the sun stood still in the sky, withering all beneath its brutal glare.

Despite the unpredictable series of lumenals and umbrals, one pattern had begun to emerge. While the days varied in length, in general they were becoming shorter, while it was the opposite case for the nights. Though Ivy had no way to measure it, she was certain the umbrals were, in the average, increasing in duration. Often, by the time a sluggish dawn crept over the world, there would be frost on the windowpanes. And of late the moorlands around the manor had turned from gray-green to gray-brown.

Sometimes, when it was dark, Ivy would dare to step out the door of the house and look up at the sky. Reading a few books upon the topic had in no way made her into an astrographer, but all it took was a keen eye to notice the changes in the arrangement of the heavens. The red planet, Cerephus, had continued to grow in size, so that it was now easily perceived as a disk by the naked eye. While not so large as the moon, it was nearly as bright, and cast a lurid crimson glow over the world.

Even as Cerephus brightened, the rest of the heavens seemed

to feel its growing influence. Other steady points of colored light, which had heretofore been sprinkled widely across the heavens, were now on the move. Each time Ivy observed them, they had traveled in closer proximity to Cerephus: purple Dalatair, pale yellow Loerus, silvery twins Acreon and Urioth, burnt-umber Regulus, and brilliant blue Anares. There were other planets too small to observe without the aid of the lens—Vaelus, Cyrenth, Naius, Eides, and far-off Memnymion. All the same, Ivy did not need to work the knobs and gears of her father's celestial globe to know that these bodies were all moving in the heavens as well. Their orbits and epicycles were gradually and inexorably altering, so that soon all of them would be arranged like shimmering beads on a single strand pulled taut. And then . . .

When twelve who wander stand as one, through the door the dark will come.

Those were the first lines of the riddle her father had left for her long ago, hidden beneath the endpapers of a book. It was the riddle that had helped her discover the key to the house on Durrow Street. The key had been revealed when she arranged the celestial globe so that all the orbs representing the planets stood in a line. As she gazed at the sky above the dark moorlands, Ivy often wondered what other doors would open when it was not just the celestial globe arranged in such a manner, but the heavens themselves.

Then she would shiver, and look away from the sky, and go back into the silent, empty manor.

Such thoughts as these, together with all that had happened, could easily have made her morbid, and caused her to lie down in some black room in the house with no intention to ever rise again. But she could do no such thing, not when Rose had need of her. Furthermore, it was the case that the immediate and constant work of sustaining themselves occupied the great majority of their time, so that she had not the luxury of letting herself be consumed in terrible thoughts. In sum, when one is cold and hungry, it is difficult to consider much of anything else.

That first night the two sisters huddled together in a corner of the front hall, holding each other for warmth beneath a musty old bearskin they had pulled down from the wall. At last both storm and night ended, and a wan morning ensued. Their first order of business was to find something to eat, for it had been many hours since they had had anything.

An exploration of the kitchen quickly revealed that they were not the first who had come here with a similar intent. There was evidence of a careless fire in the stove, and dirty plates scattered on the broad plank table—though, by the looks of it, the trespassers had been here some time ago. Their mode of entry was quickly obvious, for the kitchen door had been forced open from the outside, breaking the latch. Ivy had thought herself so clever the night before in opening the lock at the front of the house, but it turned out they could have easily come around by the back!

A perusal of the stone-walled larder off the kitchen showed that much had been looted. This had been done in such haste that several barrels of flour had been broken open to spill their contents, and pots of salted meat had been smashed. All these things were long spoiled by exposure to air and the work of rodents. But rummaging past this detritus soon revealed two barrels of flour that were undisturbed, as well as a good number of hard-rinded cheeses, a salted pork, a pair of hams, and various crocks containing dried apples, preserved apricots, olives, and even a pot of honey. Whoever had been here had not had much time to do their work, for which Ivy was grateful.

As there was still wood in the niche by the fireplace, and a tinderbox on the mantel, they soon had a fire in the stove. Ivy found a knife to slice the pork and a pan to cook it in, and she mixed the renderings with the flour to make little biscuits. They ate these with a wedge of the cheese, and some of the apricots. The result was a meal that, given their famished state, seemed akin to a feast.

The food warmed them, and lifted their spirits. After that, they had energy to make an exploration of the house. Ivy had half-feared that they were not alone here, that others might have entered the abandoned manor seeking shelter. But with the exception of spiders here and there, they encountered no other living beings.

Other than the south wing, the house appeared in much the state Ivy last remembered it, with the exception of being damper and mustier, and the air yet bore a sharp, acrid tinge of smoke. How the fire had begun, she could only guess. Though given that the shell of the outer walls yet stood while the roof had fallen in, she suspected the south wing had been struck by lightning. No one had been here to stop the fire. But there must have been a hard rain soon after the strike to douse the flames, or else the whole house would have been destroyed. That it had not been was a thing to be grateful for.

During that first day of exploring, they removed several blankets from the bedchambers and used them to make nests for themselves in the downstairs parlor. Ivy would not consider sleeping on one of the upper floors, for fear of being trapped by another fire. By the time this was done, another long umbral had commenced, though it was neither so cold nor terrifying as the first.

Over those next days, they continued to work to improve their living conditions within the old manor. An exploration of the courtyard behind the house revealed that the kitchen garden, though it had gone wild, still bore a number of herbs and greens and even parsnips and radishes which they could use to augment the foodstuffs from the larder. Though the variety was still poor, by Ivy's calculations they had now enough food to last at least a month if they were frugal.

With food and shelter secured, clothing was their next priority. It was soon apparent that their dresses, intended for a warm day in the city, were not suitable for the damp chill of the West Country. So it was they spent a great deal of time going through every wardrobe and closet in the house, looking for something suitable to wear. Then, at the end of a corridor in the north wing, in a small chamber Ivy was certain she had never entered in her prior time at Heathcrest, Rose opened a cherrywood cabinet and let out a gasp.

Ivy hurried over and saw at once the source of Rose's astonishment, for the cabinet was filled with dresses. The dresses were all of an outmoded style, with many ruffles and bits of lace, but they were beautiful all the same, made of velvet and soft wool and heavy silk in hues of gray, deep violet, and blues so dark as to be all but black.

"I wonder who these belonged to," Rose had said, touching the gowns.

Ivy had shaken her head. "I don't know."

"Look."

Rose had bent down, then picked up something from the bottom of the cabinet. It was a porcelain doll. Its face was cracked, and its taffeta dress was yellowed. But it was still a pretty thing, with glossy black hair and faded pink lips and cheeks.

"These gowns aren't very large. They must have belonged to a girl who lived in the manor long ago." She cradled the doll in her arms. "And this must have been hers as well."

Ivy thought of the large painting that hung above the first landing of the main staircase—the portrait that depicted Earl Rylend and his wife, as well as their son, Lord Wilden. And standing apart from them, almost lost in shadows on the edge of the painting, was a girl with dark hair and eyes.

"Yes," Ivy had said, looking at the doll's white porcelain face, "I think you must be right, Rose."

They chose several of the warmest dresses and took them downstairs, and then upon searching discovered scissors, needles, and thread in the old servants' quarters. Over the next several days, Rose worked upon the gowns, altering them, and using pieces carefully cut from one to lengthen the sleeves or skirt or bodice of another.

When she was done, they each had a new dress of warm wool to protect them from the chill; and as soon as she was done with these dresses, Rose began work on two more. She spent some of her time upon the doll as well, using leftover scraps to make a tiny dress for it, and employing some paints she discovered in a cupboard to smooth over the cracks on its face and brighten its lips. When she was done, the doll was so lovely that any girl might have considered herself lucky to have received it for a present.

As she observed her sister sewing in the little parlor, Ivy could only be amazed. Both Rose and Lily had been through unimaginable ordeals these last years, first knowing poverty after their father's illness, and then an even worse state following their mother's death. True, they had experienced joy and comfort in their time on Durrow Street, but it had been a short interlude—and one wrested from them prematurely.

Now they had fled to a cold, musty manor in the country. Yet throughout it all, Rose had made no complaint, and had been extraordinarily brave. Indeed, once Ivy assured her that Lily would be very well in the city, and was staying there to learn how to craft dramatic scenes for plays, the only fear Rose expressed had been for the sake of Miss Mew.

Ivy assured her the little cat would be taken care of—that Mrs. Seenly would not abandon her, and that it was better they had not brought Miss Mew with them, for there was no milk to have here. Rose agreed with this point. And though she missed the cat, her attentions were soon fixed upon the porcelain doll instead, and she kept it close always.

While Rose had been brave, Ivy could not say the same for herself—for there was something she should do, something she knew she must, but could not bring herself to. From time to time, when Rose was occupied with her sewing, Ivy would take out the small, cloudy gem that Mr. Rafferdy had given her just before their parting. He had not had an opportunity to tell her exactly what it was, yet she could not say that she did not have an inkling. For why else was she so reluctant to do as Mr. Rafferdy had instructed?

I have cast an enchantment on it that should allow you to see an echo of the things that it revealed to me, he had told her. *When you are ready, tap it three times and gaze into it.*

What thing could the gem have witnessed that day that she had not already seen herself? There was only one possibility, and she did not need to watch a reflection of that event to know that it had occurred; she felt it in her heart, which was as darkened and hollow as the husk of the manor's south wing. She would never see Mr. Quent again in this life. She would never feel the prickling of his beard against her cheek or the strength of his arms enclosing her. She was lost and alone upon a moor, powerless to stop the cold rains that lashed at her; and no matter how many times she called for him, he would not come for her again.

All the same, each time she gazed into the dim jewel, Ivy knew she should do as Mr. Rafferdy had said. Surely he had given it to her for some purpose other than to horrify her. There was something it could reveal to her, something she needed to witness for herself. Yet each time, Ivy would put the gem back into the Wyrdwood box without tapping it as he had directed.

It was the morning of their fifth lumenal at Heathcrest when there came a knock at the front of the house. The sound of it was so unexpected that Ivy hardly knew what she was hearing. For up until then she had seen no sign of any sort of human presence outside the windows of the manor: no horses in the distance, or threads of smoke rising from a croft.

Then it came again: a steady pounding upon the door. Rose had hugged the doll tightly, her eyes wide. Ivy had hesitated. Then she took up a poker from the hearth.

"Stay here," she said to Rose, then went to the front hall.

It occurred to her that this was absurd, that a band of robbers would have no fear of a small woman in a gray dress, armed with a poker or not. But then the knocking came again, and there was nothing to do but answer it, lest they let themselves in. Raising the poker, she flung open the door.

Who was more astonished, she or the dark-haired man on the other side, it was difficult to say. Ivy knew her mouth was formed into a circle much like his own.

"Lady Quent!" he said, even as she exclaimed, "Mr. Samonds!"

For a long moment they stared at each other, as if to make certain their eyes had not deceived them. But there could be no mistake. His face was perhaps a bit more tanned and weatherworn than before, but remained kind and open. At last, as if having made his own confirmation of her identity, he glanced down at the poker in her hands.

"You look very intent upon using that, your ladyship," said the farrier of Cairnbridge village.

Hastily, she lowered the poker. "I could not know who it was at the door. I feared the worst. But to discover it is you, Mr. Samonds, I . . ." She was at a loss to say anything more, and instead reached out and took his hand, and gripped it tightly. It was roughened from his work, though when he squeezed her hand in return it was with the gentlest pressure.

At last she recovered enough to invite him in, and he readily agreed, for the mist was beginning to bead upon his brown coat. It was only as he stepped over the threshold that Ivy noticed the pistol in his hand. Ivy was not the only one who had been prepared for an unfriendly welcome when the door was opened. Mr. Samonds put the pistol in his belt, covering it with his coat, and followed after Ivy.

She brought him into the little parlor, and introduced him to Rose as a fond acquaintance from her prior time at Heathcrest. Mr. Samonds's hands might have been rough, but his voice and manner were both soft, and Rose's fear was at once dismissed—though she remained shy, as she ever was around strangers, and cradled the doll on her lap while Ivy bade Mr. Samonds to sit by the fire. Ivy had no tea to offer him (for Rose had yet to discover the box of tea), but she had found a half-full bottle of whiskey in her explorations, and had brought it to the parlor thinking it might prove useful.

It did now as she offered some of the whiskey to Mr. Samonds, and he accepted it gladly.

"The lumenal has just begun, and it might be deemed early for spirits," he said after taking a sip of the whiskey. "But who can really tell what is early and late these days? The lumenals and umbrals are all a muddle."

"They are, though it seems to be more often the latter than the former here in the country," Ivy said.

"So it does. But how is it you happen to be in the country at all, Lady Quent? Given all that has occurred, I am astonished to find you here. And where is your husband?"

Ivy suddenly found it hard to draw a breath. She was mindful of Rose upon the sofa. "I'm afraid my husband is . . . not with us."

His look was startled, and he hastily set down the whiskey glass. Rose presumed Mr. Quent remained in prison in the city; she did not yet know the truth. But Ivy thought Mr. Samonds must have an inkling of it now.

"How is it that you are here yourself?" Ivy said hastily. "Back in the city, we heard of the troubles in the West Country. And since Rose and I have been here, we have not seen any sign of another soul out the windows."

"I am not surprised by that," Mr. Samonds said grimly. "There were a number of skirmishes in the county the better part of a month ago. But as I guess you know, Huntley Morden's men won out, and Valhaine's soldiers were forced to retreat to the east. By then, most of the people in the county had fled to escape the fighting. There's not a person left in Cairnbridge at the moment, though some yet remain in Low Sorrell. None of the young men, of course, for they've all joined up with Morden's army. But some of the elderly, or those who could not bear a journey, stayed there."

These words alarmed Ivy. While she knew the rebels had taken the West Country, she had not really considered what it meant until that moment. "So we are behind the line of the war," she murmured.

"Or ahead of it, depending on your point of view," he said, raising an eyebrow.

"I did not come here with the intention of taking up sides in a war, Mr. Samonds," she said. "Only to find a safe place for my sister and myself. But what of your aunt? Is she one of those who remained in Low Sorrell?"

He nodded. "She refused to go when the fighting broke out."

Ivy thought of Miss Samonds—of her crooked fingers and bent limbs, which had been affected by a childhood infirmity of the joints. "Is she so unwell as to not be able to travel?"

"No, she is well—stronger than many, despite what she has suffered in the past. She said she did not want to leave her cows, for fear they would be stolen. But in truth it was her intent to look after some of the other folk in the village who were too old or ill to leave."

Ivy could not help smiling. "She is a very able woman."

"So she is. All the same, I was concerned for her. So as soon as I was approved for a leave, I left my regiment and came directly here."

Ivy was astonished anew. Then she regarded his brown coat, and thought of the pistol he had tucked in his belt, and she realized she should not have been. Why else would a man in his late twenties, without a wife and used to working with horses, remain in this part of the country?

"You have enlisted in Morden's army," she said.

"As has nearly every able-bodied young man in the West Country, or at least those that didn't run for the east at the first sign of war." He met her gaze. "I hope you are not too dismayed at this news, Lady Quent. I think you know that by nature I am not a violent man. But in the course of my trade, I've learned that to repair a broken horseshoe, you must put it to the fire before you can forge it anew. I think Altania is broken right now. And to be whole again, I believe it must be reforged with a rightful king at its head, rather than a self-proclaimed *guardian*." He looked up at her. "Forgive me if I offend, your ladyship."

Ivy gripped the arms of her chair. Then she leaned forward, taking up the glass he had set down, and drank the rest of the whiskey herself. Never before had she imbibed such liquor, save a splash or two mixed with tea. But at that moment, she welcomed the hot fire that descended within her.

"I have no allegiance to Lord Valhaine," she said in a flat tone. And while Mr. Samonds's expression was full of questions, she expounded no further upon the topic.

After that, they spoke of the situation in the county. Mr. Samonds explained how, in Low Sorrell, a boy who had been out on the moors, trying to gather up scattered sheep, spoke of seeing a light at dusk two days past, up on the ridge where Heathcrest Hall stood. Hearing this, Mr. Samonds had feared some enemy soldiers might have been hiding out there.

Though Valhaine's forces had been driven eastward, there were some deserters from the royal army who had fled the fighting, and who had remained behind in the county. They were desperate and dangerous men and, being enemies of both sides now, they had turned to banditry to sustain themselves. Thinking such men might be using the abandoned manor as a refuge, Mr. Samonds had come to investigate.

"But you found us instead," Rose said, looking up from the porcelain doll.

"For which I am exceedingly glad," Mr. Samonds replied.

Ivy considered the signs of disturbance they had found in the pantry. "None of Valhaine's soldiers are here now," she said. "But I think such men may indeed have been in the house at some point."

"That does not surprise me," he said. "But I wonder why they should have left. This manor would have offered a fine hiding place for them."

"Perhaps the fire drove them off," she said, and offered her theory that it was lightning that had caused the fire in the south wing.

"You may be right," Mr. Samonds replied. "If so, it was a lucky stroke, and luckier still that the fire did not take the whole house."

"Perhaps it knew we were coming," Rose said, smoothing the doll's dress, "and wouldn't let itself be burned."

Ivy was used to Rose saying peculiar things, but if Mr. Samonds was disconcerted by this, he did not show it. Instead, crinkles appeared by his eyes as he smiled. "Perhaps it did at that. This is an old house, and a wise one, I would say."

Rose nodded solemnly. "Yes, it is."

Ivy asked Mr. Samonds if he would like more whiskey, but he regretfully declined. His leave was brief, and he had only time to say good-bye to his aunt before he had to ride back to his regiment, which was readying to march east. He rose from his chair, and they both went with him to the front door.

"Good-bye, Miss Lockwell," he said with a bow to Rose. Then he clasped Ivy's hand in parting. As he did, he leaned close, speaking so only she could hear. "Be vigilant, Lady Quent. If some of Valhaine's soldiers do remain in the county, they have no allegiance and nothing to lose, and so I fear are not above any action."

Ivy did not know what to say that would not upset Rose, and so only nodded. He put on his hat and went out into the mist. Then Ivy closed the door, and the two sisters were alone in the old manor once more.

B Y IVY'S BEST CALCULATIONS, Mr. Samonds's visit had been more than a half month ago. Now, in the little parlor, Ivy and Rose finished their cups of tea, brewed from the box Rose had just discovered. The hot drink did much to bolster Ivy's spirits, and she was tempted to brew another pot. Yet it was best to conserve the tea, for there was not a great amount of it.

And she still did not know how long they would have to remain here at Heathcrest.

With that thought in mind, Ivy retrieved the Wyrdwood box from the shelf in the parlor. She took out the black-covered journal, then began turning through the pages, hoping to find one that bore words she had not seen before.

Listen to your father, the man in the mask had said to her. *He will tell you what to do.*

Only so far, he had not. Ivy had checked the journal with great frequency since arriving at Heathcrest Hall, but not a single word had appeared on its pages. But some had to manifest themselves soon. After all, that was the real enchantment of the journal—that an entry would appear only when the heavens were arranged in the particular manner prescribed by her father when he wrote the words.

If my calculations are correct, even as you read this, the Grand Conjunction fast approaches, he had written in his previous entry. And, *Look for another note from me when the alignment begins.*

But it was already beginning, wasn't it? She had watched at night as the glowing sparks of the planets all began to converge upon one quadrant of the sky—the very same occupied by the red, unblinking eye of Cerephus.

Yet as she turned through the journal now, all of the pages were blank. If only there was a way to talk to her father, to ask him what she was supposed to do. But his spirit still resided in the house on Durrow Street. And as for his physical form, there was no telling where Mr. Bennick had taken him. Perhaps he had delivered her father to Mr. Gambrel—perhaps the two magicians had found some way to discover Mr. Lockwell's piece of the keystone. In which case they would have no more need of him . . .

No, she could not consider that possibility, not now. Besides, while she might not be able to speak with her father, there was someone else who *had* spoken to him.

"Rose," she said, shutting the journal.

Rose looked up from her sewing. She was cutting pieces from one of the dresses they had found in the wardrobe upstairs. The garment was of a size that it could not have been worn by a girl of more than five or six. Rose was using it to fashion a new dress for the porcelain doll—one made of silk, and of a blue so deep it was almost black.

"What is it, Ivy?"

"Just before we left the city, you said that you spoke to Father, and that he said we had to come to Heathcrest."

Rose nodded. "Yes, that's what he said. And now we're here."

"Yes, we are. But was there anything else that he said to you that day—anything at all?"

"I think so," Rose said slowly. "I mean, yes, he did say some other things. Only I don't always understand what he's telling me. Sometimes he uses words that I don't know."

Ivy sat up straight in the chair. "What did he say to you?"

"I'm not sure. Everything was all in a hurry. Mr. Rafferdy and Mr. Garritt were there, and the soldiers were coming."

"You must try to remember, Rose. It might be very important. Our father said we had to go to Heathcrest Hall. But did he say anything more? Did he say why?"

Rose shut her eyes, and a line appeared between her fine eyebrows. "He said something about the calculations, that they were off."

"The calculations?"

Still Rose did not open her eyes. "He said one of the gears in the globe was the wrong size, but that Mr. Larken was able to fix it and then adjust the clock. Only then it was too late. The others were coming."

"Too late?" Ivy said, a shiver creeping up her neck. "Too late for what?"

Rose shook her head. "It was hard to understand him. He was speaking so quickly. I think he was talking about a book—that it was too late to fix something in the book, and that words wouldn't appear when they were supposed to anymore. But that doesn't make any sense to me. How can words appear in a book?"

Ivy gripped the journal tightly and fear welled up in her. Rose could not understand her father's statements, but Ivy thought that she did. Her father had used the celestial globe to calculate the future positions of the planets, so that he could cause entries to appear in the journal at a prescribed time—entries that would tell Ivy what to do. Only some flaw had been discovered in the workings of the globe. Mr. Larken had been able to correct it, as well as the old rosewood clock, but there had been no time to rework the journal. For by then, some of the magicians of his order were coming to seize the Eye of Ran-Yahgren.

Now Ivy knew why the last entry she had discovered had appeared so briefly, and why it had faded before it even became fully visible—the heavens had not moved as her father had predicted, and had only briefly approached the required alignment. That hadn't been the case with the prior entry; that writing hadn't been gray and dim, and hadn't faded so quickly. Which meant that her father's calculations were growing more discordant as time passed.

Look for another note from me when the alignment begins, her father had written. But what if, due to the errors in the celestial globe, the heavens never aligned themselves as her father had assumed? What if the next entry in the journal never appeared at all? If it didn't, everything would be for naught; she would lack the final clues she needed to solve the elaborate puzzle her father had designed for her all those years ago.

"Don't worry, Ivy."

Rose's eyes were open now, gazing at her, and Ivy could only suppose the horror on her face had been apparent.

"I remember something else Father said," Rose went on. "I didn't know what it meant, but you're very clever at such things, so maybe you do. He said, 'Wait for the third occlusion, then open the book.' Do you know what that means?"

Yes, Ivy did—or at least she thought so. Originally, she supposed, her father had intended for an entry to appear as the Grand Conjunction began. Instead, due to the error in his calculations, it would instead appear at the third occlusion—the moment when three planets fell in line behind Cerephus. But how would Ivy know when that moment came? What if the sky was cloudy, or the planets were too dim and distant to observe?

She would have to hope that wasn't the case. But no matter what, she would need to find a good vantage from where she could view the heavens and watch their movements.

"I'm not entirely certain," Ivy said, "but I think I have an idea what Father was saying. Thank you for remembering, dearest."

Rose smiled and returned to her sewing, while Ivy put the journal back in the Wyrdwood box and set the box on the shelf.

"I think I will go upstairs to look for more candles," she said. And while that was true—for they could always use more, and there were rooms Ivy had yet to search—it was not just candles Ivy wanted to find. She wanted to see which windows might afford the best view of the night sky.

Ivy departed the parlor and ascended the stairs, passing the portrait of Earl Rylend and his family, up to the third floor. There, she moved through chambers whose furniture was all shrouded in sheets, or others that were empty. As she did, a loneliness came over her. Since Mr. Samonds's visit over a half month ago, they had seen no other living soul. More than once she had been tempted to leave the manor and to strike out for Low Sorrell. How she would have liked to pay a visit to Miss Samonds!

But it would take many hours of walking to reach the village of Low Sorrell, and she did not dare attempt it. There was no telling what—or who—she might encounter. She was no more aware of what was happening in the county than in the rest of Altania. For all she knew, the fighting had reached Invarel. Perhaps it was even over.

No, that could not be so. Surely people would have returned to Cairnbridge if that was the case, but she never saw any chimney smoke rising from that direction. Which meant the war must still be going on, and that it could not be safe beyond the walls of the manor. As a result, she and Rose only went outside for the briefest intervals, and then no farther than the well in the rear courtyard to draw water.

After some time, Ivy finished going through all the rooms on the third floor. She had collected a few more candles, but had not found a window that offered a good view of the southern sky. Unfortunately, it was the south wing that had been burned, and the windows in the rest of the manor faced in other directions. Still, she did not feel like returning to the parlor and sitting. Besides, were there not more rooms above these—rooms she had yet to explore since their return?

Since coming back to Heathcrest, Ivy had not gone up to the

attic, or to the little room she had once occupied when she was a governess. She did not quite know why. Perhaps it was due to the memory of her confrontation with the highwayman Westen there, or perhaps it was simply that she did not like to be so far from the first floor, for fear she would not be able to hear if Rose called out for her.

All the same, she now found herself going to the foot of the servants' stair and climbing up the narrow steps. She made her way along a cramped corridor down which she had once fled from Westen, then passed through a door that yet stood ajar.

A pang touched her heart. The little room under the eaves was cold and drafty, but was otherwise just as she remembered it. There was the sleigh bed, and the old Murghese rug, and the little table where she had sat alone by candlelight, penning a letter to her father—one he would never read, but which had been for herself as much as for him.

Near the bed was a heap of splintered wood—the remnants of the chair of bent Wyrdwood that Mr. Samonds had made as a boy, and which Ivy had used to entrap Westen, thus effecting her escape from the highwayman. She picked up one of the broken sticks. It was dry and lifeless in her hand. She let it fall back to the floor.

It would be better if she went downstairs, Ivy admonished herself. This was a place that could only inspire melancholy thoughts. How much she had gained since she first set foot in this room, and how much she had since been deprived of! Yet still, she endured. And she knew now that was what Mr. Quent had been trying to tell her in the dark cell beneath Barrowgate, when he related to her the story of how long ago he had given up part of himself in order to escape the Wyrdwood.

He had been telling her to let him go.

Yet Ivy wondered—was it worth giving up anything in order to survive, no matter how precious it was? What if you gave up so much of yourself that there was nothing left of who you truly were?

She hesitated, then went to the bench below the little window, sat, and looked outside. For the first time since the lumenal began, the rain had ceased, and the clouds were lifting. Pale rivulets of fog ebbed upon the landscape, flowing down from the rocky fells and pooling in low places on the moors. As the clouds broke apart farther, a dark, uneven crown appeared upon the brow of the ridge to the east of the manor.

It was the old stand of Wyrdwood, which Ivy and Rose had found themselves within after stepping through the gate on Arantus. A compulsion came over Ivy, to go to the trees and slip through the crack in the wall. It was not to step back through the gate that she wanted to do this; there was no use in such a thing, for she was certain Mr. Rafferdy would have locked the door in the gallery on Durrow Street. Rather, she wanted to touch the rough bark of their trunks, and to tangle her fingers among the crooked branches. Her father had not yet spoken out of the past to tell her what she must do now. But perhaps the trees would know. They were ancient, and they had seen the Ashen before. How else could the Old Trees have recognized their slaves, and known to fight them?

Yes, the Wyrdwood would know what to do. . . .

She started to rise from the window seat. At the same time, a dark flutter of motion caught her eye. It appeared for only the briefest moment below the window, a little distance from the house: a shadow that slipped away before it could really be seen. It made Ivy think of some lurking animal that had been unexpectedly revealed by a break in the fog, and had fled again for cover.

A dread came upon her. She had just been thinking of the *gol-yagru*, the Ashen-slaves. Was one prowling about the manor?

No, she could not believe that. The trees upon the eastern ridge stood motionless against the sky, and she could not believe that would be the case if a thing of Ashen-kind was near. More likely it was a fox slinking about.

All the same, she spent several minutes watching to see if she would spy the shadow again. She did not. But there was something else Ivy saw as the fog lifted further: the jumble of fallen stones at the far end of the ridge on which Heathcrest stood. She had read once, in a book of history, how some of the old elf circles that scattered the countryside were arranged so that their massive stones aligned with various objects in the heavens. Perhaps that had been true of this circle of stones as well; and she supposed its position on the edge of the ridge would afford it a sweeping view of the sky.

There was one way to find out for sure. Ivy rose from the window seat and departed the little room. Taking the servants' stair, she descended to the kitchen, then let herself out through the rear door. She had not stopped to put on her cape and hood, but while the air was damp and chilled, the rain had ceased, and the wool gown Rose had sewn for her was warm.

Quickly, Ivy started away from the house. She passed the well, then kept walking, following a well-worn path. As she went, she cast frequent glances around her, but she saw no other living thing. Soon she reached a solitary stone, about breast high, which stood by the path. Long ago, someone had scratched the word Heathcrest onto its pitted surface. When approached from a certain angle, the stone took on the aspect of a grotesque face gazing out over the moor.

Ivy did not stop to regard it now. Instead she kept walking while the manor dwindled in size behind her, until at last the path ended in a profusion of fallen stones.

It was the old elf circle. Despite their common name, the elf circles did not owe their origin to fairies or other fantastical beings; rather, they had been erected by the ancient people who inhabited the island long before the first Tharosian ships ever landed on these shores. For what purpose the stone circles had been raised, no one could say for certain. Yet it was clear there was some purpose or power in their arrangement; after all, it was this very place where Mr. Bennick had chosen to work his enchantment that transformed Ashaydea into a White Thorn.

Ivy picked her way through the ruin, wanting to get as close to the edge of the ridge as possible, so as to have the clearest view of the southern sky. The great slabs of stone lay strewn about, and some were cracked or broken, as if they had been scattered by some terrible force.

But had it been a natural power that had wrought such havoc, or something other? The stones bore a dark, weathered patina, and only faint remnants of the original swirling patterns carved on them remained. Yet in the places where they were broken, the stones bore rougher edges. And here and there she glimpsed symbols etched into them that were sharper and paler than the ancient, circular patterns.

Ivy reached the center of the fallen circle. She took a breath of the moist air, then looked up to see what view she now had of the southern sky. Even as she did, she felt something give a twitch in the pocket of her dress. Startled, Ivy let out a gasp. Again something twitched, as if a mouse had found its way into her pocket. Only, as she reached within, it was not warm fur she felt, but rather warm stone. She drew out the gray gem and cupped it in her palm. As she watched, it gave another jerk.

Were there still some remnants of magick here within the stone circle—faint echoes which resonated with the enchantment of the gem? Perhaps, but if so they were not so strong as to awaken the stone, for it remained dark. But she knew how to awaken it herself, didn't she? Mr. Rafferdy had told her what to do, only she had been too afraid to do it. Yet Mr. Quent had always displayed unwavering courage in the face of all things. It was time Ivy did as well. She drew in a breath.

Then, with a finger, she tapped the gem three times.

Ivy gazed down at the stone and saw that its center was no longer cloudy. Instead, it had become clear and deep, and there was movement within it—or rather, beyond it. She lifted the gem closer to her face. It was like gazing through a tiny window of beveled glass into a small, dim chamber. Only she was not seeing things that were happening there, but rather things as they *had* happened.

Horrified, fascinated, Ivy watched the minute figures in the polished facets. So this was what the gem had witnessed: a bearded man with a noble, furrowed brow, and a woman in a black dress, her face white as bone. Some agreement seemed to pass between them. The man knelt before her and bowed his head. The woman reached out her hands in what almost seemed a tender embrace. And then—

Now it was Ivy who had become a standing stone. She was rigid as a few final flickers of movement occurred within the gem. Then the gem grew dim and cloudy again upon her hand.

Still she stood there in the old elf circle, motionless. The clouds thickened again, lowering themselves toward the ridge as a mist began to fall, but she was oblivious to it. At some point, as it became slick with rain, the gem slipped from her fingers and fell to the ground, but she did not bend down to pick it up. Instead, she would stand here like the stones forever, and let the wind and rain slowly dissolve her away.

At last a sound jarred her from her stupor. It was a rhythmic, grinding noise. For a wild moment she believed it was the sound of a horse riding toward her, and she jerked her head up, thinking, *He has come!*

It was not the sound of hooves she had heard, though, but rather the noise of boots against the graveled slope of the ridge. Even as she realized this, the fog swirled and parted, and three men crested the edge of the ridge not ten paces away from her. Their boots were muddy, and moisture beaded upon their patched and dirty blue coats. Rifles were slung over their backs.

They saw her barely a moment after she saw them. The closest of the three gave a start, no doubt surprised to come upon her standing there among the stones. Then a smile parted his straggly blond beard.

"Well, good day there, ma'am," the soldier said. And he reached for the rifle on his back.

CHAPTER THIRTY

———————— ❧ ————————

𝕿HEY HAD BEEN MARCHING in the dark for nearly ten hours, according to Rafferdy's pocket watch, but still the men pressed onward.

Other than themselves, and the sound made by forty pairs of boots, the countryside through which they passed was empty and silent. A bloated moon, stained by the proximity of the red planet, was slung low in the sky. By its light they could make out the empty husks of farmhouses to either side of the road, and fields that had been reduced to ash. Here and there they passed the ruin of some cart or wagon, both its contents and horses missing, and the spokes of its wheels shattered.

At one point they encountered a lone cow, a sickly thing lowing piteously in a barren plot bounded by stone walls. One of the men shot it in the head with a pistol, and they carved what scant meat they could from its bones before marching on. But other than the cow, they saw no other living thing, nor any other foodstuffs or supplies they might have used to sustain them. Valhaine's men had burned and destroyed everything they could as they retreated east, and while their effectiveness upon the battlefield could be questioned, in this they had been remarkably efficient.

The umbral gave no sign that it was drawing to a close, and the darkness seemed only to thicken as the hours passed. Despite this, and the protracted length of their march, Rafferdy did not call for a halt. Just two days ago, they had been halfway from Baringsbridge to Dunbria in the north, pursuing the remnants of a company of soldiers that had been separated from the rest of the royal

Altanian army after a skirmish at Strayn's Fold. Then, even as Raf-ferdy was certain they were closing in on the fleeing men, a cou-rier on horseback caught up to the rebel company.

The courier's brown coat was gray with dust, and his horse's flanks were flecked with lather, for he had been riding hard all over County Baringham and its surrounds in search of any men he could rummage up. By order of Huntley Morden himself, all companies were to march for Pellendry-on-Anbyrn, some sixty miles to the east of Baringsbridge, with all possible haste. He showed them a gold seal imprinted with the silhouette of a falcon, in case they had any doubt of the veracity of the command. They did not.

After delivering this order, the courier paused only to drink some water, as well as a swig of whiskey from a bottle one of the men had removed from a corpse on the battlefield. The courier took these refreshments in his saddle. He said he was determined to ride until he had mustered every company of Morden men re-maining in fifty miles, or the horse dropped dead beneath him. With that, he dug his spurs into the poor beast's sides. It gave a scream, then lunged forward, and in a cloud of dust he was gone.

At once, Lieutenant Beckwith had expressed eagerness to turn back and make for Pellendry-on-Anbyrn. During their brief ac-quaintance, Rafferdy had not observed Beckwith to be possessed of a great capacity for patience, though there surely was not an officer to be found who was more fervent in his loyalty to Huntley Morden. Beckwith was from an old family in Dunbria that had gone in for Bandley Morden seventy years ago, and they had been stripped of title and lands after the elder Morden's defeat. Only in the last generation had the family been able to rebuild its wealth through favorable business dealings, and they now owned nearly all of their former lands.

Given their current prosperity, and their former loss, one might have thought the Beckwiths of Dunbria would be hesitant to throw in with a Morden this time around. Yet the opposite was the case, and when Morden's ships landed, Beckwith had been one of the first to enlist.

"My family has recovered its holdings," Beckwith had declared to Rafferdy not long after their first meeting, "but it is our honor we want to restore now, and our rightful king."

That had been shortly before the battle at Strayn's Fold. Beckwith's company had suffered dire losses in a previous skirmish, and so the colonel in command of the regiment had combined Beckwith's remaining men with Rafferdy's company. They had fought as a unit at Strayn's Fold, and had acquitted themselves favorably. Afterward, on the colonel's order, they had ridden in pursuit of one of the several fleeing bands of royal soldiers.

But now they had received new orders, and from a higher authority than the colonel—indeed, the very highest. Rafferdy could not say he did not share some of Lieutenant Beckwith's enthusiasm. For what reason they had been recalled, he could not know, but it had to be for some grand purpose given that it was done upon the order of Huntley Morden himself.

All the same, Rafferdy was uneasy at the idea of turning their backs upon the enemy soldiers they had been trailing. The party pursued could just as easily become the pursuer, and Rafferdy had no desire to be caught from behind by a company of desperate men. It did not matter how quickly they turned for Pellendry if they never arrived there at all.

As he deliberated, Rafferdy could see Beckwith clench his jaw, struggling mightily not to pronounce his opinion on the matter. It was not his place to do so; for while Beckwith was a lieutenant, Rafferdy was a captain, and therefore in command of the combined company.

At last Rafferdy decided there was nothing to deliberate on. Both the source of the order and its urgency meant it must be obeyed immediately. Besides, there was no indication that they had been gaining ground on the fleeing soldiers. He supposed they would keep pressing on hard, making for the garrison at Weldrick, which last he heard was yet under the control of Valhaine's forces.

So it was Rafferdy gave the command to turn for Pellendry. Beckwith barked out orders, and the men quickly came about and began marching back to the south and east. For those first several hours, Rafferdy had periodically glanced over his shoulder, looking for a telltale thread of dust rising into the air behind them. But the sky remained clear, until a swift and sudden night descended.

 S THE MEN PRESSED on through the darkness, their boots stirred up puffs of ash from the road.

Being officers, Rafferdy and Beckwith did not march on foot, but rather rode on horseback, though this was scarcely less arduous and exhausting than what the enlisted men were forced to endure. Beckwith was ever circling behind the company to keep watch on their rear, while Rafferdy scouted the road ahead. As a result they traveled twice the distance of the foot soldiers, and their backs and legs ached accordingly.

Again Rafferdy checked his pocket watch, lifting it up to read in the livid moonlight. It had been ten hours since the umbral began, and fourteen since they had stopped for anything more than a brief respite. Despite the urgency of their new orders, they could not continue on like this. Just ahead was an abandoned croft by the road, one whose roof was still largely intact. As soon as they reached it, Rafferdy raised his hand, calling for a halt.

"We'll rest for eight hours, then march again whether it's light or dark," he announced.

At once the men set to making a temporary camp, and if there was a groan or grumble to be heard, it was not due to any sort of complaint, but was simply a natural utterance that occurred when unslinging a pack from a stiff shoulder or pulling off a boot from a blistered foot. As he had been ever since assuming command of the company, Rafferdy was both astonished by these men and exceedingly pleased with them. Their behavior was not at all what he had expected out of a band of rebel soldiers.

This was not to say they weren't in general rough, poorly educated, and possessed of a deficit of manners and a surplus of superstitions. After all, they were most of them young, and up until now few had ever traveled more than twenty miles from the villages in the West Country or Torland where they had been born. Nor were any of them trained soldiers. Instead they were farmers and laborers who had taken their father's hunting rifle from the wall, or had pilfered their grandfather's pistol from an old trunk, and had gone off to enlist in Huntley Morden's army.

As a result, they were a ragtag assemblage. Aside from their brown coats, hastily sewn for them by mothers or sisters before they dashed away to war, they were outfitted with a motley assortment of clothing and equipment. And their knowledge of the world, and how to conduct themselves in it, was an equally poor hodgepodge. But if the rebel soldiers were coarse and ignorant, how were they to be blamed for it? They had dwelled the whole of their brief lives in the meanest state of poverty and abjection, and so could not be other than what they were.

Rafferdy was certain, upon first glance, that most men from the city would have thought the rebels capable of achieving little worthwhile. But observing people at countless dinners, dances, and parties had taught Rafferdy the difference between glibness and intelligence, and between mere callowness and real stupidity. From the moment he was given command over them, Rafferdy made the assumption these men were capable of a great deal, if only they applied themselves.

And apply themselves they did. In fact, the more Rafferdy came to expect of them, the more they worked to exceed these expectations. In their first engagement with the enemy, they had been overeager and fumbling, barely able to load their guns or shoot in the right direction in their excitement. All the same, with Rafferdy shouting orders, they had prevailed.

That had given them a glimpse of what they could do, and after that their shoulders straightened, their heads lifted, and their coats were kept clean and patched. Their next skirmish had been more steady, their shooting quicker and more measured, as had the one after that. Now, after more than a half month together, and with five winning engagements to their credit, they were the closest thing to veterans the rebel army had.

"Are you sure we should stop, sir?" Lieutenant Beckwith said, bringing his horse close to Rafferdy's. "The orders were to march for Pellendry-on-Anbyrn at once."

Despite his hours in the saddle, Beckwith looked ready to ride on for hours more. He was a bit younger than Rafferdy, and always full of energy: a whip of a man with fair hair and green eyes. He might have been Mrs. Quent's brother, Rafferdy had thought more than once.

"It will take us days to get to Pellendry no matter what, Lieutenant," Rafferdy said. "We'd better pace ourselves if we're to arrive in any shape for fighting."

"Is that what you think we're going to, then? A battle?" Beckwith in no way sounded disappointed by this.

"I'm only guessing," Rafferdy said.

And while this was true, it was an educated guess. If Morden's army was to win through at Pellendry-on-Anbyrn, there would be nothing to stop it. The rebels would follow the wide swath of the river valley right to Invarel, for there was no place in the broad lowlands where the royal army could make any kind of stand. They would have no choice but to retreat to the city. Of course, they could hold out in Invarel for months, and the siege could become a gruesome, protracted affair. Yet in effect it would all be over, with the war decided once and for all in the favor of the rebels.

The reverse held true as well. If Morden could not win through at Pellendry, his army would break like a wave upon a wall. Valhaine's forces in the north and south, which had been on the retreat after much harrying, would have time to regroup and go on the offensive again. They would strike at Morden's army from above and below, while Valhaine attacked from the side, and it would all be over for the rebels.

Well, however it turned out, that was days away. And unlike

Beckwith, Rafferdy was anxious to be out of the saddle. His backside hurt more than after a day sitting on the benches at Assembly.

"If we have to make camp, we'd best do it quickly so we can be done with it and move on," Beckwith said. He gave a jerk on the reins to keep his horse in place, though he might have had more success in calming it had he let them go slack. "I'll make sure the men are working with some alacrity."

"I have no doubt that they are."

"You seem very confident in them!"

"That is because I am," Rafferdy said: "I doubt anyone before has had confidence in these men, or believed they had any sort of worth. So they believed the same as well. But then Huntley Morden called to them, and told them they could have importance if they chose—that they could alter an entire nation with their actions. And now they've learned they can do it."

Rafferdy's gaze went past Beckwith, to the young men moving quickly in the moonlight, pitching canvas tents and starting fires. "I think Lord Valhaine never expected that. He thought all he had to do was give the rebels a kick to send them running. Now he's discovered that he's not facing a few dogs, but rather an army of men. And that's why he's losing."

Beckwith seemed uncertain how to reply to this. The bay gelding skittered from hoof to hoof beneath him. "I'll make sure they're clearing the perimeter of the camp so no one can come upon us unawares," he said, then spun the horse about and kicked its flanks.

Rafferdy sighed as Beckwith rode away. He was a fine young man, and his intentions were honorable, but he wanted things to happen more quickly than they were. From their conversations, Rafferdy knew that Beckwith was frustrated that he was still only a lieutenant. And while he had never demonstrated any disrespect, Beckwith could only be further peeved that Rafferdy, who had joined the rebellion just lately, was already a captain.

Of course, Rafferdy was rather nonplussed by this fact himself. To think, less than a month earlier, he had been fleeing the city, off to join the rebellion. And now he was a captain who had already led his company through a half-dozen engagements with the enemy.

It had all happened with a swiftness that would have exceeded even Lieutenant Beckwith's fanciful desires. And Rafferdy had Garritt to thank for it. Rafferdy could only wonder what other secrets his old friend was hiding. First he had revealed that he was a Siltheri illusionist, and then—far more shockingly—that he was employing his talents in service to the revolution.

Rafferdy would never have thought a being so mild as Eldyn Garritt could house the spirit of a rebel. But as Rafferdy had learned, one could not safely make assumptions based on the appearance of a man or even his history; it was his actions in the present that mattered. And Garritt's actions had saved Rafferdy that day.

As it happened, by the time Garritt brought him to a dormitory near the university, the city was already being shut. Valhaine was wasting no time, and it was happening even more quickly than Lord Farrolbrook had warned. Royal soldiers were everywhere, and the ways into and out of the city were being closed.

Fortunately, Garritt's compatriots had gotten wind of this, and they had arranged for a commotion at the Lowgate, in the form of a fire in a nearby tannery. Because water had to be hauled up from the river to douse the flames, the gate could not be closed, and in the chaos a number of men loyal to the rebellion were able to slip out of the city by pretending to be part of the bucket brigade— Rafferdy among them.

Before Rafferdy departed for the gate, the Morden men had given him information he could use to locate the rebels in the country, and they had told him the secret words to speak as he approached them. Of course, all of this presumed he would be able to find a way past Valhaine's forces and slip through the front lines. He supposed it was likely he would be shot attempting to do so, but he was determined to try it. His father was dead, and Sir Quent as well; they could no longer fight for the sake of Altania. But others were doing so, Eldyn Garritt among them—and by God, Rafferdy was not going to be patriotically outdone by his friend!

First, though, there was another matter to see to.

Due to the great confusion around the city, precipitated by the news of the fall of the West Country, Rafferdy was able to walk away from the Lowgate unmolested, and he proceeded by smaller lanes into the countryside. Finding a mode of travel other than his feet was more difficult, but at last he happened upon a farmer driving a cart of cabbages toward the city. Rafferdy explained to him he would have no luck selling his cabbages that day, and instead offered him five regals for his horse. To this, the man readily acceded.

The mare was a bony, swaybacked thing. Fortunately, Rafferdy was protected from the sharp protrusions of its spine, for the farmer had carried a saddle with him in the cart. What was more, despite its scrawniness, the horse was astonishingly spry and energetic. It seemed quite eager to leave both cart and farmer behind, and it cantered unflaggingly for hours as Rafferdy urged it southward. That was his first indication that he should not judge a being's potential by its appearance.

As he rode, Rafferdy kept to lesser-traveled bridle paths and byways, for he doubted that Valhaine's forces would treat a lord who was fleeing the city kindly—especially one who had previously been known to practice magick and associate with traitors and witches. As luck had it, though, he encountered few souls and no soldiers. Finally, as the long lumenal was sputtering out, he passed familiar fields, then rode along a colonnade of elm trees to his manor at Asterlane.

He spent only a few hours there, but accomplished several important things. The first was to assure that Lady Rafferdy was well. His mother had continued to fade, and her eyes were as colorless as her hair now. But she greeted him with a kiss, and when he asked if she wished to go to her cousin in the east, she declined, saying she would not depart this house while she lived. Rafferdy had expected as much; nor did he think she would have been much safer elsewhere. If the rebels ever made it this far east, all of their attention would be upon Invarel, not the countryside to the south.

"But will you be staying here?" she had asked him as he met with her in a candlelit parlor. A portrait of his father on the wall gazed down at them with what Rafferdy thought was a wistful expression.

"No, I cannot," he said. "There are things that I must do. And if you hear the voices of men speaking in the night, do not have a fear, Mother. They will be acquaintances of mine."

She gave him a small, fond smile. "Having lived with your father, I have gotten quite used to nocturnal comings and goings. Be assured, you will not disturb me. Do whatever you must."

He kissed her cheek, then left her in the parlor with the portrait, and he had not seen her since.

It was several hours into the long umbral when the others began to arrive. Canderhow was first, which somewhat surprised Rafferdy, for he had not thought the plumpest among them would be the swiftest. Trefnell was next, then four of the others. But two of the Fellowship never came, nor would they; for a message from Wolsted appeared in their black books, stating he and Coulten had been unable to get through the gates in time.

It is all my fault, Wolsted wrote. *My gout has made me unbearably slow, and Coulten foolishly thought to come to my aid, and so was trapped with me in the city. Do not fear for us, though. We shall keep hidden, and keep watch. And we will send you what reports we can.*

This had caused Rafferdy a pang. He had entertained some thought that Coulten would be game to come with him to join the revolution. Yet perhaps it would prove useful to have some members of their order still in the city—provided they could remain hidden from Valhaine's witch-hunters and magician-seekers.

Those seven members of the Fellowship of the Silver Circle who had reached Asterlane met in the library as the night wore on, drinking brandy and formulating plans—though these were vague at best. They had prevented Assembly from passing laws to abolish the Wyrdwood, but there was nothing more they could do upon that matter now.

"Nor do I think we need to," Canderhow said. "While the magicians of the Golden Door may wish to burn down the Old Trees, Valhaine is far too distracted with the matter of Morden to act against the Wyrdwood now."

He spoke, as usual, with a barrister's logic. All the same, Rafferdy was not convinced.

"That may be so," Rafferdy had replied, "but I cannot think they did not expect this. The High Order of the Golden Door must have some other scheme in mind to address matters. Gambrel is their real magus. He's been the one directing Davarry all this while. And from what I have learned, Gambrel is a clever and persistent man."

Trefnell's eyebrows had bristled in a fierce glower. "I suppose you are right. Destroying the Wyrdwood was an aim of theirs, yes, but not the final aim. There is one thing only which they seek."

And none of them needed to speak it, for the way the darkness seemed to press in hungrily through the windows was enough. At a recent meeting of the order, Rafferdy had described his and Lady Quent's supposition that the Ashen were preparing for the Grand Conjunction. As it happened, Trefnell's research had been leading him toward the same conclusion. Cerephus would be at its closest proximity when the conjunction occurred, and arcane energies would be at their maximum potential. The Ashen had not yet been able to enter into the world in force, so clearly they were waiting for some event that would give them this opportunity. What else could it be other than this?

The idea filled Rafferdy with great dread when he considered it. If the Ashen indeed entered the world, how could they be fought? Yet it was not the Ashen that were currently waging war against Altania; it was Valhaine's army. And that was something he *could* fight.

Weary from their flight to Asterlane, the other magicians retired, but Rafferdy remained awake. There was one more thing he had to do. He spent several hours going through his father's things.

Then, just as a crimson glow kindled in the eastern sky outside the windows, Rafferdy found what he was looking for. By means of a spell, he discovered and unlocked a hidden drawer in a table in his father's study.

Inside was a small box, fashioned of a single piece of onyx.

After that, Rafferdy slept for a few scant hours. Then he rose and, after some quick words with Trefnell, departed Asterlane. The swaybacked nag he had bought from the farmer had been given to the stable master, with instructions that it was to be cared for most kindly. In its place, Rafferdy rode a powerful gray gelding. And while his ultimate destination lay to the west, there was one last thing he had to accomplish before going there. So it was he turned toward the sun, and rode into the morning.

Some hours later, just as a purple twilight crept over the land, Rafferdy reached Farland Park. He rode up to the front of the grand house which stood at the end of a poplar-lined road, and was off his horse before the beast had fully come to a stop. Not stopping himself, he tossed the reins to a groomsman, dashed up the steps, and into the house.

This abrupt and noisy entrance alarmed the residents, and by the time Rafferdy entered the front hall he found Mr. Baydon fumbling with the flintlock on his pistol.

"Great Gods, Rafferdy, I nearly shot you!" Mr. Baydon sputtered, lowering the gun.

Rafferdy could not help a smile, noticing that Mr. Baydon had failed to properly cock the pistol. "I don't think there was any danger of that," he said, taking the gun and setting it on a table where it might cause no harm.

"But what are you doing here?"

"Something has happened in the city," Lady Marsdel said, slowly rising from her chair. "Morden's men are marching toward Invarel, I presume."

As always, little escaped Lady Marsdel's comprehension. Rafferdy bowed toward her. "You are correct, your ladyship. Lord Valhaine has shut the Old City. I only barely escaped its bounds before he did so."

Mrs. Baydon rushed forward and embraced him. "It's all so dreadful, I can hardly imagine it. But I'm grateful you were able to get out of the city. Have you come to stay with us, then?"

Rafferdy said nothing as he stepped away from Mrs. Baydon. From across the room, Lady Marsdel gave him a piercing look.

"No, Mrs. Baydon," her ladyship said. "I believe Lord Rafferdy will soon be riding westward. In which case, I can only wonder why he's come."

Rafferdy's hand went to his coat pocket, touching the hard, square object within. "I need to see Lord Baydon at once," he said.

The others exchanged somber looks, and Rafferdy grew alarmed that he was already too late. But that was not the case, for Mr. Baydon said, "I can take you to my father. However, while you may see him, he won't be able to see you. He is . . . well, you shall see."

Minutes later, Mr. Baydon opened the door of a bedchamber. The room was bright and cheerful, for a maid was lighting candles all around against the night. She departed as Rafferdy entered.

"I'm sorry, Rafferdy, but I cannot—" Mr. Baydon's voice halted as the words caught in his throat. "I will leave you with him," he said when he regained the capacity for speech, then departed.

As Rafferdy approached the bed, he understood Mr. Baydon's reluctance to enter. All that was visible of Lord Baydon was his head, for the rest of him was covered in blankets. Though for the way the covers laid almost flat on the bed, it seemed there was hardly anything at all beneath them. That part of him which was exposed bore little resemblance to the Lord Baydon Rafferdy knew. The gray mustache was familiar, but the rest was all yellowed, shriveled flesh stretched over sharp bones.

Rafferdy felt a pang in his chest, then forced himself to draw closer. Lord Baydon's eyes were shut, but his faint, rattling breaths were audible.

"It's too much, sir," Rafferdy said, his own voice becoming choked now. "They asked too much of you."

Except Earl Rylend and Lord Rafferdy hadn't known what Lord

Marsdel intended to ask of Lord Baydon—or so Rafferdy's father had written in the letter that had been locked in the drawer with the onyx box. Lord Rafferdy had explained:

Had we understood what Marsdel intended, Rylend and I would never have allowed it. He told us only that he had found an arcane artifact that could be used to remove some fraction of the curse of Am-Anaru from each of us. Yet ignorant of the truth as we were, Rylend and I were not without fault. So eager were we both to be rid of at least a portion of the dark spell which afflicted us that we readily agreed to this plan without pursuing further details.

The three of us took turns, holding the box and opening the lid just as Marsdel instructed. Though I did so for but a few moments, at once I felt a great relief come over me, and I knew that some part of my life had been returned to me. But at what cost! It was only later I discovered that Marsdel had only revealed half of the box's enchantment to us. The artifact could not contain the power of the curse permanently; in time it would escape. The only way to be sure the curse would not return to the three of us was to have another person open the box and take on the three portions of the curse within. I fear that, in Lord Baydon, Marsdel found all too cheerful and willing a subject for this unspeakable experiment.

Rafferdy could imagine what Lord Marsdel had said when he approached Lord Baydon. No doubt he had said this act would make Lord Baydon a member of their little band, the Lords of Am-Anaru. And so Lord Baydon had readily opened the box, wanting to feel like an adventurer himself.

"It is enough," Rafferdy said, bending over the prone figure on the bed. "You have done more than your share. More than you ever should have."

He took the onyx box from his coat pocket. It was hard in his hand and strangely cold. He placed the box on the covers, just below Lord Baydon's chin, and opened the lid. He spoke the runes of magick that were inscribed on the box's side. Then he watched, both horrified and entranced, as several tendrils passed from Lord Baydon's thin lips like an exhalation of black smoke and coiled into the box.

IT HAD BEEN CLOSE to a month since that day, and during that time it seemed to Rafferdy he had spent more than half of his life in the saddle. With an exhalation of great discomfort, he dismounted the big gray gelding, stumbling a bit as his boots struck the ground.

"I'll take your horse, sir," said a soldier in a brown coat.

He was so young in appearance that he made Rafferdy, at twenty-seven, feel positively decrepit. But then, given all his present aches and pains, he *was* rather decrepit at the moment.

"Thank you, Private," Rafferdy said.

He detached his small pack of things from behind the saddle, then watched as the young soldier led the gelding away. Small clouds of ash, the color of dried blood in the moonlight, were stirred up by its hooves. A chill went through Rafferdy. He wondered if that was how the Ashen had been named—if that was what Altania and all the world would be reduced to when the Grand Conjunction came and the door to Cerephus was broken open.

A barren plain of ashes.

He shivered again; the long umbral had grown cold, that was all. He went to the stone-walled farmhouse. The men had cleared out one end of the main room—the other being filled with debris fallen from the roof. They had lit a fire on the hearth and arranged a wooden bench near it. Rafferdy spread the blanket that served for his bed on the bench, then sat down. He might rather have lain down, but he could not rest yet, for Beckwith would be coming back to him soon with a report on the state of the encampment.

Rafferdy let out a grim laugh at this thought. He had never in his life wanted any sort of power or responsibility. Indeed, he had fled from it at every turn. Now here he was—a military captain in command of forty other lives, able to order them to march no matter how hungry or exhausted they were, or to throw themselves into a battle no matter how overwhelming the odds. It was utterly absurd.

Yet somehow, that was how things had transpired. After taking his leave of Lady Marsdel and Mr. and Mrs. Baydon—hardly an hour after his arrival at Farland Park—he had ridden west, giving Invarel a wide berth as he made for the front lines of the war.

That had been a harrowing experience. He had ridden through a countryside plagued by Valhaine's forces. More than once he had pulled hard on the reins, plunging his horse through the hedges narrowly in time to avoid being spotted by a patrol of blue-coated soldiers. At last he had come to the valley of the River Telfayn. It seemed far too bucolic a landscape for something so awful as war, but as he neared the region around Baringsbridge he saw evidence of recent fighting.

He waited for night, then under cover of darkness made a mad gallop to the river. There was some skirmish going on to the north, for he could see the flashes and hear the rumbling of cannon fire. It was his hope that the attention of the royal army would be turned in that direction, and in general that was the case. All the same, the flanks of the army had not been forgotten entirely, and as Rafferdy was traversing a marshy field he saw lights bobbing toward him. They were lanterns, carried by an entire company of redcrests.

There had been nowhere for Rafferdy to flee. Hastily, he had leaped down from his horse and fashioned a circle in the damp ground with his boot heel. He arranged some sticks into the shape of several runes, then hastily spoke words of magick, calling down a circle of darkness.

All went pitch-black. The stars and moon were hidden from him. There had been no time to call a circle of silence as well, but the company of enemy soldiers made a great noise themselves as they marched by. Rafferdy could feel the ground tremble, and he had been in dread that they would march right into him and thus discover him.

But they did not. At last the sound of marching feet receded into the distance. Rafferdy dispelled the circle, then mounted his gelding and rode hard for the river.

He knew he had at last made it past the front lines when he encountered a band of grim-faced young men in brown coats. Hurriedly, he called out the words Garritt's compatriots had taught him in a ragged voice. Had he been any slower about it, he would have had several rifle bullets in his chest before he finished. As it was, though the rifles were lowered, he was regarded with great suspicion, and was led none too gently to a tent to meet with the colonel in charge of the regiment.

There Rafferdy was subjected to much scrutiny. But he repeated the words he had been given, and explained how he came by them, and before long the colonel was satisfied.

"We cannot be too particular out here," said the colonel, a country lord whose large white mustache was stained yellow from tobacco smoke. "We need every man we can get, and no matter what side you might have been on, I warrant if we put a gun in your hand, you'll fire it at any fellow who bears down on you. For by God, you know he'd do the same."

After that, Rafferdy was given a rifle with a bayonet and a brown coat. He had a pistol he had brought himself from Asterlane. Rafferdy had not stated he was a lord, but that he was a man of education was apparent, and therefore it did not matter that he lacked any sort of military experience, but was at once made a corporal with ten men to command.

Not that this situation lasted for long. Two umbrals later, their position along the river was attacked in the middle of the night. Somehow the sentries had been slain without a sound being made, and a small band of the enemy had struck at the heart of the regiment's encampment, making directly for the colonel's tent.

All was in a great confusion as the rebels tried to rise up from sleep and ready themselves to meet the sudden attack. There was a volley of rifle fire, and bright flashes of light sundered the darkness, forcing the rebels to hastily fall back. It seemed utterly insane for a small band to drive right into the center of a larger force: an act that would surely result in their death. Stranger yet, several men reported that the enemy had dogs with them, vicious animals that had torn out the throats of several rebels.

Then, from his position behind a makeshift barricade near the colonel's tent, Rafferdy had seen the enemy approaching. There were three men, and slinking alongside them was a pair of humped and spiked forms. Even before the House ring upon his right hand began to throw off blue sparks, Rafferdy had been certain those things were not dogs.

What occurred then might have been a terrible massacre of the colonel and the men around him, which had surely been the enemy's plan. The rebels opened fire upon the intruders. Bullets struck their blue coats and opened holes in their necks, but still the three men lurched forward. The shadows beside them coiled in upon themselves as if to spring.

Then all at once a voice was shouting queer, harsh-sounding words.

It was Rafferdy. Using his ring, he painted blazing runes upon the black canvas of the night air, summoning a barrier of protection. The shadowy forms leaped forward—then fell back, writhing and baring curved yellow teeth. There was a smell like burning bone. Had any of the men been looking for it, they would have detected a faint blue shimmer before them, like light reflected off a pane of glass.

"Aim for their heads!" Rafferdy called out, hardly caring that the men around were not his to command. "Shoot only their heads! Fire!"

A dozen rifles fired, then a dozen pistols followed. The skulls of the three enemy soldiers burst apart in a violent effusion. Thus decapitated, their bodies stumbled forward for a few more steps, then slumped to the ground.

By then, Rafferdy was speaking more runes, redoubling the

magickal barrier he had erected. More shots rang out; the men had reloaded their rifles. The shadows convulsed and snarled. Bullets could not kill them, but they did seem to inflict pain. Or perhaps it was the power of the eldritch magicks Rafferdy had summoned that burned them. Either way, with no one to direct them now that their masters were gone, the *gol-yagru* shrank back from the barrier, then turned and loped away, vanishing into the night.

It was over. Rafferdy had slumped to the ground, trembling. Someone made a quick inventory of the men; other than the sentries, no soldiers had been lost.

By the time dawn came, much to his bemusement, Rafferdy had been branded a hero. No one who had been there understood that he had done magick. Rather, the men spoke approvingly of how he had waved a torch to blind the intruders and ward off their dogs, then gave swift and level-headed commands in the chaos, ordering a volley of gunfire, and so surely prevented further casualties. The colonel called for him, and shook his hand, and promoted him to captain there and then.

"It is only a field promotion," the colonel said, "and will require the signature of a lieutenant general to become permanent. But that's not likely to happen until this entire affair is over, so for now you may wear your stripes in confidence that they are yours for the duration."

For his part, Rafferdy had felt something less exuberant after the affair. Though they were merely bits of cloth, the stripes seemed to add a weight to his coat once they were sewn on. He had watched grimly as the bodies of four rebel soldiers, wrapped in linens rusty with blood, were lowered into the ground. After that, he had gone to the ditch into which the corpses of the three intruders had been heaved the night before.

In the dark, someone had tossed a few shovelfuls of dirt over them. Rafferdy had knelt, and brushed aside some of the thin coating of soil. As he did, he felt a compulsion to retch. The three bodies were already in an advanced state of liquefaction. It was not due to decay, though, for inside their skins was no flesh to rot, nor bones to remain afterward. Instead, a grayish sort of gelatin oozed out of their wounds. A hand protruded from the shallow grave; beneath the crust of dirt, Rafferdy could just make out the sharp black lines drawn upon the palm.

So that was why the three men, upon entering the rebel camp, had not feared for their lives. They had already been deprived of them.

Since that night, Rafferdy had not encountered any more gray men or Ashen-slaves himself. Yet he had heard rumors and tales— things that struck most of the men as oddities, but which for him carried additional meaning. He met a man who described how his horse had been attacked by a wolf—even though wolves had not been seen outside of the remotest parts of Torland in more than a hundred years—and had managed to outride the beast. The man's horse still bore the scabbed-over gashes on its side, and Rafferdy had counted them himself. There had been seven long, thin scores in the horse's flank, all drawn in parallel, as if made by a single swipe of a paw. But what wolf had seven sharp claws?

Later, he heard the men repeating the story of a young rebel who had vanished from his camp, then had returned two lumenals later. With a pistol, he had shot his closest companions in the chest, killing them all. He did this with no apparent feeling or remorse, his expression blank, before turning and walking away. Those who told the tale presumed war had driven the young soldier mad. But Rafferdy wondered if anyone had noticed the young man's hand, and if it had been marked by a dark, angular symbol.

Finally, there had been a tale recounted by a young man who joined them after traveling south from County Dorn. He had described encountering several haggard rebels who told how they had gotten lost in mountainous terrain after being separated from their company during a firefight. For days they had wandered, fearing that they would perish. Only then, in a remote valley, they had come upon a little village, and had entered it hoping to find food and shelter.

What they found instead was a thing hardly to be comprehended. There was not a grown man or woman in the hamlet, only children. These were found not in the stone hovels, which had been crusted with ancient moss, but rather locked inside wicker pens.

"It was like the children were lambs waiting to be slaughtered, or so the men told me," the young soldier had said. "They set the children free, but the wee things seemed to have no capacity to speak, and they only wandered to and fro, aimless and silent, as if they knew not what to do with their freedom. A terrible fear came upon the men, and they left the valley. At last, after much travel, they reached a more populous village at the foot of the mountains. They told the people there of the hamlet, and said the children would need help. But the villagers only shook their heads, and said that while there had once been a hamlet in the valley the men described, no one had come from that place nor had ventured there since the Plague Years more than three hundred years ago. The mountains, they said, were empty of any people. But if that was so, then how did those children get there?"

How indeed? And for what use?

Now, in the half-ruined farmhouse, Rafferdy looked at the House Gauldren ring on his right hand. It glinted blue, but it was only the firelight reflecting off its facets. Yet would the gem have flickered with a sapphire light all its own if he had ridden alongside the man who believed he was fleeing a wolf, or if he had stood in the camp when the young soldier with dead eyes shot his comrades? What if Rafferdy somehow found that lost village in the remotest mountains of Northaltia? Would the gem have blazed to life as he wandered among the ancient, moss-crusted hovels?

He could not know for certain. Yet from all these tales—and from the attack on the rebel encampment that he had helped to thwart—he could draw only one conclusion. The influence of the Ashen was not limited to a handful of occult orders in Invarel, or hidden in a few desert caves in the Empire. Rather, the forces of magick were everywhere.

Indeed, threads of the arcane were woven into the very fabric of the world. How many daemons locked in magickal prisons, or artifacts concealed in ancient tombs, had felt the growing influence of the red planet, and were now beginning to stir after millennia of slumber? Ever since the previous war—the very first war—they had been waiting for their time to come again.

And it was nearly here.

"Captain Rafferdy?"

He looked up from his ring. The young rebel soldier who had taken his horse now stood in the door.

"The cook is roasting some of the beef we found on a spit. And he's made a pudding of old biscuits and the drippings. Would you like to take a plate in here, sir?"

Rafferdy was sorely tempted to say *yes*. He was weary to the bone, and wanted nothing but to eat a little food and lie down. Then he regarded the young man's dusty, anxious face, and he knew that, in the depths of the long night, the men could use a little reassurance.

"I had better come out," Rafferdy said, making his voice cheerful. "We haven't seen beef in a quarter month, and I don't want a brawl to break out if someone thinks all they got was the gristle. Rather, if I see a disagreement, I will call for a duel at twenty paces so matters can be settled in a civilized manner, with the meat going to the victor. Just give me a moment, and I'll be there."

Now the young man was grinning. Rafferdy always thought his attempts at humor to be very poor, but the men seemed to enjoy them. "Yes, sir!" he said. "I'll tell the men to clear a path of forty paces at once."

He saluted, then departed the farmhouse.

Rafferdy found himself grinning as well. He had not believed her at the time, but as usual Lady Marsdel was exceedingly perceptive. Absurd as it seemed, given his history and habits, it turned out Rafferdy was genuinely good at being an officer. In some ways, he even found he enjoyed it. Not the countless miles spent in the saddle, of course, or the frigid sleeping conditions and miserable food. And not the long hours of boredom waiting for an engagement with the enemy to begin, or the swift minutes of blood, confusion, and fright when it finally did.

Or was it not those things, after all? No, he could not say he enjoyed them. Still, as time went on, he found a kind of satisfaction in it. Throughout his life, Rafferdy had only ever sought ways to indulge himself. He had never imagined that to deliberately deprive himself of all comfort and safety, when done for the sake of a cause greater than himself, could be more gratifying than buying every fancy coat or silk handkerchief to be found on Coronet Street. Yet it was.

Rafferdy rose from the bench. Before leaving to join the men, though, there was one thing he needed to do. He went to the corner where he had set down his bundle of things, dug deep into it, and pulled out an object contained in a small velvet pouch. Carefully, he untied the strings on the pouch, then withdrew the object.

It was the small onyx box, its glossy sides inscribed with runes and queer symbols. Slowly he turned the box in his hands. As far as he could tell in the firelight, the box remained tightly shut. But how long would that be the case? When he first found the thing in his father's study, it had been cold to the touch. Now it felt warm against his hand, and it seemed to twitch with a slow regularity like that of a heartbeat.

He could still picture the black, smokelike tendrils passing from Lord Baydon's lips into the box. As soon as they had done so, Rafferdy had clamped the lid shut. The elder lord had given a sigh, and his breath had at once grown easier and quieter. Whether he would survive or not was now a matter for the doctors, but at least he had a chance.

The same would not be true for Rafferdy if the contents of the box managed to escape while it was in his possession. Yet how could such a thing be disposed of? Inside the box were the three portions of the curse which Lord Baydon had taken from Earl Rylend, Lord Marsdel, and Lord Rafferdy. All the virulence, all the malevolence, which had eaten at the three Lords of Am-Anaru— and then had consumed Lord Baydon—over long years was now sealed within. How was Rafferdy to find a way to be rid of such a thing?

Well, he could think about it later. God knew, he would have time enough in the saddle. All that mattered for now was that the box remained sealed. He returned it to the velvet pouch and tucked it back among his things, making sure it was well concealed along with his black book. Then he left the ruined farmhouse and went to settle any disagreements over the beef.

EIGHT HOURS LATER, they were on the march again, and still the dawn had yet to come.

While Rafferdy might have thought the men would complain about traveling again so soon, they did not. Rather, the night had grown so frigid that all were anxious to move in an effort to generate warmth. Rafferdy wondered if it would snow, but the air was too dry. It seemed to cut at his nostrils with each breath, and there was a metallic taste to it.

After several hours they came to a division in the road, with one branch going direct toward Pellendry-on-Anbyrn, while the other turned due east. It was this latter route which Rafferdy chose, and the men marched after him.

A minute later Beckwith came thundering up beside him on the lively bay mare that he rode. "Shouldn't we have taken the other way?" he said. "Going by this road will take us many hours longer, and we are to get to Pellendry as quickly as possible."

"As quickly as possible, and prepared for a fight," Rafferdy said. "Before we came north, I was given a report about a cache of weapons and other goods that was hidden near Brushing Cross, in the stand of Wyrdwood there. We did not have the time to stop for it on our way north, as the soldiers we were pursuing had struck off in a different direction. But it is only a little out of our way now, and we could do with several more rifles. What's more, we are exceedingly low on powder and shot."

"True, but these things will avail us not at all if we are late to whatever is to occur at Pellendry."

"On the contrary, the most important guests are always late to a party," Rafferdy said lightly. "And they always make sure to equip themselves in all their finery before they arrive. We will do the same."

Beckwith seemed to struggle in deciding whether to laugh or frown. At last he said, "I'll tell the men to increase their pace."

"Their pace is fine as it is, Lieutenant," Rafferdy said, then noticed the agitated manner in which the young man squirmed in his saddle. So Rafferdy continued, "But if you would like to ride ahead to Brushing Cross and scout out the location of the Wyrd-wood there, and make sure no enemy are about, you may take a man and one of the extra horses to do so."

"Will there be a witch there to let us enter the grove?"

"I don't know," Rafferdy said, thinking back to the report he had read. "I know that a witch helped our men enter the grove, as it was all done under cover of night. But that was before the front pushed eastward. I would think the witch has moved on since then. But the cache is said to be just over the wall, so if we wait until daylight, we should have no fear retrieving it. The trees will not disturb us then. The Quelling will keep them subdued—as long as we do not venture within the grove and disturb them ourselves."

Beckwith's face suddenly looked a bit paler than usual in the moonlight. But he only nodded and said, "Yes, sir."

Then he wheeled his horse back around to the main company. A few minutes later, Rafferdy watched Beckwith and another man, mounted on one of the spares, canter eastward down the road.

Had it been any farther to Brushing Cross, Rafferdy wouldn't have allowed Beckwith to go. But he estimated it would only take the rest of them two hours to march there. And given how far eastward the front had moved, Rafferdy had no real fear Beckwith would encounter an enemy. Besides, this way Rafferdy could ride in peace until they reached the Wyrdwood.

Not that he wasn't anxious to arrive himself. Back in the city, Rafferdy had read in the broadsheets the rumors that rebels were making use of groves of Old Trees to cover their actions moving arms about, but he had not truly believed it until he joined the rebellion himself. Since then, he had met several officers who had spoken of retrieving weapons and supplies that, prior to the outbreak of war, had been hidden in stands of Wyrdwood in the West Country. It was these stores, cached in strategic places, which had helped the rebels advance so quickly once Huntley Morden landed in Torland.

Even more remarkable was the fact that, in each case, a witch had aided the rebels in hiding the weapons within the Wyrdwood. For this work had to be accomplished at night so it would not be seen, and that was when the Quelling was at its weakest—and the Old Trees their most restless. The presence of a witch helped to soothe the trees so the men could hoist crates of weapons and barrels of powder over the stone wall and hide them under the eaves of some grove of Wyrdwood.

Rafferdy had always thought people in the country feared both the Wyrdwood and witches. Now he understood that wasn't entirely the case, at least in Torland. Rather, the folk there had a wariness of such things, one that came from historical knowledge and direct familiarity. Yet there was also a respect for the Old Trees, and even a peculiar fondness and admiration. So it was, in the West Country, witches were tolerated, and even sought out to aid the cause; while in the city they were likely being hunted down, and perhaps being taken to the gallows. If Rafferdy needed any further reassurance he had joined the right side in the war, this fact was more than sufficient.

To Rafferdy's relief, as he rode and the men marched, the horizon ahead of them began to lighten, first from slate and then to pewter. By the time they passed the first cottages on the outskirts of Brushing Cross, the stars were fading, and a rose-colored glow welled up from the horizon. After some thirty hours of darkness, dawn was coming at last.

They proceeded through the desolate village, breath fogging upon the air, not seeing a living soul as they went. Once on the far side of the houses, they caught sight of the Wyrdwood: a ragged line upon the top of a rounded prominence some half a mile eastward.

Rafferdy accompanied the men to the foot of the ridge, then told them to halt and take a rest—a command to which they gladly assented. Spurring his gelding, Rafferdy proceeded up the slope. As he did, the eastern sky continued to brighten, turning a brilliant magenta. The trees tangled up before him, and with the ruddy light of dawn filtering through their branches, it seemed almost as if they were afire.

Perhaps he should have taken that as an omen. At that moment, though, fearing nothing was amiss, he rode right up to the wall that enclosed the grove. It was a dozen feet high, constructed of fieldstone that was thick with moss and lichen. Rafferdy could only concede that it was clever of the rebels to hide their supplies within stands of Old Trees. Nothing could be seen beyond the walls, and nor was anyone likely to climb over them—not after the stories of the Risings in Torland.

Seeing no sign of Beckwith or the other soldier, Rafferdy kept riding along the wall. As he did, a morning wind whipped up, stirring the dry grass in circles, and causing the branches that hung over the top of the wall to quiver and toss. Then the breeze dwindled and died, and the grass fell still.

But the trees continued to thrash and shudder, emitting creaking and groaning noises as they did.

Rafferdy knew at once what was happening, but still he could not react quickly enough. A branch lashed downward, snapping like a whip. It did not make any contact with him, but at the sudden sound and motion his horse gave a scream and reared up violently. Rafferdy had to leap off, or he would have been thrown from the saddle.

He staggered as his boots struck the ground, letting out a grunt of pain, then managed to catch himself. Looking up, he saw the gelding racing away down the hill, heading back in the direction they had come. His instinct was to start after it, only then he heard a voice shouting behind him. He turned and saw, just ahead, the figure of a man near the wall, beating back a twisted branch with a saber.

It was Beckwith.

Rafferdy ran forward, reaching him just in time to grab the collar of his coat and jerk him away from the wall. A moment later several branches—far more than could have been fended off with a saber—reached out over the top of the wall, groping and clutching at the spot where Beckwith had been.

"Don't be a fool!" Rafferdy cried out over the noise of the trees. "You can't stop them. It's a Rising. We'll have to abandon the supplies."

Beckwith shook his head, his face the color of ashes. "No, we can't leave. Corporal Hendry is in there!"

Rafferdy felt as if one of the branches had struck him in the chest, even though the two men were out of reach of the trees.

"Hendry is in the wood?" he shouted, incredulous. "Tell me how in the Abyss is that possible?"

"I gave him a leg up over the wall, and he was able to climb over."

"I don't mean the method that was used—I can imagine that. I mean, why in the name of Eternum would you do such a thing? I told you we had to wait until it was daylight to try to enter the wood."

Beckwith was shaking; he looked as if he was about to be ill. "We waited for an hour, and then it was very nearly dawn. I thought if we could locate the cache of weapons, we could begin retrieving them as soon as you and the men arrived, and so make our delay as short as possible."

Rafferdy swore. Damn Beckwith's unvarying impatience! He was tempted to strike the lieutenant a blow across the jaw, but instead tightened his grip on the collar of his coat.

"When did the trees start to move?"

"Just a few minutes ago. Not long after Hendry went over the wall. I heard . . . I think I heard him cry out. But I'm not sure. The noise the trees make—it's awful."

Rafferdy supposed there was a good chance the corporal was

dead already, but until they were certain they could not abandon him. He swore again, and this time it was for himself, not Beckwith. The night had been long enough to be considered a greatnight. He should have known the trees would be more restless than usual, and more easily agitated, after such a long span of darkness. But he had been dull-headed from weariness and had not even considered it.

"I'll ward off the branches to the right," he said. "You keep watch to the left. We've got to get to the wall to see if we can spot Hendry."

Beckwith nodded and gripped his saber, looking steadier now that they had a plan of action. The young lieutenant was inexperienced and overeager, but he was loyal and no coward. For his part, Rafferdy felt anything but brave; he eyed the gnarled branches, which thrust and swiped with a power and speed that was surely enough to crush bones. But this was not the first Rising he had seen.

And besides, he had powers of his own.

Drawing his saber, he spoke several runes of warding, and his House ring blazed to life. Crackling blue threads of light coiled around the hilt of his sword and snaked down the length of the blade. Beckwith's eyes grew wider yet at this display. Before the lieutenant could say anything, Rafferdy raised the glowing saber and started toward the wall. Beckwith hurried to keep up with him, and both men held their swords ready, prepared to strike at any branch that bent toward him.

None did so. Instead, the groaning noises abruptly ceased as the trees grew still. Dead leaves made a soft rustling sound as they settled all around like black snow, then came silence. Why had the grove become quiescent again? Then, as Rafferdy looked up, he understood. A thick tangle of branches unwound themselves and withdrew from the top of the wall, revealing a figure who had been hidden among them.

So, she had not moved on after all.

The branch she had been standing on bent down, and she

stepped from it, alighting onto the top of the wall. She wore only a simple pale frock, and her feet were bare beneath its hem. Leaves and twigs tangled in her fiery hair. She was, Rafferdy guessed, no more than twenty.

"Good God, who is she?" Beckwith exclaimed.

"She's a witch," Rafferdy said, then took a step nearer to the wall.

"Come no closer!" the young woman spoke. Her voice was peculiarly deep for one so small and slight of figure, and there was an echo to it, a queer sort of multifariousness, as if it were a chorus that spoke rather than a single voice. "I see the metal blade that you carry. I see the blue fire upon it. And I know who you are."

Slowly, Rafferdy lowered his saber, and he released the spell with a whispered rune. The threads of blue light were extinguished at once. But his House ring continued to throw off sapphire sparks.

"Who is it you think I am?" he called out.

"You are the ax in their hand," she said, her voice becoming a hiss. "You serve the ravenous ones—those who come from the empty place far beyond the night. They fear our branches, they know we are strong. But you would cut us, and burn us down, so we cannot stand against them." As she spoke, a black branch coiled around her waist, then snaked up and around the bodice of her gown, as if caressing her.

Rafferdy was at once horrified and fascinated. *We*, she had said, rather than *I*. The witch's eyes were the color of moss, and in them was a light, and a depth, far beyond that of any twenty-year-old woman. How long had she hidden there in the grove, waiting for the rebels to return for their supplies, listening to the trees? Long enough that she had lost herself, and had become like a tree in a forest: one of many.

A shudder passed through him. Was this what would have happened to Mrs. Quent that day at the Evengrove, had she not been able to prevent her own thoughts from being drowned out by those of the trees? Would she have writhed among the branches, and have spoken with a voice—with many voices—far older than her own?

He sheathed his saber, and held up his empty hands. "No, we do not serve the Ashen. We would fight them, like you."

"If that is truth, then why do you speak in their tongue?" she cried. "Why do you wield their power as your own?"

Their power? He did not understand. It was magick he had been wielding. But it did not matter. The first rays of sunlight fell upon the stone wall, a warm blush upon the cool stones. Dawn had finally come.

"Please," Rafferdy called out. "We have no wish to harm you, or the trees in the grove. We only wanted to retrieve some things that were hidden beyond the wall—things which were hidden with your help. But they aren't important anymore. We only want to fetch our friend who climbed over the wall and to leave."

She gazed down at him with those ancient green eyes. "You do not lie? You will take the man and then you will go?"

"Yes," Rafferdy called out. "I promise it!"

The witch was silent for a long moment as she stroked the branch that coiled around her. Then, at last, she nodded. Her lips parted to speak.

Whatever it was she said was lost in a clap of thunder.

A puff of smoke obscured Rafferdy's vision. Then it dissipated, and a horror gripped him. Atop the wall, the witch stared forward with wide eyes that were no longer the color of moss, but rather the dull gray of stones. A crimson circle stained her pale shift, rapidly expanding outward. For a few moments more she remained there atop the wall. Then the branch that had held her uncoiled and slipped away.

The witch's lifeless body fell backward from the top of the wall and vanished behind it. A shudder passed through the trees. Then they fell still as the morning sun touched their leaves.

Beside Rafferdy, Lieutenant Beckwith lowered his pistol.

"That was well done, Captain, gaining her attention like that," the young man said with a fierce grin. "She never even saw me draw my pistol. Once I was assured you had distracted her, I took my shot, and she never had a chance to induce the trees to strike us."

Rafferdy was beyond speech. He knew Beckwith was impatient, but he had never believed he was capable of so rash an act as this.

"Why?" he said, his throat ragged. "She was going to let us get Hendry. Why did you shoot her?"

Beckwith frowned. "Surely you didn't believe her! The witch had been too long in the grove, and she was beyond help or hope. You saw it for yourself, Captain. She was lost to the Wyrdwood. But she can't agitate the trees any longer, and now dawn has come. We can fetch Corporal Hendry and the arms without any fear, then be on our way."

Rafferdy was dumbstruck, and a sickness churned in his stomach. Before he could think of how to respond, the warm dawn light went to cold gray. To the east, a morning fog had risen up from fields, swallowing the sun. A chill wind rushed up the hill. The trees waved to and fro again, but this time it was only due to the force of the gale.

Suddenly came a new sound: a distant crackle that Rafferdy recognized at once as gunfire. A new fear gripped him, and he ran along the base of the wall, Beckwith behind him. He rounded a curve in the wall just as another volley of rifle fire was borne upon the wind. Below, at the foot of the ridge, a white veil hung upon the air: not fog, but smoke. Then it was torn aside by a gust, and Rafferdy had a clear view of the scene below.

Despair filled him. At the foot of the ridge, his men had tried to arrange themselves in a hasty line, but it was ragged and half formed. Marching toward them was a tight formation of men in blue coats. The fog and gloom must have obscured their approach, but now they were in plain view, and Rafferdy made a quick count. There were close to a hundred of them, the rifles held before them fitted with bayonets.

So the pursued had indeed become the pursuer. The enemy soldiers they had been following had turned about and had come after the rebels. And they had gathered more of Valhaine's men along the way. Now they advanced, and Rafferdy knew his own men were in dire peril, for they hadn't had time to form a proper defense or ascend to higher ground.

Even as Rafferdy watched, a line of bright flashes appeared as the redcrests fired their rifles. A half-dozen figures in brown coats crumpled to the ground.

"We have to get down there!" Rafferdy cried.

But his words were lost in the roar of the gale. He could just discern a shout behind him—a sound quickly cut short. Rafferdy turned around, and a sigh escaped him. He had been wrong; it hadn't been the wind stirring them. Even as he watched, the branches that had coiled around Beckwith bore his limp body upward and over the wall. Then he was gone.

So the trees did not need their witch to direct them after all. With the dawning sun obscured, they could act with a will—and a vengeance—all their own. Rafferdy reached for his saber at his hip, but there was no time to draw it, or to speak runes of power. Behind him, he heard another crackling volley of rifle fire.

Then black branches whipped down and wrapped around him.

CHAPTER THIRTY-ONE

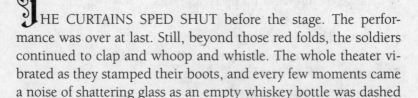

𝕿HE CURTAINS SPED SHUT before the stage. The performance was over at last. Still, beyond those red folds, the soldiers continued to clap and whoop and whistle. The whole theater vibrated as they stamped their boots, and every few moments came a noise of shattering glass as an empty whiskey bottle was dashed against the floor.

In the wing, just offstage, Riethe gripped the curtain rope and tensed his thick arms.

"Wait!" Eldyn hissed. "Not yet!"

Riethe clenched his jaw but did not pull on the rope. All around Eldyn, the other illusionists slumped upon pieces of scenery or had collapsed to the stage. They were all of them spent. They had done five performances in the last thirty hours, and Eldyn knew they were too exhausted to answer a call for additional entertainments. Were they to conjure any more illusions, they would be in danger of expending their own light; indeed, they had likely already done so. They had to rest.

Though whether the soldiers in attendance would allow it was in question. Sometimes the men departed the theater as soon as the play was over, off to seek out more drink, or to find women who were not constructed of air and light, but rather warm flesh. But sometimes the soldiers had brought ample drink and relished the sights they had been shown, and so craved more. In such cases they would continue to roar and shake the theater until the illusionists were forced to open the curtains and improvise more scenes, lest the soldiers bring the place down with their raucous exertions.

Still Eldyn waited, listening. He heard the tinkling noises of more broken bottles, and by that he guessed that they had not brought sufficient reserves of whiskey with them that night. Another minute passed, and the clapping and whistling dwindled. The roar beyond the curtain faded into a grumble. Again came the thumping of boots, but now it was the blessed sound of the soldiers getting up from their seats and departing the theater.

"By God," Mouse said from where he lay upon his back on the stage, limbs all splayed out, "if they will just leave us alone, I swear I will never drink again."

Riethe let go of the curtain rope and peered out past the edge of the curtain. "Then you'd better get used to being sober," he said, "for they are already departing."

"Already?" The diminutive illusionist sat up. "But if they were in the act of leaving the theater when I spoke, then my bargain is null, of course. Someone fetch me a cup of rum!"

No one did. Indeed, nobody even had the wherewithal to give

Mouse a thump on the head such as he deserved. Riethe leaned against the proscenium arch, shutting his eyes. Not far away, Hugoth sat upon the edge of a wooden platform that was painted to look like the parapet of a fortress, his face carved with lines.

Eldyn surveyed the rest of the players, noticing their haggard faces and hazed eyes, then he sighed. "We can't keep doing this."

He spoke the words quietly, not meaning for them to be heard, only Merrick had been standing just behind him.

"We can't, but we have to," the tall illusionist said. His cheeks and nose seemed sharper than ever in the glare of the oil lamps that lit the stage. Even so, Merrick seemed to be holding up better than most of them throughout all of this. Even Riethe, big ox that he was, appeared more worn out these days than Merrick.

"I know that you can keep going," Eldyn whispered. "And for all their complaining, Mouse and Riethe can, too. But what about the others? Hugoth's beard gets grayer every day. And even the new fellows are already beginning to look worn out."

Recently, they had hired a few men from some of the theaters that had closed. It had been Madame Richelour's hope to hire enough players so that each illusionist would be able to sit out every third performance. Only it had been harder to find illusionists willing to work onstage than they had thought, and it wasn't just because the wages they could offer were pitifully low. Rather, a large number of Siltheri had fled the city as Huntley Morden advanced. Many of those who had remained in Invarel had done so because they were older or could not travel—which in both cases meant they likely suffered symptoms of mordoth—and so were unwilling or unable to endure the risks and rigors of performing for Valhaine's soldiers.

"I don't know how we can ask them all to keep going on like this," Eldyn went on, shaking his head.

"We have to help them," Merrick said, his dark eyes grim. "You've seen what happens to Siltheri who aren't in the employ of Lord Valhaine, and who make the mistake of being seen."

Yes, Eldyn had. A few lumenals ago, there had been an impression on the front page of *The Comet* illustrating exactly this. *The Comet* was the only broadsheet still being published, and like the plays they were forced to perform at the Theater of the Moon, the newspaper contained only those images and stories which the Lord Guardian deemed to be suitably patriotic and emblematic of Altanian values and ideals.

Given this fact, it was now clear what place there would be in the nation for the Siltheri once the war was over. For the impression on the front page had depicted not just three convicted witches dangling from a gibbet before Barrowgate, but two illusionists as well. Only they had not been called such in the article accompanying the impression. Rather, they had been referred to as *stunted male witches, possessed of the most repulsive feminine characteristics, and which ought to have been born female themselves but for a perversion of nature.*

Eldyn didn't know how it mattered what sex they had been born. Either way, woman or man, if one of Valhaine's witch-hunters saw you, and glimpsed a light around you, and pointed a finger in your direction, then it was off to Barrowgate you went.

How many witch-hunters Valhaine employed to do this work, no one knew for certain. Nor were they easily spotted out in the city. They were not madmen with their eyes torn out, like the witch-hunters Archdeacon Lemarck had been trying to create. Rather, they were like Rose Lockwell—people who, for some reason, were naturally sensitive to the light that emanated from witches and illusionists. And from magicians. For it was the case that more than a few men who had been accused of practicing magick without proper approval by the government had gone to the gallows—along with any number of others who had done something that was not deemed *emblematic of Altanian values and ideals.*

Eldyn had no idea how many people there were in the world like Lady Quent's sister. He could not believe they were very common. All the same, Lord Valhaine had found at least a few. And whether they served him out of fear of reprisal if they did not, or in exchange for money, it made no difference. They could be anywhere, in any place in the city. Which meant it was not safe for an illusionist to show his face in public, unless it was on a stage in one of the few theaters authorized by the government to provide entertainment to the soldiers.

As for the women taken to the gallows—Eldyn doubted that any of them had been aware of their own nature, or had ever seen a stand of Wyrdwood except in a painting. But it did not matter. *A sibyl need not have induced a Rising or aided the illegal rebellion to have committed a crime against Altania,* the article in the broadsheet had stated. *Rather, it is the gravest sort of offense merely to be capable of witchcraft. For once brought in proximity to a grove of Old Trees, how could a witch do anything but serve its will, which is clearly bent upon the destruction of men?*

Despite all his misgivings, Eldyn did his best to effect a smile for Merrick's sake. "Don't worry. We'll make sure those who are the most weary have the smallest roles. And we'll construct more props to use in place of phantasms, just as we've been doing."

The other illusionist started to protest, but Eldyn laid a hand on his bony shoulder. "We will all of us be well, Merrick, I promise. All we have to do is keep performing. It doesn't matter how awful our plays are. There are only two other houses on Durrow Street now with enough illusionists to mount productions for the soldiers. Which means Lord Valhaine needs us."

Indeed, more soldiers than ever had been marching into the theater of late. It seemed that Lord Valhaine wanted to keep providing his troops with ample patriotic inspiration. Or was it rather that he was trying to distract them from what was happening on the battlefield? No news about rebel victories had been reported in the broadsheets since the West Country fell, but there were rumors in the city that things were not going well for Valhaine, and that Huntley Morden continued to advance on Invarel. For this reason, Valhaine was recalling more and more of his troops to defend the city.

From things Jaimsley had said, and things Eldyn had seen for himself, he believed there was truth to these rumors. And that gave him hope. It meant they wouldn't have to keep doing this interminably. All they had to do was hold on until Morden's men reached the city.

Though how long that would be, Eldyn didn't know. Soon, he hoped, looking at the weary illusionists. As for Merrick, even in the best of times his was a gloomy perspective, and he looked less than convinced by Eldyn's words. Before he could speak, though, a welcome visitor appeared upon the stage to congratulate them on their performance, as was the tradition. Only it was not Madame Richelour who came to praise them.

Rather, it was Lily Lockwell.

She wore a ruby-colored gown that surely had been taken from one of Madame Richelour's closets, and which had been liberally augmented with feathers and beads and bangles. Her cheeks were tinged pink, and her dark hair was worn in a mass of ringlets, all of which had the effect of making her look far more mature than her sixteen years.

Only it wasn't simply that she *looked* more mature. As had often been the case over the course of this last month, Eldyn was at once bemused and impressed as he watched the youngest Miss Lockwell move among the illusionists upon the stage, a basket looped over her arm. She had heartening words for each of them, and everything she said was tailored for the recipient as carefully as her red gown had been for herself.

"Your fiery crown was so bright I had to shade my eyes with my fan to look at it!" she told Hugoth, who often expressed a fear that his illusions had dimmed as he had aged. This caused him to lift his head and give a weary smile. To Riethe she said chidingly, "I believe the winged horse that bears your maiden will no longer be able to fly if her bodice should expand any farther." Which of course only made Riethe grin like a fool.

One by one, the others all received a similar compliment. "I am sure I could count every feather in the wings of the steed you conjured," she told Merrick, who was always very precise about things. And to Mouse, who was especially fond of flattery—the more grandiose the better—she said, "Your ocean was such a perfect hue of aquamarine that I hardly drew a breath, for fear that I should drown!"

This caused the small illusionist to leap to his feet. "No, for I would have conjured a crystal sphere to protect you!" he proclaimed. This won a groan all around, but Lily laughed and gave his scruffy cheek a fond pat.

"You always help raise their spirits," Eldyn said quietly when at last she drew near to him. "You're marvelous at it, really. Thank you."

Her coral-tinted lips curved upward, but she shook her head. "No, it is you who must be thanked, Mr. Garritt. I adore all of the illusions the others conjure. They're wonderful. But the phantasms you create . . ." She gave a sigh. "Sometimes when I watch them, I think it is your illusions that are real, and that everything else I can see or touch is what is false."

Like her compliments to the others, he might have thought these words were especially crafted just to please him. Yet such was the earnest light in her brown eyes that he could only think she truly meant what she said. But then, maybe she had truly meant what she said to each of them.

"Here, take this," she said and handed him a warm, damp cloth from the basket she carried.

She had been giving the cloths to each of the men so that they might wipe their faces. Eldyn lifted the cloth to his cheek. A pungent herbal scent emanated from it. He breathed in the heady aroma and immediately felt invigorated.

"What is this?" he said, astonished.

"It's hyssop," Lily said. "I read in a book that in ancient Tharos, athletes would put hyssop leaves on their arms and legs to ease their aches after a competition. And conjuring illusions seems at least as hard as running a race or jumping a vault. I searched all over until I found some growing by a grave in Duskfellow's. I knew it was hyssop at once, because it looked just like the picture I saw in the book."

Again Eldyn was astonished, but less happily this time. Despite her womanly gown, and her motherly tending of the illusionists, she was still just sixteen, and given to indulging her whims without proper thought—just as she had the day a month ago when she arrived unexpectedly at the theater.

"It was very kind of you to want to find something to help us," he said, "but you know it is dangerous to venture out into the city, especially so far from the theater as Duskfellow's graveyard."

She merely shrugged. "I am sure I was in no great peril. It was daylight, and there were plenty of soldiers about. Besides, Riethe came with me. I knew that even if I picked a cartful of hyssop, *he* would be able to carry it."

So that was where Riethe had been earlier that day. This fact reassured Eldyn, but only to a degree. Riethe's height and bulk would have dissuaded anyone from trying to accost Lily, but what if a witch-hunter had seen them? Given his appearance and manner, few tended on first glance to think Riethe was a Siltheri. Nor had Eldyn observed the light he emanated to be particularly bright; it was, like Riethe himself, goodly and expansive, but a bit dim. In broad daylight it would have been difficult to detect. But not impossible, and if a witch-hunter had paused to study him . . .

But that hadn't happened; they had returned to the theater without issue. All the same, Eldyn would have a talk with Riethe about being a willing party to such schemes. Eldyn had promised Lady Quent that he would take care of Lily, that he would see to her safety and well-being.

Only hadn't he already broken that promise? He regarded her red dress, her painted lips, and he could only believe it was so. Here Miss Lockwell was, dwelling in a theater full of Siltheri, and watching from the wings as they performed illusion plays populated with buxom women, lustful soldiers, and battles awash in illusory blood.

Of course, it had not taken long before she was doing far more than merely watching the performances. One umbral, shortly after Lily's arrival at the theater, Master Tallyroth had been gripped by particularly violent spasms, and Madame Richelour had been reluctant to leave his bedside, for she was always better able to soothe him than anyone else.

Customarily, the madam of the theater made a survey of the players before the curtain went up, and personally made any final adjustments to their makeup or costumes. That night, they presumed they would not have the benefit of such help. Only then, to Eldyn's great surprise, Lily was there. She moved among the illusionists as if this was entirely expected, retying laces, adjusting stiff paper helmets, or smoothing the greasepaint upon their faces. And while her touch was not as experienced as Madame Richelour's, her fingers were deft, and she possessed a natural flair.

While it had been gradual, ever since that night, Lily had taken on more and more of Madame Richelour's duties—even as she had begun to wear more of the madam's gowns, jewels, and face-paints. She would aid the players with their costumes before each performance started, if Madame Richelour could not, and would come to praise them when it was done.

Before long, she was assisting with the staging as well. After observing how weary the illusionists were becoming, it had been her idea to manufacture new props that could take the place of phantasms. Stars and comets needed to be conjured, but waves could be made with sheets of blue fabric undulated by the actions of people offstage. Trees could be fashioned of wood and canvas, and the same was true for mountains or castles. Once these were varnished with an illusory glow, they were nearly as beautiful and convincing as if they had been conjured entirely from light.

By means of these and other creations, the burden upon the players was lessened, and they were able to keep up the pace of the productions. It seemed nearly every performance Lily had fashioned some new piece for them to use onstage—something onto which they needed only to cast a glamour of light in order to give it the proper look. More than once, Eldyn was reminded of the tableau Lily had created for her and Rose's party last year. The tableau had been so well executed that all it took was a bit of pearly light summoned by Eldyn and Dercy to make those in attendance gasp in wonder.

It was the same here at the theater. Eldyn had observed Lily to have a remarkable aptitude for using mundane materials—paper and paste and paint—to craft astonishingly realistic pieces of scenery. He had always known the youngest Miss Lockwell had an artistic nature, but he had not realized how profound her ability was. And perhaps she had not known herself, for sometimes she gazed upon something she had made with a look of wonder that was not unlike what Eldyn had felt upon seeing the first illusions he had conjured himself.

But then, were not her creations a form of illusion themselves? Certainly by means of *her* labors, *their* work upon the stage was made easier each night. As a result, it did not take long before the other players grew used to Lily's presence at the theater, and then came to rely upon her. As for Eldyn himself, any fear he might have had that Lily's nature was akin to his own sister's had long been dispelled. While Sashie had possessed a similarly impetuous nature, she had never demonstrated such cleverness and industriousness, or such a finely developed sensibility. Nor was he the only one with such an opinion.

"Lily is the most remarkable young woman!" Madame Richelour had exclaimed to Eldyn more than once since Lily's arrival. "I have seldom seen such a theatrical eye and a gift for staging, let alone in a person of such few years. And she has such a spirit! She lifts us all up just by being here. I wonder how we managed without her. I doubt we could have done so for much longer."

That Madame Richelour had an especial fondness for Lily was evident in all their interactions. That very first day, the madam of the theater had acted as if Lily were a foundling who had been left upon the step, and had proceeded to lavish every sort of motherly affection upon her. Not that Eldyn was entirely surprised by this. Madame Richelour had never married, and so she had no children of her own. She had always mothered the young men who worked at the theater, of course, but Eldyn could imagine how she might have longed for a daughter. Now, at last, she had one she could call her own.

For her part, Lily received these affections freely and gladly.

While Madame Richelour had never had a daughter, Lily herself had been deprived of her own mother not long ago, and so their pairing was in every way natural. What was more, knowing that Madame Richelour cared for Lily reassured Eldyn to some degree, and allowed him to believe that the theater was not an entirely unwholesome place for Lily—even if Lily's change in attire and appearance was largely due to the madam's influence.

Despite the bias that naturally arose from her affections for their foundling, Eldyn was beginning to think that Madame Richelour was right, and that they would not have endured much longer had it not been for Lily's presence. It wasn't just her work upon the set pieces, or the way she had taken over some of the duties of the madam of the theater, so that Madame Richelour could spend more of her time tending to Master Tallyroth. Rather, it was Lily's spirit that buoyed them and kept them from sinking.

It was with this thought that Eldyn let go of his worries regarding the secret expedition for hyssop, and instead wiped his face with the warm cloth, letting the sharp scent clear his mind.

"Where is Madame Richelour?" he asked as he handed the cloth back to Lily.

"She is upstairs with Master Tallyroth." The pink smile on her lips faded. "He is caught in a delirium again."

Eldyn gave a sober nod. Delusions were a symptom of an advanced state of the mordoth. He had been having more and more of late.

"I'm glad she is with him," Eldyn said.

Lily sighed. "I wish I could have seen him perform. The tales Madame Richelour tells of the days when he was onstage all those years ago—it must have been magnificent to behold!"

Eldyn was sure it would have been. But it was because of the magnificence of those performances that he was in the state he was now. He had used up too much of his light, too quickly.

But all he said was "I'm sure his performances were a marvel."

Her smile returned, then she moved on to attend to the remainder of the illusionists. They were all of them grateful for her attentions, and some gave her kisses upon the cheek in return—though these were of course no more than brotherly in nature. While Lily might have been shocked to burst in upon Eldyn and Dercy that night at her party, she now seemed to understand and accept the direction in which the romantic attentions of illusionists lay—Eldyn's own included. At least, since coming to the theater, she had given no indication that her affections with regard to him were anything other than what she might have for a dear friend.

For that, he was very grateful. And while associating with illusionists might bring some discredit with it, at least her honor as a young lady could not be feared for here. Rather, she now had many elder brothers who would go to great lengths to protect her.

ELDYN SHOULD have been asleep like everyone else.

God knew, he was more than tired enough. All the same, he had not even let himself lay down on the narrow bed in his chamber, for fear he would fall asleep. Instead, he read a copy of *The Comet,* searching for any small kernels of truth among the falsehoods printed upon its pages. Only he saw nothing about how Huntley Morden's troops continued to advance in the West Country, or how here in the city redcrests had fired into a crowd of people when stones were thrown at them.

Nor was there any mention of Princess Layle, who had not been seen in over a month. Last Eldyn had heard, she was being kept in the Citadel—supposedly for her own protection. More likely she was being imprisoned. Eldyn could only wonder if Valhaine's witch-hunters had been brought to her room, and what they saw when they did.

Among all the worthless reports in the newspaper, though, there was one story that did win Eldyn's interest enough for him to read it all the way through. It was an advertising piece regarding the colony that was to be established in the New Lands. While no ships could pass eastward over the ocean at present, due to the war, reports from the initial scouting party had made it back to Altania just before the coasts were blockaded.

According to the advertisement, a suitable place for the colony had been located upon the edge of the new continent—a fecund landscape characterized by a temperate climate and vast quantities of fish, fowl, and timber ripe for the harvesting. As soon as the current conflict was concluded, the article promised, ships would be sailing for the new colony.

Once again, Eldyn fancied himself standing upon the prow of a ship, facing into a bracing wind, a lush green line thickening upon the horizon ahead. Only this time, in this vision, he did not stand alone. Rather, Dercy was there by his side, his arm draped around Eldyn's shoulders, his hair and beard as gold as when they had first met, not streaked with pewter as they had been after Lemarck had stolen his light beneath the chapel in High Holy. There was a mischievous grin upon Dercy's handsome face, and as he gazed forward, his eyes were as green and bright as the sea itself. . . .

A sharp, sudden pain pierced Eldyn's head, and the images before him wavered and dissipated. It was only as they did so that he realized he had not merely imagined the scene; rather, he had conjured it as an illusion.

That had been a foolish exertion. He was already weary from their last performance, and he had work yet to do that night. Eldyn pressed a hand to his brow, waiting for the pain to subside. At last it did. By then, the theater was quiet. He left the newspaper on the table, put on his coat, and went downstairs. Making no sound, he slipped out the rear door of the theater and into the night.

As he moved through the empty streets of the Old City, Eldyn stitched the shadows into a heavy cloak. If only it could have kept him warm like a real garment. But it could not, so he moved quickly, trying to generate heat through exertion. The umbral had been so long that the black water in the gutters was beginning to freeze. He began to fear that, no matter how thickly he wrapped the shadows around him, the white fog of his breath would betray his presence. Each time he saw a patrol of soldiers approaching down an otherwise empty lane, he would duck into a corner or alcove and cease breathing until they passed by.

At last he reached the dormitories below Butcher's Slip. He cast off his disguise, but even so it took the two young men standing by the door a few moments to notice him in the gloom. Once they saw his face, they let him pass, and he made his way down to the chamber at the end of the hallway.

As usual, Jaimsley was awake, poring over a desk filled with papers and empty whiskey glasses. His prematurely thinning hair stood above his head in wild tufts, as if he had been continually running a hand through it.

"You'd better hope that none of the Lord Guardian's men ever come in here and see this," Eldyn said, picking up one of the papers. "Copies of secret missives, maps of troop positions—this would surely win you an appointment at Barrowgate if it were ever seen."

"Don't worry," Jaimsley said with a wry expression. "All I need is a moment's notice to destroy the evidence. I've spilled so much whiskey on these papers of late that all it would take is a touch of a candle, and they'd be gone in a flash."

Eldyn couldn't help chuckling. For all that he might be one of the most important men in the city aiding the rebellion, Jaimsley was still the same homely young man who could cause people to laugh in any situation.

"So how about some of that whiskey?" Eldyn said.

Jaimsley went to the sideboard. "You're in luck. We were nearly out, but one of the boys came upon a few crates some redcrests had hidden in a house near the Morrowgate. As the redcrests shouldn't be drinking on duty, my lads decided to relieve them of the temptation."

He held out a full glass, which Eldyn accepted gratefully.

"Steady there, now," Jaimsley said, and his grin flattened a bit. "I say, are you all right, Garritt?"

Eldyn looked down. His hand was trembling, and some of the whiskey had sloshed out of the glass onto the paper-strewn desk.

Hastily, Eldyn gripped the glass with both hands. "I thought I'd sprinkle a little more whiskey just to be safe in case you have need to ignite any of these papers." Carefully he lifted the glass to his lips and drained it in one long draught. The whiskey burned his throat, but quickly diffused into a pleasant warmness in his chest.

Jaimsley watched him with close-set eyes. Then he tossed back his own whiskey in a single motion. "All right, let's get to work."

There was much to do that night, for there were several documents which their source within the Citadel—a clerk who was employed there—had managed to make copies of, and which provided key intelligence about the strength and movements of Lord Valhaine's forces.

Eldyn went to the cabinet where the tools of his trade were stored, and he drew them out: engraving plates, brushes, and a vial of impression rosin. This latter had grown difficult to obtain, until Jaimsley managed to secure a steady supply from one of the few men in the city who manufactured the substance, and who it turned out was sympathetic to the revolution.

"He said if we can keep bringing him bark taken from Old Trees, he can keep making the rosin," Jaimsley had said. Since then, rebels outside the city had been smuggling in bundles of such bark. It was taken from branches that had fallen over the wall at the Evengrove, and was brought into the city the same way messages were—through the drains, or right through the gates under the eyes of the guards in barrels of grain or blocks of tallow.

Eldyn arranged all of the materials on the sideboard. He carefully coated an engraving plate with the impression rosin. Next, he lifted one of the missives to be sent to Morden's forces outside the city. Eldyn studied it for a number of minutes, committing every letter to mind. Then he took up one of the plates, held it before him, and shut his eyes.

A green flash of light, and it was done.

He repeated these steps, and in this manner made impressions of several more letters and diagrams. A sheen of sweat broke out upon his brow as he worked, and he found himself wishing for one of Lily's hyssop-scented cloths. Instead he clenched his jaw and kept working.

"Can I get you more whiskey?" Jaimsley said as he took the last plate Eldyn had worked on and carefully wrapped it in a waxed cloth. "You look a little pale."

Indeed, Eldyn *felt* pale. Or rather, he felt transparent somehow. It was like being a windowpane: a brittle thing through which light might pass freely, but a thrown stone could shatter.

"Yes, if you can spare some," he said.

Jaimsley laughed. "For you, Garritt, we can spare all the whiskey you want. If it wasn't for you, we wouldn't be getting any messages out of the city at all these days. There are more soldiers than ever, and they accost anyone they meet. Just last umbral, one of our couriers was stopped by soldiers outside the city. They searched his satchel and found the engraving plates he was carrying, only they had no idea they were anything other than pieces of scrap metal to be sold for a coin. The redcrests confiscated his satchel, but in the end they had no cause to detain the courier and let him go."

Eldyn let out a breath of relief. The loss of the impressions was of no matter; they could be remade. But a life could not be restored if it was taken, and he was grateful the courier had not been detained. As for the messages themselves, there was little risk they could have been intercepted or read. Even if the soldiers had somehow not smeared the impression rosin in their handling of the plates, the volatile substance would have evaporated within hours. Which meant that Eldyn's scheme was working as planned.

Jaimsley handed Eldyn another glass of whiskey. It was less full this time. Still, even holding it with both hands, Eldyn had a difficult time keeping it from spilling as he lifted it to his lips.

"These documents you've gotten are all astonishing," Eldyn said hurriedly, before Jaimsely might comment on his trembling. "I can only wonder how our man in the Citadel managed to copy these."

"As do I," Jaimsley said. "We have never seen him, and do not even know his name. Nor have we ever tried to learn it, for fear of exposing him. But I will say, though he may be a mere clerk, this fellow is braver than any soldier on the battlefield, and as important as any general."

Eldyn could only grin at this, having been a clerk himself. It was strange but marvelous to think that this war could hinge not just on cannons and gunpowder, but on illusions and ink. He picked up one of the missives he had made an impression of. All of them had been fascinating. Some detailed what seemed a frantic rearrangement of troops, or reiterated urgent requests for supplies. One particularly intriguing letter made a mention that the Citadel was waiting on a report from the White Lady, but that it had not yet been received, and that her present whereabouts were unknown. Had she perhaps been captured by the enemy? If so, that would be a grave blow to the Lord Guardian, for she was one of his chief spies.

"From reading all of these, I can only start to think the Lord Guardian begins to fear he might not be victorious," Eldyn said, setting the paper down. "Morden presses relentlessly from the west, and at the same time Valhaine has to expend great effort here just to keep the city firmly under his thumb. All of these actions have something of a desperate quality."

"Yes, they do," Jaimsley said. "And there's no one more dangerous than a desperate man, for he cannot be expected to act in a rational manner, or to safeguard those things a man usually would protect. Instead, he will bare his teeth and sever his own limb if he thinks it should free him from the trap he is caught in." He unrolled a large sheet of paper on the desk. It was a map of the southern part of Altania, hastily drawn in spare but precise lines. "Look here. Our man in the Citadel managed to make a copy of this. Without a doubt, it is the most vital document he has provided us so far."

Eldyn leaned over the table. "What does it show?"

"I can't say I'm entirely certain. But do you see these?" He pointed to an arrow on the map, and to several others. "It's apparent these places are important given the way they're marked. And from other reports we've intercepted, we know that these are the very directions in which Valhaine's troops have been moving of late."

"But what are these marks beside each of the arrows?" Eldyn said, peering at the map. Next to the point of each arrow were several queer, angular symbols. They looked almost like writing, but none that Eldyn recognized.

"I'm not sure," Jaimsley said. "Perhaps they're some sort of code that states what forces are to go to these locations or what will happen there. I have to believe it's something central to Valhaine's plans. It seems mad to send his forces running willy-nilly all over the countryside like this, but there has to be some purpose in it. I can only believe he's scheming some great gambit. I have no idea what it could be, but clearly Valhaine is betting much upon it—perhaps everything. And if Morden is not prepared to counter it . . ."

Jaimsley didn't finish the thought. Instead he said, "We have to get a copy of this map out of the city at once. I'm sure as this night is long that many lives depend upon it."

"I understand," Eldyn said, and picked up another engraving plate.

The plate slipped through his fingers and shattered as it struck the floor. Eldyn stared at his hands. They were shaking violently.

"I'm sorry," he said, hastily withdrawing his hands. "I shouldn't be so careless, not when these are so hard to come by."

He started to bend down to pick up the broken pieces of metal, but Jaimsley gripped his shoulder, stopping him.

"Are you all right, Garritt?"

"I'm a little tired, that's all."

Jaimsley's face was uncharacteristically somber. "Are you sure? It seems more than simple weariness that afflicts you. All these impressions you've been making, and your performances at the theater as well—I've heard it said that doing too many such things can make an illusionist sick."

Eldyn worked his jaw, but he could summon no words to speak.

"Maybe we should take this up again tomorrow," Jaimsley said.

Again Eldyn looked down at his hands. They seemed thinner than he recalled, and for the first time he noticed how dark blue veins mottled their backs, snaking up his wrists.

You must be very careful not to create too many impressions, Mr. Garritt, Master Tallyroth had told him that last night they had really talked. *They are wondrous—perhaps the grandest sort of illusion a Siltheri can fashion. But they are costly as well. . . .*

Yes, very costly, for Tallyroth had explained how shaping the impression rosin required an illusionist to expend some portion of his own light. And Eldyn needed to look no further than Master Tallyroth to see the effects of using up too much of one's light. How many impressions had Eldyn made over the past month for the sake of the revolution? Twenty? Thirty? No, it was far more than that.

And each one had used up a little bit of his light, his life.

Promise me that you will only make another impression if it is for something truly worthwhile, Tallyroth had said that night.

I promise, Eldyn had answered. And he would hold true to that vow. But what could be more important than this?

"Hand me another engraving plate," Eldyn said, sitting at the table and looking at the map, studying its lines and markings.

Jaimsley sat down opposite him, a metal square in his hand, but he did not let go of it. "Garritt, I don't know about this."

"You said you were sure many lives depended upon a copy of this map reaching our generals."

"Yes, but what of your own life? I had suspected it prior to this, but now I am certain of it—making all of these impressions is killing you. Not as quickly as a bullet, mind you, but just as surely. I see how you get a little paler every time that you make one." He leaned over the table. "Would you throw your life away in a rash moment, like Talinger and Warrett did?"

Eldyn looked up from the map. "Talinger and Warrett didn't

throw their lives away rashly. They knew exactly what they were doing that day. They were fighting for what they believed in, and what they cared about. For our nation, and for one another. How could it ever be rash to give one's very last for the sake of such things?"

Jaimsley's mouth pulled into a flat line. For a moment he gazed at Eldyn, his small eyes unusually bright. At last he laid the engraving plate down on the map.

"Go on, then," he said quietly. "Make the impression."

And Eldyn did.

ELDYN WOKE to sunlight streaming in through the window of his little room above the theater. The umbral had been so long that he had begun to despair dawn would never come again. Only it had, and the world was filled with light.

But for how long? As he pulled on his trousers and buttoned his shirt, his gaze went to the issue of *The Comet* he had thrown on the little table by the bed. ASTROGRAPHERS PREDICT AN UNUSUAL ALIGNMENT OF THE PLANETS, read a line of large print upon the front page. And below that in slanted type, *All Citizens Should Prepare for an Umbral of Unprecedented Length.*

While the broadsheet was generally thick with misleading stories full of distorted or fabricated accounts meant to shape people's impressions, Eldyn could only believe there was truth to this particular article. If an umbral of such long duration as to seem without end was indeed to fall, and people had received no warning about it from the government, chaos would surely ensue. The very fabric of society might come apart as people rioted out of fear and desperation. Men would turn upon one another, and bonfires lit to ward off the dark and cold could leap out of control and burn the entire city to ash.

Lord Valhaine was too clever, and too desirous of control, to allow events to come to that. Over the last quarter month, soldiers had been distributing rations of candles and lamp oil and coal to people, as well as foodstuffs and blankets. These actions served to confirm the truth of the story in Eldyn's mind, as normally such supplies would be reserved for the army. Valhaine would only give them to the common people if there was great cause.

But even without all of this evidence, still Eldyn would have believed the article in the newspaper. One only had to look up at the sky to see how, each night, the various glowing points of color in the heavens grew closer and closer to the red disk of the most recent arrival. A Grand Conjunction was indeed coming. The planets would align all in a row, and the sun would be entirely eclipsed. And just how long the umbral that ensued would last was a number the astrographers had yet to calculate. Perhaps, like some said, it would never have an end.

Only Eldyn could not believe that. No matter how dark, and how bitterly cold it became, the umbral would have to end at some point. Just like this terrible war would have to end. And then what? Dawn always followed night. But what would he do when the war was over?

A spasm passed through his hands as he attempted to fasten the last button of his shirt. Eldyn winced, then rubbed his hands together to try to warm them and ease the pain in his joints. He had always assumed he would keep performing here on Durrow Street for years to come. But would he really? After all, he could hardly perform in illusion plays for very long when he didn't even have the strength to button his own shirt. How many more impressions did he have to make until he became like Master Tallyroth, tossing and turning in a delirium? And if it came to that—or rather, when it did come to that—what would become of him? Madame Richelour was always beside Master Tallyroth's bed, caring for him.

But who would there be at Eldyn's side?

He drew a breath, clenching and unclenching his stiff fingers. After that he was able to fasten the last button of his shirt and pull on his boots. Then he left his room.

Eldyn went quietly down the stairs, not wanting to disturb

Master Tallyroth, or any of the other players who were likely getting much needed rest. Evidently he was not the only one awake, though, for when he reached the bottom of the steps he heard clattering and scraping noises emanating from the theater. Thinking perhaps Riethe or Mouse was up to some bit of mischief, Eldyn ducked through a side door that led to one of the wings, then stepped past a curtain.

It was not Riethe or Mouse at work upon the stage, but rather Lily Lockwell. Her red gown had been traded for a simple pink dress, and her hair was gathered in a braid behind her neck. The only paint upon her face was the same blue color as that on the brush she held in her hand. In all, the result was a youthful look more fitting for her sixteen years.

She frowned as she used the brush to make another daub at the large canvas flat before her. Then she climbed off the wooden stool she had been standing on and dragged it to another position before the flat.

"Good morning, Miss Lockwell," Eldyn said, thinking it best to interrupt her before she had climbed back onto the stool, lest he startle her and she take a tumble.

She was indeed startled, given the expression on her face, but only for a moment. Then she smiled.

"Good morning, Mr. Garritt. Since you are here, could you give me your opinion on this? I was thinking it was silly to have Hugoth bother with conjuring ships for the seascape in the first act, for they are only ever in the background, and I was sure I could just as easily paint them. Only now that I have, I think they are rather crooked."

Eldyn approached and regarded the expanse of canvas to which she had been applying her paints. A pair of ships rode high atop swirls of blue and green and white, their gray sails billowing upon their masts.

"They are indeed listing a bit to one side," Eldyn admitted. "But that's only as it should be under the force of a gale. I think they're remarkable."

Lily's brown eyes lit up. "You do? Truly? And here I was fearing they wouldn't do at all."

"No, look." Eldyn moved his hand and conjured a wavering blue-green light. It was a simple illusion, one that took hardly any effort. Yet the effect was to make it seem as if the waves were rising and falling upon the canvas, and that the sails snapped in the wind.

"Oh," she said, and lowered her brush. "But that's marvelous."

Eldyn could not help smiling at her reaction. "It was very simple, as you had already done the great majority of work. If you keep making pieces such as these, Miss Lockwell, we will hardly have to conjure any illusions at all. Not that I am in the least upset by that idea. Rather, I thank you."

She turned away as she wiped the brush on a cloth. "You do not need to keep thanking me, Mr. Garritt. We all have our roles to play at the theater. This is mine now."

He hesitated, then took a step toward her. "Do you mean to try to make a life of it, then? Of this?"

Still she was turned away from him, so he could not see her face. "Madame Richelour told me that she is married to the theater. I think . . . or rather, I hope that it will be the same for me."

While he could not say he was surprised by these words, still he could not help but feel a shock to hear them coming from her. "You are very young, Miss Lockwell. Your opinion in such things might change."

Now she did turn to look at him, and while he had expected a petulant frown, her oval-shaped face was instead shaped into a thoughtful expression. "Do you think all of this is just a whim?"

He thought about it, then answered truthfully. "No, I do not think that. I think you feel very deeply about the theater, and also that your sensibilities are remarkably suited for it. And yet . . ." He sighed, then gestured to the shabby seats, the patched curtain. "You see this house in ill times, Miss Lockwell, but even in the best it was not much less disheveled. At night, all is beautiful beneath the glamour of illusion. But by day the blemishes are more apparent, and they are many. A life on Durrow Street is not always an easy one. It can be hard, even ugly. All the appreciation we might receive onstage does nothing to counter the contempt directed toward us elsewhere. Are you certain you would not rather give yourself to an institution that could offer you more hope of a respectable life?"

"And what institution would that be, Mr. Garritt? If you would have me wed, how can that be? I used to fancy marrying some handsome lord or earl, but I am very sure no rich gentleman would have me now. Nor do I care anymore, for I know now I could never love such a man—a man who counted coins as being more precious than the words in a poem. But those men whom I could feel such an attachment for—well, they would not wed *me*."

An ache pierced his heart, and he reached a hand toward her. "Lily . . ."

She retreated a step. "But you must not appear so sorrowful for me, Mr. Garritt! I am sure I will be very well. A fate such as Madame Richelour's would be perfectly agreeable to me, so that is what I will strive for."

In that moment, Eldyn knew he had failed in his promise to protect Lily Lockwell. Yet it had been an impossible oath, for she had been lost the moment she left her house and ventured to Durrow Street. By the time she reached the theater, the damage was irrevocable. She was severed forever from a proper and respectable society, and she was already united with the theater, as surely as if her red dress had been a wedding gown.

"Besides, Mr. Garritt, it is I who should feel sorrow for you."

He could only gape at this statement. "For me?"

"You never say his name," she said quietly. Now she no longer retreated from him, but rather approached. "Dercy's name, I mean. He was the one who was with you at my and Rose's party, wasn't he? I've heard others speak about him often, with much affection, only you never do. Do you miss him? Is that why you never speak about him?"

Eldyn felt himself listing to one side, like the painted ships on the canvas. "Yes," he said, his throat suddenly raw. "I miss him so much that I can hardly bear it sometimes."

Lily looked up at him, and despite the gloom in the theater, her eyes were bright, as if reflecting some illusory light. She lifted herself up onto her toes and leaned close. Her lips nearly brushed his, only they strayed and touched his cheek instead. Then she turned and ran from the stage, vanishing behind a curtain in the wings.

For a minute or more, Eldyn stood there, alone upon the stage. As he did, he stared at the ships painted on the canvas flat. Again he thought of his vision, of standing on the prow of a ship. And of the young man with green eyes and a short golden beard who stood beside him. Earlier that morning, Eldyn had wondered what he would do with himself once the war was finished. But he knew now.

Only why did he need to wait for the war to be over? Eldyn looked down at his hands, at the thin bones and blue veins visible beneath the skin, and he knew Jaimsley was right, that there were few impressions left in him. But he had already done his part, hadn't he? He had aided the cause of the revolution. The map he had made an impression of was perhaps the vital link to defeating Lord Valhaine. Could Eldyn not take what little life he had left and spend it how he chose—and with whom? Surely he had earned that much.

A sudden energy filled him such as he had not felt in many days, lifting him so strongly he almost thought he would fly off the stage. Instead, he dashed up the aisle between the seats. He would go to Butcher's Slip and tell Jaimsley his work was done, that he was going to use his illusions to cloak himself and slip past the guards at the gates. He would leave the city behind, and go to the country. And then . . .

"I will come to you, Dercy," he said aloud. "No matter what it takes, I will come to you."

He flung open the door of the theater and stepped into the street.

"There he is!" a voice shouted.

Eldyn thought he should have recognized the voice, for it

seemed familiar to him. He stopped short and blinked against the glare, as the sun was in his eyes. He lifted a hand to shade them—
—and a chill descended over him, as if night had fallen again. In the street before him stood four soldiers with rifles in hand, all pointing at Eldyn. He glanced to either side, but the redcrests had left little space for egress. Nor was there any use in summoning shadows; they could not hide him in the bright morning glare.

Motion caught his eye, and he looked forward again. That was when he saw the short, roundish figure standing behind the soldiers. His blue eyes were narrow and hard behind his spectacles, and his plump face, previously so bland, was now twisted in a snarl of exultation.

"Perren." Eldyn said the word, or rather moaned it in despair.

Yes, it was Perren Fynch—the young illusionist who had taught Eldyn how to make impressions, and whose awkward romantic advances Eldyn had rebuffed. Now the other illusionist advanced on Eldyn once again, but this time it was clearly with other intentions than stealing a kiss. He pointed a pudgy finger directly at Eldyn's chest.

"He's the one who made the impressions you found on that spy. I am sure of it, but if you do not believe me, you only have to compare the plates to the work Garritt did for *The Swift Arrow*."

"That's for the Gray Conclave to decide, not us," said one of the soldiers.

Please, Perren, don't do this, Eldyn wanted to say. *I have to go.*

Only before he could speak the words, the redcrests closed in, and strong hands grappled Eldyn, throwing him roughly to the cobbled street.

CHAPTER THIRTY-TWO

———————— ❧ ————————

STEADY RAIN was falling as Ivy and the three soldiers walked along the summit of the ridge toward Heathcrest Hall.

The men had slung their rifles over their shoulders, but Ivy knew those weapons could be easily returned to hand in a moment if she were to attempt to flee. Then again, she could hardly see ten steps before them given how the mist was closing in all around. If she ran from them, they could hardly have readied the guns before she was lost from view. Perhaps she would be lucky, and their shots would go wide. Then she could run down the ridge and make for the east, and the grove of Old Trees. Their guns would not help them if they should choose to enter there.

Yet even as she entertained these wild thoughts, she knew there was no point to them. For even if she escaped the men, they were not likely to pursue her through rain into the Wyrdwood. Instead, they would seek out shelter; they would make for the manor house, and there they would find . . .

"Look over there," one of the soldiers said—an ox-necked man with a single black brow that ran above both small eyes. "I can see a light in a window just ahead."

. . . Rose. She was in the manor, no doubt wondering where Ivy was. Perhaps she had determined Ivy had gone outside, and had set a lamp in the window to help lead Ivy home in the storm. But it was other eyes that saw the light now, and were drawn by it.

"Well, then, it looks like someone's home," the sandy-bearded man said. He was a small, thin-shouldered fellow with a large nose and a receding jaw. By the corporal's stripes upon his dirty blue coat, and by his manner, he was the leader of the trio. "Let's see if they're inclined to give us a warm welcome. I suspect they will, if they know what's good for them."

A knot of fear welled up in Ivy's throat. "There are some food-stuffs in the kitchen," she said. "And a bottle of whiskey. I can fill your packs, and then you can be on your way."

"Thank you, ma'am, we'll take the food," the wiry corporal drawled. "And the whiskey as well, for it's been long since we've seen such stuff. But as for being on our way—well, now, it's an awful blustery day to be turning a fellow out, don't you think? No, I think you'll do like a woman should, and fix us up that food and bring it to us, hot on a plate."

A shudder passed through Ivy, though which chilled her more—the rain or the words the corporal spoke—she could scarcely tell. Knowing there was nothing she could say or do to alter the intent of the men, she kept her jaw clamped shut as they walked. The small point of light grew brighter, and the shadow of the house loomed out of the mist.

As they walked up the steps, Ivy quickened her pace a little, so that she was the first through the front door—though the three men were right behind her.

"Rose!" she called out upon entering the front hall. She pushed wet coils of hair from her face. "Rose, we have unexpected visitors."

She did not want Rose to be surprised by the appearance of the men. And she had half-hoped that, with such an announcement, Rose's meek nature might cause her to withdraw and hide away in some room. Instead, at once Rose emerged from the little parlor.

"Ivy, there you are!" she cried, rushing into the front hall with a hurricane lamp in hand. "Is it Mr. Samonds you've brought, and his aunt? I was so worried when I couldn't find you anywhere in the—oh!" She stopped short, and her brown eyes grew large as she took in the sight of Ivy's rain-soaked gown and the three be-draggled soldiers.

Ivy took a step toward her sister, forcing herself to speak in a calm, reassuring tone. "Rose, we have visitors, as you can see. They are damp from the rain and hungry. We'll light a fire here. You go to the kitchen and put on a pot for tea. And set out the ham. When I'm done, I'll come to cut it and make the biscuits."

Rose stood frozen, clutching the lamp, staring at the soldiers. Thunder shook the windows as the rain began to sheet down outside.

"It's all right, Rose," Ivy said slowly. "Go on now."

A flash of lightning, and another peal of thunder, seemed to jolt Rose out of her paralysis. Without a word, she turned and departed the hall.

The corporal gave a low whistle. "She seems a bit simple, that one. All the same, she's near as pretty as you are, ma'am. Is that your sister, then? But where are the servants, and where's the man of the house?"

Ivy kept her chin high, but despite all her best efforts, she could not mask the horror and sorrow that were surely apparent on her face. By his own expression, the corporal saw it.

"I see, so it's just the two of you," he said, and grinned.

The thick-browed man was staring in the direction Rose had gone. "I do like ham and biscuits," he said.

The corporal glared, gripping the rifle slung over his shoulder. "You'll get powder and lead in your belly, instead of ham and biscuits, if you don't get to lighting a fire. Durbent, give him some help."

The third soldier was standing by a window, near the stuffed wolf. He had said nothing up to that point, but now he turned around and spoke. "I'm not cold."

His words were slurring and indistinct. Ivy would have thought he was drunk, except the corporal had mentioned them having no whiskey in some time. Perhaps the soldier had some speech impediment. Ivy could not get a good look at him, for his hat was pulled low, casting his face in shadow.

Next to her, she heard the corporal grumble some complaint under his breath. Perhaps he was not their leader after all. The thick-necked one clearly followed the corporal's lead, but not the other. Based upon this, Ivy made a sudden, perhaps hazardous decision.

"I would not think you would tolerate such an impudent answer," she said to the corporal, keeping her voice to a conspiratorial tone. "I do not see stripes on their coats. Are you not their commander?"

The corporal gave a grunt, as if she had prodded some sore spot. "He's not himself, that's all. He went missing in the rain the other night. He was gone until the following umbral. We thought rebels had gotten him, or he'd skipped out on us. By the time we found him, he was wandering about like his brain was addled. I think he's caught a fever, or some ague or such."

Suddenly the wiry man scowled at her, as if realizing she had induced him to confide too much. "You should keep your opinions to yourself, ma'am. Preswyn!" He barked this last to the ox-necked man. "Get that fire going. I'll keep the ladies company while they fix our dinner."

IVY MOVED STIFFLY to the kitchen while the corporal followed behind her, his hand still on his rifle. As they entered the kitchen, Rose gazed at them with a white face, standing frozen by the table. She had done as Ivy had instructed, and had set out the ham while a kettle steamed on the stove. Once again, Ivy was struck by Rose's bravery.

"Thank you, dearest," she said to Rose as she went to the table.

"Ivy, I'm frightened," Rose whispered. "Who are these men?"

"They are soldiers," Ivy said more loudly, knowing the corporal was listening. "Soldiers from Lord Valhaine's army."

Rose shook her head. "But what are they doing here?"

That was a good question. Ivy glanced at the corporal.

Again the wiry little man scowled. "We got separated from our company in a skirmish. It was as fierce a battle as you can conceive. There were rebel dogs around us, and they cut us off from the rest. We're lucky to have our lives, but we're behind the lines now. So we're keeping low until we can get out of . . . that is, until we can join up with our company again."

Ivy suspected there was some truth to the corporal's tale. That there had been a skirmish with rebels, she was sure. Just as she was sure that the three soldiers had not gotten cut off from their company, but rather had seized the opportunity to flee in the chaos of battle. They were deserters.

She made no answer, and only looked at him. By his grimace, he could see in her expression that she knew the truth of it.

"Get those biscuits cooking," he said. "We're half to starving."

He sat in a chair by the wall with his rifle across his knees and kept his gaze on the two sisters. Under these awful circumstances, Ivy prepared the meal. She cut slices from the ham and put them in a pan to fry, and mixed the flour for biscuits. When things were nearly ready, she instructed Rose to put cups on a tray. Rose did this, though the porcelain clattered for the way her hands were shaking.

"You can bring all that to the front hall and serve us," the corporal said when the trays of tea and food were ready. "I'll take the whiskey myself."

"Rose, please hand the corporal the whiskey bottle," Ivy said.

Rose took the bottle from the shelf and brought it to the corporal. At the same moment, Ivy bent to pick up one of the trays, then paused as a flash of metal caught her eye. It was the sharp knife she had used to carve the ham, lying on the table.

She cast a quick glance up. The corporal was uncorking the whiskey. As he tilted the bottle back to take a swig, Ivy made a swift motion. By the time he lowered the bottle, she had picked up the tray of ham and biscuits.

The knife was no longer on the table.

"Carry the tea tray, Rose," Ivy said, and started from the kitchen. Rose followed after, moving slowly so as not to spill anything, and the corporal came behind them.

They entered the front hall just as another clap of thunder rattled the windowpanes. Preswyn was warming his hands before the fire that now roared on the hearth. The thick-necked man had built it up to what Ivy thought was a dangerous height, and sparks leaped out into the room. The other, Durbent, still stood by a window, gazing out into the rain. His head was cocked to one side, as if he were listening to something—though what could be heard above the storm, Ivy could not imagine. She set the tray of food down on an end table, and Rose did likewise with the tea things.

"Go on and fix up some plates for us, then," the corporal said, sitting down near the fire.

Aware of the rifle he had propped by his chair, Ivy prepared three plates, and brought them to each of the men. The corporal and Preswyn both snatched the plates from her, and at once began to wolf down their food. But the other man, Durbent, did not even turn to look at Ivy as she approached. She set the plate on the window ledge by him. As she did, she caught an unpleasant odor, like the scent of spoiled meat.

Hastily, she retreated. In the meantime, Rose had poured three cups of tea.

"Put some of this in those cups," the corporal said, holding out the whiskey bottle.

Rose only stared, so Ivy hurriedly went to him and took the bottle.

"And don't be stingy with it!"

Ivy followed these orders, giving each cup a generous pour. Rose took a cup to Preswyn and the corporal, moving with exceeding care so as not to spill a drop. When she approached Durbent, though, she gave a sudden cry. The cup fell from her hands and shattered against the floor with a loud noise that made all of them jump.

All except for Durbent, who continued to gaze out the window, his head still tilted to one side.

"She's pretty enough, but she's a clumsy one," the corporal said with a snort. "Well, Durbent doesn't seem to care that his cup is gone. Don't waste any more whiskey on him. Now sit while we eat."

Ivy and Rose did as they were told, sitting on a horsehair sofa while the fire crackled on the grate, and Preswyn and the corporal ate ham and biscuits with great energy.

"Ivy," Rose whispered faintly beside her.

Ivy kept staring forward, her hands on her knees, trying to do nothing to divert the corporal's attention from his dinner.

"What is it, dearest?" she whispered in return.

"There's something wrong with him—the man over by the window. I can see it all around his edges."

Alarm surged up in Ivy's throat. "You mean you see a light around him?"

"No, it's not light."

Ivy's dread ebbed a fraction. She had feared perhaps the man was a magician—one who served the Ashen. "Then what do you see, dearest?" she whispered as the men continued to eat.

"It's like a shadow around him. I can hardly see him for it, like he's all wrapped in a cloak. Only it's more than that." A shiver passed through her. "It eats the firelight."

Now fear flooded through Ivy again, even though she didn't know exactly what Rose meant. Or didn't she? She felt a crawling on the back of her neck. An image flashed through her mind, a fragment of a dream—two figures on a sandy shoreline, struggling. One struck another's head with a stone. But it was not blood that flowed forth. . . .

Before she even thought what she was doing, Ivy stood and went to the tray of food. She took up the plate of ham, as well as the object that had been hidden underneath.

It was the carving knife.

Keeping the knife concealed beneath the plate, Ivy went to the corporal and Preswyn, offering them more meat, which they readily accepted. Then she approached the third soldier by the window.

"Do you have enough to eat?"

He did not acknowledge her, but kept his face turned toward

the rain-speckled glass. Was he looking for something out in the gloom? One of his hands rested on the window ledge, next to the plate of uneaten food. It was filthy with grime, and his fingernails were ragged and torn.

Beneath the plate she carried, Ivy gripped the knife. Slowly, she extended it outward, until the tip was but inches from his hand. Her heart was laboring in her chest. She took in a breath, and again caught the foul odor of something rotting. Then, before she could lose her will, she made a quick motion, flicking out with the knife.

The soldier, Durbent, did not flinch or move. Ivy watched as the skin pulled back from either side of the small cut the knife had made upon the back of his hand, like a lipless mouth opening. For a moment, nothing at all issued from the gap in his skin.

Then, slowly, a thin trickle of grayish fluid welled forth.

Ivy staggered backward, retreating toward the fire, only belatedly thinking to hide the knife again under the plate. The other men seemed not to notice, for they were still busily eating. The flesh upon Ivy's neck was crawling, and she felt a sickness in her stomach. She set the plate and knife back down with a clatter.

The corporal looked up with a frown. "I guess being clumsy runs in the family. Since you're there, bring me that whiskey."

Ivy took up the bottle and brought it to the wiry man. She doubted she would be able to pour it for the way she was shaking, but the corporal grabbed the bottle himself and filled his cup from it. He did not ask for more tea.

Ivy returned to the sofa and sat. Rose's hand groped for hers, and their fingers twined together.

"But you're shivering so!" Rose said quietly. "What is it, Ivy?"

What was it indeed, Ivy wondered, that was standing over there next to the window? What had happened to Durbent in those hours he had been separated from his companions? She thought of the things that Mr. Rafferdy had told her once, of the hideous transformations that had been wrought upon some young magicians, including Lord Eubrey.

Beside the fire, the corporal let out a great belch, then put his empty plate on the floor. Ivy had never seen a small, thin man eat so much. He drained his cup, then sloshed more whiskey into it from the bottle.

"Well, we've had a fire, food, and drink," he said. "All we need now is some companionship. Some womanly companionship. Wouldn't you say so, Preswyn?"

The bigger man had been prodding the fire with a poker, and his face was flushed red from the heat of the fire on the hearth. Or was it from another kind of fire? For he gazed intently at Ivy and Rose upon the sofa.

"But there's only the two of them," he said, laying the poker down on the hearth, its tip still in the coals. "And we are three."

"Well, I don't think Durbent much cares," the corporal said. His words were mushy and indistinct; the whiskey had affected him. "He's got some ague or something after his travails out in the night, and he's not fit for it. No, the only question is who gets which one."

Preswyn licked his lips. "They're both pretty."

"So they are." The corporal lurched up from his chair. "But the light-haired one's the prettiest, so she'll keep me company. You can have the other one, Preswyn."

"I can do anything I want with her, you mean?"

"Anything that stupid mind of yours can think of," the corporal said. He picked up his rifle and started toward the sofa.

New terror came over Ivy. The men had been fed, yet still there was a hunger in their eyes. Their intentions could only lie in one direction, and while Ivy's own person was surely in danger, it was only Rose whom she could think of. That either of them should lay a hand upon Rose was something that could not be allowed. But Ivy had left the carving knife under the plate; if she tried to dash over to get it, they would stop her.

If only there were some piece of Wyrdwood in the room, even the smallest bit. But there was no Wyrdwood anywhere in the manor house, except for the broken remains of the chair Mr. Samonds had made up in the attic.

No, that wasn't true. There *was* Wyrdwood in the house.

"I will give you the jewels!" Ivy cried out. "I will tell you where they are if you take them and go!"

Rose turned her head to stare at her, but Ivy tightened her grip on Rose's hand, squeezing it.

The corporal came to a stop before her, and his small eyes narrowed. "Jewels? What sort of jewels?"

"I am a lady, the wife of a well-to-do baronet. When I fled the city, I brought all my finest jewels with me, of course. They are in the parlor there. Look for a wooden box on the top shelf of the bookcase in the corner. Take the jewels, then go. You will be wealthy enough to buy anything you should ever want."

"So you're a lady, you say?" He did not sound entirely convinced, but all the same there was another sort of hunger in his eyes now. "Preswyn, go see if you can find that box. I'll keep an eye on the ladies here. And if she's lied, and there's no box of jewels— well, it will go rough for them."

He picked up his rifle and stood before the sofa, while Preswyn disappeared through the parlor. Ivy and Rose both sat motionless. The room was sweltering from the fire, but Ivy could not stop shivering. Her eyes kept going back to the rifle; more than once the corporal's finger caressed the trigger. At last, Preswyn returned to the front hall.

In his hands was the Wyrdwood box.

"I can't open it," he said, his single eyebrow drawn down in a glower. "The lid is locked. Or stuck, I mean, as I can't see no lock on it." He gave the box a violent shake.

"Stop that, you half-wit!" the corporal snapped. "If there are fine things in there, you'll break them doing that. Bring it over here."

Preswyn lumbered over with the box and held it out. The corporal sat, laid his rifle across his knees, and reached out to take the box. For a moment, both Preswyn's and the corporal's hands rested on the box.

That was the moment Ivy had been waiting for. She darted out a hand and touched the Wyrdwood box.

Bind them, she spoke in her mind.

Preswyn let out a bellowing cry and staggered back away from the sofa. As he did, he hauled the corporal up and out of the chair, for their hands were now bound together by bands of wood. Even as the men struggled to pull apart, brown tendrils coiled up their wrists and around their forearms. The rifle had fallen to the floor.

"It's alive, it's alive!" Preswyn wailed, flailing back and forth. Such was the big man's strength that these actions whipped the smaller corporal around like a ball at the end of a tether. Sheafs of paper fluttered around them, having been released as the box lost its shape and form.

"Stop it, you ox!" the corporal shouted, but Preswyn only let out another howl and spun around. As he did, the legs of the two men tangled together, and they toppled to the floor in a heap.

Ivy did not hesitate. She leaped from the sofa, then snatched up the rifle from the floor. It was heavy, but terror lent her strength. While never before in her life had she held a gun of any sort, she had seen it done enough times that she had a sense of what to do. She pointed the barrel at the two men, then put her thumb on the hammer, pulling it back.

At the telltale click of metal, the two men ceased their struggles and looked up at her. The rifle wavered in her hand, but it did not matter. At such close range, her aim hardly needed to be precise. She rested her finger on the trigger.

On the floor, Preswyn's eyes went wide, then turned to slits. "By God, you're a witch," he snarled. "You're a filthy witch."

Ivy directed the barrel of the rifle at his chest. "Don't move."

Not that they could have. The twigs that had previously made up the Wyrdwood box now bound their wrists and ankles like thin but strong cords. Some of the tendrils began to writhe and probe upward, reaching toward their necks. Preswyn was sobbing now, and the corporal's face was a grimace of pain. Then, all at once, his grimace became a smile.

"Ivy!" Rose cried out.

Ivy turned around, still gripping the rifle, and her heart ceased to beat. Durbent no longer stood by the window. Instead, he was striding rapidly across the front hall, coming directly toward her. In the brilliant firelight, she could finally see beneath the brim of his hat. His face was gray and strangely slack; his eyes were as flat and dead as stones.

"Witch," he hissed in that strange, slurring voice. He reached his hands out before him as he closed the last distance.

There was a flash of light and a loud noise like a clap of thunder. Ivy let out a gasp and staggered backward as the butt of the rifle struck her shoulder. The rifle fell from her numb fingers and clattered to the floor. For a moment she could see nothing for the haze of smoke; then enough of it was drawn up the chimney that she could see again.

Durbent lay sprawled on his back before the fireplace, staring upward with unblinking eyes. In the center of his chest was a wet, gaping hole. Ivy let out a moan, staggering back—

—and strong hands clamped around her.

"It was papers, not jewels," the corporal's voice sneered into her ear, and his sour breath washed over. "You lied to us, witch."

His wiry arms tightened around her, just as the Wyrdwood had previously coiled around him. In her terror at the sight of Durbent, Ivy had ceased calling out to the Wyrdwood, directing it. The bonds must have weakened enough for the corporal and Preswyn to break free.

Now Preswyn lumbered forward to where Durbent lay motionless. "Oh God, she shot him," Preswyn moaned. "She shot him dead." He went down on one knee beside Durbent's body, then reached out to touch the wound in his chest.

Preswyn snatched his hand back. "This isn't . . . what is this?" He stared at his hand; it was covered with a grayish ichor.

Before anyone could answer him, Durbent sat up. Then, moving swiftly, almost mechanically, he stood.

"Durbent, you're all right!" Preswyn cried out, lurching to his own feet.

Durbent did not look at him. Instead, almost casually, as if to simply push him aside for being in the way, he reached out and struck Preswyn in the center of the chest.

There was an awful crunching noise, like a porcelain cup being ground beneath a boot heel. Preswyn made a gurgling sound, and a flood of red gushed out of his mouth. He crumpled to the floor and did not move.

Durbent stepped over the corpse.

"Bloody Abyss," the corporal shouted and flung Ivy away from him. He drew his pistol. "Have you gone mad, Durbent? Preswyn was an idiot, but you had no reason to murder him! Or do you want her for yourself, then?"

Durbent said nothing. He kept walking toward them, his face without expression.

"Stop there!" the corporal yelled. "That's an order!"

Durbent took another step. The corporal fired the pistol, and again. Two more holes opened in Durbent's chest, but he did not stop. Before the corporal could get off a third shot, Durbent clamped his hands upon either side of the corporal's skull.

The struggle was violent but brief. The corporal writhed and twitched for only a few moments. Then Durbent's thumbs drove deep into the sockets of his eyes, and beyond. The corporal went limp, and Durbent let his lifeless remains drop to the floor.

Ivy stumbled back, then fell onto the sofa beside Rose. They held on to each other, beyond any capacity for speech or action. Durbent left the body of the corporal and approached the sofa. Amid the various altercations, some of the dirt had been wiped from his hands, and Ivy could just make out the black, angular symbol drawn upon the left. In that moment, while he continued to move, Ivy knew that Durbent was as dead as Preswyn and the corporal—that he had been ever since he had gotten lost in the night, and had been captured by magicians who served the Ashen. They had formed him into a weapon to serve the cause of their masters.

And now he was going to do just that.

"Witch," he said again, and reached out bloodstained hands.

Ivy held Rose tightly. She shut her eyes and thought, *Let it be swift!*

Only the blow she expected did not come. Instead, there was a hissing and popping sound, like that which the ham had made in the frying pan. Ivy opened her eyes and tried to comprehend what she saw. The glowing red tip of the poker that had been lying on the hearth now protruded from Durbent's throat, smoking as it did.

Abruptly the poker was withdrawn, and Durbent fell to his knees. A pair of hands manifested from the shadows. They wrapped around Durbent's head, then twisted it around on his shoulders. Farther his head turned, and farther still, until all at once it came free of his shoulders with a wet noise. Then both head and body fell to the floor, more of the gray fluid seeping from each, while the two sisters looked on in mute horror.

The shadows behind the body undulated, then approached. Only they weren't shadows at all, but rather folds of stiff black silk. Nor were the two pale hands disembodied entities; instead, they protruded from the sleeves of a black gown. The hands rose up and pushed back a veil, revealing the hard, white oval of a woman's face.

And Lady Shayde said, "Was either of you harmed?"

A HALF HOUR LATER found Ivy and Rose in the little parlor.

Ivy lit a candle, even though several already burned around the room. The storm had not relented, and it had grown so dark outside the windows that she wondered if an umbral was falling. The thought of it made her shudder. All her life, Ivy had ever loathed that moment when night fell and light succumbed to dark. Yet it was even more awful now that she knew what it was that dwelled in the empty spaces between the planets.

And knowing that, once night fell, day might never come again.

The flame flared atop the candle, and the gloom reluctantly

retreated a fraction. In the corner of the parlor, Rose sat in a chair, cradling the porcelain doll tightly with both arms. She was rocking softly, and her lips moved as if she was singing a lullaby. Only she made no sound.

"Are you warm, dearest?" Ivy said, adjusting the blanket she had thrown over her sister's shoulders.

Rose hunched over the doll and continued to rock in the chair. She had not uttered a word since they had departed the front hall. Her brown eyes were open wide, though they seemed to gaze at nothing.

Ivy tried to think of what she might say to encourage a response from her sister, but before she could there came a noise from behind her: a crinkling of stiff fabric. Quickly, she turned around.

"It is done," Lady Shayde said, standing in the door of the parlor. "The remains have been removed from the house."

Ivy struggled to swallow. "All . . . all three of them?"

"Yes."

Ivy could scarcely comprehend this. Lady Shayde was tall for a woman, but her figure was slender within her gown: a thing of lines and angles rather than full curves. By what unnatural strength had she been able to remove the bodies of three grown men from the house?

It did not matter; Ivy did not want to know. There were already mysteries enough for her to consider—not the least of which was why this pale being had done what she had, or why she should even be here.

Lady Shayde entered the parlor. Her dress was perfectly creased, as if she had not just been hauling corpses about.

"Is your sister well?" she said, her words just as crisp.

"Is she well?" Ivy might have laughed at the absurdity of this statement, were she not so gripped by horror. She crossed the parlor and lowered her voice. "How can Rose possibly be well? What she has witnessed can only have inflicted a profound shock upon her."

That white face, those black eyes and blue-black lips, were

without expression. "And what of you, Lady Quent? Did you not witness the same scene yourself?"

Ivy shook her head. "My sister has lived a quiet and protected life. She has never seen things such as this before. She has never seen . . . a death."

"But you have," Shayde replied, and in her black eyes was what seemed a knowing look.

A pain pierced Ivy's heart. Was the other inflicting a deliberate cruelty? Did she know about the magickal gem, and what scene its facets had revealed? She tried to draw a breath, but it was difficult to breathe.

"I must go into . . . into the hall. There is something I . . ."

But she could manage no more. She edged past the other woman, then hurried to the front hall. The bodies of the men were indeed gone, as Lady Shayde had said, though several wet stains still marred the floor. Ivy did her best to ignore these, and instead knelt to gather up the papers that had been scattered when the Wyrdwood box came apart.

As important as these objects were, there had been something of greater value in the box. Then she pushed aside a heap of broken sticks, and there it was: her father's journal, bound in black leather. She picked it up, clasping it to her breast as she stood.

"It was something precious, then," Lady Shayde said. She stood at the end of the long room, half-revealed in the dying light of the fire.

"Yes," Ivy said before she even thought to, then winced. Stories told of the White Lady's fabled power to compel others to speak, and Ivy had suffered it herself when Shayde came to interview her. She had to be careful what she said.

Only why? What use was there resisting anymore? They were under Shayde's power now; Ivy could not win a struggle against her—at least not unless they were within a grove of Wyrdwood.

"It's my father's journal," she said, still clutching the book. "It was in the box he gave me."

Shayde's dark lips moved a fraction, forming what almost

seemed the shadow of a smile—if she was really capable of such an expression. "Ah, the Wyrdwood box. That was clever of you, to identify the base desires of your attackers and play upon them. I was impressed by that, Lady Quent. You would have made a fine agent of the Gray Conclave."

Ivy stared in astonishment—not from this last statement, as shocking as it was, but from the ones preceding it. "It was you!" she gasped. "You were the shadow I saw from the attic. But you weren't just outside, were you? You were here in the manor." Ivy staggered, holding a hand to her brow. "How long were you in this room, watching?"

Shayde stepped into the firelight. "Do not fear. I would not have allowed those men to harm you or your sister. Yet you hardly needed my assistance. I can see why Sir Quent admired you so deeply as he did. You are a very capable woman, Lady Quent. You would have been able to dispatch all of the soldiers on your own, had not one of them been a . . . well, I still do not know what such things are called. But you saw what he was. Even then, you would have been successful had you but aimed for his head. It is the only way to dispatch their kind, to remove their heads from their bodies. But you could not possibly have known this."

Couldn't she have? Ivy thought of her dream, of the men struggling on the beach. But none of that mattered; she faced a different peril now.

"How did you know to find me here?" she said carefully.

"I was there at your house on Durrow Street," Lady Shayde said. "The day the soldiers came for you. I heard you say to Lord Rafferdy and his friend, the illusionist, that you would go to Heathcrest Hall."

Some of Ivy's horror was replaced by wonder. "So you were there as well. It was you the soldiers glimpsed out the window, in the garden. You lured them from the house so that Rose and I were able to escape."

"Yes, I did. Once the soldiers left the house, I told them you had fled in a carriage and ordered them to pursue you. Then I entered the house again, and I saw you step through the door, the one carved with leaves. That it was magickal in nature was apparent."

She took another step deeper into the pool of firelight. "I thought to follow you at that moment, but Lord Rafferdy had locked the door with some manner of key and gave it to the illusionist." She made a little shrug. "I could easily have taken it from him, of course, but I would not have known how to pursue you in the place where you had gone, and I might easily have become lost in the world beyond the door. So I decided I should travel overland instead. This was somewhat difficult, given the state of affairs in the country, but there was nothing that could prevent my passage. I arrived here over a half month ago, and have been watching the manor ever since."

Amid all the feelings that twisted and tangled in Ivy's breast, fascination rose up among them. "But why? Why have you followed me here?"

"I wanted to help you," Lady Shayde said.

Ivy sprang back a step; it felt as if sparks had leaped out of the fireplace and had alighted all over her. "To help me!" she cried. "How can you possibly claim to want such a thing after what you have done to me—after what you did to my husband with your own hands?"

For a moment, a discernible change altered the white mask of Lady Shayde's face. It was a tightening of flesh, a sharpening of lines, and a deepening of hollows. Ivy might almost have thought it an expression of pain. Except that was not possible, for surely *she* could not feel.

Then the moment passed, and Lady Shayde's face became utterly smooth once more. "I did what I was required to do."

"That is a lie," Ivy said, clenching her hands at her sides. "You wanted to destroy the Inquiry, to stop them from doing their work of safeguarding the Wyrdwood and the women who were drawn to it. And with my husband imprisoned, you had done so. There was no further gain to be achieved with his death. You did not have to murder him. But you did anyway—you did it because you hated him."

"Hated him?" The other woman shook her head. "No, I did not hate Sir Quent. As I have told you, hate is not a thing which I can suffer."

"Nor compassion!" Ivy exclaimed, her throat aching.

"That is true. I cannot feel compassion. Or happiness, desire, sorrow, or love—not any of these. I remember that I did feel such things once, but I cannot recall the feelings themselves. Such things were taken from me when I was made into . . . this." She lifted a white hand.

This answer in no way satisfied Ivy. "Then it was your master who ordered you to do it."

"I was indeed ordered to take Sir Quent's life. But it was not Lord Valhaine who gave me the command that I was bound to obey."

"Then who was it?" Ivy cried, the words hoarse and ragged from rage, from grief. "Who commanded you to do murder upon my husband?"

Lady Shayde lowered her hand. "It was Sir Quent himself who did."

How it was that Ivy did not collapse to the floor was a thing she did not understand. One moment Lady Shayde seemed to vanish from the far side of the hall. Then, in the space between two heart-beats, she was there beside Ivy, supporting her with cold, hard hands, and helping her into a chair.

For a dreadful span of seconds, she feared she could no longer breathe, that she had forgotten how to accomplish such a basic act. She wanted to cry out, to accuse Lady Shayde of lying. But it wasn't a lie, was it? She had seen it herself within the gem: how some exchange had passed between them, some agreement, and how he had knelt before her willingly.

At last a breath shuddered into her, burning her lungs as if she had taken in fire not air. More breaths passed in and out of her in jolting spasms; a flood of hot tears ran down her cheeks. She was weeping.

"Why?" she managed to say at last. There was so much more she wanted to ask, but all she could do was utter the word again. "Why?"

Lady Shayde was a black silhouette, standing before the fireplace. "Why did he ask me to end his life—is that what you mean? But you must know the reason for that, Lady Quent. There was never any hope that he would live. From the moment he chose to make a treaty with the witch in Torland, his doom was sealed, and he knew it.

"When I came to him in his cell, it was to tell him that he was to be tried, convicted, and hung that very day. With the grave defeat in the West Country, Lord Valhaine felt a great need to make some public demonstration of his strength and authority. But by asking me to end him, Sir Quent stole that victory from Lord Valhaine. What was more, he was assured that you, Lady Quent, would never be branded as the wife of a convicted traitor, and so deprived of all of his wealth and property, which should naturally have passed to you upon his death, having no other heir."

Ivy could only shake her head, unable to speak. It was too horrible to bear, the knowledge that he had done it for *her* sake.

"Is that what you meant, Lady Quent?" The other woman gave a shrug. "Or perhaps you meant, why did I do as Sir Quent asked of me there in his cell beneath Barrowgate? The reason is simple enough—it is because I made a promise to him long ago. In fact, it was here in this very room that the oath was made, more than twenty years ago. It was the very last day that I ever looked so."

She gestured to the staircase in the center of the hall, and to the portrait that hung above the landing. Earl Rylend, his wife, and their son, Lord Wilden, dominated the middle of the painting, while off to the side, nearly merging with the shadows, was a girl with dark hair and almond skin.

"Sir Quent was waiting for me that day when I came down the stairs. Of course, he was only Alasdare to me then. Or Dare, as I called him. He tried to stop me from going to the elf circle, where Mr. Bennick was waiting for me. I told Dare that if he would let me go, then one day he could ask anything of me, and I would do it without hesitation. I swore this to him, and he knew me well enough to know that I meant it. And so he let me go.

"Nor did anyone else in the household try to prevent me. Lord Wilden was dead; he had perished attempting a spell that was beyond him—which, despite all his tutoring by Mr. Bennick, all but the simplest of incantations were. Preoccupied with his grief, Earl Rylend had paid me no attention since his son's death, and Lady Rylend never did. And so, once Dare let me pass, there was no one to stop me from going to Mr. Bennick." She turned away from the painting. "And I did."

Ivy wiped her cheeks with the back of her hand, and she struggled to understand. Mr. Quent had only ever spoken of Ashaydea's transformation at the hands of Mr. Bennick with regret and sorrow. She could not imagine why he would willingly allow her to go to the elf circle, even if he had not fully understood at the time what Mr. Bennick planned. After all, with Lord Wilden dead, he had to know Mr. Bennick was perilous, and the two had been close since childhood. His father had served the earl, and she had been the earl's ward. From an early age, Alasdare Quent and Ashaydea Rylend had been playmates, and then they had grown up together. Given his character, it was inconceivable to her that, as a young man, Mr. Quent would simply abandon his childhood companion to an awful fate, unless—

Ivy's eyes went wide, and she sat up straight in the chair.

"You loved him," she whispered. "You loved Alasdare, only he did not return it. Not in that way, at least. For he did love you, as he fondly would a sister. But not in the way which you dreamed."

"You have keen powers of deduction, Lady Quent. Were I capable of a more usual sensibility, I suppose I would be mortified or weep with regret. But I am not. I know that I was infatuated with him as a girl, and that as a young woman I loved him—though I cannot recall what it was like to feel that love. Yet I can remember with clarity how, when I finally professed my affections to him on the same day Lord Wilden perished, he seemed puzzled by the idea.

"Nor, over those days that followed, did Dare seek me out or approach me. Thus, having been abandoned by the man whom I wanted, I resolved instead to go to the man who had a want for *me*. For Mr. Bennick had made it clear to me more than once that I was a proper candidate for an enchantment he wished to work. Dare did come to me then. But I think he knew he could not stop me from going to Mr. Bennick, not when he had refused me himself—not unless he had changed his mind on the matter. But he had not. A heart, as I know through observation—if no longer through experience—is not a thing to be easily altered; it beats in what direction it will. And so I went to the elf circle, and gave myself up to Mr. Bennick and his spells, and became what you see before you today."

That a tale of such sorrow, such pain, and such dreadful consequence should be told so flatly, and without any expression of real feeling or emotion, made it seem all the more terrible. Nor did Ivy doubt any of it. More than once she had seen the regret written upon Mr. Quent's face when he spoke of Lady Shayde—of Ashaydea. He could only have been all too aware that, had he but professed a love for her that day, her fate would have been entirely different than it was.

Only he had not loved her, at least not in that manner. Nor did Lady Shayde seem to lay blame upon him for that fact. A heart, as she had said, beats in what direction it will.

Yet what of Ashaydea's heart now? Did it not continue to function within her, however cold the blood that passed through it? Given the relentless and singular determination she had applied to her work with the Gray Conclave, in direct opposition to the labors of the Inquiry, it seemed difficult to believe she had not possessed some desire for vengeance against Mr. Quent.

Or had she?

Ivy found herself thinking of *The Towers of Ardaunto,* the book penned by Mr. Fintaur, who had surely met Ashaydea and must have known of Mr. Bennick's intention to create a White Thorn of his own.

A thorn can only pierce when it is grasped, the maiden in the story had said at the end, after plunging a knife into her lover. *Nothing can unmake me what I am.*

A thing that cannot feel cannot know what to do on its own, just as a saw or chisel cannot shape wood or stone of its own voli-tion; they required a hand to wield them. So the maiden had trav-eled to Ardaunto, to be a tool in the hand of the prince. Just as Shayde had gone to Invarel, to serve Lord Valhaine—to be a knife that he might use in any way he would. It was Valhaine's will that had directed her against the Inquiry all these years, not feelings of regret or a wish for vengeance, for she could not be affected by these things.

Upon realizing all of this, a peculiar calm came upon Ivy. Her husband was dead; here before her stood his murderer. Yet Shayde could be faulted for his death no more than a pistol could be faulted for the demise of a man who was shot by it. Neither thing had the desire for murder—only the mechanical and merciless capability for it.

Yet this new understanding only begged a new question. If Lady Shayde was the Black Dog's weapon, then why was that weapon here?

"Have you come here to kill me as well?" Ivy said. And it was strange, as she said this, that she felt almost more curiosity than dread.

Lady Shadye walked slowly to the stuffed wolf on its pedestal, the stiff fabric of her dress crackling like the now-dying fire. "You are not employing your talent for reason, Lady Quent."

"No, you cannot have come for that," Ivy said after a moment, forcing herself to think it through. "If you had come here for the purpose of murdering me, you could have let the . . . the gray man do it. Nor could you have wanted to save the deed for yourself, since it could not possibly have granted you any personal satisfac-tion to do it. If your duty was to see that I was killed, any way it was done would be as good as the next."

"Yes, that is so. Go on."

Ivy gripped the arms of the chair as if to anchor herself. "It might be your purpose to bring me back to Invarel. After all, Valhaine had dispatched soldiers to arrest me under suspicion of being a witch. He must have done that once he learned my husband was beyond him, thinking perhaps he could have some other public victory to display that day. Only that can't be it either. For you could simply have allowed the soldiers to capture me in Invarel. Instead, you misdirected them so that I might flee."

"Again, Lady Quent, your logic is sound."

Yes, it was sound. Indeed, there was only one conclusion Ivy could infer from everything that had happened. Yet it was so absurd as to be impossible. All the same, Ivy could only admit it must be the case, for no other conclusion could be reached from what she knew and what she had seen.

"You've come to help me," she said, astonished by her own words.

"Yes, I have," Lady Shayde replied. "But do you know why?"

Here the path of Ivy's reasoning ended. "No, I don't," she murmured.

Lady Shayde rested a hand upon the coarse gray fur of the wolf's back. "For twenty years, I served Lord Valhaine without question. No matter his command, I performed it without hesitation—without any deliberation upon the matter of whether it was right or wrong. A wolf does not ask if its prey deserves to be hunted, and neither did I."

"But why Valhaine?" Ivy asked, for she could only be fascinated by these words. "Why did you not serve Mr. Bennick when it was he who made you into a White Thorn?"

"Yes, it was Mr. Bennick who, taking advantage of Earl Rylend's interest in magick, convinced the earl to arrange for the old elf circle to be rebuilt. It was Mr. Bennick who researched the ancient spells and runes, and who convinced me to go there. But for all his preparations, something went awry in the working of the enchantment.

"What it was, I do not know—some flaw in the reconstruction

of the circle, perhaps, or an error in his research. Whatever the reason, the arcane powers surged beyond his ability to control them, and the stones cracked and toppled down around us. Only by terrible effort did he complete the ritual and prevent us both from perishing. When all was done, the spell was complete, and I had been remade as you see me. But the stone circle was in ruins, as was Mr. Bennick. His body was shattered, and his capacity for magick was utterly removed from him, never to return."

Ivy sat up straight in the chair, surprised by this revelation. She had always believed it was her father's old magickal society, the Vigilant Order of the Silver Eye, that had taken Mr. Bennick's magickal powers from him, as a punishment for betraying the order and attempting to steal the Eye of Ran-Yahgren. But Gambrel had said that was not the case, and it seemed he had been speaking the truth.

"In any struggle, a knife will inevitably find its way from the hand of the weaker to that of the stronger," Lady Shayde said, stroking the wolf's pelt. "Even as he slowly began to rebuild his health, Mr. Bennick remained but a shadow of the powerful magician he once was. A blacksmith might forge a marvelous sword, but that does not mean he is a knight worthy of swinging it in battle. So it was with Mr. Bennick and I. He might have fashioned me, but I required a stronger hand to wield me. So it was, in little time, I found my way to Invarel, and into the service of Lord Valhaine."

"But no more," Ivy said, rising up from the chair. "You cannot be here upon his order. Which means you serve him no longer."

"As I said, Lady Quent, a weapon will inevitably find its way to the stronger party. And over the course of this last year Lord Valhaine has . . ." Lady Shayde withdrew her hand and turned her back to the wolf. "He has grown weak and confused. Previously, it was his own vision for Altania that drove his actions. But month after month, I have watched the High Order of the Golden Door— the magicians who were purportedly his servants—turn him into their slave. How they have done this, through words or spells or some other occult influence, I do not know. But he is their plaything now, hardly more than a babbling simpleton, and is completely in their thrall. All that he does now, he does because it is *their* will, not his."

Ivy could only shudder at this. Not only had Mr. Gambrel escaped from the way station upon Tyberion, as the magus of the High Order of the Golden Door he now had complete influence over the most powerful man in Altania aside from Huntley Morden.

Carefully, she considered her next words. "If these magicians of the Golden Door have become so strong as to hold sway over your master, why did you not simply serve them instead?"

Lady Shayde nodded. "Yes, of course, I considered this. But then I rejected it. For even as Lord Valhaine had become their slave, they in turn are slaves of another, far greater power—one that, I have learned in my investigations, hails from beyond the very boundaries of this world."

"The Ashen," Ivy said, unable to prevent herself.

"Yes, the Ashen. They who are stronger than any in the realms of mankind."

"If they are so powerful as this," Ivy said, whispering now, "why do you not serve them? Is that not what you seek—to be wielded by the strongest hand, and so have the greatest force?"

Lady Shayde took a step toward her. "I told you before that I cannot suffer feelings, Lady Quent. But that is not entirely true. In general, it is in fact the case. Yet there is one sensation which I can experience, though only in certain instances. It occurs only when I am directly confronted by some power of the Ashen, or a daemon of their making. I felt it even as the gray man attacked you."

"And what did you feel?" Ivy breathed.

"I felt a fury," Lady Shayde replied, her dark eyes catching the dying firelight.

Ivy gasped. In that moment an image came to her—an image from the dream about the people in the cave. She recalled the pale woman clad in dark leathers, and how her arms had been like scythes, reaping the snarling shadows all around, and casting them down.

"What is it?" Lady Shayde took another step closer. "You know something about this, Lady Quent. I can see it upon your face."

Ivy shook her head. "I'm not sure. . . ."

"But you are sure," Lady Shayde said, moving another step. "You have great powers of reasoning, Lady Quent. And you have great power of will—I saw that for myself when I offered you a chance to free your husband, if only you would betray Lord Rafferdy. But you would not."

Another step.

"But there is more to you yet, Lady Quent. You have a mastery over the Wyrdwood—a thing which the Ashen and those magicians who serve them loathe and fear. Indeed, from the magicians of the Golden Door, we know you are a witch of especial ability. That makes you very powerful indeed. Only there is one more power that you possess, one above all others. It is knowledge. You know about things—things such as the nature of that magickal door in your house on Durrow Street, and about the Ashen themselves. How you know so much about these matters, I have not yet determined. But all the same, from your actions, it is clear that you do."

With one more step, Lady Shayde came to a halt before Ivy.

"Tell me, Lady Quent, what is it you know about me?"

Ivy shook her head again. "I'm not sure . . . it's only from a dream I've had, but . . ."

"But what?"

"I think I know what purpose the White Thorns were made for. At least in the very beginning."

A cold, white hand fell upon Ivy's arm, gripping it so hard Ivy let out a gasp of pain. The other had only to squeeze but a little more, and Ivy's bones would surely have been broken.

"Tell me," Lady Shayde said softly.

Ivy opened her mouth to speak.

"Hello?" spoke a quavering voice. "Hello, are you in here?"

As one, Ivy and Lady Shayde turned to look at the door of the little parlor. Rose had emerged from it. Her brown eyes were large in her face, and she clutched the porcelain doll in her arms.

Ivy realized the fire had died down, and the front hall was filled with a gloom. "Here, Rose," she said, stepping into the shrinking circle of firelight. "We are over here."

Rose's shoulders heaved in a visible sigh, and she hurried toward the fire. Ivy was greatly relieved to see her moving and speaking again after the shock she had suffered.

Another pale figure stepped into the circle of light, and Rose abruptly stopped, a breath escaping her parted lips.

"Good day, Miss Lockwell," Lady Shayde said and nodded.

Ivy feared that Rose would turn and flee back into the parlor. Instead, after a moment, she took several small steps, closing the last of the distance between them.

"Thank you," Rose said. "For saving us from the soldier. The one with the dark lines all around him." Then, slowly, she uncurled her arms from the porcelain doll. "I think this belongs to you."

Lady Shayde's eyes were like dark stones. "Where . . . where did you find that?"

"In a room upstairs, in a closet full of small dresses," Rose said. "I think they belonged to the girl who lived here—the girl in the picture. But you're her, aren't you?"

Lady Shayde said nothing, and Rose smoothed the doll's dress and ribbons.

"I hope you don't mind, but I touched up the paints on her face, and I sewed her a new gown from one we found in the closet upstairs. She's very beautiful, don't you think? She's been a friend to me since we came here. Only . . ." She sighed, then held the doll out before her. "I think you should have her back now."

For a long moment, Lady Shayde did not move. The last of the coals hissed and died upon the hearth. Then, slowly, Ashaydea reached out a pale hand toward the porcelain doll.

A groaning of metal hinges came into the front hall, followed by a gust of rainy air.

Lady Shayde withdrew her hand and looked up. "Someone has opened the front door of the manor."

Rose gasped, her arms going around the doll once more, and

Ivy looked toward the archway that led to the entrance of the house. Through it she could see the dull gray light of the stormy day. The door of the house had indeed been opened. But perhaps it was only the wind. . . .

The echo of boots against the slate floor came into the front hall.

What do we do? Ivy started to ask, turning to look at Lady Shayde. Only the air between Ivy and Rose was empty. Ivy looked wildly about, but she saw no one else in the gloom.

Lady Shayde was gone.

The footsteps grew louder. A moment later, a man emerged from the archway and stepped into the front hall. He carried a pistol in his hand, but he was not a soldier. Instead, he was an older man, his tall, spare frame draped with a gray suit and cape, both wet from the rain. His face was sallow, his features sharp and angular, and his eyes dark and deeply set.

These latter now turned in the direction of Ivy and Rose, even as did the barrel of the pistol. Then a smile curved the thin line of his mouth, and Ivy felt her blood congeal in her veins.

"Good day, Lady Quent," Mr. Bennick said.

CHAPTER THIRTY-THREE

NO CROWD had gathered for the hanging that day.

In the past, a throng of people would always turn out for the displays of justice before Barrowgate. Jugglers and carts selling treacle tarts would lend a carnival atmosphere. Since boyhood, Eldyn had always been astonished at how the young and old, men and women and children alike, would howl gleefully for the death of someone they did not know.

Yet in time he had come to understand. If government was the mind of Altania, arriving at verdicts and dispensing out justice based upon the cool calculations of law, then the crowds in Barrowgate represented the nation's heart. It was their fear, their hope, and their continual hunger for retribution—their desire to see someone punished for the ills that afflicted their lives—that propelled the gears of government to turn. The nation needed them, just as a brain needed hot blood to be pumped through it.

Only today, there were no throngs, and no vendors selling tarts. The people had lost their appetite for hangings, it seemed. After all, even a glutton can eat only so much, and there had been a bountiful harvest of executions of late. On some days, a score of men swung from the ropes. But today's was to be a less plenteous display. There were but four men on the gallows that morning, and none of them of any great interest—no witches or famous lords convicted of high treason by the Gray Conclave.

Given the small number of the condemned, and their low station and obscurity, the square before Barrowgate was empty of all but a few stragglers clad in dirty, ragged clothes. With so few onlookers, the number of soldiers in attendance was few as well. It was but a trio of them who marched the heavily shackled prisoners up the steps of the gibbet, where the lone hangman waited to do his work and then go home for breakfast.

"Get on up there, then," one of the redcrests barked, prodding Eldyn's back with the barrel of his rifle. "We don't have all day. Some of us have dice to roll, you know."

Eldyn stumbled, for the manacles around his wrists and ankles were heavy and painfully tight. What's more, his arms and legs had grown numb from laying for long hours in a black cell, unable to move for the chains that bound him to a ring in the floor. When the soldiers had come for him, it had been a relief. At least he was out of that fetid hole now, and would get to breathe fresh air and see light one last time before the end.

Again Eldyn tripped, but rough hands gripped him from behind, pushing him up the last wooden steps to the platform that surmounted the gallows. He was placed in position atop the trap-door, along with the three other prisoners. A noose was roughly slipped over his head and cinched around his throat so tightly he was already half-choking.

A priest in a grimy frock approached the prisoners. He mumbled some slurring words while making a few perfunctory waves of his hand before Eldyn, then moved on to do the same for the others. Once this was done, he tottered back down the wooden staircase, no doubt to return to the bottle he surely had been nursing.

The soldiers descended to the foot of the steps, while the hangman, wearing his customary hood, took his position at the lever. A scattering of onlookers, some of them swaddled in grimy rags, approached the gibbet. The prisoner to Eldyn's left was moaning some wordless plea. By the odor, the one to his right had pissed his pants.

For his part, Eldyn felt a peculiar resolve. This was not to say he was not without fear. Every man was afraid to die, in the end. And, indeed, his heart was beating wildly in his chest. He could not help wondering how much pain there would be, and what would await him when it ceased, if anything at all. Whatever it was, he doubted he would find himself in the marble halls of Eternum. Yet he did not really think he would see the fires of the Abyss, either. There would be a dark room, he supposed, and nothing more.

One feeling he did not suffer was regret. Ever since he became an adult, he had wanted nothing but to make something of himself. It was, he supposed, to compensate for how little his father had thought of him when he was a boy. To that end, Eldyn had first schemed to regain the Garritt family fortune, and then to enter the priesthood. Those endeavors had failed utterly. But they had helped lead him to the discovery of his talent as a Siltheri.

For a while, at the Theater of the Moon, Eldyn had thought he had finally found his place and purpose in the world. Yet it was only in the course of this last month that he had realized this was not so—that becoming an illusionist had been just one more step toward the role he was really meant to play. For though illusions were beautiful, lately he had been doing work that was of even greater importance. He had employed his talents to aid the cause of the revolution, and to help preserve the lives and freedom of others. What endeavor could have been of higher worth—or more at opposition with the way in which Vandimeer Garritt had lived his life?

There was none, and so Eldyn was without regret. He did not mind that he had given up so much of his own light and life to make all those impressions to support the cause. Nor did he lament that he would not be able to see the revolution through and be there to witness its end. After all, he had known from the moment he joined the rebels that he could be caught, and his life forfeited, at any moment.

Then again, Eldyn had never suspected his capture would be due to another illusionist. That Perren was a petty, selfish, and even vengeful man had already been revealed by his actions. But that he was also cruel and devoid of any sort of sympathetic feelings for other people were traits that had remained hidden. That soft, round face and those bookish spectacles had been an illusion Eldyn had not seen through.

Until yesterday, that was. Within an hour of being captured by the soldiers in front of the theater, Eldyn had been hauled before a court of the Gray Conclave. He might have expected to wait his turn behind a long line of other accused traitors to the nation, but that was not the case at all. Indeed, the proceedings moved so swiftly and efficiently—unburdened by any irksome requirement for fact or corroboration, and propelled by the cheerful clatter of the judge's gavel—that it was easy to see how a dozen trials could be held in the interval between luncheon and tea.

The captain who had arrested Eldyn presented the case against him, and called such witnesses as were required. First was a man who owned a printing company, and who had grown suspicious of the large number of engraving plates being purchased by individuals who were not known to work for the one remaining broadsheet, *The Comet.* The man had remarked upon this fact to another of his customers—one Mr. Perren Fynch.

After this, it had been Perren's turn to take the stand, which he did only after treating Eldyn to a hateful glance. He described how he had taken the information he learned to an agent of the Gray Conclave. What's more, he had reminded the agent of the ability of illusionists to create impressions. Having created such things in the past himself, Perren had described the exact manner in which impressions were made.

It was because of this, that when a spy was recently apprehended and found to be carrying metal plates, they were recognized for what they were, and were brought at once to Perren. He was able to process the plates in time, and pull prints from them, thus revealing the manner in which secret information was being smuggled out of the city and handed over to rebels. What was more, by careful study of the impressions, Perren had been certain he knew the identity of the very illusionist who had made them.

"I have brought copies of two of Eldyn Garritt's impressions that were published in *The Swift Arrow*," Perren had said to the court, a smug look upon his puffy face. "You have only to compare their details to the impressions taken from the spy to know they were made by the same man."

The judge accepted the prints, but hardly glanced at them before bringing down his gavel and pronouncing the verdict. The evidence was overwhelmingly damning. The sentence was death.

"Thank you for your efforts, Mr. Fynch," the judge had said as Perren departed the stand.

"I was only doing my duty," Perren had replied with a bow and a self-satisfied smile.

"Indeed," the judge went on, "it is good to know that, abominations though they all are, at least not every illusionist is a traitor to the nation."

That had wiped the smile off Perren's pudgy face. He had cast a furtive look back at Eldyn, and Eldyn had returned this with a slow nod, as if to say, *They know what you are now, and they will not forget.*

Perren had scurried from the chamber then, and what had happened to him after that, Eldyn neither knew nor cared. He himself was put in chains and taken away to Barrowgate, where he had spent an untold number of hours in the dank and dark. It might have been days, though he could not say for certain.

Now here he was. He supposed everyone at the theater wondered where he was. Though they would find out soon enough when they read the lists of the executed in the newspaper tomorrow.

If there would be a tomorrow, that was. For while the cool air and low angle of the sun suggested it was morning, a pall of gloom draped over the city. The sun appeared dimmer than it should have, as if something obscured part of it. In contrast, the new red planet shone more brightly than ever, as if stealing some of the sun's glow for itself.

Eldyn noted these things only passingly. Mostly he faced forward, ready to bear his fate and be done. Yet in these final moments, he realized he did hold one regret after all. And that was that he would never get to see Dercy again. He would never again look into those sea green eyes, or embrace Dercy tightly as they kissed. If he could have had any wish in the world, it would have been that.

All at once a queer feeling passed through Eldyn. He gazed down at the square below the gibbet, and he could only think that the hangman had already pulled the lever, that he was even at that moment dangling at the end of the rope while his dying brain conjured hallucinations—a few final illusions to ease his expiration.

Yet when he glanced to the side, he saw that the hangman still stood with his hand upon the lever; he had not pulled it. Indeed, he stood stock-still, just as did the three soldiers at the foot of the steps. In fact, the only people besides Eldyn who were moving were the three ragged figures before the gibbet. One of them glanced up again, and as he did he cast off his filthy cape and hat, throwing them down to the cobbles.

Eldyn could only stare, as if he had been frozen himself. No, it hadn't been a hallucination or a figment of a dying mind. The green eyes were faded, the gold of the beard was mingled with silver, but Eldyn could never have failed to recognize that beloved face.

"Dercy," he said, though the word barely had any sound to it, for the way the noose constricted his throat.

That Dercy was somehow, impossibly here was not the only cause for wonder. The two men beside him had cast off their own ragged mantles and hats. One was a younger fellow with a very high head of frizzy hair, while the other was a stout older man with ruddy cheeks and a frill of lace at his throat. The two of them held their hands out before them, muttering queer words. All of this gave Eldyn the impression that these two represented the reason why the soldiers and the hangman now stood as still as statues.

This was as much as confirmed when Dercy bounded up the steps and reached Eldyn.

"We have to be quick," he said, loosening the rope and slipping it over Eldyn's head. "Coulten and Wolsted told me they cannot work their magicks against twice their number for long. In a minute or two, the soldiers will be able to move again." He grasped Eldyn's arm and pulled him toward the steps.

"But what about them?" Eldyn said, glancing back at the other prisoners.

"By Eternum, you're still the angel, Eldyn Garritt!" Dercy exclaimed. But he grinned and hurried back to the others, removing their nooses. "Go!" he told them. "Be quick about it!"

This was easier said than done, for like Eldyn the men were still shackled, and they could do little more than hobble. Only then the younger of Dercy's two companions made a motion with his hands, and he spoke several sharp words. Red sparks sizzled around the iron manacles that bound Eldyn's wrists, then all at once they sprang open and fell away. The shackles about his ankles did the same, as did those binding the other men.

The three prisoners did not hesitate, and scrambled down the steps. Eldyn and Dercy hurried after them. As they descended, Eldyn noticed that the soldiers appeared to have altered their positions, and their rifles were held a fraction higher, as if they had been able to move for just a moment. But the younger magician with the tall head of hair had turned his attention back to them, and the redcrests were as statues once more.

By the clenching of the young man's jaw, and the perspiration upon his brow, the effort was costing him. The older magician seemed in similar straits, for his face was growing redder by the moment.

"Hurry," Dercy said.

There were so many questions Eldyn wanted to ask, but instead he gritted his teeth against the pain in his arms and legs, which was considerable now that his bonds had been removed, and clambered down the last of the steps. So weak and numb were his legs that he nearly collapsed at the bottom, but Dercy grasped his arms, preventing him from falling.

"Thank you," Eldyn said, clutching Dercy in return. "I'm not quite at my strongest at the moment."

Dercy's grin vanished, and his eyes grew solemn. "Yes, and I know why. Your hands, Eldyn—look at them. They were always so beautiful, but now they're like the hands of some old slag on Durrow Street who's on his next to last phantasm."

"I know," Eldyn said and shook his head. "I'm so sorry, Dercy, but I had to do it. I had to keep making impressions. It was for the sake of the revolution."

"No, don't be sorry. If you had done any different, you wouldn't have been you. Besides, you don't need to worry about this." He stroked Eldyn's thin hands. "I know what to do about it now."

Eldyn was astonished by these words. But he could only believe they were true, for despite the silver in his beard and the lines around his eyes—characteristics a man in his middle twenties should hardly possess—Dercy looked exceedingly well. Certainly he appeared far better than in those first days after Archdeacon Lemarck had stolen a great quantity of light from him, and the mordoth had afflicted him.

"Pardon my interruption, but may we go now?" the younger magician uttered through clenched teeth. His hands were vibrating before him. The other prisoners were nowhere in sight.

"Yes, let's be off," Dercy said, his grin returning. "We have what we came here for."

"Thank goodness," said the older, red-faced gentleman, and he let his hands drop.

Atop the gallows, the hangman staggered. He jerked his head back and forth, then he pointed down at Eldyn and let out a cry.

"Run for it!" Dercy shouted.

Eldyn ignored the pain in his stiff legs as Dercy pulled him along after the two magicians. He cast a glance over his shoulder and saw the hangman rushing down the steps of the gallows. The three soldiers were moving again as well, freed from the spell that had held them. They fumbled with their rifles, then lifted them, preparing to fire.

Dercy waved a hand, and a curtain of darkness fell down, intervening between them and the soldiers. Three shots rang out, but none of the bullets found a mark. Then the four turned down a side lane, and there before them was a black carriage. A driver sat waiting on the bench, looking rather alarmed.

"Go!" the younger magician called to the driver as they all climbed inside. "And do not spare the whip!"

The carriage lurched into motion before they had shut the door or settled in their seats. They tumbled around the interior for a moment, then managed to pull the door closed and set themselves aright on the benches. Eldyn turned around to look out the back window in time to see the three soldiers appear at the mouth of the lane. They raised their rifles. Then the carriage rounded a corner, and the redcrests were lost from view.

"I say, that was rousing," said the young man with the high column of hair, his cheeks rosy and blue eyes bright from exertion. "By the way, my name is Coulten, and this stout old fellow is Wolsted."

By their clothes and manner, Eldyn had a feeling they were in fact *Lord* Coulten and *Lord* Wolsted. Either way, he could only be grateful to know them, and he reached across to shake their hands. If Eldyn had not already seen them work magick, still he would have known they were magicians by the House rings on their right hands, the gems of which continued to throw off red and yellow sparks.

"Do you think they'll come after us?" Coulten said, now pulling on a pair of gloves to conceal his ring.

Lord Wolsted did the same. "I shouldn't think so. They won't have gotten a good look at our faces, for the binding spell would have made them blind and deaf. And with no other witnesses about to say otherwise, I would imagine the soldiers and the hangman will collude to keep the entire affair a secret. After all, if they confessed to letting prisoners escape, it would surely mean prison for *them*. Instead, they'll bribe the undertaker to dig four empty graves, and no one will be the wiser."

"I'd wager you're right," Coulten said cheerfully.

Eldyn supposed the same. But there were other matters that weighed more on his mind. "Dercy, why are you here?" he said, turning in his seat to look at the other young man.

Dercy raised a gold eyebrow. "Why, aren't you pleased to see me?"

If Eldyn had possessed the strength, he would have punched his arm. "Sun and Moon, of course I'm glad to see you! But how did you know where I was?"

"I knew because, unlike any of those dolts at the Theater of the Moon, I was smart enough to look in the newspaper to see if there was any mention about what had become of you. And there was your name, listed with the other convicted traitors to be hung today." He winked at Eldyn. "It seems you've been up to mischief in my absence. So perhaps you're no angel after all."

No, he wasn't. "But why were you at the theater?" Eldyn said, trying to make sense of all this. "In fact, why were you in the city at all?"

Now Dercy's tone and expression were no longer wry, but rather solemn. "Don't you know, Eldyn?"

"You told me you needed to go away so you wouldn't be tempted to conjure illusions—that leaving was the only way to break yourself of the habit."

"It was. And I did. But there's one craving I couldn't cure myself of no matter how long I stayed in the country." He bent his head toward Eldyn's and whispered so the other two men could not hear. "I came back for you. Or are you too much of a dolt yourself to realize that?"

After all that had happened, this was too much; Eldyn was beyond words. Not caring for the two magicians on the opposite bench, he found Dercy's hand and took it in his own, squeezing it with all his might. Dercy squeezed back.

At last Dercy released Eldyn's hand, and in a louder voice he explained how he had come to be there that day. Over the course of the last month, he had grown increasingly worried by the news making its way out of the city—how both witches and illusionists were being hunted. When he saw in a copy of *The Comet* that several Siltheri had been put to death, he knew he had to get back to Invarel at once.

Fortunately, the parish where he had been living with his cousin was to the southeast, and not behind the lines of war. Yet approaching the city was no simple task given all the soldiers on the roads. The last thing Dercy wanted was to be caught and taken before a witch-hunter, so he had used illusions to keep himself concealed as he traveled. Of course, this meant he had to go on foot rather than by horseback, which meant the journey took several days.

"But you're not supposed to be doing illusions anymore," Eldyn interrupted him. "You said you had broken the habit. Yet now you say you used illusions to get into the city. I saw you conjure another back there, when you pulled down that curtain of darkness."

"And a good thing he did, too," Coulten said, probing his frizzy crown. "I think my hair was parted by one of those bullets. If the soldiers had gotten a clearer view, I don't believe I'd be here now."

"It's all right," Dercy said, meeting Eldyn's eyes. "I won't ever be conjuring phantasms for amusement anymore—for my own or anyone else's—but I have enough light to spare for a few illusions when needed. I'll tell you about that later. For the moment, suffice it to say that a well-timed phantasm or two helped me slip through a gate and into the city."

Once inside the walls, Dercy proceeded to the Theater of the Moon, and there learned that Eldyn had gone missing. That was when he checked the broadsheets and saw Eldyn's name.

"I didn't tell the others about it," Dercy said with a sigh. "Riethe in particular would have gone lumbering like a bull into Barrowgate to save you, and would have gotten himself captured in the process. But there's one person at the theater who has some wits, and that's Lily Lockwell. I was astonished to find her there, but very glad as well. She knew I was intending to look for you, and she told me I should seek out someone she knew—a magician—to see if he could help me."

"Rafferdy," Eldyn said, amazed at Lily's good sense. "She told you to go find Lord Rafferdy."

Dercy nodded. "So she did. But when I slipped into his house in Warwent Square, I didn't find your friend there. Instead, I found these two." He nodded toward the magicians across the bench.

"And quite a start you gave us when you appeared out of the shadows like that," Coulten said with a somewhat nervous laugh.

"Sorry about that," Dercy said with a smirk that indicated he wasn't sorry in the least. He looked back at Eldyn. "I heard them formulating a plan to rescue you from the gibbet, so I revealed myself to them, and told them I was going to help whether they wanted me to or not. Though I suppose it's they who helped me, really. I'm not certain how I would have freed you without that trick of theirs."

"And I'm not certain we would have escaped without *your* trick," Wolsted replied, dabbing his brow with a handkerchief.

"Well, I'm very glad for all of you," Eldyn said. He lifted a hand to his neck, which was sore where the noose had chafed it. "But, while I do not wish to sound ungrateful in any way, I am puzzled why Coulten and Wolsted here should have given one whit about my fate when we have no connection."

"Ah, but we do have a connection!" Coulten exclaimed happily. "You are a friend of Lord Rafferdy's, correct? Well, we are also companions of his."

As the carriage raced through the city, Coulten explained how he and Wolsted had been hiding themselves at Rafferdy's house on Warwent Square ever since Invarel was closed, for they had been unable to pass beyond the wall of the Old City to reach their own abodes in the New Quarter. Just yesterday, someone had slipped a letter under the door of the house. Presuming it to be some urgent missive for Rafferdy, they decided to read it, thinking they could pass along its contents to him by means of their black books— devices, they explained, which allowed them to communicate over long distances.

Only upon reading the missive, they knew they would have to act on it themselves. The letter said it was imperative that one Mr. Eldyn Garritt, who was an acquaintance of Lord Rafferdy, be rescued before he could be hanged at Barrowgate the following day.

"But who was the letter from?" Eldyn asked, amazed by this.

Coulten shook his head. "I'm afraid we don't know. It wasn't signed, and there was no address. Yet we decided we had better act upon it."

Eldyn found this all very remarkable. "I am flattered to know I have been the subject of concern by such a mysterious personage," he said. "Yet I confess, I hardly know why I am so important as to warrant such attention."

Wolsted cleared his throat. "Meaning no offense to you, Mr. Garritt, but I believe it isn't necessarily you yourself which is of such great import. Rather, the letter referred to something in your possession. Namely, a key."

Eldyn could only frown. "A key?"

"Yes, a key that opens a particular door located within the house of Sir and Lady Quent on East Durrow Street."

All at once Eldyn understood. They could only be referring to the wooden leaf that Rafferdy had given him for safekeeping—the object that unlocked the door through which Lady Quent had passed to a place that was not upon this world at all, but rather on the moon of another. Quickly, he explained these things to the others. Dercy's eyes grew large as he did, while Coulten clapped his hands.

"That must be it!" he said. "But do you have the key with you?"

"No, it is in my room at the Theater of the Moon, on West Durrow Street."

"Then let us go there at once to retrieve it, and then proceed with all haste to the house of the Quents."

Eldyn pressed a hand to his brow, trying to make sense of all this. "But why is it so urgent that we do this? Why do we even need to open that door in the first place?"

"Because," Coulten said, his expression growing solemn, "if we do not unlock the door this very morning, then Lord Rafferdy will not be able to come through it. For the letter told us to send him a message, telling him to find a way through the door."

Rafferdy? But why would he be coming through the door? None of this made any sense; his head was filled with a fog of confusion.

Well, he would simply have to believe that whoever had written that letter knew what he was doing. After all, it was because of this mysterious person that Eldyn wasn't presently hanging from a rope in Barrowgate. He turned to look at Dercy beside him.

"What do you think we should do?"

"These two helped us greatly today, so I think the least we can do is return the favor." He grinned, his green eyes sparkling. "Come on, let's go get this key for these fine magicians."

Eldyn grinned in return, while at the same time Coulten leaned out the window of the carriage.

"To the Theater of the Moon!" he called to the driver. "And hurry!"

CHAPTER THIRTY-FOUR

AT LAST the morning fog lifted, and warm sunlight shone down upon the grove of Wyrdwood as the trees drooped and fell still.

Rafferdy slumped to his knees beside the mossy stone wall. His arms ached from raising them above his head for so long, and his tongue was as dry and cracked as the leather of his boots from speaking runes of magick over and over again. He could not stop shaking.

That he was alive was a cause for wonder. He had watched as the black branches bent down to grasp Lieutenant Beckwith and drew his lifeless body over the wall, into the grove. Rafferdy nearly suffered the same fate a moment later. More branches had cracked like whips, wrapping themselves around him, and lifting him up. He had felt his boots leave the ground.

Had the trees managed to take him over the wall and into the grove, he surely would have perished like Beckwith and Hendry. Fortunately, though the branches tangled around his limbs, they had not covered his mouth, and he was able to call out several runes of protection. His House ring had flared, and blue lines of power snaked and sizzled along the branches. As if paralyzed by this shock, the trees released him, and he had fallen hard to the ground at the foot of the stone wall.

Quickly, the branches had begun to reach out again, creaking and groaning as they bent over the top of the wall, straining to reach him. But by then he had managed to use the heel of his boot to draw a rough circle in the moist turf, and he was uttering a torrent of arcane words in an endless incantation. Time and again the branches reached for him, and time and again they recoiled as blue sparks hissed around them.

How long he had maintained the circle of protection after that, fending off the fury of the trees, he was not certain. Hours, he supposed. Whatever the duration of the ordeal, he doubted he could have maintained his efforts much longer. And even if he had, it would have done him no good; for only now did he see that the wall was riddled with cracks, and here and there stones protruded outward. Clearly root and limb had been attempting to break through the wall to reach him.

Only they hadn't. And now, in the daylight, the trees finally drowsed as the power of Gauldren's ancient spell, the Quelling, did its work.

Leaning upon the wall, Rafferdy slowly gained his feet. For a minute he stood there, steadying himself. Then he turned around and, for the first time since the trees assailed him, looked down the slope to the foot of the hill, to the place where his men had been scrambling to make some sort of stand against the approaching company of Valhaine's soldiers. He saw no lines of soldiers, no clouds of smoke from the barrels of rifles. Here and there he could make out a brown shape sprawled upon the trampled grass, but not nearly enough to account for all of the men who had been in his company. That was good. It meant that at least some of them had survived.

Unlike Lieutenant Beckwith or Corporal Hendry. Damn the lieutenant! Had Beckwith not been so impatient to retrieve the supplies—and had he not then rashly shot the witch—both he and Hendry might yet be alive. What was more, Rafferdy could have run down the hill to shout orders and arrange his men in a proper defense against Valhaine's soldiers.

Except Rafferdy knew it was not Beckwith he should be damning, but rather himself. He was the one who had allowed Beckwith and Hendry to ride ahead. He was the one who had failed to realize the enemy soldiers had indeed turned to pursue them, bolstering their numbers along the way. Rafferdy had started to let himself think he really was something of a soldier. Now he saw what that conceit had cost them.

Turning his back to the Wyrdwood, he stumbled his way down the slope to the base of the hill. He came upon a young man in a brown coat lying facedown in the grass. It was one of his own men. One by one, Rafferdy went to the other bodies scattered around. There were eleven in all, most of them wearing brown coats, but a few in blue.

He turned around in the center of the battlefield, shading his eyes with a hand, trying to understand what had happened. Valhaine's soldiers had surely had the upper hand. They had outnumbered Rafferdy's company, and they had the element of surprise. The rebel soldiers might have retreated up the hill to gain higher ground, but there were no bootprints in the moist grass to indicate they had done so.

Yet that could only be expected. The men would never have retreated up the hill, not with the trees at its summit thrashing to and fro in what anyone could have recognized was a Rising. Which meant the rebels had been trapped between the approaching soldiers and the furious Wyrdwood. They should have been slaughtered.

But they weren't, and as Rafferdy continued to survey the scene, the reason became evident. By the impressions of boots and hooves left in the soft dirt of the road, it was apparent that Valhaine's men had never finished closing the distance to the rebel company. Instead, they had turned around and gone back the direction they had come. It could only mean one thing.

They had run away from the Rising.

That Valhaine's men would turn their backs to an enemy and flee down the road astonished Rafferdy. But after all the stories that had been circulated about the Risings in Torland, and about the way Morden's forces had made alliances with witches, Valhaine's men must have feared the rebels were going to use the Wyrdwood against them. Faced with such a terrible prospect, they had turned and fled.

For their part, the men of Rafferdy's company had been no less afraid of the thrashing of the Wyrdwood. From the manner in which the mud of the road was churned, it was obvious they had rapidly departed the scene as well, making off in the direction of Pellendry-on-Anbyrn, as had been their original plan.

Amid this disaster, that was one bit of excellent news. The company could not be very far ahead of him—hours at most— which meant if Rafferdy hurried he would be able to catch up to them before they reached Pellendry. He might have a chance after all to make up for his errors, and to help his men survive what battles lay ahead.

Despite his urgent wish to catch up with the remainder of his company, Rafferdy took a while to see to the bodies of those who had fallen. He did not have the time to bury them, but he could make sure they were arranged with some degree of respect. Thus he dragged them into a line, shoulder to shoulder, and put each man's hands upon his rifle. Each soldier still had his bedroll on his back, and Rafferdy used these to cover the bodies, for he was cognizant of the crows circling overhead. He paid the same courtesy to the enemy soldiers who had fallen, though he left them where they lay.

Once he had finished this grisly task, he wiped the sweat from his brow and began his march east down the road. It was his hope he might see his horse wandering about in the aftermath of the battle, and with it under him make better time.

After only a few dozen steps his hope in this regard was at once realized and dashed, for he saw a large gray shape lying off to the side of the road. It was his horse. By its bent and bloodied foreleg and the bullet hole in its skull, Rafferdy could deduce the manner of its death. With no rider at the reins, it had broken its picket line and had run away from the dual terrors of the battle and the Rising. Only in its mad flight, it had broken its leg and foundered. As they marched from the scene, Rafferdy's men must have come upon it, and shot the beast to put it out of its misery as they passed.

Rafferdy sighed as he knelt beside the fallen horse, and he stroked its neck. Well, at least there was some small good to be gained from this ill, for Rafferdy's pack was still tied to the horse's saddle. He opened it to retrieve only the things that were most precious to him, for he needed to remain unburdened so as to travel swiftly.

Thus it was he took his cup and his knife, and extra bullets and caps for his pistol. He took the onyx box as well, which still felt strangely hot within its wrappings, and put it in his coat pocket. Finally, he dug into the depths of his pack, then pulled out his black magician's book.

The book gave a jerk, leaping out of his hands.

Rafferdy stared at the black book. It gave another twitch upon the ground. In the past, Rafferdy had sometimes heard a rattling emanate from the drawer in the writing table in his parlor at Warwent Square. By that sound, he always knew when a message written with particular urgency had appeared upon the pages of his magician's book.

The book twitched again, and Rafferdy snatched it up. Hastily he spoke the runes of unlocking, then opened the book with fumbling hands. He turned past the last few messages that had appeared on the pages of the book, ones penned by Coulten and Trefnell and the other members of the Fellowship of the Silver Circle, stating that they remained in hiding and were well.

It had been some time since these messages had appeared—so long that Rafferdy had begun to fear the others were no longer safe. But at least one of them remained free at present, for there was a new message in the book now, one that had not been there before. Then, as Rafferdy read the writing upon the page, his relief was exchanged for a concoction that was equal parts wonder and dread.

You must discover a gate and pass through it to the way station on Arantus, the message read. *Look within any stands of Wyrdwood you come upon. One of them is bound to have a gate in its midst. Your ring will lead you in the right direction. But you must make haste, for the final hour draws nigh, and she has need of you.*

Again Rafferdy read the brief message, trying to make some sense of it. Which of the magicians of the Fellowship had written it down in his black book just now, causing it to appear in all of the others' books? And to which of them had the message been directed?

The writing looked like Coulten's, but those words hardly sounded like something he would say. And as for the intended recipient, Rafferdy could only think the message was directed at him. After all, none of the other magicians in the Fellowship knew about the ancient way station on Arantus. Or at least, he hadn't thought any of them knew. But clearly, from the wording of the message, Coulten did now. Only why was Rafferdy to try to find a gate to the way station?

He didn't know, but his eyes fell upon those last words once more. *She has need of you. . . .*

Like the book, his heart gave a jerk. Who else could the message be referring to? Who else was familiar with the way station? And who else was worth journeying to a distant moon to aid?

"Mrs. Quent," he said aloud.

Rafferdy shut the book and stood. He turned and gazed back the way he had come, and at the thick stand of gnarled trees that crowned the hill. He knew that there were arcane gates hidden within various stands of Old Trees around Altania, just as there had been within the Evengrove. Like the way stations on Tyberion and Arantus, the gates dated to the first war against the Ashen in the distant past. Mrs. Quent had passed through such a gate to reach Heathcrest Hall. Or at least, that had been her intention upon stepping through the leaf-carved door in the house on Durrow Street.

Now Rafferdy had to find such a gate himself. Was it possible there was one here, in this very grove? There was one way to find out.

Your ring will lead you in the right direction. . . .

Rafferdy tucked the book into his coat pocket, then dashed back along the road to the foot of the hill. Arms and legs pumping swiftly, he climbed to the top, and soon stood before the wall again. There was not a breath of wind, and the branches of the trees drooped over the top of the wall, listless in the warm brightness of day.

Lifting his right hand, Rafferdy peered at his House ring. He shaded it with his other hand, making sure it could catch no sunlight, and gazed into the blue gem. Its center was dark and lifeless, yet he was outside the wall. Could not the thick stones interfere with any arcane energies there might be?

Hardly believing he was doing such a thing, Rafferdy applied his hands and the toes of his boots to the rough stone wall, and after some amount of scrabbling and scraping he was able to reach the top. He swung his legs over. Before him was a deep tangle of green.

Sitting atop the wall, Rafferdy cupped his left hand around his House ring and again looked at the gem. As he did, he swore a soft oath. It was faint but unmistakable: a spark of light winking in the center of the gem.

Abruptly, the spark of light in the gem became easier to discern as the sunlight dimmed a fraction. Was a fog lifting again, or had a cloud passed over the sun? No, for when Rafferdy looked up, the sky above was clear. All the same, there was now an odd cast to the light, and the shadows all around were not as distinct as they should have been in full daylight. Yet if there was no cloud or fog, what else could obscure the sun?

Understanding came to Rafferdy with a shudder. *You must make haste,* the message in his black book had read, *for the final hour draws nigh.*

So it was beginning, then—the Grand Conjunction. One of the planets had begun to edge its way in front of the sun. One by one the other planets would join it, arranging themselves in a single line before the fiery orb. And when they did, all the world would be swallowed in darkness.

His alarm growing, Rafferdy gazed at the trees. The Quelling was always strongest by daylight. But if night were to fall again . . .

There was no time to worry about such things, for every moment so spent was another moment for the planets to turn. Rafferdy turned onto his stomach, then lowered himself over the wall. He had descended perhaps halfway when his fingers slipped on the mossy stones and he went tumbling. Fortunately, a thick carpet of leaf mold provided a cushion for his fall, and he regained his feet little worse for wear. He brushed the dead matter from his coat, then began to make his way into the trees.

His immediate fear was that he might come upon the bodies of Corporal Hendry, Lieutenant Beckwith, and the witch. He had no wish to see what the trees had done to the men, or to see what Beckwith's foolishness had wrought upon the young woman who had inhabited this grove. Thankfully, Rafferdy had climbed the wall at a different point, and he saw no trace of them or the weapons cache.

Soon enough, though, another dread came over him. This was not the first time Rafferdy had walked among Old Trees, but while this grove was much smaller than the Evengrove, the air was no less dense and stifling. A feeling of oppression pressed down on him, making it a labor to draw a breath or take a step. Despite this, he clenched his jaw and moved ever deeper into the tangle of roots and branches. Daylight and the Quelling had made the trees calm, so if he did nothing to disturb them, they should remain so.

As he went, he glanced frequently at his House ring. At first the blue spark within the gem flickered like a candle caught in a breeze. Then, as the green gloom thickened, the gem began to shine more steadily, growing brighter and brighter with each step. Without doubt, there was something in the grove that emanated arcane energies. Though whether it was a gate, or some other relic of the ancient war against the Ashen, he could not say. An urge came upon him to utter runes of protection, but he resisted it, recalling how the witch had likened the language of magick to the tongue of the Ashen. He did not want to do anything that might provoke the trees.

Rafferdy pressed on, until the stone wall was lost to view behind him. In the green twilight beneath the trees, his House ring smoldered like a blue coal. Whatever it was that lay within the center of the grove, it had to be close now. Then, as he gingerly pushed aside a branch, he saw it.

A blocky shape stood in the center of a small clearing. To other eyes, it would have been no more than a jumble of old stones—the remnants of a well or chimney, perhaps. Yet Rafferdy was sure no one had ever built a dwelling in the middle of this stand of primeval forest—just as he was sure no other person had laid eyes upon these stones in living memory. For an eon or more, these stones had stood here as the moss grew upon them: dark and dormant, waiting for the touch of magick to awaken them again.

And now, at long last, a magician had come.

Fascinated, Rafferdy drew close to the gate—for he had no doubt that was what it was. The shape of the arch was unmistakable beneath a shroud of vine and leaf, and as he brushed away the moss, deep gouges in the stones were revealed: angular lines and symbols that formed words of a language older than mankind itself.

Rafferdy supposed he was exceedingly lucky that this stand of Wyrdwood had indeed concealed a gate in its center. Or perhaps it was not luck at all, and many such artifacts remained hidden within the primeval groves. Maybe it was because of these very gates that such groves had endured over the years—maybe the presence of arcane energies associated with the Ashen served to agitate the Old Trees, and to prevent them from falling into a deep slumber under the force of the Quelling. Instead they remained restless. And so, being the most likely to lash out when cut or burned, these groves were the very ones that had endured the longest.

It was an interesting theory, at least, and one worth exploring at a later time. For the moment, it was enough to know this one gate was here. As gently as he could, Rafferdy pushed the vines away from the arch and scraped the moss from the stones, so that he could discern the runes incised upon them. Once these were revealed, he studied them, making sure he recognized them all.

Then Rafferdy spoke the runes, one after the other.

As he uttered the final word of magick, his ring flashed, and lines of power crackled into being around the stones, slithering across them like little blue serpents. For a moment, through the archway, he could still see crooked trunks and gnarled branches. Then all at once they were gone, replaced by a plain of gray-green dust beneath crystalline stars and the sharp, purple crescent of a great planet.

So astounded was Rafferdy as he stared through the gate that he did not at first hear creaking and groaning noises commence all around him. It was only when these sounds became a loud roaring that he realized what it was. He turned his gaze from the gate, then swore. All around the little clearing, the trees were thrashing back and forth. Branches whipped in the air, and roots thrust up from the ground. So he had been right—the arcane energies of the gate indeed had the power to agitate the trees.

And now they were going to destroy the source of that agitation. A thick branch came whistling through the air, driving right for his skull. With a cry, Rafferdy turned and leaped through the blazing archway.

At once the roaring noise ceased. Rafferdy's boots came down not upon crackling leaves, but upon gray-green dust. Dry, metallic air filled his lungs, and cold stars glittered overhead, surrounding the large violet sickle of the planet Dalatair.

Rafferdy turned and looked back through the arch of stones. He could still see branches thrashing back and forth; there would be no returning that way until the trees grew calm again. In which case, where should he go? The barren plain around him was littered with countless stone arches—countless gates. But which one of them was he supposed to go through? The message in his book had not said.

Then, even as Rafferdy looked out over the way station, he knew the answer. There, not very far away, was an archway that was not dark, but was instead filled with warm gold light.

Rafferdy knew that ancient magicks protected this place from the frigid void between the planets. All the same, he had no desire to linger here, and he struck off quickly across the plain. In little more than two minutes, he reached his goal. As he peered through the arch into the familiar, sun-dappled room beyond, he could only let out an exclamation of wonder.

Then, without any sort of hesitation, Rafferdy stepped through the gate.

"Well, now!" Coulten exclaimed, his blue eyes going wide. "That was a fair bit quicker than we expected you, Rafferdy!"

As Rafferdy stepped over the threshold of the leaf-carved door, into the sunlit gallery of Lady Quent's house on Durrow Street, he doubted he was any less astonished than the four men gaping at him.

Three of them he knew well: Lord Coulten, Lord Wolsted, and Eldyn Garritt. Next to Garritt was a blond-bearded young man whom Rafferdy had never seen before. Though given the proximity with which he and Garritt stood next to each other, Rafferdy thought he knew this fellow as well—or at the least, knew how he was related to Garritt.

"Well, it appears that you got the message well enough," Wolsted said, beaming with satisfaction. "Coulten wrote it exactly as the letter we received specified."

Rafferdy nodded to the older lord. "Indeed, I did get the message."

"Good God, Rafferdy, what's happened to you?" Garritt said, taking a step toward him. "You look as if you've been dragged through a briar patch. Where did you come from?"

Rafferdy supposed his appearance was a bit more disheveled than Garritt was used to seeing. He flicked a dead leaf from the sleeve of his coat. "I was in a stand of Wyrdwood, on the road to Pellendry-on-Anbyrn, where my company and I were headed."

At this, Garritt frowned. "Pellendry? But how strange that you were going *there*."

"How so?"

"Because it's one of the places on the map we intercepted."

Now it was Rafferdy's turn to frown. It was clear there was much he did not know. "What map do you mean? And who intercepted it?"

"Men loyal to Morden," Garritt said. "They smuggled it out of the Citadel. A number of locations were marked on it—five in all—including Pellendry-on-Anbyrn. All of them are places where Valhaine has been gathering his troops. We're not exactly sure what it all means, but those places are important somehow."

"Yes, they are," spoke another voice. "For it is at those very places where the Ashen will enter the world when Cerephus draws near."

The voice was low and rasping, though despite its queerness Rafferdy almost thought he recognized it. He turned and saw that there was in fact one more man in the room. His curious black attire—all frilled and ruffled and gored—had blended with the shadows in a corner, but now he stepped forward. He wore black gloves on his hands, and his face was covered with a black mask that was wrought into a twisted expression. It was, Rafferdy thought, an expression of pain.

"You!" Rafferdy exclaimed. "It was you who had Coulten send me that message, and who had Garritt open this door."

The man in the black costume nodded, then took another limping step forward. "Yes, I wrote the letter Coulten and Wolsted referred to. And now that you are here, Lord Rafferdy, there is no time for delay. You must go upstairs and retrieve the Eye of Ran-Yahgren, and then you must carry it to Heathcrest Hall. For if you do not do this before the Grand Conjunction commences, all the world will be devoured."

Rafferdy took a staggering step back, as if these words had struck him with a force. "We don't even know who you are. How can we know that we are to trust you in this—that this is not something the Ashen want?"

"You should trust me because *she* has trusted me, just as her father did before her. Besides, I believe you do indeed know who I am."

And the stranger lifted his gloved hands to remove the black mask from his face.

CHAPTER THIRTY-FIVE

A DIZZYING MULTITUDE of thoughts raced through Ivy's mind as she gazed at the pistol in Mr. Bennick's long-fingered hand. How was it he had managed to get here, to Heathcrest Hall? For what purpose had he come? What had he done with her father?

And above all of these things, what was she going to do?

Ivy glanced at the splintered twigs that scattered the floor of the front hall. Was there still enough life in the ruined scraps of the Wyrdwood box for them to respond to her commands? She would have to get close enough to touch them to find out. . . .

"Do not move," Mr. Bennick said.

Ivy knew he was no longer a magician; all the same, it seemed there was a power in his deep voice, rooting her to the spot. His thumb traveled to the hammer of the pistol. Next to her, Rose let out a small cry and clutched the doll. Stretching his long, spidery legs, Mr. Bennick moved farther into the hall, keeping the pistol before him.

"Come out, Ashaydea!" He spoke in a ringing tone. "You need not hide yourself. I know that you are here."

"Yes," whispered a cold, hard voice. "I am."

Moving with a swiftness that exceeded the ability of the eye to fully perceive, a cloud of black smoke burst from a dim corner behind Mr. Bennick and flowed toward him, dark coils wreathing around his arms, his throat. The pistol fell to the floor with a clatter, but fortunately he had not cocked it, and it did not fire.

Mr. Bennick made a choking noise as his head was pulled backward. "I should have known," he said with great effort, "that I could not move more swiftly than you, Ashaydea."

"Indeed, I am sure you knew it very well," she said from her position behind him, an arm encircling his throat. "You brandished the pistol not because you believed you would have the chance to harm Lady Quent or her sister, but to force me to appear. Yet I wonder—how did you know I was here at all?"

His eyes narrowed to black slits. "I have lost my magickal abilities, Ashaydea, but I do still feel their echo sometimes. And that echo is always the most discernible when you are near." He struggled to draw a breath. "But as to why you are in this place, I have no notion."

"So, the grandson of the great magician Slade Vordigan does not possess all knowledge after all," she said coolly, then released him.

He took a staggering step, then caught himself and brought a hand to his throat. "Go on, Lady Quent," he said, giving her a nod. "Take up the gun, if you wish. I have no need of it anymore."

For a moment she hesitated, wondering if it was some trick. Then she recalled how swiftly Lady Shayde could move. Ivy tucked the journal under her arm, then darted forward and picked up the gun.

"Rose," she said in a stern tone, "go to the parlor. Shut the door and lock it once you are in. Do not open it for anyone other than me or Lady Shayde."

Rose gave a silent nod, then hurried from the hall, holding the doll tightly as she went. Once she was gone, Ivy raised the pistol.

"Be careful, Mr. Bennick," Shayde said. "I have seen for myself that she knows how to employ such a weapon."

Yes, she did. Ivy pointed the pistol at the tall magician. "Where is my father?"

"I presume that you mean, where is his physical self?" Mr. Bennick said, his voice still rasping from being choked. "For I am sure you know by now his mind still resides in his old dwelling on Durrow Street."

"Yes, I do know his presence is there," Ivy said, tightening her hold on the pistol so her hands would not shake. "It's there because he had to sacrifice himself ten years ago in order to work an enchantment of binding on the Eye of Ran-Yahgren so that you could not take it."

He gave a languorous nod, as if they were simply having a genial conversation. "Yes, I suppose that is what you must think, Lady Quent. I know that is what your husband believed of me. And you were both correct, though only in part. I would have worked the enchantment myself that day, had I still possessed an ability to perform magick. As it was, I advised your father to wait for some of the others to come, so that they could help with the binding. But there was no way to know at that point who within the order we could trust. And so your father did what he had to in order to safeguard the Eye, despite the cost to himself and to his family."

Ivy's mind whirled, trying to comprehend these statements. But why should she try when they were surely lies? "That's not true. You wanted the Eye of Ran-Yahgren for yourself. My father sacrificed his mind to keep you from getting it."

"No, I did not want the Eye for myself. I wanted to protect it, just like Lockwell did." He took a step closer. "That's why, more recently, I worked to bring you into the acquaintance of Mr. Rafferdy—or Lord Rafferdy, as he is now. I knew that, between the two of you, you would be able to enter the house on Durrow Street and renew the binding on the Eye. And so you did."

The gun wavered in Ivy's hand. "You're lying."

"No, he isn't," Lady Shayde said, a light glinting in her black eyes. She walked in a circle around Mr. Bennick. "I can discern when a man is speaking a falsehood—even a very clever man like Mr. Bennick. It is a power Mr. Bennick himself gave to me. And what he said just now is the truth. Though I would imagine it is not the *entire* truth. Mr. Bennick has ever done anything to achieve his ends, but he keeps those ends to himself."

"They are no different than yours, Ashaydea," he said, his face all angles and shadows in the gloom. "I seek to protect Altania from the forces that assail it, that is all."

"You mean as your grandfather protected Altania?" Shayde said. "Do you have such grand desires, then, and hope to drive Huntley Morden from these shores as Slade Vordigan did to Bandley Morden seventy years ago?"

He sighed and gazed down at her. "That's my Ashaydea—even as a girl, you were always an interrogator. No one in the household was safe from your questions. It is little wonder Lord Valhaine found such a use for you as he did. But you should know not to believe all myths and legends you hear. Slade Vordigan was indeed at Selburn Howe the day Bandley Morden was routed and fled back to his ships. But did the shadows which Vordigan summoned cause Morden's defeat, as the stories say? Or did they provide cover and concealment so that he could safely retreat to his ships and escape?"

Lady Shayde raised the black line of an eyebrow. "I see. The historical accounts are misleading, then. So Huntley Morden is not your enemy."

"No, he isn't. But if you wish to take me to the Citadel and deliver me to Lord Valhaine as a traitor to the realm, it will have to wait."

Lady Shayde looked away, and now Mr. Bennick's thin mouth formed into a smile.

"I see," he said. "So you are a traitor yourself now, Ashaydea. You serve no one."

She stared at him, her face hard and white, but said nothing.

"Do not mistake me," he said. "I do not mock you. Rather, I am impressed. By your nature, you are a being designed to serve. Therefore, to make such decisions as you have done—to act upon a will of your own—shows marvelous determination. That was the very reason why I chose you all those years ago, Ashaydea—out of the hope that you would one day decide for yourself what you would do with your abilities."

A buzzing noise filled Ivy's head; despite the chill in the room, she felt flushed, as if with a fever. She could scarcely comprehend all that she had just heard. But it didn't matter.

"I asked you where my father is," she said, taking another step toward Mr. Bennick, the pistol before her.

He turned to regard her. "His physical self is safe. No harm came to him in our flight from Madstone's and out of the city."

"The same cannot be said for the warden you murdered when you abducted my father."

"Murdered?" He shook his head. "No, I did not murder anyone at Madstone's."

"Then who did murder the warden, if not you?"

"The magicians that Gambrel sent, I presume," Mr. Bennick said. "I knew that he would try to seize your father, to gain his piece of the keystone, just as he did with Larken and Fintaur. Thus I moved first and took your father from Madstone's."

Ivy's head was throbbing now. "But how could you take him out of there unless you were working with the magicians yourself?"

"One doesn't always require magick to open a door, Lady Quent," Mr. Bennick said, the hint of a smile playing upon his thin lips. "For some time, I have worked to cultivate several contacts within Madstone's. Let us just say that a warden's remuneration is not so great that some increase in this regard goes unappreciated."

Ivy gaped at him. "You mean you bribed them?"

Mr. Bennick shrugged. "When magick is not available, one must resort to whatever methods work, no matter how mundane. But yes, over the last year I purchased the favor of two of the wardens. It was they who unlocked the doors for me, and who allowed me to remove your father—just in time, it seems. At present, Mr. Lockwell is safely hidden. I believe that you know Dr. Lawrent? He and Mrs. Lawrent are currently in the south, where they are staying with her family. I took your father there, and he is now in their care. So you see, you need have no fear for Mr. Lockwell's condition—though there was one small matter that required the help of a surgeon."

"A surgeon!" Ivy exclaimed. "But for what?"

"For this," Mr. Bennick said, and drew something from the pocket of his coat. He opened his hand, and on his palm lay what appeared to be a jagged-edged stone.

Fascinated, Ivy took another step closer. Yes, it was indeed a stone—or rather, a fragment of a stone. It was a deep red in color, and regular white lines scored one side of it. At once, Ivy knew what it was.

"It's a piece of the keystone," she murmured. "The piece that belonged to my father."

"Yes."

"So you did want to take it from him!"

Mr. Bennick nodded. "I did, but only to prevent Gambrel from seizing it."

Ivy could only stare, disbelieving. "But you are in league with Mr. Gambrel. Surely you intend to deliver my father's piece of the keystone to him, and your own as well!"

Mr. Bennick's sallow face was grim. "No, I am not in league with Gambrel. Indeed, he and I have ever been at odds—a fact he well knows. It is your father, Lockwell, with whom I was allied in all things. Again, look to Ashaydea if you think I do not speak the truth."

Ivy did so, looking toward that white, smooth face. Lady Shayde gazed at Mr. Bennick for a moment, then slowly she nodded.

The heat of anger died down within Ivy, even as the fire had died on the hearth leaving her cold. She stared at the pistol in her hands—then slowly set it on a table and backed away from it. For so long she had believed the very worst about Mr. Bennick; everywhere she had seen evidence of his duplicity, of his wicked intentions.

It seemed she was not so clever at solving ciphers and deducing the answers to puzzles as she had thought. While the evidence against Mr. Bennick had appeared plentiful, in retrospect it was all circumstantial as well. Yes, he had manipulated Ivy and Mr. Rafferdy, using them as a means to unlock the house on Durrow Street—just as he had manipulated the wardens at Madstone's to unlock the door to her father's cell.

But none of it had been for the motives she had presumed. She had been all too eager to find a villain in the affair of her father's illness. And so, guided by prejudice rather than reason, she had leaped to a faulty conclusion, and then had proceeded to dismiss any evidence that countered it—evidence which, now that she considered it, was plentiful, and came from the most trusted of sources.

She sank down into a chair. "My father wrote in his journal time and again how much he depended upon you, and what a true friend you were to him. I thought my father had been deceived." She shook her head. "But it was I who was deceived, and by myself. I knew my father to be among the wisest of men. I should have known that I should prefer his judgments over my own when it came to the matter of you. Only I was . . . I so wanted . . ."

"You wanted someone to be blamed for what befell your father," he said, and while his deep-set eyes were as dark as ever, they no longer seemed so hard. "As a child, you could not believe that he would abandon you of his own choosing, and so it had to have been forced by another. Then, as you grew older, the belief grew stronger."

Ivy could only nod, for it was so.

"Well, you should not fault yourself for suspecting me of such treachery," Mr. Bennick went on. "After all, I gave you little reason to think otherwise with my actions. But I knew that I did not dare become too close to you, or reveal too much, for the peril it would have placed you in. The other magicians of our order would have eagerly approached you had they thought you could help them gain what they desired. What's more, I did at times deliberately mislead you, and worked to influence events, in order to achieve an end. But it was, I hope you can see, an end of great importance."

Lady Shayde made a harsh sound that was not laughter. "That sounds very similar to what you told me, more than twenty years ago."

The tall magician turned to face her. "And you may yet play a role in achieving that end, Ashaydea. I confess, I had given up hope of that. But now I see that my hope was not in vain after all. For here you are."

Lady Shayde folded her arms, as if she felt a chill, even though such was not possible for a being like her. She turned away from him.

From the chair, Ivy looked up at Mr. Bennick. "But what is this end you seek to bring about? What is your purpose in coming here?"

"This is my purpose," he said and held up the fragment of the keystone.

Ivy clutched the journal in her hands. "My father described it in these pages, how you discovered the keystone and broke it into six, and how each of you took a piece. Only I am sure my father did not have it among his things at Madstone's, for I brought him everything he had there. I would have seen it."

"But he did have it with him. He always had it, as did the rest of us. We had to be sure no one could ever lose his piece of the keystone—something Mundy surely would have done in that rat's nest of a shop he kept. It was Lockwell, being a doctor, who came up with a way in which we could always keep the pieces of the keystone hidden, and yet never misplace them." As he spoke, he pressed a hand to his chest.

Ivy thought of the blood upon the doorstep of Mr. Larken's shop and sat up straight in the chair. "It was in him! It was inside each of you!"

Mr. Bennick nodded. "It was Lockwell who worked the magick, for we knew he had the finest touch, as well as the greatest knowledge of anatomy. By means of a spell, he could open a miniature door into a space inside the body, and so deposit the stone within. There was no blood at all." His fingers clutched at his chest. "Though I will not say there was no pain."

"So that's why you needed the surgeon—to remove the fragment from within my father."

Mr. Bennick reached into his coat, and drew out two more fragments of stone. "And from me, as well as from Mundy. Of course, magick might have been used to remove the fragments from our bodies rather than a scalpel, but neither Lockwell nor I was in any position to do so, and Mundy never had a very fine touch. Gambrel possesses such ability, but as you saw, he chose a more violent method to remove the stones from Larken and Fintaur."

Ivy gazed at the pieces of stone in his hand. "I thought Mr. Mundy had fled the city."

"So he had. But Mundy's habits and intentions were ever obvious to me, and so I was able to find him easily."

"And he gave up his piece of the keystone willingly?"

"Willingly enough. I told him that if he did not submit himself to the surgeon's knife, that Gambrel would take the stone from him by less precise means, just as he had done with Fintaur and Larken."

Yes, Ivy imagined that had indeed convinced him. "Where is Mr. Mundy now? Is he with my father?"

"No, the toad has hopped away to lose himself in the mire, as to be expected. But it does not matter, as we have what we need of him."

Throughout this exchange, Ivy's dread had gradually receded. A curious mind such as hers—one that ever sought out knowledge—could not help being engrossed by all she had heard.

"But what is it?" she wondered aloud. "What is the keystone for? I think my father intended to tell me through the pages of his journal. Only something went amiss with the calculations he had made, so that his entries were no longer appearing when he intended them to. And I fear his final words will not appear at all."

"No, they will show themselves," Mr. Bennick said. "But it is as you describe—his initial equations were off by some degree. I have reformulated them, and so have determined when his final words will appear. That is why I have appeared myself at this very moment. The last entry should manifest in the journal just as the fifth occlusion in the Grand Conjunction commences, which will be a number of hours from now."

"The fifth occlusion?" Ivy said, frowning. "But that's not what my sister Rose said. She said Father told her that I should open the book when the third occlusion begins."

Mr. Bennick seemed taken aback by this. "Your father told her this? How can that be?"

"She can speak to his spirit, in the house on Durrow Street. Or rather, I do not know if he can hear her. But at the least, she can hear him."

Lady Shayde turned around and took a step toward them. "You should believe what she says. Her sister possesses a sensitivity to the presence of both witchcraft and arcane power. I've witnessed it myself."

"And your sister told you that Lockwell spoke of the third occlusion?" Mr. Bennick said, advancing on Ivy. "Are you certain of it?"

"Yes, that's what she said."

Mr. Bennick swore an oath in a harsh language Ivy did not recognize. "Then I am not so good at astrographical calculations as I thought. I came here well before the fifth occlusion to make sure I did not arrive too late. But I fear I may have after all. For I believe the third occlusion is about to commence. Indeed, it may have done so already. Quickly—open the journal!"

Ivy was already doing so, her heart beating wildly as a panic gripped her. She turned through the pages, going swiftly, but trying not to skip any. After a few minutes she made it to the end of the book, but all of the pages had been blank.

"Again," Mr. Bennick breathed, his dark eyes intent.

Going from the back of the book this time, Ivy turned through the pages again, her hands trembling as she did. One page. And another. And—

There was a dim flutter just as she was turning a page. Hastily, Ivy turned back. No, she hadn't mistaken it. A word had appeared, and already more were following after it. They were even fainter than the last entry that had appeared, but Mr. Bennick brought a candle close, and she could make out the lines of spidery text. Rose had heard their father's instructions, and she had remembered them correctly. If it hadn't been for her, they would never have been able to read these words.

And they still wouldn't, if Ivy didn't read quickly. For hardly more than a minute after the first words had manifested, they were already beginning to fade away, even as other lines were appearing below.

"Hurry!" Mr. Bennick hissed. He came around behind her chair, and she knew he was reading frantically even as she was.

Grand Conjunction, First Occlusion,
Eides inferior to Regulus

My Dearest Ivoleyn—

There is so much I would like to tell you, but I know that time is now exceedingly precious. For if you are reading this, it means that all of Larken's calculations are indeed correct, and a Grand Conjunction of the planets has commenced even as the Red Wanderer draws close to our world.

That our little world, so minute in the great void of the heavens, is now in the gravest of perils, I suppose you can by now imagine. Just as I suppose you have learned of the Ashen, and of their insatiable hunger. Over ten thousand years ago, long before the first recorded histories of the scribes of Tharos, they nearly conquered our world. Had they done so, they would have devoured all life upon it—just as they did to their own world long ago.

For eons, the Ashen have had only one another's bodies to consume. They ever eat, and spawn, and are eaten themselves. So you can imagine the ravenous furor with which they would have descended upon our world. No light, no life would have remained.

Only it did not happen that way. The Ashen had not anticipated that our tiny world could have its own unique and inherent defenses to protect it—that is, the Wyrdwood. A union came about between women who could call to the trees and men who could wield magick. By this alliance of the first witches and magicians, the Ashen were repulsed, and their planet spun back into the depths of the Void.

Only now it has returned. And while ten thousand years ago much of Altania was covered with great tracts of primeval forest, now but a few straggled stands of Old Trees remain scattered here and there. Yet many of the old gates remain as well, relics created by the Ashen during that first war. When the red planet draws close enough, those ancient doorways will be awakened. They will open, and the Ashen will pour through in a dark flood—and there will be neither trees nor witches to stop them.

I fear this is all by design. Ever since that first alliance of witches and magicians long ago, the two have not dwelled in such harmony. For magick, you must understand, has its very origins on the world of the Ashen; it was from that world that knowledge of the arcane was brought to our own world. And while the first magicians used this power against the Ashen, it has not always been that way since. And so, throughout history, the forces of magick have sought to subjugate the Wyrdwood even as they have sought to subjugate those who might call to it and direct its power.

I fear it is for this reason that, over the centuries, women have ever been diminished to an inferior status in our civilization, constrained by the corset of society's rules, even as the Wyrdwood itself has been diminished, cut back and trapped behind stone walls. The power of magick—which resides in the Old Houses, those families descended from those first seven magicians—has ever schemed and plotted for this day, shaping and directing the wishes and actions of men, most often without their knowledge. Thus it has worked over the ages to prepare the world for the return of the Ashen, to make certain there would be no resistance this time.

And now that day has come.

But do not despair as you read this! There is yet some hope, however scant. Though it was from the world of the Ashen that magick came, that does not mean all magicians are their servants. Some have labored over the long years to bolster the defenses of this world. My own ancestor, the great magician Gauldren, was one of these. He worked the Quelling not to weaken the trees as many believe, but rather to make them slumber unless provoked, so that men would be less inclined to destroy them and more willing to simply let them be. It is because of Gauldren's work that we have any Old Trees left at all, though these are precious few all the same.

Still, it is my hope they will be enough to do what must be done. The Old Trees need not hold the Ashen at bay for long. If all goes as I have long planned, the ravenous ones will have little time to pass through the gates as they open.

It is my hope that Mr. Bennick is with you at this moment. He knows much of this even as I do, for he has from time to time spoken with the Elder One—the man in the black mask—even as I have done. It is also my hope you have found a suitable magician—the very same, perhaps, that helped you gain entry to my house on Durrow Street and bolster its defenses. It is because of what you accomplished then, Ivoleyn, in solving my riddles to you, that there is any hope at all now. It is because of this new alliance of witchcraft and magick that the Ashen may yet be defeated. For if you can call to the Wyrdwood and bid it to open the way, then your magician may master the magick of Heathcrest Hall.

Here is how it is to be done. . . .

Feverishly, Ivy read the final lines her father had written in the journal even as they began to fade. She felt a pain and pressure around her heart, as if magick had been used to place a stone within her own chest.

"Ink and paper!" Mr. Bennick said sharply. "Is there any here? Quickly!"

"There!" Ivy blurted. "In the writing table by the window."

Mr. Bennick took the journal from her and hurried to the writing table along with the candle. Ivy followed after him. He seized a pen, roughly dipped it in a bottle of ink, and scratched the tip furiously against a sheet of paper. Ivy looked over his shoulder. As she did, she saw the last faint symbols on the journal's open page flicker and vanish.

With a sigh, Mr. Bennick set down his pen. "There, I got it—though only just."

Ivy gazed at the line of runes Mr. Bennick had hastily transcribed onto the sheet of parchment. "It's a spell, isn't it? But forgive me, you have no ability to work magick anymore. How are we to use it?"

"I will show you." He set the journal atop the sheaf of parchment and stood up. "Come, we must go to the Wyrdwood—to the grove that lies to the east of the manor."

She gaped at him. "The Wyrdwood? But why must we go there?"

"There is no time to explain. I fear we have already dallied too long, and we must be there before he arrives."

And he started for the door.

Ivy hardly knew what to think. Was this all one final ruse to bring her under Mr. Bennick's power? But no, he could have already done so. Besides, she knew now that she should never have questioned her father's wisdom. Mr. Bennick may have been brusque, even harsh, in his manner. But that he was now, as ever, in league with her father, Ivy was utterly convinced. She started to follow Mr. Bennick. Only then she remembered.

"Rose," she said. "She's in the parlor still."

Lady Shayde moved toward them. "I will keep watch over her."

Strangely, Ivy found herself comforted by this. She nodded to the other woman. Then she hurried after Mr. Bennick.

By the time she reached the front door, he was already outside. She hastily put on her cape and followed him east, away from the manor. The rain had stopped, and the clouds were lifting. Despite this, the gloom upon the air had thickened into a peculiar twilight. Yet from what she could tell through the clouds, the sun was not setting, but remained high overhead.

Mr. Bennick's long legs carried him swiftly over the damp moor, and Ivy labored to keep up with him. Given the distance he maintained between them, and the fact that she soon struggled for breath, there was no opportunity to ask him anything more. They descended the ridge on which Heathcrest stood, then began to climb again. Then, just as the clouds broke apart, they reached the stone wall before the grove of Wyrdwood.

"Open the way," Mr. Bennick said.

Startled, Ivy gaped at him.

"Open a passage in the wall," he said, his voice sharp. "He will need a way to bring it through. Quickly!"

Ivy hesitated, then shut her eyes. She had not called out to many trees at once since she had been to the Evengrove, and then she had nearly lost herself in their roaring voices. But it was not so this time. This grove was not nearly as large, and while the trees spoke with many voices, Ivy found it was not difficult to raise her own above them.

You must make a way through the wall, she called out with her thoughts, shutting her eyes as she did. *Pry the stones apart with your roots. Push on them with your branches. Break the wall open!*

There was a loud *crack* followed by a brief din of rumbling and clinking. Ivy opened her eyes to see the trees give one last shudder and grow still. Loose stones scattered the ground, and in the wall there was now a dark gap large enough for a man to pass through.

This astonished her no less than the sight of Mr. Bennick grinning. "Well done," he said.

"Now what?" Ivy said, her breath fogging upon the cool, moist air.

"We wait. Though not, I think, for very long."

Mr. Bennick stood motionless, his dark gaze fixed on the wall. For Ivy's part, she needed to move to fend off the chill, and she paced back and forth, her arms folded tightly before her. The last of the clouds dissipated, but the gloom only deepened. The sky was a queer grayish purple she had never seen before, and the sun was wan and dim, like the flame of a lamp whose wick had been turned down too low. All at once a gale sprang up, roaring through the branches of the trees.

Only it wasn't a gale at all, for the heather and gorse around her were not stirred, and no breeze tugged at the hem of her cape.

"Lady Quent, you must quell the trees!" Mr. Bennick shouted. He backed away from the wall. Above its top, the crowns of the trees thrashed back and forth. "Quickly, tell them to cease!"

Ivy's urgency was such that she could not feel fear. Instead, she rushed forward, to the very gap in the wall, and flung her thoughts outward. *There is no reason to stir. You are in no peril. Hold your branches and be still!*

She repeated these thoughts, and again. Gradually, the roaring noise lessened, until finally it ceased. The branches of the trees drooped and fell still; the only motion was the fluttering of old, dead leaves as they drifted to the ground.

No, something else was moving in the grove. Ivy could hear a crunching and crackling of twigs growing nearer. Startled, she backed away from the wall. A moment later, to her great astonishment, a dim figure appeared in the crack in the mossy stones.

"Well," Mr. Bennick said, "you are only just in time."

And through the gap in the wall stepped a rather disheveled but nonetheless handsome man in a brown soldier's coat. It was only after a moment that Ivy realized who he was.

He smiled, and his face grew even more handsome yet. "Good day, Mrs. Quent," he said with a bow.

And Ivy could only exclaim, "Mr. Rafferdy!"

CHAPTER THIRTY-SIX

𝔗HEIR REUNION was joyous, but exceedingly brief. Mr. Rafferdy had but a moment to reach for her hand, and Ivy clasped his own tightly in return. It was rougher than she recalled, and stronger. The same could be said for his face. The shadow of his beard was heavy on his tanned cheeks, and the lines about his mouth and eyes had sharpened.

The effect of all this, along with his tousled hair, was to lend him something of a wild appearance—not that this was in any way unappealing. For all the grooming and impeccable fashion he had previously employed, Mr. Rafferdy had never been so striking to look at as he was that moment. Or perhaps it was merely how glad she was to see him that made the appearance of his face so welcome and pleasing.

No matter the reason, before she could speak another word, Mr. Bennick was upon them.

"Where is your companion?" he said.

Mr. Rafferdy turned and gave the tall magician a long look. Then, slowly, he nodded. Ivy could only presume he had somehow discovered the same facts about Mr. Bennick as she had.

"He is in the grove," Mr. Rafferdy said, "as is our burden. I fear the exertion of carrying it through the gate has weakened him further."

"Then let us go to him," Mr. Bennick said. "Lady Quent, will you lead us into the grove?"

Though she had no idea what to expect within, Ivy nodded. She slipped through the crack in the wall and moved into the tangled grove. Mr. Rafferdy and Mr. Bennick followed behind her. She had no need to ask Mr. Rafferdy which way to go, for he could only have come by means of the very gate she and Rose had stepped through to this place.

Whispering to the trees, she led the way deeper into the grove. Then, just as the wall was lost to sight behind them, they came to the little clearing. In its center stood an arch made of ancient stones, green with moss and worn from eons of wind and rain. A few last sparks of blue magick skittered over the stones, tracing the faint runes etched upon them. On the ground beneath the arch were two things. One was a wooden chest, which she recognized as belonging to one of the upstairs bedrooms at the house on Durrow Street. The other was a man. She could not see his face, for he was slumped forward as he sat on the ground, his pale hair draping forward. But at once she recognized his frilled and ruffled black costume.

"It's you!" she cried.

Now she knew how Mr. Rafferdy had learned the truth about Mr. Bennick. Her father had written in the journal that Mr. Bennick had known the man in the black mask—the Elder One, her father had called him.

Slowly, the man looked up. His face was high-cheeked and aristocratic, and might once have been handsome in a haughty way. Now, though, it was a sickly hue of gray, and marred by darker blotches. Despite this, the man gave a wan smile.

"You are Lady Quent, I presume," he said in a rasping but perfectly enunciated voice. "I am pleased to meet you at last."

"But surely we have met on many occasions!" she exclaimed. "How many times have you appeared to me, and spoken to me from behind your mask?"

He shook his head. "No, Lady Quent. Though I am sure you have spoken to someone inhabiting this form you see before you, know that it was not I who ever spoke to you."

Struggling to understand, Ivy looked to Mr. Rafferdy.

"It is so," Mr. Rafferdy said, meeting her gaze. "The being in the black mask who has spoken to you on occasion was never Lord Farrolbrook. Rather, he was inhabiting Lord Farrolbrook's form, for he possesses no corporeal form of his own. He was making use of Farrolbrook to come to you. In the very same way, this being used the previous Lord Farrolbrook in order to approach and speak to your own father years ago."

"But how can you know this?" she gasped.

"Because we spoke to this being ourselves but a short while ago."

Quickly, Mr. Rafferdy recounted to her the recent events that had befallen him: how a message in his black book had helped lead him from the battlefield back to the city, and to the house on Durrow Street, where the man in the black mask had been waiting for him.

"But where is this being now?" Ivy said when Mr. Rafferdy had finished. "Why has he fled?"

"Because he was forced to," Lord Farrolbrook said, then gave a cough. "When he occupies any mortal form, even one particularly suited for him as is my own, it causes that form to weaken and decay. The more he inhabits that physical body, the worse the condition becomes. It is what led my father to an untimely death."

"Then this being is wicked!" Ivy cried. She looked at Lord Farrolbrook's ravaged face with a feeling of horror, and wondered how long it would be until he followed his father to the grave.

"Perhaps," Lord Farrolbrook said, and his eyes seemed hazed with a mist. "Perhaps he was wicked, once. But now . . . ." He looked up at her. "Now I believe this being is trying to make amends."

"By injuring you in this manner? That is no way to make amends!"

Mr. Rafferdy gave a sigh. "Sometimes even a good man can do an ill thing if he is desperate enough." As he said this he reached into his coat pocket, as if to touch something there.

Ivy shuddered, but her horror was such that she could say nothing more.

"Can you walk?" Mr. Bennick said, standing above Lord Farrolbrook. "If you can go on your own, Mr. Rafferdy and I can carry the chest."

The fair-haired lord drew a deep breath. "Yes, I think I can manage, if we go slowly. But do I know you, sir? You look familiar to me."

"I have spoken with you at times when you wore the mask."

"Ah," Lord Farrolbrook said. "That is it, then. At first, I could recall nothing from those times when *he* was occupying me. It was like being in a black sleep. But lately, I have recalled a few things upon returning to myself, as one recalls vague dreams upon waking. I think that . . . no, I am sure it is his intention to come to you again, at least one more time."

"Then all the more reason for us to return to the manor," Mr. Bennick said. He reached down and took Farrolbrook's black-gloved hand, helping the slender lord to his feet. Then he and Mr. Rafferdy went to the wooden chest and picked it up. Ivy could see a glint of crimson light seeping out from the thin line between the chest and its lid.

"It's the Eye of Ran-Yahgren inside," she said. "Isn't it?"

Mr. Rafferdy's eyebrows rose. "But how did you know?"

"My father told me," she said, then turned to lead the way back out of the Wyrdwood.

᛭HOUGH IT SEEMED there should be much to discuss, they did not speak as they made their way back across the moors to Heathcrest Hall. Mr. Rafferdy and Mr. Bennick had little breath with which to speak, laboring to carry the heavy chest between them as they navigated the uneven terrain.

Lord Farrolbrook was even more strained simply to carry himself. He moved slowly, painstakingly, and often stumbled. Upon one such occasion, Ivy moved to him, as if to take his arm and hold him steady, but he shrank away before she could touch him, and he gave her such a look that she did not try again to aid him, no matter how he slipped or staggered.

Ivy had little capacity for outward speech herself. An inner dialogue more than occupied her mind as she reconsidered all that she had learned. When she had read her father's words in the journal—in what was no doubt its final entry, the culmination of all his writings and riddles for her—she had done so in disbelief, thinking it utterly impossible that such a plan could be completed before the Grand Conjunction was in full effect.

Only now, here was Mr. Rafferdy walking alongside her, helping Mr. Bennick carry the very thing her father had said was needed—the Eye of Ran-Yahgren. And there was Heathcrest Hall before them, just a short ways distant. As difficult as it was to comprehend, for they were but a few people to stand against such a ravenous horde, still logic dictated that it must indeed be possible—that they had among them all that was necessary to thwart the intentions of the Ashen.

There was only one thing Ivy did not understand. It seemed that all of the pieces of the keystone would be necessary to do what her father had suggested, yet they lacked half of them, and Mr. Bennick had said nothing about this. But perhaps in her haste to read the entry in the journal, she had misunderstood some aspect of the design.

Well, she would ask Mr. Bennick for more explanation, for he had read the entry as well. As they made their way up the steps before Heathcrest, the purple twilight thickened. And the sun, though it remained overhead, continued to fade as one by one the planets obscured it. All the same, a forceful elation rose up within Ivy. For ten thousand years, the whole of the world had dwelled unknowingly in the long shadow of the Ashen. Only now, in but a little while, that awful threat would be forever removed.

At least, so she believed for a wondrous moment. Then, as Ivy led the way into the front hall of the manor house, the flame of hope was snuffed out, and her heart shrank into a dark cinder. For all her thoughts and musings, there was one last thing she had failed to consider.

"Good day, Lady Quent," said the man who stood before the fireplace, which had been stirred up so it was blazing. The gray at his temples lent him a distinguished look, and the deep violet hue of his elegant coat complemented the large amethyst ring that adorned his right hand.

That ring flared as he made a small flick with a finger. Across the long room, near the door of the little parlor, Lady Shayde gave a jerk, like a puppet whose strings had been plucked, then stood motionless once more, her mouth open, her black eyes wide and staring.

Mr. Rafferdy and Mr. Bennick hastily set down the chest. Mr. Rafferdy started to make a move, but Mr. Bennick gripped his arm, stopping him. Then the former magician took a step forward.

"There you are, Gambrel," he said placidly. "You are a bit late, don't you think? The Grand Conjunction is already under way. Do you not need to go to your masters and grovel before them?"

"On the contrary, I've arrived exactly when I intended, *Bennick*." This last word was spoken with poisonous inflection.

Mr. Bennick nodded. "Perhaps you have. Though I imagine you have not found everything here to be exactly as you expected." He nodded toward Lady Shayde.

"It matters not." Gambrel gave a shrug, as though what he was doing required no great effort. Yet by the sheen of moisture upon his brow, and the tightness of his jaw, that was not the case. "As you can see, I have taken the sting out of the White Thorn."

"Yes, but it requires all of your will and effort to do so. You know her strength and speed as well as I do. If you turn your magick toward thwarting us, even for an instant, she will be released and will be upon you."

Given the hatred in Gambrel's eyes, these words could only be truth.

"It is but a minor inconvenience to me," Gambrel said. "Yet I wonder, had Lady Shayde not presented herself, what did you think you were going to do against me? Is this really the best you could manage after all these years, Bennick? All I see is a witch with no Wyrdwood, a magician of scant ability, and that bag of festering meat the Elder One likes to shamble about in now and then."

"Be careful," Mr. Bennick replied. "For you greatly underestimate Lord Rafferdy. The power of his House runs with great vitality in his blood, as it does in few men. He has already defeated you once—it was he who destroyed the gate in the Evengrove and trapped you for a while on Tyberion. I brought him here because I knew that, should you dare to contest him in a duel of magick, he would certainly best you again."

Gambrel did not answer immediately, and it seemed there was now a light in his eyes other than hatred. It was a glint of fear. Only then he bared his white teeth in a smile.

"Perhaps you are right, Bennick," he said. "I have been accustomed to being the finest magician in all of the arcane orders I've belonged to, but that's not to say there is none better than me. Yet while I do not have power enough to bind your White Thorn and at the same time indulge Lord Rafferdy in a duel of magick, someone has kindly left an alternative for me."

And even as the ring upon his right hand flared with purple light, he lifted his left hand and pointed the pistol at Ivy.

"The White Thorn is swift," Gambrel said, "but so is a bullet."

Ivy held her breath, staring at the barrel of the pistol.

"Lord Rafferdy," Mr. Bennick said in a low voice. "Speak a rune of binding upon him. Do it now."

"Heed that advice only if you believe you can speak more swiftly than I can pull a trigger," Gambrel said and pulled back the hammer of the pistol with his left thumb.

Mr. Rafferdy opened his mouth, but he said nothing.

"You are wiser than I gave you credit for, Lord Rafferdy," Gambrel said in a pleased tone. "Now, Bennick, be so good as to give me the fragments of the keystone. I have three, and I am sure you have the others."

"But what will you do with them?" Ivy asked. Perhaps it was absurd to voice the question. Why should he tell them anything? Yet he must have been too pleased with his plans to keep them to himself, for after a moment he did answer her.

"I will bind the keystone and use it to open the arcane gate that lies hidden beneath this manor," Gambrel said. "The gate was forged by the first magicians long ago, along with the keystone that enabled them to open and close it as they wished. Though they were far fewer in number, the magick of the first magicians was more powerful than that of the Ashen. So it is that, even now with Cerephus not yet at its closest, this gate can be opened and passed through.

"The gate leads to Cerephus itself, to an ancient city upon that world. Once I reach Cerephus, I will present myself to the Ashen, and I will introduce myself as the architect of their triumph. You see, upon my advice, Lord Valhaine has used his army to lure all of Morden's forces to various locations about Altania. It so happens that, in these same places, are other magickal gates. But unlike the gate beneath this house, these gates were not created by the first magicians. Rather, they were constructed by the Ashen during the time of the first war, and such is the design of their magick that they will awaken when Cerephus finally draws close enough—a thing it will do when the Grand Conjunction is complete.

"When this occurs, these gates will open of their own accord, bridging the void between Altania and Cerephus. A horde of Ashen-slaves will pour through, and they will devour Morden's army. Valhaine's command over Altania will be complete—as is my command over him. At my bidding, he will rule Altania in the name of the Ashen. And since there is no nation other than Altania that has ever harbored both witches and magicians in its history, it means that no other nation can possibly stand against the Ashen. Their mastery of the world will be irrevocable."

Ivy wished she had not asked the question, or that he had not answered it. She was frozen in horror. That a single man could betray all of mankind to its doom was almost impossible to comprehend.

Mr. Bennick shook his head. "And you truly believe, for this, you will be rewarded?"

"I know I will be," Gambrel said. "You see, in my studies, I have discovered secrets of their world. There are magicks there which even the Ashen themselves have forgotten, and which I can turn against them. They will have no choice but to give me what I ask for—one of the Principalities to rule as my own."

"Just a single city-state to be prince of?" Mr. Bennick said, raising an eyebrow. "What a modest request."

"You would mock me, but it is indeed modest in the scheme of all things. Yet the value of it will be incalculable. The rest of the world will be plunged into shadow—there is no way this can be avoided. But I will make my own city a haven of light: a place where art and music and science flourish. Not all of human knowledge and accomplishment need perish when the Ashen come. I can preserve it, as if in the most marvelous museum, to endure throughout time. Don't you see? Without my actions, there would be no hope of saving anything at all. But because of me, our race and our civilization will endure."

"I understand," Mr. Bennick said, his dark eyes hard. "You would willingly destroy nearly the whole of the world to save a tiny sliver of it for yourself. You are a savior indeed, of the most singular kind! But where are the other members of your arcane order? Are they not to share in your victory? Surely it is their triumph as well."

Gambrel's disgust was evident in the curl of his lip. "On the contrary, they are weaklings and imbeciles who had to be whipped like cringing dogs and dragged upon their leashes to do what simple tasks they were given. I have come here alone because there is no other who deserves to share in this victory with me. Now, bring me the fragments of keystone."

"But you won't be able to bind them together," Mr. Bennick said. "Not without knowing the precise spell Lockwell used to sunder the keystone."

Gambrel laughed. "A spell which he set down in a book—being always the practical fellow—and which someone else kindly copied down for me." He made a flick with the pistol. "Now put the pieces of the keystone on that table there. Do it, and I will ask the Ashen to show mercy, and slay you swiftly rather than force you to toil as their slaves."

"Now would be a good time to speak that rune, Lord Rafferdy," Mr. Bennick advised. "I am certain that you can stop him before he fires."

Mr. Rafferdy drew a breath, only when he did speak, it was not words of magick. "No, it's no use," he said grimly. "He has us. We have to do as he says and give him the pieces of the keystone."

Both Ivy and Mr. Bennick stared at him.

"Give him the two pieces that you have, Mr. Bennick," Mr. Rafferdy continued. "And I will give him the piece which I removed from Mr. Lockwell."

Ivy could not breathe. What was Mr. Rafferdy thinking? After all, he did not have her father's fragment; Mr. Bennick did.

"Go on, Mr. Bennick. Do as I say. Give Mr. Gambrel two pieces of the keystone."

All at once Mr. Bennick nodded. "Of course," he said, letting out a breath. "You are right, Mr. Rafferdy. Even you could not bind him so quickly as that." The former magician reached into his pocket and drew out two fragments of stone. But just two. Slowly, he walked forward and set them down on an end table, then retreated.

"Now the last piece, Lord Rafferdy," Gambrel said. Sweat was pouring down his brow. His right hand had begun to shake as his ring threw off wild sparks. "Be swift about it. My finger grows weary on the trigger."

Slowly, Rafferdy drew something from his pocket. It was not a piece of rock, but rather a small cube hewn of glossy black stone and adorned with runes. He moved to put it on the table next to the two pieces of the keystone. It was, Ivy realized, a small box.

"I put it in here, for safekeeping," Mr. Rafferdy said, then retreated.

"Get back now," Gambrel said. "All of you. Farther. I want you safely out of reach of magick."

They retreated to the far end of the hall even as Gambrel approached the table. His right hand still strained toward Lady Shayde, who remained as still as a statue. With his left hand, he set down the pistol next to the onyx box. He touched the lid, then looked up.

"If you think to trick me," he said, "and if Lockwell's fragment is not inside, I will have plenty of time to take up the pistol and shoot Lady Quent before you can come close enough to work a binding on me."

"I assure you, it is no trick," Mr. Rafferdy said.

"We shall see," Gambrel said.

And he opened the lid of the box.

It was difficult to see clearly from across the long room, but it seemed to Ivy that a puff of black smoke issued from the box, curling upward. Gambrel frowned—

—then his eyes went wide. He lurched back from the box, flinging his arms out beside him. His head tilted back, so that the cords of his neck all stood out in sharp relief, and his jaw gaped open in a silent shriek. His face went gray, and his cheeks sank inward. Dark lines snaked across his skin, like cracks upon the surface of a porcelain vase as it shattered. In mere moments he became a ghastly sight—a thing not unlike the Murghese mummies Ivy had once glimpsed behind glass in the Royal Altanian Museum.

By then, Lady Shayde was already upon him, released from the spell of binding. Only there was nothing for her to do by then. Gambrel took one more staggering step, and one dusty exhalation escaped him with a sound almost like *No*.

His purple ring flared once and went dim.

Then his shriveled form toppled over, crumbling apart as it struck the floor into a heap of sticks and sand.

IT WAS A MINUTE or more before any of them spoke. Nor did any of them move, except for Lady Shayde, who walked in a slow circle around the powdery remains of Gambrel, and then—apparently satisfied with what she saw—retreated to the edges of the room.

At last Mr. Bennick cleared his throat. "I was counting on your ability to best Gambrel, Lord Rafferdy. It was, I am aware, the most uncertain part of my plan. The better magician does not always win the duel, but I could think of no other way. And indeed, you have succeeded." He raised an eyebrow. "Though I did not know you would do it in quite this manner."

Slowly, Ivy approached the heap of dust and gray velvet that had, moments ago, been Gambrel. "But what happened to him when he opened the box?"

"The full brunt of the curse of Am-Anaru came upon him," Mr. Rafferdy said behind her.

She turned to regard him. "You mean the curse that befell the three Lords of Am-Anaru?"

"The very same."

"But how?"

"I had taken the curse from Lord Baydon and placed it in the box."

"Lord Baydon!" she exclaimed. "But how had the curse befallen him? He was never in Am-Anaru."

"No, he wasn't. But as I said before, even a good man can do an awful thing if he is desperate enough."

With a composition of both fascination and horror, Ivy listened as Mr. Rafferdy explained how he had learned what Lord Marsdel had done—how he had taken fractions of the curse's power from himself, Earl Rylend, and the elder Lord Rafferdy, and had placed them in the box. Then he had given the box to Lord Baydon, who had opened it, taking those portions of the curse's power upon himself.

It was an awful deed, the more so because it had played upon Lord Baydon's good nature, and upon his regret at being unable to join the other three men in war. Fortunately, Mr. Rafferdy had discovered the box among his father's things, and he had arrived at Farland Park in time to find Lord Baydon yet alive. He had extracted the curse from Lord Baydon, returning it to the onyx box.

"Ever since then, I have felt the dreadful power of the curse straining to be free of the box," Mr. Rafferdy said. He approached Gambrel's remains. "And now it has."

Ivy shuddered. "But why did it operate with such swiftness upon him?"

It was Mr. Bennick who answered. "I would imagine it is because the curse had worked for years within Lord Baydon, growing ever more noxious. It had done this gradually, so that his constitution could in some part acclimate to its effects. Even so, he had nearly expired from it. When Gambrel opened the box, the effects which the curse had wrought upon Lord Baydon over decades came upon Gambrel in mere moments. His physical form was not able to tolerate such a sudden and savage assault."

"But how is Lord Baydon now?" Ivy said, looking at Mr. Rafferdy.

"I cannot say for certain, for I had to depart Farland Park immediately. Yet even within minutes of taking the curse from him, his breathing eased, and his color improved. I have hope he will yet have many years before him." He looked at Mr. Bennick. "If any of us in this world do."

"That is within your and Lady Quent's power to decide now," the former magician said.

Ivy turned away from the remnants of Mr. Gambrel. "But he has still won. Even if we do as my father wrote in the journal, the gates between our world and Cerephus will be open for a brief while at least. Surely that is long enough for many of the slaves of the Ashen to come through and wreak havoc upon Huntley Morden's army. They will be decimated, and Lord Valhaine will still rule Altania."

To her great puzzlement, Mr. Rafferdy laughed. "No, Lord Valhaine won't win, and it's all due to Eldyn Garritt. Our dear, diffident friend has become both a rebel and a spy, can you imagine that? And because of his most courageous efforts, we now have a map which shows precisely where each of the arcane gates is located."

"That is marvelous!" Ivy exclaimed. "But how is that possible?"

"The rebels Mr. Garritt was working with had come by a map of Altania on which five locations were marked. It seemed a great stroke of luck, for these locations were clearly the places Valhaine was sending his troops to make a final assault. The rebels forwarded the map to Morden's generals so they could position their troops to meet Valhaine's army. Only it's clear it was not luck at all that the rebels obtained the map, but rather that they were meant to find it."

"How can you know this?"

"I know because, when I met with Mr. Garritt's compatriots, they showed me a copy of the map, and I saw at once that there were runes written next to each place marked on the map—including the rune which means *gate* in the language of magick. It can only mean that the purpose of the map was to lure Morden's army to the various locations—"

"—so that they would be near the gates when the Ashen came through!" Ivy gasped.

"Just so," Mr. Rafferdy said, nodding. "But the two armies aren't the only ones making for the gates at present. I only hope there is time enough."

"My calculations are not perfect," Mr. Bennick said. "But we are only to the third occlusion. It will be six hours I would guess, perhaps eight, before the Grand Conjunction reaches the final occlusion."

"That should be enough time," Mr. Rafferdy said. "Barely."

Quickly, he described the plans which had been set in motion back in the city. With the aid of his black magician's book, he had exchanged a flurry of messages with those members of his order who had escaped the city. As it turned out, four of them happened to be in locations which were not so very far from four of the gates—the farthest being less than fifty miles, a distance a cantering horse could easily cover in a matter of hours. The main obstacle would be passing through the front of the war, but the four magicians had been provided the necessary passwords and codes to approach Morden's commanders. Which meant, at that very moment, they were racing toward the locations of the arcane gates in the company of rebel soldiers.

"Are they going to destroy the gates?" Ivy said, breathless from the thrill of this news.

"Not quite," Mr. Rafferdy replied. "Rather, they are going to alter them. With their House rings as guides, and with the rebel soldiers to protect them, my colleagues should have scant trouble locating the gates once they reach the areas marked on Garritt's map, for these are bound to radiate much arcane energy now that Cerephus draws near. And the rebel soldiers are prepared to excavate them, for they have no doubt been buried over the eons. Then, once the gates are exhumed, Trefnell, Canderhow, and the others will carve a new set of runes upon them."

"For what purpose?"

"Do you recall the gate in the center of the Evengrove? How the arch had runes on each side so that it acted as a sort of double-lock?"

Ivy nodded. "Yes, it led both to Tyberion and to the tomb of the Broken God. That was how Gambrel intended to get from Tyberion to the tomb."

"Precisely. Similarly, my colleagues will alter the gates they dig up with new runes so that each of them bridges to other destinations."

Mr. Bennick's eyes were alight with curiosity. "And what destinations might those be?"

Ivy could only admit that Mr. Rafferdy appeared a bit pleased with himself.

"I examined a number of gates in the ancient way station on Arantus," he said. "I found a number that opened into stands of Wyrdwood, and I copied the sequence of the runes upon each of them into my black book. My colleagues will inscribe these same sequences onto the gates they uncover."

And all at once, Ivy understood. "So when the Ashen come through the gates, they will not fall upon Morden's army at all."

Mr. Rafferdy nodded. "Instead, the gates will whisk them to the corresponding doorways upon Arantus, and from there directly—"

"—into the Wyrdwood," she said in unison with him.

It was marvelous and brilliant and daring. At that moment, Ivy's only thought was to rush to him, throw her arms around him, and embrace him with all her might. Only before she could do so, a voice spoke—one that she seemed to hear with both her mind and her ears.

"If any of those plans are to have meaning, you must first bind the keystone and descend to the gate beneath this house."

As one, they all turned to look at Lord Farrolbrook. Only it wasn't Lord Farrolbrook anymore, not really. He must have been keeping his black mask somewhere in his frilled black costume, for it was before his face once more. The mask was wrought into a grimace of agony.

"Who are you?" Ivy murmured, taking a step toward him. "Mr. Gambrel called you the Elder One. But who are you really?"

Now, despite the expression of pain, the mask's mouth twisted into something of a smile. "But don't you know, Lady Quent? I have been trying to tell you that very thing for months now. Perhaps this will aid you."

With weak and trembling motions he removed his gloves. On his right hand was an ornate gold ring set with seven red gems. They caught some of the firelight, glinting brightly.

And Ivy's body went rigid. A pain passed through her—a sharp and awful rending. For months, piece by piece, she had been recalling more of the strange dream that had started coming to her at the same time as life had first taken root inside her.

Now, gazing at that glittering red ring, she at last could recall the final moments of the dream: leaving the cave, and traveling across the land with the tall man who wore the wolf's pelt across his shoulders. Moons passed, and her belly swelled. At last life had sprung forth from her, and she had cradled the infant in her arms, filled with joy.

Only then joy became horror. The tall man's body crumpled to the ground, lifeless. Even as it did, the infant boy in her arms opened his blue eyes—eyes that were far too ancient to be those of a child.

Through you, I will truly live again, the man had said as they lay together in the cave.

The man whose name was Myrrgon.

And he had done just that.

"You are the great magician Myrrgon!" Ivy cried. "Or rather, you are his father!"

He made a dismissive gesture, and the red ring flashed; though it did so feebly, like a sputtering flame on a dying candle. "Father and son—it makes no difference. The two are one and the same in my case."

Mr. Rafferdy wore a look of astonishment that Ivy was certain appeared much like her own. In contrast, Mr. Bennick had affected a curious expression, while Lady Shayde, who now approached, wore no expression at all upon the white mask of her own face.

"But how can you be Myrrgon?" Mr. Rafferdy said, touching his own House ring. "Myrrgon lived thousands of years ago."

"Yes, I did," the man in the mask replied. "Indeed, it was the one time I truly lived upon the world, and it was the same for the others."

Ivy pressed a hand to her stomach, forcing herself to breathe. "The others," she gasped. "You mean the other magicians who founded the seven Old Houses of magick?"

"Yes, Gauldren, Baltharel, Xandrus, and the rest. We had all found a way to live again upon this world. In our arrogance, we thought we could do so forevermore. Only for all our knowledge, we had not considered the price that must be paid for the manner in which we had achieved our rebirth. And we had underestimated the power of this world we had arrived at."

Now it was to her head that Ivy pressed a hand, for a pain seemed to stab there as well. "You are from Cerephus! You come from the world of the Ashen!"

For a moment, all were motionless. Then the man who was not Lord Farrolbrook nodded.

"Yes, that is the world of my origin. It is the world where I was born for the first time." He took a lurching step toward a window, as if to gaze outside, then turned the black mask to face her again. "We do not have much time left. Nor does this mortal form, I fear.

All the same, I will tell you a story, Lady Quent, since I know you are fond of them.

"Once there was a race of beings who had mastered the working of arcane powers—magick, you would call it. They used this magick to build a great civilization, making their world into a place of such majesty and awe as even your clever mind could never imagine. On the surface, it was a place of order and beauty. But beneath the surface, an endless labyrinth of engines and mechanisms and furnaces belching vapors and vitriol was required to maintain all of the wonders above. As none of our kind would deign to dwell or labor in such a place, we needed others to do this work for us. And so we used our powers to open doorways, and draw beings through from other places, other worlds. We altered them, shaping them with magick to suit our uses, and then we sent them to the foul depths below our world to labor there. The Ashen, we called them—those who stoked the blazing furnaces of magick that fueled our world. And so they did for millennia while we dwelled in ease above. Until . . ."

"Until your slaves rose up against you," Mr. Bennick said flatly.

Again the man in black nodded. "Yes, they did. And over the eons, our race had dwindled in number and strength. We could do nothing to stop them as they boiled out from below and swarmed over the world, consuming all. We had but one hope, and that was to open a great gate that was large enough to move our entire world a vast distance through the heavens in an instant, and so bring it close to another world—one which might provide a haven for us."

"You mean to this world!" Ivy exclaimed.

"Yes, this very world. But to work an enchantment of such an enormous scale was a terrible act. Our own planet was cracked and nearly sundered into pieces, while at the same time the workings of the celestial spheres around this world were disrupted and forever altered. In the tumult, nearly all of our own race perished. Only seven of us survived—the seven strongest. But even we did so only in the abstract. The essence of our spirits endured, but our bodies had been burned away and utterly destroyed.

"After this violent arrival, our world began to circle wildly around yours, growing closer yet with each revolution. Bodiless, we were able to leap across the void to this new world we had reached, and there we sought out new forms to inhabit. We observed the primitive people who dwelled on one particular island—the island you now call Altania. And we discovered, through some experimentation, that we could each force our essence into these beings, so long as we chose those who had the most powerful physical forms. Even so—even when we chose to enter the tallest and strongest of them, the dominant males of their species—we could only do so for a little while, for the physical forms would quickly begin to deteriorate and decay. And this inflicted a significant agony upon us.

"Thus it was we sought a more permanent solution, and quite by accident we discovered one. Not long after we came to this world, the Ashen began to do so as well, gradually learning to construct ever more powerful gates to bridge the way here in pursuit of us. In turn, we employed the natural defenses of this world against them. The thick forests had an inherent power to defend themselves, an ability they had developed in the distant past to defend themselves against great beasts now long extinct.

"What was more, we discovered that there were some women among the primitive people who were born with an ability to communicate with the trees. So it was we came to these women, wearing the bodies of men, and taught them to call to the forests and to turn the trees against the Ashen. This they did, driving the Ashen back as the celestial spheres continued to turn, settling into a new harmonic. In time, the planet on which we were born, which you now call Cerephus, began to circle farther and farther away in the aether, until at last it was beyond the reach of this world.

"It was during this same period, this first war against the Ashen, that Gauldren learned something remarkable. He had come, in his way, to care for one of the women whom he had taught to wield the forest—one of these first witches. Previously, we had found that if any of us were to lie with a female of this world, while in the guise of one of their males, it would mean her death. For she would inevitably conceive, and the foreign nature of the life growing within her would be as a poison to her body, and so destroy her.

"Only, in this particular case, Gauldren found this was not so. We had observed the capability of the trees to withstand the powers of magick, and it turned out the same was true of the women who had an affinity with the forest. The witch that Gauldren had foolishly cast his affections on conceived, only she was able to carry the child, and in time to give birth to it.

"As he held his infant son, and studied it, Gauldren realized the truth: here was a physical body in which was united the power of both worlds. It was a form he might inhabit without fear of it rejecting him and decaying as he dwelled within it. And so, his current form failing, Gauldren did enter into that body. It grew rapidly, far faster than a usual child. And in that form, he was able to truly live again, reborn as a man of this world—able to bind himself to any woman, to father children who looked like any others, to eat, and speak, and breathe."

Here the man in the mask paused, and Mr. Bennick spoke in turn. "So that is how House Gauldren was founded. And how the seed of magick was embedded in that line. But what of the other Old Houses? What of the rest of you?"

The man in the black garb lifted his beringed hand to the black mask as if to conceal his face, even though it was already covered. He did not answer Mr. Bennick's question. But he did not need to, for Ivy knew the answer. She had seen it herself in the dream.

"You deceived them!" she cried, and the words burned hotly as she uttered them. "You sought out some of those first witches, and you used them in the most dreadful way to make sons for yourself—sons you could steal from their mothers, and whose bodies you could inhabit without fear of pain or decay, just as Gauldren had done!"

She fell silent; she could say no more. Her horror, her fury, had made her mute; her hands were clenched into fists at her sides.

"Yes," he said at last, his voice a rasp coming through the slit in the mask. "We did just as you said. We sired the first offspring of a witch and a magician this world has ever known, and entered into those forms. But they were the last such offspring as well. For you see, we had taught the forest, and the witches, too well. In our new mortal forms, we found we could father sons—sons who inherited some of our own magickal ability. But never could we do this with a woman descended from those first witches. Their ability to fight the forces of the arcane had been increased, while our own power had been diluted. As a result, the witch's body was always able to reject the seed of magick within her. A witch could only bear a son if the father was not one of our descendants, if he had no element of magick in him. Even then, such sons of witches were not common, though they were unique in that they were males who possessed something akin to, if different than, a witch's power. Siltheri, you call them now—illusionists."

"But you can do illusions yourself!" Ivy exclaimed. "I have seen you make statues seem to move, and other such things."

He nodded. "Yes, I can do such things. After all, I am the son of a witch. But unlike all Siltheri today, I am also the son of a magician. And it is only the son of a magician and a witch who can provide a suitable vessel into which we can be reborn. But no witch has borne a son to a magician since that very first time eons ago. So it was we lived our lives, and died as mortal men do, and became things of spirit again—conscious, but not really alive." He spread his trembling arms. "Oh, from time to time we could steal into mortal form, as you see me doing now. It was easiest to enter one of our own descendants, but still they would decay. In time we wearied of it, and it became harder and harder to hold the essence of our beings together. One by one, the others began to fade away: Gauldren first, then Baltharel, Xandrus, Vordigan, and the others. One by one, they all dissipated into the aether and were gone. Of them all, of all my race, only I now remain."

Still Ivy could not speak, gripped now by sorrow from all she had heard. She could only think of the young woman in the dream. Only it hadn't been a dream at all. She had really lived by the sea long, long ago. Layka.

"So why do you remain?" Mr. Rafferdy asked, ending the silence. "Why are you still here, when all the others have gone?"

"Because there is no one else to undo the wrongs my race has committed," he said, his voice fainter now. "In our arrogance and cruelty, we created the Ashen. In our fear and weakness, we used your world as a tool to help us battle our own terrible creation. But you should not have to suffer for our errors and failings, that much I learned. That much Gauldren taught me before he faded.

"So I endured, and over the years I have labored in the shadows. Sometimes I would retreat for a millennium, only to return and sow little seeds where I could. This was not easy, for I diminished as time passed. I had to achieve things in what feeble ways I could, and always through the actions of others. I could not always find a form suitable to enter, and then was limited to go where it might, and would sometimes have to rest for centuries when I had expended too much of myself.

"Beyond that, I was forced to approach people furtively, in the most secret fashion, and give only hints and clues rather than clear answers, for fear that it would become obvious to those who awaited the return of the Ashen that I endured, and what I was scheming. For there have long been magicians who had discovered ancient artifacts from the time of the first war, or who had stumbled upon some forgotten tomb containing a daemon, and so had learned of the Ashen, feeling their power and then, twisted by it, sought to clear a way for them when in time they came again."

He took a halting step toward Ivy. "And now the time for which I have so long labored is here. You have only to do as your father instructed you in his journal, and it will be done."

He turned the dark mask to the corner where Lady Shayde stood, her dark gown melding with the shadows. "I see you forged a White Thorn, just as I advised you to do, Mr. Bennick. That is well, for you shall have need of her."

"I do not serve him," Lady Shayde said coldly.

The black mask tilted slightly to one side. "Then whom do you serve?"

For a moment Lady Shayde was motionless, as if once again she was bound by a spell. Then, slowly, her gaze turned toward Ivy.

The man in the mask nodded. "Very good. That is what your kind were first created for. That is your purpose." Clumsily, he sat down in a chair. "And now the hour is finally upon us. I will depart this form, and I will not come to you again. But know that I will be watching until it is done, and then I will fade away like the others. And know also that I thank you, and all your forebears who have ever aided in this endeavor over all the long years of this world. You deserve a better fate than what we forced upon you. It is my hope that, after this, you will discover what it is."

He gave a sigh. Then his head drooped forward, and the black mask fell to the floor, where it shattered into pieces.

Ivy clasped a hand to her mouth.

"Is he . . . is Lord Farrolbrook dead?" Mr. Rafferdy said, taking a step toward him.

Mr. Bennick bent over the chair. "No, he breathes yet. He but sleeps now, I think."

Ivy sighed and lowered her hands. She realized she could hardly see them before her. The fire had died low again, and the gloom in the hall had thickened. Outside the windows, the sky was the hue of a blackening bruise. She could make out a few cold pinpricks of stars.

"Time grows short," Mr. Bennick said. "We must go."

"Go where?" spoke a querulous voice.

They all turned to see Rose standing in the open door of the parlor. Throughout all of this, Ivy's sister had remained locked in the parlor—for which Ivy was grateful. But now she took a few steps into the front hall, her face pale in the gloom, the porcelain doll held tight in her arms.

"Where must you go?" Rose said.

"Don't worry, dearest," Ivy said, taking a step toward her. "We just need to go into the basement below the house. There is something we need to do there. But it won't take long, I promise."

"It's getting dark," Rose said. "Are you sure it's safe down there?"

Before Ivy could think of what to say, Lady Shayde moved toward Rose, closing the distance between them in an instant.

"Do not worry," she said to Rose. "I will be with them. Wait for them in the parlor. They will return soon."

At this Rose smiled and nodded, the fear gone from her face. Then suddenly she held out the doll. "You never did get to hold her. Would you like to, before you go?"

Lady Shayde—or rather, Ashaydea—seemed frozen for a moment. Then, slowly, she reached out hands that were as pale as those of the porcelain child. She cradled the doll awkwardly, gently. For a few moments she stroked its face, its hair, its blue-black dress. Then she held it out again.

"Thank you," she said.

Rose nodded once more, taking the doll, adjusting its ribbons. Then Lady Shayde turned her black gaze toward the others.

"I am ready," she said.

MINUTES LATER, they descended the stairs that led from the kitchen to the cellars. Ivy and Lady Shayde held hurricane lamps, while Mr. Rafferdy and Mr. Bennick carried the wooden chest between them. In the darkness of the cellar, the line around the lid glowed a hot red, as if the chest was filled with some molten material.

They reached the bottom of the stairs, then moved across the cellar to the farthest wall. There the rough-hewn walls gave way to smooth, black stone. Only once before had Ivy ever ventured so deep into the cellar, over a year ago, on the day she had found the painting made by the first Mrs. Quent—the one which depicted Ivy as a small child with her mother in the Wyrdwood.

Since her return to Heathcrest, Ivy had avoided coming down to the cellar, and when she did stayed close to the stairs, for the darkness below the house always weighed upon her in the most oppressive manner. It did so now as they drew close to the far wall. Its glossy surface reflected the lamplight like dark water, and a palpable chill emanated from it.

"This stone is imbued with a spell of binding and concealing," Mr. Rafferdy said as he and Mr. Bennick set down the chest. He approached the wall and ran his right hand across it. His House ring flashed a brilliant blue as he did.

"It knows your touch," Mr. Bennick said, "but that is no surprise. Both House Rylend and House Rafferdy are descended from House Gauldren. That is one reason I sought you out, Lord Rafferdy. I knew it would require a magician of that line to one day remove this barrier."

"And here I thought it was because of my charming wit," Mr. Rafferdy quipped.

Astonishingly, Mr. Bennick laughed, the sound echoing around the cellar.

"Earl Rylend had hoped his son would be the one to do this," Ivy said then. "Didn't he?"

Mr. Bennick's laughter ceased. "Yes, such was Rylend's hope. While he had little magickal talent himself, despite being descended of one of the Old Houses, his interest in the arcane was deep. It was his research that led him and his companions to the cave in Am-Anaru where they discovered the Eye of Ran-Yahgren. What was more, from his studies, he was convinced the Eye had some important role to play should the Ashen ever threaten the world again. It was his wish for his son to do what he could not, and become a magician who might be able to master the power of the Eye. But I knew from the first day that I tutored Lord Wilden in magick that he would never be the one to do this. While he possessed some talent, he had petty wants and interests, and was both impatient and easily bored. More than that, Lord Wilden was a young man possessed of both a weak character and a weak will."

"Come now, Mr. Bennick," Lady Shayde said coolly, "should you really speak so of my foster brother, and of Lady Quent's father?"

Ivy would have thought, after all that had happened that day, that she would be beyond shock. All the same, she was forced to reach out and grip the cold stones.

"Is it true?" she finally managed to gasp, looking at Mr. Bennick.

Slowly, the tall magician nodded. "Lord Wilden had a reputation for going to Cairnbridge or Low Sorrell, drinking too much wine, and harassing the young women of the village. When Merriel Addysen had a child out of wedlock, it was rumored the little girl was his. Looking at you now . . . at the shape of your face and eyes, I can only say it must be so."

Ivy felt her legs go weak, and she sagged against the cold stones to keep from falling. Only then Mr. Rafferdy was there, holding her arm and providing a warmer source of support. She drew in a breath, then after a few moments she felt steady enough to gently disengage his arm.

"Please, Mr. Rafferdy," she said. "Open the way."

And he did so. He spoke harsh words of magick; his ring threw off blue sparks that struck the wall, crackling over its surface. The stones began to fade away, as if they were no more solid than mist. Then, as the sparks vanished, the stones did as well.

Now another barrier faced them, and Mr. Bennick nodded toward Ivy. She hesitated, then reached out and touched one of the massive wooden beams that had been revealed behind the stones. The wood seemed to hum beneath her fingers, still vibrating with a memory of life, even though it had been here for centuries.

It was Wyrdwood.

These were no mere twigs gleaned from the edges of a grove, though. These were great beams hewn from the cores of ancient trees felled long ago, no doubt with the aid of magick. All the same, shaping them was little different than opening the Wyrdwood box. She formed the thoughts, sending them outward. The beams twisted themselves, bending and growing, until they parted like a curtain to reveal a flat plane of reddish stone. The stone bore no runes or etchings. The only mark upon it was a six-sided indentation in the center of the gate.

For a gate was precisely what it was.

Before they descended to the cellar, Mr. Bennick had told them what they would find down there. It was the very same thing the first Earl Rylend had found when he decided to build his house upon this ridge more than two centuries ago, and dug down into the ancient rock to lay the foundations.

Fascinated by the red slab of stone the workmen uncovered, the first Earl Rylend had undertaken a study of ancient artifacts, and this had led in turn to research into magick. Before his death, he had learned that the red stone was in fact a gate—one which led to a most perilous place—and so he labored with magicians as well as witches to erect barriers to cover it. The next few Rylend earls also maintained an interest in magick, but over time this habit dwindled in the line, eventually dying out, and the gate was forgotten for nearly two hundred years.

More recently, after stumbling upon some papers and journals left by his ancestor, the last Earl Rylend had rekindled the family interest in the arcane. His desire to learn more about the red stone slab, and its purpose, eventually led him to become aware of the Ashen, and to discover the existence of other artifacts of the first war against them—artifacts such as the Eye of Ran-Yahgren. Earl Rylend had shared much of this knowledge with Mr. Bennick, during the time when Mr. Bennick was at Heathcrest Hall, acting as Lord Wilden's tutor.

Ivy had listened raptly as the former magician recounted this history. How many things had been set in motion by that chance discovery of the red slab of stone some two hundred and fifty years ago! Or was it really by chance that it had been uncovered? Perhaps it was the man in the black mask, the Elder One named Myrrgon, who had convinced the first Earl Rylend to erect his house on this ridge and so discover the gate. And perhaps it was he as well who had encouraged the last Earl Rylend to take up his ancestor's study of magick.

Ivy could only believe it was so. After all, Myrrgon had directed her own father's actions, and those of Mr. Bennick. It was easy to believe he had done the same with the Rylend earls over time. The Elder One had claimed his power was limited, and that he had ever been forced to use the subtlest of means so as to avoid attracting the notice of those who served the Ashen. All the same, it was clear he had been able to influence and shape the actions of others over many centuries.

And it had all led to this very moment.

"The keystone, Lord Rafferdy," Mr. Bennick said.

Mr. Rafferdy reached into his coat pocket and drew out a red stone. It was as big as the palm of his hand, with six flat edges—a mirror to the recess in the gate before them.

Repairing the keystone had taken little time. They had retrieved the other three fragments from the dust of Mr. Gambrel's remains. Mr. Rafferdy had arranged them together, and had spoken the required spell which Mr. Lockwell had written down in his final entry in the journal. That was all. Now they had but to set the keystone in its place, and the gate to Cerephus, created by the first magicians eons ago, would open.

And then . . . .

"This gate leads to the very heart of one of their ancient cities," Mr. Bennick said. "When it opens, they will attempt to boil through all at once like ants from a hive." He looked at Lady Shayde. "That must not happen."

"It will not," she responded.

"And it will likely be necessary to push the Ashen-slaves away from the gate, to clear a space. I had thought originally to have Mr. Rafferdy attempt to do this by means of magick, but he will need to be ready to speak the runes of closing. Which means it is better if you do this, Ashaydea."

Mr. Bennick's dark eyes were intent upon her.

"Yes, I will," she replied at last.

Mr. Bennick nodded. "Once this is done, Lord Rafferdy and I have only to heave the chest with the Eye through the opening, making sure it passes well beyond. After we do this, Lady Quent, you are to shape the Wyrdwood to block the opening and hold them back. That will give Mr. Rafferdy time to speak the words of closing to shut the gate again."

And then it would be over. Her father had described how it

would work in that final entry in the journal. The Eye of Ran-Yahgren was itself a window to Cerephus—or a gate, really, for one could pass through a window as easily as through a door. Like the other gates made by the Ashen, the Eye had only been waiting for the moment of the Grand Conjunction to fully open.

But when it did, it would already be on Cerephus.

It is one of the very most basic tenets of magick, her father had written. *A gate must never be made to open upon itself. You see, it would be like holding up one mirror to another. The arcane energies would be endlessly reflected—until they are released in a most terrible conflagration.*

Both Mr. Rafferdy and Mr. Bennick had expounded on this, agreeing this was one of the most fundamental rules of magick. And it was a rule they were about to break in a most monumental fashion. Yet even as she thought this, Ivy realized there was one terrible flaw in the plan.

"Lady Shayde will go through the gate, to push the Ashen-slaves back and clear a space for the chest with the Eye. But at what point does she then come back through the gate?"

For a long moment, all of them were silent.

"I don't," Lady Shayde said then.

Ivy stumbled back, and a low sound of despair escaped her. It was, at the last, too much that this should be asked. She could only think of the pretty girl in the portrait that hung above the landing, of her almond skin and dark eyes. A child born of a Murghese mother and an Altanian lord—a being born of war, and of two worlds, herself.

Then Lady Shayde was there, and laid a cool hand upon her arm, holding Ivy steady.

"Do not feel sorrow for me, Lady Quent," she said softly, her white face hovering in the gloom. "Remember, I do not feel it as you do. And this is the purpose for which I was made. I am yours to command, but all the same I ask you this—allow me to go."

Ivy gazed into those black eyes. At last she lifted a hand, and touched that smooth, cold cheek. Unlike Ivy's own, it was utterly dry.

"We should not delay," Mr. Bennick said. "The Grand Conjunction approaches."

Ivy drew a deep breath.

"Mr. Rafferdy," she said, "open the gate."

CHAPTER THIRTY-SEVEN

$\mathcal{L}$ESS THAN a quarter of an hour later, they ascended from the cellar and returned to the front hall. It had grown even darker since their descent. All was an eerie purple gloom outside the windows, and the only light came from the lanterns they carried, and from the dying coals upon the hearth.

The room was drafty, and Ivy shivered. But it was not just the chill that caused her to do so. Gazing at the embers within the fireplace was not so different than gazing through the gate after Mr. Rafferdy had placed the keystone into its niche. Beyond she had glimpsed dark shapes lit from behind by the glow of a lurid crimson sky.

Then, like black eggs hatching, the shapes unfurled with terrible speed and came boiling toward the opening of the gate. Yet even as they reached it, they met with another dark shape, one that moved even faster, her pale hands becoming a blur upon the air like a deadly white mist. Those shadows that came in contact with it burst asunder.

In all, it had taken but moments. Lady Shayde had pressed through the gate, and beyond. Mr. Rafferdy and Mr. Bennick had heaved the chest through the opening. Then Mr. Bennick was shouting at Ivy to shut the way. She had laid a hand upon one of the ancient wooden beams. For a moment she gazed through the gate. The last thing she saw was the white mist being enveloped by an oily sea of shadow.

Then Ivy called to the Wyrdwood, and bands of wood wove a strong net over the door, holding back the shadows and giving Mr. Rafferdy time to speak the runes of closing. Before Ivy knew it, the three of them were moving up the stairs—three returning above, after four had gone below.

"Will they understand what it was you cast through the gate?" Ivy said, gazing at the pulsing coals on the hearth. "Will they know the doom which the Eye represents for them?"

"I doubt it," Mr. Bennick said behind her. "The Eye of Ran-Yahgren was created by the Ashen. The *gol-yagru* will only sense the power of their masters in it, and so will do nothing against it. Even if they did realize what it meant, it would not matter. The Eye is not a thing that can be easily destroyed, and nor would they have a means to send it away from their world—not until the Grand Conjunction comes, and Cerephus draws close enough for the Ashen gates to open. And then it will be too late."

Ivy let out a breath. "So it is done, then."

"Not quite. But it will be so, when the final occlusion occurs. Though I believe Lord Rafferdy yet has something he must do in the meantime."

Startled, Ivy turned away from the fireplace to gaze at Mr. Rafferdy. His face was solemn in the lamplight.

"I must get to Pellendry-on-Anbyrn," he said. "And quickly, before the Grand Conjunction is complete."

She started to ask him why, only then she understood. "You described how four magicians of your order were marching with Morden's men to find the Ashen gates and alter the runes on them. But there were five gates marked on the map, weren't there?"

He nodded. "The fifth is at Pellendry, but none of the other magicians were near to that place."

"But neither is County Westmorain!"

"No, it isn't. But the gate I came through to reach the way station on Arantus was."

At once she understood. If Mr. Rafferdy was not able to reach Pellendry-on-Anbyrn, the fifth gate would open when the final occlusion occurred, and the Ashen would come streaming through—to the very place where one of Huntley Morden's armies was marching.

"We must go back to the Wyrdwood at once," she said.

"Yes," he said, then looked at Mr. Bennick. "If I have time, that is."

"You have some hours," the former magician said. "Five, perhaps six at the most. It might not be enough to find the gate and alter it."

"It will have to be," Mr. Rafferdy said grimly. "Mrs. Quent, are you ready?"

She took up her cape. "Let us go. Mr. Bennick, will you come with us?"

"No, I believe I will stay here and watch over Lord Farrolbrook, to see if he wakes. And to be certain your sister is well."

Ivy gave him a grateful look, then turned and followed Mr. Rafferdy through the door. Outside, a preternatural twilight had settled over the world. Stars were beginning to shimmer in the sky. Above, no more than a thin sliver of the sun remained visible; the bloated disk of Cerephus had eaten almost all of it.

Neither she nor Mr. Rafferdy spoke as they raced down the side of the ridge and across the moor. To Ivy, it seemed she could feel the world turning beneath her, spinning along with the other planets as they all fell in line. Despite her gasping breaths, she did not falter, and she kept pace with Mr. Rafferdy even as they dashed up the slope to the old stone wall.

"Let me go first," she said, breathless, then passed through the crack in the wall.

Once through, she reached out her hands, touching gnarled branches. *Let us pass,* she called out. *Please, we must hurry.*

Leaves rustled, like a sigh passing through the grove. In the gloaming, Ivy could make out the faint line of a path ahead. Then Mr. Rafferdy was behind her.

"Stay close," she said, and led the way through the trees.

It did not take long until they reached the clearing in the center of the grove and the gate. The queer purple light filtered down through the opening in the trees as Mr. Rafferdy approached the heap of ancient stones. She waited for him to speak the words of magick that would invoke its power. Only he remained silent.

Ivy did not understand. Was not time of the essence? Only, for some reason, she did not urge him to go.

At last he turned around. "It is not just to the Ashen gate that I go now, Mrs. Quent. You must know, I go to war as well. It is my hope to join up with my company again, and fight with them against Lord Valhaine's army."

An ache sprang up in her throat. She wished to say something, anything, but she could not. In the dim light, it was not a fear she saw on his face, but rather a firm resolve.

"It is possible I will never see you again," he went on. "Which is why I must tell you something. You may not welcome it. You may wish that I did not speak it. Surely it is far from the proper time for such a thing, so soon after . . ." He shook his head. "But I cannot be certain I will ever have another opportunity to say it, and so therefore I must."

Still she had not the power to speak, for suddenly she thought she knew what he was going to say.

"I have never in my life given my heart to another," he said, taking a step toward her. "And I may never have that chance, depending on what happens before dawn comes again—if it ever comes at all. But if it ever did come, and if I ever were able to have that chance, then I want you to know that I would give my heart to you, Mrs. Quent. Even if you did not want it, even if you would cast it aside, still I would give it to you, and gladly."

Her own heart was beating swiftly in her chest. Around her, the trees swayed and trembled, as if they too suffered the chaotic swirl of thoughts and feelings that passed through her. Her husband was gone. The sun perished in the sky. The Ashen hungered to consume the world. How could she possibly consider anything that had to do with light or joy or life?

And yet—

"No," he said softly. "I beg you, do not answer me. If somehow I should survive this long night, if any of us should survive it, then you can tell me what your answer is. Tell me when it is day again. Until then, while it remains night, let me continue to dream."

Ivy let out a breath. The trees around the clearing grew still. She met his eyes in the gloom.

"I will see you again, Mr. Rafferdy," she said. "After the dawn."

He gave a deep bow. Then he turned to lay a hand upon the gate, and in a blaze of azure magick, he was gone.

CHAPTER THIRTY-EIGHT

FIVE HOURS LATER, Rafferdy climbed out of the pit in the ground. He clambered over the heaps of dirt that had been rapidly thrown aside by a score of men armed with shovels.

Weary, he sat down on a stone and wiped his brow. A private handed him a tin cup of water, and he drank it gladly. Around him, in the faint half light, infantrymen ran to and fro in great haste as sergeants barked orders and cavalry soldiers galloped by. It was the last press to shore up their position and form their defenses ahead of the battle.

At least now they would have but one army to fight. Rafferdy cast a glance over his shoulder, back down in the pit. At the bottom lay the arch of reddish stone that had been uncovered, seeming to glow in the eerie light of stars and planets that fell from the sky.

It had taken over two hours of furious digging until the first shovel struck red stone. Rafferdy had feared the men thought him mad as he barked orders, but the bright sparks thrown off by his ring had convinced him that they were digging in the right place. And perhaps it was the ring that had also convinced the general to listen to him, and to believe the outlandish tale he had told.

It had taken Rafferdy over two hours to reach Pellendry-on-Anbyrn, and in that he was lucky. Speaking a litany of runes, he had managed to escape the grove of Wyrdwood unharmed after appearing through the gate. After that he had started down the road to Pellendry, but he soon realized that even if he were to run the whole way, he would never make it in time. Above, the sun had become no more than a fiery corona around Cerephus. The final occlusion was approaching.

And then something else was approaching as well, something far more welcome—a company of cavalrymen coming up on the road behind him. They stopped when they reached him, and when they saw the stripes on his coat they greeted him warmly. They were riding hard for Pellendry, and they had a spare horse. In short order he was thundering down the road along with them.

As soon as they reached the rebel army, Rafferdy sought out the general's tent. He told the lieutenant outside that he had crucial information about the coming battle, and at once was shown inside. There he explained to the general what had to be done.

"If you had told me all of this a month ago, I suppose I would have had you put in confinement for a day," the general had said, stroking his gray-shot beard. "But after some of the things I've seen of late—men who do not bleed, and attacks by what seem to be wolves when there are no wolves in this part of the country . . ." He had glanced at Rafferdy's ring, which was even then glowing, and gave a grim nod. "Take a company of infantry, Captain Rafferdy, and do what you must."

So he had. And now the task was done. In the pit, timeworn symbols covered one side of the ancient stone arch, while on the other, sharp new runes marked the stones—runes carved by Rafferdy himself, copied from the symbols in his black book. The magick was done; the gate was redirected. And none too soon, given the thickening gloom.

Now all he had to do was seek out his company, which had to be here somewhere, and lead them into battle. It was rash, of course. Even without the Ashen involved, the odds were likely to be against them. Yet running headlong toward a line of Valhaine's soldiers seemed positively sane compared to what he had done in the grove of Wyrdwood near Heathcrest. What had he been thinking, to speak to Mrs. Quent like that?

Except he knew the answer. A soldier could only throw himself into the fray, no matter how mad it seemed, when it was for a cause he believed in with all his being. If he became a casualty as a result—so be it.

"Captain Rafferdy?"

He looked up, thinking the private wanted the tin cup back. Only, by the bars on his coat, it was a lieutenant.

"Yes?" Rafferdy said.

"The commander wants to see you, sir."

Rafferdy nodded and followed after the lieutenant. It was only when they approached the large tent that he realized this was not the place where he had spoken to the general. A banner with a green hawk hung by the door. That should have been warning enough for Rafferdy. But such was his weariness that it wasn't until he stepped inside that he realized it wasn't a commander who had summoned him.

Rather, it was *the* commander.

He turned from the table where he had been poring over maps of the battlefield. In the lamplight, he looked a little older and more careworn than Rafferdy expected. His red hair was touched by gray at the temples, and silver flecked his copper beard. He was not so tall as Rafferdy, though he was broad and powerfully built, and he moved with an assured and easy strength. In no way did he look like a man who had been coddled in the court of a foreign prince. This was someone who had spent his entire life preparing for war. For *this* war.

"I am told you were digging for something, Captain Rafferdy," Huntley Morden said, his voice low and touched by only the slightest Torland accent. "Did you find it?"

"We did, sir," he said, not entirely certain how to answer. "It was . . ."

The other man sensed his hesitation. "You may speak freely

with me, Captain. I would be aware of all things that occur under my command, and I will never fault a man for speaking the truth."

Rafferdy nodded. "It was a gate, sir—an artifact of magick." And he explained, as clearly and succinctly as he could, what the gate was, how it functioned, and how he had come to learn of it.

As he spoke, Huntley Morden's gaze had returned to his maps. For a long minute he was silent. "I have heard of such things," he said at last. "My grandfather used to tell me tales of shadows that prowled at the edge of the world, and of a hungering darkness from across the void—one that could never be sated. I used to think they were simply stories meant to frighten a young boy."

"And what do you think now, sir?"

The other man looked up. "Now I am no longer a boy, and I know that we should indeed be frightened."

Rafferdy swallowed. "Yes," he said, "we should."

Huntley Morden nodded. Then, all at once, he grinned. "I imagine you are anxious to join your company, Captain Rafferdy. I believe my lieutenant can tell you where to find them. I trust you and your men will help me send Valhaine's soldiers running from the field."

Rafferdy found himself grinning in return. "With their tails tucked between their legs, sir."

Morden held out his hand. Rafferdy shook it and thought, *I am shaking the hand of the next king of Altania.*

Then he left the tent and went to find his company, and to find a gun, and to fight for king and country.

CHAPTER THIRTY-NINE

EVEN AS, when the hands align themselves together on the face of a clock, an hour is struck, so it was in the heavens. The celestial spheres turned one last fraction of a degree. The twelfth planet—dim Memnymion—stood in line precisely with the others. After ten thousand years, the cycle had reached its terminus. One after the other, a shadow fell upon each of the great orbs, casting all but one of them in absolute darkness.

Only the newest wanderer, the one called Cerephus, remained alight in the firmament, and it burned like a hot coal in the void: an eye gazing with a ravenous hunger at the other worlds arranged before its gaze—particularly the orb that was closest. The umbra cast by Cerephus reached out, closing around that small, green-blue world like a burnt fist. And then . . .

The red eye flared suddenly, its crimson light now tinged with blue. For several minutes it blazed so brightly that it shone like a violent sun, drenching that little orb nearest it with a livid illumination.

Then the red eye blinked, and went dark.

At the same time, on a small green island on the small green-blue planet, the few stands of ancient forest that still remained awoke from their slumber. The trees recognized the shadows which had abruptly intruded into their silent groves. They knew these things—and they remembered what to do.

For many hours the long night endured, well after the forest groves fell still once again. A rime of white ice tinged the little green-blue world, like frost upon a windowpane. Then, at last, the celestial spheres turned another tick. The first of the orbs to have fallen into line, capricious Eides, was the first to break the ranks. The others followed suit.

The long night was over.

CHAPTER FORTY

———— ❧ ————

𝕿HE SKY WAS A COLD, crystalline blue that day.

Eldyn stood amid the throngs of people on the edges of Marble Street, not far from the Halls of Assembly. He was glad for the press of bodies around him, for despite the sunshine a chill yet hung on the air. Three swift days had come and gone since the long, terrible night ended, but still the world had not fully grown warm again.

For a while, Eldyn had feared it might freeze solid altogether. He and the other illusionists had huddled in the parlor above the theater as the darkness went on and on. They stoked the stove with coal, but it hardly seemed to make a difference. Soon they could see their breath fogging on the air, like illusory clouds, and they could not stop shivering.

Still the night continued. After thirty hours of darkness, the coal for the stove ran out, and the frost was a half-inch thick on the windowpanes. They began breaking apart wooden props and pieces of scenery to feed into the fire. Forty hours passed. Fifty. The shouts and distant screams they had heard outside ceased. To venture outside would be to perish in minutes.

The world grew utterly still, and they began to run out of stage props to break apart and burn. Sixty hours of darkness. Seventy. The final hours found them silently pressing around Master Tallyroth's chaise, attempting to keep him—and themselves—from freezing. Then, abruptly, a pink glow touched the windowpanes.

Eldyn thought at first it was some trick of Mouse's. Only as the glow brightened, he saw it was no phantasm.

Dawn had come at last.

How many people in the city had perished from the frigid cold was still not truly known, though the number could only be very high. Despite this, a carnival atmosphere now filled the city. People jostled along the street, trying to get a better view down the broad avenue. Makeshift banners of hastily dyed green cloth fastened to broomsticks snapped in a crisp wind.

From the sight, it was hard to believe that three short days ago they had all been freezing and starving. Just yesterday, warehouses down in Waterside, full of grain and other foodstuffs which Valhaine had been hoarding for his troops, had been discovered and broken into, and the goods distributed to all comers. Nor had any of Valhaine's soldiers stopped the people in this, for there were none to be seen. Once news of Morden's decisive victory at Pellendry reached the city, the redcrests either threw down their arms and fled, or they took off their uniforms and melded back in with the crowds in the city. As for Lord Valhaine himself, there had been no sign these last days, though rumors had raced through the city claiming he was dead—murdered sometime during the long dark at the hands of his own magicians.

Now people along the street laughed and clapped their hands and whistled. A rider had cantered by a little while ago shouting news—the moment they were waiting for was near. The long night was over, and the war as well. It was time for a new day to begin for Altania.

"Here you go," spoke a voice behind him. "I bought one for each of us."

Eldyn turned around in surprise. "There you are! You vanished without a word, you rascal. Where were you?"

"I went to buy you a treacle tart," Dercy said, grinning. "And you're welcome, by the way."

It was only then that Eldyn saw Dercy indeed held one of the sticky sweets in each of his hands. Some baker must have managed to get hold of molasses and flour yesterday down at the warehouses and was no doubt now selling the result for an exorbitant sum.

When Eldyn was a boy, his father had taken him to see a hanging at Barrowgate, and had bought him a treacle tart. Eldyn had not been able to eat the thing for the queasiness in his stomach that day; he had been horrified at the way the people around him had laughed and jeered at the sight of a death. But now it was for something far different that the people around him were cheering.

"Go on," Dercy said. "You could use it."

"You shouldn't have," Eldyn said. "I'm sure these cost a fortune." But he accepted the warm tart, and took a bite. The edges were crisp, and it was sweet and delicious. Surprised at his hunger, he gobbled it quickly—though no more quickly than Dercy did his.

Dercy gave a sticky grin. "Well, was it good?"

Yes, Eldyn tried to say, but suddenly his teeth were chattering, and a violent shiver passed through him. Dercy's smile turned into a look of concern.

"You're half blue with cold," he said, taking one of Eldyn's hands and pressing it between his own.

Eldyn looked at his other hand: it was thin and trembling, and the spidery lines of veins snaked up the back. He had hardly made any illusions or impressions since making the copy of the map for Jaimsley. But it didn't matter; even if he never expended another bit of light in his life, he would still always have the mordoth.

Dercy must have noticed his gaze. "Don't worry, Eldyn. We'll take care of that, you'll see. After today, it will be safe enough to leave the city. You can be sure that *he* will have made certain none of Valhaine's men are left lurking about. It won't be long before you're good as new."

Eldyn knew that wasn't entirely true. After all, Dercy himself was not good as new. There were still lines beside his green eyes, and a dusting of white in his blond hair and beard. Yet there could be no doubt that he was greatly recovered compared to those first days after Archdeacon Lemarck had stolen a great quantity of his light. He had even been able to work illusions that day when he and the two magicians had rescued Eldyn from the gallows— though after he had done so, it had seemed to Eldyn that a few more gray flecks had appeared in Dercy's beard. All the same, there was no reason to believe he couldn't recover further, or Eldyn as well.

And it was all because of the Old Trees.

It was during his time in the country that Dercy had discovered the restorative effects of the Wyrdwood. There had been a small grove of Old Trees not far from his cousin's house, and Dercy had found himself drawn to it for some reason. He would have his cousin drive him there in a surrey, and he would sit for hours at the base of the wall, drowsing as he listened to the murmur of the trees.

Only after a while, he realized he didn't need his cousin to drive him there, for he grew strong enough to walk to the grove himself. And the more time he spent in the presence of the Old Trees, the more strength and energy he found that he had. It was remarkable, yet perhaps there was a sort of sense to it. After all, witches themselves had a connection with the Old Trees. So why shouldn't their sons as well?

"We'll take you to the Evengrove," Dercy said. "We'll stay at an inn nearby so we can go to the grove every day. And we'll take Master Tallyroth as well." He squeezed Eldyn's hand, gently yet firmly. "We'll make you well again, Eldyn. And then—"

But Dercy didn't get to say what they would do next, for at that moment a great roar rose from the crowd. Eldyn looked up, and down Marble Street he saw a procession of men on horses coming, followed by soldiers in brown coats marching on foot.

The procession came nearer as the people cheered and waved their banners. At its front was a hale-looking man of middle years riding on a great bay horse. The sunlight set his hair and beard ablaze, and it glinted off the profusion of medals and bars on his green coat. One might have thought he would be solemn on such an occasion, but instead he was grinning broadly, and as he rode down Marble Street he waved to the people thronging on either side, his arm never seeming to tire.

Eldyn was sure it was impossible—after all, he was just one person in a great crowd—but as Huntley Morden rode past, he turned his head in Eldyn's direction, and it seemed to Eldyn that their eyes met for just a moment, and that the older man nodded. Only maybe it wasn't impossible, for as Morden rode on, Eldyn saw him nod in a similar fashion to others, doing so again and again, as if to acknowledge each and every one of them in the crowd that day, and to thank them.

The next thing Eldyn knew he was cheering wildly, and Dercy was doing the same beside him, even as the illusion of a green hawk went speeding into the brilliant sky.

CHAPTER FORTY-ONE

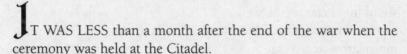

I T WAS LESS than a month after the end of the war when the ceremony was held at the Citadel.

Ivy was astonished it was all happening so soon. Yet it was clear that Huntley Morden was a man of action. Besides, no one could disagree that the nation required every source of joy and reconciliation that could be found at present, and it was clear that Princess Layle was of the same mind.

So it was, on a mild lumenal of moderate length, that Huntley Morden and Princess Layle were married at St. Galmuth's cathedral. After these vows to each other were made, further oaths were made binding them both to the nation, and they were crowned king and queen. In that act, what had been broken centuries ago was at last made whole. House Morden and House Arringhart were united, and so was Altania.

But it was not just these two who would rule the nation now—it was everyone. For in signing the papers for his coronation, Huntley Morden had granted broad new powers to the Halls of Assembly. As king he would be a strong guide to the nation—but only a guide. It would be for the people themselves to decide which direction Altania would go, and how to propel itself forward. Nor was the Crown the only one giving something up. In exchange for ceding some amount of his authority to Assembly, the king had extracted the agreement that the seats in the Hall of Magnates would no longer be inherited; rather, members of that Hall would be freely elected, just as they were in the Hall of Citizens.

The only thing more astonishing to Ivy than all these events was the fact that she had been invited to them. It seemed that Huntley Morden had been well aware of the Inquiry's efforts to protect the Wyrdwood, and so in his view Sir Quent was a hero of the realm. As such, his widow was invited to attend the wedding.

Ivy might have been in a panic to go to such an affair on her own, but fortunately she was not alone. Evidently a certain captain and magician had caught Morden's eye at Pellendry for bold and remarkable actions—both on the field of battle and off. Thus it was that Ivy found herself standing beside Lord Rafferdy throughout the ceremony in the cathedral.

It was the first time Ivy had seen him since she had taken him to the gate in the Wyrdwood. At first she had hardly recognized the tall, straight-backed man with the tanned and handsome face, for he had been so solemn. Only then he smiled, and her heart had fluttered within her, recognizing him even more swiftly than her gaze did.

There was little opportunity to speak to Lord Rafferdy throughout the ceremony—which was just as well, for Ivy hardly knew what she would have said to him. Yet to have him there was greatly reassuring—though for some reason her heart never seemed to cease in its little palpitations and flutters. Entranced, she watched as Huntley Morden and Princess Layle made their commitments to each other and to the nation. She wondered if it was possible that they loved one another. Given that they had known each other less than a month, she supposed that was not the case. Yet it was certain they both loved Altania; and perhaps that was something from which a mutual admiration could grow. What was not in doubt was that, despite the fact that neither was in their youth anymore, they made a handsome couple as they descended the steps of the cathedral while the bells rang out.

The next day, Ivy was summoned to the Citadel for another ceremony. The new king wished to waste no time pardoning those who had been wrongly condemned under Lord Valhaine's rule, and to make amends for those deeds. Though of course, some harms could never be undone.

At last Ivy heard her own name called, and she walked past the rows of stone columns to the thrones occupied by the new king and queen. There, on behalf of her husband, she accepted the pardon of Sir Quent for any and all crimes of which he had been accused.

This, Ivy had expected. What happened next she had not. For his heroic service and sacrifice to the nation, Sir Quent was being posthumously granted the title of earl of Cairnbridge, along with all pursuant lands and holdings. That in this same act Ivy herself was made into a countess was not lost upon her, and she might have swooned with all eyes in the hall upon her. Only then a strong hand took her arm.

It was the new king himself who steadied her. Though he was near to forty, Huntley Morden's face had a boyish quality to it. All the same, his blue eyes were solemn as they met her own.

"Do not look so aghast, Lady Quent," he said softly, so that in the hall only she might hear him. "Knowledge has come to me that convinces me this honor is no less fitting for the countess of Cairnbridge than for the earl. There were many battles fought in this war, and not only against Lord Valhaine's army. Your husband's actions helped to guard our nation against those other foes, the ones in the shadows, and I believe it is the case that your own actions did the same. If I had a medal I might give to you, Lady

Quent, I would. I hope you will accept these other things—this title, these lands—instead, and my gratitude as well."

Ivy was beyond words. She could do no more than attempt a curtsy. When she rose again, the king had returned to his throne. But he was grinning at Ivy now, and beside him the queen was smiling as well, her green eyes alight with approval. After that, the new countess of Cairnbridge departed the hall and made her way out of the Citadel to her abode on Durrow Street.

It was time for another kind of ceremony.

Mr. Bennick and Lord Rafferdy were already waiting for her in the front hall.

"Good day, Countess Quent," Lord Rafferdy said with a bow.

Ivy gaped at him. "You knew what was to happen today?"

He smiled slyly. "I had some idea."

Yes, Ivy imagined that he did. And she believed she now knew how Huntley Morden had learned of her actions against the Ashen. Lord Rafferdy did not wear a fashionable suit at present, but rather a brown soldier's coat. That said, the coat was exceedingly well tailored, and the bars on the shoulder were not those of a captain, but rather a major.

It seemed there was more she should say to him on the topic, but her mind was too agitated to think what it was. They had not yet had a chance to discuss what they had spoken of in the Wyrdwood, before he stepped through the gate. She had not yet given him an answer to his question. But did she know what that answer would be? Every time she considered it, her thoughts seemed to spin like the planets had in the heavens, trying to fall into some new harmonic after great disruption.

Before she could think what to say, he spoke again. "I fear that I am due back with my regiment by tomorrow, and so must depart the city as soon as possible."

Ivy drew in a breath, and now only one thought occupied her mind. She looked to Mr. Bennick. "Is everything ready, then?"

"Your father is upstairs. And I have shown Lord Rafferdy the spell he must work to remove the enchantments upon the house.

I know it well, for I helped Mr. Lockwell to devise the protections myself."

"And my sisters?"

"They are in the parlor there."

Ivy nodded. "Give me just a moment."

Excusing herself from the men, she went to the door of the parlor and peered within. The scene she found was not very different than what she had seen countless times before. Rose sat on the sofa with Miss Mew at her side, working on her sewing, while Lily stood at the pianoforte. Her folio lay open upon it, and she was applying a charcoal pencil to a page.

Yet there were some differences to the scene as well. It was not a shirt for the poor Rose was sewing, but rather a brown coat for Morden's army. And Lily wore not some pretty pink dress as she used to, but rather an elaborate gown of deep red, and her pursed lips were colored a similar hue.

In the past, Ivy would have scolded her sister for wearing a gown and paints so inappropriate for a young woman of station. Only such things weren't inappropriate for a madam of a house on Durrow Street. Lily had changed. But then, so had Rose and Ivy.

And so had the world.

"It is time," Ivy said softly from the door. "Do you wish to be there when we work the spell?"

"You're the one who knows all about magick, Ivy, not me," Lily said, not looking up from her portfolio. "I don't care one whit for it."

Her words were nonchalant, but the tightness with which she gripped her pencil belied her true feelings. She was frightened, as was Rose—though their middle sister made no effort to hide it.

"I don't want to get in the way," Rose said, her brown eyes wide. "I might knock over a candle and ruin the spell."

Despite her own trepidation, Ivy smiled. "No, Rose, you wouldn't. But you two can wait here. I don't think it will take long."

Rose nodded, and Lily kept scribbling in her folio, no doubt drawing some new scene for a play. Ivy started to withdraw.

"Oh, I meant to tell you, the gold spark is back," Rose said then.

Ivy stopped, then turned to look back at her sister. "The gold spark?"

Rose nodded. "In your light. It's usually just bright green, but there was a gold spark in it for a while. It vanished when you were ill, only it's back. I've been seeing it for some time now, only in everything that's been happening, I kept forgetting to tell you."

For a moment Ivy could only stare. Slowly, her hand went to her stomach, and pressed against it. She had been forgetting something as well in all the upheaval—a usual thing that should have happened, but hadn't. A feeling passed through her, at once a joy and a sorrow. Then, as Rose went back to her sewing, Ivy turned and left the parlor.

Mr. Bennick and Lord Rafferdy were already at the foot of the stairs. She followed them up to the third floor, to the room that had been her father's study years ago. It was still filled with his things, including the celestial globe standing in a corner. In the middle of the room was a comfortable leather chair, and in it sat a familiar figure with a cloud of gray hair atop his head.

Ivy could not help smiling. "Hello, Father," she said.

As usual, he did not answer. Rather, he sat without moving, his face slack, his faded blue eyes staring without seeing. Otherwise, he appeared well. No harm had come to him when Mr. Bennick had removed him from the city, or in his time staying with Dr. and Mrs. Lawrent and her people in the south. Ivy went to him and used her fingers to smooth his hair, knowing that despite these efforts it would soon grow wild again.

At last she looked up at Mr. Bennick. "So, what do we do?"

"Lord Rafferdy has only to work the spell," the former magician replied. "All these years, your father's spirit has been the force binding together the protections imbued upon the house. Now that the Eye of Ran-Yahgren is gone, those protections are no longer needed. And once they are removed, his spirit will be free again."

Yes, it would be free. But then what would it do? Would it

thence return to him, or would it choose to depart altogether? There was no way to know for certain; even Mr. Bennick had been unable to offer a guarantee. But for Mr. Lockwell's sake, they had to try. She bent to kiss her father's cheek, then she stepped away from the chair and looked up at Lord Rafferdy.

"Please," she said, "speak the spell."

And he did.

EPILOGUE

A Year After the War

CHAPTER FORTY-TWO

———————

"WELL, THAT'S THAT, THEN," the lawyer said, jowls waggling, and gathered up the freshly signed sheafs of paper from the table. "I must say, Lord Rafferdy, against all of my prior advice, you've made yourself a much poorer man today. You will find, when next we review the value of your estate, that you have made a significant error."

"Perhaps I have," Rafferdy said, twirling the quill pen between his fingers. "Though it is an error I hope others will soon make as well. Indeed, I rather think they will."

The lawyer gave his jowls another waggle, but said nothing further and departed the study. As Rafferdy set down the pen, the blue gem that adorned the ring on his right hand gave a bright wink. He opened a drawer in the table and took out a small book bound in black leather. Speaking a few runes, he opened the book, then turned until he reached the last of the pages which bore any writing. He read the brief message which had appeared on the page, and a smile formed upon his lips. Then he shut the book and slipped it into the breast pocket of his coat.

"Can I get you anything, sir?" his man said upon entering the study.

Rafferdy stood. "No, but you can tell the driver to ready the four-in-hand. And you can inform my mother that I will not be at dinner. I leave for Invarel within the hour."

———

$\mathcal{S}$EVERAL MINUTES less than that had passed by the time Rafferdy settled back against the cushioned bench. He watched as hill and meadow rolled along outside the window of the carriage. Until just a short while ago, all of this had belonged to him.

No longer. In the last several months, the high walls enclosing this landscape had been brought down. Now the legal barriers had been similarly removed. A great portion of the Rafferdy family lands had been parceled out and granted to those villages and parishes to which it was adjacent—with the attached legal stipulation that the land must be employed for the general benefit of the local populace.

The lawyer had claimed Rafferdy was now a poorer man, and when tallied in acres and regals, perhaps that was so. Yet previously, all of that had to balance against the care and worry which resulted from owning those lands—or more particularly, which resulted from denying them to others. Given the present lightness of his heart, he could only think the scales had now tipped in his favor. What's more, he believed that recent events would cause others to conclude as he had, and decide that the best thing to do with one's wealth, after amassing so much of it, was to give it away.

This was not to say Rafferdy had kept nothing for himself. He had—particularly those most idyllic tracts closest to Asterlane. But really, how many riches did one man need? As long as he could afford the latest style of coat, a handsome new cane, and a spry horse when he wished for it, there was nothing more he could want.

Except that was not true. There was indeed one more thing he had a want for—something he would gladly have traded all the rest of it to have. Only this was nothing that any amount of wealth could purchase. Still, it was his hope that, while in the city, he would learn if there was any chance it might ever possibly be obtained, or if it was to be ever beyond his reach.

A small grove of silver-green aspens fluttered outside the window of the carriage. They were New Trees, and thus fully in leaf.

A year ago, that had not been the case. When the Grand Conjunction occurred, a greatnight had fallen over the whole of the world—an umbral of such long duration that its equal had been recorded only in legend rather than history.

For some seventy hours, no place in Altania, the Principalities, or the Empire had known anything but starlight. A bitter cold had settled over the world, one which had caused rivers and lakes to crust over with ice and great quantities of snow to precipitate from the air. It was a dreadful time, during which people huddled together in fear as their stores of wood and candles burned low; and many of those who were caught outside, as well as a great number of animals, perished before it was all over.

At last the alignment of the planets passed, and light and warmth came to the world again. Yet the effects of the long period of cold and dark had been devastating, for as far as anyone could see, nearly every green leaf or blade of grass was blackened and withered from the bitter temperatures. At first, it had seemed as if all the world had perished.

Only that was not so, for the lumenals that ensued were exceedingly mild, and generous with light and rain in alternation. It was not long before new shoots pushed up from the ground and buds swelled forth on branches. As it happened, the very first green to be seen anywhere was upon the very oldest of trees—in the groves of Wyrdwood.

Outside the carriage window, the aspen grove fluttered out of view, and now Rafferdy gazed over a field dotted with poppies. Seeing the land like this, verdant once again, he could not help wondering if it might be the same for the human heart—if, after lying fallow for a time, new growth could spring from soil that had been rendered barren by loss and sorrow.

Another row of aspens flashed by the window, only unlike the others, these trees had never leafed out again. They stood as gray sticks beside the road; the long cold had frozen them to their core. So some hurts, then, were too great to ever be overcome.

Rafferdy turned his gaze away from the window, and did not look out it again for the remainder of the journey.

———

UPON REACHING THE CITY, he went first to his house on Warwent Square. There he found a note had just arrived for him. Reading it, he realized his timing in coming to the city was fortuitous. An event was to occur imminently—one that he would have sorely regretted missing. Yet he could not consider its happening without a fair amount of melancholy. He had not thought this day would come so soon as this!

Neither had the author of the note, for it was written quite hastily, explaining that matters had taken a sudden turn, and expressing a fervent hope that Rafferdy would be in the city.

Well, by chance or fate, he was. Quickly, Rafferdy penned a note of his own, laying out a place and time of meeting he was sure would be agreeable. After that, he composed a note for Lord Coulten. There was no need to resort to magick, for the post would do as well in this case.

Thank you for the message that appeared in my black book, Rafferdy wrote. *I hope it hasn't been too much of a burden to drive down Vallant Street each day, but I now release you from that duty. I may not have a chance to meet with you and the others of our order while I am here, depending on how things proceed, but I am certain I will see you and the rest of our little Fellowship soon enough.*

Rafferdy folded and sealed both notes, and gave them to his man to deliver. It would have been amusing to arrange a clandestine meeting of the Fellowship of the Silver Circle while he was in the city. He would have written the meeting place in his black book, a room in the Silver Branch perhaps, along with the runes to speak to be granted entry.

Of course, there was no real need for them to meet in secret anymore. The general ban upon occult orders had been lifted by the king. That was not to say that many magicians hadn't been tried and imprisoned, for they had. But each magician had been treated like any man, and had been judged upon his own actions during the war.

He supposed the Fellowship might have disbanded altogether,

had it not been for the influence of their newest member. True, ten was not so propitious a number for working magick as was nine, but when it came time for a vote, it had been unanimous, and Lord Farrolbrook had been admitted to their order.

That Farrolbrook had survived the visitations which the Elder One had subjected him to was both a relief and a wonder. At first, the physicians had given him little prospects of recovery. Yet just as those who doubted the fair-haired lord's wits had been proven wrong, so were those doctors who doubted his strength. As the months progressed, his health improved, to the point where he was now significantly recovered. All the same, it was a certainty that the length of his life had been shortened by some great amount, and he was aged beyond his years.

Perhaps it was this realization which had given Farrolbrook a wish to put what years did remain to him to good use. He had returned to his painting. And it was he who had proposed a new purpose for the Fellowship. He reminded them that, while the threat brought by the approach of Cerephus had been removed, that did not mean there did not remain relics of the two wars against the Ashen scattered throughout the world, or gateways opening to strange worlds, and some magicians might be tempted to use them for ill.

Indeed, Trefnell had heard rumors of just such an artifact, and was already on the hunt for more news of it. In which case, perhaps it was best if they did meet in secret when next they gathered, depending on who else might be searching for this thing.

Well, that would be soon enough—the next time Assembly was in session. For now, Rafferdy put on his new blue silk coat, took up his new mahogany cane, and called for his carriage.

HE ARRIVED at the house on Vallant Street a quarter hour later. As he was shown into the parlor, Mrs. Baydon looked up from the puzzle she was fitting at a table.

"Mr. Rafferdy!" she exclaimed, her blue eyes bright. "What a pleasant surprise!"

He gave a smart bow. "I understand you are just returned from your recent trip to the West Country."

"Indeed, we arrived in the city just yesterday." Her face formed into a pretty frown. "But I am astonished to see you here so soon after Mr. Baydon and I have returned. We hadn't sent a note to anybody yet. I would almost think you had heard the news by magick or some such thing."

"I am sure you know, Mrs. Baydon," he said, affecting a solemn look, "that we magicians only ever use our arcane abilities for the most important of purposes."

"Well, then perhaps you can use a spell to help Mrs. Baydon finish her puzzle," Mr. Baydon said from behind his broadsheet. "For she has complained incessantly for the last hour that there must be several pieces missing."

"But there are, Mr. Baydon!" she exclaimed. "I am sure of it."

Rafferdy sat at the table, and he spent the next little while picking up pieces of the puzzle, turning them this way and that as if utterly confounded by them, and then setting them down, as if quite by chance, right next to the place where they belonged—a fact which Mrs. Baydon would soon discover. In this way the scene quickly filled in, revealing a painted scene of wild moorlands and a manor upon a distant hill.

"So," he said, turning another piece around and setting it back down, "did you enjoy your time in the West Country?"

"Yes, very much. Lady Marsdel was the most engaging company on the journey, as you can imagine. Mr. Baydon was ill the entire time with sneezing and coughing, of course, and said he could not bear the odor of gorse. I think he simply had a cold, but he was very cross the whole time. Indeed, Lord Baydon was in far better health and spirits throughout it all. I can hardly conceive how ill my father-in-law was a year ago, given how robust he is now. He assures me that he will one day be the oldest and fattest man in Altania, and I begin to think he may well be right."

"I am happy to hear you had a pleasant time," he said, turning a piece of the puzzle in his hand.

"Are you going to fit that?" she said, and then plucked it from his fingers before he could answer, and set it into place in the puzzle. "You never wear your medals, you know."

He blinked. "Pardon?"

"Your medals," she said. "The ones you were awarded for valor and courage and all that. I am sure they would look very handsome on your new coat, but you never wear them."

No, he didn't. Why that was the case, he wasn't entirely certain. Perhaps it was that he still didn't think of himself as a soldier. Yet he had been that day at Pellendry-on-Anbyrn. They all of them had.

"I am no longer in the army, Mrs. Baydon," Rafferdy said. "I don't think it would be appropriate to wear my medals."

She looked up at him. "Dear Mr. Rafferdy, of course it would be appropriate. The war may be over, and for that I am very glad. But while you are no longer a soldier, you will be a hero forevermore. I'm afraid there's no altering that, so you might as well become accustomed to it. And don't think I haven't noticed the way you've been leaving pieces for me to fit."

She picked up a piece to set into the puzzle. The picture was nearly complete now. On its hill, the manor beckoned above the gray-green moor.

"Well, are you going to ask me, then?"

He looked up at her, startled. "Ask you what?"

"What you came here to ask me, the very moment you learned I had returned from Heathcrest Hall. Aren't you going to ask me about Lady Quent?"

At last he managed to speak the words. "And how does she fare? Is she very well?"

"You know, Mr. Rafferdy, a picture is very nice to look at." She set the final piece into the puzzle, then brushed a hand over the scene. "Yet in the end, it is far better to see a place for yourself, don't you think? For no matter how well a picture is painted or a scene is described, you can't really know what something is truly like, not unless you go there yourself."

For a moment he gazed at the landscape on the table before him. Then suddenly he rose to his feet.

"You are right, Mrs. Baydon," he said. "As you ever are. There is but one thing I have to do in the city this evening. I will leave for the West Country first thing in the morning."

"Very good." She looked up at him, her blue eyes alight. "And when you go, do wear your medals, Mr. Rafferdy."

CHAPTER FORTY-THREE

E LDYN STOLE OUT the back of the Theater of the Moon just as the curtain was rising. A familiar temptation came over him to draw the shadows in close like a cape. Instead he turned up the collar of his charcoal gray coat and drew down the brim of his hat. These actions served well enough to keep him from being easily noticed in the gloom, and no one accosted him as he made his way through the streets of the Old City.

It seemed strange not to be at the theater that night. After all, this was just the second performance of their newest illusion play, which had premiered only the evening before. What's more, it would be Miss Lily Lockwell's first night at the theater without the guiding hand of Madame Richelour there to aid her.

Not that Eldyn had any doubt Lily would do anything except manage the proceedings with zeal and confidence. After all, it had been some time since Madame Richelour had truly been running affairs at the theater. She had spent much of her time over the last year taking Master Tallyroth on excursions into the country, so that he might be near the Wyrdwood.

Eldyn, Dercy, and Riethe had gone with them on their first trip to the Evengrove, and they had feared the frail illusionist might not withstand the journey. Only he had, and Dercy and Riethe had carried him up to the grove each day, and laid him in a makeshift bed by the wall, beneath the overhanging branches.

And then, on the fifth day, Master Tallyroth opened his eyes.

Once they were assured he was no longer in immediate danger, they returned to the city. But since then, Madame Richelour and Master Tallyroth had been out to the Evengrove with great frequency. In time, Master Tallyroth regained his ability to speak in a faint voice, and even to stand and walk a few short steps. He was frail, but his eyes were bright and lively, and he remained himself.

Yet he remained ill as well. The mordoth had come exceedingly close to claiming him, and it would never fully give up its grasp. So it was that Madame Richelour had finally purchased a cottage within sight of a grove of Wyrdwood, and just that day she and Master Tallyroth had left the city for the last time, to live in peace in the country.

Over the course of the last year, Lily had assumed more and more of Madame Richelour's duties, until she had become madam of the theater in all but name. And now she was so in fact. All of the papers had been signed that morning, and the final transfer had been made. Despite her youth, she was no longer Miss Lily.

Rather, she was Madame Lockwell now.

To be madam of a theater on Durrow Street at such a young age was certainly unusual. All the same, no one Eldyn spoke to believed she did not merit it. Besides, it was generally acknowledged on Durrow Street that she had benefited from very favorable connections. Not only did she have the affections of a madam willing to sell her a charter, she also had—through her family—the wealth to pay for it.

Indeed, there had been more than enough regals, even after accounting for the theater charter, to pay for extensive renovations these last months. As a result, the Theater of the Moon, while not the largest house on Durrow Street, was now the most graceful and opulent. In addition, there were funds to hire more illusionists. That meant they could produce not only the story of the Moon Prince and the Sun King, but a second play as well.

The subject of the new play had been entirely Lily's idea. There was a book she wished to bring to the stage, she told them one night at rehearsal. And when she read from it aloud, all of them had grown excited. While they had been deprived of their master illusionist, Eldyn had worked with Lily to devise the staging for the play. Together, they had labored long hours, discussing ideas while Lily sketched madly in her folio, and then bringing the actors onto the stage to rehearse, trying this arrangement of figures or that color of light, until everything was just so.

At last, they had been ready to unveil the play. Last night, the theatergoers on Durrow Street had gotten their first look at the new production of *The Towers of Ardaunto*. And this morning, several of the broadsheets had printed stories about it, hailing it as much more than an idyll or a burlesque, but rather as a work of real art. Tonight, a large crowd had gathered outside the theater as evening fell, just as Eldyn imagined there would be for many more nights to come.

If he had any regret in all of this, it was that there was no part in the new play for himself. Not that Lily wouldn't have offered him a role had he asked; she would have. Yet while they did not speak of it, they both knew it was for the best that he didn't take to the stage. If he was ever to work illusions again, it could only be in the most sparing fashion.

True, when he looked in a mirror these days, he appeared well enough. His face was perhaps a little thinner. Faint shadows lingered beneath his eyes, and here and there was a fleck of silver in his hair. Anyone passing him on the street would have thought, *Now, there is a young man who must have been very pretty as a youth, and who still carries himself well as a man of thirty-five.*

Only he wasn't thirty-five. He was twenty-six. And if he looked at his hands, he could still easily trace the blue veins beneath his skin. Indeed, the longer he stayed in the city, the easier it became to see them there.

Master Tallyroth wasn't the only one who had benefited from visits to the Wyrdwood. On their first trip to the Evengrove, Eldyn himself had been feeble and palsied. But as they sat with Master Tallyroth in the dappled light at the edge of the Wyrdwood, Eldyn watched the blue veins upon his hands grow lighter and recede a little more each day.

Though they never went away, not entirely. And each time he traveled back to the city, they would slowly begin to return, even if he worked few or no illusions. The effects of the mordoth might be lessened, but as they had seen in Master Tallyroth, it never truly departed one. And so an illusionist still had to be careful, and to never be reckless with his own light.

Eldyn continued through the dark labyrinth of the Old City. It was just two lumenals after Darkeve, and the thin sliver of moon above shed little light on the city. Nor did the twelfth planet, Cerephus, emit any sort of visible glow as it once had done.

A year ago, at the time of the alignment of the planets, something had occurred—some catastrophic event which had affected the new planet, altering its albedo so that it was now black as pitch. Astrographers were still trying to determine what had happened. Had the conjunction caused Cerephus to draw too close to the sun or one of the other planets, resulting in this change? Many theories had been proposed, but as of yet none had been confirmed.

What had been confirmed was that Cerephus remained in the heavens, for it could sometimes be detected, by means of ocular lenses, as a black disk against the sea of stars. It was beginning to gradually recede, though—returning to the void from whence it came. At the same time, the alternation of umbrals and lumenals had steadily become less wild and abrupt over the last year. Already astrographers were able to make general predictions about the lengths of future lumenals and umbrals, and they were confident they would soon finish calculating new timetables to publish in the almanacs. Eldyn supposed that was good. For it meant everyone would once again know exactly how long they had for drinking each night.

With this thought in mind, he turned onto a familiar lane and approached a familiar door. While this was still not a particularly reputable part of the city, nor was it so grimy and fraught with menace as before. Several streetlamps threw off flickering circles of light, and at the end of the lane a hansom cab waited for a fare.

That was something he would not have seen over a year ago, when to linger in a place such as this was to go begging for a robbing—or worse. But even as the nation had grown less desperate over the course of the last year, so had its citizens. True, ills that had been wrought over generations would take far more than a year to cure. But everyone had reason to believe that, before too long, the common multitudes would gain some portion of those benefits which had heretofore been reserved only for a rarefied few. After all, the nation had two rulers now, not just one. So at least for the present, most were inclined to hope things would in general proceed better under King Huntley and Queen Layle than before.

And if not—well, the people of Altania had changed their government once, which meant they could do so again. That was a lesson Eldyn hoped both the Crown and Assembly would not soon forget.

As he approached the door of the establishment, he saw that the sign above had been newly painted, depicting as ever (though more brightly now) a green leaf pierced by a silver sword. He nodded to the doorman, then went in and proceeded to the rear of the tavern. And there, in their usual booth, he found his companion already waiting.

"It's about time, you rogue!" Rafferdy exclaimed. "I was beginning to think I was never going to have the benefit of a drink."

Eldyn grinned as he sat. "Don't tell me you're out of money again."

"Very nearly. I signed away the greater part of my lands this very morning. All for the general benefit of various townships and villages, and every nobody residing therein, and all for nothing in return. I am sure no one will so much as buy me a drink."

Eldyn was exceedingly pleased to hear this news. "I will buy you one," he said and took a coin from his pocket.

Rafferdy's eyes shone in the lamplight. "A regal! Our amusement is assured tonight. Unless . . ." He raised an eyebrow.

"Don't worry," Eldyn said. "It's real, not a copper in disguise."

He hailed the barkeep, and they soon had a pot and two cups before them. For a while they paid attention to their drink and did not talk until they had each drained their cup.

"I'm very glad you were in the city," Eldyn said, refilling their cups. "I did not think it would all happen so soon as this. But the winds are especially favorable, I am told, and everyone is anxious for the crossing."

"So you really mean to do this, then? It's not just the latest scheme of yours? Like clerking or being a priest or some such?"

"No, it's not like that," Eldyn said, wincing a bit. But then he grinned. "Or maybe it is. I suppose I was trying to make something of myself. Only in both cases, it was something other than what I really was, and that's why I failed so miserably. But with this . . ." He shrugged. "No one will care if I was a clerk or a priest or an illusionist. It won't matter where I came from, but only what I do."

"What a deviant notion," his companion said, and quaffed his punch.

Eldyn frowned. "What are you talking about?"

"I'm talking about what this world is becoming," he said. "It's absolutely dreadful, all this talk of fraternity and equality. If people cannot judge you by your name or your title or the expensiveness of your coat and carriage, what basis is left to judge you on?"

"On the basis of what lies in here," Eldyn said, reaching across the table to tap his friend's chest.

Rafferdy crumpled back into the bench, as if Eldyn had struck him a grave blow. "Yes, that's exactly what I'm afraid of."

Eldyn shook his head. After all these years, his friend could still baffle him. Rafferdy was a lord, a magician, and a decorated hero of the war. What was more, he was one of those men who had never been especially handsome in his youth, but who was growing ever more striking as he aged. Given his height, in a few years he would be positively commanding. He would be able to pass laws through Assembly on sheer presence alone.

Though at the moment he did not look very commanding, slouched as he was in the booth. They resumed their silence again for a time.

"And how is Miss Lily?" Rafferdy said at last.

"You mean Madame Lockwell," Eldyn replied.

"So, she owns the theater now?"

"Yes, it's all official. Madame Richelour is off to the country to care for Master Tallyroth. But I think she has left the theater in more than capable hands. Lily is still very young, but she has a fine sensibility and great passion. And her new play is quite marvelous."

"Yes, I saw it mentioned in *The Comet* this morning."

It was still astonishing to Eldyn that an illusion play would be discussed in such a reputable publication, and not in a derogatory way. "I must say—while it is not due to her only, of course, but also the changing times—I think Lady Quent has much to do with the favorable light in which the theaters are regarded these days. When she visited the Theater of the Moon a couple of months ago, it caused something of a sensation in the city."

"Yes," Rafferdy said. "It did."

Eldyn shook his head. "I didn't think you were in Invarel at the time."

"I read about it in the newspaper."

"Ah, yes. Well, after the famous countess of Cairnbridge went to a playhouse on Durrow Street, it suddenly became the daring and fashionable thing to do. Just like how everyone is leaving the New Quarter and moving to the Old City these days."

"She is a very remarkable woman," Rafferdy said, rather glumly.

Suddenly Eldyn realized he had been dense. He should have known at once the source of his friend's melancholy.

"So you're not going to wait until she's back in the city, then?"

"I thought I might as well go to the West Country and get the misery over with."

"You underestimate yourself, I think."

He looked up from his cup. "Do I?"

"Yes, you do. I know you never wanted power or position, Rafferdy. But that's precisely why you're the best person to have it." He gestured toward the House ring on his companion's hand. "That ring is part of you, Rafferdy. It can't be taken off, not so long as you live. So you might as well start putting it to use."

He scowled at this. "Surely you're not suggesting I try to influence her with some enchantment?"

"No, I'm suggesting you try to influence her by not worrying about who you aren't, and can never be, and instead by being who you are." Eldyn leaned across the table. "You can never replace him, Rafferdy. But nor would she ever expect you to."

Rafferdy gazed at his ring. Then, abruptly, he stood. "I think I've had enough punch for tonight, Garritt."

"I suppose I have as well."

The two men left the table and went out into the night. They clasped hands tightly, and both found it difficult to find words to speak. At last they parted.

"Well, then," Rafferdy said, leaning on his cane. "Here we each of us go, my dear old friend."

And before Eldyn could say anything more, Rafferdy turned and strolled away into the night, tapping his cane against the cobbles as he went.

IT WAS MIDDAY two lumenals later when all was ready. Eldyn had made his farewells at the theater last night, and his things had been sent ahead that morning, so the only thing left was to see to it that he arrived himself.

Given that he had plenty of time, and the day was fine, he decided to walk. He made his way down Durrow Street, past a number of theaters which had reopened in the last year, then turned onto University Street and walked through Covenant Cross. As he went, he passed a number of coffeehouses, and all of them were bustling with activity. Now that all of the copies of the Rules of Citizenship had been torn down and burned, and the colleges at the university had reopened their doors, the coffeehouses were once again bubbling pots where discussion and debate brewed.

A temptation came upon him to duck in, have a cup, and maybe see if he would run into one of his old compatriots. Only, if he were to see Jaimsley, he would inevitably be delayed. The last time they had met, Jaimsley had expounded upon a score of different things that Crown and Assembly needed to accomplish at once for the benefit of the nation. Finally, after Jaimsley had dominated all talk in the coffeehouse for an hour, Eldyn had told him he should save his wind for when he ran for a seat in the Hall of Citizens. A look of shock had crossed Jaimsley's homely face at this, but then there came a great number of *Hear! Hears!* And at this reaction, Jaimsley's crooked grin had manifested itself.

Eldyn hoped Jaimsley really would run for a seat in Assembly. He had shown both his cleverness and his capacity to lead during the revolution. The nation certainly had need of a man of his abilities at a time such as this. And if he did run, Eldyn had no doubt he would be elected.

Only Eldyn wouldn't be able to cast a vote for Jaimsley himself. And as the sun was moving a bit more swiftly than he had thought at first, it was best that he did not tarry for a cup of coffee.

He continued on, passing through the Lowgate into Waterside and heading down a narrow lane. It was only when he saw a plain, two-story building across the street that he realized his feet had followed old familiar patterns. For there was the Golden Loom, the inn where he had dwelled for a time with his sister, and where he had made a great effort to avoid the obdurate affections of Miss Walpert.

Had the innkeeper's daughter found a man on whom to lavish her plentiful, if insipid, affections? Eldyn hoped so. As for Sashie, he had managed to save her from the ruinous attentions of the highwayman Westen, only to lose her to a different sort of suitor, one whose hold upon her was now absolute.

Even as he thought this, he heard the distant tolling of the bells of St. Galmuth's. It was nearly time. He continued on past the inn, then made his way down a steep cobbled row to the docks. A number of ships moved to and fro on the broad silver river. He walked along the various piers and quays until he found the one he was looking for.

A breath escaped him as he caught sight of the schooner moored at the dock. She was long and sleek, and her sails billowed in the breeze off the river, as if she was anxious to sail. And indeed, her departure was imminent, for men hurried all over her, stowing cargo and throwing off lines.

Not long after the war, several more ships had gone east across the sea, to start the work of founding the proposed colony in the New Lands, on the shore of the main continent. Recently, the ships had returned, and unlike the ill-fated expedition to Marlstown, this one had been a great success. Now those ships, loaded with goods, were set to return to the colony, along with many more like them.

Ships just like the one before Eldyn now. Its name was the *Green Leaf*. In fact, it was for the sake of its name that he had selected this particular vessel, as it seemed propitious to him. He watched in fascination as the men worked to load the ship, marveling that it would be his entire world for more than a month. And then another world, vast and green, would stretch before him. . . .

"Waiting for someone?" spoke a voice behind him.

Eldyn was not at all startled. Rather, he grinned. "I was wondering when you were going to show yourself."

"Oh, I wouldn't miss this for anything. Say what you want, but I am going to this party with you, Eldyn Garritt."

Laughing, Eldyn turned around and gazed into sea green eyes. Like Eldyn himself, Dercy had benefited greatly from his trips to the Evengrove over this last year. So had many other illusionists. Once knowledge of the effects of the Wyrdwood spread, it quickly became common for illusionists to travel from Invarel to the Evengrove, and to walk along its edges. Many Siltheri had benefited from this.

Yet, while the lines on Dercy's face had been smoothed, they had not been entirely erased. Nor had the silver in his hair turned to gold again. And as large as the Evengrove was, there was a place where there were far more trees. Indeed, it was said the primeval forests in the New Lands stretched from one end of the continent to the other.

A horn blared.

"Well, it's time," Dercy said.

Eldyn's heart quickened in his chest. "So do you really think we can make a go of it there?"

"What do you mean?" Dercy said with a mock scowl. "There will be no finer tavern in the colony than the Two Jesters. Of course, there will be no other tavern at all when we arrive, but that only proves my point."

And all at once Eldyn could not stop laughing.

Dercy shook his head, though he was grinning himself. "An angel and a devil running a tavern. I wonder what other wonders we'll see in the New Lands? Now come along, my angel."

Arm in arm, the two made their way to the dock, and up the plank to the ship.

CHAPTER FORTY-FOUR

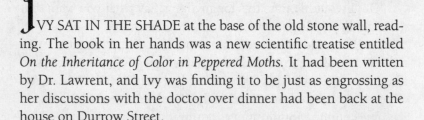

I VY SAT IN THE SHADE at the base of the old stone wall, reading. The book in her hands was a new scientific treatise entitled *On the Inheritance of Color in Peppered Moths*. It had been written by Dr. Lawrent, and Ivy was finding it to be just as engrossing as her discussions with the doctor over dinner had been back at the house on Durrow Street.

A zephyr passed through the grove, and Ivy shut her eyes, listening to the whisperings of the leaves. In their discussions, Dr. Lawrent had explained how it was possible that a trait which had existed benignly in a species for long years could suddenly become beneficial if circumstances changed. Certainly that was the case for the moths, who had put their ability to produce black spots to good use by making these spots larger and larger.

And it was true for the Wyrdwood as well. Had the Old Trees really developed that ability to move and lash out by defending themselves from enormous animals that were now long extinct? That was what the Elder One had said, and perhaps scientists would one day find the ancient bones of such creatures to prove it.

Whatever the reason for its origin, that ability of the Old Trees had become crucial again ten thousand years ago when the Ashen first came to Altania. In the millennia since, the trait became even more strongly fixed as civilization encroached upon the Wyrdwood. Only those trees which were the most likely to resist, and did so the most vigorously, survived to produce acorns and nuts. And so it was that, while there were far fewer Old Trees when Cerephus once again drew close to the world, those trees which remained were far stronger than before. That was something the Ashen hadn't counted upon.

Yet the Old Trees weren't unique in passing down an inherent trait to resist the Ashen to their offspring. Many of those first witches had borne daughters, who had borne daughters in turn, and so on—each of them inheriting the ability which allowed them to communicate with the trees. Similarly, the Elder Ones had given rise to the seven Old Houses, passing the trait of magick from father to son. So it was that the seeds to protect the world had been planted long ago, during the first war with the Ashen.

The breeze dwindled, and the grove fell silent once more. The trees drowsed in the warmth of the long day. Yet Ivy knew that, if a long night ever fell again and they were needed, they would awaken once more. Nor was there any fear that those Old Trees which remained would be cut down. They were now protected by royal decree, for King Huntley had declared all groves of Wyrdwood to be national treasures. Indeed, there was even talk of enlarging the walls around certain groves in more remote areas, to give them room to grow to a larger and healthier size.

Ivy opened her eyes and shut her book. It was time to start back, for someone would no doubt be waking up soon. Tucking the book under her arm, she made her way down the hill, away from the old grove of Wyrdwood and toward Heathcrest Hall, which loomed on the ridge to the west. For a moment her eyes searched for the sight of a horse cantering down from the ridge toward her. Only there was no horse, and no rider. Only the gorse, and the heather in bloom.

Just the other day, it had occurred to her that her time spent without Mr. Quent's company had now surpassed her time with it. Though that was not entirely true, for not a day passed that she did not think of him, or speak his name, or feel his presence. Even now, she had only to look at Heathcrest to see his countenance in its sturdy construction and stern eaves. It was not, she supposed, the handsomest manor house to be found in the country. But there was none in all of Altania that was more pleasing to her eye, or in whose walls she felt more secure.

Which was well, for Heathcrest Hall was her own now, as well as the lands around it.

After Sir Quent was pardoned posthumously, and the title of earl of Cairnbridge conferred upon him, Ivy had feared that great legal complications would arise. She couldn't help recalling how they had been ousted from the house on Whitward Street after their mother's death due to entailment. Instead, the lawyers had been able to make quick work of it all. As Sir Quent's—or rather, Earl Quent's—wife, all of the lands and possessions conferred to him, along with his existing holdings, immediately fell to her. Nor were any of these entailed in any way. What was more, there had even been some talk recently of allowing women to own property separately from their husbands, which meant a wife or daughter being ousted from their home after losing a husband or father would be a thing of the past.

Of course, there were some in Assembly who resisted such newfangled ideas, in particular the oldest and stodgiest magnates, but so much was changed in Altania now that it had become a little easier for people to give up some of the notions they had hewed to historically. As a result, Ivy had every hope that a woman would one day be able to manage her affairs as she wished in every way, to attend university, or even hold a position in Assembly. True, these notions seemed perhaps far-fetched now, but living things could change over time, so why not societies and their manners? If moths could alter their spots given enough time, so perhaps could bluff old lords in Assembly.

A pounding of hooves caused Ivy to look up. A horse was indeed riding down the hill. *It is him!* she thought wildly for a moment. Only it was odd, for even as she thought this, she didn't know just who it was she meant.

The rider rode down the slope, quickly drawing closer, and she saw that it was, in fact, Lawden. He brought the chestnut mare to a neat stop before her, then dismounted.

"Your ladyship," he said in his soft voice, his homely face solemn, "I would that you had allowed me to drive you."

Ivy could not help smiling. Of late, Lawden had been very insistent on wanting to drive her everywhere. Evidently countesses were not supposed to walk about the moors and get mud on the hems of their gowns. Or perhaps it was that he feared her not fully recovered as of yet. Though it had been nearly five months now, and in truth she felt very well.

"The weather is quite fine," she said. "And I needed the exercise."

He appeared unconvinced. "Mrs. Seenly is putting out tea. It will grow cold."

Ivy sighed, knowing she would get no peace until she consented. Besides, her legs were a bit weary from walking, and she had been gone longer than she had expected. Rose might need some assistance by now.

"Very well," she said. She allowed him to help her into the saddle, and he led the horse up the ridge and back to Heathcrest Hall.

A quarter hour later Ivy entered the parlor off the front hall. Of all the manor's many chambers, this little room was still her favorite. Knowing this, Mrs. Seenly had set out the tea things here. Ivy poured a cup and was just taking a sip when she heard footsteps behind her.

"There you two are," Ivy said, smiling. "Did everything go well while I was gone?"

"Oh yes, very well," Rose said as she entered the parlor, a bundle wrapped in a yellow blanket in her arms. "Miss Merriel slept nearly the entire time, so I got a good deal of sewing done. She only just now woke up."

Ivy set down her cup and went to Rose. Smiling, she gazed down at the baby in her sister's arms.

"Hello, dearest," Ivy said, and took the little bundle from Rose. "Did you behave for your aunt?" She cradled her tiny daughter, and kissed that soft, warm head.

Even though he was no longer here with her in this world, still Mr. Quent had managed to give her so much—a house, and lands, and security. But here in her arms was a far greater gift, one Ivy cherished above all. For Ivy had only to look at her daughter—*his* daughter—to know that he was with her yet. She could see Alasdare in the brown curls atop Merriel's head, and in the shape of her nose and the firm set of her jaw.

Then the baby opened her eyes, and it was Ivy's own eyes she saw gazing up at her, as green as new leaves.

Ivy had been shocked that day at the house on Durrow Street, when Rose said she had seen the spark of gold in Ivy's light. Only she shouldn't have been surprised. After all, the strange dream had started coming to her again, the one that began with her gathering shells along the shore.

It wasn't a dream, though; she knew that now. Rather, it had been a memory, though not one of her own. It was the memory of one of the first witches—one that had somehow been passed down from mother to daughter over the ages, just like the ability to speak with the trees.

Layka. That had been her name, the young woman who had

lived by the sea. It was she who had been used in the most terrible manner by the Elder One named Myrrgon, and who had borne him a son, whose infant body he had thereupon entered, seizing it as his own so he could be reborn. Yet despite this horror, Layka must have endured, and at some point after that she had given birth to a daughter. Like Layka, this child had possessed the *wayru*, the ability to speak with the trees, and she had passed this trait to her own daughter, and she to hers, and so on—all the way to Rowan Addysen, and to Merriel Addysen, and to Ivy herself.

And now to Merriel Lockwell Quent, here in Ivy's arms.

Why Ivy had started having the dream each time she was expecting she wasn't certain. She thought perhaps it had to do with the presence of Myrrgon himself, for on both occasions the Elder One had been nearby, temporarily inhabiting the body of Lord Farrolbrook. Just as the memories of her ancestor had been hidden deep within Ivy, so must have been the knowledge of how Myrrgon had betrayed Layka to construct a vessel for his spirit. Ivy could only think that having him close by while she herself was with child had awakened those ancient memories.

Strange though this idea was, it had to be possible. After all, was it not for the same reason that, since the time of the very first magicians, no witch had ever borne a son to a magician? Ten thousand years ago, the Elder Ones had taught both the first witches and the Wyrdwood to resist the power of the Ashen with all their might. But the power of magick and that of the Ashen was one and the same, for it was the Elder Ones themselves who had created the horror of the Ashen.

So it was that, ever after the first war against the Ashen, a witch and a magician had never been able to make a son together. Always the essence of the Wyrdwood within the witch would reject the germ of magick because of its association with the wood's ancient foe, the Ashen. And so it was that, in using the Wyrdwood to fight their enemy, the Elder Ones had defeated themselves, assuring they would never again be able to be reborn in a body that combined both the powers of this world and their own.

Yet would it ever be that way? Organisms changed over time, which surely meant they could change back. After all, if soot stopped staining walls in County Dorn, would not the moths there turn white again? It had to be so. And now, with the threat of the Ashen gone forever, resisting the power of the arcane could no longer impart any special benefit to the Wyrdwood, or to the women who spoke with it.

Which meant, perhaps one day, it would stop doing so.

Ivy's mind began to whir, like the gears of the old rosewood clock on the mantelpiece. She would write to Dr. Lawrent when she had a chance and ask him his ideas upon the theory.

But first, there was another matter of great importance to attend to.

"I imagine you are very hungry, dearest," Ivy said, gently touching her daughter's nose and cheeks, upon which Merriel let out a series of little chirps and clucks that clearly expressed this was indeed the case.

While Rose sat and turned through the pages of a folio of drawings which Lily had given to her—and which she never seemed to grow tired of looking at—Ivy draped a shawl over her shoulder and cradled her daughter close. She supposed some might think it unusual, even peculiar, that a countess would deign to perform such a chore herself, when there was surely a young woman in the village who had recently had an infant, and could be brought up to the manor to be a nurse to Merriel. Yet, no matter what propriety wished for, Ivy could not imagine surrendering such a tender joy as this to another, and so she had kept it for herself, along with many others.

When Merriel was finally content, Ivy rocked her for a time, and murmured soft songs to her. At last she kissed her daughter again, then stood.

"I believe Merriel wants for a changing."

Rose quickly set down the folio. "I can take her to Mrs. Seenly if you like."

Ivy had to confess, this was a somewhat less joyful chore, and one which she did not mind relinquishing to another from time to time. As there was someone else Ivy had a wish to attend to just then, she accepted this kind offer from her sister.

Rose took the little bundle back and smiled. "Her light is green like yours, Ivy. Only there's gold to it, like sunlight on leaves."

Ivy could only smile herself, for that was just like Rose to say such a thing. It was very good of her to spend so much time caring for Merriel. Yet her sister needed time to do things for herself as well. Tomorrow, Ivy would ask Lawden to drive Rose to Low Sorrell to see Miss Samonds.

"She eats marigolds!" Rose had exclaimed with great excitement after the first time the two of them had met.

Since then, Rose had gone to visit at Miss Samonds's house several times, and Ivy knew they greatly enjoyed one another's company. She was glad that Rose had made a friend here, since she no longer had Lily for company. Ivy missed Lily as well. But all she had to do was think of the illusion play she had gone to see at the Theater of the Moon, and of the sights of beauty and wonder she had witnessed upon the stage, and she knew that Lily was exactly where she belonged.

Rose left the parlor with Merriel, and Ivy glanced at the tea tray. There was a cup for him, but he had not come down for it. Not that this was at all out of character. So Ivy filled a cup, and then she carried it from the parlor and went upstairs. Soon she came to the room that had once been Mr. Quent's private study.

The first time she ever entered this room, a green gloom had seemed to fill it. But the vines had been pared back from the window, and now a honey-colored light spilled into the chamber. Ivy peered through the door and at once saw that she had been right, for there he was. As usual, his hair floated around his head in a white cloud, and his gray suit was rumpled and smudged with ink. He stood before the celestial globe, turning the handles and knobs as the various brass orbs spun and turned in complex gyrations.

Only then his hands fell from the knobs and grew still.

"Father?"

He did not move, but only seemed to stare at the celestial globe.

Ivy took a step into the room and said again, "Father?"

All at once he turned, a broad smile crossing his face. "Good afternoon, dear one," he said, his blue eyes twinkling. "I fear I had gotten lost in my thoughts. The new timetables that the Royal Society of Astrographers have just published are dreadful. They're rife with errors and miscalculations! I was trying to see if I could work things out any better myself."

Ivy smiled herself, then set down the teacup and approached the globe. "I am sure that you can. It's a riddle, that's all. And no one is better than you at solving riddles."

"Oh, I don't know," he said. "Mr. Bennick tells me that you are rather good at riddles yourself, Ivoleyn, and nor do I doubt him. I have ever trusted Mr. Bennick's opinion, you know!"

"Yes," Ivy said. "As do I."

"I hope Mr. Bennick will come see us soon. It has been nearly a month since his last visit, and I have quite a number of matters to discuss with him. I cannot imagine what keeps him in Torland. Now, my dear, take this knob and turn it a quarter at a time to the left to move Eides in retrograde while I adjust the azimuth of Regulus. Yes, that's it—perfect! We shall have the calculations in no time, you and I."

The tea forgotten, Ivy stood beside her father, working the celestial globe while he periodically jotted down notes or calculations, and all the while she could not recall a time when she had been happier. To have him returned to her, after all these years, was the greatest of joys. And she cherished her father all the more for how long she had been deprived of his intellect, his guidance, and his affections.

How anxious she had been as Lord Rafferdy spoke the spell there at the house on Durrow Street, removing the enchantment ʳ father had given the better part of himself to create. Then the was finished, and for a silent minute they had all watched ᵏwell as he sat motionless in the chair. Suddenly he had blinked, and his faded blue gaze had turned in her direction. Then, for the first time in ten years, he had spoken the one word she had wanted to hear him utter more than anything else.

Ivy? he had said.

During the days that followed, he had been somewhat muddled and confused. Yet bit by bit they explained to him all that had happened, and as they did his eyes grew clearer and his voice stronger. Then there had been the terrible moment when he had asked where Mrs. Lockwell was, and they had told him that she was gone. This jolt had set back his progress significantly, and he had regressed to speechlessness for several days.

Yet in time he began to improve again, and over the span of several months he became everything that Ivy had remembered him to be: intelligent, curious, playful, exacting, and above all marvelously warm and kind. After the long and awful ordeal, he was at last whole again.

Mostly, at least. For, even as he was jotting notes in his journal, his face went suddenly slack, and the pen slipped from his fingers.

Slowly, gently, Ivy touched his arm.

"Father?"

For a moment he did not move. Then all at once he blinked, picked up the pen, and went on writing as if nothing had happened. All the same, Ivy knew that they would soon be returning to the city.

Over the last year, they had enjoyed staying here at Heathcrest, or visiting Lady Marsdel at Farland Park. Yet Ivy had noticed, the longer they were away from Invarel, the more his mind would start to drift, and the more he would suffer small lapses such as this one. She supposed some portion of him would always remain at the house on Durrow Street. It was truly a magician's abode, and even as it required him, so he had need of it.

"I imagine my granddaughter wants for you, dear one," he said as he scribbled in his notebook. "You should go down to her. I'll be down soon myself to tickle her. I have just one more calculation to write out. And how the Royal Astrographers will tear at their hair when they see it!"

He ran a hand through his own hair, mussing it even further, then dipped his pen.

"Very well, Father," she said with a smile, knowing it would be past suppertime, and Merriel would be fast asleep, before he came downstairs. She kissed his cheek fondly, then left the magician to his work.

JVY RETURNED to the little parlor and there found Rose and Merriel. Rose was walking with her, and telling her the color of everything in the room, while Merriel gazed around with wide green eyes.

For a moment Ivy watched from the door, marveling at this innocent and beautiful scene. Then, imagining Rose's arms must be getting weary, she entered and accepted Merriel back. As she did, her small daughter let out a very large yawn.

"I believe someone is ready for a nap," she said.

"As am I," Rose said, yawning herself. She bent over Merriel to give her niece a kiss, then departed the room.

Ivy moved to the bassinet in the corner, then laid her daughter down and gently tucked a blanket around her. Though Merriel's green eyes drooped, she refused to shut them all the way, as if she did not want to stop looking at all the colors that her aunt had shown to her.

"I assure you, dearest, everything will still be here when you awake again," she said, touching one of those tiny hands. Then, deeming sleep more likely to come if distractions were removed, Ivy left the bassinet and went to sit on the sofa. She discovered that Mrs. Seenly had brought a fresh pot of tea, and as she had never really managed to have any earlier, she poured herself a cup.

She had just taken her first sip when, coming from the front hall, she heard the noises of the door opening, and the echoing murmurs as one of the servants greeted somebody. Moments later followed the sound of footsteps approaching.

As Ivy was not expecting anyone, she supposed it was simply someone from one of the neighboring households in the county, or perhaps the vicar from the chapel at Cairnbridge. Well, there were more teacups on the tray.

A servant appeared in the doorway. "A visitor has arrived for you, your ladyship," he announced. "Shall I tell him you will receive him?"

Ivy did not bother to ask who it was. "Of course, you may show him in," she said, and went to the table to tip the pot over a second cup.

"Well, I see little has changed since I first met you in your parlor on Whitward Street," spoke a wry, familiar voice. "For it appears you still pour your own tea."

Ivy set the pot down with a sudden clatter, then turned around. "Lord Rafferdy!" she exclaimed.

He gave a deep bow. "Your ladyship."

As he did, Ivy's thoughts turned wildly. A short while ago, she had had little trouble helping her father calculate the positions of the stars and planets, but now she could not formulate the simplest thing to speak.

Fortunately, she did not have to, as just then Merriel emitted several bright, trilling noises from her bassinet. No doubt the sound of voices had vindicated her resistance to sleeping, and she was now expressing her wish to be included in the proceedings. Knowing Merriel would not be content until she saw what was happening, Ivy went to the bassinet.

"I hope I am not arriving at an inconvenient time, Lady Quent."

"Not at all," Ivy said, at last managing to take a breath. "Indeed, this is a very good time for Merriel to meet you. As she has heard a great deal about you, she is no doubt quite eager to make your acquaintance."

Indeed, Merriel was now smiling and gurgling as Ivy lifted her from the bassinet. Her visitor slowly approached.

"But she is so tiny!" he exclaimed.

Ivy could only laugh at this. "In fact, she is a good deal larger now than she first was, and after you have held her for a time, she does not in fact feel so very tiny. Would you like to?"

He appeared startled by this suggestion. "You mean hold her? Me?"

It was amusing that a man who had bravely faced enemy soldiers, wicked magicians, and daemons from other worlds could be alarmed at the prospect of holding a small infant. Yet when Ivy held her out, he hesitated only a moment, then accepted Merriel. His actions were awkward at first as he searched for the best way to cradle her, but then he tucked her comfortably into the crook of his arm, as if he had done it countless times before.

A smile spread across his face, and his brown eyes were alight. "Well, this is utterly marvelous."

"Yes, it is," Ivy said, and she smiled herself, for somehow it seemed very right to see him hold her daughter so tenderly.

Presently, Merriel's eyelids began to droop again. Evidently, now that she was well apprised of the happenings in the room, sleep was growing harder for her to resist. Ivy took her back and returned her to the bassinet, where she gave a sigh and shut her eyes. Then Ivy went to join her visitor on the far side of the parlor.

"Is she asleep?" he said softly.

"Yes, I believe so," she replied. "But there's no need to worry about being quiet. Indeed, if we speak in our usual tones, she is much less likely to wake up than if we whisper. The sound of our voices will comfort her."

"Yours, perhaps. Mine can only be strange to her."

"On the contrary, I am certain she is very familiar with it. After all, she would have heard you on many occasions before she was born."

Now a look of wonder came upon his face. "I suppose you must be right."

"I think her willingness to sleep while you are here is proof of that."

He glanced toward the bassinet. "She's marvelous in every way, Lady Quent." Then his gaze returned to her. "Just like her mother."

Ivy could not help being pleased by these words, though she felt suddenly flustered as well. "Thank you, Lord Rafferdy," she said, a bit breathlessly. "But it has been some time since I've seen you, and in the interim it appears you've forgotten our agreement of how we are to address one another."

"I apologize for my long absence here and at Durrow Street. You see, ever since leaving my commission in the army, I have been rather . . ." He paused, then shook his head. Whatever it was that had been keeping him away, he did not say. "But I fear that you have been similarly afflicted as I. It seems that time and absence can make one forgetful of just how things are supposed to be."

"Then let us recall our proper habits, Mr. Rafferdy."

"As you wish, Mrs. Quent," he said and grinned.

As always, the expression suited him. Yet, unlike when they first met, it was no longer the case that Mr. Rafferdy was really agreeable to look at only when he smiled. True, he was very fashionably dressed, just as he had been that day at Whitward Street. Only he had no ivory cane or kidskin gloves or such regalia about him. His only adornments were the House ring upon his hand—which was in truth a rather homely thing—and the two medals, one bronze and one silver, pinned to his coat. Also, his face was at once sharper and more open now, divested of the smooth conceit which had been evident then. In all, he seemed far less concerned with his appearance.

Which is why it was paradoxical that she found his appearance to be so much more pleasing now than she had then. His hair was somewhat mussed, as if he had been riding hard. And with his wind-tanned skin, and the lines that appeared by his eyes as he smiled, there was a slight roughness—even a degree of wildness—to him that she had never noticed before. Perhaps it was just that it had been so many months since she had seen him. Whatever the reason, she could only think that Mr. Rafferdy had never been so handsome a man as he was at that moment.

"Well, then, I am glad that is settled," he said, then swallowed.

"As am I," she replied, and attempted to take a breath.

They should have clasped hands affectionately then, and sat in opposite chairs as they sipped their tea, and traded stories of their mutual acquaintances in city and country. Only they did not do these things. Rather, he continued to gaze at her. Slowly his smile dwindled, and his expression grew solemn. The light of the long day, falling through the window, caused his brown eyes to become exceedingly bright. Nor did they turn away from her, not even for a moment.

"Mr. Rafferdy!" she gasped at last, for she could think of nothing else to say. Her heart was fluttering at a rapid pace within her, as if she had just raced across the moors. Had he asked her for a cup of tea at that moment, she could never have complied, for the way her hands were trembling.

Yet it was not for tea that he had come here.

"Mrs. Quent, I am confounded!" he exclaimed at last. "I have always believed myself a man of words, but I cannot fathom how to speak to you what I must. The most ancient spell or obscure runes of magick would more easily depart my tongue."

Now he began to pace the room in the most agitated way.

"I detained myself for months, to give myself time to puzzle this out, yet that was not time enough. Then I rode all the way from Invarel, rather than take a coach, so I would have more time. Yet still it was not enough! And so I walked slowly up the steps of your manor, to think it through further. Only now I am here before you, and still I find that I do not know how such things can ever be spoken. Yet I have to speak them. I have to."

Ivy could scarcely breathe, let alone speak herself. She gripped the back of a chair, for fear her feet would cease to bear her. At last she managed to say, "Then I beg you, speak them!"

He ceased his pacing and gazed at her. For a moment, it seemed the ring upon his right hand flashed blue. Or perhaps it was only the sunlight. Then, abruptly, he took a step toward her.

"I know that previously I have agreed to call you Mrs. Quent," he said, his voice going low—and not out of concern about waking Merriel, she was sure. "But that is a promise I now wish to break. For you see, it is Mrs. Rafferdy that I would call you, if I could. But no—it is not even that. It is the name Ivoleyn that I wish to speak. So I will call you that now, even if I am never allowed to do so again. For I love you, Ivoleyn. I have always loved you, even when I was too great of a dolt to know it. That day in the Wyrdwood, I told you I would gladly give my heart to you. But that was only the half of it. For I would have your heart in return, if I could. I would spend the rest of my life with you, and with Merriel. I would belong to you both, and both of you to me, and nothing would ever alter that, unless it were to add another member to our little family. You did not give me your answer then, for I would not let you. But I ask you for it now, no matter what the answer might be. For I can no longer endure not knowing, one way or another."

Moments ago, Ivy's mind had been all in confusion. But while her heart still raced within her, it was no longer the case for her thoughts. Rather, with a perfect clarity, she knew precisely how to answer him.

"I did love you, Mr. Rafferdy," she said, moving a step toward him. "Or rather, I thought that I did. How could I not think so, given how fine and witty you were in our plain little parlor? Only then, after that, I learned what it truly was to admire a man—not because of his appearance or charm or position, but because of who he was. Because of the strength of his character, the goodness of his spirit, and the trueness of his heart. Those, I learned, are the things that are really worth being loved."

His face grew more solemn yet. "Yes, of course," he said. "I see."

He started to retreat. Only before he could do so, Ivy went to him, and reached out, and clasped his hands in her own.

"Those are the things that are worth being loved," she said. "And that is why I love *you*, Mr. Rafferdy. Truly, this time. Not because I am dazzled by you, but rather because I know you— because I have seen every one of those things in you, and far more.

Indeed, I cannot think I really deserve the love of such a man—but I will not claim that I don't want it! I do want it, more than anything—for myself, and for my daughter."

"But it is already yours," he said. "It ever has been."

He was smiling again, his face alight, and Ivy knew her own expression was a mirror to his.

"Ivoleyn," he said, softly now, as if testing the word.

And she replied, "Dashton."

Then their hands parted, but only so they might come closer, like two trees twining together to stand as one in a forest of green.

ABOUT THE AUTHOR

What if there was a fantastical cause underlying the social constraints and limited choices confronting a heroine in a novel by Jane Austen or Charlotte Brontë? GALEN BECKETT began writing *The Magicians and Mrs. Quent* to answer that question. The author lives and writes in Colorado.